The Nexus Games

[Games 1-4]

Shami Stovall

Published by
CS BOOKS, LLC

Cover Design: Darko Paganus
Editors: Amy McNulty, Nia Quinn, Celestian Rince

IF YOU WANT TO BE NOTIFIED WHEN SHAMI STOVALL'S NEXT BOOK RELEASES, PLEASE VISIT HER WEBSITE OR CONTACT HER DIRECTLY AT
s.adelle.s@gmail.com

To John, my soulmate.
To video games, for being amazing.
To Gail and Big John, my surrogate parents.
To Dan Calley, for giving a voice to the characters.
To Mary, Scott, James, Emily & Dana, for all the jokes and input.
To my patrons over on Patreon, you're the best.
To my Facebook group, for all the memes.
To RoyalRoad, it was a fun ride.
To baelrath, Namu, & NoodleMaster, for all the comments.
To Beka, forever.
And finally, to everyone unnamed, thank you for everything.

—Chapter 1—
—Stalkers—

Alex Kellan wasn't the type of person who stalkers typically targeted. He carried a loaded .45 handgun in his shoulder holster and regularly bench-pressed two hundred pounds. Most thugs could do the math—he wasn't worth the inevitable hospital bill.

Yet, for some unknown reason, a pair of men had been following Kellan wherever he went. For the last four days, his stalkers had watched his every movement from the safety of distant shadows. But each day they grew a little bolder. Each day they moved a little closer.

Curiosity was getting the better of Kellan. He had called in the suspicious behavior, and his contacts were investigating, but there wasn't much to go on.

Kellan took a swig of beer, content, for the moment, with the seedy bar atmosphere. *Nino's Place* was a rinky-dink location stuck between a Japanese restaurant and a UPS store, both of which had been closed for years.

Despite the grit and grime, there were four others seated around the establishment. One man, heavy set and bearded, sat with a trucker's posture. Another man, his hair silver and his naked ring finger permanently indented, likely drank to escape the memories that lingered.

Two others sat in the corner booth, hidden by the shadows of a burnt-out light, as silent as the broken jukebox.

There they were. Kellan's stalkers.

He decided he'd wait them out. Perhaps once he stepped outside, he could get a word with them.

A bartender walked over and offered Kellan a quizzical lift of her eyebrow. All the hair on her head had been dyed dark purple—a flashy statement that didn't match the woman's plain black shirt and unassuming jeans.

"It's Christmas Eve, ya know," she said.

"Seriously?" Kellan replied. He finished his beer with one last swig. "Huh. That explains the holiday music on the radio."

Obviously unimpressed by the sarcasm, the bartender frowned. "Don't get cute. Shouldn't you be with family? What's someone like *you* doing in *Nino's Place*?"

"Clearly, I'm here for the company," Kellan quipped.

The trucker belched.

Kellan forced himself to smile. He pushed his empty glass toward the bartender. "Pour me another."

"You on leave or something, *military man*?" the purple-haired woman asked as she filled the glass with needless showmanship, twirling it once and spinning it afterward.

He wasn't wearing a uniform, but a veteran could always spot fellow military.

The faint shrapnel scars on the woman's arms told Kellan she had once served.

"Like I said, I'm here for the company." This time, Kellan met the woman's eyes straight on.

Anything would be better than being alone on Christmas. Kellan hadn't really dated in years. His old moves—which consisted of way too many dark or sarcastic jokes—didn't usually work, but he hadn't taken the time to learn anything new.

A smirk came to the corner of the bartender's lips. She walked with a slight limp, a detail Kellan had taken quick note of when he had first entered the bar, but the other puzzle pieces of her appearance were what caught Kellan's interest. Despite her dyed hair, the freckles on her forearms and shoulders gave away her Irish lineage. He found it attractive.

"You're here for the company?" she asked as she slid over his beer. "You haven't even asked for my name."

Kellan shrugged. "I don't need to."

"Oh? Why's that?"

With no hurry, he sipped his beer. The quiet in the bar wasn't comforting. Any car that drove by could be heard through the thin walls.

But before the bartender grew irritated with Kellan's silent treatment, the trucker at the far booth scooted his mug to the edge of his tiny table. "Mavis, can I get another?"

"Your name is Mavis," Kellan said, lifting his glass in a toast.

She rolled her eyes as she ambled over to the trucker's table.

For years, Kellan had gone through special training for observation and analysis. Figuring out someone's identity without speaking to them wasn't particularly difficult, but it always impressed civilians. Mavis was a veteran, though. The cute trick probably didn't win him any points.

By the time Mavis had finished with the other patron, Kellan had downed his drink. Mavis rested her weight on the bar and gave him another questioning eyebrow.

"I'm on mandatory leave," Kellan said before she could ask again. "Trust me. I'd rather be working, but I guess Santa has a different gift for me in mind."

She whistled. "You get in trouble with the MP? That why you're not working?"

"Let's just say it was a psychologist's orders." Kellan toyed with his empty glass.

"Got cold feet? Or you another one with PTSD?"

"No, but I'm going to have traumatic flashbacks about frequenting this bar," Kellan said as a cockroach scuttled across the countertop.

Mavis grabbed a towel, but before she could shoo the insect away, Kellan slammed his glass down on the roach, breaking the quiet atmosphere with a *clack*. The trucker and the widower both glanced up, but they quickly returned to their own drinks when nothing else happened.

But the two men in the dark corner…

They neither flinched at the racket nor altered their behaviors.

Kellan couldn't help but scratch at an itch on the back of his neck when he glanced in their direction. Something wasn't right about his stalkers. They didn't act like normal men who were undercover. They didn't act like normal men, period.

"Sorry about that," Mavis said, flushed in the face as she wiped down the bar. She took his glass and thoroughly scrubbed the roach guts from the counter. "We don't usually have a problem with bugs."

"Don't worry. I'll leave it out of my Yelp review."

Mavis chuckled.

She grabbed a new glass, filled it to the brim, and slid it to Kellan. Although he had intended to drown his evening in booze, the uncomfortable feeling Kellan got from the two in the corner put a halt to his plans. His perceptions were dulled, but only slightly. Instead of drinking more, he'd keep his wits about him.

Kellan leaned forward and lowered his voice. "Hey, do you know those two over there?" He motioned with his eyes to the dark corner occupied by the two suspicious men.

"Nope," Mavis said. "But I can do a quick walk around."

Making good on her word, Mavis walked out from behind the bar and approached each customer with a smile and small talk. The two regulars chatted it up with easy topics and a jovial *Merry Christmas*.

"Do you need anything else to drink?" she asked the widower. "Sorry about the lack of music. Apparently, there are only so many times one man can listen to Jingle Bells."

"I don't need anything," the man replied. "I hate Christmas music as much as any other sane man."

Kellan gritted his teeth. The two in the corner watched his every move.

He had gotten used to having background checks run on every new acquaintance he made, as well as having his phone watched and his conversations recorded. It was for his safety as much as his unit's—there were some who would do Kellan harm simply for his position, and others who wanted to dismantle the US Special Forces from within.

Kellan watched the corner of the room through a mirror mounted behind the bar.

Mavis returned to her post behind the bar, rubbing her bad leg and grimacing. Clinking bottles together in a faux attempt to straighten up, she whispered, "Those two in the corner aren't very talkative. Just a pair of weirdos ordering a single beer each and never touching it."

"Huh."

"You're a little paranoid, is that it?" Mavis asked, giving him the once over.

"I can see why they put you on mandatory leave."

"You got me," Kellan intoned. "Kellan the Paranoid. That's me."

Mavis stopped fiddling with the glasses. "Your name is Kellan, huh? Well, I don't like this serious version of yourself, Kellan. You have an intense expression when you're quiet."

"Oh, I was just thinking about what I was going to write on that Yelp review. Maybe something along the lines of; *great drinks, but they pale in comparison to the beauty behind the counter. Ten out of ten, would visit again.*"

Mavis grew red and silent. "That was cheesy."

He shrugged. "I'm not the smoothest. You'll get sick of me."

She took a moment to gather her thoughts. "The bar closes at two," she said, her ears still a shade of pink. "We can grab a coffee afterward. I know a place."

"I have a strict schedule I need to keep. Two is past my bedtime. You understand."

Mavis nodded and turned away. "You're right. I forgot you're still active. Never mind."

"You have any days off?" Kellan quickly asked. "I'm still on leave, after all. We could get a bite to eat and *then* grab a coffee. That is, if you haven't gotten sick of me." He gave her a playful smile.

Mavis shook her head and chuckled. "I definitely should've gotten you talkin' earlier. Are you free Sunday? I have the whole day off then."

She pulled an index card from the cash register and wrote out her phone number. Then she tucked it into the front pocket of Kellan's jacket.

"You better call me," she said.

"Of course." He tossed another twenty on the counter—plenty for a tip—and gave her one last nod. Mavis returned the gesture.

"I'll see you then."

In reality, Kellan could have stayed longer, but the two in the corner booth had started gathering their things to leave. He wanted to get a good look at them before the night ended. What were they planning?

As Kellan walked by, he slowed his pace and looked them over. His open observation gave him next to no information, however. Both men wore gray hooded sweaters, dark-blue jeans, and white T-shirts. Plain. Nondescript. Lacking all personal flair.

Unusual.

Their muddy-brown hair and short haircuts also did little in the way of distinguishing them. No tattoos. No scars.

Kellan exited out onto the sidewalk and turned toward the parking lot two blocks down. He heard the door behind him, aware of the trailing stalkers.

The cold night air blanketed Fayetteville in icy fog. Closing signs hung on doors and security gates secured windows along the barren street. Black clouds blotted out the moon and flickered with the hints of a storm. If there was Christmas spirit to be felt, it wasn't in the dank alleys behind *Nino's Place.*

Kellan approached his vehicle, taking time with his keys to allow his pursuers to catch up.

When footsteps echoed between the buildings that lined the parking lot, Kellan smiled to himself.

"Finally got the stones to say something to me?" he asked.

Kellan turned around.

To his surprise, it wasn't the two men from the bar—there were four others walking out from the harsh shadows cast by the streetlamps. They all had jewelry jutting from their lips, ears, and eyebrows. The words *Fear Nothing* had been tattooed on their forearms. They were teenagers, like all local street gangs, and the four thugs approached from different angles.

"Good evening, gentlemen," Kellan said.

The four didn't reply as they advanced.

One goon withdrew a switchblade and Kellan instinctively placed a hand on his sidearm hidden in his jacket. Kellan stopped himself from drawing his gun when he noticed the teen's poor grip on his blade.

Why are they so desperate? Kellan asked himself.

The thug with the switchblade rushed in. Kellan grabbed his wrist and easily kicked out the kid's footing. Then he ripped the blade out of the thug's hand and hurled his attacker to the ground.

Two of the thugs lunged, and Kellan met the first with a solid strike to the liver—kid never saw it coming—and the shock sent the kid's internal organs on a cigarette break. The second guy got a punch on Kellan's right ear and then wrapped his arm around Kellan's neck. In a sheer display of power, Kellan flipped the boy over his body and slammed him against the asphalt.

The fourth thug, a mere two feet away, pulled a .22 handgun from the waistband of his jeans. Kellan grabbed the barrel and smashed it back against the kid's face, breaking his nose and chipping a tooth. Then Kellan tore the handgun from the kid's weak hold, backed himself against the side of his car, and watched in confusion as the first thug got to his feet.

Without a switchblade, the thug stumbled forward, his arms outstretched in a poor and ineffective mode of attack.

Kellan tucked the stolen gun away and grabbed the kid before the idiot could try anything else.

"What's wrong with you?" Kellan asked, holding back a laugh. "If you needed money this badly, you could have—"

The boy vomited, coating Kellan's arm in a yellowish mass of writhing worms and fluids.

—Chapter 2—
—Mistakes—

Kellan yanked his hand away in horror.

Worms? What the?

Kellan shoved the kid into a nearby car, his combat reflexes kicking in. He ripped off his jacket. The worms squirmed down his forearm, the sticky slime of the vomit causing them to cling to everything they touched. The sting of the worms burrowing into his flesh shocked him more than anything else.

Shaken, Kellan pulled off his shirt and raked it across his skin.

"*What was that*?" he shouted.

Kellan threw down his shirt and examined his arm, all while keeping an eye on his attackers. His skin appeared unharmed, though the phantom sting lingered on Kellan's thoughts. He twisted his forearm and saw nothing that indicated damage—no evidence the worms had even existed.

But they had, right? Kellan turned his arm around several times, pressing his fingers against his skin, hoping to feel something.

Nothing.

The thugs scrambled to their feet and then took off into the darkness.

Kellan let them go, his desire to corral them nonexistent. After a few shaky breaths, he glanced around. His gaze fell upon two figures across the street.

It was the two stalkers from *Nino's Place*. They stood under the light of a streetlamp, their hoods up, but their attention locked on Kellan. For a moment, they just stared. Without a word, they turned away and then continued down the street, leaving Kellan to his lonely parking lot.

Had they been watching the entire time?

Kellan took in a deep breath.

"I have to report this," he said with a sigh. "Goddammit."

With shaky steps, he returned to his car. He pulled his shirt back on, started the engine, and then waited in the growing warmth of his vehicle.

He pulled out his phone and dialed his commanding officer. No answer. Kellan left a message explaining the fight. He was low on energy, hating the fact that he had to report a conflict. He hadn't wanted to fight a bunch of kids in a parking lot. That wasn't why he had joined the Special Forces.

Fayetteville was half-empty for the joyous holiday. Kellan sat in his car, staring at the dashboard. He dialed Dr. Hanley, hoping he would be working. Normally Dr. Hanley was *always* working, but it was 12:30am, technically Christmas Day.

Kellan glanced at his arm.

No signs of the worms. No marks or scabs. As a matter of fact, Kellan was just as healthy as ever. He worked out for two hours every day—as per his mandated training—and jogged another hour at night, to keep his endurance high.

Kellan couldn't get the image of the worms out of his head. Where were they?

Mistakes are written in blood. That was what his old commanding officer would say. *I should've been more careful. I shouldn't have let those thugs get so close.*

"That's okay," Kellan said aloud—his shadow his only company. "Dr. Hanley will call me back soon. Everything will be fine."

Kellan looked at himself in the rearview mirror.

"What?" He narrowed his eyes. "You think that'll take a while?" He leaned back in his chair. "I can wait. I've got plenty of time."

His own joke amused him, but the silence that followed was deafening.

"Maybe I should go to the hospital."

But if the doctors *didn't* find any worms…

Kellan sighed. "Nothing would say *crazy* like raving about imaginary punk-parasites. I'd be removed from active duty permanently."

His thoughts remained on his encounter.

The worms he had seen…

Kellan closed his eyes, exhaled, and buckled his seat belt. When he opened his eyes again, he felt a sense of determination. It was his life, wasn't it? He was in control?

His old Delta Force buddies, Greer and Jones, wouldn't have wanted to hear he was alone on Christmas.

He hated thinking their names…

Kellan glanced at the time on his phone.

1am.

His joking and wits indicated good mental health, but they didn't help with the profound loneliness Kellan occasionally found himself facing.

Mavis had wanted to meet at 2am. Maybe she still would.

I've stayed up for three days in a row on several occasions, Kellan reasoned. *What's one night of missed sleep while I'm on mandatory leave?*

***

Kellan ran his fingernails over his body.

Everything itched, right down to his gums. It took a permanent piece of his brain's processing power to ignore the urge to scratch, and with what willpower he had remaining, he shoved his hands in his pockets and continued as normal.

"I didn't think we'd be seeing each other again tonight," Mavis said as she straightened her shoulder-length hair. The coffee in one hand spewed a pillar of steam into the winter air. "I thought you had a curfew. What changed your mind?"

"Let's just say it was the psychologist's orders."

With a restrained smile, she asked, "Oh, really?"

"I have a strange psychologist, I know."

"I dunno. Prescribing a date sounds like *my* kind of remedy."

Kellan scratched at his side. He *almost* called it quits, but he gritted his teeth and refused to leave. If he excused himself at the beginning of a date, he knew it would be misconstrued as something horrible. Besides, he couldn't be alone, not with his dark thoughts and a fridge full of beer. Without work to distract him, what did he have?

Kellan walked the path of the Fayetteville city park, Mavis close by his side. The place was lit and vacant, and it suffered from the cold just as much as the rest of North Carolina. He zipped up his hoodie, disappointed that his sullied jacket sat in the trunk of his car.

For their first date, Mavis had asked to grab a drink and walk through the park. Kellan couldn't believe she knew a coffee stand open on Christmas morning, at 3am, but she had proved him wrong. Mavis knew Fayetteville better than he did.

Kellan glanced around as they walked, squinting through the early morning fog. The streetlights pierced the darkness in the park, keeping it bright, but the gloom beyond the sidewalk remained untouched. He stared off into the distance, straining his ears to keep track of various voices and footsteps. How many people were in the park Christmas morning? Kellan and Mavis weren't the only ones... Could the others be his stalkers? Were they following him?

While caught in his own musings, Kellan hadn't realized how far he had gotten from Mavis. He stopped and waited for her to catch up, cursing himself for being so inattentive.

She hurried after, unable to hide her limp, and kept her gaze low.

"Let's address the elephant in the room," Mavis said once they resumed their walking.

"There's no elephant. Just us."

"Everyone asks about my scars. Everyone stares when I walk. You don't have to pretend. Let's just get it out of the way so that you don't have to speculate behind my back."

"I know why," Kellan stated. "We don't have to talk about it if you don't want."

Mavis narrowed her eyes. "You just know everything, don't you? Why don't you tell me what you *think* happened?"

"It was a grenade. Something homebrewed. If it had been military grade, you would've died, but you have too many scars, so I assume you were close, but it lacked the punch." Kellan rattled off the information with the cold tone of a dictionary. He had seen similar injuries in the past. They had ended careers.

"Yeah," Mavis muttered, turning away. "I can't believe you got all that information from a few scratch marks."

Kellan half smiled. "Trust me. It's the product of years of training."

She straightened her leg and walked a little faster. "Yeah, well, I'm not so bad.

You should've seen the others in the truck. They're chair-bound now. The medics say I was lucky I didn't lose an eye." Mavis ran her fingers through her hair, along a line on her scalp.

"Is that why you dye your hair?" Kellan asked.

Mavis pursed her lips. "You notice every little damn thing, don't you?" She huffed and then sipped her hot coffee. "Women like to have secrets, pal."

"I've heard that hair growing on or around scars can come out discolored, even gray. It's a logical conclusion that you'd dye it to cover that up." Kellan shrugged. "You probably picked the bold color to distract from your other scars. But I'll let you have your mystery."

"Yeah, okay—enough about me, hotshot. What about you? What branch are you in?"

"It's classified." Kellan smirked. "Men like to keep secrets, too."

Mavis rolled her eyes so hard, she almost lost her cup. "You're one of those *Special Forces guys*. Of course. It all makes sense now."

"*Of course*?"

"Look at you." She jabbed his side with her finger.

Kellan lifted an eyebrow.

Mavis replied by attempting to wrap a single hand around half his bicep—and failing to do so. She stared up at him with a sardonic expression. "Look at how tall you are. And look at your scruff! Grunts don't wear five o'clock shadows like you Special Forces guys." Mavis reached up and ran her knuckles along his unshaven jawline.

"Welp, you've done it," Kellan said with a smile. "You've cracked the mystery. You can expect a call from the chief of police thanking you for your dedication and investigatory skills."

"Oh, so when *you* deduce everything about my injury, you get to be all smug, but when *I* figure out your rank and file, all I get is sarcasm?"

"I told you that you'd get sick of me," Kellan quipped.

"Uh-huh. What branch of the Special Forces are you in?" Mavis touched a finger to her bottom lip. "SEAL Team Six? ISA? I bet I could guess if you showed me your gun."

Kellan didn't register her question. He stopped walking and stared across the park to the far walkway. Two men stood near a grouping of trees, their nondescript gray clothing blending with the fog. Had Kellan not been looking, he might have missed them.

His stalkers. They had to be.

Kellan broke from the path and took a few steps onto the grass before stopping.

"Hey, what's wrong?" Mavis asked.

The men by the trees… In every way they were the men from the bar except…

Kellan rubbed at his eyes and then glared. *The guys in the bar were different,* he thought. *Right?* The two men in the park had olive skin and slick, black hair. *Not* the two men from before, yet they were so very similar, right down to their hooded sweatshirts and jeans. They even stood at the same height. Were *four* men following him? Why? What was there to gain? How had they known he had gone to the park?

Mavis met Kellan out on the grass and followed his gaze. The men turned and hustled away.

"Why're you staring?" she asked.

"Don't they look familiar?" Kellan whispered. "Just like the guys from the bar?"

"No. They're different."

"Didn't you see their clothes? Jeans and sweatshirts."

"*You're* wearing jeans and a sweatshirt. What's wrong with that?"

Kellan watched the two men fade into the fog.

He itched… so much. He scratched while he stared.

The men stopped at the precipice of the fog and turned one last time, staring for an extended moment before resuming their escape. Did they want him to follow? Or were they worried Kellan would approach? Were other thugs and gangsters lying in wait around the corner? *Maybe it was a mistake to go to the park,* Kellan thought. *I shouldn't have met Mavis. Not after what happened.*

"You're seriously weirding me out," Mavis said with a forced laugh. "Those two guys look nothing like the guys from the bar. They're probably brothers, or maybe they were just enjoying each other's company. I bet you scared them off with your staring. Honestly, you look like you're ready to run them down or something."

Mavis didn't know of his stalkers, or his fight in the parking lot, or about the worms. Kellan scratched at his itchy arm while his mind mulled over the myriad of possibilities. He exhaled and returned to the park's designated pathway. Perhaps he *was* wrong, but should he take that chance?

"Sorry," Kellan said. "I got confused."

"It's fine. Just don't go freaking out strangers in the future, okay?" Mavis overhand-tossed her empty coffee cup in the nearest bin, murmuring a *swoosh* noise.

Droplets of water sprinkled over the cement. Kellan flinched when a raindrop hit his eye. He didn't care for the rain. Visibility became impaired, the constant beat of water drops drowned out all other sounds, and the slick chill made movement difficult. Perfect for a mugger or group of thugs, on the other hand…

"We should get to my car," Kellan stated. *Anything to get out of this park.*

"All right."

Kellan broke into a jog, heading straight for the street he had parked his car on. Mavis kept pace for a short distance before her foot slipped on the water, causing her to nearly trip. She corrected herself, but the grimace on her face betrayed her agony. The sudden increase in rain didn't help anything either. Her clothes soaked up the giant droplets, adding unnecessary weight.

Kellan walked back to her, but she avoided glancing up at him.

"Go on ahead," Mavis said. "I'll catch up."

He scooped her into his arms, holding her like a bride.

Mavis jerked and struggled. "Put me down," she commanded, her voice unsteady. "I don't want people thinking I can't walk."

"Trust me," Kellan said with a reassuring smile. "If anyone sees us, they won't be thinking, *that girl can't walk*, they'll be thinking, *that guy is tryin' reeeaaal hard to get laid.*"

Mavis snorted and laughed, unable to hold it back.

Kellan waited, ready to put her down if she insisted, but content to carry her if she acquiesced. Mavis relaxed in his arms and tucked her head under his chin as though the spot had been made for her. He took the gesture as acceptance and continued his way to the street.

Fourteen-mile hikes, dead drops in the middle of the wilderness, and endurance training made the walk an easy task. Kellan knew he couldn't carry Mavis forever, but what strength he had he was more than willing to share with a comrade-in-arms.

Kellan kept his alertness high as he made his way through the park. Two separate lights flickered and died, blanketing sections of the park in darkness and allowing the gloom to creep up on him.

Each light was closer to him than the last—it couldn't have been coincidence.

Had Mavis seen? The lights were going out around them!

Kellan held her tight, fearful he would need to drop her if it came to a fight. The water rushing over his skin quelled the itching, however, and his body felt more like its old self. If they were thugs like the last, they'd be sorry.

He made it to his car unmolested and glanced over his shoulder.

No pursuers.

At least, not that he could see.

"You never told me anything about yourself," Mavis whispered. "Why are you on mandatory leave?"

Placing her down, Kellan pulled his keys from his pocket and unlocked his two-door Honda Accord. Kellan opened the passenger door. As Mavis stepped in close to enter the vehicle, he stopped her.

"When you were deployed, did you ever find yourself behind enemy lines?" he asked.

She glanced up and met his humorless gaze. She shook her head in silence.

The only assignment Kellan *hadn't* aced had been three months ago. Until then, Kellan had had a spotless record.

Every mission successful.

Every hostage saved.

Every extraction perfect.

But his luck had finally failed while he had been in Syria. Kellan and two of his Delta Force teammates—Greer and Jones—had been caught inside a warehouse during a bombing. The collapsed roof had trapped them in place. Over the course of six days, Kellan had freed himself, killed the neo-terrorists who had attacked, and even dragged his two teammates all the way to the extraction location.

His supervisors had deemed him a hero, even though all he had to show for it were the bodies of Greer and Jones.

Six days in enemy territory. No food. Barely any water. Kellan had known Greer and Jones had been dead days before he'd reached American forces. He had wanted to return their bodies to their families, but carrying around two corpses…

The nightmares that had followed had put Kellan on the "at risk" list.

In order to avoid a "mental break," he had been placed on mandatory leave until Dr. Hanley supported his return to the Delta Force.

"I want to protect people," Kellan said, his voice quieter than before. "That's why I joined the military in the first place. But one time… I couldn't."

He had never told anyone outside the Delta Force about his assignment.

Kellan stepped around Mavis and made his way to the driver-side door. He shouldn't have said anything, even as vague as he had been. It was against the rules. Kellan regretted mentioning it by the time he sat down in the driver's seat, but at the same time, it felt good to tell one other human being besides Dr. Hanley. Just saying it aloud took some of the weight from his soul.

Mavis buckled herself in, her brow furrowed. "Are they making you—"

"It's not like that," he interjected. "It's complicated. I just… haven't recovered." Kellan brought his car to life and glanced between all the mirrors. Still no signs of trouble. He took an easy breath. "Where did you park your car?"

"Actually, I was hoping we could continue the evening."

Kellan lifted an eyebrow. Mavis turned away, hiding her face in the darkness of the vehicle.

"Unless you don't want to," she added.

It occurred to him that Mavis had been working the graveyard shift at a second-rate bar on Christmas Eve. Perhaps she didn't have anyone either.

Perhaps she wanted company just as desperately as he did.

"Where to?" Kellan asked.

"Do you live in the barracks or here in the city?"

"I have an apartment here in town."

"Then that's where we should go."

—Chapter 3—
—Alone—

Kellan unlocked his apartment with a quick click.

He stepped into his 700-square-foot abode and then hung his keys on the ring by the door. The sterile living room, complete with one couch, a lonely TV, and a cheap coffee table, had all the welcoming charm of a motel lobby. No pictures hung on the walls, no plants filled the corners. Everything was neat, but *everything* amounted to three plates and a fork stacked in the attached kitchen sink.

Mavis followed Kellan inside and took note of the surroundings. She walked, scanning every inch, until she stopped behind the dusty couch.

"Quaint," she said.

"Thank you. I decorated it myself."

Mavis pointed to the dark-green suede couch, the off-white coffee table, and then to the black flat-screen television. "I see you have an eye for cohesion."

"What can I say? I don't like to discriminate. All colors are equal."

Again, Mavis snorted and laughed.

Kellan peeled off his wet sweatshirt and shoulder holster, tossing both onto the kitchen counter. Mavis followed suit and removed her own sweatshirt. She had changed her outfit after work. As a bartender she wore form-fitting jeans and a black T-shirt. As a civilian, she wore a pair of low-riding cargo pants and plain *gray* T-shirt.

Not much of a difference.

He understood why the tips would be higher in her bartending outfit, but he also understood the need to be comfortable. Women's clothing baffled Kellan from time to time. He had seen torture techniques less sadistic than some fashionable high-heels, and he appreciated the fact Mavis wore a practical pair of black flat top shoes.

She gestured to the walls. "No pictures?"

"Nope."

"*None?* Why not pictures of your family? Your mother and father?"

"I thought it would be depressing to have pictures of tombstones on the wall." It was a dark joke, but Kellan couldn't take it back now that he had said it. With a chuckle, he tried to play it off.

"I'm sorry," Mavis muttered. "I didn't know."

"Forget about it."

Kellan walked over to the fridge but stopped himself before opening it. He already knew the contents. He didn't want to drink, especially given the circumstances. With a sigh, he turned away from the fridge. Kellan didn't have any cups, so offering water was out of the question.

Mavis forced half a laugh and angled her gaze to the countertop. "To be honest, I figured you would have pictures of a girl somewhere."

"So, this was a recon mission?" Kellan asked with a smile. "You didn't think I was single, and you had to make sure? Sneaky."

Mavis lifted an eyebrow. "You might still have pictures hidden away somewhere." She glanced around. "This place is really clean. Like maybe… you threw everything into a closet to hide it all."

"Huh. Perhaps. You'll never know till you search the whole apartment."

"Oh, we'll get to that." Mavis ran a hand through her hair, leaving her wet locks disheveled. "But first, I say we watch a movie. I'm sure *Rudolph the Red-Nosed Reindeer* is playing nonstop on at least three different channels."

Kellan shrugged. "Sure."

"It's cold, though. You should shut your kitchen window and we should huddle together to conserve body heat."

He chuckled, the idea of "generating heat" on the edge of his thoughts. Then he cut himself short. "Wait, what?"

Mavis threw herself back on his tumbledown couch and craned her head up to get a better look at him. "Shut the window and come join me on the couch."

The… window?

Catching his breath, Kellan whipped his head around and stared at the window above the sink. How had he missed it? The window… was open. Kellan walked over and glowered at the sill. *Holy shit,* he thought, his mind a white noise of realization. *Someone has been in my apartment.*

With unsteady hands, he closed the window. He *never* forgot to shut it. Hell, most days he never fucking opened it. Kellan could hear his own heartrate as he continued to stare. *They aren't messing around. Someone is watching me—following me—invading my privacy. How could I have let it get this far? How could I have been so unobservant?*

"Are you coming?" Mavis called from the living room, her voice sultry.

"You need to get out," Kellan stated. He turned around and went straight for his bedroom, snatching his gun from the holster on the counter as he went.

Mavis jumped up, her body stiff. "What's wrong?"

Kellan's stalkers could try to kill him. But with what?

His mind raced with ideas.

Hydrogen cyanide, sarin, and botulinum were all odorless, colorless and extremely deadly. Improvised explosives had been known to decimate entire vehicles or bedroom-sized areas with ease.

But one guy lying in wait with a gun was all it would really take, and Kellan knew he wasn't safe. He couldn't stop reviewing each and every possible situation.

Kellan kicked open the bedroom door and allowed his muscle memory to do the work. He waited a few moments, in case of possible gas threats, and shifted into the room, his back always to the wall and his gun held tightly in front of him. His bedroom—no immediate threats—had only three places to hide. Kellan kicked in the door of his bathroom. Clear. He ripped open his sparsely populated closet. Clear. He tore open a window and unceremoniously flipped his queen-sized bed over to get a better look at the underbelly. Nothing.

Mavis stood in the middle of his tiny hallway, her eyes wide. "What're you doing?"

Kellan took a few backward steps out of his room and turned to Mavis. She had her arms crossed and her hands tucked tightly into her armpits, a wide-eyed look of disbelief written across her face.

"Someone's in my apartment," he said. "You should leave."

"Your apartment only has three rooms," Mavis replied, motioning to *everything* with a sweep of her hand. "Clearly, no one is here."

From his position in the doorway of his bedroom, Kellan saw every inch of the apartment, from the kitchen-living room combo, to the cramped bedroom and bathroom. Mavis was right. No one was here.

He took a deep breath. "Someone *was* here. It's not safe. It's—"

"How can you tell?" Mavis interjected. "Unless that's why your house is so empty. Because thieves ransack the place on the daily." She half laughed and then motioned to his living room. "Thieves who leave the TV, for some reason."

"I know someone was here!" Kellan stormed into the kitchen and reexamined the window. "I never leave the window open. And… And I saw those guys in the bar and park. I know it was them—*somehow it was them.* They've been in my apartment!"

He turned around.

Mavis took a step back, her shoulders bunched around her neck. "Wow. You really are paranoid."

"I—" Kellan stopped himself short of yelling. He inhaled and exhaled with calculated breaths. "I'm not paranoid."

With slow and dramatic timing, Mavis turned her gaze to Kellan's bedroom. The mattress—overturned and smothering the collapsed nightstand—sagged and then crashed to the floor. The two stared at it a long time before Mavis returned her gaze to Kellan, her eyebrows lifting to her hairline.

Kellan shook his head. "Listen. There are these guys. Two. Maybe four. I'm not sure. It's been going on for days now. *Days.* I knew, but, I just couldn't—" He slammed his gun down on the kitchen countertop and ran both his hands through his hair. His head hurt with anxiety. He couldn't articulate his situation without taking a moment to comb through his own convoluted thoughts.

Mavis approached with a furrowed brow. She placed a hand on his shoulder. "It's okay. Calm down."

"Can *you* calm down on command?" he snapped, jerking away from her touch.

He tensed and Mavis flinched back. Kellan held his breath—a technique he had learned throughout his time in boot camp. For a moment, the apartment sat cold and silent, neither person moving. Rain pelted the roof unabated.

Mavis once again crossed her arms over her chest. "I should go." She grabbed her damp sweatshirt and threw it on. "I'll get an Uber."

"Wait," Kellan breathed. "I apologize. I…"

What explanation did he have? More ravings?

He scrunched his eyes closed. In his mind, Kellan knew what he had seen and what he thought, but when he heard his own voice, even *he* doubted. What would he tell Dr. Hanley? Anything he said about the evening would end with him being discharged from the Delta Force. A mystery group stalking him and entering his apartment to no end? What was he thinking?

"Hey."

Kellan opened his eyes, surprised by Mavis's close proximity. She stood directly in front of him, her gaze locked on his chest.

"I'll stay," she muttered. "Just take a deep breath, relax, and tell me everything you can."

Mavis wrapped her arms around his torso in a gentle embrace.

Kellan's teeth hurt. And his stomach. And his chest burned. He returned her embrace, but not without grimacing. He felt… ill. And it came on without warning. Much like the itching had.

"I'll be right back," he murmured.

Kellan grabbed his gun out of instinct and stepped around Mavis. She watched him go, but said nothing.

Once he entered his bedroom, Kellan shut the door. Mavis moved around the kitchen, likely looking for something to drink.

It had become difficult to swallow.

Kellan barely made it to his bathroom before doubling over the sink. He closed the door and waited, feeling the dry-cotton sensation that heralded vomiting. After a few tense moments, nothing happened. Kellan stood back up and ran his tongue over his teeth. He felt something stuck between two molars—a piece of spaghetti, perhaps?—and he dislodged it with his thumb and forefinger.

He examined his hand.

A yellow worm writhed around his finger. It left him pale and speechless.

Kellan threw the wretched blood-coated worm into the sink. His hands shook. He staggered back into the wall. He couldn't breathe.

Something was terribly wrong.

As if the apartment were going through the same ill effects, the lights flickered and strained. One light above the bathroom mirror burst in a shower of glass. The power drained from the entire complex with a single soft electrical sigh.

The rain ceased.

Kellan didn't move. In the darkness of his bathroom, he felt the twisting of tiny creatures beneath his skin. Squirming. Struggling. Wriggling.

Somewhere in his unconscious mind, he heard a thump in his bedroom. Then silence.

"Mavis?" he asked, his lungs devoid of air and his voice inaudible.

Kellan forced himself to breathe. Before he could call out again, the bathroom door handle turned with the slow, quiet precision of a master surgeon.

He readied his gun and waited.

The bathroom door creaked open, and the silhouette of a person emerged from the darkness of Kellan's bedroom.

It definitely wasn't Mavis. Too large. Clearly masculine. They walked without a limp.

Kellan didn't hesitate. He threw the door all the way open and fired. One shot to the chest, one shot to the head. The intruder flew back from the force of the Colt .45, crashing to the floor of the bedroom sprawled out on his back.

Then something flashed across Kellan's eyes—text that only he could see.

> **[Alex Kellan] shot [Puppet2] twice for a total of 14 damage. (9 +50% Sharpshooter Modifier)**
> **[Puppet2] stops functioning.**

It was as if the text was across the flesh of his eyeballs. It was so thin and transparent that it didn't affect his sight, but it was still clear enough that he could read.

Kellan rubbed at his eyes, his heart racing.

What the?

But he heard more noise, and his training kicked in.

Kellan stepped out of the bathroom, his gun still at the ready.

A second figure appeared at the edge of his peripheral vision. The second man lunged from the corner of the room—he had been waiting. Kellan pivoted on his heel and shot twice more.

Clean. Perfect. Efficient.

> **[Alex Kellan] shot [Puppet1] twice for a total of 15 damage. (10 +50% Sharpshooter Modifier)**
> **[Puppet1] stops functioning.**

Both men dead.

Both… puppets?

Kellan's heart raced faster than before. He didn't know what any of that meant, but at least the information was straightforward. He had dealt damage. The enemy had stopped functioning. He could give it more thought later.

He checked his body and gun.

Minimal bullets expended. He had four more shots before he had to reload.

Kellan's pulse ran quick, but his nerves held firm. Even the ear-shattering *bang* of the heavy handgun hadn't broken his concentration. He had been in this scenario too many times to choke, and his adrenaline drowned out the aching of his gut.

There wasn't any light. All the bulbs in the house seemed to have shattered.

In the past, when the power had gone out, the lights from the nearby street had always provided visibility. Kellan's attention lingered on the open window. He heard the rustle of leaves and wind, but he saw nothing in the void of black beyond the sill.

A thunderless strike of lightning illuminated the room for a fraction of a second. A rumble of power shuddered through the floor of the apartment a half second later. No other sounds. No other murmurings. In the brief glimpse of his room, Kellan identified the men. They had been the two in the park.

Kellan forced himself to take a deep breath as he moved to the living room.

"Mavis?" he asked, his voice carrying only a few feet before dying.

Nothing.

The low hum of the television caught his attention. Kellan glanced over, his arms tense and his gun up. The television sat on a channel with no programming, the white static offering a tiny amount of light to the otherwise bleak room. Kellan didn't bother to turn it off, but a small piece of his mind gnawed on the mystery of its apparent power. Everything else was dead. Why did the TV remain?

And why static? Modern TVs didn't do that, did they?

Another strike of lightning cast long shadows from the windows and trees outside. He walked to the front door and noticed it was ajar. Had Mavis left? Kellan felt the urge to look.

The inky darkness that surrounded his apartment couldn't be pierced, only the occasional flash of lightning brought about any information.

Kellan's apartment complex, a series of one-story buildings with a single pool and a laundromat, appeared empty in the brief flashes. His car was missing—*all* the cars were missing—and the nearby walls seemed half-busted and cracked. Paper trash clung to the powerful winds that blew between buildings and gathered in corners.

The short bursts of light weren't enough for Kellan to feel confident about exploring. He stood one foot outside his front door, and knew he was in a vulnerable position. What if his stalkers had cut the power to the apartment complex? They were clearly after him. If he ran around in the dark—without proper protection or gear—he was practically giving them an easy kill.

Kellan turned his gaze to the sky.

In the distance, between fog and jet-black clouds, he saw the flashing of red lights, similar to those of an airplane or a radio tower. No stars. No moon. No Christmas lights or trees. The subdued enigma of his circumstance left him on his toes and in an odd mix of pensive tension.

Was he alone?

Was he… going insane?

The wind howled.

Where had the rain gone?

Kellan stepped backward, and right before he returned to his apartment, he spotted a figure in the darkness, lit up momentarily by another flash of lightning. He readied his gun and stared.

Another flash.

Nothing there.

"Mavis?" he called out, his voice steady and loud enough to carry.

No answer.

The skittering of metal on pavement brought shivers to his spine. His training had prepared him for the unknown, but he never thought it would be used in such a dreamlike circumstance. *I should fall back to familiar territory,* Kellan thought, repeating the words of his CO in his mind.

Kellan returned to his apartment and closed the door, locking it behind him. He went to the kitchen, the apartment layout ingrained in his mind. With quick ease, and quiet movements, Kellan opened the topmost counter drawer. Two flashlights sat inside, along with a handful of batteries. He turned one on and slowly illuminated every corner of his apartment.

He was alone.

Taking a deep breath, Kellan made his way back to the bedroom. The flashlight turned his apartment into a glowing fishbowl—he couldn't see outside, but he knew the light would act as a beacon in the darkness. He kept the flashlight low and avoided shining it toward the windows.

Kellan pointed the light at his bedroom floor.

He caught his breath and tensed. No bodies.

Kellan took short breaths as he scanned the carpet. No blood. *That's not possible,* he thought. *I definitely shot them. I saw it.* He even rubbed at his eye. *The notifications had said…*

What notifications? That was insane. He knew it.

Information on his eyes?

Impossible.

Wheeling around, Kellan frantically searched the walls. To his relief, he found the bullet holes, but that led him to two conclusions…

Either the bloodless men had picked themselves up and left… or there hadn't been any men at all. Kellan had shot at figments.

Logic demanded he settle on the latter.

Am I paranoid? The thought swirled in his head. *Perhaps… Mavis left because I was just blindly shooting shadows in my apartment. And words were scrolling across my eyes like popup ads…*

The doubt clawed at his confidence.

Kellan shut his bedroom door and ambled to the window. The wind continued its howl. He tightly shut the window and locked it. Then he drew the blinds and stepped away.

"Hey, God," he said, addressing the empty room. "I know I've never spoken to you before, but… I get it. I really do. I've got PTSD. Or unresolved psychological issues. Or I was drugged by the enemy. Or whatever this is. I won't deny it anymore."

He grabbed his mattress and hefted it up onto his metal bedframe, positioning it in place. Once situated, he haphazardly threw his sheets and pillows on top.

Kellan continued with, "You've convinced me. I'm unstable. I shouldn't be in the Delta Force. I'll resign immediately." He chuckled, the sound more nervous than jovial. "What're the stages of grief again? Denial, isolation, anger, *fucked-up-hallucinations*, acceptance? Can we skip the other stages and go straight to acceptance? I'm ready now. I'm more than willing to admit whatever it is you want me to admit. I've learned my lesson."

Silence reigned supreme.

Kellan reached into his pocket and pulled out his cellphone. He dialed Dr. Hanley, but the device beeped with an error message.

No service.

"Of course not," Kellan murmured, unable to stop another anxious chuckle. "That would've made sense. Who needs *sense* when you have trauma-inducing nightmare scenarios to deal with?"

His mind overflowed with history lessons of soldiers from Vietnam who came home with terrible nightmares and horrific delusions, all of which were brought about by the reality of war and death. They spoke of *seeing things* at all hours of the night and *hearing voices*. Tragic tales. None of them ended well. Most, in fact, ended in suicide.

Kellan glanced down at his gun. The idea that he still had control over whether he lived or died gave him a small bit of reassurance. He had control over *something*, at least. With a deep breath, Kellan calmed his excitable heart rate, switched off his flashlight, and stared into the darkness of his room.

"I'm going to sleep," he announced. "And when I wake up, I'll be well enough to visit Dr. Hanley. No more hallucinations. Deal?"

Kellan sat down on his bed—fully clothed and uncomfortable with the idea of undressing, even in his own home—and rested back, his head cushioned by his lumpy pillows. He inhaled, closed his eyes, and placed his handgun on his chest.

The minutes dragged.

Outside his window, the wind moaned, and tree branches scratched the glass of his windows. He gripped the blankets, refusing to investigate, and instead, focusing on sleep. He had to sleep. Everything around him was nothing more than a nightmare brought about by stress.

It would disappear in the morning.

Kellan laughed to himself. "Was *Mavis* even real?" he asked aloud. To no one.

Knowing my luck, she wasn't. He half-smiled. *The first girl I've connected with in a long while was nothing more than a figment of my imagination.*

The silence of the apartment seeped into Kellan's spirit.

He lay motionless, only daring to open his eyes after what felt like an eternity. Sweat pooled around him. What would he do in the future? How would they treat his illness? Would he ever be normal again? Kellan had never heard of a case of severe anxiety being "cured" as much as being "dealt with" via copious amounts of drugs. Would that be his new reality?

His body itched. Kellan felt squirming just behind his eyes. He had a knife—in the drawer of his nightstand—and the idea of digging into his skin and removing the struggling worms just beneath crossed his mind.

Kellan laughed again—dark and sardonic. "Nothing is more insane than cutting yourself to remove illusionary worms."

They weren't real. They couldn't be.

Sleep never came, only new worries and possible outcomes. Kellan stared at the ceiling, watching the reddish gray hue of the dawn break through the darkness and creep past the drawn blinds. The clouds—fog?—weakened the intensity of the light.

"Good morning, Fayetteville!"

Kellan jerked upright, his gun tumbling into his lap. The energetic announcement had emanated from the living room, like a ringmaster was somehow in his apartment.

"This is the morning news! I'm your designated host, here to deliver you information straight from the Arbiter."

Confused and disoriented, Kellan leapt from his bed, threw back the blinds, and glanced out the window. The fog obfuscated everything. He could make out the hints of trees and the black of the street, but not much else. Kellan rotated his arms. He was stiff from the long night of tension, never having managed to relax.

His mouth dry, Kellan walked out of his bedroom and headed straight for the kitchen. The television had remained on for the entirety of his "rest"—the news program had started on its own—and the volume allowed for the voices to carry throughout the tiny apartment. Kellan ignored it and went straight for the fridge.

Although it wasn't a *breakfast of champions*, Kellan withdrew a beer. He uncapped the bottle and drank the thing in one long take, guzzling the drink as fast as he could without choking. He needed to numb his thoughts.

Kellan gasped for breath once done and grabbed another. He hesitated for a moment, holding the second bottle in one hand. He turned it over in his hand. The drink was warm. Kellan stared into the fridge. The light was off. He clicked the switch on the side of the fridge door. Nothing.

Right. The power was out...

But how did the television remain on?

"—and now that the *Conflux* is upon us, a curfew has been levied across the city," the TV continued. "Those found out on the streets at night will be punished! What a time to be alive."

Kellan ambled over to the couch, his eyes fixed on the television.

The news anchor, a thin and narrow man with sharp features, sat manacled to a metal desk, his wrists raw and his fingers blistered. He wore a suit with a uniform color scheme of black and white, stitched tight enough to constrict the man's breathing, but it was clean enough to be brand new.

Across the man's face, snug over his eyes, was an ivory blindfold, the same high-quality fabric of the man's white tie. The man had dark-red hair, matted with dried blood, creating a disheveled and unkempt appearance from the shoulders up.

Despite his bizarre appearance, the man smiled with perfect white teeth, his voice strong and confident. "Remember, those interfering with the duties of a

Pestbyter will *also* be punished! And—most importantly—those who defy the orders of a Justice will be *severely* punished! No one is to interfere in this year's competition! It's much too important. *Much too special.*"

The background of the "news" program was just a rusted wall. No TVs with displays. No scrolling words. It was just… an ominous room, with a blindfolded man chained to a desk.

Kellan almost dropped his warm beer.

What the hell is going on?

—Chapter 4—
—The Nexus—

The blindfolded news anchor smiled wide—his teeth brilliant.

"Remember, my faithful viewers, if you *are* going to be insubordinate, make sure to do so in front of the cameras! The punishments for interference this year will be extreme, but that makes for *damn good* entertainment!"

The blindfolded man laughed and then yanked on his shackles. He… couldn't seem to free himself. His raw skin bled a bit, but the news reporter hid the damage by tugging his sleeves over his wrists.

Kellan slumped onto the couch, engrossed in the broadcast. Was this some sort of PTSD-fueled dream? What did it say about his mental state? Or perhaps he was beyond help now…

"This week's forecast is filled with rain," the anchor said. He brought a manacled hand up to his blindfold and stroked just over an eye socket, a splotch of crimson ever-growing beneath his fingertips. "Finding a place of shelter is recommended, especially considering that, from what I've seen, this Conflux will be very… exciting."

Again, the man laughed, this time even throwing his head back as he did so.

Kellan grabbed his remote and switched the channel, curiosity driving his actions.

The first few stations were white static, but the third had loud music and whimsical colors. Kellan stopped switching and focused on the show in front of him. A group of children, vagabonds in appearance with ratty brown clothes and dirty faces, sat in a semi-circle around a fully grown man dressed as a clown.

The clown's clothing, just as strange as the news anchor's, consisted of a yellow and red jumpsuit with wide frills and fingerless gloves. He hopped about, dancing to the children's clapping, and then disappeared off the side of the screen.

The clown returned with a four-foot-tall purple teddy bear. He flung the bear into the center of the semi-circle of children—the thing landed with a heavy thump—and he handed each child a plank of wood or baseball bat.

The children shrieked with delight, jumped to their feet, and whaled on the teddy bear with all their might. They screamed *outsider, outsider* with each swing, relentless in their brutality.

At first, Kellan thought the bear inanimate, but amidst the thrashing, he could have sworn the bear lifted its arms in defense, shielding its bear-head, and silently cowering from the blows. The bear "suit" was too small for an adult…

Kellan switched off the television.

He had seen enough.

The programming left him feeling uneasy. With a tightness in his chest, he pushed off the couch and shuffled through the apartment.

"The hell is going on?" Kellan whispered to himself.

Scratching at the door drew his attention.

Kellan readied his gun, lunged for the handle, and then threw open the door. Fog rolled over the streets, the pavement cracked and broken. The morning light, red because of the ominous fog, barely illuminated anything.

A dog stood at the door, its tail tucked between its legs. It whined and backed away a few steps.

Had it been the one scratching at the door?

Kellan stepped forward.

The dog bared its teeth and scrambled backward.

Kellan held his gun close, his breath slowing as he took in information. The dog's teats hung low and swollen, milk dripping onto the pavement. Its golden fur was riddled with mange and its gums bled. The pathetic animal shook from malnourishment, its eyes wide in fright.

The dog had recently given birth.

She had puppies somewhere nearby.

"Were you the one knocking?" Kellan quipped, his anxiety never truly leaving him. "Now isn't a good time."

The dog offered a growl in response.

Kellan shifted back into his home. His fridge had nothing but beer, but one of the cabinets had some leftover beef jerky. He grabbed the bag and returned to the front door. The dog stared at him with wide eyes. Kellan threw the jerky onto the ground.

"There ya go," he muttered. "At least one of us won't be miserable, right?"

The dog—a golden retriever—devoured the meat. She went from piece to piece, her tail wagging. Kellan carefully stepped forward and then knelt. He stroked her head, trying to reassure her with gentle whispers, careful not to touch the raw and hairless areas near her ears. The dog didn't protest the gesture.

Once the dog had finished her meal, she turned and trotted off.

Kellan stood and then tensed. Dread took hold of him as the dog's silhouette faded in the fog. He didn't want to be alone, and an irrational part of him thought that if he lost sight of the dog, she might disappear forever. Despite knowing his actions were against protocol, he jogged after the animal.

The mother dog perked her ears up at his company.

Newspapers swirled around Kellan's feet. He bent down and snatched up a small scrap. The article was written in logograms—characters that represented whole words and phrases—common for Asian languages. Kellan recognized a handful of the Chinese hanzi, at least the simple ones he had taught himself on the side. He regretted not learning more, if only because the pictures next to the article showcased odd pieces of machinery that made no sense out of context.

Kellan grabbed another piece of newspaper. Again, the writing was in Chinese. Why? Fayetteville had never had a substantial Chinese immigrant population. He glanced up at a street sign as he walked by. It had large white hanzi characters scrawled across the standard government green.

He turned his attention to the apartment buildings and took note of their ramshackle condition. Walls sat busted and in disrepair. Windows were boarded up. Some walls were just… free standing. The roof and other three walls had been knocked down.

No one lived in the complex. Or if they did, their presence remained hidden.

"Merry fucking Christmas," Kellan quipped.

The dog looked over and tilted her head.

Kellan let out a single laugh. "Ya know, Scrooge got three ghosts and Susan met Santa Claus. Where's my Christmas miracle, huh? I'd settle for anything other than *dystopian Christmas teaches man to appreciate modern amenities.* That's not too much to ask, is it?"

The dog continued on her way.

Kellan followed closely, shaking his head. *Here I am talking to a dog,* he thought.

The dog barked, and Kellan jumped for cover without a second thought. He slammed his back against a nearby crumbled wall, his gun readied and close to his chest. The wall, unsupported by a building or roof, acted as the perfect cover. Kellan glanced around, catching sight of the dog. He followed her gaze.

The hum of power cut through the fog.

Kellan stared in horror as a sphere of metal machinery hovered up the street, physically parting the water molecules by taking in air and ejecting it out the sides in its apparent ability to stay afloat midair. Radio antennas sprouted from the top of the metal sphere like spines, and four thick electrical cords hung limply from its underbelly—an underbelly painted with a thick black substance that contrasted harshly with the clean silver found everywhere else.

The machine-sphere was roughly the size of a motorcycle, completely suspended in the air, its electrical cords almost four feet in length.

A single camera "eye" swiveled in front, stopping only once it "caught sight of" the dog.

When Kellan stared, another box appeared in his vision—words on the surface of his eyes.

Personal Ability—Blitzkrieg Analysis

The mage has keen sight and can comprehend visual information faster than others.

The mage can see *basic* details of other magical beings and objects upon first glance without the need to spend mana.

Kellan rubbed at his face and then stared again. This time, he saw words and numbers around the ball of machinery, like a reticle on his eye had homed in on the object.

Name: Pestbyter #32
Race: Semi-Sentient Construct
Magics: Metal, Eclipse
Rank: Impossible
Armor Rating: 5
Health: 20/20
Stats: Concealed
Abilities: Concealed

"*Hello,*" the ball of machinery—the Pestbyter—said to the dog. The machine's voice, singsong in tone, sounded like a young girl with joy in her life, but it dragged on a fraction of a second too long, betraying its artificial nature. "*Who are you?*"

The mother dog barked again. And again. She ran to a nearby pile of trash, standing over it and growling with the ferocity only a mother could exhibit.

"*Stand down while scanning commences,*" the Pestbyter said.

A red wave of light swept the area up and down. Kellan pulled back behind the wall, avoiding what appeared to be LED lights scouring the nearby broken building. He didn't know if the machine had the ability to detect heat or movement, or how well it detected sound, but he knew now wasn't the time to get caught.

Did the machine have weird sight like he did? Could the machine see numbers and damage and *health*?

He needed more information—and he needed it fast.

Kellan waited, focused on observing the science-fiction monster hovering over the dog.

"*You are not authorized to be here. As punishment, your belongings will be given to the Arbiter.*"

One cord hanging from the machine tensed with life and stabbed down at the dog, piercing her head through the eye in one violent motion. The dog twitched and stumbled over, a whine escaping her throat in a long, drawn-out, breath.

The Pestbyter's other cords shot into the belly of the dog, ripping open her stomach and gathering up organs. The machine-sphere plucked each one at a time, ripping membranes from flesh in quick and efficient movements. A compartment opened on the underbelly of the sphere, and the Pestbyter stuffed each harvested organ deep within its motorcycle-sized body. The blood that splashed on its metal frame added a new coating of "paint" to the black that lingered.

Once done with the dog's body, the Pestbyter scooped up the puppies hidden in the trash and shoved them deep within its metal confines as well.

The puppies whined and barked…

But no one came.

Kellan shifted in place, his body itching, and his willpower divided with all the new information he had taken in. He accidentally scraped his boots across a broken piece of cinderblock.

"Who's there?" The Pestbyter swiveled in the air, its camera-eye zooming and focusing.

Kellan froze.

"Please reveal yourself," the Pestbyter said, its synthesized tone "sweeter" than before. "*I won't hurt you.*"

Kellan knew bullshit when he heard it.

The hum of the Pestbyter hovering remained a constant in the otherwise-silent atmosphere. The sphere didn't move, it just remained floating on the other side of the street. Kellan held his breath. At the end of a five-minute standoff, the machine-sphere turned away, floating through the fog, seemingly having given up on anyone revealing themselves.

Kellan rubbed his eyes. They weren't giving him any more information.

The Pestbyter didn't search, nor had it detected him when he sat only thirty feet away behind a plaster wall. The machine might as well have been a man in terms of capability, and Kellan knew how to deal with men.

He jumped to his feet, but he didn't know where to go.

How many of these *Pestbyters* were in the area? Who controlled them? Who had made them? What was their purpose? Who was authorized to be in the area and why was *he* here? Kellan heard his commanding officer's words ringing in his ears. *Know yourself. Know your enemy. Know victory.*

The dog gave birth and nursed her pups for a few hours at the very minimum, he reasoned. *Which means if the machine is patrolling the area, it isn't doing so often, or else it would've caught the dog long before now. I can probably move around without getting caught... at least for a few hours.*

As the sun made its long march into the sky, the fog dissipated.

Kellan turned his gaze upward, looking for anything he could climb to get a better view of the surrounding territory. He spotted a two-story building—a rundown gym with a fire escape ladder mounted to the masonry—and made his way over to it, slinking between rubble and decimated buildings. Shoving his gun in the waistband of his jeans, Kellan mounted a nearby fire escape ladder and yanked himself up.

Kellan leapt onto the gravel of the roof and instantly lost track of his previous thoughts.

The last of the fog cleared with the heat of the sun, revealing the world around him all the way to the horizon. Kellan stepped to the edge of the building, his eyes locked on the sight of Fayetteville.

Well...

Not really.

It was Fayetteville... if Fayetteville had absorbed both LA and New York City into its metropolitan area. The sprawling cityscape breathed the smoke of industry into the sky, blotting out most of the light. Skyscrapers—hundred-story skyscrapers unheard of in Fayetteville—dominated the skyline.

Kellan glanced up farther, his mind almost unable to take in everything all at once.

Zeppelin-style airships hovered overhead, red lights blinking at either end. More perplexing were the floating islands they were tethered to—chunks of rocks with buildings, trees, and grass suspended in air without any apparent machinery or technology to explain the phenomenon. The islands, large enough to be aircraft carriers, cast long shadows over the buildings far below.

The sky's wicked shade of red persisted past the dawn, no doubt the result of the lingering smog and pollution.

"I see my puppets failed," a voice from behind said.

Startled and already tense, Kellan drew his handgun and whipped around, inches from firing. He jerked his firearm to the side the moment he spotted the speaker.

A little boy, age ten at the most, stood at the other end of the roof. Had he been there the entire time? Kellan had been too preoccupied with the sight of the city—he hadn't investigated the roof before turning away from it—a rookie mistake. *I should've looked. I should've kept careful track of my surroundings.*

Kellan's eyes flashed with the same reticle that had appeared with the Pestbyter. This time, it focused in on the child.

Name: Sun Sen the Puppetmaster
Race: Human
Magics: Mind, Body, Soul
Rank: Concealed
Armor Rating: —
Health: 6/6
Stats: Concealed
Abilities: Concealed

Kellan rubbed at his eyes, trying to shake away the images. They faded after a moment.

The boy wore a long, sleek black robe meant for an adult, the bottom crumpled in a pile at his feet, but the neck—a turtleneck—fit snugly up to his chin. He lifted the bottom of his robes like a duchess lifted her dress and then crossed the roof in no real hurry.

"I shouldn't be surprised," he continued with a sneer. "But I thought you would've *at least* been incapacitated."

The actions of the Pestbyter and the people on the television left Kellan wary. He kept his hands on his weapon and took a step back when the boy drew close.

"Hello," Kellan drawled. "Where's your mother?"

"Hmpf!" the boy grunted with a huff. "What a patronizing thing to ask. Where is *your* mother?"

Kellan smirked. "You're a little precocious, aren't you?"

The boy swished his long, black hair back over his shoulder. His heritage was undeniable, but his eyes, dark and discerning, flickered with something more when catching the light. He looked Kellan up and down, his gaze lingering in a way no child's should.

"What're you doing still holding that?" the boy asked, motioning to the gun. "We both know you won't shoot a child."

Taken aback, Kellan gripped the handgun tighter. He narrowed his eyes. "You know what's going on here?"

"Of course."

"Then start explaining."

The boy let go of the bottom of his robes, allowing them to once again pool again at his feet. Then he held his arms wide. He cleared his throat. "Welcome to the Dread Nexus, where every reality meets! Every outcome and possibility, be it high-tech, war-torn, or prosperous. Every reality you could ever fathom, and the ones you can't—realities with magic, sorcerers, AIs, and witches—*every* reality converges here and forms this world."

Kellan waited and absorbed the information at a slow rate.

Was any of this real?

Did it matter? He needed the information. Whatever this was, he would have to report it all. Whenever he made it home.

The boy continued, "Enchantment and technology meet for mayhem and harmony. Those born here are natives, those who come here—people like us, people from *other* realities—are *outsiders*."

Kellan stole a glance back at the massive cityscape. Despite the distance, he could see the signs of poverty and extreme industrialization. And his thoughts returned to the machine-sphere that had eaten the dog…

This can't be real. It just can't be.

"Let's say… I believe you," Kellan said with a soft chuckle. "And let's say this is *every reality ever*. Shouldn't this place be nicer? Where are all the prosperous realities?"

"They're here."

"Help me out then. I don't see them."

The boy stared up at Kellan with a harsh edge of seriousness. "Imagine the convergence of realities is similar to mixing paints. You use whites, greens, blues—those are the prosperous colors—the prosperous realities. Then you also use browns, grays, and yellows—those are the unprosperous colors, representing the unprosperous realities. Then you stir them all together on your canvas. Do you know what happens then?"

"I'm no painter."

The boy smiled. "They turn black."

—Chapter 5—
—Tyranny Worms—

Kellan glanced back at the cityscape, his mind reeling as he grappled with his thoughts. Everything had happened so fast—what was real and what wasn't? Could everything be a dream? Was it just a series of hallucinations brought about by stress?

The smell of smog and industry burned his nose.

It all *seemed* real. And if it was, what were his plans?

"Why can I see things on my eyeballs?" Kellan asked. "What's with the boxes of information?"

"I told you," the boy replied, rolling his eyes. "This is *all* realities. Unlike yours, most realities operate with more concrete rules to their universe. The magic stems from numbers, because numbers make up everything."

"What do you mean?"

"I mean, you're made of cells. A certain number of them. And they're made of atoms. Finite numbers of atoms. Even atoms have atomic *numbers*." The boy crossed his arms and shook his head. "Listen, I don't have all day to discuss this. Let's just say—you have magic now. And magic is a little more precise than you might think."

This was all an unknown.

During Kellan's advanced training, his CO had stressed the need to gather intel in unknown situations. He had drilled it into Kellan's head so deeply they had a mnemonic: SALUTE.

Size. Discover the strength of the enemy forces.

Activity. Discover the goals of the enemy forces.

Location. Map out the territory controlled by the enemy forces.

Unit. Discover the average team configuration of enemy forces.

Time. Determine the timeframe the enemy forces are operating under.

Equipment. Discover the types of maps, sensors, and surveillance tech the enemy forces use.

Then again, if he were trapped behind enemy lines, his CO had stressed another mnemonic: SERE.

Survival.

Evasion.

Resistance.

Escape.

The basic steps to return home. And as far as Kellan was concerned, this new "black paint" dimension was filled with enemy forces, which meant he was in enemy territory. SERE would be his priority, and SALUTE would be his secondary objective. If this dimension was the size of Earth, then no location was safe. He needed to find a way out of here—to whatever paint color he had originated from—and leave all of this behind.

Kellan lowered his gun and exhaled.

"You're taking this remarkably well," the boy said with a smirk. "I knew I chose the right man."

"I'm sorry, who are you?" Kellan rubbed his temple, remembering the name *Sun Sen* that had appeared with the "basic" information. "Apparently, you know me, but last I checked, I'm not friends with many kindergarteners."

"You may call me *Sun Sen the Puppetmaster*." The little boy had a flair to his words, bordering on grandiose. "Or you may simply call me *Sen* or *The Puppetmaster*, whichever is the most appropriate custom to show respect in your culture."

Kellan snorted. "Puppets? Like, the wooden toys?"

Then he remembered the men in his apartment… *Puppet1 and Puppet2.*

"All kinds of puppets." The boy—Sen—didn't seem bothered by the question. He had answered as though his profession were one of great importance. "I bring them to life. And then control them."

Kellan wasn't sure if he could trust *Chinese-Pinocchio*, but he needed as much information as he could get and the kid was providing it, free of charge.

After a few controlled breaths, Kellan took in the surrounding territory with a critical eye. His apartment complex, once home to eighty Fort Bragg personnel, stood barren. Only his residence, separated from the others by a long crack in the ground that encircled the building, appeared habitable. Rusted barbed wire adorned a tall, brick wall that surrounded the community of apartments—a wall taller than Kellan remembered.

No matter the similarities and details, he knew the area around him wasn't his home. It mirrored his apartment complex, but it was something else. Something foreign.

Something sinister, Kellan thought, his attention caught on a stain of blood smeared across the road below.

"How did we get here?" Kellan asked, his gaze returning to the sprawling factories and collection of hovels just beyond the wall of the complex.

"I brought you here."

Kellan jerked his attention back to the boy. "*What*? Why?"

"The Conflux is upon us," Sen replied. "My sister wishes to participate in the competition, and we need one more outsider before our team will be official. You have a certain set of abilities and perks that will make you invaluable."

Kellan stared down at the boy for a long moment.

Some *child* had brought Kellan to a nightmare realm in order to participate in a competition? Now Kellan knew he wasn't insane. He wasn't creative enough to think up such a bizarre situation.

Sen sighed and rolled his eyes. "I imagined our first meeting to be quite different. I had a speech planned out… But you're not as frightened as I had expected. A pity. I had rehearsed a fine bit of theatrics."

He flipped his hair back and sighed. "No one appreciates theatrics anymore…"

Footsteps echoed around the empty and shattered buildings. Kellan tensed and lifted his Colt .45 back into the ready position. No matter what was happening—either he was insane, or it was all real—he had to be on alert, lest he fall victim to the horrors and succumb to terror.

"We don't have time for this," Kellan stated. "This place isn't safe. We should fortify a secure location and discuss everything then."

Kellan took three long steps toward the ladder.

Before he could leave, Sen cleared his throat and said, "You will go nowhere."

Kellan's legs locked mid-stride and his chest tightened with an uncomfortable pressure. Everything hurt—mildly, like a sunburn, but deep beneath the skin—and Kellan gasped in unexpected shock. Even his heart felt squeezed and strained beneath some sort of oppressive force.

What is this?

He inhaled and exhaled, his mind focusing on the tautness of his body. Nothing itched, and the squirming had ceased. After a moment of realization, Kellan turned his head and glared back at Sen, his muscles stiff and filled with knots.

"What's going on?" Kellan asked, his voice a harsh rasp.

Sen stepped closer, and Kellan pointed his gun. His torso prickled with strange sensations as he twisted himself to face the boy. Kellan's body fought against everything he did, but with great effort, he could still force himself to move.

You will go nowhere.

The boy's command echoed in Kellan's thoughts… like his muscles were screaming the words back at him.

Sen offered a smug smile. "It seems my *Tyranny Worms* have matured enough to become useful."

"You're doing this?" Kellan asked, his voice strained. "Whatever this is—*stop*."

Sen took another step closer, his confidence unfaltering. Kellan held the barrel of his .45 pointed at Sen's head, Kellan's finger gripped on the trigger. His heart pounded and his vision darkened into a tunnel. The boy was so young! Just a child and…

Heavy boots hit metal as people climbed the building's fire escape ladder.

Sen combed his glossy, black hair with his fingers and waited. "Are you fighting it?" he asked. "You will not shoot me."

Kellan couldn't move.

"Just as I thought." Sen kicked his long robes aside and stepped up next to Kellan. "You should settle into your new—"

With fast but rigid movements, Kellan wrapped his arm around Sen's neck. He lifted the child up with the hold, cutting off his air and restraining him against Kellan's chest. Sen was small—a third Kellan's size—and easily manhandled. Kellan held the choke, unwilling to let the boy speak, and then pocketed his gun.

Kellan didn't know what was going on, but he could put one and two together.

The boy had been the cause of the worms. He had admitted to taking Kellan from Fayetteville. Well, *normal* Fayetteville. He had even demonstrated some *power* over Kellan. For all intents and purposes, Sen was Kellan's enemy, even if just a child.

Kellan wouldn't allow the boy to run the situation.

"You're going to take me back," Kellan said, suffering the blows of the boy's weak kicks as he struggled. "I don't care how."

Kellan's vision failed him as searing pain flooded his body.

[Puppet1] used *Draining Touch* on [Alex Kellan] and inflicted -1 temporary fortitude loss.

The notification appeared in his mind, even if his eyes were closed.

Powerful hands yanked him backward, and Kellan lost his footing. He dropped Sen in the process.

Stand down, his body whispered. *Don't resist.*

Kellan's sight returned in time for him to spot his attackers—the two hooded men from the park—the same men who had invaded his apartment.

His stalkers.

Sen stumbled forward and rubbed the length of his neck through his oversized robes. "Ruffian," Sen said. "I don't need to speak to control my worms!"

Kellan's stalkers slammed him onto the gravel of the roof. Kellan attempted to jump to his feet, but his body wouldn't respond properly. He rolled to the side and half-stood, his movements sluggish and his skin gushing sweat.

Sen dramatically waved his arm. "Enough!"

The two "men" heeded his command and leapt away. Again, Kellan went to stand, but Sen glowered down at him.

Kellan got to one knee, but he couldn't seem to force the rest of his body up.

The boy brushed himself off and offered Kellan a glare. "It seems not all my Tyranny Worms are mature… But it's only a matter of time now. You won't be able to fight forever." He glanced over at the two stalkers and his dark eyes went wide with concern. "Look what you've done!"

Kellan stared in horror the moment he got a good look at his attackers. They had holes in their bodies—one in the chest and one in the forehead each—holes that matched the damage of a .45 bullet. Their faces were ripped and torn, the damage radiating from the gunshot holes like shattered pieces of glass, and their eyes stared off in different directions, vacant.

The men shambled close to Sen as he gingerly examined their "injuries."

Kellan saw no blood on their jeans or sweatshirts, but their inner workings were a mass of raw flesh, string, metal, and sinew.

Like… robots.

No. They really were *puppets.*

"My poor babies," Sen muttered, frowning. Then he glared at Kellan. "You've damaged them. Why couldn't you simply roll over like the others I had infested? The others gave me no trouble!" He exhaled with a huff. "*And somehow you resist my worms.* Perhaps you're *too* strong. I can't have you escaping during the competition…" Sen stroked his narrow chin. "I may have miscalculated."

Kellan couldn't offer a response. He stopped resisting and allowed himself to catch his breath. *What's wrong with me? What're these worms doing?*

"Don't worry, I'll fix you later," Sen said, patting the "puppet men" on the head and shooing them away with a motion of his hand.

The mannequins took several steps back and said nothing.

Sen turned to face Kellan, but unlike the last time, he kept himself at arm's length when he approached. "As for *you*—it's impossible to go home anytime soon. Don't bother trying to force me to take you back. It just won't work."

Kellan rubbed at his side, wondering how the worms operated. Was there a medication he could use to kill them? He knew he couldn't ask, so he decided for something Sen might actually answer. "What do you want from me?"

"I already told you," Sen said. He fussed with his oversized robes. "My sister, Lady Mage Sun Xiang, wants to win the Nexus Games, a competition held here in the Nexus once every ten years or so."

Control over Kellan's body returned in small increments. At first it was his feet, then it was hands, then his elbows. He moved and rotated as much as possible, frustrated by the disgusting parasites floating around his body.

Kellan shot the boy a glare. "So, you *infected me* with these worms in order to get me to help?"

"I didn't *infect* you," Sen said with a wave of his hand. "Tyranny Worms live in your bone, blood, and muscle, but you shouldn't fret. They're there to help you as much as they are to control you."

"What're you talking about?"

"They won't let their host die that easily," Sen replied with a smirk. He lifted his arm and stroked the crook of his elbow. "Maybe, one day, I'll let you meet the queen." A bulge appeared from under his skin—extensive and thin like a vein—reaching from his arm all the way up his shoulder and disappearing under his robes. It writhed beneath the surface, twisting, as if enjoying Sen's strokes.

Oh, fuck me.

"Don't make that face!" Sen huffed and turned away. "As long as the Tyranny Worms connect us, you'll gain access to my unique skills. Some people in your dimension might even call it *magic*, but where I'm from, that's not the term we like to use." Sen rolled his eyes like this was all one big childish game.

Kellan still found it hard to believe he was taking instructions from a kid who looked like he had to steal hair from his father's razor in order to have a beard.

"Am I ever getting back home?" Kellan asked.

"Home?" Sen lifted an eyebrow. "If you live through this competition—*and heed my commands without further incident*—then I'll send you back. You might not want to return, however. Not when you see the prize for the winners."

"Prize?"

Although Kellan had little interest in the Nexus Games, he did want as much information as possible. What prize was so valuable that it required kidnapping people and forcing them to join a team?

Kellan stared at the roof gravel. A small piece of him was reassured by the fact that they would be entering a game. Games had rules, didn't they? Once he knew what to expect, perhaps this wouldn't be so difficult. Perhaps he could find some loophole and escape the games early.

"What's the prize?" Kellan reiterated.

Sen gathered his robes up and walked over toward the ladder of the building. "If you want a full explanation of the prize, you should come with me. There will be announcements soon. All teams will have to gather at the starting point. The number of keys we'll have to retrieve will be determined once everyone has entered."

Keys?

"Wait." Kellan got to his feet and held out a hand. "How can I trust anything you say? You could be telling me anything. I don't know what you are. Even your appearance is a lie. I mean, you *look* like a little boy, but you're clearly something else. Children don't act like *this*."

Sen snorted and turned on his heel. "Perhaps we should put some of my claims to the test." He walked to the edge of the roof and pointed to the ground below. "I command you to jump off the building."

Kellan caught his breath. "What? We're more than twenty-five feet up!"

Before Sen could retort, Kellan felt himself compelled to follow through with the command. His body jerked against his stubbornness, zombie-walking to the edge. Sen only offered a smirk when Kellan glanced over. Was he enjoying his torment?

Unable to stop himself, Kellan walked to the edge and then jumped, his heart stopping for the second it took to plummet to the ground. The windows on the building flew by as the asphalt raced up to meet him.

He rolled upon impact, using his momentum to cushion the landing, but it wasn't enough. One leg slammed up into his chest, winding him. He tumbled across the unforgiving asphalt with pain radiating from his knee and thigh.

[Alex Kellan] took 5 falling damage.
[Tyranny Worms] restore [Alex Kellan] for 1 damage every 6 seconds.

Kellan rolled onto his back and stared at the red sky above, certain he had fractured a bone, perhaps cracked his sternum. It took him several minutes to realize he wasn't dead. *People have died from falls like that. What if Sen had ordered me to shoot myself?*

Kellan held back a grunt of pain as his leg twitched. But within moments, the agony subsided. With a shaky hand, he felt up his thigh. Nothing. He wasn't injured. Shock took hold of his thoughts, freezing them in place. He sat up and glanced down at his legs.

[Alex Kellan] has recovered all health.
[Tyranny Worms] return to *Infestation Mode*.

Kellan got to his feet. His legs didn't fail him.

His eyeballs—the weird messages in his mind and sight—were telling the truth. The worms really *had* saved him.

He hadn't seen Sen and his puppets get down from the roof, but they stood on the sidewalk, watching as Kellan examined his body for further injury. Kellan found nothing out of place other than his scuffed clothing.

"The worms use their own bodies to mend your flesh," Sen said from across the street. His matter-of-fact tone was like listening to a dictionary speak. "They die so that your bones and skin and muscle can be repaired nearly instantaneously. However, the more that die to keep you alive, the less there are until they breed and repopulate your body. You don't want to put them through too much stress for too long."

"What're you doing?" a man shouted.

Kellan snapped his attention to the noise, his hairs standing on end. They were in a hostile environment, why would anyone draw attention to themselves by yelling?

He readied his handgun, prepared for combat.

Then he spotted the person who had shouted.

It was… a man. At least, sort of. He was humanoid in shape, but from what Kellan could see, the man was covered in fur, like a classic werewolf. Most of the man's body was swaddled in heavy cloth, and the wolf-man wore a hood that half-covered his face, but not entirely. He had a canine-snout and long fangs, just like any frightening wolf out in the woods.

His clothing, brown and caked in dirt, rang with the clink of metal on metal as he stomped forward, though no metal adorned the outside of his outfit. He walked with a hunch, his head hanging lower than his shoulders, but even that didn't diminish his impressive height.

The fur… It was reddish-brown and poked through any holes in the cloth wraps. The man's hands had fingers, but they ended in black claws that shone with a keen point.

Again, a reticle appeared, targeting this new "man" and feeding Kellan information he wasn't sure yet what to do with.

Name: Husker Linis
Race: Rennic
Magics: Wyld, Magma
Rank: Concealed
Armor Rating: —

Health: 9/9
Stats: Concealed
Abilities: Concealed

Sen regarded the werewolf with a formal bow of his head. "Ah, Husker. You're just in time."

The wolf-man snorted and growled at the same time—an odd noise, but it was deep and threatening. "Sen. You disappoint me." Husker motioned to Kellan. "I told you not to take *this one*. He's too dangerous."

Sen shook his head. "The man is skilled, isn't he? We can't risk losing by entering a teammate we can't rely on."

"You're letting your emotions blind you. You could have flesh-sculpted one of the other warriors instead of taking *the strong-willed one* simply for his *passing resemblance* to—"

"*Enough*," Sen snapped. "You said your piece. I disagreed. I have our new warrior under control, and he won't have the option to fail us." Sen shrugged. "It's perfectly safe."

"What will your sister think?"

"She won't dwell on the matter because she won't know of the matter, do I make myself clear?" Sen glared at the wolf, even though he was a good two feet shorter. He pointed at the beast with one child-sized finger. "*Don't* tell my sister anything about our new warrior. She left me in charge of finding someone suitable, and I did just that."

Kellan hated how much louder they were becoming. He had a PTSD-style flashback to the Pestbyter patrolling the area. With his gun held close, he said, "You two should keep your voices low."

"I am not loud," Sen said as he stomped his foot on the sidewalk. "This is a commanding tone, not an argumentative one."

"Indoor voices."

Sen threw back his hair and crossed his arms. "I won't be treated like a child. I'll have you know that, despite my appearance, I'm thirty years old."

"Uh-huh. Then I'm sure your parents' Google history contains a lot of things like, *how do you abort a middle-aged baby*."

The werewolf man, Husker, chuckled at the comment, his voice gruff and low. When he straightened himself to full standing height, he was nearly nine feet, his shoulders broad and his muscles defined, even through the heavy clothing.

"He's talkative," Husker said. "That'll be fun, but your sister won't like it."

Both of Sen's puppets—the men with the weird bullet hole wounds—turned in unison. A set of soft footfalls echoed down the empty streets.

Kellan held his breath. Both Sen and Husker went silent.

"Kellan?" someone called out. "Is that you?"

Mavis stepped around the corner of a building, her eyes wide and her clothing just as dirty as Husker's. The moment she spotted Kellan, a hopeful smile graced her freckled face. She limp-ran forward, pushing through her injury until she reached his side. Up close, Kellan saw that not every fleck on her skin was a freckle—she had a fine mist of blood splattered from her elbow to her ear.

And Kellan's eyes—his *Blitzkrieg Analysis*—once again gave him information.

Name: Mavis Cartwright
Race: Human
Magics: Magma, Metal
Rank: E, E
Armor Rating: —
Health: 7/7

Stats:
Strength—2
Dexterity—3 [Accurate]
Fortitude—1 [Hobbled]
Charisma—2
Manipulation—2
Intelligence—3
Perception—4 [Mystic]
Wisdom—2
Willpower—4 [Tough]

Abilities:
Personal—[Rebuilt]—The mage can develop their physical stats (strength, dexterity, fortitude) for half the arcana cost.

Mavis shook her head and the green of her eyes mixed with the red hue of the light, creating a bright gold yellow. The purple dye in her hair looked amazing under the crimson sky.

"Mavis…"

Kellan didn't know what to say. He had almost convinced himself that she wasn't real, but now that she was here, it was almost worse. Was Mavis trapped in this world with him?

"We need to get out of here," Mavis said, grabbing Kellan's arm tightly. "This place isn't safe." The edge in her words betrayed her panic. "I don't know what's going on, but I think I'm hallucinating—see numbers over my eyes or something. Everything is different. It's not right."

"You brought *two*?" Husker asked with a growl, his fangs fully visible with his speech. "That's unacceptable, Sen. We only needed *one more.*"

Mavis got an eyeful of the werewolf man and nearly lost her skin in fright. She paled—whiter than most snow—and Kellan held her tight. Although the werewolf was intimidating, Kellan suspected he would handle bullets like Swiss cheese. *Then again, I don't have silver*, Kellan mused. *Might have to get creative.*

Although she wasn't entirely sanguine, Mavis stayed close to Kellan's side, her wide eyes fixed on the wolf-man.

Sen crossed his little arms. "That woman was a mistake. I never intended for her to accompany us."

"Are they mates?" Husker asked.

"I suppose that's a logical explanation. I figured our warrior would be alone at night during the transition to the Nexus, but I guessed wrong. He had been alone every *other* night I observed him, though."

Mavis turned away and stared up at Kellan, determination in her gaze. Without speaking, she motioned with her head to the street. She pulled his arm again. Kellan shook his head.

"I can't," he murmured.

His muscles burned with his resistance. *Stay where you are*—the instructions echoed in his mind. Kellan couldn't move his legs. Mavis furrowed her brow and shook her head.

"What's wrong?" she whispered. "Do you know those two?"

Before Kellan could answer, Husker snorted. The clinking of metal, like chains, rang out. With each odd noise, Kellan grew more nervous. How long before the machine-sphere returned? Would it rob everyone here of their organs?

Husker motioned to Mavis with his giant, clawed hands. "Sen, take care of this. Order our warrior to kill the woman. Then we'll see how much control you really have over him."

—Chapter 6—
—Pestbyter—

Kellan shoved his .45 into Mavis's hands and then pushed her away before Sen could give him any commands. "*Shoot the little boy,*" Kellan shouted, practically tripping over his words in his haste to speak.

He didn't blame Mavis for answering him with an incredulous stare. Last they were together, Kellan had raved about stalkers. Why trust his assessment of the situation when he could be a paranoid lunatic?

Sen glowered at the exchange. "Restrain the woman!" he commanded.

Kellan's body twitched into action and so did the two puppets, as though they were synchronized to Sen's commands. Kellan stepped forward, against his will, but he fought against each movement, slowing his body.

Sen said the worms died to help me heal, Kellan reasoned. *It should be easier to resist since they just mended my broken legs.*

Sure enough, he could stop himself from moving if he focused hard enough.

The other two puppets weren't resisting, however.

Mavis leapt back and held the gun with all the familiarity of a US soldier. Her expression twisted in disgust at the sight of the puppets when they drew near—the exposed wet flesh dangling out the holes of their bodies could churn even the hardest of stomachs.

She shot them both once in the head—the bang of the gun louder than the arguments Sen and Husker had been wrapped up in. When that didn't stop the puppets, Mavis shot twice more at their legs, blowing out one kneecap each.

Fantastic aim.

Kellan had to take a moment to admire that—but also took note of the fact that the damage boxes didn't appear whenever someone *else* attacked. His eyes were just… normal eyes in those situations.

The puppets fell to the ground, one leg useless, but that didn't stop them. They crawled forward, faster than Mavis had been expecting, like speedy zombies hungry for ankles. She aimed for their chests and pulled the trigger, but the gun only answered with a weak *click.*

Kellan's magazine had been half-empty when he had handed it over.

Thankfully, Mavis was a soldier at heart. She tossed the useless gun to the side and then withdrew a Ka-Bar from a hidden pocket on the inside of her jeans.

The Ka-Bar was a standard issue US Navy utility knife, seven inches of sharp steel that had never let Kellan down.

When the puppets scuttled close, Mavis stabbed down into one's neck. The knife cut through their fake flesh and inner workings. The puppet-man made a hissing noise as it grabbed her ankle. Mavis stabbed again, and that time, it was enough. The doll stopped functioning.

The second one grabbed her weak ankle and bit down.

Mavis growled a curse under her breath before whipping around and stabbing the puppet multiple times. Compared to before, her aim had worsened. She just stabbed wildly, creating puncture wounds across the mannequin's body. It still didn't take long before it stopped functioning.

"Fascinating," Husker growled. "You brought *two* warriors."

Sen huffed. "Quiet, *you*. I'll handle this." He glared at Kellan. "I said *restrain the woman*."

For some reason, the command struck Kellan hard. He lunged forward and grabbed Mavis by the shoulders. She stared up at him, her eyes wide, the Ka-Bar gripped tightly in her hand.

"Stab me," Kellan said, knowing he'd be "fixed" by the worms afterward. "And then run! You need to get out of here."

He tried to throw her to the ground—well, *he* didn't. Kellan didn't want to comply, which made the fight clumsy. Mavis's injured ankle and weak leg only added to the awkwardness. She refused to stab him, and instead, Kellan and Mavis circled around the street, each struggling to knock the other over.

"Kellan," Mavis muttered between strained pants. "What's… going on?"

Through gritted teeth, he replied, "You can't trust me. Just escape."

"I'm not… leaving you behind."

Something about the way Mavis spoke reminded Kellan of his "incident." Both Greer and Jones had been adamant about never leaving anyone behind. Just remembering the two of them… It caused Kellan to lose focus.

The worms forced him to trip Mavis and then slam her on the pavement. Winded, Kellan easily took the knife from her hand and pressed it against her throat. He then knelt on her—his knee trapping her arms against her chest.

"He's controlling you?" Mavis whispered, her gaze searching Kellan's. "Is that… Is that what's going on?"

Although Kellan couldn't nod, he could at least reply with, "Yes. You should've run."

"How is this even…?"

"You should've shot the boy when you had the chance."

"No one is shooting me," Sen said, flouncing over to his "dead" puppets. He stared at them for a long time, his lips pressed so tightly together, they had become a single white line.

Then he turned his attention to the discarded handgun. With a sneer, Sen picked it up with his forefinger and thumb, like it was something disgusting. "Didn't you say you wanted to go home? That won't be happening without *me*."

"*Finish this*," Husker stated. "We're already late, and your sister wouldn't tolerate this dithering."

Sen glowered at the handgun. "Finish what?"

"Order our warrior to kill the woman."

Kellan held his breath, mentally ready to resist whatever command Sen sent his way. He wouldn't kill Mavis. He just wouldn't.

"You think too small, Husker." Sen tucked the handgun into his gigantic robes. Somehow, the weapon disappeared into the folds of his oversized outfit. "Outsiders are commonplace during the Conflux. We don't need to kill the woman. *She's also a warrior.*"

Husker groaned. He ran a clawed hand up his long canine snout and then back down again, ruffling his red fur. "An *enemy* warrior. You don't understand. They'll be trouble for us. Mark my words."

"No, they won't." Sen turned his attention to Kellan and smiled. "Give the woman our worms."

At first, Kellan wasn't even sure what Sen was asking. Yeah, he had worms. But how was he supposed to—

His stomach twisted and lurched. Kellan grabbed at his sides, almost cutting Mavis's throat with his jerked movements. She stared up at him, her lip curling in disgust.

"Are you about to vomit?" Mavis whispered. "Please tell me you're not going to—"

Kellan wanted to apologize in advance—he really did—but his mouth went dry, and the contents of his stomach came before he knew what to do with them. Just like in the parking lot outside of *Nino's Place*, Kellan vomited up yellow worms. They spewed out his mouth like half-digested spaghetti, writhing and slithering the entire way.

They landed on Mavis's neck and collarbone, and she jerked her chin up to avoid anything getting near her mouth. It didn't matter, though. Kellan knew they had entered his body through his arm—they were definitely going to enter Mavis's body through her neck.

It was a weird day, to say the least.

"You rely too heavily on those worms," Husker said with a growl. "Don't you know the stories? They say you can't control them forever. The queen gets too big."

"Those are fairy tales!" Sen walked back to the werewolf man and patted his side like a good little puppy. "They didn't give me the title of *Puppetmaster* because I fail at controlling my puppets. This will be fine. Look." He pointed at the two puppets on the street. "She destroyed them. Those two together counted as a single teammate for the Nexus Games. Now she can take their place."

Husker pushed Sen away, almost causing him to fall to the ground. "Don't be a fool. Those *pieces of wood* you called people could've been used to set off traps or help us with puzzles. Now we've lost that advantage." He huffed and turned away, his fangs visible as he clenched his wolf-like jaw.

Kellan wished he could see more of the werewolf's face. The canine's hood remained mostly up, covering his eyes and ears. Kellan couldn't fully determine his mood outside of the werewolf's blatant anger.

After wiping the worm juice from his chin, Kellan finally regained the ability to act on his own. He stood, allowing Mavis to get up, and then tried to clean his shirt.

Mavis leapt to her feet and half-stumbled when she put weight on her weak ankle. Then she straightened herself and felt around her neck. The worms were gone—buried deep into her.

"What's going on?" she asked.

"I'll explain in a second," Kellan said as he took hold of her arm. He pulled her close and then glanced down the streets. "But there's a robot nearby. A sphere-robot. It's called a Pestbyter. It must've heard the gunfire. We've got to avoid it at all costs."

Husker's canine ears twitched. He turned to face Kellan. "You know what it's called?"

"Yeah," Kellan said. "My *eyeballs* haven't lied to me yet. If they say it's called a Pestbyter, I'm sure it is."

"You can see its name?" The werewolf's fur stood on end. He whipped his attention to Sen, his fangs bared. "*There's a Pestbyter nearby?*"

Before Sen could answer one way or the other, a terrible sound of humming filled the empty streets. Kellan's heart sank as he turned his attention to the half-ton spherical robot. It floated around a corner and turned its camera on them in an instant. The eyes glowed a sinister red.

"*You are not authorized to be here,*" the Pestbyter said, its sweet-little-girl voice disturbing Kellan to his core. "*Outsiders, and outsider mages, must present themselves to the Arbiter. All those found in restricted areas will be punished.*"

Kellan grabbed Mavis's hand and whispered, "We need to go. The damn thing is going to steal our organs."

"Wait, what?" Mavis asked.

"Trust me. We have to go."

He backed away, never taking his eyes off the enemy. Kellan didn't know what it was capable of, but his vision seemed to have some sort of magical, or technological, scanning abilities, and Kellan intended to make full use of *that*.

Husker also backed away, his head lowered, and his hackles raised. "A Pestbyter shouldn't be here."

The floating machine advanced, faster than it had moved with the dog. The hanging cords gently tapped along the ground, and Kellan briefly wondered what the machine was searching for. When it was ten feet from Kellan, the Pestbyter stopped and maintained a slow hover, stirring the papers on the ground.

Sen stepped forward. "We're here for the Nexus Games. We will present ourselves to the Arbiter as soon as our team has assembled."

"*Outsider mages are not permitted here,*" the Pestbyter said. "*As punishment, you will be eliminated.*"

The machine sphere opened itself up, as though splitting in half. It revealed a glowing red crystal, no bigger than a finger, connected to wires and mounted to the interior of the machine. The crystal pulsed in rhythm, similar to a heartbeat.

Then the machine revved. It turned to angle itself toward Kellan—and he didn't need any further warning. He shoved Mavis aside and attempted to dodge, but the Pestbyter was too accurate. A red beam—some sort of laser—shot out in an instant, power crackling from the blast as it scorched the very air.

It looked as though it would strike Kellan through the chest, but then a shimmer appeared around him. A barrier? The beam of crackling red struck him in the chest and sent him to the ground, his skin burnt enough that it smelled like BBQ. The notification that flashed across his eyes was tinted red.

> **[Sun Sen] used *Shield Ally* on [Alex Kellan], reducing the next attack's damage by 90%.**
> **[Pestbyter #32] used *Arbiter's Breath* on [Alex Kellan], dealing an automatic 50 damage.**
> **[Alex Kellan] suffers a total of 5 damage.**
> **[Tyranny Worms] restore [Alex Kellan] for 1 damage every 6 seconds.**

Kellan rolled to his side, unable to breathe. His hands shook as he attempted to stand. Everything was blurry, even when Mavis hustled over and offered her hand.

"Holy shit," she muttered, though it was hard for Kellan to hear. "What's going on?"

He glanced down at his body. A hole—more like a divot—had been carved into his chest. Writhing worms squirmed around his insides. Before his eyes, and in a matter of six seconds, the worms melted into his flesh, becoming muscle, skin, and bones like Tetris pieces falling into place and then becoming solid.

Although blood wept onto the asphalt, it wasn't long before Kellan's thoughts returned to normal. He could move again. He stood on shaky legs, his thoughts more frantic than his pounding heart.

50 damage? So far, the creature with the highest health had been the Pestbyter itself, and it only had 20.

If I hadn't had that shield—could the worms have even saved me? Can they put me back together when I'm literally nothing?

Exhaust and steam wafted off the Pestbyter. Its red crystal pulsed a little slower, and the cords hanging from the underside of the sphere grew limp.

"*As punishment, you will be eliminated,*" the Pestbyter said, its little girl voice a harsh juxtaposition to the situation.

"Wait," Sen said, his hands up. "We're participants! You shouldn't be attacking us."

Without warning, the Pestbyter shot another red laser, so bright it hurt Kellan's eyes. He shielded his gaze, fearful he'd been targeted a second time. Fortunately, he hadn't been. No notifications flashed in his mind or across his eyes.

Instead, the Pestbyter had targeted Sen.

A shimmering shield shot up in front of Sen, but the laser practically blew through his barrier and then through his little body, leaving a smoking hole the size of a quarter right through his lower torso. Sen hit the asphalt and collapsed, his arm wrapped over his stomach, covering the wound in his body.

"*Damn the eternal void*," Husker growled.

He rushed forward, using his hands as feet, like a four-legged dog. The clink of chains followed him like a second shadow. He scooped up Sen and hefted him over his massive shoulder.

The Pestbyter's red crystal dimmed. Then it descended a few inches, as though its hovering could no longer sustain its weight. The machine was losing power.

Kellan saw an opening.

"C'mon!"

He yanked Mavis and ran for the broken buildings. Husker carried Sen and followed, his movement fast due to his large size. Together, they ran into an empty alleyway between buildings. The Pestbyter fired a *third* time, damaging a corner of the apartment building in an attempt to kill them.

Kellan dodged a downpour of falling bricks, and once they had settled, he scooped Mavis up into his arms and held her close to his chest. Husker dashed ahead, easily leaping over a dumpster while keeping Sen on his shoulder the entire time. He seemed to move with superhuman strength and speed—and Kellan took note of the werewolf's stamina.

When they reached the exit of the alleyway, Husker darted to the left and made his way down the road. Kellan went right, and the moment he could duck into another alleyway, he did.

Goodbye, Puppetmaster.

The foul fog lingered in the air, making everything hazy. Kellan knew that he shouldn't run recklessly into enemy territory, but he see any other options.

He couldn't return to his apartment. Sen knew where he lived, and he could control Kellan through commands. Sen had even demonstrated the ability to control him through *thoughts* and Kellan didn't want any part of that. He'd find his own way home.

Kellan glanced at his chest. The injury was gone—all thanks to the Tyranny Worms. Mavis leaned her head on his collarbone, and he offered her a confident smile.

She returned it.

Together, they exited the alleyway and ran along a broken road toward Nexus-Fayetteville.

If this was every reality mixed together, surely someone else could return Kellan home…

He stepped up onto the broken sidewalk and then headed north, to a part of the city with a small parking lot and a landscaping business, complete with a flower shop. He still hadn't seen anyone else—no humans or *other races*. It was just him and Mavis.

Kellan wasn't sure why. Weren't there other people around?

Then he heard the terrible hum of another Pestbyter.

His heart seized up as he realized Pestbyter #32 wasn't going to be the only one.

The hovering mechanical sphere floated out from around the other side of the flower shop. Its cords hung low, and its eye camera tilted and swirled until it landed on Kellan and Mavis.

"There are more?" Mavis whispered, her grip tightening on Kellan's shirt.

"*Hello,*" the Pestbyter said, its voice the exact same as the last's. "*Who are you?*"

—Chapter 7—
—Mages—

Kellan set Mavis down and then stepped in front of her. He no longer had his handgun, or the safety of his apartment, but he knew he wasn't going to let anything happen to Mavis. In a matter of seconds, he took stock of the surroundings.

Broken sidewalk.

Cracked windows on the flower shop.

But the fog obscured his vision…

"Stay behind me," Kellan whispered. "When the machine attacks, run for it."

"Wait. I have an idea." Mavis gently squeezed the back of his shoulder. "Keep it distracted."

The landscaping business was just as cracked and messed up as Kellan's apartment complex. Unlike the complex, however, the building didn't have Chinese characters—they were English. Easy to read. The side of the building read: *OK Flowers and Gardening.*

Apparently, in some dimensions, things were just mediocre.

When Kellan focused on the Pestbyter, his eyes filled with the same information he had gathered before.

Name: Pestbyter #56
Race: Semi-Sentient Construct
Magics: Metal, Eclipse
Rank: Impossible
Armor Rating: 5
Health: 20/20
Stats: Concealed
Abilities: Concealed

Rank: Impossible?

What did that mean? Was it similar to a military rank? Did it indicate hierarchy in a structure? Authority? Capability? Command? Kellan wanted to ask, but he knew the sinister machine wasn't here for that. It was some sort of area-control device. It kept things *out* or *in.*

"*You are not authorized to be here,*" the Pestbyter said.

Kellan held up his hands. "Oh, you know what? This isn't where I parked my car. My bad."

The moment the camera eye focused solely on Kellan, Mavis pushed away from him and dove into the flower shop through the front door. It was only ten feet from her, but the awkward hobble of her gait drew attention.

The sphere of machinery hovered closer, its camera eye turning toward the shop. "*Outsider mages must present themselves to the Arbiter.*"

"Oh, right," Kellan said as he stepped forward. Then he sarcastically whapped himself on the forehead. "Completely slipped my mind. See, I was just heading there, but I got lost." Kellan stepped closer until he was mere feet from the sphere. He could see his reflection in the scarlet lens of the camera eye.

The machine didn't back away or hesitate.

It smelled of blood, and its underside was stained with blackish crimson.

"*You are not authorized to be here.*" The Pestbyter gave Kellan its full attention. "*As punishment, you will be eliminated.*"

Kellan held his breath. As soon as the sphere began to split apart and open—revealing the red crystal within—Kellan knelt and grabbed a chunk of the broken sidewalk. It felt like a brick in his hands. And as soon as the Pestbyter was fully opened, Kellan didn't hesitate.

He smashed the broken bit of sidewalk into the pulsing crystal, attempting to shatter the whole damn thing in a single blow.

[Alex Kellan] struck [Pestbyter #56] with a rock for 6 damage (3 +100% bonus for striking a vulnerable spot).
[Pestbyter #56] reduces damage of each hit equal to its armor rating of 5.
[Pestbyter #56] takes a total of 1 damage (-50% accuracy for cracked core).

Although Kellan was familiar with the notifications and information, he could put one and two together. The machines were sturdy. They didn't take all the damage they normally would—not even their "vulnerable" crystal centers.

Dammit.

A laser shot from the machine, but this time, Kellan knew what to look for. With the reflexes of a jungle cat, he leapt through the cracked window of the flower shop, shattering the glass and tumbling across the tile floor. The laser itself blasted through a part of the wall and several pots of roses.

Petals, soil, and water spilled across the floor, some of which was on fire. Kellan jumped to his feet, both dirty and wired on adrenaline. *The Pestbyters have 20 health?* Kellan glanced around and found several impromptu weapons—hoes, spades, bricks, pots—and tensed himself. *Nineteen more strikes. Maybe I can do it.*

Kellan grabbed a spade and hid behind a counter, hoping the machine would float itself inside.

Where was Mavis? He hadn't seen her in the shop. Hadn't she run inside?

The Pestbyter didn't enter the establishment. It stayed outside and fired another laser.

Kellan hit the ground and rolled into the shadowy corner of the shop. The laser carved through a portion of the front desk, destroying a vase and mangling the cash register. The laser seemed capable of ripping through stone and even partially melting steel. After just two laser shots, the entire flower shop looked like a demolition zone.

Embers wafted through the air, landing on wood and plants and slowly creating a blaze.

"*Are you still there?*" the Pestbyter asked sweetly. "*Outsider mages are not permitted here.*"

Kellan glanced at the spade in his hand and thought back to the last Pestbyter. It had gotten weaker after each shot. With a smirk, Kellan threw the spade across the flower shop. It hit a bucket of tulips, knocking them over and spilling them to the floor.

The Pestbyter shot another laser in the bucket's direction, incinerating the flowers with its powerful blast of destruction. The hum of its hovering body lessened. Kellan got to his feet. He grabbed a hoe with a long handle and then leapt over the counter. When the machine caught sight of him, the crystal pulsed again.

The laser was bright, but Kellan skillfully leapt to the side, avoiding the red beam as it once again sliced up the flower shop. With as much speed and power as he could muster, Kellan ran over and smashed the red crystal with the metal edge of the hoe.

A small fragment of the crystal broke off.

[Alex Kellan] struck [Pestbyter #56] with a hoe for 8 damage (4 +100% bonus for striking a vulnerable spot).
[Pestbyter #56] reduces damage of each hit equal to its armor rating of 5.
[Pestbyter #56] takes a total of 3 damage.

Damn, Kellan thought. *A hoe is a better weapon than I thought it would be. I need to keep that in mind.*

The crystal pulsed with a weaker luster.

"*Attacking an agent of the Arbiter is forbidden,*" the Pestbyter said—its voice no longer sweet and innocent, but mechanical and dark.

The machine's new tone startled Kellan for a split second. The Pestbyter's cords lashed out and tried to grab him, but Kellan knocked the cords away with his hoe. When the crystal pulsed again, he leapt out of the way. A *fifth* laser pierced the air, scorching the flower shop and adding to the ever-growing fire and devastation.

As Kellan stood, he realized his shirt had been singed in the process. He had almost been hit—and he suspected a single hit would be the end of him.

The Pestbyter slowed. Its laser obviously cost it a hefty toll in energy.

Before Kellan could come up with another plan, the rev of a loud and powerful engine caught his attention. A truck drove around the corner of the flower shop. It had the words *OK Flowers* written along the side—and Mavis in the driver's seat.

She only had about twenty feet worth of parking lot to gain speed, but the massive vehicle—more a tiny semi-truck—managed to accelerate at a surprising rate. Kellan had a second's notice to get out of the way. Mavis drove the vehicle straight into the sluggish Pestbyter.

The resulting impact smashed the front of the truck. The Pestbyter hit the parking lot and scraped across the ground, creating sparks. The truck dragged the machine sphere a good fifty feet, creating a line of black and white skid marks.

The truck eventually screeched to a halt, stalled by the machine under its engine.

Mavis stumbled out the driver's side and then hurried toward Kellan, her bad leg giving her trouble, but not much. She pushed through it.

The truck jostled and moved. The cords of the Pestbyter weakly thrashed.

"Are you okay?" Mavis asked once she was close.

Kellan gripped his hoe and stepped around Mavis. "It's not dead."

"We should just leave it!"

"No. It's stuck."

Kellan strode over to the truck. The fog at the edge of the parking lot swirled, as though something were in it. Kellan knew he had to end this confrontation as quickly as possible. What else was here? What other dangers were lurking in the darkness?

When he reached the smoking engine of the smashed truck, the Pestbyter lashed out with a cord. Kellan allowed the cord to grab his arm. The Pestbyter dragged him toward the ruined engine—its split-open sphere body wedged into the twisted steel.

Kellan swung with his hoe and struck the pulsing red crystal. Notifications flashed on Kellan's eyes as he hit the Pestbyter again. And again.

The crystal tried to flare to life to shoot a sixth time, but the machine's core finally shattered on the seventh swing.

The Pestbyter stopped moving. Its cord released Kellan.

While Kellan gulped down air, trying to catch his breath, his attention was drawn to the red crystal. It was shattered into multiple pieces, lying inside the machine. They glowed brighter than before and then disappeared.

Kellan gritted his teeth and gasped.

He stumbled backward, his body tingling with untold power. A new notification flashed across his eyes.

[Alex Kellan] absorbed 3 arcana.

He rubbed at his eyes, stunned by the power. It felt… so right. Like the type of satisfaction found at the end of a long workout multiplied by ten.

He dropped his hoe.

Then, when Kellan took a deep breath, a whole series of information flashed in his mind and on his eyes.

Alex Kellan
Magics: Eclipse, Body, Metal
Rank: E, E, E
Mana: 5/5
Health: 7/7
Unspent Arcana: 3
Strength—4
Dexterity—4 [Accurate]
Fortitude—3 [Tough]
Charisma—3
Manipulation—1
Intelligence—2
Perception—5 [Keen-Eyed]
Wisdom—1 [Broken]
Willpower—10 [Defiant] (Halved)

Abilities:
Personal—[Descended from Zenith]—The mage has the raw magic of Zenith in their blood and has no rank maximum. The mage can also develop one "unknowable" magic.
Personal—[Blitzkrieg Analysis]—The mage can see *basic* details of other magical beings and objects upon first glance without the need to spend mana.
Training—[Sharpshooter]—The mage adds a 50% bonus to gun damage.

Flaws:
[Greater Attachment]—The mage suffers greater from personal loss than normal. Whenever the mage loses someone close, the mage's wisdom is reduced to 1 and their willpower is temporarily halved.

Magical Skills:
None

When Kellan exhaled, the information left him. He rubbed his chest, baffled for a moment while he tried to analyze everything. Magics? Ranks? Abilities? He closed his eyes and thought everything over.

He still didn't understand what the magics and ranks meant, but now he had a better grasp of *abilities.* They were special traits that affected the person who had them.

The… mage?

"Am I a mage now?" Kellan whispered.

"What?"

Kellan flinched. Mavis stood next to him, her eyes narrowed in concentration. She gave Kellan the once over.

"Are you okay?" Mavis asked. "You weren't moving for a few seconds."

"I'm fine. Are you?"

"Well, the truck is fubar, but I'm fine."

"I keep seeing information." Kellan rubbed at his temples. "I think I'm a mage. Well, to be more accurate, *we're* mages. Whatever that means."

"Information on your eyes?" Mavis half-smiled and half-laughed. "I keep seeing it, too! Whenever I do anything, there's, like, *a narrator* who describes my every action but with numbers."

"Like a video game," Kellan muttered.

"Exactly! But it also describes things. I don't understand everything." She scratched at her arms. "It's all so strange."

Kellan nodded along with her words. "It's magic, apparently. That's how it works."

Mavis ran her hands through her dyed-purple hair. "How do you know?"

"Magic is made of numbers." Kellan chuckled and then paced in a small circle. "*Everyone knows that,*" he sarcastically muttered. "The world is numbers." He motioned to the dead Pestbyter. "Even when I was fighting that *thing*, I thought to myself... *I can kill it if I hit it a certain number of times.* Numbers. All numbers."

"Like our health."

He nodded. "Like the... *arcana* I have now? I think it's a power source. Or a building block? Not sure yet. The magic doesn't seem to care if I understand—it just provides data and seems to assume I'll know what to do with it. Like seeing the solution to an equation without seeing the equation first. The magic does the math for me, but it's not about to show its work."

"My high school teachers would be so fucking pissed," Mavis quipped.

For some reason, the joke got Kellan chuckling. Then she followed suit. But it didn't last long. Mavis's expression hardened.

"I don't understand," she whispered. "How do *you* know anything about numbers magic?"

Before Kellan could answer, more laughter echoed out over the parking lot. But it wasn't theirs.

Then the edge of the fog swirled and moved. The laughter was... cruel and cold and dark. Kellan didn't recognize it, but he knew it was trouble.

He pulled Mavis close as distant footfalls closed in on their location. They were lazy and casual—no running or hustling.

Kellan stared at the movement in the mist.

C'mon, eyes. Don't fail me now. What's going on?

Three individuals exited the fog. Men. All of them. Confident in their strides, their clothing thick with armor, and somehow biker-gang in style. Two men were normal—humans—but the third was a man with black feather wings. He walked with a slight hunch, his hands in the pockets of his jeans. It was as if the wings were so heavy, they'd affected his posture.

The first man who strode forward was tall, nearly seven feet, with a shaved head and piercings on his eyes and lower lip.

Kellan's eyes didn't need to tell him he looked like an old-world Persian thug.

But his eyes did give him another readout.

Name: Nasir Warren the Butcher
Race: Human
Magics: Entropy
Rank: B
Armor Rating: —
Health: 7/7
Stats: Concealed
Abilities: Concealed

So many things are concealed. Kellan clenched his jaw. *The only person who hasn't had information concealed was Mavis… Which is probably because she doesn't know anything about magic. And this world.*

Like me.

Kellan gripped his shirt as the men approached, his heart beating loud enough that he could barely hear the outside world.

I'm probably walking around just broadcasting my capabilities. Everyone else has taken steps to conceal themselves, probably for a good reason. I need… to fix this.

The men stopped laughing as they drew near.

The one with wings stretched them out. His wingspan was massive—nearly fifteen feet—and even if the bones were hollow, Kellan imagined they'd be heavy.

His analytical eyes told him the rest.

Name: Kin Line the Raven
Race: Niav
Magics: Storm, Wyld
Rank: B, C
Armor Rating: —
Health: 6/6
Stats: Concealed
Abilities: Concealed

Then Kellan turned his attention to the third man. He was Kellan's height, with pale skin and short, dark hair. He wore the thicker biker clothing—a metal pauldron on his shoulder, over the jacket—and boots with steel toes.

The man's right eye…

It was a machine. Like a high-definition camera but glowing in the center with a soft blue light.

When Kellan stared at the third man…

Name: Concealed
Race: Concealed
Magics: Concealed
Rank: Concealed
Armor Rating: Concealed
Health: Concealed
Stats: Concealed
Abilities: Concealed

Nothing? How is that possible? Not even his name?

The three men stopped a few feet from Kellan and Mavis, their expressions similar to sharks who had already been fed but could still fit a bit more in their stomachs. The bald man and the raven smiled widely. The last one—the nameless one with the weird eye—stared at Kellan with a disturbing intensity, his laughter gone, his eyebrows knitted.

Kellan didn't like any of this.

The bald one—Nasir—glanced at the busted Pestbyter and chuckled. "Ya know, I thought the two of you were dead the moment the Pestbyter found you." He shrugged. "But I guess you're a little more resourceful than I assumed."

"Doesn't matter, though," the winged guy—Kin—said. "Fighting a Pestbyter is against the rules. Destroying one is far worse. And the Arbiter isn't the forgiving type." When he flapped his black-feathered wings, the fog cleared away from the parking lot. "Every Justice in the city will be agitated now."

Nasir held a hand up and rubbed his fingers together. "Enough of that." He turned his dark eyes on Kellan. "I saw you gathered some arcana from the kill, didn't you?"

His tone wasn't friendly. Kellan held his breath, wondering what he could possibly say to defuse the situation. He didn't have threats, or weapons, or any robot allies. Could he outrun them? While carrying Mavis?

Kellan's silence wasn't taken well.

The corner of Nasir's lip curled upward. "What? Not gonna talk to me?" His tone switched to something softer and darker. "That's fine. We can do this the hard way if you want. I *always* prefer the hard way."

—Chapter 8—
—Arcana—

Kellan's mouth fished for words, unable to land anything. Then Mavis stepped around him, her head held high. "Aren't you human?" She glanced between Nasir and the unnamed man. "Can you help us? Please."

The bird-man flapped his wings a second time, his yellow eyes narrowed on Mavis. He said nothing, but Kellan suspected he was offended with being left out of Mavis's plight. Perhaps he had once been human? Kellan had no idea how most fantasy creatures worked.

"They're outsiders," the unnamed man said, his attention never leaving Kellan. The single glowing mechanical eye constricted and dilated, like a freakish camera lens.

It unnerved Kellan, but he never allowed his unease to show on his face.

"I know they're outsiders," Nasir growled. "Outsiders are the easy pickins." He motioned to Kellan. "You aren't going to need that arcana. You're not even gonna make it until the end of the week." With a laugh, Nasir returned his gaze to Mavis. "So maybe you two should help me… And not the other way around."

"Kellan and I just want to get home," Mavis said. "Is there some sort of arrangement we can make? Maybe you can take us to a portal? Or something similar? And we can give you whatever you want?"

Nasir snorted and then laughed once. He pulled a tin container from his pocket—something the size of his palm—and Kellan stepped around to Mavis's side, fearing an attack. Instead, Nasir withdrew a black cigarette from the container and then lit it with a built-in lighter on the side of the tin.

He tucked it all away as he took a drag on his smoke.

To Kellan's surprise, his eyes flashed with a reticle of information.

Magical Item [Consumable]—Hane Cigarette

The mage gains +2 perception and mana recovery while the hane remains in the mage's system. Highly addictive.

"What're we doin' with these two?" Kin asked. He scratched at where his wings were attached to his body. "We shouldn't take too much time. We have to register for the games."

"I want more arcana," Nasir said as he exhaled a line of smoke. Then he eyed Kellan. "I can't take you two home—that's not in my power." He cracked a smile, the smoke dangling on his lips. "You're not gonna find anyone with that ability, either. It's rare for a mage to have travel magic."

"So, you can't help us?" Mavis asked.

"No."

"Then… we'll just go."

Nasir took another long drag on his smoke. "No. You won't be doin' that, either. Either you hand over the arcana, or I'll carve it out of you." Nasir snapped his fingers and flashed Mavis a cruel smile. "But since you're *human* and I'm *human*, I'll make sure it's as painless as possible. How does that sound?"

The bird-man laughed, Nasir chortled—but not the machine-eye-guy. He remained quiet and serious.

Kellan had already made deductions about the arcana. It was used as fuel or power, and it was obviously valuable. A random man was going to kill him for it. That was always the measure of something's value: how much trouble was someone willing to endure in order to get it. And clearly, Nasir would go through a lot.

But Kellan didn't know how to give it away. And if he asked, he'd reveal his ignorance on the matter. Was that the best course of action?

"Well?" Nasir asked, his breath laced with smoke. "I'm not going to ask again."

The motto of the US Special Forces was: De Oppresso Liber. It meant *To Free the Oppressed.* Kellan thought of it whenever someone tried to manipulate him through force and fear. These punks and their low-level thug behavior angered him more than normal.

"Let's say I decided to give you my arcana," Kellan said, trying to keep his voice neutral. "How would I do that?"

He couldn't avoid asking. He had to know.

"Hold out your hand," Nasir said, smiling. "And you can make them appear in your palm. Just hand over all your arcana, and we'll *graciously* leave you alone."

The machine-eyed-punk tightened his hands into fists. He seemed tenser than before, his whole body stiff. But Kellan didn't know what to say to him.

Mavis glanced up at Kellan. For a brief moment, they stared into each other's eyes. Mavis had a look of worry—perhaps she wanted him to submit?—but Kellan couldn't bring himself to go down without a fight. He furrowed his brow, and she must've known his intentions.

Mavis stepped aside, her hands shaky.

"I'm not going to give you my arcana," Kellan said.

Nasir exhaled a mouthful of smoke. "Oh? What's that? But we're both human, right? Shouldn't you be helping me?" He chortled at his own sarcastic joke.

"I'm not just an average human." Kellan offered the man his own snide smirk. "I'm the kind who knows how to kick ass."

"What's his problem?" Kin asked, his feathers ruffled.

Nasir laughed. "What's it matter? He's a *dead man.*"

Without warning, Nasir threw a punch. Kellan leaned back, dodging the blow. For some reason, the man's hand was covered in a dark, shimmering energy. Although Kellan wasn't sure what that meant, he could take an educated guess.

It was bad.

Nasir leapt forward, his hand outstretched. Kellan stepped to the side and tripped the man. It was a simple trick he had learned during his grappling classes—using the enemy's momentum against them.

With a stumble, Nasir caught himself by grabbing on to the crumpled hood of the truck. Rust and rot spread from his fingertips, wasting the metal of the car away into fine dust.

The rot spread to the entire hood, slowly destroying everything.

Kellan caught his breath. What would he do against someone who could destroy a truck by simply *touching* it? A sudden realization struck Kellan—Nasir wasn't going to "rough him up." The man was aiming to kill him.

"Holy shit," Mavis said as he stepped away, her attention glued to the destroyed truck.

Kellan held an arm out, trying to shield her from the rot-touch bastard. He hardened himself to the reality that he might not live after an attack like that. He grabbed his hoe off the ground, hating the fact that he didn't have his sidearm.

I don't want to be in grappling range of this guy.

"Wait," the machine-eyed punk said.

Nasir stepped away from the truck. He ran a hand over his bald head, and his tongue darted out to lick some of his lip piercings. "Why should I wait, Jace? These two are pissin' me off."

The previously unnamed man—now Jace—brought an unsteady hand up to his nose and pinched at the bridge. "You're not going to believe this, but he's Alex Kellan."

Silence settled over the foggy parking lot. Then Nasir and Kin exchanged amused glances.

"It's a coincidence," Kin said. "Humans share names all the time. Parents name their children after themselves, like self-absorbed lunatics. This is just *one* Alex Kellan."

"No." Jace shook his head and then shot Kellan a hard glare. "It's not a random Alex Kellan. He has the *Descended from Zenith* ability."

The raven-man fluffed again, his beady eyes wide. Even Nasir seemed spooked, like this wasn't the information he'd wanted to hear. He gave Kellan the once over, almost in disbelief. "No. Impossible. *Him?*"

"It has to be." Jace shrugged. "That means he was probably *brought here by someone intentionally.* He's not a standard outsider whom we just stumbled across during the Conflux."

The three of them exchanged knowing looks. Kellan didn't like that. When he glanced at Mavis, she lifted an eyebrow, like he might know what was going on. Unfortunately, it seemed everyone knew more than he did. It was frustrating.

Nasir laughed, his smile wide, showing off his sharp canines. Even his molars seemed more pointed than normal. "Oh, this is amazing. I can't believe it. These Nexus Games are gonna be brutal." Nasir turned his attention to Kellan. "You're entering the games, aren't you? You have a team?"

Kellan didn't know how to answer. Sen had said something about joining a team, but Kellan wasn't excited to be a forced participant.

"I've got some friends," Kellan said, at least trying to imply that perhaps he shouldn't be messed with. "I take it the three of you are entering?" He held his hoe close, ready to strike at the man's head like a piñata if he got any closer.

"We're part of a team," Jace said, his mechanical eye still scanning Kellan. "We'll see you in the games, most definitely." Then he hesitated, holding his breath as he reached into his jean pockets. He withdrew a necklace. Kellan recognized them as dog tags.

US military dog tags.

"I apologize for Nasir's behavior," Jace muttered. He handed the dog tags over. "We didn't know it was you when we approached. Take these and… try to stay safe until you raise your rank a bit. Gather more arcana. Learn some useful magical skills. You're way too weak to be walking around alone."

Too weak?

Kellan gritted his teeth, irritated at the comment. Despite that, he liked Jace. He seemed different from the other two. With a quick motion, Kellan grabbed the dog tags and shoved them in his pocket.

"Thank you," he said.

Mavis pointed to Jace. "How do you know Kellan?"

Jace's face reddened, and then he took a step backward. "No. I don't know him." He gestured to the edge of the parking lot. "C'mon, fools. We need to see the Arbiter before the registration closes down. Let's go."

Before anyone could offer any further commentary, the three biker thugs headed out of the parking lot. Nasir and Kin whispered the entire way, chuckling as they went, amused by their own commentary. Jace glanced over his shoulder several times, his brow furrowed.

On the backs of their jackets was the same elaborate coat of arms.

They had a sword, a handgun, and a manticore stitched into the leather jackets. The words, "Win, Conquer, Execute" were stitched underneath.

Once they were gone—so deep into the fog that Kellan couldn't see them anymore—Mavis brushed off her pants. Only the smell of Nasir's black cigarette lingered.

"What was that?" she asked.

Kellan shrugged. "I don't know. Apparently, people already know me. And they think I'm going to enter the Nexus Games."

"What are the Nexus Games? *Survivor* or something? *The Hunger Games*?" She glared at him. "Are we going to have to kill each other? Because if we are, I'm out."

"It's a team competition," Kellan muttered, his gaze drifting to the asphalt as he mulled over the new information. "Mages group together to do *something* and gain keys. The prize is worth killing for, at least according to the kid."

"Keys?" Mavis crossed her arms and exhaled. "Okay. Well, the next question is: do we trust those guys? They said we wouldn't be able to find a way back. Do we keep looking for one anyway?"

Can we trust them?

Kellan reached into his pocket and withdrew the dog tags. He turned them over until he could read the information. His heart stopped for a brief moment, his hands shaky.

The tags read:

Kellan, Alex
991-93-6789
O Pos
Catholic

The random biker punk had my dog tags? Kellan stared at them, his vision tunneling. He hadn't really worn his tags since his time in the army. Once he had joined Delta Force, he hadn't needed them anymore. He wasn't supposed to wear anything that could easily identify him.

"Are those your tags?" Mavis whispered as she stared at the necklace.

Kellan only replied with a nod.

"He said he didn't know you… But he had your tags?"

Jace had been the only one whose information had been completely concealed. And he had been the only one with friendly advice. Kellan was willing to bet Jace knew more than he had said, but was it worth chasing after them?

"That guy kinda looked like you," Mavis muttered.

"No, he didn't." Kellan touched his own dark hair and thought back to Jace's appearance. "He was scrawnier than me."

"Less muscle, yeah. But otherwise…"

"What does it matter?"

Mavis shrugged. "I don't know. Maybe we should team up with them?"

Kellan didn't want to team up with men like *Nasir*.

He didn't want to team up with a kid like Sen, either.

And he still didn't know what he was going to do about the games in general. Would he really be forced to participate? Was it the only way home?

He put the dog tags on around his neck. He had missed the feeling of them.

"I think we should just do what Jace suggested," Kellan muttered. "Gather *arcana* and get stronger." He glanced over at the ruined truck. "Laser beams, rotting touch… People have some powerful skills. *We* should have some, too."

"We had to smash a Pestbyter to get arcana, apparently." Mavis twirled some of her purple hair on a finger. "But it could've easily killed us. Maybe… we could find something easier?"

"Perhaps."

Kellan hadn't obtained the arcana until the machine had stopped functioning. And Nasir had wanted to take the arcana—by killing Kellan if necessary. Which meant acquiring arcana would likely be a violent affair from start to finish. Unless there were other ways to gather it? Kellan wished someone would just answer his questions.

"Ah! There you are!"

Kellan and Mavis turned on their heels. The fog at the edge of the parking lot swirled again. This time, Husker and Sen emerged from the mist. It was easy to identify them. Sen was short and dragging his robes behind him like a child dressed up as one of his parents. And Husker was a hulking werewolf with a heavy cloak and hood.

They were the oddest of all odd couples.

Sen hurried forward, his giant ruined robes billowing outward. "What kind of fool are you?" He glowered—his child-like face scrunched in irritation. "I'll find you no matter where you go. My Tyranny Worms connect us. Now get over here, *warrior*. You'll serve me with no further incident—*or else*."

—Chapter 9—
—Get Your Bets In—

"Stop yelling," Kellan said. He motioned to the Pestbyter corpse lodged in the rotted truck. "You're going to summon more creatures to us."

Sen's eyes went wide as he drew close, his attention on the busted machine. "Harming a Pestbyter is against the rules! Look at what you've done!"

"*For the love of all that's holy.*" Kellan ran a hand down his face, silently asking whatever number-deity ruled this nightmare to give him strength. "You sound like a dead brain cell when you walk around shouting."

With a gentle graze of his fingertips, Sen touched the broken Pestbyter. Then he knelt next to the machine and stroked the bloodstained cords. *At least he's doing it in silence,* Kellan sarcastically thought to himself, though he was ultimately confused by Sen's apparent sadness. *We all need to feel bad for the murder-bots?*

Husker walked up, his tall and imposing frame difficult to miss. He sniffed at the ruined truck and then snorted. "One of you piloted this vehicle?"

Mavis replied with a nod. "I did. I drove trucks for the army. Some bigger than this."

"Hm." Then Husker turned his attention to the rotted hood. The rust had gathered in piles, and some of it flew off with the breeze. "This was done with entropy magic." Husker glanced between Mavis and Kellan. "Who did this? It wasn't either of you."

"Some mages here for the Nexus Games," Kellan replied. Then he motioned to the truck. "How can you tell what type of magic was used? I feel like that kind of information would be useful."

"Entropy is the magic of decay, loss, and death." Husker curled his lip, flashing his canine fangs. "I don't know who you met, but you shouldn't trust entropy mages. Whatever those mages said to you—ignore them."

Mavis narrowed her eyes. "Why? You have to give us a reason. Kellan and I don't know what's going on."

"Because the type of magic you develop is based on your personality—your inner soul and desires. Mages only develop entropy magic if they're monstrous and autocratic. Rogues. Pirates. Assassins. Thugs. Bullies." Husker's fur stood on end. "And the worst of all: tyrants and despots."

Kellan tried to think back to his own magics. He had seen them for a brief second—when he'd killed the Pestbyter, a whole host of numbers of information had flashed before him. What had it said? He closed his eyes, and to his surprise, the same chart appeared in his thoughts, like it had been a letter tucked away in a mental drawer, and now he had it in his hand.

Alex Kellan
Magics: Eclipse, Body, Metal
Rank: E, E, E
Mana: 5/5
Health: 7/7
Unspent Arcana: 3
Strength—4
Dexterity—4 [Accurate]
Fortitude—3 [Tough]
Charisma—3
Manipulation—1
Intelligence—2
Perception—5 [Keen-Eyed]
Wisdom—1 [Broken]
Willpower—10 [Defiant] (Halved)

Abilities:
Personal—[Descended from Zenith]—The mage has the raw magic of Zenith in their blood and has no rank maximum. The mage can also develop one "unknowable" magic.
Personal—[Blitzkrieg Analysis]—The mage can see *basic* details of other magical beings and objects upon first glance without the need to spend mana.
Training—[Sharpshooter]—The mage adds a 50% bonus to gun damage.

Flaws:
[Greater Attachment]—The mage suffers greater from personal loss than normal. Whenever the mage loses someone close, the mage's wisdom is reduced to 1 and their willpower is temporarily halved.

Magical Skills:
None

After examining the information, Kellan shook his head and dispelled the chart. When he opened his eyes again, he turned to Husker. "What about eclipse, body, and metal magics? What do those say about the mage?"

"Eclipse mages are typically solitary creatures," Husker muttered as he thought over the question. "They form few social bonds and tend to keep themselves hidden. They're the loners who develop invisibility and the like. Body mages are the type who excel at physical activity or prefer to care for others. Healers. Warriors. Athletes. And metal magic…" Husker snorted. "That's the magic of civilization, hierarchy, and technology. Individuals with a soldier's mentality typically develop metal magic. So do individuals who have an affinity for high-tech wonders." He shrugged. "I know little about technology. And care less."

Kellan wanted to protest. This almost sounded like those ridiculous *zodiac signs* he hated so much. But there was a core of truth to some of the things Husker had said. Kellan *didn't* have many bonds or relationships. He had the others of the Delta Force—and that was it. And he *did* enjoy physical activity. And… he was a soldier. His magics fit him to a T.

Which meant if he found *others* with eclipse, body, or metal magics, he would likely have things in common with them, since their personalities would be similar.

Now it was all starting to make sense.

"And entropy magic allowed that mage to destroy the truck?" Kellan asked, staring at the rust.

"That's right."

A shame. Kellan crossed his arms. *It would've been useful if I could develop that ability.*

The entire conversation, Mavis scratched at her arms, legs, and sides. Itching. Itching. Itching. Kellan recognized the first signs of the Tyranny Worms.

Sen stood and fidgeted with his ruined robes. The Pestbyter's laser had left a hole in the silk, right over his chest. Kellan had the same problem—he felt a little silly with his holey outfit, but it wasn't a pressing issue.

Sen glanced away from his clothes and then fluffed his hair. "We have a problem. We need to speak to my sister *right away*. By destroying a Pestbyter, you've put us in a dangerous situation. We'll have to answer to the Arbiter. If he… deems us criminals… we'll never be able to enter the Nexus Games."

Husker grew still and quiet.

"Who is this *Arbiter*?" Mavis asked, one hand on her hip. "He's the guy who runs the games, right?"

"Silence!" Sen flounced away, heading for the edge of the parking lot. He hurried with the agility of a child. "We must go immediately!"

Husker turned to follow. Then he glanced over his shoulder. "Stick close to us. I'm impressed two E-rank mages could handle a Pestbyter, but there are far more dangerous things around. Now that you're both part of our team, I wouldn't want to see you get hurt before the games even begin."

For a long moment, Kellan thought about protesting. He didn't want to associate with Sen, but at the same time, Husker and Sen *did* have answers to his many questions. When Mavis stepped to his side, he gave her a quick nod. *We'll just have to work around this for now. Perhaps Sen's sister won't be such a child.*

Together, Mavis and Kellan followed Sen. They entered the fog, left the parking lot, and then continued down the cracked road toward Nexus

Fayetteville. Mavis walked the slowest, but Sen's legs were so short, it didn't matter. They weren't speeding through the streets.

The closer they got to the main city, the more noises floated across the winds. Honking. Shouts. Even gunfire. Somewhere in the distance, there was a commotion. It kept Kellan on edge.

The fog cleared a bit to reveal a makeshift barricade of broken cars, barbed wire, and cement dividers. A caution sign was nailed to the barrier for good measure, which amused Kellan. At least the citizens were being honest.

Sen hurried to a narrow entrance in the barricade. There were no guards or Pestbyters to protect the entrance—it was just a gap in the barricade.

Husker entered after Sen, and Kellan stepped in third, Mavis close behind. The moment they got into the city, a terrible odor rushed over them like a foul disease. It smelled of sewage and grime. Kellan lifted his arm up and covered his nose, his eyes watering at the edges. In cases like this, he would usually use a gas mask, but he didn't have any of his equipment.

To his surprise, there were people around.

Four people huddled around a garbage can. Another four were across the street, around a fire inside an oil barrel. They wore winter clothing—scarfs, fingerless gloves, and heavy coats. It took Kellan a moment to realize some of them weren't human. One was a scrawny werewolf person—dressed in the same winter clothing as the rest of the apocalypse-hobos.

Kellan kept waiting for his eyeballs to give him information, but nothing came.

He stepped closer to Husker, narrowing his eyes. "Why aren't I getting any information?"

Husker snorted. "Probably because these people aren't mages. Divination abilities only trigger when magic is around."

While Kellan wasn't entirely sure what that entailed, he could at least deduce a couple of facts. The people here didn't have magic, which meant they were less of a threat. However, Kellan had learned the hard way that *anyone* could be a threat at any time, and he kept his guard up, never trusting the denizens of the twisted city, even when they glanced his way with fear in their eyes.

Mavis pointed to the skinny werewolf in the thick brown coat. His ears were mottled and pockmarked, as though they had been chewed.

"Do you know him?" she asked, scratching her shoulder.

Husker glanced over. "You think all rennic just know each other, is that it? We all look the same to you?"

"Well… I-I don't know. I'm sorry."

Then Husker looked away and laughed. "I'm givin' you a hard time. I know him. That's Weese. I spoke to him the first time I arrived here. He's a hane addict. Best to avoid him unless you've got something to trade."

Weese's ears stood on end, as though he had heard his name and homed in on the conversation. Kellan didn't like the desperate look in his bloodshot eyes.

A few shops along the road had large windows packed with dozens of TVs. The bars over the windows made it difficult to see the screens clearly, but Kellan didn't need many details to know what was happening.

It was the creepy news anchor. The one chained to his desk. The man with the bloody blindfold who had laughed the entire presentation earlier in the morning.

Kellan jogged over to the window, eager to hear what the anchor had to say.

Unlike last time, the news show wasn't in a grimy newsroom. The blindfolded man sat at a desk in a large studio, with several flat-screen TVs behind him, each playing footage of individuals doing *something*.

One screen showed a man skinning a deer.

Another screen displayed a woman fighting in a war.

A third screen showcased a man in a trench coat standing in front of a forest.

"Registration is almost over, ladies, gentlemen, and everything in between." The news anchor smiled widely, his perfect white teeth an odd contrast to the dimly lit—and mostly gray—studio. His hands were still cuffed to the desk, and he struggled with them, though he never commented on his confinement.

"Our high rollers will be pleased to hear that the infamous Brenner Hawke, traitor to all humanity, has added his name to the roster of competitors this year." The blindfolded news anchor motioned to the screens behind him. They all switched at the same time, showing a dozen of the same image.

A man in a powered exoskeleton suit—Brenner Hawke, Kellan assumed—walked down a narrow corridor, like someone was filming him with a tiny camera pinned to their shirt. The metal suit gave Hawke a few inches of height and completely covered him from head to toe in gray-steel armor. The suit was sleek and deadly. It looked agile, even if each step sounded like a skyscraper going for a stroll.

Whoever was filming tried to back away from the approaching power suit.

He wasn't fast enough.

With lightning speed, the man in the power suit withdrew a sword—something straight out of a science fiction movie. One side of the blade was metal, and the other side was super-heated plasma, neon red in coloration. Then the man slashed at the camera, clearly ending whoever had been holding it.

Kellan had no idea why—there was no sound to the video or any explanation attached to the action.

A few of the Nexus-hobos cheered from the other side of the street, obviously watching the news from afar and delighted with whatever had happened on screen.

Perhaps they just love violence? Kellan shook his head.

"Isn't Hawke fascinating?" the news anchor asked. "Hawke's laser sword can cut through anything." The man lifted his hand as far as the cuffs would allow, and then slammed his fist on the desk. "What I wouldn't give to be sliced in half by the legendary *Brenner Hawke*. What an honor. What a delight." He threw his head back and laughed. "I can't wait for the sweet release of death! It'll be glorious."

Kellan watched with morbid curiosity, unable to look away. Just like before, he had no idea what was going on or why such a production even existed.

The news anchor rubbed at the blood splotches on the blindfold. "Sorry, everyone. I got caught up in the moment. Let's return to the reports, shall we?" He smiled and placed his cuffed hands on the top of the rusted desk. "Over fifty teams have registered for this Nexus Games. Over twenty teams have the bare minimum of five teammates, but at least six teams have the maximum of *ten members*. So high. So risky. They'll have to get more keys—one key per member in your team. *That's the rules.* Even if a member dies, the teams of ten will need ten keys."

Again with the keys.

Kellan wasn't entirely sure why they were needed, but perhaps it didn't matter. What he could gather was: the keys were required to win the game. Every team had to gather the number of keys equal to their *starting teammates*. So, the fewer teammates, the faster a team could finish. In theory.

Kellan still had too many questions, and not enough answers.

"We have a lot of S-rank and M-rank mages this year," the news anchor said with a laugh.

The screens changed behind him, showcasing soldiers, warriors, fighters, and pilots. Kellan couldn't keep up with the information, but he saw a few creating firestorms or controlling blizzards, and a few even disappearing from sight with some sort of invisibility. They all had incredible powers—obviously magic, though some seemed technological in nature.

The anchor shook his head. "Remember to get your bets in! Everyone wants some arcana. Myself included!"

Some of the screens flashed with words and lists. Some were Chinese hanzi. Some were in Farsi. Some… Kellan didn't recognize. Finally, he found a screen displaying the information in English.

Arcana Bets

First Mage to Die—10:1
First Team to Obtain a Key—5:1
First Team to Break the Rules and Be Disqualified—4:1

Kellan didn't even read the rest of the list. He got the picture.

People were going to watch the games to bet on various things that would happen. And was arcana being used as a form of currency?

"Remember, if you lose and can't pay, the Arbiter will always accept lives," the anchor said, as though answering Kellan's unspoken question. "He loves lives! Fresh blood is the best blood, ladies and monsters."

The homeless individuals whispered among themselves. Kellan glanced over his shoulder, watching them all debate the information. Would they bet arcana? Did they even have it? Kellan would've bet against it. He'd had to kill one of the Pestbyters just to get *three* total arcana. He suspected if that was the bar, it was difficult to procure.

"Get all your bets in soon," the anchor said, nothing but overwhelming joy in his voice. "And keep an eye out for the last few teams to register! I'm told we'll be having a surprise guest."

"What're you doing?" Sen shouted from the other side of the rundown road. "We must stay together! Watch TV when we're resting!"

Kellan pulled himself away from the news report and hurried back over to the others. Mavis eyed the TV as well, her attention on the laughing figure of the news anchor.

"Careful what you take to heart from that show," Husker muttered. The clink of chains rattled every time he took a step. "The reporter, Bitso, isn't what he seems."

"I have two functioning eyes," Kellan quipped. "I can tell the man isn't right in the head."

"That's not what I meant. Bitso is *Descended from Zenith*. From what I heard, he developed one of the unknowable magics, and was punished by the Arbiter. Bitso has no loyalty to the truth, or even to reason."

Punished for developing a certain type of magic?

"I thought you said the magics were based on your personality," Kellan muttered. "So, *Bitso* didn't really have a choice, right? It was his personality?"

"The unknowable magics are different in this regard. They *must* be learned and developed. They're difficult, complex, and rare. You must have the Arbiter's blessing before you can obtain one."

"What kind of name is *Bitso*?" Mavis asked.

Husker snorted and laughed. "I ask myself a similar question that every time I hear a human's name."

The dark clouds overhead threatened to wash the street with frigid rain. Kellan and Mavis walked close together. The deeper into the city they got, the more it became an amalgamation of buildings and concepts. Some stores were broken-down buildings. Others were machine-like and futuristic, with neon lights on the sides and no windows.

Kellan spotted a robot standing outside of a door, its metallic body covered in a blackish grease. Its eyes were LEDs that shone green. It gave Kellan the once over before turning away.

More people milled about the street, but none of them activated Kellan's Blitzkrieg Analysis. He ignored most of them—they were humans in shabby clothing, all avoiding his gaze—but a couple caught his attention.

Another person with wings.

Another werewolf.

One man carried a backpack that was twice as large as his torso. It seemed filled to the brim with objects, and face masks hung off the side. One of the masks *did* activate Kellan's magic-sensitive eyes.

Magical Item [Armor]—Mischief Maker's Mask

The mage gains +2 dexterity, conceals his magics and ranks to basic divination, and resembles a certain famous character from a franchise in some other universe. It's stylish.

Kellan rubbed at his face and almost ran into Husker, who had stopped dead in his tracks. Sen stood in front of an odd building—a sandstone establishment with silk curtain doors, a brick fence around the property, and tiny circular windows. It reminded Kellan of opium dens he had seen in India, but with an odd Arabian feel.

Smoke wafted from the tiny windows at a constant rate. The people who went in and out of the place kept their heads down and hoods up.

The neon sign outside was written in Chinese hanzi—it was the only one *not* in English.

"Here we are," Sen stated. "My sister is waiting for us inside." He shot Kellan and Mavis a sneer. "You two look miserable... But we don't have any more time." He walked over and smacked both Kellan and Mavis on the side of the leg. "Straighten up. Speak clearly. Don't embarrass me in front of my sister."

Mavis grimaced at the touch and stepped away. "*Watch it.*"

"Perhaps you should speak to your sister first," Husker growled. "I'm telling you: she's not going to be happy with your choices."

"No, she'll love it." Sen stared up at Kellan, his eyes slowly narrowing. "Well... On second thought... Perhaps I'll take in our warrior, and then I'll bring up the fact that my puppets were mangled and report that we have a second warrior to take their place."

Husker grumbled something under his breath, but Kellan didn't catch it.

With a dramatic wave of his hand, Sen turned and headed for the front door of the building. "Follow me, *Alex Kellan.* It's time you meet the leader of our team—my dear sister, the Lady Mage Sun Xiang."

—Chapter 10—
—The Illusionist—

Sen walked into the bizarre establishment through the silk-curtain front door. The silk was a vibrant red, and it shimmered when it moved, like playful scarlet water.

Kellan followed after, tense in every regard. The Nexus wasn't a place of predictability, and he hated entering an unknown place without a reliable weapon or teammate. However, he wasn't ready to fight the issue, either. Now was the time for answers, and Kellan suspected the Lady Mage Sun Xiang would at least have a few.

The building smelled like a hive of hippies.

With his breath held, Kellan glanced around. The front room was decorated with soft pillows and silk. A werewolf man stood at a desk, his claws around a glass of water. His white fur highlighted his dark eyes perfectly—though some of his fur poked through his butler uniform.

The wolf-man's ears went straight when Sen and Kellan entered. "What can I do for you two?"

There weren't any chairs or tables. Just pillows. Piles of pillows in the corners like the place was meant for a giant slumber party of stoners.

"Fool, we don't have time for discussions!" Sen proclaimed as he hurried through the lobby and straight for a door marked with the stairs sign. "You will pack Sun Xiang's things *immediately*."

The white wolf snorted and laughed. "Oh. You're with the Illusionist. Right."

Then he didn't move. He just sipped some of his water, like there was no rush in the world. The place could be on fire, and this guy would still be casually drinking.

Kellan walked by, giving the man a hard stare. His eyes told him nothing.

A non-mage, then.

Kellan went to the stairs and followed Sen up to the third story. Every door was a silk curtain, and from inside the building, Kellan heard the sounds of merriment and eating. The farther he got away from the lobby, the more the place smelled like BBQ. Kellan breathed a bit easier.

With haste in his steps, Sen rushed into the third-story corridor. He hurried to a curtain door at the very end and then gestured with his short arm. "Here."

Kellan stopped at the precipice and hesitated. For some reason, he had an odd sensation flood him right before entering. Sen threw open the silk curtain and stepped inside—Kellan followed once the feeling had waned.

The small sitting room was drowning in a haze of incense.

Various plants filled the corners, stuffing an extreme amount of life into the tiny living space.

There were two more curtain doors—one to a balcony, and one to a bedroom. Kellan wondered if there was a bathroom nearby. Perhaps the Nexus was so twisted that it didn't have those.

Kellan laughed to himself at his own joke.

"Sister?" Sen called out. "I've returned with our warrior. Come see."

The curtain to the balcony rustled.

Sen turned on his heel and glared up at Kellan. His child-like face made him look like he was throwing a tiny tantrum.

"Kneel," Sen commanded.

The worms in Kellan's body writhed around at the command. The sensation of a hundred tiny creatures in his system made Kellan grimace. He could fight against them—and the command—but he decided to wait. He actually wanted to speak with Sen's sister.

Without his control, Kellan knelt on one knee.

"*Really*?" Kellan hissed under his breath. "You could've *asked*."

Sen didn't even glance at him. "Silence. My sister deserves your respect."

Before Kellan could offer up a retort, a woman opened the curtain to the balcony.

Sun Xiang was beautiful—not like a model, or an actress, but the kind of regal beauty found in an oil painting or statue. She wore a robe with sleeves too long to be practical. They fell all the way to the floor, covering her arms and hands. When she walked, her long black hair swayed with the movement, silky enough to rival her elegant robes.

The white of her outfit highlighted the inky wonder of her hair. Everything seemed thought-out and perfect—the woman could've been photoshopped.

Name: Sun Xiang the Illusionist
Race: Human
Magics: Mind, Soul, Concealed
Rank: Concealed
Armor Rating: —
Health: 7/7
Stats: Concealed
Abilities: Concealed

Xiang and Sen were related. Kellan could see it in their facial expressions.

But when her eyes landed on Kellan, she stopped mid-step.

"*Sen*," she whispered. "What have you done?"

After clearing his throat, Sen stepped forward, almost tripping over his robes.

"This is for the best, Sister. I told you I'd find a warrior worthy of us, and here he is! We just need to get him a weapon, some arcana, perhaps some armor… You'll see."

Xiang shook her head, her eyes glazing with water. Kellan slowly stood, unsure of why tension in the room was rising.

She turned away. "I can't believe you've done this."

"Aren't you pleased? I thought you'd enjoy this, truly." Sen waved at Kellan with one arm. "You know we can build him up to be powerful enough to win."

"You're a fool." She took a deep breath. "And we don't even have the time required to fix this mistake."

"It's not a mistake." Sen moved closer to his sister and offered a smile. "This is *perfect.* Trust me. Look! He has the Descended from Zenith ability. Isn't that what you wanted?"

Xiang said nothing. She kept her back to the room, her attention on the balcony that overlooked the road. A gentle breeze subtly played with her hair and kept the room cold.

"I have control of him," Sen continued, his voice becoming shaky as he continued. "He won't betray us. I used our father's Tyranny Worms. See? He can't leave us now."

"Sen."

He froze, obviously caught off guard by his sister's icy tone. "Y-Yes?"

"Leave us."

Sen rubbed at his arms. For a prolonged moment, he did nothing. Then he glanced up at Kellan, offered him a glower, and turned for the curtain door. He dragged his feet as he went, glancing at his sister like he might say something.

He never did.

Sen pushed his way out of the curtains and into the hall. After another few moments—where Kellan listened to Sen's distant footfalls—Xiang finally turned back around.

"Kids, am I right?" Kellan quipped.

But then he caught his breath.

Xiang wiped a stream of tears from her elegant face, her sleeves soaking up all the water on her cheek. Once she had rubbed at her eyes, she walked farther into the room, circling around Kellan. Along the way, she touched the leaves of the plants, her hands never emerging from her outfit.

When Xiang stopped, she met Kellan's gaze, her eyes still red but no longer crying.

"I apologize," Xiang said, her voice graceful and confident. "My brother can be insensitive. I think he's flesh-crafted himself too many times. All that changing of his shape and appearance has messed with his thoughts and affected his common sense."

"I don't think I know what's going on," Kellan said as he crossed his arms.

"Sen never should've brought you here."

"We can agree on that."

Xiang studied his facial expression. Her eyes became glassy a second time, but she looked away and took a deep breath. "I should… apologize once again. That emotional outburst earlier was unbecoming of me. You must be confused and frightened. This world is new to you. Allow me to introduce myself."

"You're Sun Xiang the Illusionist," Kellan said. He sarcastically motioned to his face. "My eyeballs told me all about you."

She nodded once. "You have a keen perception, and your personal ability allows you to know the details of magical people and objects." Xiang held her wrist to her chin, her sleeves hanging low, as she thought of something. "How has your stay in the Nexus been so far?"

Kellan couldn't help but chuckle. "My experience? I feel like my default emotion has been, *What the hell is going on?* Followed closely by, *Oh no, not again.* A person can only take so much O-face before their jaw gets tired, if you catch my drift."

"I see. And has my brother… Has he been good to you?"

Good to me? Kellan had to think over the question for a long moment.

"Your brother seems to have enslaved me for the purposes of playing a deadly game," Kellan said, unable to keep his sardonic tone out of his words. "I don't know what messed-up reality you come from, but where *I'm* from, that's not appreciated."

Xiang tightened her jaw and glanced away.

With a wave of her sleeve, the plants in the room vanished. All of them. And then the curtain over the balcony—and the curtain for the other door. The room was barren. Devoid of all furniture and welcoming warmth.

Kellan flinched and glanced around, taken aback by the sudden change in their surroundings.

"I will speak with my brother," Xiang muttered, her gaze vacant as she stared at the distant wall. "Again, I apologize for what he's done. He never should've dragged you into our affairs. I never wanted this."

Kellan's eyebrows went to his hairline as he examined the empty room. There was nothing around them. Nothing. "Let me guess. Everything was an illusion? That's how you got that fancy title of yours?"

"In a word, yes."

"Look, I don't care about your brother's lack of common sense, or the games he wants to play, or how crazy this world is." Kellan rubbed at the hole in his shirt. "I just want to go home. Send me and Mavis back, and I'll chalk this all up to a fever dream and never think about it ever again."

Xiang closed her eyes and exhaled.

When she didn't say anything, Kellan lifted an eyebrow. "What's wrong? I know you or your brother can do it. He said you had the capability."

"*I* have the capability." Xiang turned to him. "But please reconsider."

Kellan half smiled. "Reconsider staying?" He motioned to the balcony. "I don't know if you're aware, but there are murder-robots floating around the streets ready to beam a fool down just for existing. It's not really my kind of place."

"We need your help for the Nexus Games."

"I'm sure you can find someone else."

"I *could* find people," Xiang said matter-of-factly. "But I need talented individuals if I'm to have any hope of winning the games."

Kellan forced a quick sigh. "What's the prize? *Ten bajillion space-dollars*? Or whatever you people use for currency? Arcana? A medal that cures cancer? It better goddamn blow my mind if it's worth all this insanity."

"The prize is access to Zenith."

Kellan waited for her to follow that up with an explanation. When she didn't, he rotated his hand around in a circle, urging her to continue.

"Zenith is a dimension unlike any other," Xiang said with an amused smile. "Everyone who goes there is filled with magic beyond compare. It's a wonderland of arcana, resources, longevity, technology, and prosperity. It is literally *perfect*."

"So, you're going to compete in the Nexus Games so you can win a weekend getaway to a resort dimension?" Kellan scoffed and then shrugged. "I'm not buying it."

With a slight hint of anger, Xiang stepped up to Kellan, her eyes narrowed. "This isn't about power or seeing Zenith with my own eyes. This is about the people who are there."

Kellan held his breath, both angered and intrigued. "People?"

"Ten years ago, my mother won the Nexus Games," Xiang stated. She took a breath, and then continued with, "She was supposed to send me magical resources from Zenith so that I could use them to fix our nation—a land being ravaged by corruption—but she never contacted me. I fear… something is wrong. I must find my mother, and the only way to do that is to get to Zenith myself."

"Your mom might be too busy enjoying herself," Kellan said with a shrug.

Xiang moved away from him, her demeanor once again calm.

"My mother would never abandon her people. The only reason she entered the Nexus Games was to get to Zenith and find a solution for our suffering." Xiang held a hand to her chest. "I have to find her. If I don't… my homeland will crumble. It's already on the verge of collapse. Not from politicians or mismanagement. It's from a hex. A type of corrupted magic." She shook her head and turned away. "I know… you know nothing of magic. But please believe me. Hexes are the worst form of magic. They're a rot that festers from the inside and destroys everything you love."

"There's no other way to deal with hexes?" Kellan asked.

Xiang shook her head. "No. Once they've formed, they're like a cancer that will never relent. Husker understands. That's why he agreed to help me."

Kellan crossed his arms and then uncrossed them, uncertain of what to do. Xiang was right—he didn't know anything about hexes, or why they were so terrible. He didn't know anything about Xiang's homeland, either.

He understood patriotism, though. And wanting to protect things that mattered to him.

At least on those topics, he felt sympathy.

"Let me get everything straight," Kellan said, one hand up. "You want to compete in these games so that you can find your mother and save your homeland."

Xiang met his gaze and slowly nodded.

"You need *my* help because you're out of time and options."

Again, she nodded.

"And if you *don't* succeed, your homeland will crumble, and you'll never see your mother ever again?"

"Correct," she said. Before Kellan could say anything more, Xiang added, "And if you help me win, *you'll* also gain access to Zenith. You'd become more powerful than you've ever imagined. The magic of Zenith flows so freely, it empowers all who live there. They become immortal."

Immortality?

The more Kellan heard, the more Kellan became suspicious. A perfect dimension where everyone lived forever as a powerful wizard? Seemed too good to be true. Then again, robots that stole the organs of dogs was never something Kellan had thought would happen, so perhaps anything was possible.

"I don't care about the immortality," Kellan stated. "But I suppose power wouldn't hurt in this situation." Anything to avoid being rotted into dust, like the truck.

"Then you'll help me?" The hope in Xiang's voice cut Kellan deep.

Kellan rubbed at his jaw. "Listen—what makes you think we'll win? Mavis and I were dragged here against our will. We don't know what's going on. You want a team where forty percent of the members are clueless?"

"That can be fixed with time and explanation. It's your potential that…" Xiang shook her head. "It's your potential that *Sen* thought would be an asset to us."

"Sen is trying to control us with worms." Kellan tensed, trying to keep the conversation civil. "If he really wants us for potential, he wouldn't have us in metaphorical chains."

Forcing people into servitude was always a recipe for disaster. Drafting soldiers typically resulted in deserters, mutinies, and insubordination, but soldiers who freely joined were typically more loyal and resourceful.

"Tell Sen to remove the worms," Kellan demanded.

Xiang frowned. "Sen is afraid you'll betray us if he has no means to control you. And not just in the voluntary sense—there are several magical means to control someone, but if Sen maintains hooks, he can always bring you back."

Nothing about that explanation eased Kellan's worries—if anything, it made them worse. The enemy could control people? Were there other puppet masters?

"I will try to find a way to free you of the infestation," Xiang said. "For this, you have my word."

Kellan sighed and nodded once. "All right."

"In the meantime, your magics can be grown with more arcana, and with enough power, you can remove any obstacle in your way."

"And that makes you think we have a chance to win the Nexus Games?" Kellan had no idea what was required of the games. Physical tasks? Magical ones?

Getting a rose from a potential significant other? What were the obstacles of this hyper-magical reality show?

"I think we'll win because you're not the only one with potential."

Xiang once again waved her hand.

But instead of flowers appearing around them, the entire room vanished. Kellan no longer stood in a dinky room of an opium den. He stood at the edge of a cliff overlooking a dozen waterfalls.

The rush of the water, the mist in the air, the scent of forest and pine—it all assaulted him at once.

Kellan stumbled backward and almost tripped on a rock. He glanced around, his heart racing. Where were they? Rainbows filled the waterfalls, a trick of the light. The brilliant sun, shining overhead, made everything vibrant and wonderful.

Birds… herons, specifically… flew overhead in beautiful V formations.

As far as Kellan was concerned, he and Xiang were out in the vast wilderness, all alone. When he glanced over at her, she smiled and laughed into her sleeve.

"What's so funny?"

"You're always so tense," she said, more jovial than she had been before.

"Oh? You talk like you know me."

Xiang's smile dropped. In a serious tone, she said, "We've never met before. I've just… known someone who is similar. I apologize. I shouldn't act as though I'm familiar with your mannerisms."

She held out her hand. "Let me show you something."

Kellan brushed off his clothing. The water from the falls irritated his nose. He stepped over the rocks with careful precision and then placed his hand on Xiang's. Her palm was soft, and her fingers delicate.

"Okay," Kellan muttered.

Xiang closed her eyes, and information was sent to Kellan's thoughts, in a manner similar to when his eyes activated.

Sun Xiang's Abilities:

Personal—[Descended from Zenith]—The mage has the raw magic of Zenith in their blood and has no rank maximum. The mage can also develop one "unknowable" magic.

Personal—[Master Manipulator]—The mage is a master of manipulation and trickery. Their illusions are always considered 5 ranks higher (even beyond maximums) in order to avoid detection and divination.

Kellan ripped his hand away from her. For some reason, seeing her abilities… It made him feel slimy. Like he had touched something he shouldn't have. Or that something was…

It wasn't right.

"Well?" Xiang asked. "You saw it, didn't you?" She waved her hands at their surroundings. "That's why your Blitzkrieg Analysis didn't activate when I created our false environment. My illusions are beyond compare."

Kellan slowly nodded along with her words, his attention on the rainbows and birds. He really couldn't see the difference. Even the scents seemed real.

He didn't know *how to compare* this ability to *normal* illusions, but if Xiang—who was familiar with this world and its rules—was confident, Kellan suspected she knew best.

"With my brother's ability to alter flesh and control people, and Husker's raw talent for destruction… I think we stand a good chance of acquiring the keys we need." Xiang threw her hair over her shoulder and smiled. "Please. Help me."

Her beauty seemed more suspect to Kellan now that he knew the truth. Was Xiang even showing her true self? It made him wonder.

But he didn't really care.

If what she had said about her mother and nation was true, Kellan wanted to help. It was his default setting, deep in his core.

And although he didn't know *all* the aspects and rules of the Nexus Games, he did know a few harsh facts. First off, he needed Sen or Xiang to get back to his home dimension. Secondly, if he refused to help, they could just force him regardless, due to the Tyranny Worms. And lastly, if he wanted any chance at all to gain their trust—and ultimately learn everything about this twisted dimension and its people—he couldn't fight against them too hard now that he was neck-deep in their business.

Kellan sighed. "All right. Fine. I'll help you."

—Chapter 11—
—Eyes of the Arbiter—

"Thank you," Xiang said, her expression softening.

With a twirl of her hand, the illusions melted away. The room returned to its original appearance—green plants in every corner. A pleasant aroma of flowers. No one would ever suspect that the room was actually a drab, empty space devoid of decoration.

Kellan glanced around, still amazed by the detail of Xiang's illusions. "And once we win, if Mavis and I want to return to our dimension, you'll take us there, right? We don't have to accompany you to Zenith?"

She nodded. "But I don't understand why you would avoid it. Whatever life you had before, you can have a better one in Zenith."

"Yeah, but maybe I *liked* my life before." Kellan felt the depression in his own voice. Had he really been happy? "Mavis needs the choice, too. I don't want to decide anything for her."

Xiang lifted a perfect eyebrow. "To be honest, I'm not entirely sure who *Mavis* is. I'll have to discuss this all with my brother." She stepped away from him, her long white robes flowing with her movements. "And… I need some time to process everything. Please speak to Sen about acquiring arcana. You should have some abilities before we enter into the games, and we don't have much time left."

"Wait," Kellan said. "I have a couple of questions."

Xiang stopped near the balcony curtain, but she said nothing. In silence, she waited.

"I killed a Pestbyter, and Sen seemed to think that was the wrong move. What's going to happen?"

"We'll need to avoid the Justices until we can speak to the Arbiter himself. Destroying one of his creations is a crime that only he can absolve you of. It'll make our trek to the AVU Palace difficult, but I'll handle it."

"Okay. And who is the Arbiter?"

"An ancient and powerful mage who has ruled the Nexus since history has been recorded here. He is, perhaps, part of the dimension itself."

That didn't help Kellan as much as he had hoped it would.

"What is a *mage*, exactly?" he asked.

"An individual with a soul who is capable of improving their magic." Xiang combed her fingers through her inky hair. "You are a mage. I'm a mage. Husker is a mage. But the Pestbyters are not. They are semi-sentient constructs, incapable of improving their magic and completely devoid of a soul."

"How did I become a mage?"

"Crossing into the Nexus," Xiang answered matter-of-factly. "There's a percentage chance every time a soul crosses from one dimension to the other. One percent, the soul perishes. Eighty percent, the soul is touched by the Sea of Chaos and is granted magic. A nineteen percent chance the soul is granted lesser magical powers—they become a half-mage or something weaker."

Kellan almost laughed. There were hard percentage numbers for when someone was granted magic? Was the *Sea of Chaos* an ancient algebra teacher who wanted the chance to say, *I told you that this would be important! But did you listen? No!*

"Wait." Kellan could barely contain his anger. "There's a one percent chance someone *dies* when they jump between dimensions?"

Xiang nodded. Then she glanced over her shoulder. "Does that upset you?"

The reckless disregard for his life bothered him, but Kellan wasn't sure how angry he could get now. Sen had risked Kellan's life. It hadn't been a huge risk, but it had still been a risk.

"Can you just tell Sen to stop controlling me and Mavis? That way we can attempt to work together?" Kellan wanted that more than anything. The Delta Force wasn't a team made up of nine talented individuals and one imprisoned enemy soldier. The Special Forces units only worked because they all trusted each other.

"Please," Xiang said, fatigue in her voice. She looked away from him, her brow furrowed. "I need time. I told you I'd speak with my brother, but now… isn't the right moment." She held on to the silk curtain. "If you could give me some space… I would appreciate that."

After a short sigh, Kellan muttered agreement and then left the room. He stepped into the hall and turned to the right, only to almost trip over Sen. Kellan stopped and stared down at the kid, wondering when Sen had wandered back, and how much of the conversation he had overheard.

Without a word, Sen hurried down the hall, his expression neutral. Kellan followed, but the same feeling of tension returned. Something was wrong between the two siblings, though Kellan wasn't sure what. And it was obvious to him that the sister hadn't wanted Kellan around.

For some reason.

"Xiang seemed upset by my presence," Kellan said as they reached the staircase. "I think she was crying."

Sen stutter-stepped to a halt. He waited at the edge of the first step, not moving. Then he inhaled and continued on his way. "You needn't worry about that. I will speak with my sister. She's just had a rough time lately. *Nothing to dwell on.*"

"Okay, well… Xiang said you would teach me about magical abilities." Kellan followed after Sen. "She mentioned arcana. That is how I develop magic, isn't it?

Arcana?"

Sen huffed as he took the steps one at a time, his legs short and his enthusiasm less than before. "Arcana is the crystalized form of someone's essence—their *soul*, if you will."

The information stopped Kellan in his tracks. "Wait," he said, desperate to understand. "I found arcana in the Pestbyter. Xiang just said it was a construct. It had no soul."

Sen chuckled. He stopped on a step, turned around, and smiled. "Oh, you're so young." He straightened his robes. "The Pestbyter is capable of moving because of the power of the arcana. Think of it like a battery. The Arbiter made toys—the Pestbyters—and then powered them with the arcana."

"The souls of… other people?"

"That's right."

"And that doesn't disturb you?" Kellan asked with a single laugh.

Sen shook his head. "Of course not." Then he turned back around and headed down the stairs. "Reality is harsh, and the strongest rule. The dead don't need magic power—and once their arcana is gone, they're done forever."

Kellan listened, but the cold way Sen spoke rubbed him the wrong way. Kellan had never handled death well—that was what his therapist had said, anyway.

And apparently, that's what the magic says as well, Kellan thought with a chuckle. Apparently, he had a "flaw" which showed up any time he "examined" his own magical numbers. What had it said?

Kellan closed his eyes as they went down the last of the stairs, his nose filled with the thick smoke of the hippie den.

His flaw…

> **[Greater Attachment]—**The mage suffers greater from personal loss than normal. Whenever the mage loses someone close, the mage's wisdom is reduced to 1 and their willpower is temporarily halved.

"What is the number next to my wisdom on my… on my magic stats?" Kellan asked as they entered the entrance room of the building.

The white wolf butler-man at the front counter gave Kellan and Sen a brief glance. "Lucky blessings, mages."

"Good day," Kellan awkwardly muttered, unaccustomed to the awkward phrase.

Sen didn't even bother answering the man. He waved a short arm and said, "Your wisdom score is a representation of how well you make decisions or snap judgments in dire situations. The higher a mage's wisdom, the more they can resist stress, heat-of-the-moment violence, and impulsive self-gratification." Sen clapped his hands together once. "It also represents their long-term planning, and it's the skill used for long-term magical abilities."

Again, Kellan wanted to protest, but the more he thought about it, the more that made sense. His wisdom score was a one—likely due to Greer's and Jones's deaths—and ever since then, Kellan had felt lethargic and prone to self-destructive decisions. Like drinking excessively. Staying away from the rest of his family.

Sen threw open the front curtain and strode out into the gloomy weather of the Nexus. The sky was tinted red, and the fog had migrated upward, like a low-hanging cloud or a patch of smog. Noise from the busy city bounced between buildings, creating a song of civilization.

Husker and Mavis waited out on the sidewalk, deep in conversation. They didn't stop until Kellan and Sen drew close, and even then, it was reluctantly.

Mavis offered Kellan a smile, and he suspected she was okay.

"What did your sister say?" Husker asked, his voice a growl.

"She was upset," Sen said matter-of-factly. "But she seems better now. Our warrior has agreed not to fight against us anymore. He's part of our team."

"Really?" Mavis turned to Kellan, her purple hair fluttering in the breeze that rushed down the road. "You want to stay here? *In this place*?"

"I don't *want* to stay here." Kellan sighed. "It's a little complicated. Apparently, Sen and his sister need help. They want to see their mother and help their nation."

Husker slowly turned his attention to Sen, his lip curled downward. The little boy said nothing in response.

"We can talk about this on the way to our destination," Sen said. He threw his arms out to the side and dramatically stepped onto the black asphalt of the cracked street. "I will summon transportation."

Kellan held his breath.

How did someone *summon* transportation? Would there be a magical circle that appeared on the ground, like when someone summoned a demon in a movie? Would the space-time continuum open and reveal a twisted chariot? Kellan's imagination ran wild, thinking up the craziest possible situations.

Instead, the sound of tire streaks came from a distant road. A limo turned around the corner and headed to their location. The vehicle slowed and then came to a stop in front of Sen. The tinted windows prevented Kellan from seeing inside—but once he got close, he didn't want to see the inside. The limo was scuffed and rusted at points, like it had just escaped an impound.

That was it? No demon? No carriage pulled by unicorns? It was just a rusty limousine?

Kellan really didn't understand the Nexus.

Sen smiled. "Ah, this is the way to travel."

"You can't be serious," Husker growled. He turned and tugged at the hood of his cloak. "We can't take this. The Arbiter won't allow it."

"I doubt he'll prevent us from using his transportation."

"Heh. Then test it. Have our warrior step inside."

Sen huffed, tossed back his long black hair, and shuffled over to the limo's back door. He opened it up and then waited. With a tight turn on his heel, he faced Kellan. "Would you do me the honor of sitting inside?"

"Why?" Kellan asked, glancing between Husker and Sen. "What's going to happen?"

"The Eyes of the Arbiter are going to get upset," Husker drawled.

Kellan crossed his arms.

"It might not," Sen said. "We should try it, at the very least."

With a sigh, Kellan decided to give it a try. He took a seat in the limo. The inside was alive with neon green and pink lights, like the limo had been designed in the 80s. If the driver turned out to have huge puffed-up hair that reached the roof, Kellan wouldn't have been surprised.

But then an eyeball opened on the roof of the limo—straight out of the fabric and nearly the size of a golf ball.

Kellan tensed, his gaze on the eye that never looked away, never even blinked. The eye was fleshy and clear, but also machine-like. The camera at the center constricted and dilated, focusing on Kellan.

Information rushed to Kellan through his magical senses.

Magical Item [Semi-Sentient]—Eyes of the Arbiter

An observation tool used by the Arbiter to keep tabs on the citizens of the Nexus. They appear across surfaces with electronic components. Can see through moderate levels of obfuscation. It's rather creepy.

"The eyes are here," Kellan muttered, unable to look away. "Now what?"

Husker snorted. "Get out of the vehicle."

But then the eye on the roof of the limo closed with a wet *click*. The roof returned to its normal state—fabric and half-ripped. Kellan held his breath, unsure where the eye had gone to. Could it move? Or was it just under the fabric? He reached his hand up, his fingers trembling as he went to touch it.

Then a clicking sound unnerved him. *Click, click, click.* He had heard it before.

An igniter.

Kellan's heart stopped for the split second it took him to leap out of the limo. He managed to roll out of the limo *right before* the entire inside was flooded with flames. The seats burned, the floorboards caught fire, and the entire vehicle looked like a crematory for a short six seconds.

Sen held up an arm to shield his eyes.

Mavis just stared, dumbfounded.

But none of this seemed to surprise Husker. He laughed for a moment and then sighed.

With shaky limbs, Kellan got to his feet.

Sen exhaled. His irritation was comically apparent. "Very well, we *won't* take the Arbiter's transportation." He waved his arm, and the limo took off down the road, its insides still alight with fire. "We'll have to hurry, then. We'll head to the outskirts of the city and search for a yami."

"What's a yami?" Mavis asked, rubbing at her arms. "Is it as bad as random eyes trying to kill us?"

"Yami are monsters born of corrupted magic," Husker replied. "If you kill the big ones, you can harvest their insides for small amounts of arcana." He shifted a bit, his chains rattling. "Since our warrior already has some arcana, we'll only need to strike down one or two in order to get him enough to develop some magical abilities."

"What about me?" Mavis turned to the werewolf creature. "You said I was talented enough to develop magic, and that I should."

"Hm. You are, but if we manage to arrive at the AVU Palace without much difficulty, we can get easier—and more plentiful—arcana. It would be the safer route to ensure you're not harmed further."

Mavis nodded along with his words. "All right. That sounds reasonable."

"Since when did you two become friends?" Kellan quipped.

She shrugged. "He's rational. I like him."

"He suggested that Sen order me to kill you. You remember that? When we all first met?"

"It was a precaution," Husker said before Mavis could respond. "If you weren't under our control, it could spell disaster for us all."

That wasn't the best explanation.

But apparently, Husker was on their team—and if Kellan was going to help them win, he'd have to get along with the werewolf-man.

Sen hurried down the road, toward the edge of the city, and back to the barricade. "Come. I know a place where yami dwell. Those odd panthers who stalk the darkness. They will provide us with the necessary arcana to give our warrior an advantage in battle."

—Chapter 12—
—Magical Abilities—

Kellan didn't see much of their surroundings as they left the barricade. The hane-addicted hobos of the fringe society gave him odd looks, but their gazes never lingered long. Kellan wasn't the type of man most considered mugging.

The TVs weren't alive this time. The screens remained dead as they walked by.

But there was a pulse to the city that Kellan hadn't felt before. Like a steady current of electricity was shooting through the cement. That was insane—he knew that wasn't how conductivity operated—but it was hard to describe.

It was like the city was alive.

Once beyond the barricade, Sen stopped walking. The harsh winds blew by, and above their heads, a giant Zeppelin flew into the city at a slow and steady rate. The giant airship cast a long shadow, and Kellan held a hand over his eyes to get a better look at the ship.

"What's that?" he asked.

"Another last-minute team," Husker replied with a sigh. "We're going to have a lot of competition."

Mavis held her long hair back in one hand. "Damn. How many teams are there going to be?"

"I suspect close to a hundred."

Which means at least 500 people, if each team has to have a minimum of five members. Kellan found it harder and harder to believe that their team would succeed. *If everyone here knows what's going on, they'll have the advantage.*

The Zeppelin continued overhead, the entire airship nearly 800 feet long. It casually entered the city, the sound of the engines reverberating off the skyscrapers of the twisted Fayetteville.

"So, do we have any equipment?" Kellan asked, acutely aware he didn't have his sidearm anymore.

Husker tugged at his hood. "Equipment?"

"Gas masks? Weapons? Body armor? Vehicles of our own? Boots?" Kellan circled his hand. "Something that will give us an edge?"

"We have Xiang. Her illusions are second to none."

"That's not going to save us in every situation, will it?"

Perhaps it would? But Kellan didn't like being unprepared. His CO would've ripped him a new asshole if he had thought he could go into enemy territory without having some sort of backup plan or tools with which to escape an untenable situation.

Sen slowly exhaled. "We can get equipment… Normally, I just order my puppets to do that."

"Don't command Kellan to do anything," Mavis snapped. "Explain it to us."

"I'll try," Sen drawled. "It's not normally my style, but since you are both *teammates—*" he used air quotes for the word, "—I'll try to remember you're not my creations."

Kellan waved away the comment. "Where do we get equipment? I'm interested. Please tell us."

"Well, my sister gathered several locations of interest for us." Sen reached into his oversized robes and withdrew a piece of paper. The tiny print on the page was more Chinese hanzi. Sen read from the page. "There are places in the Nexus where things *come over* from other dimensions. My sister knows how to find these worm holes, if you will."

"Okay. And what comes through to the Nexus?"

"People, objects, buildings." Sen glared at the paper. "What we need to do is head to the closest location with—" He stopped himself mid-sentence. Then a smile crept onto his face. "No. I found something. We'll get you *Sevriss.*"

"No," Husker growled. He lowered himself onto his hands and stood like a wolf. Now that his eyes were closer to Sen's, he glared at the child. "Not that. You've already taken too many risks. Let's find something easy—nothing magical—and get back to Xiang."

Sen scoffed as he stuffed the paper into his robes. "Your inability to take risks is why you're hexed, Husker. Let me and my sister do all the decision-making." He waved him aside and then walked off the road and onto the scrublands just outside Nexus-Fayetteville.

Then Sen hurried out toward a grouping of trees in the far distance, far from the buildings and roads. It looked like abandoned woodland—the kind of place where someone would film a horror movie—and Kellan already felt his muscles growing tense.

Once Sen was out of earshot, Husker stood back on two legs. "Be careful," he whispered. "There are some dimensions so distorted by violence and power that even one of their simple teacups can lead to downfall and despair."

Mavis couldn't stop herself from laughing once. "I guess that's our new destination, huh? *Land of deadly teacups*?" She offered Kellan a smirk. "I can't wait to see you deal with that."

***

The "wilderness" around Fayetteville was a mix of an abandoned mobile home park and a haunted forest. Trees were scattered around everywhere, including jutting through mobile homes, right in the middle. Moss, leaves, and mushrooms grew over most surfaces, including the deflated tires of the white trash abodes.

The smell of gasoline and rot irritated Kellan's nose, but he didn't let that distract him. He kept his eyes open, hoping they would trigger on *something*. Unfortunately, he only got notifications on some of the plants.

Magical Item [Plant]—Deathweed

A potent leafy vine filled with remnants of arcana. When consumed, it enhances magical capability. Once the bonus fades, the mage loses 1 to all stats. If any stats are brought to 0, the mage passes out for thirty minutes.

The deathweed didn't look appetizing. The black vine, and half-wilted leaves, made it seem… dead. Kellan frowned at the few he came across, wondering how many people ate the plant out of desperation.

Sen pushed through the mobile home park, walking around the rusted vehicles and even pushing over a lawn chair in his attempt to get from point A to point B. He wouldn't tell anyone the destination, however. Kellan, Mavis, and Husker followed behind, but at a slow pace, due to the fact that Sen had short legs.

It was quiet.

Kellan stayed alert. Mavis seemed to do the same.

"Sevriss is a semi-sentient magical weapon," Sen said without warning, causing Kellan to tense. Sen continued with, "My sister found it just over this way."

"It's cursed," Husker growled.

"Our warrior said he wanted equipment, didn't he? It'll be perfect for him."

"He doesn't even know what a curse is. You can't expect him to make an informed decision."

"I don't care. All I need to worry about is—"

Something leapt out of a nearby mobile home. A beast. The monster lunged for Sen so fast and furious, you'd think it was Vin Diesel, but Kellan had been prepared. The moment the monster emerged, he ran for a lawn chair and snapped off one of the aluminum legs, ready to bash the creature if needed.

The monster was some sort of black bobcat.

"Some sort" was the best descriptor Kellan could think of. It wasn't really a cat—it had the body of one, complete with a short tail, common on bobcats—but its head looked to be stitched to its body.

And not professionally stitched, but awkwardly and gruesomely. Like a blind person who had never held a needle and thread had looped the flesh of the cat together.

And the head wasn't right—it was a wolverine or bear. Something with a long snout and too many teeth. Its slimy saliva poured from its gums like a waterfall of mastication, and it snapped with powerful jaws at Sen's face.

Sen hit the ground, startled. The bobcat monstrosity dug claws deep into his flesh, staining his giant robes with scarlet.

More information darted across Kellan's sight.

Name: Fanix
Race: Lesser Yami
Magics: Wyld, Entropy
Rank: Impossible
Armor Rating: —
Health: 7/7

Stats:
Strength—3
Dexterity—3
Fortitude—2
Intelligence—1
Perception—4 [Vigilant]
Willpower—1 [Animal]

Abilities:
Pounce—The yami doubles its dexterity whenever attacking a target that hasn't yet detected it.

With as much force as Kellan could muster, he golf-swung at the monster's messed-up head. The aluminum of the lawn chair bent upon impact, but it was enough to smash half the creature's face and send a bloody fang twirling into the dirt.

[Alex Kellan] struck [Fanix] once for 3 damage.

The notification didn't help anything.

Yeah, I got it. I saw the blood. Get out of here.

Husker backed away from the violence, his clawed hand trembling as he tugged at his hood, shielding his face and eyes.

Mavis didn't bother ripping off the leg of a chair—she brought the whole damn chair to the fight like a WWE wrestler. When the bobcat turned its disgusting head to face Kellan, she was already there, ready to join the fray. She swung from the side and battered the cat's body.

The monster hissed with all the deep tone of an actual bear. It startled Kellan a bit, but not as much as the beast projectile-vomiting.

In one quick motion, Kellan leaned away, dodging the sludge. It hit one of the mobile homes, and the same rotting power that Nasir had used to destroy the truck was now at work on the decayed vehicle.

Sen scrambled away, holding the injury on his body. "It's a yami," he said in a cold, calm, and matter-of-fact way. "Destroy it before it summons more."

The bobcat rushed for Kellan, its black fur on end. The eyes of the beast were bulging and jiggling, like a dead fish, but it somehow could "see" Kellan. When the monster came, Kellan readied his bent aluminum chair leg.

"*Come on,*" he taunted. "I'm ready for another round."

Bobcats were typically small—they weighed an average of twenty pounds—but this beast was at least sixty. Its claws were long enough to be knives, and it hissed again as it swiped.

Kellan swung at the creature's wolverine head. He struck one of the eyes, and it exploded like a ripe zit.

[Alex Kellan] struck [Fanix] for 2 damage.

What? No special modifier for its eye?

With a shudder, Kellan stepped back.

While the beast thrashed its head and screamed, Mavis moved up behind it and bashed with the chair. The yami growled and then hit the ground, its body gushing blood at a fierce rate. With a whine and a screech, it twitched its legs, but couldn't stand.

It had run out of health.

Kellan took a deep breath, both his hands still gripped tightly around his impromptu weapon. When the monster didn't move, he shuffled closer to it and glared.

A red shining crystal floated out of the monster's body on a river of blood. It spun into the gory mud and glittered like a star on Earth. The red of the crystal seemed eerily similar to the carnage all around them.

Sen struggled to his feet. "Husker! How dare you." He grabbed at his robes and stumbled a few steps. "You incompetent rennic… You didn't even help!"

"You know I'm not about to get involved for something like *this,*" Husker snapped. He waved a clawed hand around, his fur on end. "This isn't worth my abilities. Our *new warriors* clearly had it handled."

"Hmpf!" Sen held his injury—a solid bite to his side—his body trembling. "If I die, we won't be able to enter. Don't you understand?"

"You seem alive to me."

The statement ended the conversation between them.

A part of Kellan knew their lack of camaraderie would be a problem. If they were a team, how were they going to get through anything if they were bickering constantly? Then again, Kellan understood Husker's frustration. No one wanted to deal with the kid.

Kellan knelt down and picked up the red crystal—the arcana. It soaked into his skin a second later, filling him with a sense of power and wonder.

Then he saw the information again, only this time truncated.

Alex Kellan
Magics: Eclipse, Body, Metal
Rank: E, E, E
Mana: 5/5
Health: 7/7

Unspent Arcana: 4

What was he going to do with four arcana?

As if asking the question provided an answer, a flood of information filled his mind and sight, causing him to stumble to the side. He grabbed at his head, trying to come to terms with everything he was seeing.

In his mind, he knew he had a "limited selection" of skills based on his actions…

Eclipse—E-Rank Powers

Illuminate [1 arcana]

An extremely early light-based power, this allows the mage to make an object give off illumination; it leads to far more powerful things later…

The mage spends a mana, and an object is made to glow with light equal to a torch for thirty minutes.

Shadowed Edge [2 arcana]

The mage causes solid shadows to briefly manifest along an attacking edge, widening it and rendering it sharper, for greater damage.

The mage spends a mana, reactive to a successful brawl or melee attack, and adds +4 damage to the attack.

Flash [1 arcana]

Rather than a steady glow, a low-rank mage can release a powerful pulse of light.

As an attack or a reactive action, the mage can spend a mana and release a flash of light into an opponent's eyes. The mage uses their perception vs. the target's perception or manipulation, whichever is higher. If the mage succeeds, they blind the target for the round.

Pierce the Darkness [3 arcana]

Mastery over light and dark includes the ability to pierce the shadows…

The mage can always see in the dark.

The eclipse magic… Kellan somehow knew this was the magic of light and darkness. Kellan couldn't explain it, but the information filtered into his thoughts at a slow rate.

Body—E-Rank Powers

Adrenaline [1 arcana]

One of the simplest processes of the body is the obvious way the adrenaline floods the system, producing the fight or flight reflex. The mage with this ability learns to hyper-accelerate this process, including flushing it back out of his system.

As a reactive action, the mage spends a mana and immediately boosts all physical stats by one for six seconds as magically charged adrenaline floods the body.

Ignore Pain [1 arcana]

Body mages learn to control the autonomous functions of their body, one of the simplest of which is pain.

The mage spends a mana to ignore agony for thirty minutes. This power ceases if the wound itself disappears.

Skin of the Dead [1 arcana]

A few mages learn to control their autonomous functions to the point that they can shut themselves down, appearing dead.

A mage spends a mana point and a temporary willpower and enters an extremely reduced state of body activity, similar to suspended animation. During this time, they appear dead to all but the most advanced medical checks. They can set this time for any amount of time they wish, from a few minutes to a hundred years. At the end of that time, they will wake up having needed neither food nor water nor air. [Note: not immune to things like maggots eating them and do not sense tactile stimulation].

Improved Body, rank I [3 arcana]

Body mages learn to enhance their physique in many ways.

The mage gains an additional point of health.

Body magic… It had dominion over flesh and healing. And strength. Kellan could almost hear the promises of speed and power, but he couldn't quite grasp everything.

Metal—E-Rank Powers

Mold Metal [1 arcana]

The most basic metal mage power, and one that is quite useful. This power represents control over metal in its most limited form; the mage can shape it.

The mage spends a mana, and for thirty minutes, they can mold metal as though it were clay.

Repel Metal [1 arcana]

Metal mages can also repel metal, with a rudimentary but powerful form of magnetism, forcing it away from them.

The mage spends a mana as a reactive action to being attacked, and gains an advantage when dodging anything made of metal.

Laser, rank I [3 arcana]

Metal mages rely on light, or "laser," energy in their attack. This power is, weirdly, shared by eclipse mages.

The mage gains "laser" as an energy type and may spend a mana to shoot a destructive beam from their hand. The damage dealt is equal to metal magic rank (E = 1, D = 2, C = 3, etc.) + half the mage's dexterity score.

Metal Skin, rank I [4 arcana]

Metal mages can gain a slight covering to their own skin; while not as easy or as efficient as magma mages, they can still protect themselves quite well…

The mage gains +1 armor rating.

Metal magic… It was the magic over civilization and technology. Bending metal, controlling electronics, and military strategy and leadership. It was the magic of growth for all, if Kellan was understanding the whispered words inside his head.

It was too much. Kellan pinched the bridge of his nose and forced the information to disappear. What was that? Powers? Abilities? Spending mana? He tried to take everything in, but it all seemed to slip from his thoughts and swirl together like leftovers down a sink drain.

"Kellan? Are you okay?"

He opened his eyes to see Mavis standing close enough to touch his shoulder. He replied with a slow nod, but it obviously wasn't enough for her.

"What happened?" Mavis asked.

"I was… bombarded with a bunch of information. Something about spending this arcana."

"That's how you develop magical abilities," Husker said as he turned away from the bloody scene. "You use the arcana to infuse the magic into your body. Right now, you're the lowest rank of mage: E rank. You'll only have access to a limited amount of magic. You'll see the options. Maybe you have the choice to see in the dark. Maybe you can pick to breathe underwater. Either way, you have to determine what's best for you—and then use your arcana to gain that power."

Kellan nodded along with the werewolf's words. That made some amount of sense. It was like ordering from a menu. He had cash—the arcana—and now he was going to determine what sandwich he wanted to have with him, just in case he got hungry.

"Why didn't I get any arcana?" Mavis asked, glaring at the freakish bobcat.

Sen finally finished patting down his soiled robes. "Because there's only a limited amount of arcana to go around. That's why it's valuable and sought after. *Everyone* wants more magical abilities. Wait until you see the higher ranks of magic—some of those powers cost twenty, thirty, or even *fifty* arcana, and they're worth it."

"Wait," Kellan said, holding up his hands. "And people *bet* with arcana in the Nexus Games?"

Sen nodded. "Correct. You learn quickly."

"So they become powerful mages without fighting?"

"Again, you're a quick student."

"That's bullshit," Mavis said, crossing her arms. "We could just *gamble* our way to Merlin-level magic? What're we even doing out here in the swamp? Let's go back and play some blackjack."

Sen huffed and turned away, his black hair clumped with blood. "Fools. The gambling dens see more death than an average battlefield. If you ever lose more arcana than you can pay, *you're* harvested on the spot. The Arbiter doesn't like to hand out loans. Which means only the lucky—and sadistic—become powerful through gambling."

While Kellan wasn't opposed to gambling, per se, he did agree with Sen's statement. Risking life and limb to get some arcana, when it was found in the bodies of the nearby monsters, seemed a little extreme.

"But I bet they get a lot of arcana quickly," Kellan muttered.

Husker snorted. "You either level to A rank or end up in a body bag. But some people like the rush of gambling their lives away."

"What's the highest rank?"

"M rank. It goes E, D, C, B, A, then S for specialist, and then M for master." Husker shrugged. "Some say there are ranks beyond that, but only in Zenith."

Sen clapped his small child-hands once. "Yes! In Zenith, you can achieve higher ranks than M. In Zenith, arcana rains from the sky. In Zenith, *all* magical abilities are obtained at once." He hardened his expression to something sardonic. "Don't you fools know anything?"

Mavis sighed. "I feel like I know less and less the longer we travel through this twisted landscape."

"I'm right there with you," Kellan muttered as he rubbed at his chin.

But now I have to decide what magical abilities I'm going to acquire. It seems I should choose wisely. I might have a hard time coming across more arcana.

Sen removed his hand from his injury and stared down at his body. "Ah. Fixed. Perfect." Then he turned on his heel and resumed his walk. "Come along. Our new weapon is waiting."

—Chapter 13—

—Equipment—

The odd mix of trees and mobile homes intrigued Kellan. *A group of adventurers, walking through the White-Trash Forest, were jumped by a zombie cat,* he mused, entertaining himself as they went. *But how long have we been out here?* He glanced upward, his vision obstructed by the branches of the oak trees.

The sun was high in the sky, and pillars of light shone down around him. When did they need to register for the Nexus Games by?

"Which abilities did you acquire?" Husker asked, breaking the silence with his gruff voice.

Kellan crossed his arms and then shrugged. "I'm not sure. The few that stood out to me were the ability to mold metal, something to ignore pain, and the ability to shoot lasers from my hands."

Mavis snapped her attention to him. "*Lasers*? Why are you even hesitating? I need to see that."

"Well, there was this ability that flashed in my mind called *Skin of the Dead*." Kellan half-smiled. "It allows me to pretend to be dead, apparently. That's amusing, right? I'm a mage, and the first ability I learn is on par with training a dog to lie down when you say *bang*."

With a twirl of his hand, Sen threw back his long black hair. "How dare you. This is a serious affair. *Skin of the Dead* is a cowardly ability picked up by low-tier body mages who want to avoid confrontation as much as humanly possible. You should develop an attack—since that's what you're good for—or a utility ability to better protect me and my sister. Every other *joke* ability should be forgotten."

Although Kellan wanted to argue, he agreed with Sen's overall assessment. Apparently, everything here wanted to kill them. His best bet was to either have a strong offense—to kill everything first—or a strong defense and utility, to better combat the unknown.

And there was a lot of unknown, as far as Kellan was concerned.

"Why are we in the middle of a mobile home forest?" Mavis asked. She glanced around and frowned. "Reminds me of my childhood."

"This is the effect of the Conflux," Husker drawled.

Sen scoffed. "Haven't you figured it out already? The Nexus is where parts of other dimensions collide. During the Conflux—" he clapped his hands together once, "—things are mashed together. Clearly, a forest and this trash heap were fused to become this one area."

"I don't like it." Mavis rubbed at her arms. "It's unsettling."

"What a profound thought," Sen quipped. "Surely you must've been a philosopher on your world."

"Hey, careful with your sarcasm. Didn't your parents ever teach you any manners?"

Sen's frown deepened. "I regret all the decisions that brought you here."

While they argued, Kellan took a deep breath and then closed his eyes. He didn't want to remain blind too long—not when monsters could apparently leap out at any moment—so he tried to focus on a magical ability he wanted.

Molding metal?

Shooting lasers?

There was an ability that would give him a point of armor rating, which seemed useful…

Another ability would give him a health point.

Kellan shook his head. He hated indecision, and he wasn't going to let it stall his actions here. What he wanted was something that was versatile.

Mold metal… He could make impromptu weapons. Or escape from places with metal. The more he thought about it, the more he wanted to try. What was the harm? The ability to mold metal only cost a single arcana. It was the perfect "training" ability.

Kellan willed himself to take it.

His mind flooded with information again.

> **E-Rank Metal Powers:**
> **Mold Metal**—The most basic metal mage power, and one that is quite useful. This power represents control over metal in its most limited form; the mage can shape it. The mage spends a mana, and for thirty minutes, they can mold metal as though it were clay.

"Okay, I got this mold metal power," he said as he opened his eyes. "Now what?"

Sen exhaled and then rolled his eyes. "Not the most useful ability… But I suppose it'll do. You just need to spend mana to activate the ability. Then you can use it to your heart's content."

Before Kellan could try anything on the rusty mobile homes, they reached a fence.

The chain-link barrier separated them from a swamp of mud and twigs. Amid the sludge was a ruined airplane. Not just *any* airplane—a 1960s Gulfstream II. It was a two-engine business jet. A smaller version of a modern commercial aircraft, with circular windows and a pointed cockpit.

The airplane had been smashed in half, though.

Kellan walked to the fence and laced his fingers through the chain-links. He stared at the plane, his brow furrowed.

A large serpentine skeleton was wrapped around the airplane, as though it had been in an epic fight with the airliner. The serpent's ribcage was hooked around the outside of the rusted jet, and Kellan wondered how long the bones, and the plane, had just been sitting there in the mire.

That serpent must've been huge… At least the size of a freeway. What's going on?

"Tell me there aren't interstate-sized yami around here," Kellan muttered.

Husker snorted. "Shouldn't be."

His tone wasn't as confident as Kellan would've liked.

"There it is," Sen declared. He pointed beyond the chain-link fence, straight at the ruined airplane and the massive skeleton. "Sevriss is in the skull." He motioned everyone over the fence. "You go. I'll wait here."

"Is it because you're too short?" Kellan asked.

"N-No." Sen crossed his arms and smirked. "If I wanted, I could order you to carry me. I would just prefer to wait here while the rest of you do the dirty work." He fluttered his robes out in a dramatic fashion. "This task is beneath me."

He looked like a child with a god complex. Kellan still couldn't figure out how Sen appeared to be eight when he was supposedly thirty.

But he didn't have time to question things. He grabbed the fence, determined to leap over, but then stopped himself halfway. *Wait. I have magic now.* He smiled to himself as he thought about using mana. *Clearly, mana is another form of currency. I spend it to use my skills.*

Without much effort, a surge of power rushed through him, like a jolt of electricity from a discharged AAA battery.

Somehow, he sensed he had gone from five mana to four.

Kellan gently touched the chain-link of the fence. Then he squeezed his hands. He almost laughed aloud when the fence squished between his fingers. It reminded him of Play-Doh. *I can actually mold metal. That's… such a useful ability.* Kellan ripped a part of the fence away with ease.

Mavis's eyebrows shot for her hairline. "Is that your magical ability?"

Kellan pulled another chunk of the fence away, clearing a small hole for them in a matter of seconds. "That's right." He yanked a fistful of metal from the fence and held it in his palm. The silver steel wire looked hard when he examined it, but the moment he closed his hand, the metal gave way, completely defeated by his magic.

"Okay, okay," Sen said, rolling his eyes. "Stop looking at yourself in *amazement.* That is a *basic* metal mage power. Literally every metal mage has it." He snapped his fingers. "*Go.* Get the weapon. You can pat yourself on the back after you've done something."

Kellan wanted to remind the kid that he had almost been eaten by a bobcat, but he held back the comment. "Fine."

He stepped through the hole in the fence, prepared to step onto the mud, but then sank farther than he ever expected. His shoe went into the grime, followed by his ankle, then his calf, until finally Kellan hit solid ground—his knee was almost completely submerged in mire-like mud.

The fart-like *squish* that accompanied his step just added the cherry atop the disgusting sundae.

Husker snorted back a laugh.

"Are you okay?" Mavis asked, frowning.

"Very," Kellan drawled.

He stepped forward with his other foot and it, too, sank into the mud, all the way to his knee. When he tried to step forward with his first foot, he had to tug and struggle. When he finally got his foot up, he lost his shoe to the disgusting sludge.

Gnats and flies buzzed around.

A smell of sewage wafted up to his nose.

Kellan glanced over his shoulder. "Sen—you didn't want to get the sword because you didn't want to walk through this, is that it?"

The little kid half-smiled. "Perhaps." Then he pointed at the plane and serpent skeleton. "But hurry. We really don't have much time."

"Walk through the watery parts," Husker said, motioning to the more lake-like mud in the middle of the area. "It'll be easier."

After a heavy sigh, Kellan did just that. He trudged his way through the grime, losing his other shoe in the process. In all his time with the Delta Force, he hadn't gone through any mud-pits, but during basic training, there had been several obstacle courses that had involved moving through water and dirt. Once he got the hang of moving, he made it to the water without much more trouble.

And then something cut his leg.

Kellan flinched and backed away. With his breath held, he lifted his left leg. He gritted his teeth, both hating the sight and angry with himself for being careless.

Barbed wire had cut through his jeans and was hooked into his calf. Worms wriggled along the injury, trying to heal his flesh but unable to because of the metal.

[Alex Kellan] took 1 cutting damage from rusted barbed wire.
[Tyranny Worms] restore [Alex Kellan] for 1 damage every 6 seconds.

Kellan reached out with a shaky hand and batted away the spare worms. They fell into the mud, writhing and squirming, each one more putrid yellow than the last. Then he used his *mold metal* ability to unhook the barbed wire. He almost laughed—it was so easy to remove.

Thank the stars I picked up this ability, he thought as he threw the mangled barbed wire to the side. *But this confirms it's only my hands that use the ability—my legs didn't mold the metal. I have to touch the metal with my fingers and palms if I'm going to manipulate it.*

"Are you okay?" Mavis called from the fence.

"Yeah." Kellan stepped forward a few more times. With careful movements, he tried to "search" the mud for more barbed wire. "Apparently, a *war zone* and a *swamp* were fused together here to make a *fucked-up pit of despair.*"

His leg touched another patch of barbed wire, and Kellan silently cursed to himself. He couldn't see the wire beneath the surface of muddy water—but it was there. Tons of it. Waiting to shred his legs.

"Hurry," Sen called out. "Just finish this up."

If Kellan could have his way, he'd throw Sen into the swamp and never look back.

Unfortunately, reality had a different plan.

The ground quaked. At first, Kellan couldn't really feel it, but he saw the ripples rushing across the surface of the brown water. Although he wasn't sure what was causing it, he already knew it wasn't good.

"Damn," he whispered under his breath.

Husker placed a clawed hand on the fence. "*Run.* Get out of there." He pointed. "There's a yami in the waters. It's heading toward you."

Although Kellan didn't want to see, he glanced over. The top of a scaled creature was poking out of the muddy water, half-covered in grime and circled by a swarm of gnats. The creature didn't swim like a shark or a serpent—it moved like it was walking, causing quakes in the swamp with each movement.

An alligator? Perhaps a *giant* alligator? Kellan wasn't sure.

The massive creature took several steps, faster and faster, disturbing the swamp as it headed for Kellan.

"*Run,*" Husker ordered again. "That beast will drag you beneath the surface and drown you."

"I can't fight it?" Kellan called out, estimating a distance of a hundred feet between him and the monster.

"I wouldn't recommend it. That yami is a hassle for most B-rank mages." Husker motioned to the airplane. "Thankfully, it won't leave water."

More ripples and splashes. The muddy alligator moved through the swamp with the grace and speed of a drunken frat boy—but it never changed its target. The beast headed for Kellan, and once it was eighty feet away, it popped up two eyes to get a better look at its prey.

That was when Kellan finally got information.

Name: Queen Hexiton
Race: Greater Yami
Magics: Wyld, Metal, Entropy
Rank: Impossible
Armor Rating: 5
Health: 45/45

Stats:
Strength—10 [Strong-Jaw]
Dexterity—2

Fortitude—12 [Sturdy]
Intelligence—1
Perception—2
Willpower—1 [Animal]

Abilities:
Death Jaw—The yami can maintain a hold and grapple with a target, even when dead. The jaws lock in place.

Kellan nervously chuckled to himself. *I hate this place.*

The yami picked up its pace, stomping closer and closer to Kellan.

He turned to run, but immediately cut himself on barbed wire just beneath the surface of the brown water. It hurt—he grimaced—and yet another notification of the damage flooded his vision.

He could deal with the boxes of info. He could deal with the injury. But the barbed wire *burned.* He had to run through at least two hundred more feet of swamp and metal before he reached the airplane, and he knew the sheer amount of pain he'd experience would hinder his escape.

"*Go,*" Mavis called, panic in her voice. "It's almost on top of you!"

Kellan stepped forward again, and the wire cut his other leg. With his jaw clenched, he took a deep breath.

What other magical abilities did he have access to?

Ignore pain.

E-Rank Body Powers:
Ignore Pain—Body mages learn to control the autonomous functions of their body, one of the simplest of which is pain. The mage spends a mana to ignore agony for thirty minutes. This power ceases if the wound itself disappears.

Kellan spent the arcana, and then the mana.

He was down to only three mana.

I don't care what it takes—I'm not getting caught by this damn slow-moving alligator. He ran forward, occasionally reaching his hands into the swamp water to mold the metal away from his legs. The barbs cut his legs, and sometimes his arms, but Kellan didn't feel any pain. He felt the prick—the physical pressure and sensation—but much to his delight, no agony whatsoever.

Although his blood filled the water, he also didn't care.

Notifications about the worms kept informing him that he was being healed.

The alligator stomped faster, but never fast enough. Kellan dragged himself up onto the destroyed airplane long before the mighty beast could catch him. Unfortunately, his jeans were shredded, and he had no socks or shoes anymore, but at least he didn't have to deal with the monster.

"Hurray," Kellan sarcastically said to himself.

Mavis clapped from her location near the fence. "You had me worried," she said with a laugh. "Thank goodness."

He waved to her. "Yup. I'm fine. I'll be back in a moment."

It was then that Kellan realized something dreadful—he'd have to run through the swamp a second goddamn time.

I really hate this place.

With a sigh, Kellan stood and walked along the rusted and broken pieces of the airplane. It was smaller—the type of aircraft meant for fewer than thirty people—and he hopped from one damaged area to the next, hoping that nothing would break. The deeper he went, the darker it became.

He found the skull of the serpent near the cockpit, shrouded in shadows. Kellan slowly shuffled his way over, hating the fact that he couldn't see Mavis and the others.

A few times, he stepped on broken glass and discarded bolts, but it never hurt. *The perfect magical ability to step on Legos with*, he thought to himself, amused. *Mundane uses for extraordinary abilities.*

The serpent's skull was as large as a truck. Kellan walked up to the mouth and glanced at the person-sized fangs before heading into the cranium.

To his shock, there was already someone there.

That was a lie. A person's *skeleton* was there. The boney hand of the individual was holding a sword—a blade pierced into the roof of the serpent's mouth.

A black blade.

Had the wielder of the sword died fighting the serpent? Kellan couldn't come up with any other explanation. He glanced around, hoping he could find another weapon that wasn't a blade. *I don't know how to swordfight, dammit…*

The plane quaked, and Kellan could've sworn he heard someone shout. Was the alligator on the move? *What the hell am I doing? I have to get back to them.*

Kellan hurried over, pushed the human skeleton out of the way, and then yanked the black sword out of the serpent's skull. The moment it was dislodged, Kellan received a notification.

Magical Item [Semi-Sentient Weapon]—Sevriss

A mythical weapon that is said to appear once in every dimension. Powerful and versatile, it transforms to match the preferred weapon-type of its wielder. It's also cursed. Weapon damage varies depending on the weapon. Has a 10% chance to double arcana when used to make the finishing strike.

Cursed?

The hilt of the blade pulsed in Kellan's hand. His chest tightened, and he stumbled backward, caught off guard by the odd sensation coursing through him. It was as if the weapon had an emotional range that Kellan could suddenly detect.

"*Will you wield me?*" a strange voice whispered in his ear—in his mind.

"Excuse me?" he asked aloud.

"*Will you wield me?*"

Kellan exhaled. "Maybe."

"*I will grant you power, and the ability to destroy your enemies. But as punishment, you will be doomed to die a bloody and violent death.*"

"Lovely," Kellan quipped. "Anything else I need to know?"

"*You will not know the embrace of loved ones, or the warmth of a winter bed. You will only know pain and suffering for the last few moments of your existence.*"

The dead man inside the serpent's skull suddenly made a little more sense to Kellan.

He took in a ragged breath.

"*Do you accept?*" the ghost-like voice asked, a mere whisper in Kellan's mind.

That was when Kellan heard it again.

More screaming. The sound of metal twisting. Mavis shouting something.

Were they in danger? Kellan couldn't see.

"*Do you accept?*" the voice asked again.

"Yes." Kellan held the weapon close. "Now let's go help the others."

—Chapter 14—
—Hexes—

Kellan leapt over the few chairs of the busted airplane and made his way to a rent in the side of the wall. He glanced out across the muddy swamp, all the way to the ruined chain-link fence. The "alligator" was there—Queen Hexiton—and Kellan caught his breath at the sight of it out of the mud.

The yami was a massive alligator the size of a flattened bus. It had six legs, each with an extra joint, bizarre human-like hands, and razor-like claws. Its underbelly and "hands" were all metal. The scales were a mix of steel, copper, and shiny aluminum, and the claws themselves looked to be jagged tin. The top part of the alligator was green and tan, with muscles so bulging, Kellan would've sworn the beast was on steroids.

The monster had emerged from the mud, smashing the fence, and was now lunging for Mavis and the others. Sen and Husker fled, but Mavis lingered behind to slow the beast.

With animalistic rage, the alligator crashed into one of the dilapidated mobile homes. The puny dwelling didn't stand a chance. It crumpled under the beast's massive weight and size, some of the metal paneling sparking when it came into contact with the alligator's copper underbelly.

Mavis stood her ground, throwing random junkyard objects. A lawn flamingo. A brick. A blue plastic kid's swimming pool. When she struck the beast's eye, it flinched and then snapped its jaws in her direction.

Mavis threw a lawn chair.

The alligator caught it with its massive jaws. In a single bite, the piece of furniture was crushed in half.

Husker and Sen stopped and turned, watching the combat without interfering. Sen occasionally screamed something—*he was the one screeching the whole time?*—but Husker said nothing.

"*Kellan*!" Mavis shouted. "Hurry!"

With his breath held, Kellan examined Sevriss. It was… a short sword, or maybe a gladius. Kellan had taken enough world history courses to know he didn't have anything particularly unique or linked to a culture.

"Dammit," he muttered to himself. "I really don't know how to use a sword."

The blade pulsed with an eerie energy, somehow discontent. Kellan chuckled.

"You got any ideas?"

No words filled Kellan's ears, but he felt a desire from the sword… A desire to be set down. Eager to comply with the magical object, Kellan placed the sword on the floor of the ruined airplane. He thought it would slip down into the mud—because the plane was at a slight slant—but something stranger happened.

The blade disappeared into the shadows.

Sevriss completely left his field of view, as though the darkness were liquid, and the sword had sunk below the surface.

In a panic, Kellan reached down to grab it. To his shock, his hand plunged into the shadows. His fingers twisted around an object. He pulled up, half-surprised and half-elated to see he no longer had a sword.

He had an assault rifle.

Kellan laughed once, the happiest he had been since entering the nightmare world. The darkness wasn't quite as terrifying when Kellan felt like he could defend himself against the night terrors.

For just a couple of seconds, Kellan examined his new weapon. The Mk-17 SCAR was standard issue for Special Forces agents. Kellan had held hundreds. This one—black in design and with a rail system on the barrel—was lighter weight than he remembered. When he tried to check the barrel and the magazine to count the number of rounds, nothing opened.

"What is this?" he muttered to himself, even as the rumbles and sounds of shouting continued across the muddy field.

Sevriss never answered with words, only feelings. It felt… happier now. Perhaps bloodthirsty. And maybe even… judgmental. Like it wanted to see what Kellan brought to the table.

Magical Item [Semi-Sentient Weapon]—Sevriss [Mk-17 SCAR-H Mode]

A mythical weapon that is said to appear once in every dimension. Powerful and versatile, it transforms to match the preferred weapon-type of its wielder. It's also cursed. Weapon damage varies depending on the weapon [SCAR, (7 + dexterity – target's dexterity) and doubles the bonus from firearms-enhancing abilities and magical skills]. Has a 10% chance to double arcana when used to make the finishing strike.

The black—cursed—rifle was the type meant for standard-range engagements. The massive alligator was a few hundred feet away, which was within easy range. Kellan braced the rifle and then took aim.

He didn't need long.

When he fired, the SCAR rifle had less of a kick than the standard version he used back home. The bullet slammed into the fleshy part of the alligator.

[Alex Kellan] shot [Queen Hexiton] for 18 damage. (8 +100% Sharpshooter Modifier + Sevriss Bonus)
[Queen Hexiton] reduces damage of each hit equal to its armor rating

of 5.
[Queen Hexiton] takes a total of 13 damage.

How much health did it have? Forty-five?

Although Kellan wasn't the biggest fan of quick math, subtraction was an easy game. He glanced at the rifle, wondering if there was any need to watch his ammunition. Normally, his rifle held twenty rounds. Sometimes, if he used a belt of ammunition, he could have more, but with the magical weapon, he had no idea what to expect.

The giant yami stomped its six legs, causing a minor quake throughout the area. Trees shook, and leaves filled the air like a green snowstorm. Mavis fell to the ground, as did Sen. Kellan grabbed part of the airplane to keep his balance, but the ruined aircraft bent and creaked.

After a jolt, and the sound of metal being twisted, the passenger section of the plane tilted further, becoming a makeshift slide. Kellan held on to the side of the plane, his fingers getting stuck in the metal. He had forgotten about his ability to mold metal like clay, but he was quickly realizing it had plenty of applications.

It's only limited by my cleverness.

"Kellan!"

The alligator charged for the downed Mavis.

Without a second thought, Kellan let go of the plane. He slid as he took aim, but it was just enough to get several shots almost in the exact same spot.

Kellan landed in the mud, sinking to his knees.

This chump can't handle a gunner. It's just an animal. I could kill it with ease, so long as I maintain a good distance.

For some reason, the alligator's scales stitched themselves back together, as though it were healing its injuries. Did it have worms? Or was this some sort of ability it had?

I spoke too soon. What if this thing can heal forever? I have no clue what these things can do.

The beast had already taken over twenty damage, yet it didn't flinch or thrash around. It grew angrier and angrier, roaring into the forest and disturbing the branches. When it pounded its metal feet, everything shook again.

Kellan rapid fired. More hits. More damage. But the healing happened faster—more desperate. And the creature seemed stronger for it, like it was going into a berserker rage.

Then it rushed for Mavis, its jaws wide open.

She tried to stand, but her bad leg made her movement slow going.

Kellan mentally prepared himself to continue firing, but he knew Mavis likely wouldn't last long against an angry magical beast. *One that I enraged!*

Thankfully, the monster never reached her.

At some point while Kellan had been focusing on Mavis and the yami, Husker had joined the fray. In one dramatic motion, the werewolf-man threw off his cloak. His reddish-brown fur reminded Kellan more of a fox than a wolf. His pointed ears had black tips, and part of a chest and stomach had white fur. He wore a pair of trousers, ratty from use, but not dirty. Manacles were around his upper arm, wrists, and ankles, however. Bits of chains hung off each, and the links of the chains shone with glowing writing.

The writing became more intense as Husker leapt for the alligator. He collided with the beast's jaw. Husker latched on to the alligator, even as the monster lifted its long snout into the air. Husker's claws sank into the beast's flesh—beyond the scales—and purplish energies pumped into the monster.

Little by little, cracks formed in the monster.

Husker's eyes glowed the same purple, his fur on end. He panted loud enough that Kellan could hear all the way across the field of mud and on the busted airplane.

Although Kellan couldn't "see" the damage being dealt, he was a witness to the utter obliteration of the monster's scales, muscles, and face. Whatever the purple energy was, it didn't like the alligator.

The yami thrashed, trying desperately to dislodge the werewolf. At one point, its half-rotted back slammed Husker against one of the mobile homes, denting the side. Husker groaned, but never released the monster.

When the yami slammed him a second time, blood exploded across the side of the mobile home. But it was too little, too late. After the second slam, the monster staggered on its six legs.

Kellan held up his rifle and fired. He didn't even look at the notification. He just watched as the monster collapsed to the ground, its body breaking apart and its blood pooling under it.

For some reason, the rifle felt… satisfied.

Without waiting for instruction, Kellan walked across the muddy swamp. Unlike last time, he took his time, using his hands to feel for the barbed wire. His magical ability was still in effect, allowing him to mold the wires whenever he came into contact with them. His ability to ignore pain also made the swamp an easy trek. No matter how many sticks and rocks he stepped on, Kellan felt fine.

He yanked himself out of the sludge and headed for Mavis. She stood in the blood puddle around the yami, her eyes on the crimson arcana glittering in the gore. With a shaky hand, she knelt down to examine them.

Kellan walked over, splashing through the blood as he made his way to her side. Six arcana crystals sat in a pillar of light streaming down from the forest's canopy.

"Six?" he balked. "The Pestbyter was scarier, and it only gave me three. Not that I'm complaining. Apparently, we need this stuff."

"I'm not sure why it gave us six," Mavis muttered. "It's larger? And it did seem… powerful."

"Take them."

She glanced up, one eyebrow raised. "All of them? I think you and Husker deserve a few."

At the mention of the werewolf, Kellan turned his gaze to the other side of the alligator corpse. Husker was on the ground, curled in the fetal position, his breathing rapid. The purple energy was no longer flowing from his claws and fangs, and his eyes had returned to their normal darkness.

Without his cloak, he seemed thinner than Kellan had thought he would be. Emaciated.

Kellan walked over, and Mavis decided to join him.

"What's wrong?" Kellan asked.

Husker closed his eyes and remained still, his shallow panting the only noise he made. The chains and manacles around his limbs had stopped glowing, but the writing on each remained prominent. Kellan couldn't read any of it—it was in a language he didn't understand.

"Leave him alone," Sen said as he stormed over. "Don't touch him."

"What's going on? How did Husker kill it? The alligator looked like it was getting stronger for a moment…"

"It was," Sen stated. Once he was close to Husker, he placed his hands on his small hips. "Wyld magic has control over animals, vegetation, and primal urges. It's the magic of *the beginning*, and most wyld mages develop feral powers—red of tooth and claw. It's the same with the yami. Yami are just beasts of corrupted magic, so they get even deadlier versions of normal powers."

"It *was* berserk?" Kellan asked, his eyebrow raised.

"That's right. A normal wyld mage can do the same thing—once in a berserk state, they heal faster and their damage is increased, but they also lose rational judgment. This beast is known for killing people by surprise. Once it's taken enough damage, it starts its mayhem cycle."

Mavis knelt next to Husker. When she reached out to touch his reddish fur, Sen slapped her hand.

"*I said don't touch him.*" With a child-like glare, Sen stepped between the werewolf and Mavis. "Are you secretly two people? Because one person couldn't possibly be this dumb. It was a simple instruction."

Before anyone could speak, Sen huffed.

"Did you get Sevriss?" Sen stared up at Kellan with a frown. "Tell me that gun is what we're looking for."

Kellan held the rifle close. "Yeah, but it said it was cursed."

"No one cares about that."

"I think I do, little man. It said I would die a violent death, far from loved ones."

Sen scoffed. "Listen, if we make it to Zenith, all curses and hexes will be lifted. *That's why we're going in the first place.* Both my sister and Husker are under the effects of terrible hexes, and we have to get that fixed."

"What's the difference?" Mavis asked, almost with a laugh. "Between a hex and curse."

With the matter-of-fact tone of a dictionary, Sen replied with, "Curses are weaker, and can be lifted through tedious means. They also only affect a person *once*. For example, Kellan will suffer a violent death. Obviously, there's no other effect, and it can't happen again. It's a *onetime deal*."

Mavis nodded along with the words.

"Hexes happen *multiple times*. For instance, look at Husker." Sen gestured to him with a quick wave of his hand. "Technically, Husker was given powerful death magic—a mix of entropy and meta. He can destroy most magical creatures so long as he can maintain a firm grip. He drains mana and life at a shocking rate. But every time he uses his *Reaper Touch*, the hex takes a terrible toll."

Before Sen finished the story, Kellan glanced over. The werewolf seemed dejected. His tail was between his legs, and his hands trembled. It almost seemed like he didn't want to continue living. He just stared at the grass in front of him, his gaze glassy.

His fur was matted with blood, and his ribs seemed awkward—like they were broken—but otherwise, the man seemed healthy. What was wrong?

"What happens to Husker?" Mavis asked, obvious concern in her voice.

Sen crossed his arms. "Every time he uses his ability, a member of his family dies."

—Chapter 15—
—I Thought You Had a Problem—

"*A member of his family dies?*" Mavis repeated, her brow furrowed.

"They disappear," Husker said, his voice so faint, Kellan almost didn't hear it. While still on the ground, Husker sighed and continued with, "*They vanish from existence.* Never to be seen again."

Sen slowly nodded. "However, there's a small bit of hope. Perhaps we can find a way to search them out once we reach Zenith."

Kellan suddenly understood why Husker wanted to avoid confrontation at all costs.

"And Husker will be completely cured of this hex if he reaches Zenith?" Mavis asked.

"Yes." Sen flipped back his long hair. "That's why he agreed to join our team for the Nexus Games."

"Why doesn't he just kill himself?" Kellan asked, though he knew he came across as callous. He was curious—and it would've been his own solution to the problem if he had any family left.

"If Husker dies, the hex is transferred to someone in his family," Sen replied, no emotion in his response. "His is a hex of dynasty. It will haunt his bloodline until they have all disappeared… Or until Husker solves this little problem. We must reach Zenith."

Kellan glanced over to Mavis. "Zenith is the realm of high technology and perfect magic."

She nodded. "I know. Husker told me about it when you were speaking with Sen's sister."

"Perfect," Sen said. "Since we're all on the same page, why don't we discuss the arcana? Apparently, we have six. Two go to Husker, two go to me, and two go to Mavis? Or maybe Husker should get all of it… Due to the circumstances."

In Kellan's mind, Sen hadn't done jack shit, and therefore deserved nothing. But Husker…

He really did deserve the majority, at the very least.

Husker remained on the ground, unmoving. When the others turned his way, he closed his eyes again and sighed. "I want none of it." There was a finality in his voice that bothered Kellan. Did Husker consider the arcana tainted? Someone in his family had died to obtain it, so now Husker couldn't touch it?

"You two should split it," Sen stated, gesturing to Mavis and Kellan. "You're our weakest mages. Even one or two abilities will take you a long way."

With a curt nod, Kellan glanced over at Mavis. She offered a shrug. "I haven't gotten any yet."

"You take five," Kellan said. "I'll take one." *That way, we'll have gotten an equal amount.*

After a brief second of contemplation, Mavis nodded. "All right."

The two of them returned to the giant pool of blood around the massive alligator. Despite the fact that they had been talking for several minutes, the beast was still gushing bodily fluid at a fierce rate. Kellan wondered if there was a second dimension hiding inside the belly of the gator—a dimension that led straight to blood.

Once they were out of earshot of Sen and Husker, Kellan lowered his voice. "Are you okay, by the way?"

Mavis glanced up at him and forced a single laugh. "I don't know."

"That's it? You got nothing else?"

"Everything is so surreal." She ran a hand through her dyed hair. "You don't think it's crazy that it's still technically Christmas? I mean, I should be home watching *It's a Wonderful Life* for the twentieth time, but instead, I'm here, fighting monsters in a trailer park forest."

"I meant *are you physically okay*," Kellan said. "But I guess I can play therapist, if you need."

Mavis snorted. "Do you always use sarcasm as a deflection tactic? Or is it just with me?"

"Oh, *you* want to be the therapist?" Kellan smiled as he leaned down and touched one of the scarlet arcana. "I'm down with some roleplay."

The arcana absorbed straight into Kellan's body through his fingertips. The sweet sensation of power filled his being, like a hit of a satisfying drug.

Mavis knelt down to collect her five arcana. The moment she touched one, she shivered and closed her eyes. "This is… weird. I like it. But it's weird."

"That's what all the girls tell me," Kellan quipped.

When Mavis opened her eyes again, she had absorbed all the glorious arcana. She stood—but it was slow, so as to not put any pressure on her bad leg. "Are *you* okay, Kellan?"

He lifted up his new assault rifle. "I've never been better."

"See? There you go again. Deflecting." Mavis rubbed her hands together and glowered up at him. "You just *agreed* to help these lunatics win a game you know nothing about. Are you seriously so down on your luck—or looking for thrills—that you don't care about your life? Shouldn't we focus on just getting out of here?"

For a long moment, Kellan said nothing. He mulled over her comments, wondering if there was a kernel of truth behind them. The fact of the matter was: he didn't have much going for him. No family. No friends outside of the Delta Force. Had the decision to stay and help out with a nightmarish game been so easy because…

"If you want to leave, I'm sure you can find a way on your own," Kellan muttered.

Mavis shook her head. "If you're staying, so am I."

"Why?" He hefted his weapon close. "Are you so seriously down on your luck—or looking for companionship—that you'll cling to anyone?"

He hadn't meant his statement to sound so harsh, but he couldn't take back the words now that they were said. Mavis locked up like she had been slapped, unmoving, her breath held.

Silence festered between them. Mavis finally looked away, her gaze drilling a hole in the dead trailer park grass.

Kellan rotated a shoulder. "Look, never mind that. Clearly, neither of us should pretend to be a therapist. We have bigger problems." He motioned to the giant alligator with Vanna White-flair. "I give you exhibit A. *Monsters*." Then he dramatically motioned to his ripped-up jeans and bare feet. "I give you exhibit B."

"Bare feet?" Mavis quipped.

"No. *A complete lack of armor and supplies.*"

As if he had been eavesdropping the whole time, Sen called out, "We need some protective gear if we're going to make it to the AVU Palace. Stop playing with the yami's blood and get back here!"

"Is it just me, or has he been angrier lately?" Mavis whispered.

Kellan shrugged. "Puberty will do that to you."

Together, Mavis and Kellan walked around the shallow pool of blood and made their way back to Husker and the kid. To Kellan's surprise, Husker was still on the ground, unmoving. Had he given up on life? His hex *was* horrific…

"Ah!"

Confused, Kellan tensed.

Sen's eyes went wide the moment he caught sight of Kellan's bare feet. The little kid ran over, his adult-sized robes dragging across the grass.

"What're you doing to yourself?" Sen practically shouted. He knelt in front of Kellan and touched his feet.

Kellan jerked away. "Watch it, kid."

"Sit down," Sen ordered, no mirth in his voice.

The worms…

They writhed and moved, fighting against Kellan's desires. But they were weaker… Possibly from the barbed wire? Kellan held his breath and decided to play along. If Sen tried anything funny, he'd just jump up and surprise him.

Kellan took a seat on the grass, his rifle still in hand.

"Let me see your feet," Sen commanded.

After a long sigh, Kellan allowed the kid access to his bare feet.

"Look at this!" Sen shrieked.

He grabbed at Kellan's foot and then molded the skin and muscle—like it was clay. Kellan almost pointed the rifle at Sen's head, but the kid quickly reached into Kellan's foot and withdrew a thin shard of glass.

Mavis uttered a quick *yikes* and Sen held the glass in a pillar of light shining through the trees. The crimson blood made the glass seem stained.

Then Sen tossed the glass off to the side and "molded" Kellan's foot around a second time. Kellan couldn't feel anything, and as his heart pounded against his ribs, he remembered why.

His ignore pain ability.

"You can't treat your body like this," Sen said as he withdrew a second piece of glass. "Do you understand how complex you are? You're a vessel for your brain, and each part feeds into another. If you neglect something as important as your *foot*, you're going to struggle with everything else. *We're a system. A machine. A computer.*" Sen huffed and practically shouted, "*We're a flesh computer!*"

"Calm down," Kellan growled. Then he held up a hand. "Quiet. Please. I'm listening. No need to yell."

"How are you… twisting his flesh around?" Mavis asked, her attention glued to Kellan's morphing feet.

"Our warrior has *mold metal*, but I have *mold flesh*," Sen said matter-of-factly. "Body magic has domain over most things blood and bone. For years, I altered the faces and features of mages in our court."

He continued to "sift" through Kellan's foot. He withdrew another piece of glass, and one screw. Once he was done, he shaped Kellan's feet back to how they had been—perfect and undamaged.

A few times, Kellan swore he saw worms squirming to escape his body, and he wondered why. Sen had the queen… Were they trying to return to her?

Sen sighed. Then he glanced up at Kellan. "Have you looked at your more advanced abilities? You should be able to see D-rank possibilities now."

Although Kellan was still fascinated by the fleshcrafting magic, he decided to turn his attention inward. Like before, he saw a list of abilities. But… there were a few more.

Metal Magic Rank D Cost: 5 arcana

Metal—D-Rank Powers:

Repair [1 arcana]

One of the most common and most useful abilities, this power allows a metal mage to return something to its proper, ordered state, taking the inherent structure of an object, and returning it to that base.

The metal mage spends a mana, and any single, non-magical object of up to person size is repaired.

Blades [2 arcana]

Metal mages are able to manifest metal on their bodies as a transformation, taking on the forms of knights or even stranger automatons. Early on, however, it manifests in smaller ways, which allows blades to spring from the arms of the mage, allowing them to always be "armed."

The metal mage spends a mana and gains blades from his arms for thirty minutes. These deal strength + 4 damage.

Intuitive Tech [2 arcana]

The metal mage quickly understands how machines, vehicles, and foreign computers work…

The mage spends a mana, and for thirty minutes, he has a "phantom" understanding of machines. He can temporarily pick locks and use most vehicles, firearms, planes, and computer terminals as though he has trained with them before.

Systems Check [2 arcana]

Metal mages can sense the true form of objects, the perfect state that they should be in… and where they currently are. This allows them to see where the deviance is for even the largest objects, including cars, radio towers, and battleships.

The metal mage spends two mana, and instantly knows where damage or disrepair is (not things like microfractures that might someday lead to damage, but actual, causing problems at the moment, damage). There is no limit to the size that can be checked, but it must be a distinct unit (spaceship) as compared to a concept or network (a city, or the internet).

Laser, rank II [3 arcana]

Metal mages rely on "laser" energy in their attacks. This power is, weirdly, shared by eclipse mages, thought by many to be an "opposite" typing. This tends to be excellent for beams, and weak for nearly everything else.

The metal mage gains "laser" as an energy type, and the damage dealt is equal to metal magic rank (E = 1, D = 2, C = 3, etc.) + the mage's dexterity score. This stacks at half rate (round up) when added to any other light power.

Servos [Cyborg] [1 mana drawdown/5 arcana]

Metal mages who have taken "Cyborg" abilities gain multiple options, including servos, in which the mage generates a system throughout their body that instantly controls muscles with feedback to more closely mirror the mage's intent, increasing precision of force applied, and increasing the rate at which they react to minute changes in the physical environment.

The mage gains +1 dexterity.

Phantom Excalibur [Metal/Eclipse Rank C] [4 arcana]

Metal and eclipse mages can make metal weapons supernaturally hard and sharp, and give them sheaths of light energy. The result is a weapon that is extremely dangerous.

The mage spends two mana, and a mana every six seconds, and manifests metalline and light properties onto a weapon as one bonus. This adds +4 damage and ignores 4 armor rating. This can also affect a mage's "Blades" power.

Kellan could hardly believe it.

Some of his abilities were fascinating, but in a way he hadn't expected. The ability to repair things? Metal magic… It was the magic of civilization and technology. Of order. Or hierarchy. And, of course, metal.

The more Kellan understood, the more he liked it.

Sen turned to Mavis. "You need to determine what abilities you'll be taking. You're a metal and magma mage, correct? Magma has plenty of offensive abilities. Fire. Heat exhaustion. Controlling the earth around your opponent's feet. Surely you can pick something suited to your fighting style."

For a brief second, Mavis went still and quiet. She stared at nothing in the distance, her gaze vacant.

Is that what I look like? Kellan mused.

"Now that you have your weapon, we need to get you some armor." Sen glared at his bare feet. "We can't have you showing up to the AVU Palace looking like a drug addict."

"Yeah, we wouldn't want that," Kellan quipped.

"This is serious. We need to ask the Arbiter for forgiveness. You destroyed one of his Pestbyters, or have you already forgotten?"

Kellan sighed. "Trust me. I'm never going to forget."

With a dramatic swing of his arm, Sen pointed at Husker. "Help carry him. We need to hurry. We haven't much time."

Although Kellan didn't want to drag a giant werewolf man around, he knew they would probably need him. Kellan got to his feet, walked over to Husker, and then knelt. The half-man, half-canine, jerked away from Kellan's grip, his reddish-brown fur on end.

"I… I can walk," Husker growled. With shaky hands, he pushed himself off the ground.

But then he slipped.

Kellan grabbed him and held on. With as much strength as he could offer, he helped Husker to his clawed feet.

"Why'd you do it?" Kellan asked as he held the other man steady. "Why'd you use your ability if it was going to hurt your family?"

"The yami would've killed Mavis." Husker's ears went down as he sighed. "And we don't have enough time to find another teammate. Not even Sen could make new puppets in the small amount of time we have left…"

"Competing in the Nexus Games is that important to you?" *He risked everything to save Mavis for that?*

"It's my only solution," Husker said, his voice hollow. "I've tried everything else to break the hex. If the magic in Zenith can't do it… I have nothing left."

—Chapter 16—
—Inbred Mages—

Husker smelled of wet dog and cologne.

What an odd combination, Kellan thought as he half-carried Husker's weight. He was a werewolf-thing—his race was a rennic?—and was larger than most humans, but Kellan didn't mind. He could handle escorting Husker for a while. With one arm, he helped carry Husker, and with the other hand, he carried his rifle.

Kellan searched his rifle until he found a strap secured to the side. He unhooked it, and then hefted the rifle up on his shoulder. It made everything easier.

"Thank you," Husker said as they turned around one of the deserted mobile homes.

"Don't mention it." Kellan had his arm around Husker's body securely. "These Nexus Games are cooperative, right? We're a team now? In my experience, it's better if we get along."

"Hm. Where I come from, in the Batonka Jungles, the Immortal Rarn teaches us the importance of family. Not just families of blood, but families of profession and craft. The shipwrights are a family. They all pour their sweat into the ships they make. The leatherworkers are a family. They all work with the same pelts and tools, caring for the same environment."

"That's not really the sentiment held in my homeland," Kellan said with a smirk.

"Our families are smaller," Husker growled. "My kin and home are a fraction of your homeland's population. It's easier to know and care for three hundred people than it is to care for three hundred million."

"Makes sense, I suppose."

Husker turned to him, his foxlike ears twitching. "We will need to be like family if we have any hope of surviving these games."

Surviving.

Kellan had avoided asking about the death rate for a few specific reasons. He hated hearing the odds—he much preferred to focus on the current obstacle in front of him, rather than a nebulous chance of failure.

While they walked, Mavis veered off toward a patch of red tulips. She stopped and stared, her eyebrows knitted together. "Some of them are dead."

Kellan glanced over and noticed some of the *deathweed* that he had seen before. The deathweed had a distinct wilted-vine appearance. The black weeds complemented the bright red of the tulips, though, like a ladybug-themed garden.

Information about the weed came back up for Kellan, but he waved it away.

"Don't bother with that," Sen said. "*Leave it.* We must hurry."

No one bothered to argue.

Mavis moved away from the plants and hurried to catch up with the others, even if she limped slightly to do so.

As they reached the edge of the White Trash Forest, Sen stopped walking and froze. Kellan followed suit the moment he noticed why.

A strange man was rummaging through the wreckage of the trailer park. It didn't take long before the man noticed them.

He was a ratty-looking man in a pair of stained sweats, and a moth-eaten tank top. Had the man dressed himself out of a dumpster? Kellan could think of no other explanation.

But the stranger was holding a plastic grocery bag filled to the brim with deathweed.

The man glanced over and spotted them. His eyes were so far apart, it was as if they were trying to escape his face.

Kellan couldn't tell if the man was twenty-five, fifty, or just deformed.

Kellan's magical sight gave him a bunch of other information.

Name: Brenty Flinn
Race: Human
Magics: Wyld
Rank: D
Armor Rating: —
Health: 7/7
Stats: Concealed
Abilities: Concealed

"Hello, *Brenty*," Kellan said, confused by such an odd name. He released Husker and placed a hand on the side of his rifle, hoping this wouldn't turn violent.

Brenty caught his breath. He had a scruffy beard and no shoes—the epitome of a homeless man. And then he clutched his bag of deathweed close. "You… You're all outsiders."

"We're not here to hurt you." Kellan pointed to the nearby deathweed. "Look. You can have all that."

"You're… You shouldn't be here… You're no good. Bad luck."

Kellan almost laughed. *Did this weirdo miss the giant dead alligator? I'm pretty sure I'm bringing good luck to this whole area.*

That was when Mavis stepped in. "Let's pretend we didn't see each other, okay? No bad luck then."

With a shaky hand, Brenty grabbed a fistful of deathweed out of his plastic bag. As he brought it to his mouth, Kellan thought back to what his eyes had told him about the substance. What did it do? Just thinking that question brought the information back.

Magical Item [Plant]—Deathweed

A potent leafy vine filled with remnants of arcana. When consumed, it enhances magical capability. Once the bonus fades, the mage loses 1 to all stats. If any stats are brought to 0, the mage passes out for the remainder of the scene.

Enhances magical capability?

Kellan lifted his rifle and fired before Brenty could put the strange plant in his mouth. Kellan hadn't aimed for the man—but for the deathweed. The power of his rifle practically splattered the weed in one brutal go, and it took part of the man's hand with it, leaving Brenty with only three fingers.

"You aimed for *his hand*?" Sen balked. He motioned to Brenty. "What're you doing? His *head* is the most logical spot."

With confusion and fear, Brenty shivered. Then he took a single step backward, his freakish eyes glancing down at the bag and then up at Kellan more than eighty times a minute. He never even reached to cover his hand—it wept blood at a steady rate.

"Take your stuff and go," Kellan stated, his rifle up and his finger on the trigger.

Brenty caught his breath.

Then the bleeding of his hand stopped. While Kellan watched, bits of Brenty's flesh stitched themselves back together—bone formed, muscle twisted into place—and soon, Brenty had *four* fingers.

With his good hand, Brenty picked up his grocery store bag of deathweed and then hustled away, glancing over his shoulder with twitchy paranoia.

"What's wrong with you?" Sen turned and placed his hands on his hips. "Half the reason I brought you here is because you're a cold-blooded killer." He waved his hand. "That hobo was probably worth an arcana or two."

"I'm not *a cold-blooded killer*," Kellan stated with a sneer. He slung his rifle onto his shoulder and then offered Sen a glare. "I'm a soldier—a special agent. Someone who completes specialized tasks for the greater good of their nation. I'm not about to murder a coke-head for the fun of it."

Sen slapped the back of his hand into the palm of the other. "We need arcana. This is a matter of life or death. Trust me—if we don't have enough power for the Nexus Games, we're all going to die. Do you think *Coke-Head* has anything going for him? Of course not. We need that arcana more than he does."

With an indignant glance, Kellan turned to Mavis and Husker for help.

"I agree with Sen," Husker said. He held his side with one clawed hand, his red fur matted with dried blood. "If someone has to die, I'd rather it be *Coke-*

Head, as you so lovingly put it."

Mavis shook her head. "I don't agree with murder. If we can get arcana from monsters, let's just leave the people alone."

"*Coke-Head* won't fight back, though," Sen said with a sigh. "I thought the two of you would understand the strategic genius of easy arcana." He waved away the comment. "It doesn't matter. You'll soon come to agree with me. Since we're *outsiders*, the locals will always want us dead."

"Locals?" Kellan asked.

"People born in the Nexus. They see outsiders as corruption. The Conflux is a season of bad omens to them. Everything that crosses over into their dimension is considered evil and must be done away with."

Kellan pointed in the direction Brenty ran. "And he was a local?"

"Correct. You can tell. The man was so inbred, he was practically a sandwich."

Without another word, Sen headed for the city. His robes were dirty from their adventure in the trailer park, but that didn't seem to bother him. Kellan and the others followed close behind.

"Wait," Mavis said as they walked. "If that man was a local, why was he speaking English?"

Husker snorted. "He wasn't speaking English. You can just understand him. That's a side effect of the Nexus—since so many places, dimensions, and times touch this one world, the magic is in flux. Everyone can understand the spoken language of others."

"I can't read half the signs," Mavis muttered.

"Because it's not spoken—the words remain as they did in their home dimension."

The process of entering the city was the same as it had been the last time. A strange barricade—more hobos milling around the entrance, each with wide eyes and salivating lips. Apparently, there was a competition between mages somewhere in the city, yet Kellan hadn't seen it yet.

He wondered why.

Husker forced himself to walk over to a battered shopping cart. In a quick move, he yanked a grubby trench coat from a pile of festering clothing. Despite the odor, Husker threw it over his shoulders and then pulled it tightly around his body.

"What're you doing?" Mavis asked, scrunching her nose.

Husker returned to the group. He had the appearance of a 1920s dime novel detective. Who was also a werewolf.

"I have to hide the shackles," he said, his foxlike ears twitching.

"Why?"

"They're manifestations of the hex. They give me my powers to kill others—but they also mark me. Other mages who understand the terrible nature of hexes will likely want me dead, for fear I can spread the hex to them."

"Can you?" Kellan asked, stopping dead in his tracks and turning around.

Husker snorted. "If I use my ability on someone, and I *don't* kill them, I can pass the hex." He growled, showing his sharp fangs. "But that won't remove it from me. I'd just be spreading the poison—like a sickness. I don't want to infect anyone, but the other mages won't even want to take a chance. It's best if we just hide this for now."

That all made sense to Kellan, but his gut told him it wouldn't be that simple. Something would happen unless they found a better disguise.

"This way," Sen said as he turned down a narrow alleyway with the rank stench of sewage.

With reluctance in his step, Kellan followed after. Mavis and Husker lingered behind, each whispering to the other. Kellan almost wanted to linger and join their hushed conversation, but he decided to stick close to Sen instead.

The kid will get into trouble far faster than the other two.

Their footfalls echoed in the narrow space. It made it difficult to listen for enemies. Kellan kept his hand close to his weapon.

"So," Kellan said, keeping his voice low. "I noticed Brenty somehow healed some of his injury."

"*Who*?" Sen shot him a baffled look.

"Coke-Head. He healed part of his hand."

"Oh. Him. He isn't worth remembering. Clear that from your mind."

"But how did he heal himself?" Kellan almost wanted to shake the kid. "I just want to know that answer."

"All mages can heal themselves. It's just inefficient without a body mage." Sen patted his own chest. "I'm a fantastic healer, for example. With my body magic, I can heal most injuries. I fixed Husker's broken ribs, if you hadn't noticed." He tossed back his hair. "You can thank me later."

"Back up. I thought I needed *Tyranny Worms* to heal. I *don't* need them?"

Sen shook his head. "Technically, each mage can spend one mana to heal one point of damage, but since mana is also how you use the majority of your magical abilities, that's a problem. The Tyranny Worms heal you without the need to spend mana. They're superior in every way."

"Superior to… what? A bullet to the head? I'll agree with that."

"Body mages learn healing early on. Trust me."

The long and dark alleyway seemed empty. Kellan sighed and closed his eyes, trying to think of his own body magic abilities.

Body Magic Rank D Cost: 5 arcana

Body—D-Rank Powers:

Heal the Body [2 arcana]

This power is the simplest manifestation of the body mage's well-known ability to heal others.

The mage may spend a point of mana to heal another of three points of damage.

Brutal Reaction [3 arcana]

Another simple manifestation of the body mage's ability to improve their body with direct magical infusing. This power relies on a sudden spiked infusing of mana directly to the twitch muscles of the mage. Although extremely effective, this sudden influx to the muscles, without proper compensation, is damaging to the body of the mage.

The mage may spend two mana in order to jump into immediate action. For thirty seconds, the mage moves at twice the speed, and for double their strength. However, this is extraordinarily damaging, and inflicts three unavoidable points of damage that take effect during the course of the thirty seconds.

Increased Strength, rank I [4 arcana]

As the body mage increases in rank, magic comes to permanently infuse their musculature, granting them increased strength.

This increases the mage's strength by +1.

Increased Dexterity, rank I [4 arcana]

As the body mage increases in rank, magic comes to permanently infuse their musculature, granting them increased speed and control.

This increases the mage's dexterity by +1.

Increased Fortitude, rank I [4 arcana]

As the body mage increases in rank, magic comes to permanently infuse their bones and muscles, granting them increased resistance and durability.

This increases the mage's fortitude by +1.

Jolt-Resistant Muscles, rank I [4 arcana]

Body mages who rely on rapidly infusing their body with magic soon learn that even when their bodies can perform amazing feats, they rip themselves apart when doing so. The mage with this power learns to compensate to some degree, reinforcing their body in such a way as to inhibit the damage they take from their powers.

When using body powers that inflict damage on the user, the mage takes a point less damage.

Ragged Edge of Mortality [Body/D-rank Entropy] [2 arcana]

The mage with this power understands both life and death deeply. They gain the ability to both harm and heal in the same attack, allowing them to meticulously control the damage inflicted.

When a mage hits somebody with an attack that would kill, the mage may spend a mana to keep the individual alive with exactly one health.

"Rank D of body seems interesting," Kellan muttered.

"You should focus on that magic," Sen stated. "It suits you. Pick up some fighting powers—but leave the healing to me."

"Hm."

Kellan had three unspent arcana. It required five arcana to "rank up" to D, and it seemed that all the D-rank powers would be locked until he managed the advancement.

Kellan didn't get much time to ask about the powers, however. Sen stepped out the other side of the alleyway and then pointed across the shattered asphalt of the wide road. A large warehouse stood across the street. Unlike most warehouses, with windows and cracked doors, this one was made of reinforced steel, even the roof.

It was more a shipping crate than a building, but Kellan spotted several doors and a single skylight window on the slanted roof. In his mind, the building seemed… sleek. And futuristic. Some odd words were written on the side, but in a language he didn't recognize.

"Why're we here?" Kellan glanced at the sky. The red hue of an angry sun was his only prize. "I thought you said we don't have much time."

"This used to be a supplies locker for shock troops." Sen gave him a sideways glance. "I'm pretty sure it's been picked through, but some of the weaker supplies—or maybe even cursed supplies—should still be left. We'll outfit ourselves and then meet my sister at the AVU Palace."

—Chapter 17—
—High-Tech Armor—

Sen led everyone to the side door of the warehouse. The solid construction told Kellan that Sen was probably right—this was a place for valuable equipment. No one secured a warehouse with a steel door, reinforced walls, and tall roof unless they had something worth protecting.

The walls of the building had to be thirty feet tall, all without windows. Clouds gathered in the sky, some so black they looked like they were going to a funeral.

Sen motioned to the door. "See if you can use your new ability to mold metal. Open the door."

"All right," Kellan drawled.

He walked over and placed his hand on the steel of the door. Instead of bending to Kellan's will, and molding like clay, the metal wouldn't yield. Kellan pressed his hand against the surface and struggled. Had it been longer than thirty minutes? He hadn't thought so.

"I can't." Kellan gritted his teeth. "Why not?"

"It's as I suspected. The building is infused with magic. You can mold metal, not magic—altering the composition of the material used in construction is a preventive measure against low-rank metal mages. This warehouse obviously came from a dimension where magic is prevalent. Places without mages wouldn't have thought—or been able—to do this. That means the contents of the warehouse, if any are left, will probably be high-tech or magical."

Sen gestured for Kellan to move aside.

With an exhale, Kellan stepped out of the way. He watched as the eight-year-old-looking man placed his little hand onto the door. Then Sen closed his eyes. When Sen removed his hand, the door slid open with a *whoosh* akin to a soft sigh. It was like the door was straight from a Star Trek set—perfectly moving on its own and fitting into the wall.

Stale air wafted out of the dark warehouse.

The building clearly had power—the door had just opened—but no lights came on. Sen stepped aside and pointed Kellan in. With a few hesitant steps, Kellan moved into the building, keeping his back to the wall.

He held his rifle close, his attention on the metal of the grip and magazine.

I couldn't use my mold metal ability on the gun, either, Kellan realized. *My power doesn't affect anything magical, just like Sen said.*

When Kellan reached a set of light switches, he tried to illuminate the cold warehouse. He clicked the switches into place, but nothing happened. The darkness remained thick. The only light came from the single skylight in the roof, and it wasn't enough to see anything.

Squeaks echoed throughout the warehouse.

Hundreds. Of. Squeaks.

Kellan held his breath, straining his hearing. What did the sounds remind him of? *I'd give the remainder of my shredded pants for a pair of field goggles,* he thought, his jaw clenched. If he had night vision, the warehouse wouldn't be a problem.

Wait. Apparently, I'm an eclipse mage. Something about eclipse magic…

He thought about the powers available to him. He could make things glow, he could create shadowy blades, cause a flash in someone's eyes, or… see in the dark.

The others waited at the edge of the darkness, all around the warehouse door. Mavis poked her head inside. "Kellan?" she whispered. "Are you there?"

"Yeah," he said. "There's no light."

"Okay. But what's that noise?"

The squeaking persisted.

"I don't know." Kellan rubbed at his temple.

"What're we going to do?"

I have three arcana. I could purchase the ability to see in the dark—which sounds amazing—or I could purchase the ability to create illumination, which would help the group, but also alert the enemy to our presence.

The dilemma ate at him for a moment, but again Kellan didn't want indecision to hold him back. Illumination was cheaper—a single arcana—which he'd likely recover quickly, at the rate they were killing things.

When he spent the arcana, a sense of electricity flooded him. He had the ability to make something glow like a torch.

Kellan bent down and searched the floor. His fingers touched something hard—a steel pipe—and he picked it up. His mold metal shaped it oddly, but not too bad. He spent a mana.

Only two mana left.

The pipe suddenly lit up like a bright white glowstick, as though the object were comically radioactive. It was like a lantern flashlight, and Kellan held it high above his head.

The warehouse was a storage facility for metal crates, wooden boxes, and a ton of machinery that Kellan was unfamiliar with. Bits of broken machines were scattered around the floor, but Kellan still couldn't spot the source of the squeaking.

"You can make pipes glow?" Mavis asked as she stepped inside, her eyes squinted as she stared at the glowing pipe. "Sorry… I just used some arcana in order to do this."

She held her hand out and flames sprouted from her palm. The fire flickered with a powerful inner heat, and the reddish-white embers provided a decent amount of light. It didn't compare to the pipe, though.

"I can create fire now," Mavis said, awe in her words. She stared at the fire, half-smiling. "Magma magic, apparently. I can, uh, make rocks on my skin, too. If I want armor rating, apparently."

Sen pushed his way into the warehouse, almost knocking Mavis over. He glanced around at the piles of boxes and broken machines. "Let's navigate this junk maze and get to the armor in the back."

"Do you know what that squeaking is?" Kellan whispered.

After a short pause, Sen frowned. "It sounds like something *you* should handle, warrior. That's your lot in life. Handling noises like this."

Husker stepped into the warehouse, his disgusting trench coat dragging along with it a smell like a second shadow. He kept his head down, his mood still subdued after the incident with the hex.

"Eclipse magic is useful," he said, staring at the pipe. "Eclipse mages can bend light at will, even around them, granting them invisibility."

"Don't encourage him." Sen huffed. "We want him to rank his body magic first."

Kellan hated the way Sen seemed to think he could dictate everything. In an act of defiance, Kellan was almost ready to just exclusively focus on every magic *but* body. "Why shouldn't I learn invisibility?"

"I didn't say you *shouldn't*—I said you should focus on body magic *first.* Whichever magic you rank up to D will become your primary magic. No secondary magic can be ranked higher than your primary, which means you can't rank anything higher. So, if you go to D-rank eclipse, but then later want to go to C-rank body, you're going to have to raise eclipse magic first, does that make sense?"

Kellan nodded. "Sure. Yeah. I get it. The first magic I improve is my favorite for life."

"Good," Sen said with a hint of smug satisfaction. "I can explain things to you, but I can't understand them for you—let's hope you never grow confused."

The squeaking grew louder and more desperate. Hundreds of squeaks. How many things were in the warehouse?

Mavis, Sen, and Husker all turned to face Kellan.

I guess I have to discover the cause of the noises. Kellan smiled to himself. He used his rifle's strap to tie the illuminated pipe onto the barrel of his weapon, creating a makeshift flashlight.

Now that I have an eclipse power... Shouldn't I be able to see the D-rank powers?

Eclipse Magic Rank D Cost: 5 arcana

Eclipse—D-Rank Powers:

Laser, rank I [3 arcana]

Eclipse mages rely on light, or "laser," energy in their attack. This power is, weirdly, shared by metal mages.

The mage gains "laser" as an energy type and may spend a mana to shoot a destructive beam from their hand. The damage dealt is equal to eclipse magic rank (E = 1, D = 2, C = 3, etc.) + half the mage's dexterity score. Stacks with other "laser" powers.

Photosynthesis [4 arcana]

Light can be a power, and it can be a power source. In some places, it is the only readily available power source…

The eclipse mage gains an hour of "rest" and 3 mana for every hour they are near naked in relatively high levels of daylight. In blazing hot deserts, they gain four mana per six seconds.

Shadow Tools [2 arcana]

The eclipse mage with this power causes the nearby shadows to form into solid objects… Small, precise, and fragile objects.

The mage spends two mana, and for thirty minutes they can create small tools made from pure darkness. Light destroys the objects.

Eyes of Light and Darkness, rank I [4 arcana]

The mage is simply better at noticing subtle things, whether it be a blush, a shifting of the eye, the movement of a shadow, or even the time of day based on the light.

The mage gains +1 perception.

Sentient Shadow, rank I [4 arcana]

The eclipse mage's shadow gains a slight amount of sentience as it's infused with magic. This power makes the shadow have a physical aspect, and it moves to help block and hold.

The mage gains benefits when dodging and brawling, but they lose 5% to their familiar's growth.

Thick Shadows, rank I [Sentient Shadow, rank I] [2 arcana]

The mage's shadow jumps in the way of all damage, protecting their "person" at all costs.

The mage gains +2 "living shell" to their health. The shell must be broken before the mage can be harmed. The shell is reformed whenever the mage sleeps.

Empower Shadow, rank I [3 arcana]

The mage can "boost" their shadow.

The mage spends two mana, and a mana every six seconds to hold, and their shadow gains increased fortitude. This gives the mage +1 armor rating until their shadow is destroyed.

Dammit, Kellan thought. *Sen was right. I'm not even a few ranks into this mage thing, and already I can't get enough arcana to purchase everything I want. And the cost just keeps going up.*

"What're you waiting for?" Sen asked. He clapped his hands once. "Come, come. Those noises are irritating, and I want them dealt with."

Kellan moved forward, and to his surprise, Mavis hurried after him, her flame in hand. She offered a smirk, and he acknowledged it with a quick nod.

"You've got bare feet," she whispered. "You'll need some backup. That's me."

"Thanks."

Whatever awkwardness had come between them in the trailer park had faded. Kellan continued forward, stepping around a machine the size of a large house. In the low light of the warehouse, with only his impromptu flashlight and Mavis's fire, he couldn't tell what the machine's original purpose was. Maybe it dug in the ground? It had "claws" and a small driver's seat.

The squeaking became louder.

Mavis and Kellan reached an intersection of boxes and broken equipment. Shattered guns—rifles, shotguns, and even a few empty magazines—were scattered across the floor. To Kellan's disgust, blood was smeared across the concrete. The splatters were consistent with a struggle…

And then a body being dragged.

Red blood. Not black. Which meant it was fresh.

"I'll go this way," Mavis murmured, motioning to the left of the boxes. "This place is huge."

Kellan shook his head. "We're not splitting up."

"Aren't we supposed to be hurrying? We can search the whole warehouse quicker."

"I don't care. Haven't you ever seen a horror movie? C'mon. Get your head in the game, soldier."

Mavis half-snorted and laughed. "All right. We're a team."

"Okay, then we're going to the right."

"Why?"

"That's where the squeaking is coming from."

Mavis replied with a single nod. Together, they headed around the boxes and broken equipment. Kellan took point, his rifle held close. Technically, he'd use a different gun for close combat encounters, but the Mk-17 SCAR was still suitable for close firefights.

More boxes. More machines the size of houses. The further they went in, the more Kellan's blood pressure rose. And the squeaking just kept getting louder—and angrier. Like the buzzing of bees.

Kellan didn't speak, he just glanced at Mavis and mouthed, "I'll go first." Then he walked around another set of metal crates and lifted his rifle.

The sight shocked him. Kellan stumbled back, his shoulder hitting one of the giant crates. The sturdy storage unit didn't move—he just slammed into it.

Rats.

Hundreds of rats.

They swarmed over bodies. Dead bodies. People of all ages. Adults. Children. No clothes, just chewed flesh, blood, and dirt. It reminded Kellan of Holocaust pictures he had seen in high school.

The rats chewed at the bodies, ripping apart the flesh. Everything soft on the corpses was devoured first. Eyes. Guts. Brains. The insides of the bodies were strewn across the floor. The black-furred rats fought each other over the organs, playing tug-of-war with human tissue.

The bodies… They reminded Kellan of his time in Syria, a recent memory he didn't wish to relive.

Kellan stepped back around the boxes, his body stiff, unable to breathe. *Calm down,* he repeated to himself. *Dr. Hanley gave you relaxing exercises for a reason, dammit. Just calm down.*

"You okay?" Mavis mouthed, no voice, her brow furrowed.

He nodded. "Y-Yeah," he whispered, his voice shaky. "I don't think we need to worry about the noises. They're just rats. Let's just… go the other direction."

Together, they left the scene of the rats, but Kellan couldn't block out the noises they made. Mavis and Kellan returned to the fork in the "road" and continued to the other side of the warehouse. Pods and lockers were lined up against the metal walls. Although there was foreign writing on everything, Kellan recognized military equipment when he saw it.

The pods had full suits. Head-to-toe sleek equipment, like some sort of space marine under suit. The lockers had weapons and armor that Kellan recognized. Vests. Leg guards. He understood what to do with everything there.

His eyes flared to life on some of the objects. *Magical items.* Most just provided armor rating, but a few added to dexterity or fortitude.

More squeaking drew Kellan's attention. He pointed his rifle and flashed light on more rats gathered around a locker. He couldn't see any bodies, but the red on the floor told him there had to be *something* nearby.

"I don't think we're in a horror movie," Mavis whispered, staring at the rodents. "I feel like this is a twisted comedy, where someone just wants to see our reactions."

"Oh, this is a horror movie."

"Yeah? How do you think it's going to end?"

"I'm going to die. Sen is *definitely* going to die. Husker will probably go tragically. Sen's sister is probably the killer, let's be real. But you—you'll live. You'll just be haunted by all our deaths as you return to college to try to piece together your broken life."

Again, Mavis smiled. "But we have magical powers." She held her hand up, the fire still flickering. "That doesn't happen in horror movies."

"Haven't you seen *The Shining*? Magical powers mean we'll probably die faster, and because we went insane. If we ever get out of here, and make it back home, we'll have to have a marathon of all the classic horror flicks."

"Sounds like a date," Mavis said, her tone a mix of hope and melancholy.

Would they make it back?

The squeaking grew in agitation, drilling into Kellan's thoughts. And while he enjoyed the conversation with Mavis—and the ease with which they could talk about nothing and have fun doing it—the rats swarmed around the locker as though they were trying to tunnel through it.

Kellan pointed his rifle around until he found a shattered portion of the floor. Rats were pouring into the warehouse through the crevice, climbing over each other to get inside.

"Let's get Sen and Husker, get our equipment, and then get out of this place," Kellan muttered. "Knowing the Nexus, the rats will be filled with diseases, or more sentient worms, or *hexes.*"

As if the dimension wanted to prove him right, the *wall* moved. It pulsated, as though alive. The metal warped, and shifted, and Kellan didn't want to take any chances. He grabbed Mavis and yanked her back around a few crates, his heart beating fast. When he chanced a glance, he didn't need to shine his light to see what it was.

It was an Eye of the Arbiter.

The gross half-flesh, half-machine object had *appeared* on the wall. Its iris shone with inner light, like a red LED. With slow and calculated movements, the eye scanned the nearby area, stopping only on the pile of rats, examining the rodents for a long sixty seconds before disappearing back into the wall.

Then it was gone, just as quickly as it had come.

"What was that?" Mavis whispered.

"The Arbiter, apparently." Kellan took shallow breaths. "His eyes can appear on any surface with electronics—which I guess means the walls of this hellhole."

Mavis sighed. "This is one big snafu."

"You're telling me."

Without wanting to drag anything else out, Kellan guided Mavis back toward the entrance. The warehouse was "secure," but they weren't really safe.

Sen and Husker waited patiently at the front door—no conversation between them. The moment they spotted Kellan, they moved forward.

"Did you handle the problem?" Sen asked.

"It's just rats," Kellan replied. "For some reason, there's a stack of bodies in the building. I have no explanation for that. I haven't seen any people here. Just a crack in the ground that I suspect leads to the outside, and one of the Eyes of the Arbiter. The rats are using the hole as an entrance."

Sen sneered. "Bodies? Must be the locals."

"Show us the bodies," Husker said. "I can smell the difference, even when they're dead."

Smell the difference?

Kellan shook his head and led them through the machine graveyard. The angry squeaking led them just as much as the bloody path. Even before they reached the corpses, Husker stopped and snarled.

"They're locals. Ten of them."

"Why?" Kellan asked. "Who would pile a bunch of bodies here?"

Sen rolled his eyes. "Remember when I wanted you to kill Coke-Head? I'm not the first person to have this idea. Sometimes, outsiders who are familiar with the games come to harvest some of the stray locals. Those inbred mages and half-mages are easy pickings. Sure, they only give you a single arcana if you're lucky, but when they barely fight back, most don't mind getting their hands dirty."

The rats continued their chorus of anger and feasting.

"This way to the armor," Kellan said, leading them away before he had to see the carnage a second time. "Keep an eye out, though. If someone was murdering a bunch of a random people, he's probably nearby. The blood is fresh."

Sen, Husker, and Mavis stuck close. Mavis's fire illuminated their faces like the haunting glow in an eighteenth-century church oil painting.

Despite Kellan's fear, they found nothing else. They arrived at the pods and lockers without incident. The rats continued flowing from the crack in the ground, heading toward their mysterious locker, or rushing for the pile of bodies on the other side of the warehouse.

No more Eyes of the Arbiter.

"Ah, thank the north star," Sen said with a smile. "This is exactly what we need!" He hustled over to the armor and weapons. "We'll take whatever we want, and then head straight to the palace."

"Your sister wanted you to gather armor from reliable places," Husker growled. "You shouldn't have spent so much time following *Alex Kellan*—you should've given that up when I told you months ago."

Sen snapped his fingers. "Enough. We made our decisions. This is where we are now."

"This is junk left over by everyone else. You should've listened to your sister and just done things right."

"This is better than nothing, isn't it? Gather the armor. Put it on. Only magical items, though. If you wear non-magical gear, it'll be destroyed within seconds during the games."

Husker flattened his ears against his head, displaying anger like only a canine could. "The magical items will all be cursed, mark my words."

"We're going to make it to Zenith, aren't we?" Sen rubbed at both his temples. "I swear to the dark stars that if you don't stop chiding me about these decisions…"

Husker never responded.

"I'm going to search around," Kellan said as he backed away, his tension still high. "I'll stay close. Call out if you need me."

While Sen and Husker tore the lockers apart, Kellan glanced around the darkness, shining his magic-enhanced pipe at every corner. The rats continued their march on the corpses, but when Kellan flashed them with light, they scattered around, their red eyes alight with murder.

"Warrior! Here, now. We have the perfect armor for you."

Kellan returned to them, silently wishing he had picked up the *Pierce the Darkness* ability to see in the dark. At least then he would be able to spot whatever villain was lurking nearby.

When Kellan returned, Sen was waiting for him with a tiny rectangle of black held in one of his kidlike hands. "Look at this," Sen said. The tiny rectangle was barely the size of a Band-Aid. "You'll like this. It attaches to your spine, and enhances eclipse and metal magic. Perfect for you. See? I know what I'm doing."

Kellan stared at the magical object and allowed his analysis to determine the significance.

Magical Item [Armor]—Shadow of a Dying Star

Uniform armor worn by the stealth gunners of the Flestiss Dominion. Sturdy and reliable, this piece of armor attaches to the mage's spine and requires a mana to activate. Once activated, the armor covers the mage completely and grants +2 "living shadow shell" armor defense, and +2 armor rating. The mage can deactivate the armor at will. It's also cursed.

Hurray. Another curse for me. How pleasant.

Kellan exhaled and mentally shrugged. *Might as well. We're either winning or we're all suffering the consequences, apparently.* And while Kellan wasn't a fan of randomly taking detriments, he couldn't think of another way to acquire armor and weapons. Sen was his only source of information, as much as he loathed to admit it.

He snatched the armor from Sen. The moment he touched it, another whispered voice filled his mind, like a ghost was so close it was scraping its teeth on the shell of Kellan's ear.

"*Will you wear me?*"

Kellan nodded once.

"*I will grant you protection, and the ability to slip through shadows. But as punishment, you will lose at a game of chance. The dice will not fall as you want them.*"

"That's it?" Kellan quipped. "No doom or gloom? I don't have to pay with the blood of my firstborn child?"

"*It will happen when you least expect it. A chance encounter will not go your way.*"

While Kellan hated everything about the curses and hexes, he at least knew now that the curses were a one-time occurrence. He would lose one "game of chance" that involved dice. Couldn't he just avoid dice?

But I don't know jack shit about the Nexus Games. Maybe they're entirely played with dice.

"How often will we be rolling dice in the Nexus Games?" Kellan asked, giving Sen a narrowed glance.

"Never," Sen stated. "At least, that's never been one of the challenges in the past games."

Kellan held his breath.

"*Do you accept?*" the ghost-like voice asked, a mere whisper in Kellan's mind.

"I accept." And then Kellan brought the tiny square to the back of his neck and pressed it against his flesh. He waited for a few seconds—wondering if he had done it right—when the pressure of needles entering his flesh caused him to shiver.

When he removed his hand, he rotated his shoulders.

The armor… felt cold and powerful. A steady sensation ran down his spine.

And then a siren pierced the quiet of the outside.

"*Registration for the Nexus Games will soon close,*" a metallic and robotic voice blared throughout the area. The thick metal walls muffled the words, but they couldn't drown them out. "*All outsiders who fail to register within the next twenty minutes will be branded a menace. The Justices and Pestbyters will remove you from the city—dead or alive.*"

—Chapter 18—
—My Father's Arcana—

"Look what you've done," Husker growled. He flashed his fangs at Sen. "How do you plan to get us to the AVU Palace?"

Sen pointed to the many lockers, and then gestured to the darkness of the warehouse. "Quickly gather some things. Boots. Pants. Knives. Pack it in the bags in the back of the locker. We'll figure everything out later."

Husker didn't question the kid. He gathered the supplies, hastily shoving them all into two backpacks. The rats were in the way, but the werewolf shoved them aside with clawed hands. "How are we going to make it? We can't take any of the city transports, not with the Eyes of the Arbiter looking for our warrior. It'll take too long to get to the palace."

"We'll take the Lightning Lift," Sen said matter-of-factly. "Once we reach one of the lifts, it'll only take us a minute to travel to the palace."

"Have you forgotten it *costs arcana* to travel on the Lightning Lifts?" Husker threw on a backpack and then threw one at Kellan. With a grunt, Kellan caught the pack and then slung it over one shoulder.

"I can pay the costs," Sen said, his volume rising, damn near shouting.

Kellan held up a hand, his teeth gritted. "*Quiet.* What's wrong with you? There's a lunatic murderer nearby, and you can't ever seem to control your volume."

"We just have to reach the main road," Sen said, taking a deep breath and then exhaling. "Everyone stay calm… but also remember that we'll die a terrible death if we fail this." He pointed forward and then snapped his fingers. "Let's go."

Rushing around enemy territory—*unfamiliar* enemy territory—wasn't Kellan's idea of a sound plan. He hated every second they rushed through the dark warehouse and out into the stormy weather gathering overhead.

Something else caught Kellan's eye. The moment they exited the warehouse, he spotted lights in the sky. Lasers, spotlights, and even glittery effects filled the clouds. The lights came from the city itself, like there was a premiere happening nearby. The spotlights swirled around, and the multi-colored lasers danced alongside them.

"Are we at an 80s laser light show?" Mavis asked, her eyes narrowed at the weather. "What is this?"

"It's from the palace," Sen stated. "Let's go. Down that alleyway over there." He turned to Husker. "Carry me."

The canine-man growled something in irritation, but then stooped and picked up the boy. He carried him alongside the backpack, and then took off down the alleyway Sen had pointed at. It was wider than the last, and lined with dumpsters.

Kellan hated the smell, but he didn't have time to note it. He stepped on something. With his bare feet.

A nail.

Pain flared through his calf and leg, practically up his spine. The nail had gone straight into the heel of his foot. He sucked in his breath and half-fell onto one leg.

Goddammit. I guess that means my 'ignore pain' ability is over…

Husker continued forward, running faster down the alleyway the longer he went. Mavis was the only one to glance over her shoulder. When she noticed Kellan, she stopped.

"Are you coming?" she asked.

Kellan waved her on. "Keep going. I'm going to put on boots."

"But—"

"*I'll catch up to you.*"

Kellan was confident he could catch up with the group, so long as he had protection for his feet. Mavis must've thought the same, because she replied with a nod and pushed herself to catch up with Husker, her limp slowing her a bit.

With a few swift movements, Kellan unslung his backpack and dragged a pair of boots out. They weren't the right size, but at least they were larger than needed, and could fit on his feet and then be tied securely. He slammed his feet into them, but cringed when he slid his injured foot into the leather of the boot. The blood made everything slick.

Should I heal this? I only have two mana left.

He stood, and tested out his ability to walk. *It hurts, but I can make do. I should probably conserve my magic.*

Screams echoed down the alleyway, but not from the direction of Mavis and the others. The shouts were coming from behind him.

Kellan tensed and whipped around. Were the shrieks coming from the warehouse? At first, he turned to ignore them, but then he heard words being shouted.

"*Don't touch my sister! Leave us alone!*"

Another scream.

"*Help!*"

The paralyzing couple seconds left Kellan drained. He held his breath, his chest tight. They sounded like kids. Could he leave them? Were they running from the mass murderer who had butchered all those people in the warehouse?

The thought of leaving…

It bothered Kellan to think he would just abandon people calling for help.

"Damn," Kellan whispered to himself as he hurried back to the warehouse.

The laser light show continued overhead.

Kellan exited the alleyway, and it was everything he had feared.

Two kids were huddled next to a giant pile of trash. They were no older than ten, both wearing sweat-stained jogging pants and oversized T-shirts. One was a boy with a lump on his face, just over his left eye. A tumor? And the other, a girl, had so many teeth they were fighting to stay in her mouth.

Were they locals of the Nexus?

A rennic loomed over them—a werewolf that looked like a black and white Siberian Husky. He wore military cargo pants and nothing else, like a thug from an old-school gang movie. Crimson blood dripped from his massive claws. He wiped the blood off on his pants as he smiled a fang-filled grin at the kids.

"Leave our f-family alone," the boy shouted, his right eye streaming tears, but his left eye—the one under the tumor—too milky white to even move.

Kellan was only fifteen feet away from the whole scene. Kellan's analysis gave him some info on the werewolf killer.

Name: Griss the Black Wolf
Race: Rennic
Magics: Wyld, Magma
Rank: C, D
Armor Rating: 2
Health: 9/9
Stats: Concealed
Abilities: Concealed

The Black Wolf?

The rennic swiped his claws at the children, cutting the boy on the arm. When the kid screamed, the werewolf chuckled, his sadistic enjoyment plain for all to see.

The little girl cried.

Kellan didn't know the kids, and he suspected they were the children of "inbred mages," but he didn't care. He refused to sit by and do nothing while a lunatic cut down kids for arcana.

"*Hey*," Kellan shouted. "Leave them alone."

The wolf glanced over his shoulder, his fangs showing. "Beat it, punk. I found them first."

"I'm not a lunatic who kills children. I said, *leave them alone*. Or I'll make you."

"Heh. I'll rip your throat apart, human. I need the arcana."

Kellan lifted his rifle, took aim, and fired. The shot hurt his ears and startled the rest.

[Alex Kellan] shot [Griss] for 10 damage. (4 +100% Sharpshooter Modifier + Sevriss Bonus)

[Griss] reduces damage of each hit equal to his armor rating of 2.
[Griss] takes a total of 8 damage.

The werewolf's head practically exploded off his body. The rennic hit the ground soon after, splashing in the chunks of flesh and blood.

Kellan half-smirked. He hadn't expected his shot to be so damaging. *Sevriss is paying for himself, I guess.*

The children stared on in horror. First at the gore, and then turning their misshapen eyes on Kellan. He grimaced, well aware that he probably looked just as frightening as the rennic had.

Kellan moved forward, prepared to end the rennic and ultimately save the kids, when something unexpected happened. Despite missing half his brains and most of his face, Griss got to his feet. Without warning, the bloody rennic unleashed a torrent of flame—like he had a flamethrower, only the heat and fire came straight from his padded hand.

Kellan used his weapon to shield his face, but it wasn't enough.

[Griss] hit [Alex Kellan] with a beam for 3 fire damage.
[Tyranny Worms] restore [Alex Kellan] for 1 damage every 6 seconds.

Kellan tried to quickly duck away, but he leaned too much weight on his injured foot and half-stumbled. His burnt arm was stitched together by the worms. Before he could react to the situation, the werewolf was already on top of him. Griss ripped Kellan's rifle out of his hands and threw it to the side.

To Kellan's horror, the rennic's head and face were "growing" back in place, seemingly made from nothing—or perhaps mana, he wasn't sure.

With supernatural strength, Griss slashed Kellan across the chest with two-inch-long claws. Kellan hit the ground, his vision tunneling.

[Griss] used *Berserker's Rage*, temporarily boosting physical stats and gaining regeneration.
[Griss] slashed [Alex Kellan] for a total of 3 damage.
[Tyranny Worms] restore [Alex Kellan] for 1 damage every 6 seconds.

Kellan only had seven health.

Griss had dealt six damage. The worms had healed two.

But doing math was the least of Kellan's worries. Without his rifle, he struggled to come up with a plan. The werewolf—overcome with wyld-magic rage—howled at the sky, his scream half-drowned out by the crack of thunder that followed.

I have two mana, Kellan reasoned, his heartbeat loud in his ears. *I can mold metal, ignore pain, make things light up… or…*

Kellan closed his eyes and remembered the armor Sen had just given him. He spent a single mana and the magical item attached to his spine—the Shadow of a Dying Star—activated.

Black shadows wrapped themselves around Kellan in an instant. Cold power covered his body from head to toe, breathing new life into his sore muscles. He could see through the shadows over his face, but he somehow knew they protected him completely. They were… a part of him. Like a third arm. A third eye.

When the rage-infested werewolf attacked again, the shadows *leapt* from Kellan's body to block the blow, even going so far as to try to knock the clawed hand away.

[Griss] slashed [Alex Kellan] for 3 damage.
[Alex Kellan] reduces damage of each hit equal to his armor rating of 2.
[Alex Kellan]'s living armor takes a total of 1 damage.
[Tyranny Worms] restore [Alex Kellan] for 1 damage every 6 seconds.

I healed up to four health.

But Kellan was still on the ground. When Griss came in with claws again, Kellan grabbed a broken pipe on the ground.

Only one mana left.

He activated his *mold metal* ability—spending the last of his mana—and then gripped the pipe. He squeezed it on one side, flattening it until the pipe had become a blade. He struck at Griss as the wolf came in for an attack, hitting his side. He cut through the wolf's fur, spilling blood across the cement. But Griss wasn't even fazed.

The wolf slashed with powerful claws, hitting Kellan to the side and slashing his arm.

Information flooded Kellan's senses, but only two things really stood out to him.

[Alex Kellan]'s living armor takes a total of 2 damage and then breaks.
[Tyranny Worms] are unable to restore [Alex Kellan] and return to *Infestation Mode*.

Kellan tumbled across the ground, his heart pounding.

The shadows around him broke, but some of his armor still remained, leaving him disorientated. The worms *couldn't* heal him anymore? Had he been damaged too much? And too often? Were the worms weak?

Griss stalked over to Kellan, saliva dripping from his blood-soaked maw. He barely functioned—his berserker rage seemed to take all higher thought from him.

Kellan pushed himself to his feet. Griss lashed out again, but Kellan managed to just barely dodge, his legs shaky. He still had his makeshift knife, but it obviously wouldn't matter if the wolf could regenerate.

Think. What am I going to do?

Griss swiped again, this time with so much power, he almost knocked himself over. With simple movements, Kellan dodged aside. He knew a chance when he saw it. Kellan stabbed into the beast's ribs as Griss tried to regain his footing. Then Kellan dodged away.

Again, the wolf healed.

Kellan waited, his own injuries a mild distraction, but he pushed it all aside to focus on the fight. When the werewolf attacked again, Kellan had an idea. He stabbed into the beast's ribs and molded the knife *onto the wolf's ribs,* jamming the metal inside the man before he could regenerate.

Griss roared and backed away. With animal intelligence, he clawed at his own body, trying to rip the metal out of his ribs. His regeneration didn't seem to include "ejecting foreign objects out of the body" so the metal prevented Griss from healing the injury.

It bled. Constantly.

Enraged, Griss turned to Kellan. He rushed in with his mouth open, and then he crunched his fangs on Kellan's shoulder.

[Griss] bit [Alex Kellan] for a total of 3 damage plus bleeding.
[Alex Kellan] reduces damage of each hit equal to his armor rating of 2.
[Alex Kellan] takes a total of 1 damage, plus 1 from bleeding.
[Alex Kellan] is bleeding. [Alex Kellan] will suffer an additional damage every 90 seconds until healing is received.

Without his worms, and at two health remaining, Kellan hit the ground, his vision spinning.

Through the confusion and suffering, Kellan spotted a piece of broken machinery next to his head. He grabbed it, molded the metal, and when Griss came to kill him, Kellan leapt up and stabbed the murderer in the neck.

More notifications, but Kellan ignored them.

Griss swiped with claws, but Kellan leaned away, dodging the attack, only to lean forward again and then mold the metal of the machine. He stabbed it into Griss's neck. Kellan then molded the metal to hook it to Griss's spine, preventing the werewolf from healing the injury to his throat.

With the intelligence of a brick, Griss clawed at his own neck in an attempt to dislodge the metal. He screamed as he dug his claws deeper and deeper into his own fleshy body, completely out of control due to the magical rage.

It wasn't long until the werewolf collapsed to the ground, both pieces of metal still jabbed into his body, causing him to bleed out on the concrete. The beast huffed and tried to take in ragged breaths, but everything sounded wet and strangled.

Kellan exhaled. While he had been in many dire situations in his life, he had never felt so out of sorts. The numbers from the magic gave him an accurate way to gauge effectiveness, but they also acted as a harsh reminder of his own mortality.

He wasn't sure he enjoyed thinking of himself as having a "limited amount of health," even if that was the reality.

With shaky legs, Kellan forced himself to his feet. *I need my rifle.* He stumbled over to his weapon—the black Mk-17 SCAR on the ground—and then scooped it up. The gun seemed pleased to return.

But Kellan had no mana.

No means to heal.

No way to use any of his abilities.

Then Kellan turned his attention to the two kids. Their deformed faces stared back at him, eyes wide. The boy clutched a grocery bag close to his chest.

"P-Please," the boy said. "Don't hurt our family."

Kellan shook his head, and then motioned them away. "Get out of here," he said, his voice breathless. "Before some other murderer shows up. Hurry."

The boy with the face tumor turned to the little girl with the crooked teeth. They regarded each other with a long and confused glance.

[Alex Kellan] suffers 1 damage from bleeding.

Kellan collapsed back to the ground, his heart racing.

He had one health left.

No mana.

The death march was real—and fast. With shaky hands, he tried to remove his shirt so he could tie it over his injuries and staunch the bleeding. But he couldn't manage it.

The little boy and girl hobbled over. Both of them had mismatched legs, one longer than the other.

"You need to heal," the little girl said, her voice a whisper.

"Can't," Kellan breathed. "I don't have any mana." Then he waved them away again. "Go. C'mon. Get to safety." *I took all this damage for you. At least get away. At least live.*

The boy glanced over at the dead rennic. Two arcana glittered in the pool of blood. The boy scooped them up, his hands scarlet, and then handed them to Kellan.

Without hesitating, Kellan grabbed the glowing red crystals. They sank into his flesh as he absorbed them, but what good would that do? He didn't have any abilities he could purchase that would help in the situation. All the healing from body magic was in D rank—at least, the magic he could see.

"Can you increase your magical rank?" the little girl asked.

She had muddy blonde hair and watery gray eyes. Her tannish skin was discolored in areas, like she was diseased. Even then, her eyebrows wrinkled together in genuine concern.

"I can't," Kellan said through a ragged breath. "I only have… four arcana…

It takes five for me to rank." *What good would it do anyway?*

"You get more mana when you rank up," the girl said, answering Kellan's unspoken question.

The little boy stared at Kellan with his one good eye. His tumor eye—milky and unseeing—never blinked.

Time was running out.

The boy placed the grocery bag on the ground. A chorus of tiny clinks reached Kellan's ears. It sounded like the kid was carrying around glass.

When the boy opened the bag, Kellan caught his breath.

Arcana. All of it.

At least fifteen.

"This is our family," the boy said as he sifted through the arcana. Then he grabbed a specific red crystal and held it to his misshapen ear, like he was listening to the ocean inside a shell. "My father wants to thank you… for saving me and my sister. He wants you to live."

The boy held out the single arcana.

"I can't," Kellan said, his whole body twisted in anguish as his vision faded more and more.

"He wants you to live," the boy repeated, thrusting the arcana closer to Kellan. "Please. Before it's too late."

Without many other options, Kellan held out a shaky hand.

The arcana… It *had* been red, but the moment Kellan's fingers got close, it glittered with an inner golden hue. The arcana shifted color completely to a bright gold, just as Kellan absorbed it.

He didn't know why, and he didn't care. If he wanted to live, he had to do something.

Now, with five arcana, he could rank one of his magics, gain mana, and then heal…

But whichever magic he picked would become his primary.

Eclipse, the magic of light and dark.

Body, the magic of flesh and physical improvement.

Metal, the magic of civilization and technology.

Kellan had no time to dwell. He went with his gut instinct, and just ranked the one he thought would help him the most…

—Chapter 19—
—Primary Magic and Focus—

Sen had wanted Kellan to focus on body magic. While it had merits, Kellan just felt a defiant edge that wouldn't let him take it. *Maybe this is my "low wisdom" speaking, but I don't want to give him the satisfaction of being right,* he thought.

Metal magic…

Eclipse magic…

The shadows had protected Kellan during the fight, and since he was running out of time, he went with his gut instinct. Eclipse magic. He didn't care anymore. He spent his five arcana and a surge of power flooded his body.

Kellan's new maximum mana went to ten.

With the first mana he recovered, he healed himself, but at the same time, his mind and vision were flooded with a new option. *A focus.*

A focus.

What did that mean?

More information. More words whispered into his mind from some sort of helpful source. What was a "focus?" It was a magical ability Kellan needed to pick now that he was D rank. He would only ever get one—something that would guide his choices through magic as he continued to rank. The focus would empower him, even now.

He only got one…

And then he saw them. Since he had ranked in eclipse magic, he would need to take an eclipse focus. Kellan somehow knew he would never be able to pick his focus ever again. What would he take? What would be the most useful?

He didn't have anyone to ask…

Eclipse Focuses

The Thug

The mage's sentient shadow gains the "menacing" property, and can stun opponents for 6 seconds if they fail their willpower check. Gain the title "the Thug."

The Hidden

The mage may become invisible without mana cost, but any quick or violent actions reveal them. The mage is also considered 2 ranks higher to avoid divination, and their stats are also concealed. Gain the title "the Hidden."

Shadow Warrior

The mage gains "Sentient Shadow, rank II" for free, gains +1 effective rank to sentient shadow, and the shadow gains an additional attack every six seconds, at either base damage or rank + mage's wisdom, whichever is higher.

Light Warrior

The mage gains +6 light damage to their lasers, increased accuracy, and may use "Flash," if possessed, as a reactive action to being attacked by a melee or brawl attack once every six seconds.

Shadow Master

The mage gains the C-rank power "Shade, rank I" for free (creates a shadow-copy of the mage with half stats). The mage also gains +1 Shades at all times, and all "Shades" are considered a rank higher.

Void Agent

The mage gains the C-rank power "Shadow Step" for free (the ability to step into the shadows, move their full distance, and then exit the shadows). Diving into the "void" of darkness only lasts 6 seconds, but the mage may travel anywhere that a shadow could fit through.

Dark Paladin

The mage gains the ability to have his shadow wrap around him as armor, and to also form a sword. The mage may do this without spending mana, but once the armor and weapon are destroyed, the mage must spend 4 mana to rebuild them. The armor grants +4 armor rating, and the sword deals strength + 4 damage (all shadow blade abilities can stack onto this).

Living Shell [Eclipse/Body]

The mage's sentient shadow has life equal to his combined ranks in body and eclipse, and heals at half the mage's self-healing rate (or one per day).

Demon [Entropy/Eclipse]

The mage gains a single additional shadow attack for sentient shadow (does 3 damage or damage equal to the mage's wisdom score, whichever is higher), and gains "Entropic Tentacles" for free. Everything rotted by the

> mage's shadow is considered to have been killed by the mage. The mage can sense nearby red arcana.

A combination of magics?

Kellan gave serious thought to taking the eclipse and body focus, but his mind went straight for the "Void Agent." A small part of him liked it only because of the word "agent" in the title. When he was younger, he wanted to be a secret agent. It had led him to joining Delta Force, though he had never admitted his childhood fantasy to anybody.

Stepping into the darkness… and moving through it…

Kellan knew that mobility was crucial in warfare and combat. Those with the mobility advantage often won.

Invisibility also seemed tempting…

Although he wasn't an expert on magic, the faint whisper of information told him that the higher rank he was in eclipse magic, the more powers and abilities he would have access to. Even if he didn't take invisibility as his focus, he could use arcana to gain it later.

Void Agent.

Kellan picked it without another thought or regret. That was what he wanted, and he didn't have any time left to debate. Once he had selected, he gritted his teeth as cold power seeped into his body, like icy rain penetrating his skin and chilling him to the bone.

But then the sensation left him.

He had chosen. Eclipse was his primary magic, and Void Agent was his focus.

With a heavy breath, Kellan pushed himself off the ground. He was still very injured—only two health, and four mana. The Tyranny Worms weren't going to help him for a while.

The little boy stared with his odd eyes, one so milky it seemed blind. The little girl tugged on his arm.

"We should run," she whispered. "Now that he's better, he might hurt us."

Kellan picked up his rifle and slung it on his shoulder. "I'm not going to hurt you. Take your… family… and get out of here. It's not safe."

"You're an outsider?" the boy asked, his tumor practically jiggling as he spoke.

Kellan nodded once. "Sorry, kid."

"My father thinks you're a good man."

A simple question struck Kellan. "Why was… your father's arcana gold?"

"Red arcana means it was taken by force. Gold arcana means it was freely given."

The little girl patted her ratty hair. "*Gold arcana cleans the soul,*" she said like she was reciting a nursery rhyme, "*red arcana takes its toll.*"

The boy repeated her little song. "*Gold arcana cleans the soul, red arcana takes its toll.*"

Although Kellan would've *loved* to get more information on this, the laser light show overhead was bothering him. He leaned down and met the gaze of the little boy. "Hey, you live here, right? Do you know the fastest way to the

Lightning Line?"

"You mean the Lightning *Lift*?" the boy asked with a tilt of his head.

"Yeah. Whatever. The Lightning Lift. Do you know where it is?"

Both the kids nodded their heads. Then they held hands—the boy keeping his grocery bag filled with arcana close—and headed for another alleyway. Not the one Sen had gone down. Kellan chased after the kids, using two more mana to heal some of his injuries as they ran.

He didn't have a watch, but he knew he had spent more than eight minutes fighting Griss.

If I make it in time, it'll be another goddamn Christmas miracle.

—Chapter 20—
—The AVU Palace—

Kellan followed after the misshapen children. They dove into an alleyway, and a few feet in, they turned straight into a brick wall. Kellan thought they might comically slam against it, but that wasn't the case.

The kids ran through the wall as though it didn't exist. Poof. Straight through.

Although Kellan didn't want to slam into a brick barrier, he didn't have much time to debate his course of action. He charged through the wall, right where the children had disappeared. He tensed right before he "hit," expecting to slam his face into the wall and get some sort of comical notification across his eyes about the rules on concussion damage.

Instead, Kellan stumbled through, unharmed by the wall.

When he glanced backward, the wall was still there.

An illusion, Kellan mused, his thoughts returning to Sen's sister, Xiang. She had been capable of grand illusions…

"Hurry!" the boy yelled.

Kellan glanced around. The two kids were deep inside a dimly lit warehouse. Boxes, lit barrels, and tents were everywhere. It reminded Kellan of the underpasses in LA—the ones filled with homeless encampments.

Dozens of people milled around, each one more misshapen than the last.

Kellan didn't stare. He ran by the tents and the barrels, holding his breath so as to not breathe in the smell of human stench.

The kids dove through the crowd of people, weaving between groups. Kellan matched their pace, keeping up with them as he went.

"An outsider," someone said from the warehouse.

"He's with us," the boy shouted. "Let us pass!"

The throngs of inbred homeless slowly cleared away. The boy and girl dashed to the opposite wall, and Kellan chased after. Once again, the kids jumped through an illusionary wall. Kellan followed behind them, never questioning the logic.

They exited out into another alleyway. The boy and girl jumped into the next building, shifting through a third illusion.

When Kellan followed this time, he almost froze in place. They had entered a normal house, with a small kitchen, complete with a stove and microwave. He stumbled into a table, knocking over a drink onto the floor.

"There are illusions everywhere?" he called out.

The girl and boy were in the attached living room, staring at Kellan with wide eyes.

"Of course there are illusions," the little girl said. "It's to protect us from the outsiders."

The boy nodded once. "Most outsiders can't see through the illusions. We try not to leave… but sometimes we have to."

Kellan walked around the table and then hurried after the children, even dodging around a ratty sofa. The kids opened a door and ran down a long hall. Kellan didn't even question it anymore. There were pictures on the wall, and music humming from a nearby room, but he ignored it all and instead counted the beats of his heart.

He could keep track of the time if he counted his heartbeats.

One more illusion wall.

And then another.

Finally, the boy and girl leapt through a wall and then stopped. Kellan tumbled into the boy and grabbed him. He muttered apologies as the boy hugged his grocery bag of arcana, the tiny red crystals clinking like glass.

They stood on the edge of a dark parking lot. Across the way, a grouping of buildings was squished together like crooked teeth slammed into a tiny mouth.

"The Lightning Lift is around that building," the little girl whispered. She rubbed her hands across her dirty T-shirt. "You need arcana to ride it."

The boy hugged his bag. "You can't have any more."

"That's fine," Kellan said as he stepped around the children. "Thank you for bringing me here." He glanced at the illusionary wall, knowing they had taken a substantial shortcut. "I appreciate your help."

The little boy touched the tumor over his milky white eye. "My name is Hua."

"My name is Twi," the girl added.

Hua and Twi, Kellan repeated in his mind, confused by their odd names. But he shook the thought away. *Everyone has odd names here. Who am I to judge?*

"Call me Kellan," he said as he started his jog across the parking lot. "And stay out of trouble, all right? Next time I might not be around to chase off the rennic."

Hua and Twi stood their ground at the edge of the parking lot. They held hands and watched as Kellan went all the way around the building. They never said a word—and the emptiness of the area felt colder than it had before.

But Kellan realized something disturbing.

They weren't alone.

There were illusions over most of the buildings. And people were inside. Watching. Fearful. Trying not to leave.

The thoughts swirled around in Kellan's head as he rounded the building. To his surprise, Sen stood near the front door. It was a diner, complete with a sign in English that read, "Breafast Starting at 9.99!!"

Yes, breakfast was, in fact, misspelled without a 'k.'

What a terrible sign.

Sen's eyes went wide. "There you are!" He waved his arm and pointed to the side of the building. "Hurry! Quickly! We haven't much time remaining!"

A tall metal pole, similar to a telephone pole, was attached to the diner. It cracked and hummed with inner power. Bars and pipes jutted out of the pole at different heights, and it stretched up a good twenty feet into the sky.

Kellan's eyes informed him of its purpose.

Magical Item [Permanent Structure]—Lightning Lift

The mage may spend a single arcana to ride the Lightning Lift. The mage can choose any other Lightning Lift on the same dimension and travel there—no matter the distance—in thirty seconds. The mage must spend a single arcana each time they want to ride.

"Come, come," Sen said as he hustled to the base of the metal telephone pole.

Kellan, still flooded with thoughts of his encounter, stared at the top of the pole. "Hey, Sen. Have you ever seen gold arcana? Do you know how—exactly—it's different than red arcana?"

Sen stopped once he reached the pole. He glanced at Kellan with a sneer. "What're you talking about? Arcana doesn't come in *other colors*. It's red."

"I saw one that was gold."

"You were mistaken. You probably saw a sparkly crystal, or a bottle cap—who knows. It wasn't arcana." He pointed to his feet. "Now get over here before a Pestbyter or some lonesome inbred mage finds us. We need to reach the AVU Palace and we're already pushing our luck!"

His volume couldn't be contained. With each word Sen shouted, he got louder and louder. Kellan couldn't stop himself from dwelling on the small bit of information. He knew something about magic that Sen didn't. Gold arcana. What did it mean?

Kellan strode forward, his eyes still fixed on the top of the pole. How did the Lightning Lift work, exactly? His eyes hadn't told him more than the basic information. Obviously magic was involved, but…

"I went to D rank in eclipse magic," Kellan said as he reached Sen's side. "And I have a focus now, apparently. Some sort of one-time magical power."

"*Eclipse*?" Sen dragged his hand over his face. "What a waste. You should have ranked in body magic. Now you're going to be some sort of shadow warrior. Urg." He placed his other hand on the lift. "I hope you took a good focus. Like *Dark Paladin* or something useful. So far, your magical abilities have been underwhelming, and my sister already thinks you were a mistake."

Kellan followed Sen's lead and also placed his hand on the lift. "How is this my fault? It sounds like your sister wanted you to find someone who knew more about magic than *not at all.*"

Sen said nothing, his narrowed eyes and deep frown speaking a thousand words.

"Well?" Kellan asked. He glanced at the lift. "Are we going?"

"Very well. Close your eyes."

"What? Why?"

A pulse of energy shot through the pole. It spread from Sen's hand and shot through the metal like a wave of warmth. Kellan reveled in the sensation. It reminded him of… hot chocolate on a cold night. It was comforting, and relaxing.

And then lightning struck the pole.

Hot pain seared through the palm of his hand. White light flashed in his eyes. He closed them—but too late. He was blinded by the brilliant bolt of electric power. A tingling sensation went through Kellan's body, and then he stumbled away from the pole, disorientated and confused.

He stumbled a few steps before someone grabbed him.

The fur on the man's arms told Kellan it was some sort of werewolf person.

"Everything is okay."

Husker.

He had a distinct voice. His words had the edge of a growl on them.

"Kellan? Are you okay?"

Mavis. Her voice was a comfort when compared to the onslaught of madness that was the Nexus.

But Kellan still couldn't see. He rubbed at his eyes, but his vision remained purely white. With a groan, he pushed away from Husker's arms and stood on his own feet, though the world swayed.

"I told you to close your eyes, fool. This is your fault."

Sen's voice had a grate that could irritate the dead. Kellan would recognize it anywhere.

The ground shook beneath Kellan's feet. No—*shook* wasn't the right word. It vibrated from the forces of a powerful bass. Music played close by, like techno and rock had a child and it was celebrating its twenty-first birthday.

Kellan had always preferred country and rock over other types of music, but techno wasn't so bad.

"What's going on?" Kellan asked, still rubbing at his eyes.

"It's the AVU Palace," Husker replied matter-of-factly. "There's always a celebration whenever the Nexus Games start. This year seems to be grander than ever."

Kellan's eyesight returned in spots. First, he saw dots of color, then he saw images. The Lightning Lift—a metal telephone pole with pipes and steel rods—stood across a four-lane street from a massive set of stone stairs. It reminded Kellan of the Lincoln Memorial, though larger. The memorial only had fifty-eight steps, but this was at least one hundred.

Probably one hundred and twelve.

At the top of the stairs was a colossal building. Literally a palace worthy of kings. Kellan had seen similar buildings in Europe, especially when he went to visit Versailles and the Kremlin. The building was designed around a dome amphitheater, and around the building was a gargantuan garden and tall iron fences.

It was the size of a football stadium, and two Zeppelins floated in the sky around it, shining in the laser light show.

The lights—lasers and spot lights—shone from the base of the massive palace. They flickered and moved, creating a rhythm of movement that was almost hypnotic.

Dozens of people stood around on the front steps, most of whom were dressed in long flowing gowns, or formal military uniforms. None of them were deformed, and Kellan's half-blinded eyes filled with more notifications.

He ignored them, and tried to focus on the palace.

"It's a party?" Kellan asked. "Here?"

Husker stepped into his limited vision, his fox-like ears twitching. "That's right. The Arbiter throws a grand celebration. All the mages who are participating pay their respects. In the morning, the first games begin."

Sen clapped his hands. "Come. My sister is waiting for us at the door."

The four-lane street was jammed with rusted cars and broken machinery. Sen shuffled between the junk in order to make his way to the opposite sidewalk. Mavis, Husker, and Kellan followed, but Kellan tried to glance around.

The sky was dark, and the streetlamps weren't in working order. The nearby skyscrapers prevented Kellan from seeing much. Were they in the heart of the city? The Lightning Lift could've taken them anywhere.

But the Zeppelins… He remembered those.

We must still be in the Nexus-Fayetteville. Kellan pinched the bridge of his nose. *And this AVU Palace… There's no building on Earth that corresponds to it. Fayetteville doesn't have anything like it.*

The individuals on the front steps of the palace gave Sen odd glances. Some even whispered things, each one pointing, but only for a short moment. Kellan didn't know what they were all so excited about, and he wasn't about to ask.

They only had a few more minutes to register before it would become "open season" on them. Husker must have felt the same mounting pressure, because he hurried up the steps, his trench coat pulled tight.

Halfway up the stairs, on a large stone platform with benches and a fountain, was Xiang.

Kellan wouldn't forget her. She was more beautiful than the lasers in the dark sky, or the sparkle of the water in the dragon-shaped fountain. Her black hair fell like inky waterfalls over her shoulders, and when she glanced over to the group, her white robes flowed around her, silhouetting her slender shape.

"Who is that?" Mavis asked, her eyes wide.

"Sister," Sen said as she hurried over. "We've done as you wanted. Both our warriors have gathered some arcana and now have magical abilities."

Xiang turned her perfect gaze to Kellan. She didn't meet his gaze—she avoided it—and instead stared at his ripped-up jeans and bloody boots.

I look like I belong with all the homeless mages, Kellan mused to himself.

After a long inhale, Xiang motioned the others closer with a gentle motion of her wrist. "Please, gather round. This will already be one of the most embarrassing moments of my life, but I at least want to mitigate the humility."

"This won't be embarrassing," Sen said. "You'll see. I guarantee it'll get the attention you want."

"Oh, we're going to get attention," Husker sarcastically muttered.

Xiang held up a hand to silence her brother. "I can already hear the ridicule. Please. Brother. Listen to me this one time. If the other teams try to goad or taunt us, we aren't to respond. We have a plan, and we must adhere to it."

With a short exhale, Sen nodded. "Very well. What do you want from us?"

"Get closer. I'm going to cast an illusion over all of you for the celebration. Then we'll go inside and deal with… the fallout of your terrible decisions."

—Chapter 21—
—Alex Kellan the Defector—

Once everyone was close, Xiang waved her hand.

Her illusions worked in an instant, wrapping around each person completely. Xiang gave everyone a new outfit and altered their natural appearance but didn't actively conceal their identity.

Mavis's jeans and shirt had been replaced with a military uniform. Not any military that Kellan was familiar with, but he recognized the uniform conformity of insignias on the shoulder and collarbone. Mavis still wore pants, but now she had a long-sleeved jacket complete with a vest and undershirt. Fancy, and colored mostly black with white accents.

And her faint scars were gone.

Her purple hair was more reddish and "naturally colored." And while Kellan already found her attractive, Mavis lost any and all imperfections.

Sen's robes became a beautiful red and gold. They flared with color, shimmering like the soft reflection of water. While they didn't shorten, they seemed more liquid and ethereal, flowing around his kid-like body.

Husker now wore a coat made of luxurious furs. Thin chains hung from some of the pockets, each attached to an illusionary pocket watch. Had Xiang created them to hide the sound of his actual chains? Kellan thought it clever.

When Kellan examined himself, he was both surprised and intrigued. His military outfit was covered in shadows. It reminded him of his cursed armor. The darkness moved around with his movements, like a shadowy echo. He wore the same outfit as Mavis—mostly black, with slight white accents—but his insignia and "rank" were different.

Mavis had one jasper-red bar on her collarbone and shoulder. Kellan had two silver bars.

"What is this?" Kellan asked, pointing at the bars.

Xiang combed her inky hair with delicate fingers. "It indicates your highest rank of magic. You're D-rank eclipse. Silver is the color of eclipse magic. Your *friend—*" she said the word with a strain in her voice, "is E-rank magma. Red is the color of her magic."

Xiang motioned to her long white robes. On her shoulder, she wore five slate-gray bars.

"And you're A rank?" Kellan surmised.

"Correct."

"And gray… is the color of mind magic?"

Xiang replied with a slight smile. "Exactly." Then she smiled at the rest of the group. "Don't fuss with your clothing or worry about my illusions failing. You're protected when you're with me. I've even taken the liberty of hiding your basic information from those with analysis abilities."

When Kellan turned his attention to Sen and Husker, he took note of their ranking as well. Sen had four sandstone-tan bars. B rank. Tan for body magic. And when he glanced at Husker, the wolf had three bars of emerald-green. C rank. And green had to be for wyld.

"But we have multiple magics," Kellan stated. "Why aren't those colors included?"

Xiang dismissively waved away the comment. "You needn't worry. Etiquette only requires a mage to announce their primary magic. We don't have to announce any of our other talents."

She turned, her whole body a work of art as she glided across the platform and around the glittering fountain. The last half of the stairs awaited them. Xiang didn't call or demand they follow, she just made her way up to the massive palace.

The bass continued to pulse through the ground, sending rhythmic waves through the soles of Kellan's boots.

It was odd. He *felt* the blood in one boot, but when he glanced down, he couldn't see it. Obviously, his new clothes were just illusions—and not really there—but his mind kept trying to play a trick on him.

It was unsettling.

Kellan walked with the others around the fountain. While Mavis and Husker admired the fixture, Kellan turned his attention to the few other guests. They also wore bars of various stones and colors on the collars of their outfits.

Three gold bars.

Four black bars.

Two green bars.

Kellan dwelled on the information. While his analysis gave him information, most of the time it was concealed. The bars were just clothing. Anyone could wear anything, couldn't they? *Would people lie about their magic and rank?* Kellan wondered.

Then Kellan noticed something else. Each person on the steps of the AVU Palace had something tattooed on the back of their left hand. A number. He couldn't get close enough to see the number *exactly*, but he could tell most had different numbers.

Why?

He decided to keep quiet for the time being, and followed the others up the steps.

Thirty stairs from the top, Mavis slowed. Although she looked perfectly healthy, she did slow her pace and rub at her bad leg. When Kellan walked up, he offered his arm.

"Thank you," Mavis said with a half-smile.

"Anything for a fellow soldier," he replied.

Mavis took hold of his elbow, but they only made it a few steps before Xiang stopped and turned around.

"Don't stand near each other," she stated. "This will already be painful enough." Then she pointed to Husker. "Help our other teammate if she's having trouble. Once we start the games, we can find a reconstruction facility and Sen can help her rearrange her stats."

Husker bowed his head slightly. "As you wish." He walked down the steps and took Mavis from Kellan's arm. "Don't fret. Soon this won't be a problem."

Although Kellan wanted to protest, he stopped himself from doing so. Xiang rubbed at her face and turned away, her sullen expression more of a mystery than an irritant.

When they resumed their trek, the music from inside the palace became louder and louder. Sen lingered until he was close to Kellan. Together, they walked side by side up the last few steps.

In a quiet voice—that was almost drowned out by the music—he said, "Don't speak to anyone inside. And don't do anything to embarrass my sister. We won't be joining the festivities, so all you have to do is be good, and quiet, until our registration is complete. Is that understood?"

Kellan crossed his arms, his shadowy illusions adding to his menacing appearance. "Ya know, we'd probably get along a lot better if you stopped talking to me like an unruly punk."

"We don't need to get along well. You just need to heed my advice."

"You'd much rather just command everyone like a puppet, I take it."

Sen tapped the side of his head. "It's infinitely easier when I don't have to explain my to people who have IQs sitting squarely at room temperature."

"What's that supposed to mean?" Kellan growled.

"I meant *in general.*" Sen threw a hand up. "People aren't taking enough action. They hesitate too long, and it's not my style." With a dramatic swish of his robes, Sen added, "I'm a strategist."

The instant Kellan stepped on the top step, another message flashed across his vision and in his mind. It was so prominent and imposing, he was forced to pay attention.

The AVU Palace Oasis

You have entered an Oasis. While inside this non-conflict area, all mages are forbidden from initiating direct violence. Offensive magical abilities are limited. Any who attempt to circumvent this rule will answer to the Arbiter himself.

An Oasis?

Kellan snorted and laughed to himself. The palace prevented people from attacking? *All the denizens of this dimension should stay here.*

There were two sets of double doors into the palace, each made of thick wood with designs of dragons carved into the center. Pestbyters hovered around each of the doors, their spherical machine bodies hard to miss.

Neon-colored lights flashed from within, the rock-techno continuing to increase in volume. The entire place felt like a rave, but Kellan couldn't help but stare at the architecture. The palace was a mix of Gothic and Rococo design.

The palace was grand, theatrical, and had sweeping archways. The windows were large enough to drive a truck through, but also held together with iron bars and crafted with stained glass. Gargoyle-like statues of dragons were on most corners of the roof, and tall walls added to its imposing presence.

It was like five different time periods had smashed together into one building.

Xiang walked inside, ignoring the Pestbyters as she went.

Kellan didn't feel as bold.

When the machines turned their camera-eyes on him, however, they didn't attack or rush forward. They simply scanned the crowds like they were waiting for something. Kellan wasn't that something.

With unsteady steps, Kellan made his way inside with Husker, Sen, and Mavis.

The moment they crossed the threshold, Kellan had to take a second to absorb everything all over again.

There were hundreds of mages inside.

Kellan's eyes flashed with so much information, he had to forcibly ignore it.

The Gothic interior was somehow mixed with machine-like parts. Clockwork walls, futuristic doors, and neon lights made him feel like he had stepped onto the set of the Matrix. Tables and luxurious chairs were placed throughout the gigantic entrance foyer, as though this was a place to socialize before going deeper into the palace.

And there were two sets of stairways to higher levels, and at least half a dozen doors that led into the building. Kellan wasn't sure where to even begin.

A loud voice pierced through the music, its pleasant tone a harsh juxtaposition to the terrible information.

"*Registration for the Nexus Games will soon close. All outsiders who fail to register within the next five minutes will be branded a menace. The Justices and Pestbyters will remove you from the city—dead or alive.*"

Despite the colored lighting, it was easy to keep track of Xiang. Her white robes, and striking beauty, could be seen from across the city.

She walked to one of the massive doors—another one guarded by a hovering Pestbyter—and strode through. Husker and Sen hurried to keep up. Kellan and Mavis gave each other odd glances as they passed by other mages.

Most were human, but the rest ranged in all shapes and sizes.

Kellan even spotted a few machines. Androids? He wasn't sure. He decided now wasn't the time. They only had five minutes remaining.

But they were gathering attention… More and more mages were turning their way and pointing. Even the robots. Even the oddly colored werewolves. Hell, even the Pestbyters swiveled their cameras over, watching as Kellan and Mavis walked through the door.

The beat of the fast-paced music heightened Kellan's anxiety.

Something was wrong.

He didn't know what, but there was clearly something everyone else knew—and he didn't.

The room he entered was quieter than the foyer, and the music was different. It was some sort of slow tempo jazz, chill and unhurried. The room itself was large—practically a ballroom in size—with betting windows across the back wall. Numbers were on screens overhead, including the number of mages and teams currently in the Nexus Games.

Dozens of mages stood around, most smoking black cigarettes.

Hane. Kellan had seen it before.

"Oh, look! If it isn't Sun Xiang."

The hyper voice matched the person it came from. A woman with an athletic build stepped out from a grouping of mages, her smile bordering on manic.

She had a Mohawk, her black hair spiked in all directions, and she wore a sleek suit of armor that reminded Kellan of a pilot's outfit. It was a complete jumpsuit that hugged her body, with hexagonal plates of metal over most vital areas. The suit effortlessly moved with the woman, never hindering her, despite how much it should weigh. The whole suit was black, except for one arm, which was colored a hot pink.

Her shadow… it moved on its own. It even had a face—like a mask at a theater, with eyes that curved upward to display a smile. It waved to Kellan when he stared at it.

The woman's ears and face were pierced with enough metal for a hardware store.

But Kellan didn't care. All he wanted to see were the bars of rank on her collarbone.

Six black bars.

Black…

Kellan didn't need anyone to explain. He already knew.

Entropy magic. The same kind that had almost killed him. And when his eyes gave him the basic analysis, he knew he had guessed correctly.

Name: Ysa Voight the Wraith
Race: Human
Magics: Entropy, Eclipse
Rank: Concealed
Armor Rating: Concealed
Health: Concealed
Stats: Concealed
Abilities: Concealed

"Greetings, Ysa," Xiang said as the woman walked over. "If you don't mind, I haven't much time left."

Ysa smiled wider, her gaze so intense, it was as if her pupils were always moving. Twitching. Kellan wanted to say she was touched by madness, but he really didn't know what was wrong with her.

Her shadows swirled around her feet, waving and smiling the entire time, regardless of what Ysa was physically doing.

"It's a shame you don't have your mother here to help you out," Ysa said with a slight laugh. The few mages behind her exchanged laughs and whispered comments. "Although… since her other team died in the last Nexus Games, maybe she isn't the best coach, huh?"

Xiang only offered a slight smile in response.

"Have you seen?" Ysa held up her left hand. She, too, had a number emblazoned on the backside. Hers read: 42. "All registered. Team 42."

"Fantastic for you," Xiang said, curt. "If you'll excuse me, I'll do the same."

With a manic giggle, Ysa pointed to the screens above the booth. "I'm on the same team as your ex. Haven't you seen? I think that's rather hilarious, don't you? *Maybe if you had just listened…* You could've joined us. We could've won this whole thing together."

Xiang said nothing, her silence cold and icy.

"We're here to enjoy the night before the games begin," Ysa said, her voice more high-pitched than before. "Maybe you should have a few smokes on us before we have to fight? I swear we'll treat you to some amazing—"

The woman glanced over at Kellan and caught her breath midsentence.

Kellan glanced over his shoulder, worried some sort of yami monster had wandered into the palace somehow. But there was nothing.

When he turned back around, Ysa was still staring, the side of her lip now twitching. Even her shadow stared, its "eyes" just shadow-puppet circles, like it was shocked.

"You didn't," Ysa whispered, her delight growing with each second. "*You. Didn't.*" When she burst out into laughter, it drew the attention of everyone in the betting room. The other mages, who had been minding their own business, were now focused on the commotion.

"Isn't that Sun Xiang?" someone muttered.

"Daughter of the former winner, and one of the Descended from Zenith," another chimed in. "The illusionist. You've seen her. I hope she's not entering."

"Wait, who's that with her?"

"Damn. She must be entering. That's her team, I assume. Oh, wait…"

Ysa's cackle grated on Kellan's nerves. When he turned to Xiang, he noticed she had become as still as a statue, her posture stiff. She waited, like this was inevitable.

Once Ysa had her laughter under control, she rubbed at her watering eyes. Even her shadow did the same, though it never made any noise.

"You found some *alternate dimension version* of your ex to compete with you in the games?" Ysa said, loud enough for everyone to hear. "Sun Xiang, that's so pathetic. *I had no idea you were that obsessed.* Oh, this makes everything thirty times more hilarious."

Her laughter resumed.

The shadow pantomimed laughing as well.

Kellan stiffened, his focus on the conversations around them.

"Wait, Sun Xiang sifted through other dimensions to find someone like her old fiancé?"

"That's sad. I have to tell Jonsie right away. He'll love this."

Laughter haunted the corners of the room, like every group of mages was watching with rapt amusement. Even Kellan felt embarrassed and awkward, and he wasn't entirely sure what was going on.

Ysa instantly snapped out of her chuckling and smiled, like a light switch had been flipped and now she was ready to talk about something else. She pointed to the screen above the booth. "You think *the real Alex* is going to stand for this? The moment we find you out in the games, *we're going to smear the entire arena with your little faker's blood.*"

Kellan turned his attention to the screens.

Then he read the roster for "Team 42."

Leader: Brenner Hawke, Traitor to Humanity
Member: Alex Kellan the Defector
Member: HR-8
Member: Ysa Voight the Wraith
Member: Viniss Tarkin the Vanguard Queen

With understanding dawning in her eyes, Mavis turned to Kellan.

"There's another one of you here?" she whispered.

Kellan tensed, unsure of what to say. When he glanced at the other teams—99 others—he noted that his name never showed up again. No one else's did. There wasn't a second Sun Xiang or Sun Sen or Husker or even Mavis.

His name was the only one up there.

Ysa laughed again, this time icy and cruel. "Oh, this is so perfect. Your Alex didn't come from a dimension with magic, did he? *He has no clue what's going on.* Xiang, be serious—did you actually think you were making a statement with this stunt?" Ysa poked her cheek and giggled. "Or did you think you were going to make him jealous?"

Her shadow dashed around the floor, no longer laughing. It seemed… angry.

But Xiang never answered.

Sen fidgeted with his long robes. Kellan hadn't noticed until then, but his face was red and his hands unsteady.

"*Registration for the Nexus Games will soon close. All outsiders who fail to register within the next minute will be branded a menace. The Justices and Pestbyters will remove you from the city—dead or alive.*"

Xiang finally swept past, her expression unchanging. "Forgive me, Ysa. Perhaps we can speak later. Right now, I need to register."

"Go ahead!" Ysa laughed again as she turned and headed for the door out of the betting room. "I can't wait to tell the others. This is so perfect. I couldn't have asked for anything better." Her cackling echoed throughout the room as she left.

Without much time to ask questions, Kellan hustled to Xiang's side. "Are you going to explain?"

"Once registration is finished," she replied, cold and calm.

They approached a window flanked on either side by Pestbyters. Kellan felt himself involuntarily tense as they neared. The android behind the counter had no eyes or face. It was a series of machines, vaguely shaped like a person. When it spoke, it did so with an old-school radio-like voice, complete with static crackle.

"Hello there, boys and girls." The android jerked from side to side. "You may register a team here. Please wait while I give you the disclaimers."

Everyone waited, and then the android spewed a few sentences so fast, it would've given the Micromachines commercial a run for its money.

"Once you register for the Nexus Games, you will be unable to quit. All members of your team must be present to register. Once registered, your team will be assigned a number. You may register a team between five members and ten members, but one of them must be designated the team leader. If the team leader dies at any point, the whole team loses, but members may die, and the team can continue to participate in the games. Additionally, the number of members determines the number of keys required to win. In theory, any number of teams may win the Nexus Games, but to preserve fairness and transparency, I'm obligated to inform you that no team, in the history of the games, has ever made it through with all their starting members, nor have multiple teams shared in the prize at the end. If your team loses the Nexus Games, the punishment is death at the hands of the Arbiter. Lastly, you agree to have your name and likeness broadcast throughout the Nexus, and are painfully aware that the Arbiter sees and hears everything. Any attempt to cheat or avoid the rules or harm the Pestbyters and Justices will be met with punishment as determined by the Arbiter."

The android concluded its speech with a little spin.

Xiang placed her left arm on the counter of the booth and slowly slid it toward the machine. "My name is Sun Xiang, and I'm registering as the leader of our team."

The android placed his hand over Xiang's, and a crackle of energy zapped her arm. In an instant, a number was branded on her skin.

Team 101.

Xiang stepped out of the way and motioned for Kellan to take her place.

Although the copious number of warnings were still ringing in his head, Kellan hesitantly stepped forward. He placed his hand on the counter and slid it closer to the android. The machine-man spun around again, and its old radio voice darkened.

"I apologize, you cannot register for the Nexus Games. You've already broken the rules and harmed a Pestbyter."

The two Pestbyters guarding the window turned to face him. They lashed out with wire-like tentacles and grabbed both of Kellan's arms before he had much time to react.

"Hey," he barked. "Wait!"

"We're here to speak to the Arbiter about that!" Sen called out from Kellan's side.

The android nodded once. "That's good. Because I'm going to have you escorted to the Arbiter right away. He'll determine if you can enter the Nexus Games or not."

The Pestbyters jerked Kellan away from the window. He struggled, but he couldn't seem to do anything... violent. A passive thought came over him, like violence was something he couldn't even fathom.

"*To the Arbiter,*" one of the Pestbyters said, sweet in all regards.

—Chapter 22—
—The Arbiter—

The Pestbyters dragged Kellan through the halls of the AVU Palace.

To Kellan's mild fascination, the gigantic building seemed to be divided into distinct sections. The music and décor changed with the area. The entrance was a techno rave, but one grand ballroom was an indoor swimming pool meant to look like a lake, complete with waterfalls and soothing music.

Kellan only got brief glances, though. Another section of the palace was mostly darkness and smoke, with the distinct smell of lust wafting into the hallway. When Kellan tried to free himself from the grips of the Pestbyters, they held him in place, their wire tentacles tightening around his arms, threatening to completely cut off his blood circulation.

"So, what's the Arbiter like?" Kellan sarcastically asked, forcing a smile. "He a Christmas guy? Or Is he more into Hanukkah?"

The Pestbyters didn't answer. They swiveled their camera-eyes to stare at him, and then returned their gaze to face forward.

The trek was longer than Kellan had been expecting. The final minute he had before registration ended was surely up. Would they allow him to register now that it was over? Kellan wasn't sure, and his anxiety grew with each passing minute.

Rumbling quaked the palace with enough force that paintings and television screens mounted to the walls shook. Kellan managed to crane his head to the side enough to look at some of the screens.

It was that same newscaster… Only this time he was standing in the middle of a football-sized field. He walked around the edge of a massive circular pit. The pit itself had to be the size of an Olympic swimming pool. And Kellan knew he was feeling nervous since he was mentally measuring everything in terms of sports fields.

"Exciting news, all you sad sacks within the Nexus!" the news anchor, Bitso, said to the crowd. "This round of games is about to begin! We have so many exciting players this year. It's the largest ever! The Arbiter is pleased."

More rumbling. The newscaster shook, and Kellan felt it through his boots. Was the football stadium close?

The pit… It was dark and ominous, with a slight amount of steam rising up from the void-like depths.

The news anchor wore his blindfold, even as he danced around the edge. With a microphone in one hand, he gestured to the stadium. "Are you all ready?"

Cheers erupted from the distant stands. Who was watching? What were they doing?

"Are we heading to the pit?" Kellan asked the Pestbyters.

They didn't answer.

"The Arbiter isn't a sentient pit, is he?" Kellan quipped. "Because I know the Nexus is weird, but that would definitely take the cake."

Again, the Pestbyters didn't answer.

Then the Pestbyters turned down a hall, and Kellan lost sight of the screens. The rumbling of the floor added to his increasing heart rate, and he took a moment to inhale and exhale. All his calming tactics were required to steady his thoughts.

When they slammed through a pair of metal doors, Kellan had to blink back a wave of intense light. The thunderous noise of a sports stadium bombarded Kellan all at once, catching him off guard. The Pestbyters dragged him onto the same football field that Kellan had just seen on the screens.

The lights came from the domed ceiling—the same one he had seen while standing in front of the palace.

The stands around the field seemed filled with individuals, but they were so far away, and not bathed in light, that Kellan couldn't make out any details. When he glanced up, he spotted a hole in the domed roof—the same shape and size as the pit.

When Kellan turned his eyes downward, he spotted the blindfolded news anchor strolling around the edge of the now-infamous pit. He kept the microphone close to his mouth as he made exciting declarations to the crowd, but Kellan couldn't seem to hear him.

His heart was pounding in his ears, the echo drowning everything else out.

The grass of the field was perfectly trimmed, but there were no lines for football or any other sports. Occasionally, Kellan spotted a few stains of red, which only added to his nightmarish thoughts.

"People don't get thrown into the pit, do they?" he asked.

And once again, the Pestbyters said nothing as they hovered along.

Two other people were on the field. Kellan hadn't noticed them until the Pestbyters stopped and held him in place.

The other two people were also held by Pestbyters—restrained in place, and unable to flee, just like Kellan. They stood twenty feet away, one on Kellan's left, and one on Kellan's right.

The man on Kellan's right was shaky and dappled in sweat. He looked like he had escaped a Ren Faire—a place where everyone dressed as medieval squires and knights—or perhaps Comic-Con.

The girl on Kellan's left was freakish. She was mostly human, but her hands, arms, feet, and shins were covered in reptile scales. The scales themselves were metallic copper, which matched her tanned skin. Her black hair—short enough to defy gravity—was spiked in multiple directions, either through gel or terrible sleeping, Kellan wasn't sure which.

And the girl had a thin lizard-like tail. It was flattened, like the body of a centipede, and the same copper color as the rest of the scales on her body.

She wore jeans and a black jacket, but otherwise, she had nothing else.

Her lithe body and panicked expression made Kellan think she was young, perhaps in her twenties.

Technically, Kellan received analytical information on each of the people next to him, even Bitso, but he could barely focus on it.

Numbers. Names. His mind was swirling. All he deduced from it was that they, too, were magical.

"Before we begin the games, the Arbiter wants to remind everyone that certain rules must always be obeyed," Bitso said, gesturing to Kellan and the other two. "As always, the Arbiter must judge those who damage his property. It's a terrible crime to harm his Pestbyters and Justices! Lots of *beautiful arcana* went into creating them, after all."

Cheers and boos mixed in equal parts as the crowd gave their opinion on the matter. Kellan strained his eyes to see them, but they were just too far away, and shrouded in too much darkness. Again, he regretted not taking the ability to see in the dark.

The rumbling across the football field became intense. Kellan would've fallen over if it hadn't been for the Pestbyters holding his arms.

Bitso stumbled around, laughing the entire time, his voice carrying across the stadium through the speaker system. "Whoa, there! It seems the Arbiter is ready to pass judgment. Please, everyone stand for the Lord of the Nexus!"

Kellan held his breath as the steam from the pit rose out in columns.

The audience in the stands grew quiet. It felt like the whole world was holding its breath as the ground quaked and shifted.

Then it emerged.

A clawed hand.

And not any claw—but a mechanical hand the size of a tennis court. It slammed onto the field, the blades of the claws digging deep into the dirt.

Then a second claw emerged. It, too, slammed into the ground and dug deep.

The strain of metal, and the whirl of gears, rocked the entire football stadium. From the pit emerged a dragon. A completely machine-made dragon. Servos. Pistons. Gears. Wires. Lights. The beast had no flesh—just the mechanics of an android made into the shape of a lizard with horns, wings, and fangs.

No eyes, though.

Its massive head, covered in sharp corners, and antlers like spikes, had no eyeballs with which to see. Its mouth, large enough to fit a hockey rink inside of it, glowed bright radioactive green, like its insides were shining constantly.

The dragon didn't fully pull itself out of the pit. It remained half in the ground, and half out, resting its weight on its massive elbows as it leaned its head over the football field.

The crowd cheered, their delight filled with an edge of fear.

"Here he is," Bitso screamed, his voice barely audible above the crowd's fearful jubilation. "The Arbiter!"

Kellan swallowed hard. When the notifications came up this time, he forced himself to pay attention.

Name: Lord of the Nexus, The Arbiter, Keeper of the Gates to Zenith
Race: Primordial Dragon
Magics: Mind, Metal, Entropy, Travel, Meta, Fate
Rank: Concealed
Armor Rating: Concealed
Health: Concealed
Stats: Concealed
Abilities: Concealed

When the Arbiter exhaled, his breath was laced with heat and the stench of oil.

Kellan tensed, his body so stiff, he didn't know if he'd be able to move, even if the Pestbyters released him.

The Arbiter was gargantuan. His body almost took up half the field, and when he moved his head, a gust of air pressure whipped by, almost stealing Kellan's breath. *That's the beast who's going to decide my fate?*

Bitso waved his hand, and a pair of spotlights focused on him. A dozen shadows cascaded around his feet as he walked further out onto the field.

Floating television screens hovered out around him, each so large, they could be a theater screen. They flickered to life with footage from around Nexus-Fayetteville.

"Well, the Arbiter is ready! Let's see what these mages have done to garner his ire!" Bitso pointed to one of the gigantic screens, despite the fact that he was blindfolded tight.

Could he actually see?

Kellan wasn't certain.

The screen flared to life.

It was a video of the Ren Faire guy. He was running through an alleyway when a Pestbyter hovered into the man's path. The angle of the camera… It was like it was mounted on the alleyway wall.

The man with the bizarre Ren Faire clothing unleashed a powerful crackle of lightning from the palm of his hand. It struck the Pestbyter, and the machine-sphere tumbled through the air.

"Oh, no!" Bitso shouted. "That poor Pestbyter. It was just *doing its job* when this homicidal maniac accosted it!"

The crowd booed and threw things, but they never reached the heart of the field.

The Ren Faire man yelled and yanked on his restraints. "I didn't know! I swear! I didn't know!"

"Ignorance is no excuse!" Bitso pointed to a second screen.

It showed the man shocking the Pestbyter a second time. And then a third time.

Finally, the Pestbyter hit the ground and its arcana was exposed. The man walked over, absorbed the red crystals into his hand, and then hurried from the alleyway, like he was running from something.

Kellan's heart beat hard against his chest.

Okay. Well, I hope the Arbiter is a forgiving dragon… Because that's exactly what I did.

Bitso wheeled around on his heel and pointed to the massive machine dragon. "Arbiter, what is your final decision? Will the man continue to suffer, and live here in the Nexus? Or will you grant him the sweet, sweet release of death?"

Again, the crowd voiced their opinion with thrown items and shouts.

The Arbiter lifted one of his massive claws.

The Pestbyters released the Ren Faire man. With panicked steps, the man turned away and ran in the opposite direction, his arms flailing as he tried to steady himself.

He didn't get far, though.

The Arbiter brought his claw down in one massive strike. He slammed the field hard enough to damage the surrounding area, creating a crater so deep, someone could make a pond out of it. Kellan would've toppled over from the aftermath—the air, the shaking of the ground—but the Pestbyters continued to hold him in place.

The Ren Faire man was dead.

When the claw was removed, his arcana—and his blood splatter—were clearly in the crater of the attack.

The two Pestbyters gathered up the man's arcana and then hovered over to the edge of the pit. They dropped the arcana down into the dark void, where the dragon had emerged from.

Then Bitso turned his attention to Kellan.

"Yikes," he said with a manic—almost lunatic-style—laugh. "*That* was quick! What a trial. That's how I want *my* death to go, that's for sure!"

Kellan wanted to shout *wait*, or *can we talk about this*, but his throat was so tight from anxiety that he couldn't seem to find the words.

Bitso touched the blindfold over his face and blood sprouted across the white cloth. "Well, well! On to the next *lucky chump* who incurred the Arbiter's wrath! Let's all turn our attention to the screens to see what this boob did, shall we?"

When the screens turned to face Kellan, all he could hear was the constant beating of his anxiety-ridden heart.

—Chapter 23—
—Offspring—

The first screen played a recording of Kellan…

Inside of a limo. The same rusty, neon-lit vehicle that Sen had tried to summon for them to ride around in. The camera filming was mounted to the roof, and pointed straight at Kellan's bemused face.

That was the Eye of the Arbiter, Kellan thought, the realization hitting him hard.

The huge theater screen, hovering around the football field, changed the recording to show Kellan and Mavis in front of the flower shop. An Eye of the Arbiter had been recording him from across the parking lot, mounted to some sort of streetlamp.

Kellan watched himself slam the open Pestbyter with a rock, cracking the red crystal inside.

"Wow," Bitso said over the microphone, his voice filled with amusement. "What an unbridled act of aggression! This sad sack just *attacked* the Pestbyter right in the metaphorical groin. What a low blow."

Booing filled the dark audience of the stadium, their disapproval creating a rumble all its own. When the Arbiter shifted his position on the edge of the pit, Kellan felt the tremor of his weight and power.

The video continued.

Mavis drove a truck around the side of the building and slammed into the Pestbyter going as fast as she could.

"What's this?" Bitso asked as he grabbed at his blindfold. "Did our sad sack have an accomplice?"

The irritation from the audience spread like wildfire. Were they calling for Mavis's head as well? Kellan craned his head around, trying to find someone to reason with.

There was no one.

He was in the middle of a gigantic field, watched over by a colossal machine dragon, held in place by two hovering sphere robots, while a lunatic news anchor narrated everything like he was a ringmaster in a circus.

Who was there to reason with? Who could Kellan beg to spare Mavis?

The enemies of logic were all around him.

"What's that?" Bitso said as he glanced up at the massive dragon. Hot steam gushed from the Arbiter's mouth as the dragon exhaled. Bitso smiled wide. "Don't worry, ladies, gentlemen, and everything in between! The Arbiter has decided that the accomplice needn't be questioned. She wasn't the one who dealt the killing blow."

Had the Arbiter spoken? Kellan hadn't heard any words, just the low groans of gears and pistons. Could Bitso interpret what that meant? Did the audience understand the Arbiter? Kellan wasn't sure.

Then Kellan watched himself use a garden hoe to repeatedly strike the Pestbyter. Over and over. Until the Pestbyter finally stopped moving and gushed out its three arcana. Then the screen showed Kellan kneeling over the machine and absorbing the arcana for himself.

"Oof," Bitso said, tugging at the collar of his suit. His eyes were *still* blindfolded, yet he reacted to every detail on the screens. "That looks pretty cut and dry. What a blatant rule violation. This chump must want to die about as much as I do, am I right?"

Bitso motioned to the Arbiter.

With his breath trapped in his chest, practically burning his lungs to escape, Kellan waited, unable to exhale.

Then the floating screens flickered and flared to life with another recording.

"What's this?" Bitso moved around the field, the spotlights following him. "We have *more* footage the Arbiter wants us to see?" Bitso placed a hand over the microphone and "glanced" in Kellan's direction. "Did you kill *two* Pestbyters or something? Look, I don't want to tell you how to commit suicide, but just putting a bullet in your own head might've been more efficient. I'm just sayin'."

Confused, and still mired in dread, Kellan watched the screens with rapt fascination.

The video played a scene from the back alleyways of the futuristic warehouse.

Kellan spotted the black wolf man attacking the two kids, Hua and Twi—the boy with the tumor, and the girl with teeth so misshapen, he could even see them in the recording.

"Leave our f-family alone," the boy, Hua, shouted.

The audience in the football field quieted as everyone watched Kellan step out of a narrow alleyway. Kellan lifted his cursed rifle and fired, striking the wolf. The resulting fight wasn't something Kellan was proud of…

The beast wheeled on Kellan, knocked his gun away, and then proceeded to rip him apart. Kellan molded the metal into the werewolf's body, and managed to prevent his regeneration, but most of the fight involved Kellan on the ground, bleeding to death.

Even at the end, crimson wept from most parts of Kellan's damaged body as he staggered around.

"P-Please," Hua said on screen. "Don't hurt our family."

Kellan shook his head and waved his hand. "Get out of here. Before some other murderer shows up. Hurry."

The Eye of the Arbiter had been recording the fight from above, at an angle

Kellan hadn't seen. The Eyes… They really were everywhere.

Watching.

Listening.

Kellan wanted to glance around the football stadium to see if he could find any more, but he knew it was currently impossible.

The video continued on until the kids ran over and handed him a single arcana. But right before they handed it over—and it became golden—the video ended. Blip. No more footage.

The Arbiter exhaled another mountain of hot steam, his machine-body clanking from the movement of gears.

Bitso, awash in the mist for a long moment, chuckled. "Wow, what an interesting turn of events." His voice boomed across the silent crowds. "It seems that even the Arbiter can feel sentimentality for his children. That's right, folks—most forget that the denizens of the Nexus descend straight from the Arbiter himself!"

Descend from him? Kellan thought, his eyebrows knitted. *They're his offspring?*

For a short, hesitant moment, Kellan glanced up to stare at the Arbiter. The dragon had his head angled in Kellan's direction, steam rushing between the cracks of his sharp fangs. Was the beast trying to speak to him?

Kellan couldn't understand, and he quickly glanced away, hoping the dragon didn't take offense to the staring.

With a showman's flair, Bitso lifted a hand into the air and smiled. "The Arbiter will allow this sad sack to compete in the Nexus Games! What a sad turn of events—*but at least it'll be interesting for the rest of us!*"

The cheering that rose to meet his statement hurt Kellan's ears. He finally exhaled, his lungs threatening to burst. With deep breaths, Kellan felt his tension and anxiety leave him, though not enough to feel comfortable. The Pestbyters kept their hold on his arms absolute.

Bitso strode across the grass and walked over to Kellan's side. His sleek suit didn't match his bloodstained blindfold, nor did it complement Bitso's pointed molars—the news anchor had a sharp smile that looked similar to a shark's.

Now, when he wasn't so panicked, Kellan managed to see the information of his Blitzkrieg Analysis.

Name: Bitso, Unwilling Servant to the Arbiter
Race: Human
Magics: Storm, Fate
Rank: A, A
Armor Rating: —
Health: 7/7
Stats: Concealed
Abilities: Concealed

With a twist of Bitso's hand, the Pestbyters released Kellan.

Bitso moved the microphone away and leaned in close. The smell of his expensive cologne filled Kellan's nose.

With curious pokes and pats, Bitso felt up Kellan's upper arm. "Trembling still? A tough guy like you? That's adorable." He chuckled and poked at Kellan's shoulder. "You're filled with *disgusting* Tyranny Worms, though. You'll regret that once you're in the can. A pity."

Kellan managed to calm himself, but not enough to regain his full composure. The crowds out in the shadowy stands were still filling the arena with noise. Were they angry that Kellan had gotten to go free? Or were they intrigued? Kellan couldn't tell.

"Listen, between you and me, the Arbiter doesn't care *that* much about his mutant children—they're a little past their expiration date, if you catch my drift." Bitso smiled wide, his face inches from Kellan's. "But the Arbiter *is* impressed you managed to get some *gold arcana*. Good job. He *really* liked that. Keep it up, and the Arbiter might even call you back here for some prizes, you get me?"

Kellan didn't know what to say. He stared at the other man, still reeling from the dread of the over-the-top trial.

"Oh, and if you ever find me outside of an Oasis…" Bitso sighed wistfully. "Would you mind killing me? I've got sixty arcana for you if you manage to plant several bullets of your *cursed rifle* right between my eyes. Good deal, right?" Bitso patted Kellan's upper arm. "I won't even fight back. It'll be amazing for the both of us. I promise."

"I…"

"Just think about it. And why do you look so confused? Like an envelope without an address."

"Can I… even still register?" Kellan whispered, his voice nearly drowned out by the Arbiter's machines and the shouts of the audience. "Time's up."

"Ha! So punctual. Don't worry about it, sad sack. You'll get your chance to jump in the blender. The Arbiter has given you his blessing."

Before Kellan could reply, Bitso brought the microphone back up to his mouth.

"Do you have any words for us, sad sack?" His voice once again boomed across the stadium. "Something to instill fear into your competitors? Or maybe to entertain the masses watching at home? Something insightful?"

Bitso practically poked Kellan in the face with the microphone—like he couldn't see, because of the blindfold—but Kellan was still confused on the issue.

"Merry Christmas," Kellan said into the microphone, literally unable to think of anything clever to say.

The response from the audience was mixed. Excitement. Anger. It was incoherent. Kellan couldn't tell what had upset them.

"Huh," Bitso said. "I'm not familiar with that phrase. Is it a *thank the good stars I'm not dead* saying from your world? Merry Christmas indeed, am I right, sad sack?" Bitso slapped Kellan's arm again, and then pointed to the far end of the field—beyond the bloody crater and to the metal double doors. "Now get out of here. I have work to do."

Kellan stumbled one step, and then managed to turn around and head for the doors. The heat of the overhead lights beat down on him worse than summer sunshine. He was already sweating by the time he moved twenty feet away.

"Next up, we have this unruly girl! A real degenerate, if you ask me. Play the footage!"

More cheers. More rumbling.

Kellan stopped walking and glanced over his shoulder. The floating screens played footage of the girl with the copper scales and tail. She leapt from one dilapidated roof to another, clearly searching for something. The camera didn't have a good angle—it was on a light pole, far from the lizard-girl.

With claws on her hands and feet, she scurried over the roofs. Her jeans and jacket combo restricted some of her athletic movement, like she was unaccustomed to the clothing, or as if they were too small.

Then a Pestbyter showed up on the screen.

But it was injured and cracked… Sparks flew off the machine in irregular spurts. It barely spun through the air, creeping toward the lizard-girl. She froze—like an animal caught in headlights—but when the Pestbyter attacked, its laser hit a nearby building, breaking some bricks and actually damaging *itself* with falling debris.

The girl then leapt forward and attacked with her claws and fangs, biting at the red crystal inside the open sphere of the machine. That was the last of its health, apparently. It collapsed shortly afterward.

The girl had barely done anything.

Kellan turned around, waiting to hear the decision. *She doesn't deserve death for that.*

"What a bizarre series of events," Bitso said with a laugh. "This Nexus Games is going to be more fail videos than epic duels at the rate we're going. Or maybe just a series of one-sided beat downs. With men like Brenner Hawke around, you know we're going to have a bloodbath!"

The audience laughed, cruel, dark, and manic.

Bitso motioned to the Arbiter. "What say you, *Lord of the Nexus*? Has this punk sullied your beautiful realm?"

The crowds went silent as they waited.

The Arbiter turned, his gears and pistons grinding with hateful metallic sounds. But the dragon didn't turn his attention to the girl—he faced Kellan.

Bitso whirled around, smiling wide. "What's this? Sad sack stayed to watch the death of his competitor? *Good news!* The Arbiter said you saved *two* of his children, so he'll let you decide the fate of this punk!" Bitso rubbed his hands together, more blood staining his blindfold, turning the white fabric a dark red.

More spotlights homed in on Kellan. He shielded his eyes, but it was still entirely too bright to see.

Bitso walked over to the lizard-girl. She was restrained by two Pestbyters, her arms held above her head. With wide eyes, she glanced over her shoulder to get a good look at Kellan, her whole body trembling.

Bitso yanked her left hand from the grip of the Pestbyter. "What's this? She's part of Team 89? Yikes. Losing a member this early in the games is a terrible turn of events! *How hilarious!*"

More laughter.

It was starting to grate at Kellan's sanity.

He stepped forward, his breathing ragged. "Let her go," he shouted. His voice barely penetrated the cacophony of the arena.

But Bitso heard.

He immediately stopped laughing and turned to face Kellan. "What was that, sad sack?"

"Just release her," Kellan said. "If I get to decide—that's what I want. I want her to go free."

The crowds obviously hadn't heard his decision yet. They continued to laugh and cheer, like they might finally get to see more blood.

Bitso stepped forward, his smile waning. "She's your competitor. Surely you want to have an advantage against her team, don't you? That's just good sense."

Kellan couldn't even deny that. It probably *was* good sense. But he really didn't know. He didn't know the details of the Nexus Games, or what was expected of him—or the lizard-girl—or anything else going on. All he really knew was that he didn't want to watch her get smeared across the football field like the Ren Faire guy had.

And if saving the two kids had paid off for him, perhaps this would as well?

"Just let her go," Kellan said. "*That's what I want.* I don't care who she is."

The Arbiter gushed more steam onto the field. But instead of doing anything further, he slid back into the enormous pit he had emerged from. His exit left a wake of wind, disturbing the floating screens and even the Pestbyters.

The pit remained a black void with occasional smoke wafting up from it.

The audience didn't understand—their confused shouts and questions rang throughout the football stadium.

The Pestbyters released the lizard-girl. She stumbled forward, clawing at the grass to get her footing.

Bitso held up his hand, trying to gain the audience's attention. "Apparently, the Arbiter is sparing two people so they can participate in the games! What an unusual—and terrible—gift!"

The hot spotlights and frantic shouting still bothered Kellan. He turned away and jogged for the far doors, hoping to make it back into the halls of the AVU Palace.

If I'm lucky, I'll never have to see the Arbiter ever again…

—Chapter 24—

—Brenner Hawke, Traitor to Humanity—

Kellan stood in the long corridor of the AVU Palace, his dread lingering. The sounds of the stadium were muffled by the thick walls. The screens mounted to the hall walls were set to a low volume, creating an echoing effect. The cameras followed Bitso around the football field as he made declarations about the Nexus Games.

With little focus, Kellan hurried on his way, passing door after door. Each room sounded like a party was raging inside. He was desperate to find a place where he could gather his thoughts—somewhere calming and safe. *Peace and quiet—for two seconds—that's all I'm asking. It's not much. Please, Baby Jesus.*

As if the universe had a cruel sense of humor, someone shouted down the hall. "Hey! Wait! Please!"

Kellan stopped and turned around. The lizard-girl with the copper scales ran to his side, her black hair stiff, like it had product in it—or it was coarse. The girl jogged over and stopped next to Kellan, her amber eyes wide.

She was so thin, and only five and a half feet tall. How old was she? Kellan had no idea.

The information his analysis ability provided flashed over his eyes.

Name: Levvy Torrin
Race: Rezrah
Magics: —
Rank: —
Armor Rating: —
Health: 7/7

Stats:
Strength—2
Dexterity—2
Fortitude—2 [Scaled]
Charisma—2

Manipulation—2
Intelligence—2
Perception—3 [Keen-eyed]
Wisdom—2
Willpower—2

Abilities:
Personal—[Vampiric Fangs]—The rezrah can drain mana from a target whenever making a bite attack that deals damage.
Half-Mage Power—[Lucky]—The half-mage has fortunate events happen to them (once per fifteen minutes) in minor and major ways.

"I'm Levvy Torrin from Arkirn," the girl said as she knelt on one knee and bowed her head. "Th-Thank you so much for helping me."

Kellan motioned for the girl to stand. She got to her clawed feet, practically standing on her tiptoes. Her scaled tail swished from side to side as she stared up at Kellan—now silent and waiting.

"I'm Alex Kellan," he finally said, realizing this was an introduction. "You don't need to thank me. As a matter of fact, forget this. I… I need to go." He turned on his heel and resumed his walk down the hall.

Levvy didn't say anything. She followed Kellan as quiet as a shadow, sticking close—only two feet away. When Kellan glanced over his shoulder, she met his gaze with a smile.

"Merry Christmas," she said.

He narrowed his eyes. "You celebrate Christmas?"

"W-Well, I thought it was a phrase from your country that meant you were grateful to be alive? Isn't that what Bitso said?"

Kellan ran a hand down his face, already regretting his statement. He didn't reply to the girl, hating the fact that she was still following him. "Aren't you a little young to be part of the Nexus Games?"

"I'm twenty years old, long considered an adult in Arkirn," Levvy said, slight irritation in her voice. "And I didn't want to take part in the Nexus Games… I was accidentally sent here during the Conflux. I was happy living in Arkirn, learning the art of silversmithing. This world… It's unkind."

Twenty years old? Kellan could barely believe it. But then again, she wasn't *human*. Were rezrah just smaller as a race? He had to assume that was the explanation.

"The Conflux brings random people here?" Kellan asked.

Levvy nodded once. "That's how half the people in the games got here. They had to join, or be marked an enemy by the Arbiter, and be hunted down by Pestbyters and Justices. I… I had to join."

Before Kellan could say anything further, a door opened, almost striking him. Kellan jerked to a stop. Levvy stopped next to him, practically running into his arm.

Two individuals stepped out from the palace room, followed by a waft of smoke and the thump of heavy music. Once the door shut, the song became muffled, and the smoke died off.

Kellan recognized the two men.

Nasir Warren the Butcher. The seven-foot-tall bald biker with the lip piercing. He was distinct in a thuggish way. *And he has entropy magic*, Kellan recalled, still trying to gather all his chaotic thoughts.

The other man was *Jace*.

No title. No other information.

He was the thug who had given Kellan his dog tags.

Jace was Kellan's height, with pale skin and short, dark hair. He wore an honest-to-god metal pauldron on his shoulder, over his leather jacket. And Kellan would've said he was "normal" except for Jace's machine-eye. The center of the eye glowed with a blue LED, like it was some sort of camera.

"Kellan," Jace called out, half-smiling. He stepped closer, smelling of smoke. "I saw the whole trial on the viewscreens. The Arbiter's judgments have never been that dramatic before."

Nasir snorted. "What's wrong with you, Jace? We shouldn't be associating with *sad sack*." Then Nasir laughed and shot Kellan a glare. "Right? That's your new name now? I bet ya ten arcana that Bitso makes it your title once the games start."

Kellan gritted his teeth. While he didn't know what was going on half the time, he really didn't want *Alex Kellan the Sad Sack* as his title.

"You cur," Levvy said, a hiss on her voice as she stepped around Kellan. Her copper scales were flaring as she moved closer to the two men. "Alex Kellan is a noble knight. He deserves your respect."

"What's that, girlie?" Nasir asked, straightening to his full and impressive height. He was practically two feet taller than the girl. "I saw your pathetic fight on the viewscreen. *You're weak.* Just a half-mage. Watch your mouth before it gets you killed early."

Kellan placed a hand on Levvy's shoulder before she mouthed off again. She glanced up at him, her eyebrows knitted. When he pulled her back, she allowed him to step forward.

Kellan was prepared to just walk by, but Jace stepped in his path, his machine-eye focused on him. "Wait. I wanted to speak to you. About the games. About… if we met out on the field."

Nasir scoffed and then rolled his eyes. "Jace, you're making a mistake." He held up his left hand. The number 77 was inked just below his knuckles. "We're going to win. We got the lucky number."

"Lucky number?" Kellan asked, on the verge of laughing. "Are you serious?"

"Deadly. The last person who won had the number *77*." Nasir shoved his hands into his jean pockets. "And the last winner before that was on team 37, so I submit to you that the *7* is the luckiest part."

Jace rubbed at his own hand. He, too, had a black 77 marked on his body.

Although Kellan didn't really want to make plans with random competitor teams, he was curious about Jace. He had given Kellan his own dog tags… and he did look familiar.

"Are you me?" Kellan asked, finding it an awkward question. "As in, are you Alex Kellan the Defector? Me from another dimension?"

"No." Jace rubbed at the back of his neck, turning his intense eyes on the floor instead. "Look, you'll recognize yourself the moment you meet him. You two share the same… appearance."

"But not the personality," Nasir said with a huff. "The other one is *way* more intimidating."

"I'm not here to talk about the other you." Jace took a deep breath. "Look—"

A chill rushed down the corridor. Nasir and Jace both grew still and silent. They turned their attention to the end of the hall—opposite the doors to the field. For a long moment, they just stared.

"He's coming this way. Shit…" Nasir opened the door to a random room and slipped into the smoke and music, not uttering a single word about his disappearance.

When Kellan turned to ask Jace, he caught his breath.

Jace had vanished.

No sound. No indication he had left. Just… *poof.* Gone.

"You should be careful," Jace's disembodied voice said. "I think he's coming to see *you* specifically."

Kellan couldn't see Jace—was he invisible?—and Kellan whirled around, his gaze searching. *Who're they afraid of?*

And then, when Kellan turned around to speak to Levvy, he noticed she had left as well, the sound of a door clicking shut the only evidence she had fled. *What's going on*? Kellan took a step backward, wondering if he should leave the corridor as well.

It can't be worse than the Arbiter, he reasoned. *And this place is an Oasis… No one can do any violent actions here. Why would the others be spooked?*

Someone rounded the corner at the far end of the hall.

It was a man.

Just an ordinary man.

Well, perhaps not *ordinary*. He wore cargo pants, military boots, and a tight tank top, his muscles on full display. When the man strode forward, it was with the swagger of someone so confident in their abilities. He moved with the strong gait of a fighter, and the casual speed of someone who just didn't give a damn.

Kellan waited, tense and uneasy. No matter how much he just wanted to rest, the Nexus wasn't about to let him.

The other man… When he drew close, the chill intensified. It matched the man's cold exterior. He had sandy blond hair, swept back, with dark eyes that could disturb the dead.

The stranger smiled, but he had all the welcoming warmth of a morgue.

Kellan's eyes flashed with the analytical information he had become accustomed to.

Name: Brenner Hawke, Traitor to Humanity
Race: Human
Magics: Body, Metal, Entropy, Travel, Meta
Rank: A, S, S, A, D
Armor Rating: 15 + 10 Shielding [Metallic]
Health: 55/55 [Cyborg-Enhanced]

Stats:
Strength—20 [Cyborg-Enhanced, Iron Grip]
Dexterity—18 [Cyborg-Enhanced, Pinpoint Accuracy]
Fortitude—20 [Cyborg-Enhanced, Tireless]
Charisma—5 [Controlling]
Manipulation—11 [Dark, Occult]
Intelligence—8
Perception—14 [Cyborg-Enhanced, Keen-Sighted]
Wisdom—6
Willpower—11 [Ambitious]

Abilities:
Personal—[Overconfident]—The mage can never hide their basic information, but if they are ever in combat with an enemy mage who does, this mage's physical stats (strength, dexterity, fortitude) are doubled.
Hex—[Wielder of Arondight]—The mage is capable of wielding the legendary laser sword, Arondight. As punishment, the mage must kill one member of a sentient race every seven days (the counter starting after each death), or the wielder dies.
Hex—[Apex Growth]—The mage gains double the arcana from all his kills. As punishment, the mage suffers from *mana burn* (mana use burns them, dealing damage equal to mana spent).
Hex—[Exarch's Power]—The mage gains an immunity to a magical energy type (fire, ice, lightning, laser, phantasmal, entropy, or phase) and becomes immune to all *mana burn* effects. As punishment, the mage's permanent mana pool is cut in half every time they rank to S in a magic. If the mage ever drops below 20 permanent mana, they die.
Hex—[Connected to the Sea of Chaos]—The mage's mana pool is doubled, and they gain access to the unknowable magics, capable of ranking them as any other. As punishment, the mage's soul cracks each time they use a C rank or higher power (and after an unspecified number of cracks, the mage's soul shatters, killing them).

Kellan could barely get through all the information. *How many hexes does this guy have?*

But he knew the name. *Brenner Hawke.* The one Bitso had seemed excited for.

"Here you are," Brenner drawled, no hurry in his voice. He slipped his hands into his pockets. "I'm glad I managed to find you before anything happened."

Kellan glanced over his shoulder, surprised by the desert around him. Not a single soul was around—except for maybe Jace, who was invisible—but otherwise they were alone. When he turned back to Brenner, the man was giving him the once over.

"You have a lot of hexes," Kellan said. "Is that why you're in the games?"

"I'm in the games to get to Zenith. The hexes are just to acquire the power necessary to guarantee my victory."

"Acquire the power?"

"That's right. That's why people agree to hexes in the first place. For the power—some sort of magical item, ability, or great boon the hex offers."

Kellan slowly nodded, absorbing the information. Husker's hex allowed him to kill people. What did Xiang's hex do? And Brenner's… Brenner had so many, he might as well be drowning in them.

"I saw your trial on the viewscreen." Brenner smirked. "And how you fought that rennic in the alleyway, defending the two inbred kids."

"Oh, yeah?"

"It was pathetic. You almost lost to a C-rank chump. That's not like the Alex Kellan I know, which means… You have no idea what's going on here, do you?"

Kellan crossed his arms, unsure of how to respond.

"It's okay," Brenner said with a lazy chuckle. "If anything, this is my fault. Xiang summoned you here because she can't stand losing to me."

"What do you mean?"

Brenner held out a hand, like he wanted to shake Kellan's. "I'm Admiral Brenner Hawke, with the United Earth Defense Force." When Kellan didn't take it, Brenner returned his hand to his pocket, no hint of irritation or offense. "Listen, Xiang and I have a long history, and I apologize that you got caught up in all this."

"Oh?"

"Let me make it up to you. You haven't registered for a team, correct?"

Kellan lifted an eyebrow. "Not yet."

"Then join mine."

He caught his breath, stunned by the offer. "Are you serious?"

"We already have five members—" Brenner shrugged, "—but I'll make an exception for you. The other Alex Kellan is a good friend of mine, after all."

Kellan mulled over the statement. He glanced at Brenner's hand. Sure enough, he had a black 42. He *was* on the same team as Kellan's doppelganger.

"You… want *me* on your team?" Kellan asked. "You just said my fighting was pathetic."

"You're rather weak. But you don't have to worry about that. Haven't you seen the numbers? I'm favored to win the games."

Brenner waited, like he wanted some sort of reaction—or perhaps a congratulations. Kellan didn't offer either. He just wanted the man to get to the point.

With a sigh, Brenner continued, "Listen, if you do what I say, and keep your head low, you might just live long enough to win the Nexus Games with me."

"Lucky me."

Brenner smiled, though it wasn't anything genuine. "It's better than joining Xiang's team. She's a snake—a manipulator. I guarantee she won't even make it to the third round. You have a much better chance with me."

Kellan rubbed at his arms, the chill in the hallway worse than before.

"Let me get this straight," Kellan said. "You and Xiang had a falling out?"

"That's right. She thought she could win the games without me, and now I want to make sure she regrets every decision that brought her here." Brenner motioned to Kellan. "And if I convince her old flame to join my team over hers—*for a second time*—it'll be an amusing blow to morale." When he smiled, it was more wicked than Kellan had seen before.

"So, you want to recruit me to get back at Xiang?" Kellan huffed and forced a laugh. "That's embarrassingly petty."

Brenner's smile didn't wane. "Petty? No. It's *thorough*."

The venom in his voice seemingly came from nowhere.

Kellan tensed, like the conversation could become a fight.

"I can't just *beat her at the games*," Brenner said, his volume increasing a bit with each word. "Xiang and I had a deal—and she broke it. So now… I need to break her. Mentally. Emotionally. *Physically*." Brenner lowered his voice, his body tense and controlled, right down to how precise he blinked. "I'll *thoroughly* make sure she regrets crossing me, and if you join my team, it will be yet another blow to her ego. She'd only have four members of her team, and she'll be forced to recruit some bum from the streets."

Kellan kept his arms crossed, his fingers digging into his arms.

Despite the fact that Kellan wasn't answering, Brenner continued, "And I already told you—if you join me, you'll likely win the games. There's no downside."

Kellan smirked. "Look, I've known you for a grand total of ten seconds, and already I would prefer the company of a murderous clown. There's so many red flags coming off you, I can barely see."

Brenner didn't react. He didn't say anything—his facial expression didn't change. But when he spoke, it was slower and vicious. "Is that right?"

"I don't know Xiang very well, but from what I know of you, I'm not interested."

There was a prolonged moment of silence.

Then Brenner said, "I'll give you one more chance. And think about it, Alex Kellan. I know you. You're a solider. A man who wants to do a job—and he wants to do it right. Xiang is going to use you. You might not know for what, but I promise you, she's not being truthful."

Before Kellan could answer, Brenner held out his hand a second time.

"Join me, Kellan. I'll introduce you to your counterpart, and we'll discuss our path to victory. I promise you won't regret it."

—Chapter 25—
—Twelve Magics—

Kellan stared at Brenner's hand, caught in a loop of thoughts that yanked him back and forth.

On the one hand, Brenner was right. Kellan preferred to work as a soldier in a hierarchy that was straightforward with him. And Brenner reeked of military. On the other hand, there were two kinds of military people, in Kellan's experience—the kind who valued loyalty, defense, and self-sacrifice, and the kind who valued power, control, and authority over all others. Brenner was clearly the latter. Kellan had never much cared for those kinds of military people.

And there was also the matter of surviving an unknown game filled with obvious magical and technological dangers. Kellan didn't trust Xiang—she had asked for his help, but Brenner was right again. She was shady, and Kellan knew he wasn't entirely in on whatever secrets she had.

And they were probably substantial secrets, considering everything that had already happened. *And* her brother forced him into the competition with magical worms. It was still a contention between them…

So, what would it be?

Play the deadly game with Xiang, an illusionist who didn't trust him and clearly had a past that would come back to haunt them all?

Or play the deadly game with Brenner, a man with an obsessive need to win and dominate, who was potentially a sociopath?

Although no option was Kellan's ideal, he knew he still had another obligation, and that was to Mavis. The only reason she was in the Nexus was because of him. Kellan couldn't stand the idea of abandoning her or competing on a team without her. It didn't matter how much everyone thought Brenner would win, Kellan wouldn't abandon Mavis.

"Sorry," Kellan said. "But I'm sticking with my original team."

Brenner put his hand down, like he wasn't surprised with the outcome. "A shame. But that's fine. It's not like you're a threat. And killing you will be just as morally debilitating as taking you on my team—it's just not going to be as amusing."

"What a shame," Kellan quipped. "It sucks when your petty revenge schemes can't be *amusing*."

With a casual shrug, Brenner once again slipped his hands into his pants pockets. "Well, it's obvious you don't really know what's going on here, so I'll let most of this slide."

"How gracious."

"I'll see you around." Brenner turned and walked off, no hurry in his step, no other words or even a glance over his shoulder. Once he turned and disappeared from the hallway, the chill dissipated.

Kellan glanced around, trying to see Jace. He couldn't—the invisibility was perfect.

He did notice an eyeball on the ceiling, however. Large, half-flesh, half-machine. One of the Eyes of the Arbiter. Even now, the Arbiter was watching.

A shiver ran down his spine.

"You still here?" Kellan whispered.

"Yeah," Jace responded, his disembodied voice on the other side of Kellan. "I wasn't going to miss that."

Kellan turned in Jace's general direction. "What was that? Why was it so cold? He just has an ominous aura?"

"It happens when you start taking on so many hexes. Those taint the soul like nothing else, and after a couple, anyone sensitive to magic can feel them."

Kellan crossed his arms and then uncrossed them, his thoughts wrapping around the concepts of *curses* and *hexes*. Sen had told him the difference, but Kellan still hadn't fully grasped the situation…

Curses and hexes were the cost of acquiring either powerful items or powers.

"Brenner took a bunch of hexes in exchange for phenomenal magical abilities? And a laser sword, apparently?"

Jace dropped his invisibility, appearing out of thin air, casually leaning on the wall of the AVU Palace. He offered Kellan a shrug. "I'm pretty sure he went out of his way to find a bunch of specific powers to help him win the Nexus Games. Double arcana from kills? Wielding one of the legendary weapons? Immunity to a magical energy type? Too convenient to be random. Brenner planned this out long in advance. Not sure how he found so many beneficial hexes…"

"Do other mages do that, too?"

"Sometimes. But typically, just one hex—hexes usually have such a terrible negative side effect, that no one wants to take them." Jace glanced over, his machine eye's iris constricted. "You have a couple curses. Nothing serious. You might want to consider taking a hex to give yourself an edge. You're so weak, otherwise."

"Thanks," Kellan muttered as he turned away. "I'll keep that in mind."

"It's just friendly advice." Jace pushed away from the wall. "And one more piece of advice—you should go register before something else happens. You never know around here."

Although Kellan was suspicious of almost everyone in the games, Jace was the only one who seemed genuinely helpful, and with seemingly no strings attached. It made Kellan wonder. Why? But he didn't really want to go into it now.

He still felt exhausted.

With heavy feet, Kellan headed down the hallway, trying to retrace the path the Pestbyters had taken to the field. The music within the palace rumbled the walls and floors, even shaking the chandeliers. Some rooms were quieter than others, and Kellan appreciated the mellow attitude.

I'd take a hex just to get a solid eight hours of sleep.

Despite his fatigue, Kellan managed to find his way back to the door that led to the betting room with all the counters and windows. He pushed his way in and found the same quiet area that he had left. Soft jazz music played over the speakers as people walked up to the windows to place bets.

Kellan searched for Mavis, but he didn't spot her. The only one from his team who still remained was Xiang. She was the most striking and beautiful individual in the room, her elegant grace superhuman. It was like comparing a supermodel to a bunch of terribly drawn stick figures.

He strode over to her, a million questions swirling in his head. When he approached, she regarded him with a neutral expression.

Xiang smoothed her long, silky white robes. "I'm glad you've returned. The Arbiter has given you his blessing?"

"Do you know what the Arbiter looks like?" Kellan asked as he stepped close to her. He tried to keep his volume down, but his anger made it difficult. "He's a damn *machine dragon*. The size of a skyscraper! No eyes." Kellan motioned to his face. "Nowhere. Just steam. And radioactive green insides."

Xiang brought a slender hand to her chin. Her gaze fell to the carpeted floor. "If you believe the legends, the Arbiter clawed his own eyes out to gain true sight over his domain. The Eyes of the Arbiter were his actual eyes that he imbued with life."

"After everything I've seen, I believe it."

Xiang motioned to the registration window. The same android from before was waiting—a machine person without any sort of facial expression or presence. "We should finish. Then we can go meet the others. It's imperative we rest before the first game."

Although he still had questions, Kellan went straight for the window. He placed his left arm on the counter.

"Welcome," the android said with an old-timey radio voice. "The Arbiter has made an exception for your registration. Which team would you like to join?"

"Team 101," Kellan said.

"A good choice! They have yet to register a fifth member, and they were close to being disqualified." The android grabbed Kellan's left arm and then ran its machine-hand over his skin.

It hurt for just a second. A quick jab. Then a black number blossomed across his skin.

101.

Kellan removed his arm and stared at it. The odd tattoo marking almost seemed… capable of movement.

"Congratulations," the android said. The sound of poppers and confetti rang out from his tiny speakers. "You have successfully registered for the Nexus

Games. In the morning, at exactly 9am, your team leader will be given a prompt to choose your style of game. All instructions for the specific game will be given to you at that time."

"Thanks," Kellan muttered, his attention still on the number.

"Please follow all the rules given to you at the start of each game. Failure to abide by the rules could lead to punishment at the hands of the Arbiter."

Kellan nodded.

"I feel compelled to remind you, given your earlier violence, that you aren't allowed to attack the Pestbyters or the Justices."

"Oh, don't worry. I learned my lesson."

"Good." The android spun around. "Good luck in the Nexus Games!"

Kellan stepped away from the window. His arm felt normal. No pain, no differences. He walked back to Xiang's side, now prepared to get more answers.

"Some lunatic named *Brenner Hawke* approached me," Kellan said. "He wanted me to join his team."

Xiang had no reaction. She motioned to one of the far doors, and walked with Kellan toward it. "I take it he told you that he would win the games, and you should join him to have a chance of winning yourself?"

"Something like that."

When they approached the door, Xiang motioned with her hand. The door seemingly opened by itself, moved by some unseen force. Xiang and Kellan walked through and entered another hall through the palace.

"He also said you were a manipulator," Kellan muttered. "And after seeing your specialized ability about illusions, I'm leaning toward believing him."

"Hm."

"You wanna tell me what's going on?" Kellan lifted an eyebrow and glanced at her.

Xiang threw back some of her inky-black hair. "It's an uninteresting story. I was with Brenner. We made plans to compete in the Nexus Games, but during our planning, and gathering of arcana, I fell for someone else."

"*Me*?" Kellan quipped.

"Yes and no." Xiang pointed to a door in the hall, and headed straight for it. "He's you, but his dimension is so far removed from yours, that you two really aren't the same people. You look alike. But that's where the similarities end."

Kellan nodded along with her words. Was this a nature versus nurture situation? Was the other Alex Kellan different because his universe was strange?

When they approached the next door, Xiang once again flicked her wrist. The door opened, they stepped through, and then it closed behind them. The next room was an aquarium—several tanks filled with jellyfish, rays, and sharks were scattered throughout the dimly lit room.

A few other mages milled around the area, staring at the exotic fish. The ceiling was twenty feet up, and some of the tanks went all the way up.

One of the fish… was a seahorse, but so large, it might as well have been an actual horse.

As they walked through the blue lights glowing from the tanks, Xiang half-smiled. "Well, after I… left Brenner to be with someone else… He didn't handle that well. We had some disagreements, and after some *violence*, we went our separate ways."

"Wow. That's the vaguest story I've ever heard." Kellan stared at a glowing green jellyfish. It had a red dot inside its bloom, like the immortal jellyfish. "Do you care to add any details?"

"That's as specific as I'm going to get."

"Okay. Well, Brenner declared he's going to win, but not before completely destroying you. I'm pretty sure he's out to murder you in the most psychotic way possible."

They walked to the other end of the aquarium, away from the other mages, and toward a door in the darkened corner of the room. Xiang stepped up to the door and stared at the handle. Kellan waited, wondering what was going through her head.

The door opened, but not from Xiang's influence. Sen stood on the other side—his child-like size a slight shock as Kellan had to glance down just to see him.

"There you are!" Sen said once he planted his eyes on Xiang. "I was beginning to worry. He shot Kellan a glare. "I saw what happened on the viewscreen. You're completely reckless. I'm surprised the Arbiter rewarded that behavior."

Without a word, Xiang walked around her brother and into a second hallway. Sen followed close behind her, fussing with the hem of her sleeves. When Kellan followed, he tried to ignore "the kid" but he found it difficult.

"Why are you upset?" Sen asked, his brow furrowed.

Xiang shook her head. "I'm okay."

"I know you, Sister. You're not. Was it something our warrior did?"

Kellan gritted his teeth. "I'm just asking questions. I don't think it's unreasonable to expect a few answers, especially considering that I'm going to be risking my life for *our* victory."

"You don't really understand magic," Xiang stated matter-of-factly. "So it's difficult to even begin to explain."

"I'm picking things up."

Sen rolled his eyes. "Please, warrior. Quiet. You've been bumbling your way through everything so far. You don't understand anything. Do you even know how many magics there are? Or their basic properties?"

"I do," Kellan stated.

Xiang glanced over, her dark eyes calculating. "From one day in the Nexus?"

"That's right."

Sen scoffed. "Tell us, then. Please. I can't wait to hear."

The new hallway was mostly empty, but a thin cloud of smoke milled around the ceiling, creating a BBQ aroma. Kellan hadn't realized how hungry he was until then, but he hoped they'd find a room soon.

"Well?" Sen snapped. "Or were you lying?"

Kellan stopped walking. The other two did as well.

"There are twelve magics," Kellan said.

He had seen them during the party. He had counted everything he saw, from his analysis, and the metal bars on people's outfits.

Kellan continued, "And those twelve magics seem to be broken into four groups of three. The first group of three are storm, magma, and eclipse. They're all magics related to elements."

Sen's eyebrows slowly crept to his hairline. Xiang waited, her gaze sharp and intelligent, like she was silently grading his performance.

"The second group is body, mind, and soul," Kellan stated. "Since they're all related to someone's physical being."

Xiang smiled slightly.

"The third grouping of magics are wyld, metal, and entropy, and I think they're related because they have to do with the flow of life. Birth, civilization, and then death."

"They're known as the *destiny* magics," Xiang added with a nod of her head. "And you're correct. They're the magic that stems from the circle of life. Growth, progress, and death."

"And the last set of magics are the *unknowable ones*, aren't they?" Kellan half-laughed. "The only people who had them were Bitso, the Arbiter, and Brenner Hawke. And they were travel, fate, and meta. Something about these make them special—or maybe more powerful—than the rest."

Kellan had paid special attention to how frequently he saw the magics. *Tons* of mages had at least one elemental magic. Storm, magma, and eclipse magics appeared everywhere. A good portion of the mages had body, soul, or mind, and few had wyld, metal, or entropy.

But travel, fate, and meta were basically unseen, except for the three Kellan had listed.

"They're known as *ascendancy magics* to those who are educated," Sen said matter-of-factly. "Travel magic allows individuals to teleport or slip through dimensions. Fate controls luck and allows you to see into the future. And meta is the magic *of* magic. You can empower things or change magic fundamentally. These magics are too powerful and complex for most mages. Those who can learn them are thought of as ascended."

He spoke as though he was caught in a moment of awe, happy to discuss the topic with anyone who wanted.

"And there are energy types associated with different magics," Kellan stated.

His magics had told him about the lasers, Mavis had used fire, and the Ren Faire man who had attacked the Pestbyter had used lightning. Which meant different magics offered different typings.

And then there was Brenner's hex… The one that granted him a magical typing immunity. It listed all the different types, but it made logical sense to connect them to certain magics.

"Storm magic has ice and lightning typing," Kellan said, trying to logically grasp at which magic each would have. "Magma has fire. Eclipse and metal seem to have lasers… Mind has phantasmal." The mind magic was a guess, but he wasn't about to admit that. "Entropy has entropy, obviously, and then there's phase damage, and it comes from one of the unknowable magics."

"Travel," Xiang said. "Phase damage is the typing that breaks things apart."

Kellan pointed at her. "There. I know the magics. I know they offer different skills, and have numerous magical energies."

"Did someone tell you all of this?" Sen demanded.

"No. I just paid attention."

Xiang smiled, but she quickly lifted her hand to cover half her face with her sleeve. After a moment, she said, "Maybe you and your counterpart aren't so dissimilar."

"Well, since I know what's going on, are you two going to answer my questions?" Kellan crossed his arms and clenched his jaw. "I think I deserve to know. Why is Brenner so obsessed with killing you? And is there anything to do about it? I feel like we need a plan for a man like him."

Xiang lowered her hand and nodded once. "Very well. You're right. You're more competent than I originally expected. But… my personal history really is of no consequence."

"That's right," Sen said.

"And I already have a plan for Brenner. You needn't worry yourself over him."

"Oh?" Kellan lifted an eyebrow. "What're we going to do?"

"Have you seen Husker use his power of decay and destruction?"

"The thing he used on the yami?" Kellan thought back to the beast in the bizarre swamp. Husker had rotted away its life in a matter of mere seconds.

"Brenner doesn't know about Husker's hex," Xiang stated. In a quiet voice, she added, "The reason I reached out to Husker was because he wanted to get rid of his hex… And because I knew his power could kill Brenner within a matter of seconds. His hex deals more damage to the target based on the power of the target itself. The more powerful the mage, the more destruction it does."

Kellan half-laughed. "Really?"

Xiang smiled. "If Brenner comes for us, I have an ace up my sleeve—and that ace is Husker."

—Chapter 26—
—Team 101—

Kellan followed behind Xiang and her brother as they headed for an elegant staircase made of polished wood and marble. The twenty steps to the second floor were a breeze for Kellan, but each one was its own adventure for Sen's short kid-legs.

When they reached the second floor of the AVU Palace, Kellan almost asked one of the thirty-eight other questions he had at the tip of his tongue, but Xiang waved her hand and another door opened.

"Here," she said, calm and graceful. "This is where we'll stay for the majority of the Nexus Games."

Kellan stepped around her and entered a glorious suite, comparable to any penthouse he had seen. He hadn't ever spent the night in a penthouse, but several of his missions had required him to protect politicians staying in them.

This suite was the kind straight out of a brochure—the perfectly immaculate room for all the photos and advertisements.

Lush crimson carpets, leather couches, and a grand dining table filled the entrance room. Four doors led to bedroom and bathroom combos, and a restaurant-sized kitchen was positioned near the back, adjacent to a palatial balcony.

"This is the suite reserved for legacy players," Sen said as he hurried into the suite. He waved his short arms around. "Since Xiang's mother won the last Nexus Games, she's allowed to stay here for her time during the games."

"Xiang's mother?" Kellan lifted an eyebrow. "I thought you were siblings."

Xiang entered the suite and then closed the door with a flick of her wrist. It shut with a quick *snap*. "We have different mothers."

"So, you're half-siblings."

"You catch on so quickly," Sen quipped.

He hustled to the center of the main room, between two gigantic couches. A large TV was mounted on the far wall, and Sen stopped to stare at his reflection on the dead black surface. Then he touched his face, his fingers lingering on his puffy cheeks.

Xiang waited by the front door.

Before Kellan could get another comment in, Mavis and Husker stepped out of a bedroom.

Husker had ditched his trench coat and opted for just his pants—and his chains. Where had Xiang's illusions gone?

Kellan glanced down at his own body. His ratty tank top, shredded jeans, and bloody boots were a surprise. He felt his body up, wondering when the illusions had disappeared.

Mavis wore her black T-shirt and jeans, her limp still noticeable, but not so much when she carefully moved about. The moment she spotted Kellan, her eyes went wide. "You made it!"

He nodded as she made her way over. "Yeah. Somehow."

"I saw what happened on the TV." Mavis patted his arms and chest, like she was searching for some sort of hidden injury. "That trial was insane. I can't believe a dragon killed a man."

"I think I lost a few years off my life from pure fright alone," Kellan said with a forced chuckle. "But apparently, the Arbiter liked that I helped his kids and gathered some gold arcana."

Sen wheeled around, glaring. "Are you still going on about *gold* arcana? I told you, that's not possible."

"The Arbiter liked that I got it—and wants me to keep gathering it."

Sen stomped across the wide-open space and then frowned. "I saw the whole trial, even the footage of when you gallivanted off to play with children. There was no gold arcana anywhere to be seen."

Kellan opened his mouth to rebut the statement, but caught his breath short. The videos *hadn't* shown the arcana. They had all abruptly ended right after the children came over to help him. Kellan had thought it odd in the moment, and he wondered if it had been done intentionally.

But why?

"There was gold arcana," Kellan muttered. He knew he wasn't insane—at least, he hoped not.

"If it exists, I'm sure we'll see it again," Xiang said, disinterest in her voice.

She practically glided across the suite, her steps making no sound and barely disturbing the carpet. When Xiang reached a bedroom, the door opened for her. She stopped in the doorway and turned around.

"At 8:30am tomorrow, the rules for the Nexus Games will be recited over the Arbiter's channel. We should be awake for that."

Husker shook his head, like a dog dispelling water. Then he smoothed his fur and nodded. "I agree. We shouldn't miss that."

"Until then, I recommend you take a dip in the spa, and then get some sleep. We should be well rested before the first games begin."

Xiang didn't wait for acknowledgement. She stepped into her bedroom and shut the door behind her. The click of a lock told Kellan she wasn't expecting to emerge before the morning, though he did wonder why she wasn't strategizing with them more.

Why weren't any of them strategizing?

"Shouldn't we be discussing the games more?" Kellan asked, the mounting pressure eating at him more than his fatigue.

"They're difficult to talk about," Husker muttered. "There are different types of games for each round. The team leaders pick which game their team will participate in, once they're prompted. Until then, we don't know what the game will entail."

Oh, fantastic. Just what I've always wanted. No information whatsoever.

Kellan kept his sarcasm to himself.

With a wide swoosh of his robes, Sen turned, headed over to Mavis, and then stopped by her side. He glowered at her leg, and she stepped away, frowning.

"What're you doing?" she asked.

"Sit on the couch," Sen commanded.

With a grimace of pain, Mavis jerked and turned. It took Kellan a moment to recognize the signs of the Tyranny Worms at work. They controlled Mavis until she did as instructed and sat down. Once situated, she shook her head and grabbed at her temples.

Sen walked over and pointed at her leg. "Take off your pants."

On the edge of being enraged, Kellan stormed over and grabbed Sen by the shoulder. He whirled the kid around, much to Sen's shock.

"What're you doing?"

Sen flailed around until he dislodged himself from Kellan's grip. "How dare you! Don't touch me. I'm not here for you to push around—I'm here to use my puppetry and fleshcrafting abilities! Our *second warrior* is hobbled. You think that will help us in the games, cretin? *I need to fix her.*"

Confused and uncertain of what was going on, Kellan stepped away from Sen. "You can fix her?"

"*Of course I can!*" He motioned to himself with dramatic flair. "I'm Sun Sen! A talented mage of esteemed repute."

Mavis scooted to the edge of the couch. "Well, if you really can, you didn't need to command me. I would've let you heal me at any time."

"Just remove your pants so I can see the injuries." Sen turned back to her, his eyes hardened and his focus intense.

Mavis did as she was asked.

Her legs…

Both had scars, but her left leg was much worse than the other. It was gnarled and shiny with twisted skin that had healed poorly. Her knee was the worst part. It looked like it had gone through a blender and then been slapped back on her body.

In an attempt to be polite—but still see what was going on—Kellan moved around to the back of the couch, so that he could see Sen, but not most of Mavis's body. Husker joined him, his hulking werewolf form smelling slightly like wet dog.

There were no words exchanged; Sen simply touched Mavis's knee and his hand slid into her flesh as though it were clay. Mavis shuddered as Sen's fingers ran through her muscle and tendons, and then through her kneecap and bones.

"You were damaged by… shrapnel," Sen muttered, his focus absolute. Then he yanked his hand out of her leg, leaving it slightly twisted, as though it had been deformed. "You're missing pieces… Curse the good stars."

After a long sigh, Sen pulled his red robes off his shoulder, exposing his own skin. Then he scooped at his body—physically removing a bit of his being—and held it in his hand like Play-Doh. With careful movements, he brought the flesh-ball close to Mavis's knee and slowly kneaded them together, like a baker smooshing dough.

Kellan and Husker watched with rapt attention, never glancing away.

The chunk Sen had taken from his own body didn't remain a giant hole in his body. Instead, it filled in with more flesh, seemingly coming from the rest of Sen's physical being. It didn't look like the work of the Tyranny Worms…

Kellan didn't dwell on the mystery long.

It was intriguing the way Sen moved his fingers and molded Mavis's knee back into a perfect form. It reminded Kellan of watching a master sculpture. With every movement of his fingers, Sen shaped Mavis a perfect leg, removing all scars and returning her to perfect health.

Before he was done, he shaped her right leg as well, scraping away the blemishes.

"You should take better care of your body," Sen muttered with the authority of an angry teacher. "It's the flesh cage that holds your mind. You don't want it to break, do you?"

Mavis rubbed at her left knee. "Trust me, I didn't want to get injured. It just happened."

"Make sure that was the last time. I… don't know if I can keep doing this."

Sen stepped away from her and then pulled his robes back over his shoulder.

He appeared younger than before.

Perhaps a bit shorter.

Like a seven-year-old.

After a shaky breath, Sen walked back over to the TV. He glanced at the black surface, his reflection staring back at him. With slow movements, he touched his cheek again, examining the puffiness.

Examining his youth.

Mavis stood from the couch, put her jeans back on, and then twirled around. A laugh escaped her, high-pitched and giddy. Then she stopped and turned to Kellan.

"Do you believe this?"

He shrugged. "If an alien descended from the sky and said he could turn us all into llamas, I'd believe it at this point."

Mavis slapped her left knee. "Stop joking around! *Do you see this*?"

"Yeah. It's amazing." Kellan walked around the couch. "I'm glad. I just…" He focused his sight on her, wondering if the numbers had changed…

Name: Mavis Cartwright
Race: Human
Magics: Magma, Metal

Rank: E, E
Armor Rating: —
Health: 7/7

Stats:
Strength—2
Dexterity—3 [Accurate]
Fortitude—2
Charisma—2
Manipulation—2
Intelligence—3
Perception—4 [Mystic]
Wisdom—2
Willpower—4 [Tough]

Abilities:
Personal—[Rebuilt]—The mage can develop their physical stats (strength, dexterity, fortitude) for half the arcana cost.

"You gained a point of fortitude," Kellan muttered. "And it doesn't say you're hobbled anymore. It seems like he actually fixed you."

Mavis smiled and nodded. "That's insane." Then she turned around, laughter in her words as she said, "Thank you, Sen. Just… Thank you."

The kid remained focused on the TV. He didn't answer.

Mavis quietly walked to his side, clearly determined to speak with him.

Unwilling to disturb Sen, Kellan glanced around for Husker. The werewolf man was already in the kitchen, and heading for the sliding glass door that led to the massive balcony. Kellan jogged after him, wanting answers to so many questions.

He crossed the kitchen—the smell of lemon and sugar igniting his hunger—but he pushed past it until he came to the balcony door.

Then Kellan caught his breath.

It wasn't just a normal balcony. It was a spa. The whole balcony. With water that fell from the far edge, like a waterfall, down to the gardens below. Hot steam wafted off the surface of the water, mists caught in a gentle breeze.

The water glowed a gentle pink. The lights on the floor of the spa gave the entire thing a mystical and ethereal appearance.

The spa had to be large enough to allow for a whole herd of elephants.

Husker opened the sliding glass door. Then he undid the belt of his pants, carefully stepped out of his clothing, and then into the spa. He sighed as he sank into the depths, all the way until the water reached the bottom of his canine chin.

His chains seemed to hold him down, sinking immediately to the polished marble bottom.

"What is this?" Kellan asked as he stepped to the edge of the water.

He couldn't fully articulate his feelings, but the water called to him.

"It's a mana spring," Husker said as he closed his eyes. "Step in, and your mana will be restored."

Kellan hesitantly reached for the bottom of his tank top. He stared at Husker. The man had enough fur to hide anything questionable, but Kellan wasn't so lucky. Then again, the high-tempo music and joyous screams could be heard on the chill winds around the palace. Perhaps this was a "party place" that didn't care about clothing.

The sound of scraping drew Kellan out of his thoughts. He glanced upward and spotted someone on the side of the palace, just above their balcony.

Kellan reached for the rifle slung on his shoulder, but he stopped himself once he recognized the copper scales and flat tail.

It was Levvy, the rezrah.

She was hanging on to the side of the palace like a freakish half-human, half-gecko creature. With a few awkward movements, she slid down the wall toward the balcony, and then unhooked herself the last few steps and fell onto the small walkway to the mana spring.

"I finally found you!"

Husker's fur stood on end as he straightened himself. "What's this?" he asked with a growl, his fangs bared.

"It's okay," Kellan said, holding up hand. "She's with me."

"You know a rezrah?"

"I wouldn't say that. She's just… the person I saved from the Arbiter."

"I'm forever grateful." Levvy stood next to him, her jeans and black jacket more scuffed up than before, like she had slid through the dirt at a baseball game. She held up a clawed hand. "I wanted to see you before the games began."

Kellan glanced at the water, then back at Levvy, debating whether or not to try the mana spring. "We're on different teams. Shouldn't you be with your friends? Preparing for tomorrow?"

Levvy tapped the tips of her clawed fingers together, her gaze falling to the floor. "There isn't much to discuss. I've, um, been designated the Straggler."

Finally making up his mind, Kellan ripped off his boots. Then he stepped into the spring, unconcerned with his pants, and opting to keep his tank top. *I doubt anyone will care if I swim fully clothed*, he thought.

"Straggler?" Kellan asked, only half paying attention to Levvy's statements.

"That's right. So… I thought I would come and spend time with you."

The soothing power of the water soaked straight into Kellan's body. He happily sank into the waters, just as Husker had, and allowed himself to absorb all the magical goodness the spa had to offer.

A notification filled his mind.

[Alex Kellan] has recovered all mana (10/10).
[Tyranny Worms] enter *Hive Mode*.

Kellan jerked into a standing position, his breathing ragged.

He rubbed at his face, his hand wet, and the warm water soothing his tired eyelids. "I can never just relax," he whispered with a dark chuckle. "It's always *something*. Worms in my body. Dragons about to crush me. Madmen bribing me to kill them. Can I get *one thing*, Universe? Just one moment of relaxation. I'm begging you."

Levvy leaned close to the water. After staring at the calm surface for a long moment, she unzipped her leather jacket and removed it. She wore nothing underneath, and her copper scales only covered the sides of her ribs.

"What're you doing?" Kellan demanded. He held up a hand to shield his vision. "Put your damn clothes on."

"Is-Is something wrong?" Levvy stepped away, her voice shaky. She grabbed her jacket and wrapped it around her body.

Husker rested back into the water and huffed out a laugh. "Nothing is wrong. Humans are just odd creatures. They have little dots on their chests that they don't want anyone else to see. It's shameful for them."

"R-Really?" Levvy pulled the jacket away from her body—just a small amount—and stared at her own flat chest. "Rezrah don't have dots."

"Of course you don't!" Sen shouted as he stepped out onto the balcony, his volume so loud, Kellan was sure the Arbiter could hear it in his pit. "Those *dots* are mammary ducts from which milk is secreted. Humans feed their young from their own glorious bodies, whereas rezrah chew food and regurgitate it for their children—who hatch from eggs, like disgusting lizards."

Kellan slapped a hand to his face, somehow a mix of embarrassed, baffled, and frustrated. For some reason, the universe had answered his plea for relaxation with an interdimensional sex-ed class.

"What're you doing here, anyway?" Sen asked Levvy, his volume ever-increasing. "You're a spy for Brenner, aren't you? You stink of treachery."

The rezrah girl moved away from him, her scales flaring. "I came to see Alex Kellan. I… I wanted his advice for the games."

"You won't speak to him." Sen pointed to the waterfall edge of the balcony. "*Leave us*! You're not welcome here, snake."

Levvy hugged her jacket close. Then she turned and ran to the edge of the balcony—to the last part of the walkway—and leapt off toward the gardens below. Kellan wasn't concerned since he had just seen her scuttle around like a gecko, but he couldn't help but feel like she had been trying to explain something to him.

"Was there a reason you did that?" Kellan asked.

"She's just a half-mage." Sen sighed and rolled his eyes. He, too, stepped into the mana spring fully clothed. The pink water soaked into his adult-sized robes. "Next time, only use your boons for people who might be *useful* to our operations, understand me? Half-mages aren't worth our time."

"They have half the magic or something?" Kellan quipped.

"No, fool. Half-mages are incapable of ranking magics. They have a single magical ability, *and that's it*."

Husker leisurely waded through the tranquil waters, his voice calm and relaxed. "Half-mages sometimes have a useful ability, though. They're random.

Each half-mage has something unique. Some make them glow in the dark. Some allow them to destroy building-sized objects. If we found the right half-mage, they could be useful to us."

Kellan thought about Levvy's abilities. *She was lucky? That was her half-mage power? And that was all she got?* Kellan almost felt bad for her. If that was her only magical ability, how would she survive in a world with monsters both machine and humanoid?

"Well, that rezrah wasn't useful," Sen snapped. Then he sank too far, and his head dunked below the surface. When he reemerged, his black hair was wet and clinging to his face. He could've starred in one of *The Ring* movies. After a few coughs, he shouted, "Who designs these? There's no reason for them to be so deep!"

The sliding glass door snapped shut. Kellan glanced over to spot Mavis standing next to the spa. She offered Kellan a smile as she tugged off her own shoes and then stepped into the water—again, fully clothed.

It was now becoming a tradition.

"Sen," she said as she sank down in the water, all the way to her chin. "Do you have a moment? I… I want to know more about our numbers… These stats, as you called them…"

—Chapter 27—

—Rules for the First Games—

"The numbers you see are just a representation of your abilities," Sen said as he dragged himself to the side of the spa. "Strength is obviously raw physical strength. It represents your ability to deal physical damage. Dexterity is your fine motor skills and speed. It represents your precision, ability to aim, and dodge."

He spoke with the engagement of a dictionary.

"And fortitude must be your stamina and endurance?" Mavis asked, interjecting. "I get it. I don't need an explanation of the *words*. I don't understand the *numbers*. What does a *2* mean for strength? A 2 out of *what*? Is this like a score for a movie?"

Sen held onto the side of the spa and sighed. "Look, most sentient races are born with limited abilities. Humans tend to start with stats between 1 and 5. If you have a 1 in strength, you're weak. At the bottom 10% of noodle-y arms."

"And what does a 2 mean?" Mavis asked.

"A 2 is considered average. Most humans fall into that range." Sen held up a hand in dramatic fashion. "*But a 5 is legendary!* A 5 would be the strongest human you can think of! A titan among humanity. A person with muscles in places most people don't even have places."

"Curtis Blaydes?" Mavis asked.

"Arnold Schwarzenegger from the 70s?" Kellan quipped.

"Sure, whomever those are." Sen put his arm down and sighed. "You can use magic and technology to elevate your stats beyond 5. If your stat is between 6 and 10, you're in a new category of power and recognition. 11 through 15 is the next tier of power. 16 and above is considered some of the best of the best."

Kellan hadn't seen many people's stats. He had his, Mavis's, Levvy's, and… Brenner's. Of those, Brenner's were ridiculous. He had 20 in both strength and fortitude. *I only have 4 and 3 respectively*, Kellan thought. *Which means I have a long road if I'm going to compete.*

"What about willpower?" Mavis asked. She moved through the glowing pink water until she was next to Sen. "It seems different than the other stats."

Sen smiled. "How perceptive of you. Unlike all your other stats, willpower is a representation of your inner drive. It can't be altered through magic or technology—it can only be increased through your own actions and perception of reality. Think of it this way—the more you believe in yourself, and follow through with your own plans and ambitions, the higher your willpower will become."

With a huff and a laugh, Husker said, "Self-doubt and depression often cripple a mage's willpower. And willpower is your ability to defend yourself from some magics and mental afflictions. It's best to keep a positive outlook."

Kellan sardonically laughed to himself. In a nightmare world, the brightest thing around was the radioactive glow from the Arbiter's mouth. The Nexus was the epitome of gloom. How was he supposed to maintain a positive outlook?

With a quick touch of her leg, Mavis smiled. "Well, I know I got down on myself after the grenade… But now that you healed it, I feel like a whole new woman."

"Fantastic," Sen drawled, very little caring in his voice. "I'm so glad you feel better."

"I mean it. I really appreciate what you've done. I've never seen anything like that."

For a long moment, Sen said nothing. He just hung onto the side of the spa, his small child-like hands gripping the marble. With a small exhale, he leaned a cheek on the stone.

"Thank you," he muttered. "I specialized in the study of anatomy specifically to master flesh crafting and puppet creation. Very few people understand the costs associated with such skills."

Mavis sank into the water, all the way to her chin. Her dyed purple hair spread away from her, flowing into the spa. "You gave me a point of fortitude. Why not give me points to all my stats? Why not do it for everybody?"

"Because it permanently takes from *me*," Sen snapped. Then he pulled himself out of the spa, his robes half-clinging to his body and half-dragging behind him, like a drowned bride. "Every stat I give someone not only costs me a year of my life, but an arcana, *and* one of my own stats. I can't just *make people better*."

He slowly marched back into the suite of the AVU Palace, no more words for anyone.

Mavis glanced over at Husker. The wolf offered a shrug.

"It's best we get inside," he eventually said. "While the spa is comforting, we don't want to be outside for too long."

Kellan didn't need to hear any more. He didn't like being outside—not when their enemies were all around them. Apparently, several people wanted to see Xiang fall, and that meant they wanted to see *him* fall.

With quick movements, Kellan leapt out of the spa. He went to offer Mavis a hand, but she smirked at him and then leapt out of the spa as well, clearly proud of her regained ability to just *stand*. With a twirl, dripping pink water everywhere, she motioned to her leg.

"Refurbished," she joked.

"Now with extra flesh from a kid's shoulder," Kellan added in a salesman's voice. "Just what everyone is lookin' for."

With a chuckle, the two of them turned to Husker. He dragged himself out of the spa, his wet fur and chains weighing him down. Once out, he shook his whole body like a dog, flinging water everywhere. Kellan shielded his eyes and frowned.

Then Husker tugged on his pants and headed for the suite, still dripping water.

"You're not concerned about getting the place dirty?" Mavis asked.

The werewolf shook his head. "It'll be cleaned. Don't worry about that."

He walked inside, headed for a random bedroom, and then disappeared into it without another word. The silence that followed reminded Kellan of too many horror movies. Even the celebrations outside seemed to have calmed down. The music was soft and distant, and there was a stillness in the air that betrayed a collective nervous tension.

Mavis turned to him, half her purple hair wet. "Can I stay with you tonight?" With a flustered twinge to her voice, she added, "Not anything serious. I just don't want to be alone here. You understand, right?"

"Of course," Kellan said. And although he didn't voice it, he didn't feel like being alone at the moment, either.

He motioned to one of the unoccupied rooms, and together they crossed the giant living space. Mavis opened the door, and they entered a luxurious room that was just as posh as the central living room. Black rugs, a four-poster bed, thirty pillows, and a mattress the size of a small island.

But unlike a normal bedroom, with a dresser or some sort of personal space, this room had nothing. Except a gigantic TV mounted to the opposite wall of the bed. It had to be at least eighty inches. Kellan stared at it as he strolled inside.

While Mavis patted the soft blankets, Kellan tapped the power button on the bottom of the TV.

It flickered to life.

Kellan recognized the scene. It was Bitso's newsroom, this time more advanced and clean than before. Bitso's desk was silver and shiny, his cuffs had been polished, and the screen behind him played images of people using magical abilities.

Someone created a storm.

Someone else disappeared and reappeared elsewhere.

And then someone slid into the darkness, slithered across the ground, and emerged from the shadows a moment later. Kellan watched that bit with intense interest. He hadn't yet tested out his focus ability.

"—and based on past accomplishments and training, we currently have the top three teams," Bitso said with his usual flair. He fixed the white blindfold over his eyes, so that it was a bit snugger than before. "Obviously, we have Team 42, whose leader is none other than Brenner Hawke, the man who has a kill ratio of one-to-seven-billion. Too bad he didn't get arcana for all those kills, am I right?"

Bitso laughed and then turned to his left, like he was supposed to have a co-anchor, but no one was there.

Not even an empty chair.

When Bitso's laughter finally calmed down, he turned his "gaze" back to the camera. "Team 5 is the second team of the top three teams likely to win the games. Their leader, the Nexus resident who goes by the name *Nosferatu*, is the only Nexus resident M-rank mage registered for the event."

The screen behind Bitso showed a deformed man wearing a stylish Italian-style suit. He stood in the middle of a destroyed city, bodies and wreckage intermingled in piles all around.

The man's deformities consisted of boils, lumps, and lesions, though nothing wept pus or blood. His hair was thin—barely there, like the hair on a cactus—and the man's eyes were milky pale.

He had all the charm of a corpse.

"Nosferatu is such a classy individual," Bitso said. He rubbed his own clean suit. "It makes me sick." He slammed a fist down on his desk, smirking. "This is one of the few times the Arbiter has allowed a resident of the Nexus to compete."

Then Bitso tensed and glanced around.

"What's that?" he asked.

But no one said anything. Even the screen behind him, showing off the footage, was muted.

"You want to know what magic he's M rank in?" Bitso held a hand to his ear. But again, no one was talking. "Oh, that's simple, my friend. *Metal* magic. Rare for someone of his breed, I know, but Nosferatu has made a name for himself crafting magi-tech. He has some of the most powerful artifacts I've ever seen."

Mavis hopped on the side of the bed, her damp clothes squishing as she moved. The bed was so gigantic, she barely disturbed the mountain of pillows. "Are you enjoying that?" Mavis patted the blanket. "Come see this. I've never seen silk like it."

"I'd like to know more about the other teams," Kellan absent-mindedly said. He kept his attention on the TV as he backed up to the bed. Once his legs touched the edge of the mattress, he sat down. "You don't find this fascinating?"

"I find it a little morbid." Mavis reclined on the bed, her gaze on the ceiling. "Husker said that in some of the games, we're going to have to fight each other. I don't really want to imagine it just yet."

Kellan watched as Bitso played more footage of Nosferatu, but he didn't understand it. The deformed man was just holding objects—little avocado-shaped metal orbs. What were they? Why bother filming it?

"You don't want to know what we're up against?" Kellan muttered, his brow furrowed.

"Apparently, we get stronger by killing things." Mavis crossed her arms over her chest. "I just get the feeling this is going to get… It doesn't matter. Husker said we should focus on resting. If I think about it, I won't be able to sleep at all."

"You and Husker getting along?" Kellan couldn't pull his attention away from the TV.

"You know that hex he has? His father took it. His father wanted to kill someone, so he accepted a legacy hex that would kill everyone in his family. And once his father died, Husker inherited the problem. He doesn't seem like a soldier. He reminds me of a scholar. I feel sorry for him."

Bitso slammed his hand on the desk. "The third team most likely to win is none other than Team 101." He motioned to the screen behind him, and an image of Xiang flicked into existence. "Sun Xiang's team is a ragtag band of *randos*, from what I hear. As the daughter of the last winner, most bookies placed her *number one* to win this round of the Nexus Games, but her complete lack of magical advancement over the last few years has hurt her chances."

With a dramatic frown, Bitso turned to his imaginary co-anchor. "Maybe she's sad she lost her mommy."

Silence.

Then Bitso threw his head back and laughed. It died down into chuckles before he managed to add, "Oh, yes. That's a good point. Maybe it's because she lost her family, her lover, and her mentors, all in one fell swoop." He shot the imaginary co-anchor some finger guns. "But don't worry. I'm sure she has a few tricks up her sleeves."

Mavis ran her hands over the silky blankets. She stared at the folds and wrinkles. "I'm serious, Kellan… Do you see this?"

Although he didn't want to look away from the TV, he managed to glance back long enough to see what had excited Mavis so much.

The silk sheets…

They shimmered. Beautifully.

Then information flashed across Kellan's eyes.

Magical Item [Object]—Dreamweaver's Blanket

This blanket is made from dreamweaver silk. Upon touching it, the mage makes a hidden willpower check. If the mage's willpower is lower than the dreamweaver the blanket was crafted from, they become entranced. Every six seconds, the check is made again, but the dreamweaver's willpower is considered 1 higher (which continually stacks, +2 after twelve seconds, +3 after eighteen seconds, and so on). This occurs until the mage is eventually entranced.

It's so soft. You just want to sleep on it.

"Mavis," Kellan muttered.

"Yeah?"

"I think… the bed might not be good."

"Hm? What's that?"

But…

He couldn't really look away from the blankets. They were black, and silvery, and so soft. Too soft. Invitingly soft. Kellan rested back on them, his breathing evening out.

So luxe. So kingly. Kellan loved this bed. He didn't normally care for beds, or random material objects, for that matter, *but this bed…*

He would die for this bed.

That's such a stupid thought. Kellan laughed to himself. *The bed… It's already tricked me. I…*

Kellan closed his eyes. And then sleep took him.

***

"Good morning, Fayetteville!"

Kellan jerked upright, his breathing ragged. Where was he? With wild movements, Kellan glanced around, confused by the dark rugs, posh bed, and gigantic TV. His dreams had been so pleasant and vivid, that he thought the Nexus had been a nightmare.

Unfortunately, he was still in the AVU Palace.

"This is the morning news!" Bitso shouted from the TV, all smiles and laughter. But his suit was wrinkled, his wrists were bloody around the cuffs, and his blindfold was smudged with darkness. Had he been hosting the news *all night*?

"I'm your designated host, here to deliver you information straight from the Arbiter." Bitso giggled and then motioned to the screen behind him. "It's 8:30, and it's time for the rules of the first games. Is everyone ready?"

Kellan stood from the bed, his whole body crusty and grimy with oils from sleep. He slapped his cheeks, trying to shake his grogginess. Fatigue clawed at his thoughts.

"Each team leader will have three game types to choose from," Bitso said, excitement in his voice, even if he appeared ragged. "The first game is *Seek and Destroy*. What a fun one! The rules are simple."

Bitso waved to the screen behind him.

It displayed a cityscape, much like Fayetteville, but it was all a simple diagram. Tiny houses. Little roads. Nothing more than a display.

"The Arbiter will hide *five keys* inside the bodies of five bunnies. He'll then set them free within the designated area. Each team who participates in this game will have a single day to find a bunny and extract a key."

Mavis sat up from the bed, her purple hair all over the place. She rubbed at her head, her eyes crusted with sleep. She groaned as she turned her attention to the TV.

Bitso snapped his fingers. "But there are a few interesting *twists!* The Arbiter loves twists, after all. The first is the Net. Like most games, the play arena of the *Seek and Destroy* game will have a Net around it."

The screen displayed a crimson net around the city. It created a dome shape, but as Kellan watched, the dome… shrank. It became smaller and smaller, narrowing until the play arena was just a few blocks wide, instead of a whole city.

"The Net is fun," Bitso said with a laugh. "Any living flesh that touches it… instantly dies."

The screen showed an animated bird running into the crimson net. The moment the bird came into contact with the net, little Xs appeared on its eyes, and then it collapsed to the ground, upside down.

"But non-living objects are unharmed."

The net slid over buildings, but nothing changed afterward.

"Additionally, each team will need to pick a Straggler." Bitso held up a finger.

"Just one. And this is the funny part. Listen close. The Straggler will be hunted by a *Kuji*." With a lunatic-style giggle, Bitso clapped his hands together once. "I love the Kuji. They're so delightfully creepy. *And silent*. They'll stalk the Straggler until they die. And once they do, the role of *Straggler* will be automatically passed to another on the team. Until they're eventually all dead."

Mavis stopped rubbing her eyes. She stared at the TV, her mouth slightly agape.

"There's sad news, though." Bitso sighed. "Once a team finds a key, their Kuji will die. Boo."

Kellan watched the screen, hoping he would get a glimpse of a "Kuji," but nothing ever appeared. What were they? Could they be killed?

"One more rule," Bitso said. "*Seek and Destroy* is strictly PvE—*player versus environment.* Teams cannot fight each other. If you do, the Arbiter will decide your fate."

"Wait," Kellan said. "That means…"

"Which brings us to the second game this round. *PvP Seek and Destroy.* That's right! PvP—*Player versus Player.* In this mode, the Arbiter will hide *forty* keys in forty bunnies! All the other rules still apply, except, the instant you find one, you must defend it for one hour. Once you do, you win! That's right. Teams can fight each other. Find a bunny? That might be too hard! Kill another team instead!"

Forty keys? Kellan already knew why there was a difference. If all one hundred and one teams did the PvE Seek and Destroy, only five of them would walk away with keys. Not enough for everyone. But there were so many keys in the PvP game… If fewer than forty teams signed up, there wouldn't even be a need to fight each other.

"The last game is a game of chance," Bitso said with a grin. "It's called *There Are Four Doors and One of Them Has a Key, But Another One Has Certain Death, Have Fun With That.*" He slapped his hand on the desk. "Not very creative, I know. But the Arbiter loves his chance games. And only one person has to open the door. Guess who? That's right! The Straggler! The suspense is so delicious."

"Is this guy serious?" Mavis whispered.

Kellan half-shrugged. "I think so."

—Chapter 28—
—The Straggler—

The TV continued to play footage, and Bitso waved his arms around with the energy of three teenagers, but Kellan heard nothing. His thoughts fought with each other to take priority, and his grogginess wasn't helping anything.

A game of chance?

Sen specifically said we weren't going to play any chance games... Kellan gritted his teeth, his thoughts dwelling on the fact that his cursed armor would cause him to dramatically fail a game of chance at the least opportune moment. *Maybe I should try to trigger the curse before we play any games.*

The other problem was the issue of "the Straggler." What was that? Levvy had mentioned it earlier, out in the mana spa. Kellan had been too distracted by the rejuvenating effects to ask pertinent follow-up questions.

As if Bitso could read his thoughts, the bizarre, blindfolded man pointed to the screen behind him.

"Remember, each team must designate one of their members as the *Straggler.*" Bitso smiled, showing his sharper-than-average teeth. "The leader can never be chosen for this role. And once the Straggler is chosen, there is no way to remove the designation. Well, except through death. Once the Straggler dies, another member of the team is designated, all the way until the leader runs out of teammates..."

Mavis walked over to Kellan, a hand tangled in her purple hair. "What was happening with that bed? I swear it knocked me out."

"Yeah," Kellan muttered. "It did."

"The last winner of the Nexus Games lost each one of her members, one by one," Bitso said as he rubbed at his chin. "If I recall correctly, the Straggler on her team always died during the bonus rounds. Up until she didn't have a team left." He laughed and slammed his fist on the metal table. "She played the last game *alone* and somehow won the whole thing. Amazing."

Xiang's mother.

Kellan watched the TVs in the background, hoping to glean to just a little more information. What did the games look like? How did the Stragglers die? Kellan wanted more knowledge, but it seemed like everything was determined to keep it from him.

The Nexus denizens had been forthcoming with info. Kellan had asked a question, and they had answered.

They had even known all about the gold arcana…

And not even Sen or Xiang seem to know anything about that.

Kellan tightened his hands into fists. *As soon as I get the chance, I should search for more Nexus citizens. Maybe they can tell me what's going on. If I just knew a bit more…*

"So each team has a leader," Mavis said as she turned to Kellan. "And the leader gets to pick everything that happens to the team?"

He nodded once.

"And each team has a *Straggler*? And that member is… the unlucky one? Who gets hunted by monsters or has to participate in the chance games? Until they die?"

Kellan nodded again. "And then a *new* Straggler is chosen."

"But… why?"

"To cull the weakest players of the team," Kellan muttered, more to himself than to Mavis. "From what I've seen, the strongest player is the leader, and if they die, the whole team automatically loses. But if the Straggler is killed, nothing happens other than a new Straggler is chosen, all the way until it's the leader left. This is a game mechanic solely meant to kill off people."

"That's sadistic." Mavis crossed her arms and then uncrossed them, her nervous energy infectious.

Kellan shoved his hands into the pockets of his pants in order to keep from moving around too much. He glanced over his shoulder at the bed, and caught sight of his rifle. Had he put it there? He couldn't remember unslinging it from his shoulder.

The blankets had basically hypnotized him.

Kellan grabbed his weapon, threw the strap over his shoulder, and kept it close. Supposedly, the first game would start in less than thirty minutes. He didn't want to be caught flatfooted.

Then he gave the blankets a second glance. They hadn't hurt him—they had caused him to fall asleep. And then once he had awoken, he could leave them.

Seemed useful. But how could he utilize them? Even touching the blankets caused him to start making willpower checks. If he could somehow use them against other people…

"Kellan?" someone from the main room yelled.

Finally awake and ready, Kellan exited the bedroom with purpose. Husker was waiting in the gigantic front room, standing by one of the black leather couches. He had several piles of clothes and bags, separated into four stacks. With a motion of his clawed hand, he pointed to a pile with cargo pants, a jacket, and a tactical backpack.

"For you," Husker said. His fox-ears twitched as he added, "I guessed at your size, but I thought you'd appreciate this."

Kellan wandered over to the clothing. A pair of socks and a pair of shooting gloves were under the pants.

"You got these for me?" he asked.

Husker slowly nodded. "The first game is about to begin. We'll only be allowed to take what we're wearing, so please change."

Only take what they were wearing?

Kellan picked up the backpack. "If we have supplies inside the pack, we can use those, too?"

"That's right."

Thankful for the supplies, Kellan gave the man a nod and then hurried back to the bedroom. Mavis watched him with a lifted eyebrow as Kellan ripped off the blankets and sheets from the massive bed.

"Husker has new clothes for us," he said. "You should change. The first game starts at 9am. We should be ready."

"All right," Mavis said. She walked out of the room, but she glanced over her shoulder several times, watching Kellan manhandle the bedding. "Don't take too much time with that."

Kellan examined the sheets. They had the same *dreamweaver* effect as the blankets. With quick movements, he grabbed the sheets, folded them up, and then shoved them into the backpack before he could succumb to the ill effects.

Then he ripped off his shredded jeans, and kicked off his bloody boots. He changed into his new clothing, thankful they had *someone* on the team who was concerned with keeping them well-equipped.

Kellan glanced around the room. The TV continued, even as Kellan tried to find something else he could use in the games. Unfortunately, nothing else in the room seemed useful. No weapons. No other magical items.

"—and once the games begin, I'll be announcing each winning team, each death, each bonus round gained, and each challenge round found." Bitso slammed his hand on the desk again, drawing Kellan's attention. "Last Nexus Games, the bonus rounds really played a huge difference in the winning team. Obviously, most of the mages at the beginning of the games are weaker—barely any magic, limited arcana gain—*but the bonus rounds change all that.*"

Kellan stared at the TV, waiting to hear the catch. He needed more arcana, that much was certain, but he wasn't entirely sure what the best way to go about collecting it was.

"Those who compete in the bonus rounds often find themselves flush in arcana." Bitso turned to his imaginary co-anchor and waited, as though in the middle of a conversation. The silence grated at Kellan's nerves, but right before he looked away, Bitso threw his head back in a laugh. "Yes! That's right. Those bonus rounds are more for the clever, and less for the brute. The Arbiter loves his puzzles."

With some sheets packed in his backpack, Kellan exited the bedroom. Husker remained in the middle of the room. All the piles of clothing had disappeared, and everyone else was near the front door, new clothing and packs in hand.

Xiang and her brother mumbled to each other, speaking in whispered words, but fast and sharp enough to tell Kellan it wasn't a pleasant conversation.

Mavis walked over to Kellan. Her new clothing—a thick jacket, blue jeans, and snow boots—fit perfectly. She gave him the once-over. "You okay?"

"Yeah," he said. "But do you hear that?"

"Hear what?" Mavis held her breath.

Besides the shushed argument of Xiang and Sen, there was nothing. Even Husker's breathing was louder than anything else.

"Not even birds," Kellan muttered. "It's just… quiet."

One of Husker's ears turned to face Kellan before the rest of his canine face. "There's blood in the air. Even though this is an Oasis… someone has brought a corpse to this place. Perhaps more than one."

The room—the suite—and Kellan's bedroom were spotless. What was Husker smelling?

Xiang held up a hand, and her brother silenced himself. When she stepped forward, everyone turned to face her.

"Before we start the first game, we need to determine who will be the Straggler," she said. "I've decided it will be Husker."

The werewolf offered a low growl from his throat. "I thought you wanted me close to you at all times."

"The reason I picked you was because of your power, not because I want you dead." Xiang threw back some of her long, perfect hair. "The Kuji won't stand a chance against your ability, which means we won't have to worry about losing a member of our team during the first game."

Mavis held up a hand.

Momentarily confused, Xiang stared at her. Then she motioned to Mavis. "Do you have a question?"

"How many games are there?" she asked as she put her hand down.

"There are ten rounds to the Nexus Games. After two rounds, there's always a challenge, for a grand total of fifteen chances to gain keys." After a long sigh, Xiang clarified, "We need a number of keys equal to our team members. Even if one of you dies, we will always need five keys in order to win the games. Unfortunately, most teams do not find keys during the games. The chaos, danger, and traps tend to deter weaker mages. Or they die. Either way, if we manage to go five rounds, and get five keys, we will be the first ever to do it."

"Wait, so there's a chance we might not find the key?" Mavis asked.

Sen scoffed. "Of course. Imagine if we pick the *door game* for this round. Out of four doors, only one has a key. And if we picked wrong, the game would be over, and we'd have nothing. Or perhaps a dead teammate. Then we'd head into the second round of games without a key."

"So, if we don't get keys for seven rounds, we'll have basically lost." Kellan walked closer to the suite's front door. Then he shot Sen a glare. "And I thought you said there weren't any *games of chance* during the Nexus Games? What's wrong with you?"

"*We're* not going to pick those games." Sen threw one of his small arms into the air. "It's a fool's errand to take any games of chance. First off, a twenty-five percent chance to win is terrible. Secondly, there's no chance to gain arcana during those games. We need all the magical power we can get, so obviously we want the other games."

Mavis stepped close to Kellan. "Are we going to join the PvE game? Or the PvP game?"

"Player versus Environment," Xiang answered matter-of-factly. "We're much too weak to handle some of the other teams. And…"

"And some of them are gunning for you?" Kellan asked, sardonic and dry.

"Yes."

Xiang motioned for Husker. "Come. That's the second reason you must be our team's Straggler. Brenner has promised me that he'll kill our team, one by one. He'll assume whoever I designate as *Straggler* is the weakest—which means he'll target you first if he ever gets the chance."

Husker walked to her, his tail swishing. "And you want me to kill him the moment I can?"

She smiled. "Just like we discussed. Once Brenner is dead, his whole team will fail. And after that, we won't have anything to worry about for the rest of the game."

The two stared at each other for a long moment. Then Husker lifted his clawed left hand—the number 101 marked his red fur. Xiang brought her own marked hand up to his. Once they touched, Husker gained an additional mark.

A skull.

It looked like the skull of a dog, and it appeared under the 101.

"You're the Straggler," Xiang said as she removed her hand. "Thank you, my friend."

Husker bowed his head. "Thank *you* for helping me overcome this terrible hex."

"The games are about to start," Sen said. "Have you *really* decided which game we'll play in? No last-minute change of heart?"

"I wish to speak with the Arbiter first," Xiang stated. She turned for the door. "Once I've spoken to him, I'll finalize our decision."

"What happens once you pick?" Kellan asked.

"We'll be teleported to the game arena and locked under the Net. Then we'll be trapped there until we find a key, or until the allotted time is up."

Kellan rubbed at his knuckles as he mulled over the information. They didn't have any food or water with them—at least, not that he knew of. If the game lasted twenty-four hours, wouldn't they need supplies? *Perhaps I can gather something while Xiang speaks with the dragon.*

With a flick of her hand, Xiang opened the door to their suite.

Mavis flinched away, and Sen's eyes went wide. As Kellan stepped forward, he noticed Husker's fur was standing on end.

The hallway…

Kellan held his breath as he exited the suite. The entire corridor smelled of copper and flesh. Blood was smeared over the rugs and walls.

Two bodies were lying on the floor. Kellan recognized them both.

Hua and Twi. The two children he had saved in the alleyway. They had been cut up, and their insides thrown around the hall.

A message had been written on the wall in their dark-crimson blood.

It read:

Join the PvP game or else

"Who did this?" Mavis asked from within the suite.

Sen stared at the floor. "Brenner."

—Chapter 29—

—Seek and Destroy—

Kellan stared at the bodies of the two kids, his mind numb and his body icy. There had been several times in his military career that he'd had to deal with corpses, but ever since his last mission, he really couldn't stand the sight of them.

Especially when they were people he had known.

"Brenner did this?" Kellan whispered as he turned away from the gruesome sight. Blood had soaked into the rugs and dried to a dark color. "Why? How did he even know them?"

Husker snorted and then growled, "These are the children the Arbiter showed on the viewscreen..."

Everyone had seen it—Kellan helping the children. Had Brenner singled them out *specifically* to agitate him?

"Can other teams attack us between rounds?" Kellan asked as he carefully turned his gaze to the gory message written on the wall.

"Once the games have started, the only official way to kill people is in the games themselves. Or, I suppose, with the Arbiter's blessing."

"And the Arbiter doesn't outlaw the killing of his own... offspring?" Kellan had no better term for them. The residents of the Nexus were his family, weren't they? How could the Arbiter allow them to be killed?

"The Arbiter has no rules against killing the inbred mages," Sen stated. "Only against harming his machines."

Xiang stepped into the hallway, her attention lingering on the dead children for only a moment. Then she headed for the stairs, giving no indication she could even smell the horror show around her.

"Why do this?" Kellan demanded.

Sen hurried after his sister. "To get under our skin, no doubt. Brenner has a way of agitating everyone."

He's taunting us, Kellan realized with a dark chuckle. *That arrogant SOB. He's planning on torching everything until we come to him.*

"Shouldn't we bury them?" Kellan wasn't sure of the etiquette in the Nexus. Leaving them in the hallway seemed disrespectful.

Husker shook his head. "The Pestbyters handle all dead bodies. Leave them."

He turned to face Kellan. "And don't worry. The Eyes of the Arbiter miss nothing. He saw what happened here."

Mavis placed a hand on Kellan's shoulder. He flinched and wheeled on her. With half a smile, she gently asked, "Are you okay?"

"Yeah," he said, his voice raspier than he wanted. Kellan ran a hand down his face, clearing away the sweat. "Let's go. Let's just... go."

He hated the idea that he could've been tangentially related to the deaths of Hua and Twi. They had been so helpful, and forthcoming with information. And so young. Did Brenner really have no compassion or empathy? Kellan wanted to speak to Xiang about the matter, but she seemed aggressively uninterested in discussing the topic.

Husker followed closely behind as Kellan and Mavis made their way to the stairs. Mavis kept her eyes on her legs most of the time, staring like she was marveling at how well she walked.

Kellan just focused on holding his breath until he was down half the flight of stairs. Anything to distract him from the fact that he was leaving a trail of bloody footprints behind.

Xiang had already headed off for the Arbiter, leaving the whole group behind. It was her modus operandi at this point—leave the team and isolate herself. Kellan didn't understand why.

"The keys," he said, trying to steady his voice. He glanced over his shoulder at Husker. "There are forty in the PvP version of *Seek and Destroy.* Since we only need five, couldn't we just play that game until we had them all? And win the Nexus Games *instantly* in that case?"

The werewolf man snorted. "You don't understand. We need five *different* keys. The forty found in Seek and Destroy will be the same key. All Seek and Destroy games will be that way, even if they're offered in future rounds."

"So, we can't just collect a million keys in one round?"

Sen hopped down the last of the stairs. Then he came to a halt. "We can gather extra keys if we want to prevent other teams from getting them. That's happened several times in past games."

"What a delta-bravo move," Kellan muttered.

"Delta-bravo move?" Mavis lifted an eyebrow.

"D-B. For *douchebag.*" He shrugged. "Just a nicer way of saying it."

With an amused smirk, Mavis patted his shoulder. "You don't need to worry about your language."

"It's just a habit." He shrugged off her touch, hating the idea of human contact. "Listen—I just want to beat this game as quickly as possible. I'm not accustomed to madmen threatening me four to five times in a single day. It's only a matter of time before one of them sticks."

He reached the bottom of the stairs and stood next to Sen. When the others reached them, they just milled around, standing in the lavish hall of the AVU Palace. Soft music played in the halls, and the place smelled like a casino in Vegas.

Kellan didn't like it.

He was about to voice his concerns when the 101 numbers on his left hand shook around on his skin. He lifted his arm and stared at the black mark. It practically vibrated, and then went still.

"It's time," Husker said, eyeing his own mark. "Xiang must've chosen."

Kellan touched the mark on his hand. It was a tattoo. Never moving. No texture. How had it moved?

"She spoke with the Arbiter already?" Mavis asked, her brow furrowed. "But she's barely been gone and—"

Kellan lost his breath.

A strange feeling jolted through his body.

Like the Lightning Lift.

He closed his eyes, and the mark on his left hand burned for only a moment.

Then Kellan was teleported, along with the others.

***

Kellan stumbled forward, his breath returning to him like a wave hitting a beach. He gulped down air and steadied himself. Then he opened his eyes, surprised to see he was standing in an urban jungle of skyscrapers and mismatched technology.

Large pipelines were jutting out of the streets—huge metal tubes, as if the sewer had gone haywire and decided it wanted to be above ground.

Trains—all kinds of trains—were scattered about the roads. Coal-powered trains. Bullet trains. Trains Kellan had never seen in his life. Steam powered? The engines were tipped over and the boxcars were wide open.

The shadows of the skyscrapers stretched over the roads, creating a dark shadow of civilization. But the sky… It wasn't blue. It was red. A web had been "thrown" over the city, creating a dome with a checker-like pattern of webbing. The dome had to be more than a mile above them, arching down to the ground, creating a playing arena.

The Net.

Kellan stared at the red sky, his eyes wide with disbelief. Bitso had explained everything. Any living thing that touched the Net would die. And it would start closing.

"Kellan?"

He glanced around, surprised to see the rest of his team on the same devastated street.

No one else was around, just Sen, in his long robes, Husker in a coat and pants, Mavis in her new jeans and jacket, and Xiang…

She wore something different. A white pantsuit with all the authority and legal flair of a high-powered attorney. Her black button-up shirt matched her shiny heels. Her long hair had been tied in a bun, secured in place with decorative butterfly pins.

The 101 on her left hand was prominently displayed.

"Sister," Sen said as he approached her. "The Arbiter was fair with you?"

"He was." Xiang glanced to her side. A shop with a broken window display had several TVs facing the street. They flickered to life, seemingly for no reason, only to display Bitso's messed-up news program. "The Arbiter has given me his blessing."

"It's 9am," Bitso said with a laugh, his voice haunting and echoing with so many TVs playing the same thing. "And the first games have begun. Of the one hundred and one teams participating this year, fifty-one of them have decided to *play it safe* and go with PvE Seek and Destroy."

Bitso motioned to the screens behind him. Several videos were cutting in and out of all the teams in the same bizarre city-train-sewer playground as Kellan.

"Forty-three of them decided to take the risky path and play the PvP version." Bitso smiled wide. "I like these ones. They're already my favorite." Then he snapped his fingers. "And seven teams decided to go the fast route. They get to open doors. Who will get lucky? Who won't? It'll be fun to see!"

Gunshots rang throughout the broken city.

Kellan glanced around. He didn't see anyone. He could see several blocks in each cardinal direction, but the trains and sewer tunnels were everywhere. He saw no signs of people, just the war-torn cityscape.

"The first game has officially begun," Bitso said over the many TVs. "Will people find the bunnies? *Will we see helpful doors?* Let's find out!"

Kellan watched the screens long enough to see a video screen display a nightmarishly dark room with four freakish doors made of metal and coated in rust. A person, some man, stood in front of the door, dressed in apocalyptic armor scraped together from the dumpster of a military supply store.

He went to the first door, his hand shaky, and then pulled away at the last moment.

Then he went to the second door and pulled it open in dramatic fashion.

Nothing happened.

There was nothing behind the door. Just an empty room of darkness and sadness.

"Oh, unlucky," Bitso said, shaking his head. "Of the four doors, there are two with nothing behind them. One has the sweet release of death, and the last a key. I guess Team 65 gets *nothing* this round. Now they just have to wait."

Kellan tore his gaze away from the TVs. He didn't want to watch the other teams pick doors. One of them would find the *death door*, and Kellan had no interest in seeing it.

"They've released the Kuji into the city," Husker muttered, his nose twitching. "We should get going. I don't want to have to use my ability if we can avoid it."

Xiang held up her hand. Everyone went silent, but the gunshots and sounds of distant war still rang out through the empty streets.

"Husker, you take one of our warriors and search the east side of the city. The bunnies… They'll be small. Perhaps dead, I'm not certain. In the last Nexus Games, the Arbiter had them find *ducks*, and all the ducks were different. One was alive, one was a wooden carving, another was a sign…"

Husker nodded along with her words. "I'm glad we have someone who knows the ins and outs of the competition."

"I intend to win," she firmly stated. "What you need to do is pay attention, and travel quickly. I picked the PvE route so we wouldn't have to worry about attacks just yet. Once we've gotten a bonus round, things will be different for us… But for now, just search. We *must* have a key by the end of the first round. *Must.*"

Must?

Kellan didn't understand. Didn't they have multiple rounds to try for keys? Her urgency seemed panicked. Or desperate.

Husker motioned to Mavis. "Will you help me?"

Her eyes went wide, and for a brief moment, she hesitated. Then Mavis stepped forward and nodded once. "Yeah. I'll help."

"Good. You have the reliability of a mercenary soldier. I worked with several when I lived in Aracor."

"O-Oh. Thank you?" Mavis gave Kellan—and then Sen—an odd glance. She said nothing else, though. She took her place next to Husker.

"Sen, you will search the city and look for something to puppet." Xiang glowered down at him, her voice filled with the sting of irritation. "You and some sort of golem can search the south."

Sen said nothing. His small shoulders slumped, and he stared at the street. When Kellan stared for a moment, Sen shot him a glare, as if this were *his* fault.

"Kellan, you'll search with me," Xiang said. "We'll head north. Throughout the day, we should all move west until we meet at a place closest to the Net. Don't worry about staying in contact throughout the game. The moment we find the key, we'll all be teleported out of the Net and back into the AVU Palace."

Husker snorted. "What if we run into yami? Even if this isn't the PvP arena, the monsters will be hostile. And some of them are large."

"Avoid them," Xiang stated. "They'll be weaker this round. The Arbiter is merciful that way."

"Shouldn't we stay together?" Kellan asked.

Xiang shook her head. "There are only five keys here. We can't afford to dawdle."

"What if the other teams find them first?"

For the first time since the game began, Xiang smiled. She turned to Kellan with a hint of amused confidence. "The other teams will find nothing—at least, not while I'm here."

She waved her hand.

And then hundreds of bunnies appeared. *Hundreds.* Some of them alive. Some of them toys. Some of them signs. And when Xiang waved her hand a second time, they scattered around, littering the entire city. The "live" bunnies hopped away, jumping into the sewers and boxcars, and the toys and signs were placed around like the whole city was a book of *Where's Waldo?* and everyone had to find the real bunnies out of the hundreds of fakes.

All those illusions…

Xiang had filled the city with a million red herrings, likely to drive the other teams insane.

"You will know when you see an illusion," she said to Husker. "Trust me. I've made them so that you'll recognize the difference. The other teams will not be so lucky. While they're distracted, find the real ones."

"How will I know the difference?" Kellan asked.

Xiang gestured for him to follow. She walked down the broken street, her heels clicking. "*I* know the difference. Come. The sooner we find it, the sooner we can return to safety."

—Chapter 30—

—Merry Christmas—

Kellan held his rifle close, the barrel pointed at the ground.

The bizarre city didn't remind him of Fayetteville. The buildings were closer together, and the street signs, shops, and public notices were all written in kanji, hiragana, and katakana—all pictograms and alphabets used in Japan. Occasionally he saw words in English, like a coffee shop with the words, "Happy Happy," written on the window.

The distant sounds of conflict kept Kellan on guard.

Once he and Xiang turned down a street, he couldn't see Sen, Husker, or Mavis, which also worried him.

"Does the Nexus not have cellular towers?" Kellan asked. "Having phones would make this easier."

"They won't work," Xiang muttered.

"What about short-wave radios? We could use things like walkie-talkies to stay in touch."

"The Net prevents the use of that kind of technology."

Kellan half-laughed. "The TVs are working fine. Obviously, some tech works."

"The images you see on the TVs are projections from the Arbiter." Xiang glanced around, a slight frown on her perfect face. "Most communications from the Arbiter work no matter what, so long as it's within the Nexus. If you took those TVs to some other dimension, they would lose all usefulness. Even as televisions."

Kellan ran a hand through his hair, irritated that everyone seemed to know important details about their surroundings, but they didn't care to share. He wished he had more details about the rules, and what they needed to do to win.

Skittering—the rapid scrape of something on metal and asphalt—caught his attention. He lifted his rifle and pointed at the nearby alleyway, some narrow space between two cracked buildings with wooden boards nailed over the windows.

"What was that?" he whispered, unable to see anything down the dark alleyway.

Xiang stopped and turned, her expression never shifting away from *disinterest.*

"It's a Kuji. You needn't fret. A Kuji won't attack unless you're marked as the Straggler."

Kellan kept his weapon up regardless. Apparently the Kuji were the killer monsters out to cull teams. They had to be dangerous.

"What does it look like?" Kellan stared at the alley, but he saw and heard nothing. No movement. No more skittering.

"It has the look and shape of a spider."

"Whatever made that sound was too big to be a spider."

"Very well." Xiang smiled to herself, a chuckle on her breath. "It's a *large* spider." She crossed her arms, her expression distant. "I had forgotten how much you like to argue semantics and word choice."

A shiver went down Kellan's spine. First off, he hated spiders. And secondly, he didn't like the way Xiang thought she knew him. Whoever *Alex Kellan the Defector* was, he wasn't him.

"The Kuji won't attack?" Kellan asked, his voice low.

"No."

"Then one second. I'm going to get a look at it."

Xiang didn't reply. She stood in the middle of the street, her attention on the surroundings. A couple of her illusionary bunnies hopped by, both with white and brown fur, like rabbit-shaped cows.

What kind of spider was in the alleyway? Kellan wanted to know what to look out for. And he wanted his eyes to give him more information on the beasts. Why were they so spooky? Surely, they couldn't be too dangerous.

With careful movements, Kellan approached the alleyway. Two dumpsters, a dilapidated couch, and three trash bags were the only objects in the alley. A cold breeze washed through the narrow walkway as Kellan glanced around. The darkness in the shadows made it difficult to see the fine details.

He *could* light something up with his eclipse magic, and again, Kellan cursed at himself. He wanted the ability to see in the dark. It would make everything so much easier.

Kellan inched into the alleyway, only a few steps, when someone stepped out of the shadows, seemingly from nowhere. On instinct, he held up his rifle, ready to fire, but he relaxed once he saw who it was.

Jace.

His machine-eye glowed in the darkness, the light-blue hue almost a reassurance. Jace was one of the few people Kellan classified as *sane* within the world of the Nexus.

Jace held up a finger to his lips and offered a quiet *shh*. Then he pointed up.

Kellan followed his gesture until he spotted a portion of the wall and window that wasn't boarded up.

"A Kuji is nearby," Jace whispered. "They don't like it when people go looking for them."

Kellan lowered his weapon and pointed it at the ground. "Xiang said they wouldn't attack."

"They won't, but they can make your life difficult even without killing you.

Trust me. You should get out of here and focus on finding a key."

"Oh, yeah?" Kellan didn't like the tone of his voice. "Why's that?"

"I've bet arcana that your team gets a key in the first round." Jace smirked as he stepped back into the darkness. "You wouldn't want me to lose arcana, would you?"

Before Kellan could respond, Jace was gone. Or invisible. Kellan wasn't sure. He just knew that the mysterious man always seemed to be close by. Was Jace… following him? He still hadn't unraveled the mystery of the dog tags.

Kellan touched his tags as he backed out of the alleyway.

"Are you satisfied?" Xiang asked.

He turned and jogged to her location. "Not really." Once he rejoined her, Kellan tightened his grip on his rifle. The city seemed so massive, and he wasn't sure where to begin.

As if having the same thought, Xiang said, "If one of the keys is in a live rabbit, it's likely underground. It's winter, and they prefer to burrow. We should head into the sewers to look." She pointed to one of the many tunnels jutting out of the ground. "We don't have much time. The Net is already shrinking."

"Where are we? Exactly?"

Xiang glanced around. "By the look of the language, I'd say we're in some sort of parallel to Japan."

"We were teleported here, right? And that happens instantly?" Kellan glanced up at the sky. The morning sun filtered through the crimson of the Net, giving the whole city an eerie aura.

"That's correct. Teleportation happens instantly."

"Then we're not in Japan."

Xiang lifted an eyebrow. "Why do you think that?"

"Because it's still morning." Kellan pointed to the low light of the sun. "It was morning in Fayetteville. Which means we're still in the same time zone. If this were Japan, it'd be night."

"Why does it matter where we are?"

"Because *bunnies*," Kellan used air quotes around the word, "have different behaviors depending on where you are in the world and depending on whether we're talking about hares or rabbits. *Hares* stay above ground. No burrowing. *Rabbits* burrow. Eastern cottontails—which are found on the east coast of North America, near Fayetteville—don't burrow. They live in forests and thickets, usually next to open fields. So we probably shouldn't check the sewer first."

Xiang brought a hand to her chin, her eyes narrowing. For a prolonged moment, she said nothing, she just mulled over the information. Finally, she asked, "Why do you know so much about bunnies?"

"I had to take several field survival courses," Kellan replied with a sigh. "I thought that information would never really come in handy, but this is the second time I've had to utilize everything I've learned, so I'm sure the universe is having a good chuckle."

Xiang fidgeted with her nails before finally nodding. "This is an urban area, but perhaps there's a park we can investigate."

"What? You don't have some retort about how the bunny is actually part of the Arbiter or something?" Kellan chuckled at his own joke. With sarcastic jazz-hands, he added, "*The Arbiter pulled out his kidneys in order to make mammals for his misshapen children, and anyone who touches the hopping organs will be thrown in a pit with a million giant spiders.*"

Xiang gave him no reaction.

With a sigh, Kellan slung his rifle onto his shoulder. "Listen, if there's something magical about the bunnies, it would be great to—"

Searing pain ripped through his back.

[Sinsidious Chick #3] used talons to stab [Alex Kellan] for 3 damage. [Tyranny Worms] restore [Alex Kellan] for 1 damage every 6 seconds.

Kellan shouted as he stumbled forward, caught off guard by talons ripping through his flesh.

A bird had attacked him.

No. Not a bird.

A monster.

It was some sort of raven, but it was the size of a large dog. Somehow, it had swooped down, silent as nightfall, and dug its talons straight into Kellan's back. The bird had metal parts—mechanical in nature—and when it flapped its wings, the strength of its flight was enough to lift Kellan off his feet.

Without much thought, Kellan lifted his rifle and shot up at the monster.

[Alex Kellan] shot [Sinsidious Chick #3] for 18 damage. (8 +100% Sharpshooter Modifier + Sevriss Bonus)

The beast shrieked and then released Kellan. When it was about to fly away, Xiang waved her hand. *Another* bird appeared—an illusion—and it flapped its giant wings in front of the monster, confusing it. The beast slashed and shrieked, unable to see through the fakery.

Name: Sinsidious Chick #3
Race: Lesser Yami
Magics: Eclipse, Wyld
Rank: Impossible
Armor Rating: —
Health: 1/19

Stats:
Strength—5
Dexterity—5
Fortitude—1 [Hollow Bones]
Intelligence—1

Perception—2
Willpower—1 [Animal]

Abilities:
Stealth Fighter—The yami can cloak itself in a bubble of silence and a shroud of invisibility while in flight. The bubble and field break when the yami takes violent action.

It only has one health left.

Kellan shot the beast. It flapped its wings, unable to support itself until it eventually crashed to the ground. The bird twitched and flapped as its screeching gradually died along with it.

Kellan took a deep breath as he stared at the dying monster.

"Number three," he muttered, his back on fire from the damage. The freakish Tyranny Worms stitched his skin back together, but Kellan already knew there were more nearby.

He glanced at the sky. There had to be more. He couldn't see them.

Xiang walked over to the corpse of the bird, and then knelt. The black oil-like blood glittered with two pieces of red arcana. She grabbed one, and it disappeared into her flesh, practically melting into her.

Right as Kellan was about to say something, another bird suddenly became visible. Its bubble of silence popped as it swooped for him.

Without conscious thought, Kellan stepped backward.

And then disappeared into the darkness. He *sank* into the void, out of reach of the bird. The talons hit the road, but Kellan had vanished into the shadows and "stepped" away through the darkness, like swimming in cold ink.

When Kellan wanted to emerge, he stepped up, like quickly walking out of a pool of weightless water. He was a good ten feet from his original position, and his "shadow-step" had happened so fast, even the second bird seemed confused.

"*Void Agent,*" Kellan muttered to himself as he stared at his hand. His focus in eclipse magic… He closed his eyes for a moment to think about it.

Void Agent

The mage gains the C-rank power "Shadow Step" for free (the ability to step into the shadows, move their full distance, and then exit the shadows). Diving into the "void" of darkness only lasts 6 seconds, but the mage may travel anywhere that a shadow could fit through.

Stepping through the darkness? A tactical godsend.

When the bird screamed and lunged for him again, Kellan willfully stepped back into the shadows. Diving into the safety of the darkness was interesting—but he couldn't experience it long. It was like his breath ran out in just six seconds. He had to emerge, but he stepped out behind the beast as it slammed into the road.

Kellan stood, lifted his rifle, and fired.

The raven screamed as the bullet ripped through most of its frail body. The machinery wasn't as delicate, but the moment the bird started bleeding, it obviously wanted to get away. The raven took to the sky, and Kellan let it go.

But when he glanced up, to follow the trail of the monster, he had to crane his head back to see the top of a fifteen-story building. On the roof was the largest damn bird Kellan had ever seen in his life. The bird's body was so swollen and bulbous, it obviously couldn't fly.

It had to be the size of a single-family house. Maybe larger.

Its eyes had ruptured and wept blood. Its feathers were mangled and falling out onto the roof of the building. Visible bulges of flesh—they were so large, Kellan suspected they were the size of a person—pulsated and popped, gushing out pus with the consistency of cottage cheese.

"What is that?" he said, breathless.

Name: Sinsidious
Race: Greater Yami
Magics: Eclipse, Wyld
Rank: Impossible
Armor Rating: 5 [Layers of Disease]
Health: 60/60

Stats:
Strength—15
Dexterity—2 [Bloated]
Fortitude—20 [Layers of Disease]
Intelligence—1
Perception—0 [Blind]
Willpower—1 [Animal]

Abilities:
Immaculate Conception—The yami lays fertilized eggs that hatch within ten minutes.

"Ten minutes?" Kellan said aloud. He whipped around, his heart rate going up. "We need to get into a building."

Xiang glanced around, and then hurried for a door in a building across the street from the massive beast. With a wave of her hand, the door popped open. She entered.

Before Kellan followed, he rushed for the corpse of the single dead bird. He scooped up the arcana from the black blood, and then absorbed it.

[Alex Kellan] absorbed 1 arcana.

He ran for the building with Xiang, and as he went, a dozen more of the birds appeared in the sky, all swooping for his location. Kellan leapt into the darkness just before the next set of talons would have ripped into his body. He traveled through the darkness and emerged inside, next to Xiang.

The building was some sort of office complex. A receptionist's desk, along with waiting chairs and a couch, were all positioned around the walls.

The dozens of birds screeched, and two flew for the windows, shattering glass.

Xiang sighed. While rolling her eyes, she waved her hands and created more illusionary birds, the same kind she had used to distract the first. The fake birds fought with the real ones, distracting them.

Once the birds weren't clawing at the building, Kellan managed to catch his breath. The worms finished their work, and Kellan no longer felt the sear of pain.

"Creatures like that are common in the games," Xiang said. "It's meant to distract us. We need to leave it and focus on the bunny."

"We could gather some arcana." Kellan rotated his shoulders. "The birds weren't difficult to kill."

"They'll swarm you. That's their tactic."

A box fell off the receptionist's desk.

Kellan whirled on his heel and brought up his gun.

"It's one of the inbred," Xiang said with a frown. "Kill that if you want arcana."

Kellan lowered his weapon, disgusted with her flippant disregard for sentient life. He didn't want to kill any innocents trapped within the twisted confines of the Nexus.

"Come out," Kellan said. "I won't shoot you."

For a short moment, nothing happened.

But then someone crept out from behind the desk, their odor reaching Kellan before he truly saw them. The soft stench of forgotten garbage wafted throughout the room. The person's filthy clothes were ripped and tattered. It was a man—maybe more a teenager—with lumps on his body, a beach of a forehead, and no hair on his face, not even where eyebrows should've been.

"I-I'm not here," he said, spittle flying out as spoke. "I was j-just trying to g-get home. I w-won't interfere with your g-game."

Kellan hesitated. He slung his weapon over his shoulder and motioned to the room. "It's just me and… and this lady." He stepped forward, but just once. "Look, do you mind if I ask you a few questions?"

"Are you really asking it questions?" Xiang stepped closer to the front door and glanced out the windows of the office building. "The birds are retreating to their mother. We can leave soon."

Kellan ignored her.

The misshapen man remained on the ground, half on his knees, half poised to stand. Kellan motioned him up, disappointed his analysis didn't see anything.

Which meant the resident wasn't a mage or half-mage.

"What's your name?" Kellan asked.

The man pulled on his dirty coat. It was brown, either from soil, or because it started brown, Kellan wasn't sure.

"My n-name is Cash."

"Really?" Kellan said, immediately regretting the question. "I mean, that's not important. Sorry. I just need to know a few things. I'm Alex Kellan, and—"

The man's eyes went wide. He had no eyebrows for further emotional shock, but Kellan got the picture.

"Oh, you're Sad Sack!" Cash said as his lips twitched into a smile. "M-Merry Christmas! I'm happy to be alive, t-too!"

Kellan sighed and then dragged a hand down his face. "Jesus."

"The Arbiter s-sent out messages of wh-what you did." Cash rubbed his hands together, the skin on his knuckles flaking off, revealing raw scabs. "You saved Hua and Twi. Such good kids. Their p-parents didn't make it."

Kellan wanted to ask, *You knew them?* but his throat tightened when he remembered the hall. He shook his head, dispelling the thoughts.

"W-Wait." Cash held up a hand and then stepped forward. His smell became ever more prominent. "Can you help me? The y-yami… The Arbiter has given it life once a-again, but the chicks are a-attacking. They'll find our h-home and kill us all."

"We don't have time," Xiang stated.

Once again, Kellan ignored her.

"If I help you, do you think you could help us find the key for the game?"

Cash hesitated. He rubbed his hands together at twice the speed. "The Arbiter has f-forbidden us from helping outsiders." He stared at the ground, avoiding Kellan's gaze. "F-Forgive me."

"It's fine. Never mind. Do you think you could help me find more gold arcana?"

Xiang gave the conversation her full attention, her keen eyes locked on Cash. She waited, expectant, but remained quiet.

"Gold arcana…" Cash hugged himself. "If y-you kill the bird… I think I m-might know someone who w-will offer up their a-arcana."

"And arcana freely given is gold, right?" Kellan asked, hoping Xiang was paying attention.

Cash nodded once.

With a sardonic glance, Kellan turned to Xiang, and then motioned to himself, and then to Cash. "I told you. There is gold arcana. Hua and Twi even sang a song about it."

"*G-Gold arcana cleans the soul, red a-arcana takes its toll.*" Cash didn't sing as well as the kids, but even he seemed to know the little rhyme as soon Kellan invoked it.

"The key is more important than your quest for gold arcana," Xiang stated. She returned her gaze to the window. The skies seemed calm, but Kellan knew it was all a farce. "And killing the mother will take a considerable amount of time."

Kellan held his breath. He had an idea on how to deal with the bird. It was a tactic he had used while in the Delta Force several times.

"If I can kill the bird, I will," Kellan said.

Cash's eyes grew bloodshot and glassy. He smiled, despite himself, and then bowed his lumpy head several times. "Really? Oh, praise you. Merry Ch-

Christmas! Thank the Arbiter!"

Without a word, Xiang headed toward the exit. How much time did they have left? Kellan was certain they had plenty. Her desperation bothered him, but he figured she would change her tune as soon as she heard his plan.

—Chapter 31—
—Mind Magic—

Kellan stepped closer to Xiang.

The red light of the sun through the Net created a burning hue throughout the office building. More shouts and gunshots echoed throughout the city, punctuated by periods of quiet.

"Listen, I have an idea," Kellan said. "We'll destroy the building. When it collapses, the creature will fall and die. And I've brought buildings down before. We used explosives to—"

Xiang held a hand up, and Kellan stopped speaking.

"It's cute you want to solve everything like this is a mission back on your dimension, but we don't have time to decimate a building." Xiang touched Kellan's upper arm. "We're mages." In a sarcastic tone, she added, "It means we can solve problems with magic."

"So, we can blow up the building with magic?" Kellan quipped.

"As in, magic has other solutions. Explosions aren't necessary."

"With my magic… I can mold metal, shape it into a knife, make that knife glow like a flashlight, and then stab myself with it, all while feeling nothing because I can ignore pain." Kellan held up a hand. "Oh, and I can step through shadows. None of those things compare to a good ol' fashioned explosion, though."

"Your poor choice in magical abilities can be fixed with enough arcana." Xiang dragged her fingers up to his shoulder. When Kellan glanced to stare at her touch, she removed her hand. "Listen—you saw the yami, didn't you? Its high fortitude and armor?"

"Yeah."

"Physical attacks will be damn near useless, but *magical attacks* can easily deal with the monster. Fire, for example, has an interesting side effect. It can *exhaust* targets, causing them to lose fortitude, or destroy their armor completely."

"Well, Mavis isn't here. She's the only magma mage I know."

Xiang crossed her arms and sighed. "Fire was just an example. I'm a mind mage. We needn't focus on physical attacks."

"I don't know what mind mages can do." Kellan gestured to the world around him. "I don't know what anything can do, really. I'm relying on my *eyeballs* to give me constant information."

"Sen didn't explain more of the magics to you?" Xiang hardened her expression. Her voice practically became dull as she muttered, "I told him to instruct you before the games began."

"He told me some vague things. Like how magics relate to personality, but nothing I could use to strategize with."

Xiang glanced around, her intelligent eyes landing on a door with two squiggly kanji. "Perhaps I should just show you what mind mages are capable of." She strode over to the door, her heels clicking the entire way. "Come. If you want to waste time on this yami, I'll indulge your curiosity, but only so you can understand more of my abilities. After this, we must focus on acquiring the key… and nothing else."

With another wave of her hand, the door opened, revealing a stairwell that led up. The office building wasn't as tall as the one with the bird yami—it was just ten stories—and Kellan glanced upward, counting the many steps that went upward in a square, all along the wall.

He could see up the middle of the stairs, all the way to the ceiling.

Xiang didn't head for the steps. Kellan didn't blame her. Who wanted to climb ten stories in heels?

But it did make him wonder what was going to happen.

Cash, the inbred resident of the Nexus, followed them into the stairwell and closed the door. He stood tall, though his tattered clothes practically fell apart as he moved. He left a trail of threads behind as he walked.

Everything echoed up the steps and against the plain gray walls, even a slight sigh. Kellan held his breath, waiting to hear someone—or something—lurking nearby. Cash and Xiang didn't move. To Kellan's surprise, he heard nothing.

Only the increased howl of the wind outside.

"Mind mages are capable of many feats," Xiang said as she stepped into the middle of the stairwell. "Telekinesis is fairly common. It's the ability to move objects with your mind." She lifted her hand, and then her whole body lifted from the ground. She continued upward at a steady pace—not fast, though.

She had the speed of a lazy elevator.

Kellan ran up the first flight of stairs and beat her to the second story. Xiang didn't seem to mind. She continued upward, riding her invisible elevator, her feet hanging, her toes pointed toward the ground.

"If you can fly, why aren't you doing this all the time?" Kellan asked as he leaned onto the railing.

"The answer to your question is *mana*. It's a finite resource, and unless we have a way to replenish it, I don't want to waste any. It costs me mana to use more than five pounds' worth of force with my telekinesis. Small objects, or doing minor tasks, like opening doors, requires no mana."

"I see."

Xiang continued her silent ascent. Kellan ran up the next set of stairs, keeping pace with her now, waiting for the next lesson on the strange magic.

Cash followed them up the steps, his movement surprisingly quiet. He tried to stay out of sight, even going so far as to hug the walls and keep his hands from the railing. Perhaps he knew something about magic, but he didn't say.

"Mages gain a *focus* at D rank, and then a *specialist* ability at S rank, and a *mastery* ability at M rank." Xiang spoke without any strain in her voice. Her telekinesis didn't seem to distract her in the least bit. "These extra abilities tend to reduce mana cost. For instance, my illusions are almost costless to manifest. I only need mana for illusions that are larger than a multi-story buildings, and even then, my illusions are always cheaper."

"Yeah, I can step into the darkness." Kellan spoke the words as his gaze wandered to the next set of steps.

Instead of climbing them, he dove into the shadows. The inky void of cold power welcomed him. He traveled through the darkness, going up the steps of the stairwell in a matter of seconds. Kellan exited the darkness on the fourth floor and had to take a deep breath.

"Did you see that?" he called out over the railing.

"Y-Yes," Cash replied. "Impressive."

"The ability to step into the shadows is a very common ability among eclipse mages," Xiang said as she lifted up beyond the fourth story and continued to the next. "What you need to do is focus on developing the *laser* ability. As an eclipse and metal mage, you have the perfect synergy already set up."

"Oh, yeah?" Kellan slipped into the darkness another time. He exited on the fifth story, exhilarated by his power. He felt like a dolphin, diving into the void. "What if I just want to focus on eclipse magic?"

"Then I recommend invisibility and creating shadow shell armor. Eclipse magic can harden darkness and use it like a physical object. So long as the light is dim, you'll have a great advantage."

They went all the way to the ninth floor, Kellan practicing his shadow-stretching ability, Xiang casually floating to her destination with her telekinesis, and Cash following with silent determination. Once they were almost to the top, Xiang's tone shifted to one of amusement.

"Laser damage can become powerful," she said with a smile. "But phantasmal damage—the kind created by mind magic—is the trickiest."

"Why is that?" Kellan stopped at the last set of stairs.

"Because instead of targeting a person's fortitude to deal damage, phantasmal typing targets a person's willpower." She floated to the tenth story and then landed with the grace of a falling leaf. With a flick of her wrist, she pushed her dark hair over her shoulder. "The damage I deal with my *mind blast* is based on how much willpower I have over my target."

Kellan stepped into the darkness, but instead of slipping over the steps like a quick shadow, he slithered across the wall. He exited the shadows on the tenth floor, stepping out of the wall and marveling at his ability.

"Wait," he said, his thoughts returning to the conversation. "What do you mean?"

"If I have one or two willpower over my target, I deal one damage with my mind blast. And if I have three or four, I deal six damage… And if I have five or six higher, I deal fifteen… And finally, if I have seven or higher, I deal thirty. The target soaks the damage only with their willpower—no armor rating."

Kellan rotated his shoulders. "You can bypass the armor rating?"

"That's right." Xiang headed for the door to the roof. "Now you understand. Each magical typing has its advantages and disadvantages. Fire will reduce the armor and stats of the opponent. Lightning will stun. Ice will slow and freeze. Phantasmal will attack willpower only. Entropy will permanently maim. Phase typing will ignore all armor and shielding."

"What about laser damage?" Kellan asked.

"You'll have a lot of damage," Xiang said, her hand hovering above the handle. "Since two magics share the typing. And its range is by far the greatest of all magical types."

The door to the roof flew open. Xiang walked out, Kellan shadowed her steps, and Cash quickly ran up the last of the stairs to join them. A harsh wind rushed over the roof, and Xiang shielded her eyes as she strode to the edge of the building.

The disgusting bird was across the street and above them, perched atop the fifteen-story skyscraper. It howled and spread its diseased wings, losing more feathers. The fat blob of a bird moved its head around, but without any eyes, it obviously couldn't see.

Eggs were pushed from its bloated body, slime-coated and sticky.

Kellan lifted his gun, ready to attack the fell beast, now that he was closer. Xiang placed a delicate hand on his elbow, and then gently pushed the weapon down.

"I told you—that's not a sound tactic." Xiang smiled. "Allow me to demonstrate my abilities."

Without a word, Kellan jerked his elbow out of her grip. She offered a frown at the gesture.

Kellan stepped in close and lowered his voice, making sure his back was turned to Cash. "Why did you assign me to search the city with you?" he whispered to Xiang. "Because I don't have any interest in becoming *Alex Kellan the Replacement*. You can keep your love triangle. It doesn't need to be a love square."

A prolonged moment passed between them.

Xiang stepped away and rubbed at her temple. "I brought you with me so that you wouldn't be ordered around by *Sen*. Isn't that what you wanted? You were concerned about his Tyranny Worms, weren't you?"

Kellan caught his breath, mulled over the comment, and then nodded.

"Next time I won't take your desires into account." Xiang turned on her heel, her beautiful hair flowing in the wind. "And trust me—looking at you doesn't set butterflies free in my stomach. It sets them all on fire. I just… needed to make sure the Arbiter caught sight of me touching you once or twice."

The mere mention of the Arbiter bothered Kellan. He glanced around, and within moments, spotted one of the creature's freakish eyes. It was poking out of a billboard on the top of a nearby building. The electronic sign was blinking an advertisement for spaceship-shaped cola, but the Eye of the Arbiter was just sitting in the middle, staring at them from afar.

Watching.

Recording.

Why did she want the Arbiter to see? Kellan couldn't even think of a reason.

Cash grunted and then pointed to the bird. "More! M-More!"

With his rifle still in hand, Kellan glanced back at the monster. He figured more of the chicks would start attacking, but that wasn't what Cash was pointing at.

Other people were attacking the gigantic bird.

They leapt around the roof of the building, the flash of their magic lighting up the sky and practically reflecting off the crimson Net overhead. They moved around the beast so quickly, Kellan didn't get a good glimpse of them.

The crash of windows and the rattle of automatic gunfire drew the attention of the invisible birds. With swarm intensity, they flew for the roof, attacking everything around their mother.

Kellan counted over two dozen dog-sized ravens. They thrashed around their mother, fighting the other participants of the Nexus Games. A couple died—their bodies plummeting to the ground—but most were bloodthirsty and desperate.

"Aren't we going to do something?" Kellan asked.

Cash rushed to the edge of the ten-story building. He leaned against the ledge, his bloodshot eyes wide. "It has to die… It *has* to."

Wounds appeared across the yami and its blood splattered off the edge of the skyscraper and down to the streets below. Xiang smiled to herself as she watched the carnage from afar.

Who were the mages attacking the monster? And why? Kellan wished he could get some data on them. They continued their fight with the beast while drowning in enemy chicks.

"They're going to kill it," Kellan muttered through gritted teeth. "If *we're* going to get the arcana, we need to do something."

"Phantasmal damage doesn't have the range of lasers," Xiang said. She held up a hand, her fingers outstretched. "But now that we're on this roof, the beast is within my grasp. And those fools have weakened the beast considerably. Stand back, and marvel at the power of phantasmal damage."

Kellan stared at the bird, wondering what phantasmal damage would even look like. Gray fire? Or something ghostly?

But he saw nothing.

And then the head of the bird exploded.

Brains flew out in all directions, its last few cries a jumbled mess of sounds, like its body was releasing its own confused gurgle as the head was completely demolished. The phantasmal damage had been a straight attack to the brain—nothing more. No collateral damage. No area of effect. Just a one-on-one target.

And the monster only had one willpower.

What's Xiang's score? Kellan wondered. But he already knew she likely had seven over the monster.

The yami spasmed and twitched, its massive body flailing. Then it crashed to the roof of the skyscraper, the last of its eggs cracking under its dead weight.

Xiang flicked her wrist, and ten scarlet arcana crystals flew off the roof, carried by the invisible hands of telekinesis. They glittered as they sailed through the sky and straight over to Xiang.

"A flawless victory," Xiang said with a smirk as the arcana then floated around her, orbiting like tiny moons.

"Hey!" someone yelled from the skyscraper. "*That kill was ours.*"

Cash scrambled over to the door of the office building. He could physically hide himself rather well, but his odor prevented any chance of him remaining fully incognito.

"You want that g-gold arcana, right?" Cash asked from the safety of the stairwell. "Bring the yami's a-arcana. We should h-hurry."

But Xiang didn't listen to the man. She stood her ground and waited as two mages from the enemy team flew over on hawk-like wings.

—Chapter 32—
—Prize Room—

Kellan recognized one of the winged men. He was the raven-winged man who was part of Jace's team. As soon as he landed, Kellan was confident in his assessment. The man wore biker clothing—a leather jacket, jeans, and a black T-shirt—and his left hand was marked with the number *77*.

Kellan used his sight to confirm.

Name: Kin Line the Raven
Race: Niav
Magics: Storm, Wyld
Rank: B, C
Armor Rating: —
Health: 6/6
Stats: Concealed
Abilities: Concealed

He has lower permanent health, Kellan suddenly realized. *But why*?

The other person who flew over was a woman with hawk wings. She glided down, landed, and then shot the dead yami and its dozens of chicks a harsh glare. She, too, wore biker clothing, and her hand had the mark of Team 77.

Name: Vila Line
Race: Niav
Magics: Wyld
Rank: B
Armor Rating: —
Health: 6/6
Stats: Concealed
Abilities: Concealed

Vila and Kin, huh?

The two bird-people stalked closer. Their wingspan was a good fifteen feet, but once they tucked in their feathers, and hunched a bit, they were compact enough to walk around without hitting anything.

The woman with hawk wings brushed back her pixie-short brown hair and smiled. She had a thin, striking beauty to her. It didn't work so well with the biker outfit—she was slender, almost the exact opposite of a classic burly gangster.

"Oh, here you are," Vila said, her brown and red feathers flaring for a bit. "You and your *boy toy* out gathering arcana?"

Xiang said nothing.

The ten crimson arcana crystals orbited around her in a perfect circle, just inches from her body. She watched Vila and Kin with a passive, almost disinterested, expression.

When nobody spoke, Vila stepped forward. She was a few inches shorter than Xiang, but she opened her wings slightly, and Kellan suddenly understood why animals did it in the wild. Vila did look a little more intimidating with her wings spread, and her gaze narrowed in a glower.

"You already have enough enemies in this contest, you really want more?" Vila asked. "*We* damaged the beast—give us some of the arcana, and we'll consider this even."

Kin, the raven man, stared at the monstrous birds. The chicks were consuming the body of their mother. He shuddered and then returned his attention to the conversation.

"Leave us," Xiang commanded. "And I won't kill you the first chance I get in the coming games."

The icy cold statement shocked Kellan.

He hadn't expected her to escalate the situation.

"Are you serious?" Vila said with a smirk. "You have no allies, no advantages, no great teammates to lean on… And you *still* want to cause trouble?"

She flapped her wings once, sending a strong gust of wind over the roof. The debris and dirt kicked up, but Kellan was ready. He had his arm up, shielding his eyes as he maintained his focus.

"I thought this wasn't a PvP game," Kellan said, drawing everyone's attention. "We're not allowed to fight, right?" He held his rifle close, though—waiting for something to happen.

Kin snorted and shrugged. "Oh, don't you worry." He stepped back, as did the hawk-girl. "We're not going to fight you. The Arbiter wouldn't allow that. But you're gonna run out of time. Eventually you'll *have* to play a PvP game, and when that happens…"

Vila snapped her fingers. "Everyone is gunning for you. You and your boy toy aren't going to last long."

Although Kellan didn't want to admit it, there was a feeling of drowning that crept into his thoughts. Like everyone here *did* want them dead, and the longer the games went on, the worse it would become, like swimming out in the ocean with no land in sight.

Eventually, the inevitable reality would sink them.

So why wasn't Xiang at least looking for allies?

Kellan glanced over at her. She said and did nothing. No reaction to the threat, no words in retort. She merely offered a slight smile.

A harsh scream cut through the city. A bird? A person? It was too high-pitched and pained to tell. The Net—red and glowing—pulsed for a few seconds, similar to a heart beating. Kellan stared at the phenomenon, confused and uncertain.

The misshapen man, Cash, hurried for the door back into the building. Kellan had almost forgotten he existed.

"Oh, no," Cash muttered as he fled. "Th-They're angry…"

Another scream, this one louder than the other, and deeper. It was different.

Vila and Kin spread their wings and took to the sky, their attention on the yami. The dozens of birds swarmed around their dead, half-eaten mother. Then the Net pulsed again, and Xiang turned her attention upward.

"What's going on?" Kellan asked.

"There are only a certain number of greater yami in each game." Xiang turned on her heel and headed for the door. "Whenever one dies, the rest become empowered, and often enraged. It's the Arbiter's way of keeping things interesting."

She stopped at the door and twirled her hand.

The ten arcana floated over to Kellan.

"Don't absorb them," Xiang stated. "Put them in your pack if you want to play the deformed man's game."

Kellan hesitantly reached out and grabbed one of the red crystals. The warmth surprised him. He had an urge to absorb it into his body, but he denied the feeling and gently placed the arcana into his backpack, along with the bedsheets from the AVU Palace.

These are someone's soul, he thought as he tucked eight more into the pack. *It's odd to hold them.*

With the last arcana, Kellan stared at the crystal.

Xiang didn't wait for him. She opened the door and headed for the stairwell, following Cash.

But Kellan thought back to the children he had rescued. They had… held the arcana up to their ear. That thought struck him, and instead of hurrying after Xiang, he did the same. He lifted the arcana to his ear and closed his eyes.

The screaming of the monsters seemingly faded…

And the whispers of the arcana echoed in his ear canal.

Sad…

Frightened…

Whispers…

Kellan kept his eyes closed tightly, trying to decipher the words. He could almost place them. Like they wanted to say something, but they were too far away.

Help… Monster… Help…

Then the building shook.

Kellan snapped his eyes open and glanced around. The Net pulsed, and then the building quaked. He tried to run forward—to reach the door—but the street down below cracked open, and gas spewed into the air in giant pillars. He placed the last arcana in the backpack.

The building cracked and rumbled. The windows of all nearby buildings shattered outward, raining down on the sidewalk—and down around Kellan—in a torrent.

His first thought was about armor, and his second thought was about the curse he had taken to gain his shadow armor.

He spent one of his ten mana and activated his armor.

Glass rained upon him, but the shadows sprang up and shielded him. The darkness wrapped around his body, creating a sleek suit of armor that attempted to shield him from all damage.

[Alex Kellan] suffers 4 damage from falling glass.
[Alex Kellan] reduces damage of each hit equal to his armor rating of 2.
[Alex Kellan]'s shadow shell absorbs 2 damage.

No damage.

But before Kellan could celebrate, the roof cracked open.

He lost his footing, and right as he was about to tumble down, he willed himself to step into the darkness. He wanted to walk through the shadows, just like he had done in the stairwell, but that was when he realized something terrible.

He was falling. The roof had broken apart.

And the darkness couldn't jump from one piece of debris to the other. His movement was limited to that of a shadow. He could stretch across the ground, or under cracks in doors, or even through tiny holes, but a shadow couldn't fly through the sky.

Which meant for six seconds, he fell with the piece of the roof, hidden away in the darkness.

The piece of cement crashed through the floor below, and then through the floor below that. More glass. More destruction. Metal beams even twisted and broke through barriers, devastating the structural integrity of the building.

Three floors down, Kellan had run out of time. He exited the darkness and tumbled through the chaos. As soon as he could, he dove back into the shadows. The rumbling and quaking continued, but as long as he was in the inky void, it seemed nothing could actually hurt him.

At least, Kellan hoped not.

He fell one more floor before the shaking stopped.

He stepped out of the darkness and coughed. Dust and debris hung on the air like a fog. The building groaned, promising it would topple soon, but not just yet. Every window had blown outward, covering the street below in a minefield of glass shards.

Kellan waved his hand around his face, wishing he had some sort of protective face covering. He missed his old military pack. That thing had every bit of survival gear he had ever wanted.

"Oh, hey, hey, hey! It's your lucky day!"

A floodlight came on, piercing its way through the dust and lighting up the demolished floor with a bright white spotlight.

Kellan grabbed his rifle and took several steps away, unable to see beyond the light.

Two other floodlights sprang to life—one red, one yellow—and they shone around the destruction, swirling in a playful and exciting way.

"Congratulations! You found a *prize room*!"

With his weapon still up and ready, Kellan wheezed again, clearing his lungs of the worst debris. Then he tapped his chest. "What?" he barked.

"A prize room. You found a prize room. Rejoice!"

Kellan rubbed at his face. The building shuddered as everything began to settle around him. With a shaky hand, he patted at his body. He still had full health. His shadow armor—and the ability to dive into the darkness—had saved him.

"What's a prize room?" Kellan asked.

"A room where you get prizes."

The voice… It sounded like it came from something small. And possibly cute. It was hard for Kellan to imagine—a child? No. It sounded more mature. As though an adult had swallowed helium and was now speaking with a regal tone.

"I understand the words *prize* and *room*," Kellan sarcastically replied. "What happens here? You just give me a prize?"

The floodlights pointed away, allowing Kellan to see where the voice was coming from. A tiny desk—something shaped for a housecat—sat near the opposite wall. The cracks in the wall threatened to widen, but for the moment, the building had stopped shattering.

A small person sat at the tiny desk.

No. Not a person.

A devil-like creature. A humanoid with little horns and bat wings.

An imp.

Its golden eyes had the pupils of a goat—a straight, horizontal line.

The little imp, with red skin and black horns, wore a small suit that perfectly fit its pintsized body.

Name: Prize Imp #5
Race: Semi-Sentient Construct
Magics: Mind, Fate
Rank: Impossible
Armor Rating: —
Health: 2/2
Stats: Concealed
Abilities: Concealed

"The Arbiter hides rooms like this all throughout the games," the imp replied.

"He likes it when the participants find them. As a reward for your diligence and curious nature, you can win a fabulous prize."

Kellan glanced around, figuring it all had to be a trick. "My diligence and curious nature? You saw I fell through the roof, right? I didn't even know prize rooms existed until right now."

"I'm not here to question how you got here." The imp shrugged. "Besides, what do you want me to do? Send you away? C'mon. That's no fun. You've got to take your prize."

"What is it?"

Kellan slowly walked toward the cat-sized desk, careful about his footing. The floor sagged, but it didn't give out. He made it to the desk, but he wasn't confident about the situation.

"I can't spoil the surprise," the imp said. "You have to discover the prize yourself."

Kellan glanced out the shattered window. "Yeah, well, before that… What caused the earthquake?"

"Angry yami."

"One?"

"The plural of yami is yami. And when I answered, I meant several." The imp flapped its little wings. "There's a big one sleeping under the city. When the Net shrinks a little more, it's going to burst out and eat everyone."

Kellan caught his breath, his body tense.

Literally everything about this game is designed to get us to rush, he realized. *If we don't get the key, then the city will collapse, the Net will shrink, and a million monsters will attack us.*

He forced himself to exhale.

Xiang is right. We shouldn't be wasting any time.

Kellan glanced over at the imp and met its gaze. The creature's strange pupils unnerved him.

But the imp had been very helpful so far.

"Hey," Kellan said. "Do you know how to get rid of Tyranny Worms?" He wanted to rid himself of the control—and he wanted to do it without letting Sen know. Sen had a way to make more of them, after all…

"I do," the imp said.

"Can you tell me?"

The imp flapped its wings. "Look, the Arbiter doesn't like when I give out too much information. We're already chatting *way* too much. Most people walk in, answer my question, grab their prize, and walk out."

Kellan hesitated for a moment.

"Fine," the imp groaned. "Instead of a physical prize, I can tell you the answer, if you want."

"Sure."

"Okay." The imp sat straighter, and then smiled with sharp teeth. "Answer my question, and then you'll receive your prize!"

Kellan nodded once. "Hit me."

The imp cleared his throat and then asked, "*What's the name of the bar you met Mavis at?*"

"What?" Kellan balked.

"*What's the name of the bar you met Mavis at?*"

"How do you know that?"

"I have fate magic given to me by the Arbiter," the imp said. "It allows me to search through time for the answers..." It waved its hands around in a mystical manner. "And I searched through your history to craft this question. An obscure detail you thought was unimportant. *Now it comes back to haunt you.*"

"How much of my past do you know?"

The imp shrugged. "I dunno. About... three hundred and eighty pages of a book, if we had to quantify it. But that's not important. Just give me your answer! Your prize awaits!"

Kellan hadn't thought about his time in Fayetteville until that moment. He closed his eyes, hacked back some more dust, and tried to remember the name of the bar.

It was...

"*Nino's Place*," Kellan said, confident in his answer.

The floodlights flashed around for a moment, and the imp clapped its tiny hands.

"Correct! That's right!" Then the light settled, and so did the imp. "I have a prize for you, or you can take your information. Which would you like?"

"The information." Kellan didn't even hesitate.

"Okay." The imp held up a hand. "Tyranny Worms are killed in several manners. First, you can kill the queen, which is typically in the body of the controller." The imp held up its other hand. "Or you can kill the hive of worms in the body, usually by injecting the person with venom. I suggest hydra venom, for the best result. Careful, that way is likely to kill the person as well as the worms."

"Where do I find venom?"

"Hmm." The imp stroked its chin. "I don't know if I can answer *two* questions... But since this is a weak prize, I guess I'll allow it. You can find venom in the Pan Town Oasis. There's a shop there, run by a resident of the Nexus, who has venom for sale. Careful—they don't like outsiders in Pan Town."

Kellan nodded once and then stepped away from the desk. "Thank you."

The imp gave him a sarcastic salute. "No problem. I look forward to seeing you in another prize room."

Before Kellan could reply, the lights, desk, and imp all vanished in a puff of glitter and smoke. *Poof.* Gone. He glanced around, confused for a moment, but the longer he looked, the more certain he was.

Nothing here. Not even a trace of the imp and its lights.

Bizarre.

Kellan backed out of the ruined room and headed for the stairs, ready to end this game as fast as possible. *I need to get the venom, trade this arcana for gold, and then get the key with Xiang. No more delays. No more prize rooms. Just straight to victory.*

—Chapter 33—
—Travel Magic—

The ruined stairwell had twisted in on itself. Kellan stood at the edge of the cracked steps, staring at the crunched cement and protruding metal beams. The longer he evaluated the situation, the more he knew he wouldn't be able to walk down.

But the shadows.

Kellan knelt down and examined the cracks in the cement. His ability to move like the darkness could—in theory—allow him to slip through the cracks in the rubble. If there were pockets of space large enough to hold him, he could dive into the shadows, resurface for a moment in a pocket, and then dive back in until he reached the bottom.

Confident he could do it, Kellan stepped into the darkness, sinking into the cold protection of the void. He moved with the ability and ease of shadows—right through the cracks of the cement, over the busted metal beams, and closer to the ground floor. When his six seconds were up, he emerged in a cramped and crumbling place.

This whole damn building is going to fall apart. I have to get out of here as soon as possible.

Kellan took a breath, and then dove back into the darkness. When he emerged the second time, he was at the base of the stairwell, on the ground floor. He stepped onto the ground, his attention drawn to the sea of shattered glass and broken bits of buildings.

To his surprise, Xiang stood near the exit of the building. Kellan walked over, careful about his footing.

"Where have you been?" Xiang asked, her impatience clear in her tone, but not her neutral expression.

"I found a prize room, apparently." He offered a shrug. "But I eventually made it—"

"A prize room?" Xiang gave him her full attention, her eyes wide. "What prize did you get?"

"I just asked for information."

The long moment of silence that followed wasn't reassuring.

"Nothing else?" she asked.

Kellan shook his head. "I just asked for the information, and the imp gave it to me."

Xiang clenched her jaw and then pinched the bridge of her nose. After a long inhale, she slowly sighed. "Next time, ask for an item. *Prize rooms* can either give predetermined items, or they can sometimes give you anything you ask for. The imps are empowered by the Arbiter himself. If they let you ask for a prize, ask for something specific and powerful."

"Listen, unless I'm asking for a dirty nuke, I'm not sure what I *can* ask for that would be helpful in this situation." Kellan motioned to the area. "What would you suggest? Can I ask for a key? Can we win by finding prize rooms?"

Xiang pursed her lips. "No."

"Then what? What should I have asked for?"

"Next time you find a prize room, ask for Excalibur or the Green Dragon Crescent Blade. Both are legendary weapons—unbreakable and awe-inspiring. Powerful prize rooms can summon them for you. Weaker rooms… You might get a cheap copy, but at least it'll be an improvement."

Kellan almost couldn't believe her suggestion. "You want me to ask for a *sword*? I don't know how to wield one."

"They're sentient," Xiang said with a sigh, as though Kellan should already know this. "They give their wielder the basic skills to use them. Trust me. Always ask for a legendary weapon. It's the safest bet—even if you don't want it, you can sell it to someone else."

Another rumble through the street put Kellan on edge. He glanced around, looking for Cash, but he never found the deformed man. Was he okay? Kellan searched the nearby area, frantic in his movements.

"Cash left for Pan Town," Xiang said as dust and debris rained off the damaged buildings.

Kellan stopped and turned to her. "We should head there as well." The imp had been kind enough to provide all the information, though Kellan silently cursed himself for not asking for something more elaborate.

I wish people would've told me this ahead of time.

Xiang held out a hand. "Come. I'll take us there. *But hurry.* I don't want anyone to see this."

Kellan jogged back to Xiang. She brushed off her white suit, using her illusions to cover the dirt stains on her collar. When he drew near. Xiang took him inside the stairwell again. The windows were gone, the stairs were ruined, and there was no sign of life.

"Hold your breath," she commanded.

Kellan did as he was told.

And then he felt a powerful pressure tighten around his chest. It felt like… sinking deep into the water. Unable to breathe. Unable to move.

And then the pressure vanished, and Kellan stumbled forward. He gulped down air and then glanced around.

The Pan Town Oasis

> You have entered an Oasis. While inside this non-conflict area, all mages are forbidden from initiating direct violence. Offensive magical abilities are limited. Any who attempt to circumvent this rule will answer to the Arbiter himself.

Another Oasis…

Kellan rubbed at the back of his neck. He checked his backpack and his weapon, his training kicking in at every move. He needed to secure himself before he could secure his surroundings.

Once he knew he was safe, he took stock of his surroundings.

It was a massive sewer system. Giant tunnels under the ground, made of cement and large enough to drive a truck through, spread out in the four cardinal directions. There was no water or sewage, thankfully—just hobo tents, barrels with fires, and wooden boxes that had been converted into seating.

Nexus residents milled about, walking around and chatting with each other—each as misshapen as the last. One woman had ears the size of her shoulders. One man had eyes sinking into his skull, practically engulfed by the skin around the sockets.

When the ground rumbled, dust fell from the sewer ceiling, but everything was so secure, nothing fell out of place.

Kellan and Xiang were a good twenty feet from the Nexus residents. Lanterns, high-powered flashlights, and power generators kept the tunnels bright, but somehow Xiang and Kellan were in a spot of darkness set apart from the underground town.

"How did we get here?" Kellan whispered, still disorientated.

"I teleported us." Xiang glanced over, her eyes narrowing into an icy glare. "I would prefer if you said nothing about my capabilities. It's important that very few people know I can do this."

Kellan stared at her long enough to get the information across his eyes.

> **Name:** Sun Xiang the Illusionist
> **Race:** Human
> **Magics:** Mind, Soul, Concealed
> **Rank:** Concealed
> **Armor Rating:** —
> **Health:** 7/7
> **Stats:** Concealed
> **Abilities:** Concealed

Mind, soul, and concealed… Now I know—her third magic is travel.

"And only certain people can learn travel magic?" Kellan asked. "Right? Because it's unknowable?"

Xiang grabbed him by the upper arm and held him close. "*Don't.* We can't discuss it here. If you want to know more, we can speak in private. *Away from the games.* Do I make myself clear?"

She sounded like an angry mother.

Kellan wasn't amused, but he understood the need for secrecy. "All right. I'll wait."

She released him and went back to patting down her white suit. "Thank you." Then she smoothed her long hair and said, "I apologize for the outburst, but we've already wasted so much time. I wanted to be done with the game by now."

"Already?" Kellan asked. "Why?"

"Because Brenner is likely done," Xiang intoned. "And it would be best if I didn't look to be falling behind."

"And because the monsters are getting restless."

"That, too." Xiang offered a smile. "You learn quickly. The Arbiter punishes those who take too long in the games."

"What a bro. Really helping the underdogs."

Xiang turned on her heel. "Your sarcasm isn't needed here, Alex. Focus. Trade away your red arcana and show me your mythical *gold* arcana so we can leave this dumpster fire."

Alex.

He didn't like being addressed by his first name, but he also didn't have time to quibble about nonsense. With intent and purpose, Kellan strode forward, into the light of Pan Town, and toward the hobo encampments.

The moment he revealed himself, the many eyes of the residents went wide. They scattered into their hovels, hiding behind tent flaps. Some of them seemingly disappeared into the walls…

Illusions.

Kellan remembered how the two children had pulled him through multiple walls—doors upon doors hidden away so that the residents could escape.

"This is an Oasis," someone called out, their voice echoing in the sewer tunnels. "You can't fight here."

"Don't worry, I'm not going to," Kellan said.

It occurred to him then that there were dozens of people here. Even if all of them only had *one* arcana, it would be effortless for him to raise up some of his magical abilities. That was disgusting—he wasn't in the market for butchering a bunch of innocent people, and it completely went against everything he held dear—but he understood why disgusting lunatics would search out the Nexus residents.

They were easy targets.

Why would the Arbiter abandon his "children" like this? Kellan wasn't sure how they were even related, but if they were, it didn't make much sense to him. Was the Arbiter dead inside? As cold as the machines that ran his body?

He shook the thoughts away, uncertain how he would find the answers.

Hefting his rifle strap onto his shoulder, Kellan strode deeper into the sewer settlement. Eyes watched him from the holes in the tent flaps. He tried not to dwell on them as he headed for an obvious stand.

A terrible cardboard sign hung on the wall. It had four sets of languages written on it. Thankfully, one set was English. It read:

Item Shop
No Outsiders Allowed

An old woman stood behind a particleboard counter, her back hunched so much, she was practically doubled over. Her wispy gray hair hung limp around her sagging face, but the laugh lines around her eyes put Kellan at ease. Her ratty and stained dress, on the other hand, had seen better days.

"Hello," he said. "Do you know where I can find a man named Cash?"

Kellan's gaze drifted to the three objects the woman had for sale. His analysis gave him all the information he needed, even though the woman had taken the time to write out each item's description.

Magical Item [Consumable]—Hane Cigarette

The mage gains +2 perception and mana recovery while the hane remains in the mage's system. Highly addictive.

Magical Item [Consumable]—Perfume of the Damned

Perfume that makes the wearer smell like a Straggler. All effects that say "only target the Straggler" also target those who wear this perfume. Lasts for six hours.

Magical Item [Consumable]—Hydra Venom

Potent venom. Lethal. Upon contact, the mage makes a stamina check (against a hidden number). If their stamina is two lower than the check, the mage dies. If one lower, the mage is paralyzed for one hour. If the mage makes the check, they are nauseous for twenty-four hours. If the mage surpasses the check, the venom has no effect.

The venom and perfume were in glass vials—each smaller than a finger.

The cigarettes were just on the table, a small stack of ten.

"Cash?" the old woman asked. "He's down that tunnel, speaking with our father."

Our father? Kellan thought about that statement for a long moment. The woman looked to be in her eighties. Cash didn't appear nearly that old—perhaps in his thirties? How were they siblings?

Kellan pointed to the wares. "Can I buy something?"

The woman smiled, her laugh lines giving her a pleasant appearance—for an elderly person. "A prize imp came to see me not too long ago. Said a fool boy didn't ask for a prize, just information."

Kellan held back sarcastic commentary.

The woman continued, "The imp paid for this venom. Said I should give it to the fool who came asking for it. I think the imp felt bad you left emptyhanded."

With a gentle push, the woman moved the vial of black liquid closer to Kellan.

He picked it up and examined the stopper. It was a rubber seal.

"Careful," the woman said, her voice shaky. "It's quite dangerous. Not many can survive."

Kellan stared at the venom in his hand. The hane cigarettes allowed a mage to restore mana. He needed that. And the perfume… It seemed useful. Not to wear for himself, but he could imagine a few situations where it could come in handy.

"How much for these other things?" he asked.

The woman touched her sagging cheek. "Normally, I don't serve outsiders… But Cash had pleasant things to say. I'll sell you anything you want for three tael."

Tael?

Kellan patted his pockets. He didn't have that currency.

"I have sheets made out of dreamweaver silk." Kellan pulled the black sheets from his backpack and draped them over the shop.

The woman stared at the sheets with her pale gray eyes. "Oh, so much. What fine craftsmanship. I'll take just half. You take the rest of my wares. That's more than fair." She pulled a pair of rusty scissors from a pocket of her grimy dress. "Here, here."

With a few quick snips, the woman sliced the sheets clean in half. She handed Kellan one side, and then quickly pushed the sheets under her makeshift stall.

"Don't want to touch them too long. They'll put me to sleep." The woman smiled at Kellan. "Take your things."

Kellan scooped up the hane cigarettes and the perfume. He stuffed them in his pack, along with the other half of the sheets. The woman pointed to a tunnel, and he followed her directions, hoping to find Cash.

Although the sewer had no waste, it still smelled of sweat. There were too many people living in close quarters.

When Kellan arrived at the entrance of the tunnel, he realized there weren't any lights within. Thankfully, Cash was there, standing near the entrance, his entire body trembling.

"Th-There you are," Cash stammered. He waved Kellan into the tunnel and then pointed to the darkness at the very back. "Here is the m-man who wants to trade you arcana. I s-spoke to him about w-what you want."

But Kellan didn't see anyone.

It was just… a black void.

Kellan stepped forward, a tad confused. Once again, he opened his backpack, but this time he withdrew the ten red arcana. He held them out in a pile, seemingly at thin air.

"Hello?" he called out.

No response.

Cash stepped up to Kellan's side and pointed into the blackness. "There he is." When nothing happened, Cash beckoned to the shadows. "I told you. He killed the yami. He has the bird's arcana."

"*I see that*," a slimy voice hissed, so thick and harsh, Kellan almost reached for his weapon.

A shiver went up his spine. "Hello?" Kellan asked again.

The darkness replied, "*The yami was made from the arcana of my associates. Give them to me, and I will give you* my *arcana in exchange.*"

Cash smiled and urged Kellan to do as he was told. Kellan stared at the glittering crimson in his hand and then stepped forward again. He held the crystals out. For a long moment, nothing took it.

For the love of all that is holy, please don't let this be a crazy monster that sucks me into a hellish pit.

A hand reached out of the shadows—too large to be human, but somehow human shaped. The fingers ended in claws, the thumb was larger than it should be, and the skin was wan and grayish.

Kellan almost jerked away, but the monster took the arcana from his palm.

With gleeful giggling—something only a lunatic could muster—the creature lifted its hand up, and then threw the ten pieces of arcana onto the cement floor.

The arcana shattered.

The red glitter held within each crystal sputtered and flew into the air, disappearing like dust on the wind. A soft cry, almost inaudible, reached Kellan's ears. A short scream of suffering, and then silence.

"*I told them I would have the last laugh,*" the thing in the dark said with a giggle. "*They thought they would escape me, but they were wrong! Now look at them!*"

The fragments of the arcana disturbed Kellan, but he wasn't sure what to say. Weren't they already dead?

Laughter echoed in the tunnel as the beast cackled at ever-increasing volumes. It took a solid minute before it gathered the mental fortitude to quell its amusement.

The monster held out its freakish hand, palm down. Kellan offered his hand, and the creature tensed. Seven pieces of glowing gold arcana sprouted from the wrinkles of the creature's palm. They landed in Kellan's grasp, and he gently drew them closer.

"*Thank you,*" the creature said, its body still concealed by the blackness. "*You may have a fraction of my soul—I want you to live, slayer of yami. You clearly know which side to take in this war.*"

The statements unnerved Kellan, but he didn't voice his concerns. Instead, he held the crystals close and then muttered, "Thank you. I have to go." He backed out of the dark tunnel, never turning around. He was too afraid to face his back to the shadows—and the monster.

Cash didn't follow. The deformed man just offered a wave.

Kellan took in a deep breath, and then walked back through Pan Town, the many eyes following him a second time as he returned to Xiang's location on the outskirts of the hobo town.

The gold arcana glittered in the darkness, like stars in the sky, brilliant and unyielding. For some reason, they felt calming and happy. Had he just helped a murderer commit some sort of heinous deed? Or had he helped someone seek justifiable revenge? Kellan had no idea.

When he approached, Xiang's eyes went wide.

Kellan held up his prize. "See? Gold. I told you."

Xiang stepped close, the reflection of the arcana in her eyes.

When she reached for the crystals, however, something strange happened. Her fingers came close to the crystals, and the golden color faded. The arcana shifted color to crimson—fast and angry, the glowing glitter within swirling like angry bees.

Xiang jerked her hand away, and the arcana slowly shifted its hue back to gold.

The arcana knew she wasn't meant to have it.

It's like the arcana… is still a person. Still alive. Somehow.

"I've never seen this before." Xiang stepped away and crossed her arms. "But I don't see the advantage. You traded ten arcana for seven. What else does it do?"

"I don't know," he muttered.

"Absorb it. Pick some more magical abilities. Then I'll take us to the park." She tossed her black hair over her shoulder and glanced away, her curt movements unusual.

Kellan had never seen her so agitated.

As he absorbed the gold arcana through his palm, he felt a warmth spread from his hand to his elbow, to his shoulder, and then to his chest. It comforted him, almost. A strange feeling.

[Alex Kellan] absorbed 7 gold arcana.

Kellan had been distracted by his impending death when he last absorbed gold arcana—he hadn't seen the notification that said it was gold. Was there a difference? Or was Xiang right? It was all for nothing?

"Pick abilities," Xiang demanded. "Quickly."

Normally, her impatience would've bothered him, but Kellan already knew the magical abilities he wanted.

The ability to see in the darkness. An E-rank eclipse power that cost three arcana. He purchased it immediately.

Pierce the Darkness [3 arcana]

Mastery over light and dark includes the ability to pierce the shadows…

The mage can always see in the dark.

He still had five arcana left—one red, four gold. They weren't separated whenever he glanced at his own abilities, though. It was just a static number. Five arcana.

It didn't matter. Kellan knew what he wanted to do next.

"Xiang," he muttered, keeping his voice low.

She turned to him, her eyebrow raised.

"I can learn one of the unknowable magics, can't I?" Kellan ran a hand over his chest. "Because of one of my abilities."

He thought back to the listing when he looked at "himself."

> **Personal—[Descended from Zenith]—**The mage has the raw magic of Zenith in their blood and has no rank maximum. The mage can also develop one "unknowable" magic.

Xiang nodded once.

"How do I do that?" Kellan asked.

"You need to save some arcana, and then have someone to teach you." Xiang sighed. "But those magics are difficult to master, and you need the Arbiter's blessing."

"I think I'll get it," he said, the warmth of the gold arcana still in his body. *He wanted me to get gold arcana… and now I have it. He let me kill one of his Pestbyters for less.*

Kellan met Xiang's gaze. "If I get his blessing… Will you teach me?"

Xiang held her breath. For a short while, she said nothing. But when she turned away, she smirked to herself. "You're always so surprising. Pleasantly so. I love it when you come up with schemes."

"Will you?" he demanded, not wanting to be compared to his alternate-self.

"Yes. But only where no one can see."

That was good enough for Kellan.

If he had access to one of the rare and powerful magics, perhaps even low ranks would provide him the edge he needed to really compete.

Xiang held out her hand. "Come. Let's find our key."

Kellan grabbed her wrist, and the two teleported out of the Pan Town Oasis, a pop of air the only signal they had left.

—Chapter 34—
—A Bunny—

Kellan appeared between two oak trees in a vast park.

He stumbled forward, regaining his balance after a few moments, and then swallowed air. The teleportation process was instant, but his body felt the pressure of moving from one location to another long after—the feeling of air being pushed out of the way so he could exist in a space he previously hadn't was odd.

After a deep breath, Kellan asked, "Can you teleport into solid objects?"

Xiang frowned. "What did I say about discussing my powers?"

The park around them was active with life, and Kellan backed up until he was right beside Xiang. Shouts, gunshots, and the crackle of magical energy created a song of chaos.

And the park had seen better days, even before the fresh bullet holes. The shabby benches were pushed over, the trashcans had been dumped over the grass, and Kellan spotted more than one police-tape murder scene.

He also noticed several elementary school desks, pencils, and chalkboards lying around the area.

It reminded Kellan of the mire and the barbed wire. So many things were merged in one, that the environment had become a freakish amalgamation.

Nearby movement caught Kellan's attention. Groups of individuals ran between the trees and over the fields of grass, all of them chasing bunnies. At least five teams had entered the park, the numbers on their left hands giving away their participation in the Nexus Games. The illusionary rabbits zipped away from them, fleeing in all directions. Xiang's magic made them indistinguishable from normal animals.

"Get it!" someone screamed. "*It has to have a key!*"

"That rabbit is ours!" another person added.

"Grab the other one! Chase it this way!"

And to Kellan's amusement, all the fake bunnies turned and headed back for the city, abandoning the park altogether. The people chased after, like some sort of Alice in Wonderland metaphor.

An odd detail also stood out to him…

The shadows of the trees, the darkness of far-off alleyways—he could see perfectly in them. It was like light shone over everything, flooding the park with illumination. It was his magic, his ability to see through darkness, and Kellan marveled at how much it improved his perception of the world.

Kellan stood next to Xiang, rifle at the ready, waiting until the groups had put some distance between them. When he was certain no one was around—not even the Eyes of the Arbiter—he glanced over at Xiang.

"Well?" he asked. "Can you teleport into solid objects?"

After a long exhale, Xiang tossed her hair over her shoulder. "No." She strode over the grass and dirty patches until she came to a stone walkway. "If I can't fit in the space, I can't travel there."

"And if I had that magic, I'd be able to zip around?"

She smiled as she brought a hand up to her chin. "There's an amusing ability in this magic called *blink*. It allows the mage to occasionally avoid all damage from attacks as you teleport to safety."

"Interesting."

"I think it would suit you."

Kellan half-smiled. "Don't say that. The defiant part of me wants to pick something else, now."

"Even your alternate dimension selves are stubborn," Xiang said with a chuckle. "It must be genetic. Which is why you should *definitely* learn to blink. It'll keep you alive in a desperate situation."

"A good strategist tries to avoid desperate situations." Kellan thought back to his CO, and how many times he had drilled in the importance of making wise decisions. "Ideally, we'd never have to use our last resort plays."

Xiang's expression hardened into something neutral. In a quiet voice, she said, "Yes. Your soldier instincts serve you well." She sighed and then turned her attention to their surroundings. "Let's search. While everyone else is distracted by my illusions, we should be able to investigate the park without interference."

Kellan glanced around, wanting to secure their new area, but the bizarre landscape made that difficult. The school desks and bookshelves created barriers, some a few feet high, like they had been dumped out of the bed of a truck into one forgotten pile.

"Sister!"

The shriek of Sen's voice caused Kellan's hair to stand on end. He turned and spotted the man-boy hurrying toward them. Sen's face—round and pudgy, like only a child's could be—was knitted in concentration. He brushed off his robes as he approached his sister, sticks and leaves caught in the longer parts.

"I have a single temporary puppet, but it's an observational tool at best." Sen pointed to the red sky. A small black drone hovered far overhead. "I took control of the machine." With a huff and a smile, he finished with, "And there are bunnies nearby."

The drone was nothing more than a camera on flying equipment. Kellan had seen plenty at his local Target. *That* was Sen's puppet? Kellan was almost disappointed.

Xiang barely acknowledged her brother. She nodded once and walked into the park, her gaze on something in the distance.

As she walked off, Sen turned his gaze up at Kellan. "What have you two been doing?"

"Nothing," Kellan said. "We fought a yami, I found a prize room, and then we hit an Oasis."

When he listed it out like that, Kellan realized they had already spent a lot of time in the first game. *No wonder Xiang's so anxious.*

"A prize room?" Sen's voice practically left him. His eyes went wide as he moved closer to Kellan. "What did you get? Tell me."

"I got perfume." Kellan tapped his backpack. He wouldn't tell Sen what he actually got—not now, not ever. He fully intended to kill the worms in his body, he just wasn't sure how and when. "Perfume of the Damned."

"That's *it*?" Sen raked both hands through his hair as he ground his teeth.

"Let me guess." Kellan sarcastically rubbed his chin. "You wished I had asked for a sword."

"*No.* I don't care about *swords*, you buffoon! If you find a prize room, and they let you pick your prize, ask for Langarren Clay! Can you remember that? *Langarren Clay.* Say it with me."

Kellan held his rifle close and smirked. "What's that? Play-Doh for adults?"

"Fool—it's the most magical flesh you'll ever see!" Sen flailed his arms around, almost like he didn't know what to do with his pent-up energy. "If I had even a handful of that, I could make someone great! And if I had a little more… I could craft my body back to its former glory." He glared at Kellan. "Just remember to ask, all right?"

"You're not going to command me?" Kellan asked, dark and serious.

Sen gritted his teeth. "My Tyranny Worms don't work on *long term* commands. They're more immediate, and physical. I can't make you think about things days from now." He turned on his heel, his dirty robes fluttering behind him. "And if you don't want me to command you, then I suggest you start searching the park! My sister is already ahead of us."

With no urge to argue, Kellan walked alongside Sen into the junkyard of a park. At a few points, Kellan had to step over bike racks, and even help Sen get over, though the little man wouldn't acknowledge the assistance.

The shadows and darkness…

Kellan stared at the cold, forgotten corners of the park, amazed by his ability to see everything as though it were bright and sunny. It wasn't like using night-vision goggles, or any of the other tech devices he had used when on assignment. He just *saw* everything, as though the darkness were more of a color shade than something that obstructed vision.

The park was larger than Kellan had been expecting. By the time he and Sen had caught up with Xiang, they had been walking for nearly five minutes, the distant buzz of Sen's drone a constant reminder that it was there. They came across an old elementary school building—a one-story disaster with yellow walls, caged windows, and a disgusting cat mascot half-faded on the front sign.

It reminded Kellan of plastic lunch trays and old schoolbooks.

The plants of the park grew around it, practically becoming one with the building. Some of the trees even jutted in through the windows.

Then the ground rumbled.

Kellan steadied his stance, but Sen fell over immediately. Xiang almost fell, but Kellan stepped forward to assist. She took his arm and remained upright, though she refused to look him in the eye.

Once the shaking was over, Xiang stepped away from him. Without commenting on his help, she pointed to the Net above. "It's shrinking."

Sure enough, the crimson dome over the city constricted and moved slowly closer. The distant red "walls" didn't move at breakneck speeds, but it was fast enough to be alarming. Kellan tried to calculate their distance from the Net, but it was too difficult to do properly from his angle.

More than half a mile, at least, he thought. *We should be fine for now.*

"Check the building," Xiang said, pointing to the elementary school. "Quickly."

The nearby area was devoid of life. No animals. No people. Kellan didn't even see any of the Nexus residents. But he wasn't going to question her urgency—obviously, Xiang wanted this over and done with as fast as possible.

Kellan jogged over to the building, keeping his movements quick and quiet. When he reached a window, he carefully glanced through, making sure to keep ample distance between himself and the glass. The last thing he wanted was a surprise attack.

His dark vision allowed him to see into the depths of the elementary school. The remnants of classrooms were scattered across the inside—throughout the halls, closets, and all the rooms. It was as if someone had taken the building and shaken it. An elementary school snow globe.

Kellan moved to the next window, making sure to duck under the previous one before moving on. If someone was inside, he didn't want them to know he was here.

When he glanced into the second office, he spotted something odd.

A bunny.

Black. Watery. Like it was physically made of ink.

That's it. It has to be. The bunny we've been looking for.

Kellan watched with amazement as the creature moved around the ruined classroom with the silence of a corpse. The animal sniffed at the desks and poked its nose into the paperwork on the ground. It didn't have any features—no eyes or whiskers or even a mouth—it was just an inky puddle in the shape of a rabbit, complete with long ears and a puffy tail.

Kellan shifted his weight to one foot, and the rabbit froze. Before Kellan could fix the situation, the cute little creature dove into the shadows, moving through the darkness just like Kellan could. The rabbit left the classroom in an instant, the shadow zipping under the crack in the closed door.

Animals can have these abilities?

With careful movements, Kellan hurried back to Sen and Xiang. Once in their presence, he pointed to the window. "The rabbit is inside, but—"

"You're certain?" Sen interjected, his eyes wide.

"—I think I might've scared it." He shook his head. "The rabbit dove into the darkness and moved through it. I'm not even sure if it's still in the building."

"No problem." Sen snapped his little fingers. "We'll handle this."

The drone buzzed and flew over the school, hovering at a height too high to really see anything. Kellan glared at the drone, and then turned his attention to Sen. The little kid was waving his hand around, controlling the machine with just his gestures.

"What're you doing?" Kellan asked. "Where's your phone? How are we going to see through the camera?"

"I can see what the drone sees," Sen muttered, his attention never leaving the drone. "That's one of the benefits of my puppets…"

"You can see through the camera?"

"Yes… Which is how I know that our rabbit has exited out the back door."

Kellan cursed under his breath. "Is it running?"

Sen's brow furrowed. "No. It's just… sitting there. Picking at the grass growing on the side of the wall."

Determined to get a visual on their target, Kellan hurried around the outside of the building, diving into the shadows as often as he could to hide his own footsteps. The ability to slide through the darkness was a handy tool, and right as he was approaching the back corner of the school, he stopped and glanced at the roof.

It would be easier to spot the rabbit…

Kellan stepped into the shadows, traveled up the side of the building, and then exited on the roof, a smile on his face. *Having magic isn't so bad.*

The drone overhead was high enough that the buzz wasn't irritating, but Kellan still hated it.

With slow steps, Kellan made his way to the edge of the building. When he glanced at the ground, he spotted the inky bunny in an instant. The creature hid in the shadows of the twisted building, nibbling on the grass with its "mouth." Kellan was still convinced it had nothing, but the ink seemingly absorbed things.

It had a physical body.

Kellan dove into the darkness and exited on the ground, around the corner. He again returned to Xiang and Sen.

"Well?" Sen asked. He motioned to the park around them. "What're you waiting for? We're the only ones here. Grab the bunny."

"I think if I go for it, the thing will escape into the darkness." Kellan knew from experience that his shadows allowed him to travel in all sorts of bizarre ways. "But I have a different plan."

Xiang lifted a perfect eyebrow. "Oh?"

After slinging his backpack off his arm, Kellan knelt and rummaged through the contents. "Trust me. If we work together, this bunny is as good as ours."

—Chapter 35—
—The First Key—

Kellan withdrew the dreamweaver sheets. He kept the other items in his backpack and returned it to his shoulders. Careful not to hold the sheets too long, he set them down on the ground.

"You can make illusions, right?" he asked.

Xiang forced a smile. "I consider myself competent."

"Do your illusions have smells?"

She tilted her head to the side. "Of course. My illusions even have tactile sensation—I can trick the brain into thinking it's feeling something. I've taken every improvement for my illusions that arcana can purchase."

"Fantastic." Kellan spread the sheets out across the dirt and then backed away. "Can you create some rabbit food? Preferably something odiferous?"

Sen glanced from the sheets, to Kellan, and back to the sheets again. With a sneer, he walked over, glared at the black cloth, and then crossed his arms. "What're you…?"

"We'll put the food on the dreamweaver sheets."

Both Sen and Xiang had a look of realization the moment Kellan uttered the words. Which meant they were familiar with the effects of the magical sheets. That saved Kellan the hassle of convincing them that his plan would work.

It was simple, really. If the inky bunny got onto the sheets, it would be subjected to the dreamweaver powers. If the bunny's willpower was low—and according to Xiang, animal willpowers were—then it would quickly fall asleep. Kellan had experienced the sheets in the AVU Palace. At no point had he felt the magic taking hold of him. Which meant the bunny would likely be taken by surprise, but by then, it would be too late.

Then Kellan could retrieve the key.

From… inside of it?

He wasn't sure.

"I approve of this plan," Xiang said.

Sen scoffed and looked away. "It's a decent plan, I suppose."

Xiang twirled her hand. A pile of leafy greens appeared in the middle of the silky black sheets. Their odor was enough for Kellan to smell from afar.

"There." Xiang smoothed her suit. "These should do the trick. Animal noses are sensitive to the smells of fresh vegetation."

Kellan motioned them away from the sheets. The three walked further around the bizarre elementary school in the middle of the public park. Once safely behind a pale tan wall, Kellan glanced around the area. The red hue of the Net overhead gave the park a sinister glow.

He had, sadly, gotten used to the horror show atmosphere.

Rumbling caused the ground to shake, but only slightly. Kellan kept his rifle close. The other Nexus Games participants didn't seem to be nearby. In the distance, he heard their shouts, their gunshots, and their bursts of magic, but near the elementary school, it was mostly still.

He could thank Xiang for that. Her initial distraction—creating hundreds of bunnies—really *had* worked in their favor.

Maybe we can win, Kellan thought to himself. *If we avoid most of the other competitors, and Xiang continues to use her illusions in clever ways, it seems logical we could win…*

Then again, every time he *thought* he knew what was going on, Kellan always found himself discovering something new. And not in a pleasant way.

Kellan glanced around the corner of the elementary school. He could just barely see the black sheets with the piles of greenery on top. He wasn't sure where the inky bunny had gone, but all they had to do now was wait.

Sen's drone hovered overhead—far above them—but Kellan could still hear the buzz of its motors.

"Could you turn that off?" he asked.

Sen frowned. With a wave of his hand, the little machine twirled down to the ground, growing louder and louder as it got close. When it finally landed, the motors instantly shut off.

The drone sat on the ground, unmoving.

Sen picked it up. The machine was as large as an old-fashioned phone book.

"That's not really a puppet," Kellan muttered.

"Anything you control is a puppet." Sen pursed his lips. "Most of my magical abilities revolve around fleshcrafting, healing, clairvoyance, and physical manipulation. I specialize in creating puppets with enhanced capabilities—like draining the physical lifeforce of others—but since you *smashed them*, I wasn't able to bring them along in the games."

"You're the one who sent them into my apartment. What did you expect me to do?"

Sen glared. "I had hoped you would be too mentally frail to handle the situation. And my puppets would've incapacitated you, and then I could've brought you to the Nexus with little trouble or backtalk."

"*Mentally frail*?" Kellan had never felt his blood pressure rise quite like with Sen. The child-man had a way of getting under his skin like a bamboo shoot.

"Enough," Xiang said, her tone harsh.

Kellan returned to observing their surroundings. They weren't out in the open, but they weren't hidden, either. Standing against the front wall of an elementary school was not how he had imagined getting the first key of the competition.

Sen and his sister said nothing. They waited with patience and poise, never once complaining or fidgeting.

"Why do yami have arcana?" Kellan asked, breaking the silence. "You said yami were born of corrupted magic. But when we destroy them, arcana comes out."

Sen went to answer, but Xiang lifted an elegant hand. She answered with, "Arcana *is* magic. Yami are either born from corrupted arcana, or they're made by the failed rituals of mages, or occasionally by the Arbiter himself. In all three instances, the arcana is the heart source of the creature."

"Someone else's soul?"

She nodded.

Kellan wrestled with the concept for a long time.

"This is it," Xiang whispered. "The creature is nearing our trap."

After a deep breath, Kellan glanced around the corner of the building. Sure enough, the void bunny was at the edge of the sheets, staring at the illusionary food. It looked so realistic, Kellan didn't blame the creature for being fooled.

When the bunny stepped onto the sheets, Kellan held his breath.

He watched it move forward. One step at a time.

And then the inky bunny stretched and lay down. Even before it reached the food.

It was asleep.

"We got it," Kellan whispered with a smirk.

He stepped into the darkness, snaked across the ground, and then stepped out of the shadows right next to the sheets. The bunny didn't move. It had practically become a puddle of ink while it slept.

Kellan knelt to grab the creature, but then something strange happened.

The shadows lifted from the ground, becoming tendrils and tentacles. With surprising speed, the darkness grabbed the inky rabbit and lifted it up before Kellan could grab it.

Kellan lunged, hoping to wrestle the bunny from the shadows, but he was too late. The darkness lifted the creature to the roof of the elementary school.

A haunting laugh filled the area, and Kellan actually recognized the voice.

Jace, the man with the machine-eye, dropped his invisibility and showed himself. He stood at the edge of the roof, one foot on the ledge, one foot down. The shadows gave him the inky bunny, and the man crushed the creature between his fingers, the black ooze gushing over his hand.

"I knew you'd find one of the keys first," Jace called out with a smile. "Thank you for this."

Kellan's heart practically stopped. He had considered Jace an ally, but he quickly realized the man had been following him this entire game.

Just to steal whatever key they found.

Kellan rapid-fired his rifle, but the shadows flared up to block the bullets. Each tendril and tentacle were a physical object that blocked the bullets, shielding Jace from the shots. They became damaged, but it would take too long to chew through the barrier of darkness Jace had created.

Frustrated, Kellan slipped into the darkness and darted for the roof. When he emerged from the shadows, he witnessed Jace pluck a piece of electronics from the bunny. It reminded Kellan of a USB drive, but smaller.

That was the key?

The moment Jace had the electronic key in hand, he offered Kellan a smug smile. "My team wins this game."

"No!" Xiang shouted from the ground.

She lifted her hand and the force of her telekinesis ripped down half the wall of the school. Kellan and Jace almost fell off of the roof, but Xiang's attack hadn't been fast enough.

Jace disappeared. All that Kellan heard was a pop of air as Jace teleported away in an instant.

Kellan cursed under his breath. Then the ground rumbled harder than ever before. Worried about the others, Kellan leapt into the shadows and snaked his way back to the group. When he emerged next to the others, Xiang was glaring at the ground.

"I can't believe him," she said, venom in her words. "*That ingrate.*"

"I think we should go." Kellan took hold of Xiang's arm and urged her away from the building. "I don't know what's going on, but I don't like it."

"The Net is shrinking," Sen said through gritted teeth. He dropped his drone. "And the yami underground are on the move… Every time one of the keys is found, that entire process accelerates."

More fun news.

"We should get out of here," Kellan said, waiting for Xiang to teleport them to a new location.

But she shook her head and glanced over at the other teams in the park. They were hundreds of feet away, yet she still didn't want to risk them seeing her use her abilities. Kellan didn't know what else to do but run.

He turned to face the tree line when creatures emerged from the ground. The beasts burst out of the grass and soil, all while hissing like only insects could. It reminded Kellan of cicadas, or a whole hive of angry crickets.

To his horror, centipedes the size of people clawed their way out of the dirt, each with three eyes. The eyes seemed more human than insect, but Kellan didn't have time to give a damn.

Name: Quixit #5
Race: Lesser Yami
Magics: Magma, Body
Rank: Impossible
Armor Rating: —
Health: 10/10

Stats:
Strength—4 [Strong-Jaw]

Dexterity—4
Fortitude—2 [Slender]
Intelligence—1
Perception—2
Willpower—1 [Animal]

Abilities:
Centipede Toxin—The yami injects toxin into the victims it bites. If they fail a fortitude check, they lose 2 from all physical stats (strength, dexterity, fortitude).

Their red bodies and black underbellies reminded Kellan of the Nexus itself. Their long legs ended in sharp spines—sharp enough to rip through the ground and carry them forward. Their giant maws were filled with pincers, and when they came for Kellan, he groaned.

He leveled his rifle and fired at the first one to cross his path. They had low health compared to some of the creatures they had fought, and when Kellan unloaded, his various bonuses with the rifle more than gave him the advantage.

With a few carefully aimed shots, Kellan blasted the heads off two. They screamed and collapsed to the ground, but four more erupted upward, all hissing into the air.

It was like with the ravens…

There had been dozens of "baby" yami nearby, and one large "mama" yami spawning them all.

If we fight here, we'll be mired in enemies. We either need to get out of the park or destroy the mother. Kellan glanced around, his heart racing as the earth tore open all around them. Ten more centipedes were jutting out of the dirt. *I have no idea where the mother is…*

Xiang nimbly avoided the pincers of a centipede and headed for the trees, her sights focused, but her expression set to an icy anger. She still hadn't gotten over Jace taking their key, apparently…

When Kellan glanced over his shoulder, he noticed Sen was having more difficulty. He was too small to outrun the centipede beasts, and he was generally uncoordinated. When one centipede lunged for him, Kellan whipped around and fired his rifle, blasting a hole clean through the insect's chest.

When the yami hit the ground in a pool of its own blood, the shimmering glitter of two arcana appeared.

"Help me!" Sen commanded.

Kellan's muscles tensed on their own.

The Tyranny Worms gripped his insides, compelling him to fire on the next centipede that rushed for Sen.

"I was already helping you!" Kellan shouted through gritted teeth. "Ordering me to do it isn't beneficial!"

Sen ran to his side and grabbed the side of his cargo pants. "Like I would trust you to stay! You've already betrayed Xiang and me once before. I won't make that mistake again."

Kellan grabbed the kid by the shoulder and then ran around two more centipedes emerging from the ground. As he ran, Kellan knelt and plucked the two arcana he had spotted out of the pool of blood.

[Alex Kellan] absorbed 2 arcana.

"I'm not that other Alex Kellan." Kellan pulled Sen toward the trees. "*I've* never betrayed you!"

"*It's only a matter of time,*" Sen growled. "You're just like him!"

Xiang had already made it into the trees—even in heels. Kellan was mildly impressed, but he couldn't dwell on it long. The ground rumbled, and the dirt shifted.

I need to use the shadows…

Kellan held onto Sen and then dove for the darkness.

And then they both crashed into the ground like bumbling baseball players looking to eat some dirt. Kellan felt the pain of the crash in the back of his neck. He groaned and rolled to his side, baffled by the turn of events.

He hadn't slipped into the darkness at all…

Why not?

Sen coughed out grass and then rubbed at his face. "Did you try to shadow-step with me in your arms? You're not strong enough for that! You're just a D-rank mage!"

Kellan stumbled to his feet just as a centipede caught up with him. The beast lunged and caught Kellan's ribs with one of its pincers. Kellan cried out as agony burned through his system.

[Quixit #7] sliced [Alex Kellan] for 4 damage.
[Alex Kellan] reduces damage of each hit equal to his armor rating of 2.
[Alex Kellan] takes a total of 2 damage.
[Tyranny Worms] restore [Alex Kellan] for 1 damage every 6 seconds.

Kellan grabbed at the injury, the wriggling of the Tyranny Worms almost a welcome sensation. *Ironically, they've been my most reliable ally,* he thought bitterly.

When the centipede went to attack a second time, Kellan brought his rifle up and fired, damn near point-blank. The creature's chitinous armor shattered, and the beast hit the ground in a splatter of blood and innards.

Kellan grabbed Sen and hauled him to his feet. "Look, since I'm literally the only one fighting these things, cut me some slack. I thought I could take you into the darkness."

"Just don't—" Sen gasped and grabbed onto Kellan's arm, similar to an actual child.

The ground cracked and then sagged, opening wider as the hissing of the insects intensified. Kellan slid toward the crack in the ground. Unable to use the shadows—at least, not if he wanted to keep Sen—he tried to run for the trees, but he lost his footing.

Kellan half-tripped but stayed upright. Sen was throwing off his balance, as was the constant and ever-growing earthquake.

Then the ground opened up fully, revealing sewer tunnels that ran underneath the park.

Kellan and Sen tumbled down into one of the tunnels filled with darkness and beetles.

—Chapter 36—
—The Kuji—

Kellan hit the floor of the tunnel shoulder-first. Something about damage flashed across his vision, but he didn't care. His shoulder throbbed in agony as he rolled over the thousands of insects swarming in the tunnel. Beetles the size of quarters squirmed over, under, and through his clothing.

In that moment, Kellan almost regretted picking up the ability to see in the dark. Now he could see the mass of maggots, worms, beetles, and millipedes that surrounded them. He would've preferred if it had stayed a mystery.

With a groan, Kellan quickly pushed himself to his feet. His body ached, but the writhing of the Tyranny Worms told him they would soon repair the damage.

The yami centipedes headed for the surface. Pillars of light broke into the tunnel at various points, but the quaking caused the ground to shift, closing most of the small holes and caving in the tunnel.

I need to get out of here before we're buried alive.

Kellan knocked some of the bugs away with shaky hands. When he glanced around, he found Sen lying on his back, the swarms covering most of his small body. Kellan waded through the insects and scooped up the kid, carrying him like a parent would a child.

"Let's go," Kellan said, his vision perfect, even though there was no light.

The sewer tunnel extended to a four-way intersection. The grit and grime—and the foul odor of feces—told Kellan this had once been an operating sewer. Thankfully, it wasn't any longer. Determined to free himself from the stench, he hurried down the tunnel, his boots crunching the bodies of the insects as he went.

It sounded like he was running across corn flakes.

"Wait!" Sen commanded.

Kellan's body locked up. The grip of the Tyranny Worms hindered his movement. His muscles became stiff, and it pained him to even lift his legs.

"What're you doing?" Kellan demanded.

Sen rubbed at his head. Blood dribbled down from his hairline. "Do you even know where you're going?"

"I can see! Stop ordering me to do things. I'm trying to get us out of here."

The ground shook with earthquake intensity. Dust and debris rained down throughout the tunnel.

"Take me to the surface," Sen commanded.

Once again, the worms in Kellan's system flared to comply. With his irritation building, Kellan stomped forward. He had already intended to get them out of the sewers, but now he almost wanted to do an incompetent job, just to spite Sen and his need to control everything.

Kellan crunched his way to the underground four-way intersection. To his surprise, two individuals stumbled their way toward him. They obviously couldn't see a thing—they dragged their hands along the tunnel wall, their eyes unfocused, and their feet unsteady.

One was a man, and the other a woman—both humans in their early twenties. They wore jeans, jackets, and hiking boots. When their information flashed across Kellan's eyes, he realized they were both E-rank magma mages, though everything else was concealed. The boy, Hank Gardener, and the girl, Fern Garcia, had numbers on the backs of their left hands.

Team 80.

But the girl also had a skull on the back of her hand.

She was the team's Straggler.

"Hurry," Hank said. He lifted his hand and flames burst to life, providing him a limited amount of illumination. "Before the yami catch us." He coughed into his elbow, and his fire flickered.

Fern rubbed at her curly hair. Dirt was caught in her tiny curls. "Which way?" She, too, coughed and wheezed, the dirt and dust obviously bothering them.

Kellan stepped forward. "Not this way." With only two choices left, Kellan motioned to the southern tunnel. "Follow me. I think I know how to get us out of here."

He was fairly certain—though not entirely—that the Net was to the north of them. If they wanted to avoid the wall of death, they would need to maintain their trek in the opposite direction.

"Who are you?" Hank asked, holding up his fire.

Sen squirmed in Kellan's arms. "Don't help them! They're an enemy team!"

Without bothering to answer anyone, Kellan stormed down the southern tunnel. If Team 80 followed, great. If not, that was their problem. Kellan didn't want to get bogged down in monster-infested territory, and Sen was basically correct. Hank and Fern *were* competitors.

The two from Team 80 decided to follow along, however. They matched Kellan's pace, trekking along behind him, stepping on the dead bugs he had squashed.

"Now I know what it's like to be in an anthill," Fern muttered.

Hank nervously chuckled. "I'm smashing every anthill I see from here on out."

"Stay quiet," Kellan said. "We don't know what's down here."

The crunch of their footsteps wasn't helping, but Kellan didn't know what to do about that. He tried to ignore the hundreds of bugs, but there were so many, they got into his boots, his socks, and pants—some clawing up his pants and onto his shirt.

It took most of his willpower to just press forward.

I can swat them away later.

They made it a good 200 feet when a fourth set of sounds echoed in the tunnel, causing the hair on Kellan's neck to stand on-end. What was following them?

When he turned around, Kellan caught his breath, all the blood draining from his face.

A giant spider walked behind Hank and Fern, in the darkness just beyond Hank's flame.

Not a normal spider, but a freakish monster straight from the land of nightmares. It had a human face with needle-sharp teeth and eyes that bulged and jiggled like a dead fish.

The monster's eight legs ended in human hands, and the fingers curved in fish-hook claws. The monster had to be the size of a bus, but because of its spindly nature, it easily fit in the tunnel, its legs on the ground, wall, and ceiling. The monster's mouth was large enough to fit a human head inside, and its tongue had the length and dexterity to twist itself around.

Kellan couldn't move.

Something was preventing him from stepping away, or dropping Sen, or even lifting his rifle. And when he tried to struggle against it, something flashed over his eyes.

[Alex Kellan] has been paralyzed by [the Kuji of Team 80]'s *Haunting Sight*.

Hank and Fern—completely unaware of the demon behind them—almost ran into Kellan. Hank stopped an inch before, his expression twisted in confusion.

"What's wrong?"

Sen shook in Kellan's arms. "Now isn't the time for resting!"

No one else saw it. The freakish hell spider crawled forward, lifted one of its hook-clawed hands, and as silent as the night, stabbed Fern in the shoulder and neck.

Fern gasped and tried to scream, but the monster's fingers curled around her throat and proceeded to puncture terrible holes into her flesh. The gurgle of Fern's shriek echoed in the tunnels as the Kuji dragged her back to its needle-fanged mouth.

"Fern?" Hank asked as he whipped around, his eyes wide.

But he couldn't see through the darkness.

The Kuji bit down on Fern's head, its strength enough to sever it straight off her body. A clean decapitation.

"What's going on?" Hank demanded.

The moment the Kuji tilted its head to gobble down the rest of Fern's body, Kellan felt himself regain control of his body. *It was the eyes.* If he met the Kuji's gaze, he would become paralyzed all over again.

"*Run!*" Kellan shouted.

He grabbed Hank, yanked him away from the nightmare spider, and then dashed down the tunnel as fast as he could. Carrying a child and pulling a full-grown man limited Kellan's speed, but he didn't care. The Kuji was *clearly* strong enough to end any of them in a single strike, and Kellan wasn't going to sit around to fight it, not when the creature had the ability to render him helpless.

"What's going on?" Hank asked again. He tried to free himself from Kellan's grip. "Where's Fern?"

"She's dead! We have to go!"

The Kuji…

Kellan heard it chasing them.

The beast wasn't even hiding its movements anymore. It was crunching the bugs along with them, moving with eight legs when Kellan only had the two.

Sen twisted his fingers into Kellan's shirt, his whole body trembling. Did he know what was chasing them? Or was he just afraid because of the circumstances? Kellan couldn't tell.

When they came to another intersection, Kellan saw one tunnel was smaller than the others. The roof had partially collapsed, making it a narrow passageway that would require them to snake their way into. Which was perfect.

Kellan dashed straight for it.

"Watch yourself!" he called out, his voice echoing.

He dove for the tunnel and jammed his way into the crack-like passage, Sen crushed up against his chest as he went. Hank followed close behind—so close, Kellan swore he heard the man's heart beating in his chest.

Kellan went a few feet before the tunnel opened up. That was when he saw it—far down the tunnel, hidden in the dark, was a ladder. *Thank God for my dark sight.* He immediately ran for it, wanting to get to the surface as desperately as a stranded fish headed back for the water.

Hank followed close, his breathing becoming more and more frantic.

The insects weren't in this tunnel. Their footfalls were quieter.

Kellan couldn't hear the Kuji anymore.

When Kellan reached the ladder, he stopped and set Sen on the ground. Hank slammed into his back and they both almost toppled over. Kellan maintained his footing and whirled around.

"Get ahold of yourself," Kellan said. "There's a ladder here."

Hank's fire went out, leaving them all drowning in darkness. It didn't bother Kellan, but Sen and Hank both glanced around, their eyes wide.

"I can't focus on my magic," Hank said, gulping down air. His brown hair, chestnut in color, was drenched in sweat and clinging to his face. "My hand… The skull… It appeared there… Fern is dead."

And now Hank was the Straggler.

Kellan cursed under his breath. "The Kuji is after us."

"*Us?*" Sen balked. "No, no, no! Was that why you were running? What's wrong with you! That Kuji isn't after *us*. It'll only hunt the Straggler of a specific team. Ditch this simpleton and we'll be perfectly safe!"

Hank grabbed Kellan by the front of his shirt and clung for dear life. "Don't leave me! P-Please. Someone in our team already died. They just vanished! Fern became the Straggler… I don't know what to do!"

Kellan placed a firm hand on Hank's shoulder. For a long moment, he didn't say anything. He just squeezed his grip on the man, trying to reassure him through physical means.

"Take a deep breath," Kellan said. "Slowly."

Hank did as he was instructed. He inhaled, then exhaled, all at a slow rate. After a moment, he was calm. He released Kellan's shirt, his hands shaky. "I'm sorry. Just please don't leave. I don't want to be alone. Please."

"It's fine. Just stay close to me, all right? We'll get out of this."

Sen scoffed. "Are you listening to me? We should leave this man!"

With his teeth gritted, Kellan turned and then knelt in front of Sen. The kid couldn't see him, but he knew Sen would be able to hear better if he were down at his level.

"You want me to ask for that *Langarren Clay* in the next prize room, right?" Kellan asked.

Sen hesitated. After a short moment, he finally responded, "Yes."

"Then shut up and let me do my job, all right?" Kellan grabbed his arm and pulled him close. "I'm going to get you, and this rando, out of the tunnels, and then we're going to get ourselves a bunny, and we're going to get out of the game. Understood?"

Sen's eyebrows knitted. "Why the rando? *What's wrong with you*? He's not one of us!"

Hank nervously shifted his weight from one foot to the other. He couldn't see, but that didn't mean he was deaf.

"You said the Kuji isn't going to kill us, right?"

Sen nodded once.

"Then what does it matter if I try?"

"The Kuji will stop anything that gets between it and its kill," Sen stated matter-of-factly. "If we just leave this man to his grave, we have nothing to worry about."

Kellan shook his head. "Fine. Let me take him with us, and if the Kuji is about to get him, I won't stop it. Deal?"

"This is insanity."

Hank offered a snort and a laugh. "This is my *life*, man."

"Deal?" Kellan insisted.

Sen rolled his eyes. "Your backwards strategies will get us killed…" Then he just shook his head. "Get us out of here! I don't care what you do. No more waiting."

Satisfied, Kellan wrapped his arm around Sen and lifted him off the ground. Then he turned for the ladder. It was difficult carrying someone and hoisting himself upward, but Kellan could manage. Fortunately, Hank didn't need any assistance.

When Kellan reached the top, he had to push open a manhole cover. Light spilled in from the surface. He crawled onto the street, pushing Sen onto the asphalt first. Once Kellan hefted himself out of the underground, he turned and cursed under his breath a second time.

A gargantuan centipede scuttled across the street, hundreds of legs, a thing of legend.

Clutched between its pincers was a dead bunny.

—Chapter 37—
—The Second Key—

The massive centipede had yet to spot them. Kellan hesitated, the lower half of his body still in the sewer, his elbows on the street as he stared, breath held.

Name: Quixtitan
Race: Greater Yami
Magics: Magma, Body
Rank: Impossible
Armor Rating: 10
Health: 60/60

Stats:
Strength—14 [Strong-Jaw]
Dexterity—10
Fortitude—3 [Slender]
Intelligence—1
Perception—8
Willpower—1 [Animal]

Abilities:
Death Grip—The yami will not release its pincers until it dies.

The bunny in the creature's grip…

It wasn't real. It was a stuffed animal. The centipede carried the bunny across the street, the wave-like movement of the centipede's legs both disgusting and hypnotizing. Although Kellan didn't know for sure, he was confident the stuffed animal had a Nexus Game key.

That has to be it. It's a seek and destroy game… The Arbiter wants us to destroy the yami.

The beast was at least 400 feet away, and it was large enough that it could easily fit across a four-lane road. How fast was it?

Sen grabbed Kellan's shoulder and tugged him toward the surface. "Quickly!"

The harsh shrill of his youthful voice attracted the yami. And then Kellan got to see the monster's speed. The centipede whipped its head around to face them, its legs picking up speed, and its tail lifting, similar to a scorpion. A stinger shone in the scarlet lighting.

"Goddammit," Kellan breathed.

He hefted himself out of the sewer, but by the time his feet were on the street, the yami was already 100 feet closer.

Too fast. Kellan couldn't carry Sen, and protect Hank, while outrunning the monster. It was an impossibility.

"Run!" Sen commanded. "There! Take me into that dwelling." He pointed to a two-story house across the road, the kind of thing found in cookie-cutter American suburbs.

The Tyranny Worms didn't care that this was a terrible idea. They clawed at Kellan's insides, compelling him to grab Sen. The centipede monster rushed closer, and Kellan gritted his teeth, knowing this would result in disaster.

"No," he growled.

But the pain of the Tyranny Worms…

They fought against him, trying to fulfill Sen's demands. Kellan didn't care.

He spent a point of his mana—bringing him down to eight—and activated his *Ignore Pain* ability. The clawing of the worms didn't irritate him anymore. Even though it felt like he was slogging through mud, he could move himself without listening to Sen.

The yami was within 50 feet.

Instead of running across the street, Kellan leapt back down into the sewer. He missed the ladder, fell past Hank, and then hit the ground rolling. He probably hurt himself—some sort of damage notification flashed across his vision—but he felt great. No agony. No impairment to his vision.

Kellan got to his feet, his movements sluggish from the worms, or broken bones, he wasn't sure.

Sen flailed around in his arms.

"What're you doing, you cretin! How dare you disobey me!"

Hank quickly climbed down the ladder, his eyes wide and his hands sweaty.

The centipede slammed at the manhole, but it was too wide to fit through, just as Kellan had expected. But that didn't deter the beast. It screeched as it slammed its head and pincers against the hole, cracking the cement and widening the hole.

The stuffed animal remained in its grip, even as the monster rearranged the street.

Kellan dropped Sen and brought up his rifle. He fired at the beast, his bullets impacting the centipede's armor. He dealt some damage—breaking into the soft center of the monster—but it wasn't nearly enough. The centipede cracked the manhole open and fit half its body into the underground before Kellan could even manage to deal ten damage.

"We're going to die," Hank shouted as he backed away from the ladder, trembling the entire way. "*We're going to die.*"

"You should've listened to me!" Sen yelled, adding his voice to the chorus of panic.

The yami broke the manhole open enough that the beast fell into the sewer, a rain of debris and dust coming with it. Kellan shoved Sen out of the way and then leapt back himself, putting a small amount of distance between him and the beast.

But the centipede lashed with its tail. A curved stinger cut Kellan along his side.

Four damage.

Kellan felt none of it. He felt his own hot blood, however. It soaked into his shirt and pants, causing him to shiver.

Without any other words, Sen ran over and touched the back of his leg. A flood of warmth filled Kellan's entire being. The damage disappeared—his skin stitched itself together long before the Tyranny Worms could do anything.

"Keep fighting!" Sen barked.

Kellan was beyond tired of the obvious commands.

The centipede coiled the front half of its body while its tail thrashed around the cramped space. The stinger caught Kellan a second time—three damage—cutting up Kellan's gut and slicing part of his ribs. Again, Sen healed him before his insides were on the floor, but Kellan knew Sen's mana had a limit.

They were losing too fast.

"We're going to die," Hank said, clearly so mired in dread he couldn't come up with any other words to express himself.

"*No one is going to die*," Kellan stated.

Defiant and determined, he unslung his backpack and rummaged through the inside.

The centipede swung its tail, slashing some of the wall, busting half the ladder, and carving a furrow in the floor. Its bullet holes wept blood, and that was all Kellan cared about.

The monster had low fortitude.

The hydra venom had said it was lethal if the target failed its fortitude check—but Kellan's Blitzkrieg Analysis hadn't told him the exact number for the check. He had intended to research it later, but he wasn't going to have a *later* if he didn't get out of the current situation.

Unencumbered by Sen's presence, Kellan stepped into the darkness, and slipped across the floor with the ease of a shadow. He exited the void next to the yami's head. After removing the stopper, Kellan tossed the tiny vial of hydra venom. The dark liquid splashed across the beast's injuries—a tiny trickle, barely anything.

The gargantuan centipede shuddered.

Its tail thrashed once more.

And then it collapsed to the floor of the sewer. Dead.

Ten red arcana sprouted from the small puddle of blood around the beast's head. They glittered with inner power, even in the dark.

Kellan let out a long breath. Then he ran both his hands through his hair, more adrenaline in his veins than blood. He rubbed his eyes and smiled to himself. At least it was over. He had done it.

No casualties.

Hank laughed. It was nervous and awkward, but genuine. "No one died?" He laughed again, did a twirl, and then pumped a hand in the air. "Hot damn! *You did it*! That's how you make spaghetti and meatballs, right there!"

What a bizarre saying. Kellan refused to comment, but he was glad Hank was happy. "You're welcome."

"Thank you, man. Thank you. Seriously, thank you."

"Wait, was that hydra venom?" Sen hurried over to the corpse of the centipede. He placed his small hands on the carapace of the monster. "You used *hydra venom*? Where did you get that? When did you get it?"

"In Pan Town," Kellan said.

"Why?"

"I purchased it just in case I would need it."

Sen held his breath for a long moment. Then he finally whispered, "You were going to kill me, weren't you? That's why you got this." He stepped away from the centipede. "That's why you didn't tell me about it!" His volume had increased with each accusing word.

After a sigh, Kellan shook his head. "I wasn't planning to murder you. I was planning to murder the Tyranny Worms." He ripped the stuffed bunny out of the centipede's pincers, delighted to finally have some of his goals in his hands.

"You pathetic liar. The hydra venom would've killed you if you injected it." Sen threw his long hair over his shoulder. "Joke's on you. My body magic makes me immune to poison and venom. *Your plan never would've worked.*"

"I wasn't going to kill you," Kellan said. He shot Sen a glare, but something drew his attention.

A spindly arm had reached through the narrow pathway in the far tunnel. The fish-hook claws and disgusting human hand belonged to none other than the Kuji. Before Kellan could call out, the long arm reached all the way over to Hank. The Kuji dug its claws deep into Hank's shoulder.

The man screamed as the Kuji jerked him backward. He fell to the sewer floor, and the spider dragged him toward the narrow passageway.

The Kuji was clearly too large to get into their side of the sewer, but if it pulled Hank through the narrow walkway, it would have no trouble decapitating him just like the Kuji had done with Fern.

Kellan shoved the stuffed animal into the waistband of his pants and then dove into the darkness, fueled by desperation. He leapt out next to Hank, his heart pounding. He grabbed Hank's arm with one hand and hefted his rifle with the other. Although his aim was off, Kellan didn't care. He fired at the Kuji's arm.

The bullets…

They didn't seem to harm the beast. The spray of fire lit up the sewer, and the echo of the shots would've hurt Kellan's ears, but he still couldn't feel pain.

Nothing happened to the Kuji. Was it just too strong? Did magic protect it?

Kellan didn't understand.

The Kuji continued to drag Hank toward the pathway, its hook-claws deep in Hank's flesh. Hank continued to scream. He kicked, and flailed, and grabbed at the ground, trying to free himself, but it wasn't working.

Kellan pulled on his arm.

The Kuji's claws ripped deep furrows in Hank's body. Then they hooked into Hank's collarbone, which made everything difficult.

"Help!" Hank screamed. "*Help! Don't let it take me!*"

Kellan pulled harder, but the Kuji wasn't being deterred.

"Leave him!" Sen called out from down the sewer. "He's not worth it!"

Again, defiant and determined, Kellan refused to give up. He had told Hank he wouldn't let him die. He had told him.

Just like…

Just like he had with his fellow Delta Force teammates, Greer and Jones. But in that case, Kellan hadn't been able to save them. He had failed. It haunted him. It did. He hated to admit it—because nothing was supposed to haunt him—but he just couldn't let it go.

Kellan pulled the stuffed animal from his waistband and shoved it into Hank's hand. "Reach inside! *Do it*!"

The command had been so loud and thorough, Hank seemingly managed to wrangle the last of his courage. Hank ripped open the bunny just as the Kuji pulled him to the narrow opening. Then, with a look of confusion, Hank withdrew a small USB drive from the guts of the stuffed animal.

The second key.

Right before he was crunched by the needle fangs of the Kuji, Hank was teleported away. A pop of displaced air echoed in the sewer. The Kuji's hand was empty. The clawed hand gripped at the air before withdrawing to the other side of the narrow pathway.

Kellan's heart continued to pound against his chest.

Again, he had done it.

No casualties…

"Tsk, tsk, tsk," a voice whispered in the depths of the sewer. "I remember…. everyone who takes away my prey…"

The Kuji?

Kellan smiled to himself. Somehow, even *he* was making his team enemies. The voice didn't add anything else. The monster spider disappeared into the stench of the sewer, leaving Kellan alone with a centipede corpse and a man-child.

Light from the broken manhole shone down around them.

Sen stared at the location where Hank used to be. He held up a hand. "Did you just give him the key? The second key? Seriously?" He shook his head in obvious disbelief. "You somehow found *two* keys, and you lost them both? I'm just… I'm at a loss for words."

Kellan walked back over to Sen's side, his mind dwelling on the reality of the situation. There were only five keys in this game, and almost half of them were gone. What would they do if they couldn't find any more? What if they ran out of time?

What if *their* Kuji started killing them all?

Kellan cursed himself under his breath. He hadn't thought about that while Hank had been screaming. All Kellan had thought of was saving the man.

"Let's head to the street," Kellan muttered.

The ground rumbled.

It was happening again. The Net was moving, and the yami in the game area were being disturbed. Now that two keys were gone, everything was going to get harder. On shaky feet, Kellan headed over to the half-ruined ladder. Sen hurried after.

The rumbling waned.

"You disobeyed my worms," Sen said, anger in his voice. "What's wrong with you? If you had listened—"

Kellan whipped around, tense. "*Listen*—running from the monster would've lost us the key, too, all right? And we probably would've been ripped to shreds in the meantime." He motioned to their surroundings. "At least my plan got us a dead yami. Maybe, before you go ordering me to do stupid shit, you should remember I'm the team's *warrior*—" he used air quotes, "—and I know a thing or two about fighting. Trust my judgment."

"I don't trust you at all."

Kellan placed his hands on his knees and bent over to get down to Sen's height. "That's the problem, tiny."

"How dare you." Sen scoffed as he grabbed the ladder. "You don't even know what's going on here. I know this competition, and I know you. My judgment is sound."

Kellan grabbed him and yanked him back. Sen stared with wide eyes. "Did you think I would give Hank that key to save him?"

Sen opened his mouth, but for a long minute, he said nothing. Then he pursed his lips, his brow furrowed. "No. I didn't think you would do that."

Kellan stood up straight, his point made. "I'm. Not. The other Alex Kellan. I don't know what that delta-bravo did to you, *but I'm not him.* Stop this. Stop hindering your own team. Stop fighting me. If I don't know something, teach me. If we're in the middle of combat, trust me."

There was a moment of silence between them. Sen took several shallow breaths, his gaze drifting down to the ground. He seemingly mulled over the conversation, unwilling to comment.

But the rumbling started again.

After a short exhale, Kellan motioned Sen to the ladder. "Let's go."

Sen grabbed the lowest rung. "You… weren't going to kill me with the hydra venom?"

"If I was, I would've done it the moment we were alone in the sewer," Kellan stated, no hesitation. "I could've said some yami got you and been done with it. But I didn't. Because that's not why I got it."

As the ground quaked, Sen nodded once. "Fine. Maybe I was wrong about you. But that's all I'm admitting." He lifted himself up the ladder. "And we don't have time for this. We need to reunite with my sister and fix this mess you've made."

—Chapter 38—
—The Net—

Kellan reached for the ladder and then hesitated. He walked over to the ten arcana shining in the centipede's blood. When he knelt to absorb them, Kellan briefly contemplated the origin of the glittering crystals. Was the Arbiter using people's souls to make monsters? Just to fill his games?

What kind of sadist lunatic was that machine dragon?

Kellan absorbed the arcana, bringing his total up to seventeen. It seemed like an outrageous amount, up until he thought about his eclipse powers.

Eclipse Magic Rank C Cost: 10 arcana

He couldn't even rank to C without spending ten arcana.

And for some reason, he couldn't preview the abilities like he had with D rank. When he thought about his magic, all he managed to see were the E- and D-rank powers.

Kellan sighed as he headed back to the ladder. Somehow, Sen's short legs had taken him all the way up to the road, even though the top rungs were damaged from the yami attack. Kellan climbed up to the surface, wondering whether he should spike up eclipse to gain more useful powers—similar to his ability to slip through darkness, or even better—or if he should just save his arcana for travel magic.

In the end, he decided to save. Travel magic was just rarer and stronger. The only person in the AVU Palace Kellan had seen with it was Brenner Hawke. Apparently, Xiang had it as well, and perhaps a few people with their magic concealed had it, but they were few and far between.

Kellan stepped up to the road. The air hung heavy with humidity, drenching him in sweat. Afternoon light streamed through the red Net overhead, the aura of crimson straight out of a horror movie. And the Net pulsed as it moved, shrinking around them, even as Kellan stared.

The top of the Net touched the roof of a nearby office building, the red dome washing over the fifteenth floor, harmlessly passing through the cement and metal. A pair of pigeons, who had been sitting on the edge of the roof, were caught by the silent movement of the Net.

The pigeons didn't go up in flames or burst like a balloon—they disintegrated. Within a couple seconds, the living breathing birds were nothing more than dust on the wind.

"Why is everything here a nightmare show?" Kellan asked, his attention glued to the ashes.

Sen rubbed his cheek. "I told you. The Nexus is made of every other dimension and—"

"Yeah, yeah. But that doesn't explain why the Net has to instantly cremate life."

"It's instant and not painful. That's the Arbiter being kind."

Kind.

Kellan couldn't believe it was a word used to describe the bizarre dragon. Then again, it could've been worse. The Net could've killed them slowly from the inside out. Or it could've been a nightmare spider that chased them around the game arena, looking to hook-claw them when they least expected it.

His heart skipped a beat, and his stomach twisted with anxiety. "We need to find Mavis and Husker," he whispered.

"*No,*" Sen snapped. "We need to find a third key! Focus. The moment we have a key, we'll be teleported out of here. *That's* how we'll help our teammates."

Kellan glanced at the sky. The Net continued to move. Tremors disturbed the ground, softer and softer, but ever present. He knew they had to keep out of any instant-death traps.

"Let's go this way." He pointed toward the center of the city.

Sen nodded once.

Together, they headed down the road. Kellan kept his rifle close and his backpack tight on his back. He didn't have much in the way of supplies. Some black hane cigarettes and a vial of perfume. Kellan didn't have any other surprises or tricks, and it made him nervous. They were coming down to the wire.

To Kellan's surprise, the road ended in a giant loop driveway. At the opposite end of the driveway was a neoclassical building, reminiscent of American government institutions. White walls. Pillars. Giant dome at the top. The entire thing was probably larger than it needed to be, but that was no doubt a specific design choice.

But the sign outside was written in more Chinese hanzi—characters that Kellan had no familiarity with. He cursed under his breath, wishing he knew something other than Arabic.

"We should go around," Sen said, narrowing his eyes. "Although we might find a prize or puzzle room inside, we'll be at a disadvantage if we run into any trouble."

"You don't think a bunny will be inside?"

Sen shook his head. "We found a bunny in the park—somewhat in a building. The Arbiter doesn't usually hide them in similar locations."

"What if—"

And then an earthquake hit. Kellan almost lost his footing. Sen hit the ground with both hands, scuffing his palms. The Net pulsed faster.

And then it started shrinking down in a dramatic fashion, narrowing down toward the center of the city. Kellan couldn't believe it. The Net started moving fast. Then faster than that. When he glanced back at the office building, he realized the Net had shrunk down enough to wash over the eighth story.

The Net hadn't been close enough for Kellan to see down the street, but now he could. The bubble of death was rushing toward them.

"What's going on?" he asked, his breathing shallow.

Kellan could fight yami, but he couldn't fight the Net. If it came for them, what was he going to do? What *could* he do?

"Someone must've found the third key," Sen said, still lying on the ground. He brushed his black hair out of his eyes, blood smearing his forehead. "We're running out of time!"

Kellan glanced around. To his dismay, he saw no vehicles. He would've given a finger for one of those Lightning Lifts. Instead, he had only a few options if he wanted to head away from the approaching Net.

He could walk around the neoclassical building.

Or he could go through.

The shortest distance between two points was a straight line. But the earthquakes were getting worse. What if the building collapsed on top of them?

"We're going inside." Kellan stepped forward, grabbed Sen by the back of his robes and then hauled the kid into his arms. With confidence in his gait, Kellan jogged toward the front stairway. Despite the shaking of the ground, he managed to keep his balance.

"Maybe we can go over," Sen said.

At first, Kellan was ready to argue, but then the words sunk in. *That's not a bad idea.* Going over the building would be the safest—and it would eliminate the chance they would get lost inside, or have a roof come crashing down on top of them. And government buildings almost always had utility or emergency ladders on the outside.

There was a dome on the building, but there were flat portions of the roof all the way around.

Once Kellan made it up the front stairs, he stopped by one of the pillars. Then he set Sen down and examined his surroundings. No ladders would ever be on the front—where the public could see. They were on the inside, near the front entranceway, usually behind doors secured by sheriffs or local police officers.

Kellan had seen it hundreds of times. But he didn't want to waste time searching around inside.

"Wait here," Kellan said. He moved toward the wall of the building.

When the ground shook again, Sen fell over. He gritted his teeth and looked up. "Don't leave me," he commanded.

The worms flared to life once again, and Kellan jerked to a halt. But his *Ignore Pain* was still active. He knew he could power through, if he needed to.

Kellan glanced over his shoulder, trying hard not to yell. "I need to find a way up. *Let me go.*"

"I don't want... you to go too far on your own. You have no idea what you're doing."

"I'll be right back, I promise you."

There was a prolonged moment between them. The Net was moving, the ground was practically threatening to break underneath them… Even the pillars of the building were cracking.

"Okay," Sen said with a sigh of defeat. "*Fine.* Go. Just come back. Please."

Without wasting time, Kellan dove into the darkness. He moved with the freedom of shadows, going up the wall and then exiting on the edge of the roof, right at the end of his ability. When Kellan stumbled forward, he slammed into the side of the dome. Cracks—starting at the base—cascaded upward, forming lightning-style lines all the way to the top.

Now on the roof, it would be easier to find the access ladder than from inside. Kellan ran around the dome, keeping his eyes open for Sen's way up.

A small part of him contemplated moving on without Sen—Kellan could easily leave the kid behind—but he knew he wouldn't. He wouldn't even let *Hank* die, and Kellan hadn't even known the bastard. He just couldn't stand the thought of losing people.

Then Kellan spotted it.

The ladder access point. A large metal door.

He ran over and grabbed the handle. Locked. He shook the door, frustrated. Could he shoot through the handle with his cursed rifle? Then Xiang's voice echoed in his thoughts. *I'm a mage. I don't have to solve things the traditional way anymore. I can solve problems with magic.*

And Kellan had the power *Mold Metal.*

He spent a single point of mana.

Which brought him down to seven remaining.

With his magic activated, Kellan touched the metal door. He scooped out the door like it was made of Play-Doh, effortlessly dismantling the handle and lock. Once he could, Kellan opened the door and headed for the ladder. Instead of going down the metal ladder—and potentially molding each rung—he dove into the darkness and zipped down the ladderway.

When Kellan emerged, he was in some sort of security room. He couldn't read the hanzi, but he recognized the lockboxes, security cameras, and paperwork. He ran to the next door, carved out the lock again, and then ran out into the front foyer.

The rumbling and earthquakes had ruined the beautiful architecture with debris and cracks. Kellan dashed for the front doors and once again molded the metal so that there were no obstacles between Sen and the ladder.

The moment he burst outside, Kellan was greeted with a terrible view of the moving Net.

It swept down the road, heading straight for them.

Sen struggled to get up, and Kellan ran over to the man. Again, with little effort, he scooped the kid up and carried him into the building. Tiles rained down from the decorated ceiling. Each tile shattered when it hit the floor, creating mild hazards.

Kellan didn't stop for anything.

He slammed into the security room, and then set Sen down by the ladder. With some encouragement, he pushed Sen up the starting rungs. He watched the man go, and once he was at the top, Kellan used the darkness as an elevator. When he stepped out of the shadows, he was on the roof of the building, the humidity waiting there to greet him.

"Thank you," Sen said, his voice shaking.

Kellan smirked. "Don't get soft on me now. We're not out of the woods."

"Yes, well, we've got to keep moving. That's always the key. Keep moving."

But Kellan hadn't heard a word the man said. His attention had been drawn to the top of the dome. Something gold, glinting in the red light, circled around the peak of the building. What was it?

He stared, squinting, until he realized it was a buzzing gold machine.

In the shape of a bunny.

Kellan's heart sank to his feet. The Net was quickly coming up to the loop-around driveway. They were literally running out of time.

"There it is," Kellan said, pointing. "The *fourth* key."

—Chapter 39—
—A Toy Shop—

Sen glanced up and squinted. Then he held up his small hand, his fingers fanned out. At first, Kellan wasn't entirely sure what the kid was doing, but then the gold machine jerked in the sky and turned straight for them. The buzzing of its little propellers grew louder as it descended.

When it got close, Kellan was surprised by how tiny it was. The machine—it looked like a gilded wind-up toy—was a toy bunny. The legs had springs, the propeller was on top of its head, in the shape of long ears, and its arms moved up and down in a quick cycle.

The bunny flew straight into Sen's hand and then shut off. Even though the building rumbled and shook, Sen managed to stay upright.

"How did you do that?" Kellan asked, balancing himself on the side of the dome. "I thought we'd have to climb up there or something."

"I have the title *puppetmaster* for a reason." Sen held the toy close. "Non-sentient machines are easy to control. Simple computers are the same way. Bodies without a mind who fights back are perfect."

"You know that sounded creepy, right?"

Sen motioned to the far back of the building. "Carry me while I break into this device."

After a short sigh, Kellan scooped Sen up into his arms and headed for the back of the building. Sen wasn't heavy, but Kellan hated being his horse. He hadn't minded being Mavis's horse. He would've been Mavis's ride until the end of time. But Sen…

Not Sen.

The earthquakes wouldn't relent. Twice, Kellan almost tripped. He stumbled and slowed, and just before the roof gave out, he made it to the back of the building. He glanced around, hoping to find another ladder, but there was none.

"I'm going to throw you," Kellan said, his attention drawn to a large tree growing close to the walls. "The branches will hurt, but you can heal, right?"

"What?" Sen barked. "You can't *throw me.*"

"Oh, I definitely *can.*" Kellan ran over to the tree, trying to judge the distance to the ground. They were at least thirty feet up. They'd survive.

"I'm not a ball!" Sen held the gilded machine close to his chest. "Don't you dare throw me!"

"I either throw you, or you fall with me when I throw myself."

Kellan stopped at the edge of the building, mere feet from the tree. There were no leaves, just empty branches poking in all directions, some of the twigs pointier than Kellan would've liked.

Sen grabbed Kellan's bloody shirt. "I'll… I'll stay with you."

Although the fall intimidated Kellan, he knew his *Ignore Pain* ability was still in effect. He exhaled, and then leapt from the building. He hit the tree—and several branches—as he plummeted to the ground. And despite the fact it hindered his ability to roll, Kellan kept Sen cradled in his arms. He protected the other man as much as possible, even when he hit the ground back-first.

Winded, but feeling no agony at all, Kellan struggled to get a breath.

Sen clutched Kellan close. He coughed, then rubbed at his face, and finally crawled out from under Kellan and stood. "I really dislike these games…"

After a moment of recovery, Kellan stood and brushed himself off. "Open the damn bunny so we can get out of here."

"Ah, yes… The bunny."

Sen caught his tongue between his lips as he fidgeted with the small machine. For several long seconds, he adjusted and twisted the toy, seemingly taking it apart one piece at a time. Kellan waited and watched, fully aware of the rumbling and the shrinking of the Net.

But he said nothing. He knew Sen wouldn't appreciate any commentary, and it would just lead to them fighting.

Finally, Sen popped the machine in half. "I did it!"

Kellan clapped his hands together once. "Fantastic. Get the key. Let's go."

But Sen didn't find a key inside the machine. Instead, he withdrew a small piece of paper. It was rolled up like a tiny scroll, held together with a piece of string. Sen undid the string and rolled it out in his hands.

A map.

Sen stared at the drawing, his eyes following the vague lines. Kellan knelt closer. He didn't understand all the symbols, and the writing around the legend was in a language he didn't even recognize.

"What's this?" Kellan asked.

"It's written in Eastern Psian," Sen stated matter-of-factly. "It says the key we're searching for is in a toy shop."

Kellan cursed under his breath. He stood straight and almost laughed. Of course—they would never find their way out of this.

"The good news is that we're close." Sen pointed down the road. "This way. Come. We're heading in the right direction."

"You're sure?"

"Yes, *fool.* I know how to read maps." Sen snapped his fingers. "Now let's not delay. We're short on time as it is, and I don't—"

Kellan scooped the kid up in his arms and took off in a run. His legs didn't work as well as usual, and he suspected he had twisted his ankle, or perhaps cracked a bone… But since he couldn't feel the pain, he didn't know how or what was damaged. And he didn't care. If they made it to the toy shop before anyone else, they could finally escape the game.

And Kellan still had seven more mana. He could use his *Ignore Pain* ability again, if needed. Anything to get them out of here.

But it became a moot point. Sen placed a hand on Kellan's chest and a flood of warm healing energy entered Kellan. He breathed easier as he continued to run down the street, his legs returning to their normal functionality.

"Thank you," Kellan said between controlled breaths.

Sen didn't reply.

Gun shots and screams rang out in the city. Kellan pushed them from his mind. Although he wanted to check out the sudden outburst of fighting, he knew it was a terrible idea. He had already saved some people—it wasn't his job to protect *everybody.*

I need to focus on my team. Save them first. Then worry about others.

The rumbling and quaking stopped. Kellan smiled to himself.

Thank you, sweet Baby Jesus.

The Net was still shrinking, unfortunately.

Thankfully, Sen had been correct. The toy shop hadn't been far. Kellan ran five blocks, all while carrying the kid, but that was when he spotted the neon lights in the shape of a video game controller and a sailboat. That had to be the place.

Kellan's stomach grumbled—almost louder than the distant gunfire.

He hadn't eaten in… so long. The toll of everything was finally catching up with him. Toy shops had candy, and Kellan found himself fantasizing about M&Ms and Snickers bars. What would they taste like mashed together? Kellan wanted to find out with every fiber of his being.

"We're almost there," Sen said, pointing to the neon sign. "That's it!"

Kellan slowed his run to a jog as he approached. To his dismay, he spotted movement inside the building, just beyond the giant display windows. People were searching through the aisles, knocking over stacks of blocks and board games.

"People are here," Kellan said as he approached the front door. That was when he sat Sen down. "What're we going to do if they find the key before us?"

"We're going to start searching for the fifth key," Sen said with a sarcastic edge.

"No other plan?"

Sen pointed to the glass doors. "My *plan* was to find the first key and be out of here already. Since you lost it, I say you get in there and deal with these chumps. Scare them off. Or threaten them. Or something."

Kellan wasn't going to do that. He knew whatever he said, he probably wouldn't follow through with, and he still thought it was a terrible idea to antagonize everyone around them.

But he had to do *something*. Kellan stepped forward, prepared to just search harder and faster than everyone else. He walked past the half dozen cash registers and straight into the toy shop, enjoying the smell of fresh-cut wood and clean floors. It reminded him of the local stores near his apartment.

For some reason, even the mundane seemed exciting, like he would never experience it ever again.

And then Kellan spotted the two individuals in the shop.

Mavis and Husker.

Right as he saw them, they both noticed Kellan.

"Is that really you?" Mavis asked. She ran out of her aisle and straight to Kellan. With a smile, she threw her arms around him in a tight hug. "I'm so happy you're okay!"

When they separated, Kellan realized she had her own rifle—a semi-automatic Springfield SAINT. A hunting rifle, but a nice one. Kellan wasn't surprised. Although Husker was apparently capable of dealing out lethal hex-based damage, Mavis needed something for protection as well.

She tucked some of her purple hair behind one ear and smirked. "You're never going to believe what happened to us."

Husker came walking out from an aisle, his fitted coat looking a bit unfortunate for him. The humidity bothered Kellan, and he couldn't imagine living with both the heat *and* fur. Husker was practically panting, and his pointed ears were pressed back on his skull.

"I have a lot to tell both of you as well," Kellan muttered.

"Where is Xiang?" Husker cut in. "Wasn't she with you?"

"I, uh, lost her." Kellan turned to the door. "Sen! Come in here. It's our team."

The kid hesitated for a second, but then crept into the toy shop through the front doors. He peered inside, and then hurried beyond the cash registers. As soon as he could, Sen headed straight for Kellan and stood right next to him. "Finally! Now we're in good company."

"We stumbled across a puzzle room," Mavis said as she smacked Kellan's shoulder. "It had traps, and riddles, and Husker and I had to, like, outsmart the building in order to escape. We almost died. It was intense. I mean, I was scared in the moment, but afterward, I was riding a high like you wouldn't believe."

"Oh, I can believe it," Kellan muttered with a chuckle. Then he smacked her back. "I found a prize room. It wasn't flashy, and I didn't die, but there was an imp."

"You found a *prize room*?" Husker stepped forward, his fox-face in shock. "What did you get?"

Kellan half-shrugged. "Look, it's not that big of a deal."

"Oh, it's a huge deal. Those prize rooms can sometimes have the most wondrous of items." Husker stepped even closer, his damp fur sticky with sweat. "If you find another one in the future, you should request a *divine egg*."

Kellan choked back a laugh. Xiang wanted a sword. Sen wanted clay. And now Husker wanted *an egg*? He almost couldn't believe the requests. "Sure, sure. An egg. Anything else I need to add to the grocery list before I find another of these prize rooms?"

"I'm serious," Husker said with a growl. "A divine egg will hatch into a powerful familiar. Since none of us are bonded to one, it would be a great boon. Those creatures add to your magic—and they're rare in the Nexus."

Kellan stopped his joking and nodded once. A familiar? He knew the term. Wizards and witches had familiars. Well, he thought they did. He wasn't entirely sure. Mages needed familiars, didn't they?

"All right," Kellan muttered. "I'll remember that."

Sen shot him a glare, but otherwise said nothing.

"We haven't found any keys yet," Mavis said, ignoring everyone else's commentary. She just continued to smile up at Kellan. "But we found this golden toy bunny. Husker could read the writing on this map, and it brought us here. You felt the earthquakes, right? Husker said that was because people were finding keys."

Kellan nodded along with her words. "Yeah. I know."

"Have you found anything yet?"

Sen snorted and laughed. "Oh, we found some keys." Then he crossed his arms, his eyes narrowed in a glower.

With an amused lift of her eyebrow, Mavis gave Kellan a questioning look.

"We found a key." Then Kellan sighed. "Two keys, actually."

"Really?" Mavis's eyes went wide. "What happened?"

"He lost them both," Sen interjected.

Kellan could barely look at Mavis and Husker as he said, "Yeah. Yeah. That's what happened. I lost them."

Husker flashed his fangs. Then he smoothed his reddish fur and exhaled. "How? What happened?"

"Some other guy on one of the enemy teams appeared out of thin air and grabbed the first key before I could. Then… the second key… It was in this stuffed animal. And I gave it to some other guy so he wouldn't get killed by the Kuji."

The story wasn't elegant or well told, but it had all the relevant details. Mavis and Husker waited, like they wanted to hear more, but Kellan wasn't sure what he would even tell them. There wasn't anything else. He offered them another shrug.

"That's it," he said, ending it lamely.

"Wait," Husker said. "A stuffed animal? Like a toy?"

Kellan nodded once. "Yeah. It was a toy."

The werewolf man turned and walked to the back of the toy shop. Mavis, Kellan, and Sen followed. Although the store was dim, and barely lit, Kellan didn't have any trouble seeing. He thanked his magic again, loving the ability to see through the thickest of darkness.

Husker stopped near the back wall.

Something had obviously tunneled into the store. The wall was destroyed, and a whole display of stuffed animals had toppled over…

The bunnies were ripped to shreds.

Had the centipede yami come through here? Kellan knelt near the stuffed animals and cursed under his breath. They looked identical to the rabbit he had ripped out of the mouth of the monster.

"What's wrong?" Mavis asked.

"Oh, nothing. Situation normal—all fouled up." Kellan stood and then ran a hand through his hair. "We're going to need to find another key location."

"You're sure?"

"Pretty positive."

Sen threw his arms into the air. "Oh, Hakael, give me strength. Have you forsaken me?"

"Now isn't the time to be prayin' to gods," Husker growled. He grabbed Sen by the robes and practically dragged him into the air. "Where's Xiang? She can solve this problem. I know she can."

"We lost her," Sen stated. Then he ripped his clothing out of Husker's clawed hands. "In the park. But I'm certain that my sister is still searching for the keys, just like we are. She doesn't give up."

Kellan wasn't sure what else they could do, however. Didn't Xiang know everything about the Nexus Games? Wasn't she prepared to find keys, and fight the others? Why wasn't she—

The number on the back of Kellan's hand—the 101—stung his skin. Had his *Ignore Pain* worn off? He rubbed at the number, but the agony intensified. The others rubbed at their hands as well…

And then Kellan and the rest of his team were teleported away.

—Chapter 40—
—Alex Kellan the Rulebreaker—

Kellan stumbled forward and found himself in a casino-like building with lush red carpets and club-style techno music. The walls were covered in abstract paintings, some with red skies, some with spaceships, and others of dragons eating machinery.

The AVU Palace Oasis

You have entered an Oasis. While inside this non-conflict area, all mages are forbidden from initiating direct violence. Offensive magical abilities are limited. Any who attempt to circumvent this rule will answer to the Arbiter himself.

The smoke that hung on the stagnant air of the AVU Palace was a welcome aroma. Kellan took a deep breath, pleased they were no longer in the twisted landscape of the first game. With a smile, he glanced around.

Husker, Mavis, and Sen stood close, each with wide eyes and half smiles. They glanced around their surroundings, obviously a little confused. They were all in a large hallway, far from the main casino and dance floors, and nowhere near their room.

When Kellan turned around, he almost choked on his own breath.

Xiang stood in the hallway with them, her white suit completely drenched in crimson. The blood splatters coated her from neck to toe, and even the ends of her hair and one cheek were dripping with scarlet.

She looked like she had been hit with thirty water balloons, each filled with the fresh blood of a murder victim.

But in her right hand was none other than the USB drive key. Somehow, she had secured a key for their team, teleporting everyone out of the arena and away from the many dangers.

With a flick of her delicate wrist, Xiang used her illusions to hide the blood. It "vanished" underneath a façade of pristine white. Then Xiang smoothed her long, black hair, and took a deep breath.

When she glanced over, Xiang took a moment to look everyone in the eyes. "I'm glad to see you all made it."

Kellan slowly nodded. "Are you okay?"

"Another flawless victory," Xiang said, her voice devoid of emotion. "The first game isn't going to stop me."

Judging by the copious amount of blood, Kellan was positive it hadn't been as flawless as Xiang wanted people to believe. But he wasn't going to call her out on anything. If she wanted to pretend everything was handled, he would let her.

Sen ran to his sister's side. "I was worried about you. We should definitely get you to a mana spring right away."

Xiang didn't reply. She swayed on her feet, almost falling over.

Both Kellan and Husker leapt forward to catch her. Husker reached her first and held Xiang with his large paw-like hands. Xiang shook her head and rubbed at her temple. Then she shoved Husker away.

"*I'm fine,*" she stated. "There's no need for theatrics."

Again, Kellan could tell something was wrong, but he didn't know what to say.

Before he could think of anything, Mavis placed a hand on his shoulder. He glanced over, and she smiled up at him.

"We lived!"

He smirked. "I guess we did."

"We need to celebrate."

"You took the words right out of my mouth."

Unfortunately, the far doors at the end of the hallway slammed open. Kellan and Mavis turned around just as two Pestbyters hovered into the corridor. Their spherical bodies and wire tentacles gave them the appearance of dislocated eyeballs. The soft rumble of their hover bothered Kellan—he hated those machines more than he suspected he should.

The Pestbyters moved around Xiang and Sen, and then went straight for Kellan.

"*You have broken the rules of the Nexus Games,*" the first Pestbyter said, sweet and girly. "*You will need to speak with the Arbiter regarding your misconduct.*"

Both the Pestbyters wrapped their wire tentacles around Kellan's arms and jerked him forward. He didn't struggle against them, because he knew it was pointless, but he did voice his frustration.

"I didn't break any rules," he said, biting back a curse. "I swear. It wasn't me."

"*To the Arbiter,*" the second Pestbyter said with a giggle.

Xiang whirled around on a heel and held up a hand. "Wait. I'm the team leader. I demand to know where you're taking him."

The two Pestbyters stopped, their wires still firmly around Kellan's upper arms. Without turning around, one said, "*To the Arbiter, of course. If you wish to contest his sentence, you will need to speak with him after.*"

With a huff and dramatic swish of his arm, Sen added, "There wasn't any rule breaking! I wouldn't have allowed it. This man is my puppet."

Kellan would've preferred his defense to be anything other than *he was a puppet,* but he couldn't take the words back now. Instead, he just waited, his heart beating fast. Would the Arbiter crush him this time?

No, he thought. *I didn't do anything wrong this time. I didn't mess with any of the Pestbyters. What could the Arbiter possibly be mad about?*

The two Pestbyters didn't wait around for more arguments. They dragged Kellan down the hallway, hovering at a quick pace. Then they slammed through a set of double doors and headed down another corridor, this one filled with tall candle stands and suits of full plate armor, like they had entered an old-world castle.

"So, what if the Arbiter is wrong?" Kellan asked as they continued to yank him.

But the Pestbyters didn't respond.

Instead, Kellan focused his attention on the AVU Palace. He wasn't familiar with this part of the building. The Pestbyters took him through another set of double doors, straight into a casino floor filled with card tables and buffet spreads. The smell of food caused his stomach to grumble all over again.

Would he ever get to eat again?

Kellan worried he never would.

Then the Pestbyters dragged him up a set of stairs, through more doors, up a long, straight staircase, and finally, to another set of large wooden doors.

Kellan was sick of seeing them, but he knew now the Pestbyters weren't taking him to the football field in the center of the palace… They were taking him someplace new.

"Is the Arbiter here?" he asked as the Pestbyters hovered in front of the door.

Again, they didn't answer.

Finally, one of the Pestbyters opened a door. Then they shoved Kellan inside and shut the door behind him, leaving him in a large office room without any windows.

Just… none.

It felt odd, and weirdly claustrophobic, to be in a room with no way to see outside.

There was a desk in the middle of the room. A desk made of metal and rivets. A single chair was on one side, and Bitso sat on the other side, one of his wrists chained to the edge of the desk. Two large TV screens were mounted on the far wall, each eighty inches, at the bare minimum.

No other furniture decorated the room. No paintings. No bookshelves. No other places to sit. There weren't even that many lights—just one long bulb over the desk, flicking every few seconds.

Bitso had the same outfit he always had. A dark suit and a white blindfold, all decorated with slight smears of red. When Bitso smiled, his sharpened teeth practically gleamed in the fluorescent lighting.

That was when Kellan noticed all the eyes.

The ceiling and two of the four walls were covered in the Eyes of the Arbiter—giant half-spherical machines that stared at him through flesh-like lenses. They were the size of a human head, all unblinking and watching him with a strange intensity.

Kellan counted two dozen.

"Ah, if it isn't my favorite player!" Bitso held up his free arm. "Come. Sit down." He touched his white blindfold, fixing it in place.

With hesitant steps, Kellan made his way over to the empty chair. It was a rickety thing with no cushion. The Eyes of the Arbiter watched his every movement, the lens of their cameras staying with him.

Kellan sat down, his anxiety making it hard to articulate his many grievances.

"Oh, wait a minute," Bitso muttered. He leaned on his desk, getting closer to Kellan. "You're not my favorite. You're that knock-off alternate dimension version of my favorite. You're not even in my top ten."

"Thanks for that," Kellan quipped. "Can you tell me why I'm here?"

Ignoring Kellan's question, Bitso leaned back in his chair—something leather, luxurious, and soft. "Congrats on living through the first game, sad sack."

"The Pestbyters said I broke the rules. What's going on?"

Bitso snickered. Then he exhaled and swayed in his chair. Blood stains appeared on his blindfold—soaking up from his face—but the man didn't indicate he was in any pain. Bitso just chuckled to himself, amused by something Kellan wasn't aware of.

"I want to know what's going on," Kellan demanded.

Bitso frowned. Then he sat straight and placed both his hands on the desk. "You're just all business, is that right?" He tapped his fingers on the desk. "Listen, I don't get much company in this place. Let's just take our time, all right? Relax. I'll get to your punishment soon enough. Trust me, the Arbiter was fairly disappointed with how you behaved."

Kellan narrowed his eyes, his chest tight with worry. "What're you talking about? What punishment? Why?"

"What did I just say about that? *We'll get to it.* For right now, let's watch some of your game footage, shall we? That'll be fun. I do love judging people."

Bitso laughed and then snapped his fingers. The two TVs on the far wall flared to life. They both displayed Kellan in the Nexus Games, running around the game arena, fighting the yami or using his shadow-stepping ability.

Bitso pointed to the left screen, and it flickered over to footage of Kellan using his *Mold Metal* power on the doors of the neoclassical building.

"You know what's weird about you?" Bitso asked. He didn't even turn around to look at the screen as he muttered, "You're using *Mold Metal.* And you have the ability to make things *glow*. And you also *Ignore Pain.*" The TV flashed over to Kellan fighting the centipede.

The TVs had no sound, but Kellan could still hear the way Hank kept shrieking, *We're all going to die*. It was ingrained in his memories.

"What's your point?" Kellan asked. "Is it against the rules to pick up those particular powers or something?"

Bitso smiled wide. Then he leaned forward on his metal desk. "What's wrong with you? Don't you understand you're supposed to pick up powers that synergize?" He pushed away from the desk and his handcuffed wrist strained against his restraints. With a sigh, Bitso sank a bit in his chair. "Most mages pick a lane and run with it. Lots of damage. Evasion. Something. It's almost like…

You're just picking things at random. You want to win this thing, right? You want to get to Zenith?"

"I like the versatility."

Bitso smirked. "Ah. Yes. You did take the Void Agent focus. And you were a Special Forces soldier, weren't you?" With more pep in his voice, Bitso pulled himself closer to the desk. "Let's watch your fight together, shall we? I had fun with this one." He snapped his fingers and the fight with the centipede started all over again.

The moment the centipede cut Kellan across the stomach, Bitso held up a hand. The video paused.

"Right here—look at this." Bitso pointed to Sen. "Your teammate has the *Shield Ally* ability, but he didn't use it *at all.* That could've saved you from taking a whole lot of damage." With a laugh, Bitso waved his hand. "Look at his face! He's panicking. And he made poor choices while frightened."

Sure enough, Sen's face was twisted in panic. Kellan hadn't noticed at the time—he had been too busy fighting a damn monster—but Sen was just flailing around during the fight.

"But look at *you*," Bitso muttered.

The TV showed Kellan diving into the darkness and then emerging near the monster. He threw the hydra venom on the creature, and then it spasmed and died.

"You didn't panic. You made fantastic decisions." Bitso giggled as he yanked against the handcuffs. "I love it when I find people who are good at murdering things." Bitso slowly rubbed his free hand over his chest, tugging at his white tie. "I could watch this all day… It makes me feel good in the most tender part of my loins."

The TV looped the footage of the centipede dying. It spasmed and hit the ground of the sewer, collapsing with a silent groan since the TV was muted.

Kellan wasn't sure if Bitso was just insane, or if death was somehow a fetishistic fascination for the man. He definitely wasn't going to ask.

"I guess you can be my eleventh favorite player," Bitso finally said. He snapped his finger and the loop stopped. Instead, the video continued to play until Kellan and Hank were dealing with the Kuji.

"Does this have anything to do with the rules I broke?" Kellan asked.

Bitso slammed a hand on the desk. Kellan flinched, but only because he hadn't expected it.

"What was *this*?" Bitso asked as the TV showed Kellan handing over the second key. "Do you even understand how the Nexus Games work, sad sack?" Bitso turned his blindfolded face in Kellan's direction and frowned. "You're supposed to get the keys for yourself. Instead, you were the best player on Team 80, and you didn't even get anything for it. What's wrong with you?"

"I… didn't want him to die." Kellan scooted to the edge of his seat. "Look, they said multiple teams could win the Nexus Games. Why can't they win, too?"

"Oh, multiple teams *can* win. They just never have. It gets a little cutthroat near the end, which is amazing." Bitso laughed and slapped his knee. After a moment, he rubbed at his temple and calmed his mirth. "Wait, is that your goal? Have everyone *win*? What a terribly misguided vision of the future you have. It's almost adorable."

Kellan glanced around at the eyes on the ceiling and wall. They watched him—and only him. Kellan exhaled and tried to ignore them, but he wasn't sure what he should be doing. Relaxing with Bitso while he replayed the whole match as though it were a home video?

"Oh, and here's where you found a prize room!"

Kellan returned his attention to the TV. Sure enough, it was a video of him speaking with the prize imp.

"You are a fascinating player," Bitso said, tugging harder on his tie. "You completely botched your prize request."

"Look, I didn't even know prize rooms existed." Kellan placed a hand on the desk, his anger quickly replacing his anxiety. "And if I did break a rule, it's probably because I wasn't aware of it. As far as I'm concerned, this entire game is arbitrary and random, and it's not my fault I didn't know what to ask for in the damn prize room!"

He hadn't meant for his voice to get so loud, but he couldn't help it.

None of that fazed Bitso. He rubbed at his chin, mock-contemplating the situation. "So, what you're saying is… you want a rule book, is that right?"

"I…" Kellan sighed. "A rule book would be nice, yeah. Do you have one?"

Bitso shrugged. "Sure. I'll send one to your room. Just for you, sad sack. Since you're so good at killing."

"Thanks."

"Oh, and because I like you so much, I'll let you in on a little secret." He laced his fingers together and chuckled. "Next time you're in a prize room, and the imp lets you pick a prize, ask for the blood of Councilor Zero."

"Who's that?" Kellan asked.

"Who *cares*?" Bitso laughed harder and then leaned on the desk so far, he was almost lying across it. "Zarr Mantis gave himself the title of Councilor Zero when he was kicked from his homeland—*because he's a dramatic edgelord*. But all that *really* matters is that he infused his blood with the void of black stars. That's right, his blood runs like ink, and if you drink some, it'll give you a minus twenty percent modifier to rank eclipse magic. That makes it cheap and easy to gain power—and everyone loves cheap and easy, baby."

Kellan opened his mouth to say something, but then thought better of it. Instead, he lowered his voice. "Is that guy here?"

"You ask too many questions." Bitso slid back into his seat. "And *no*. Of course not. He's on some other dimension, probably brooding. You know other dimensions have their own histories and mages, right?"

"I'm starting to get that."

"Just trust in me." Bitso rubbed at one of his sharpened molars. "Have I ever led you astray? You definitely want some of Councilor Zero's blood. Just remember it for next time."

Kellan tried to keep his questions to himself, but every time someone told him about the prize room, they had a completely different suggestion for the prize at the end. Which was the best? Kellan wasn't sure—but he also didn't want to think about it right now. He had been dragged into the room for breaking the rules.

But what rules?

"Okay, let's finally get to the heart of the issue." Bitso clapped his hands and the TVs switched to footage of the first key.

Kellan watched as he put the dreamweaver blanket on the ground.

"Was it because I took the blanket from the AVU Palace?" he asked. "If it is, I'm sorry. I—I didn't think I was stealing it. I thought… it was ours. Honestly."

Bitso laughed and slapped a hand on the metal desk. Then he turned to Kellan, his smile more sinister than it had been previously. "That's not it, sad sack. The Arbiter doesn't care if you take *some blankets*. No one does."

"Okay… Then what?"

Bitso pointed to the TV, his blindfold secured over his eyes, to the point it looked like it might hurt. How was he watching anything?

But then the TV showed footage of Jace appearing. Jace grabbed the rabbit off the sheets and yanked the animal to the roof of the elementary school. Kellan fired at him, and shadows lifted up, blocking the bullets.

"There!" Bitso held up a hand, and the footage paused. "There it is. Tsk, tsk, tsk." Bitso chuckled as he leaned back in his seat. "The Arbiter was very disappointed in you."

Kellan stared at the TV, trying hard to think of what he had done wrong. "Shouldn't *Jace* be in trouble? He stole the key from me."

"Oh, stealing keys is totally within the rules. But attacking another player in a PvE game… Well, that's just straight-up cheating."

Kellan caught his breath. He hadn't thought about that when he had shot at Jace. He hadn't been thinking at all, really. He had just been trying to get the key back.

"And don't you dare say *I didn't know the rules.*" Bitso snickered as he waggled a finger. "It was in the title of the game. *Player versus Environment Seek and Destroy.* You knew you weren't supposed to attack anyone. Admit it."

"I…"

There was no way around it. Kellan knew, deep in his gut—he had broken the rules.

"*Say it.*"

Kellan exhaled. Then he wiped his sweaty palms off on the top of his pants. "Yeah. I knew I wasn't supposed to attack anyone."

Bitso didn't laugh or giggle—he just smirked. "You should've done what your team leader did." He pointed at the TV, and the footage played forward.

Xiang used her telekinesis on the building around Jace's feet, obviously trying to cause him to fall. But she never used her abilities on Jace directly.

"That's allowed?" Kellan asked.

Bitso nodded. "Xiang is very good about following the rules. Her mother almost got in trouble during her time in the Nexus Games… It was quite an ordeal."

"So… What's going to happen to me?"

"First off, you're getting your first title." Bitso clapped his hands together once. "Alex Kellan the Rulebreaker. It has a nice ring to it." He leaned back in his chair. "The Arbiter thought it amusing."

"Anything else?"

"Of course." Bitso laughed again, dark and icy. "Since you're so trigger happy about attacking others, the Arbiter has decided that your team will be forced to participate in a PvP game for this next round." He rubbed at his blindfold. "Lucky you."

—Chapter 41—
—The Price of Kindness—

"My whole team?" Kellan asked, his volume increasing. "But no one else broke the rules. It was just me. You shouldn't force them all into a PvP match."

As though sarcastically agreeing, Bitso slowly nodded along with Kellan's words. "Hm. I see why you might be frustrated, but this is a team competition. Teams are typically penalized as a unit."

"But—"

"The normal punishment for attacking someone in a PvE match is death," Bitso said, cutting Kellan off. "But the Arbiter spoke to Jace about the event, and Jace apparently asked that the punishment be lighter for you. How generous. Right, sad sack?" The man smiled. "But I suppose… if you *want* death instead of a team PvP match… I could make that happen."

Kellan caught his breath, unwilling to make any further comments. Although *he* had created the problem, he wasn't sure dying would actually solve anything. Would leaving his team down one member be better than forcing them to fight other teams? Kellan wasn't so sure. And Xiang had made a big deal about how she could win the Nexus Games—even PvP matches—so long as Husker was on their side.

"Oh, what's that?" Bitso held a hand to his ear. "You *don't* want to die? I guess you're going to have a PvP match, then." He put down his arm and yanked on the handcuff. He had done it so much his wrist had become raw and bloody. "Welp, that's everything. Remember the rules. Don't break them."

After a long exhale, Kellan got to his feet. What would he tell Xiang? Would this mess with her overall plans? He could already hear Sen's shrill screams.

Kellan glanced around and noticed that most of the Eyes of the Arbiter had disappeared. Only one remained. It was positioned on the ceiling, directly above them, its camera pupil constricting and dilating anytime Kellan moved.

Bitso pulled on the cuffs again, drawing Kellan's attention.

"You know, I can free you from that." Kellan stepped closer and pointed to the cuffs. His ability to reshape metal could easily destroy the restraints. "Do you want me to remove it?"

Bitso placed a hand on his chest and leaned his head back. "Oh. How cute.

You really *do* have a hero complex. You know what? Just for that, you'll be my *second*-favorite player in the Nexus Games this time around."

Kellan narrowed his eyes. "You… don't want me to help you?"

With a smirk, Bitso motioned Kellan close.

Against his better judgment, Kellan got closer to Bitso, going so far as to place his hands on the top of the cold desk. When Bitso motioned him even closer, Kellan tensed. Was this some sort of attack? A joke?

Bitso lowered his voice. "Listen. I'm going to let you in on a secret."

"Okay…"

"I'm not trapped to this desk. I'm not trapped in this room. I'm not even trapped in the Nexus." Bitso chuckled as he said, "I'm trapped in my own damn body. So, unless you're prepared to put a bullet in my head, there's nothing you can do to *save me*." He put the last two words in air quotes. Then he leaned away from Kellan and chuckled. "Sorry, sad sack. But I really appreciate the effort. You're the only one who's ever offered to help."

"Sure. Okay." Kellan stepped away from the desk. He rubbed at his hands, surprised by how chilly the desk had been. But then remembered *why* Bitso was here—Husker had said it was punishment for learning one of the "unknowable" magics without the Arbiter's permission.

Bitso tilted his head to the side. "You have something else you want? I don't have long. Once the game ends, I need to do all my fabulous broadcasts."

"You have fate magic?" Kellan asked. His eyes told him everything—Bitso had storm and fate—but he wanted to make sure before proceeding with his last line of questioning.

"Fate magic is one of the best," Bitso replied with a smile.

"I wanted to know… would the Arbiter allow me to learn it?"

Bitso laughed so hard it echoed in the windowless room. He tried to spin his chair, but his handcuffed wrist prevented him from going far. Once his mirth had reduced down to a chuckle, he rubbed at his blindfold. "You couldn't handle fate magic! Do you even know what it does? Of course not. It'd drive you insane. Trust me." Bitso tapped a single finger against his temple.

"What about travel magic?"

"Hm. Maybe. If you had someone to teach it to you."

"I do." Kellan glanced up at the single eye on the ceiling. "So, can I learn it? Do I have permission?"

The Eye of the Arbiter said nothing. It stared with freakish intensity.

"The Arbiter says he'll allow you to learn travel magic to C rank," Bitso said with a sigh. "But if you want to learn higher than that, you need to collect *at least* two more gold arcana."

Kellan returned his attention to the blindfolded news anchor. It was odd the Arbiter made such a big deal out of the gold arcana, especially since none of the other contestants seemed to be gathering it. Why did the Arbiter want that? For what purpose?

Everything about the Arbiter confused Kellan. He was certain that he was missing something—the dragon's motives weren't apparent.

"Why can't I hear the Arbiter?" Kellan asked, pointing to the eye on the ceiling.

Bitso touched his lower lip and sarcastically *hmmmed* for a second. "You don't know anything about magic, do you? You probably come from one of those dimensions where no one is a mage and you all live dreary, mundane lives."

Holding back his own sardonic commentary, Kellan nodded. "Yeah. That's right. Hence why I ask all the questions."

"Well, rest assured that I accurately report on the Arbiter's decisions." Bitso offered a shrug and a smile. "He just doesn't feel like talking to you. Maybe in the future, if you actually follow the rules, the Arbiter will grace you with his invasive mind magic. Then you'll *really* know how powerful he is, when he's clawing around your mind." Bitso snorted and laughed. "What an experience. I can't wait for you to have it."

"Sounds excellent," Kellan drawled. "I'm gonna go." He inched toward the door, hoping to escape the room before the Arbiter changed his mind and started speaking to him.

Out of everyone in the Nexus, Bitso really was the only person who answered all of Kellan's questions… even if the man did so in an insane and flippant manner. So, if Bitso said the Arbiter's speech was like taking a rake to the mind, Kellan believed him.

Kellan backed out of the room and shut the double doors behind him. To his surprise, the two Pestbyters were waiting outside, their spherical bodies hovering in the stairwell.

"*Hello,*" one of them said in a cutesy voice.

Kellan lifted an eyebrow and said nothing in return. He didn't like the Pestbyters. At all. He hated the fact that he was on their side, apparently. Without even a gesture of acknowledgement, he moved around the machines and headed down the stairs, taking the steps three at a time. When he reached the bottom, Kellan jogged back to the corridor he had teleported into.

The pulse of the AVU Palace was increasing with every minute. More and more voices rang out in the larger rooms, and Kellan suspected other teams were finishing with the games. Music filled the halls, and the smell of fresh baked bread hung in the air.

Again, Kellan's stomach demanded to be heard. He rubbed at his gut as he picked up his pace. Kellan desperately wanted to return to his team and fill them in on everything he had learned.

And he wanted to spend his seventeen arcana.

Travel magic…

His only real advantage.

Kellan made it back to the starting corridor—he recognized the old paintings and lush red rugs—but his team was nowhere in sight. Desperate to find them, Kellan jogged further down the hall, opened a set of doors, and just searched through the AVU Palace, even though he had no idea where he was within it.

Room after room.

He slammed open doors, pushed aside divider curtains, and checked most closets for any sort of secret pathway. Unfortunately, he didn't recognize most of the areas. He even found a hospital-style room, complete with bedpan and EKG monitor. Why would that be in a palace? Kellan suspected the Nexus was some sort of twisted inspiration for a *Where's Waldo?* book.

Finally, Kellan slammed through a door and found himself standing in the registration room. The counters, display screens, and bizarre androids were all familiar to him. He slowly walked forward, glancing around, trying to get his bearings.

Groups of people stood around the room, some dressed like they were at a cocktail party, others dressed in military combat gear, like they had just returned from the games. Kellan recognized some of the people—he had seen them in the palace the day before.

"I can't believe what he's done," one man in a tuxedo said. He pointed to the screens above the registration counter. "It should be a crime."

"I believe it." A woman in a sleek dress—the same color as her pale flesh—slid up next to the man. "Brenner isn't one known for subtlety. Didn't you see the vids?"

"Seems extreme. I had bets on some of those teams. He just killed them outright."

"I told you that you shouldn't diversify this early in the game. Way too many of these mages are going to die."

Kellan turned around and stared up at the screens. The teams were listed by number and then by members. Some of the listings were either crossed out, blank, or filled with white static. It took Kellan a moment to understand what he was looking at.

It was an updated list for teams who had lost their leader, were still in the game, or for those who lost every single member.

Team 42—Brenner Hawke's team—was confirmed to have succeeded.

With twenty-three of the forty keys offered in the PvP Seek and Destroy match.

Kellan gritted his teeth, disgusted by the information. That team had intentionally prevented others from gathering the key they needed. And from all the crossed-out lines on the registration board—as well as the static teams—it seemed that Brenner and his murder crew had wiped out a solid chunk of the competition in the opening round.

A terrible thought floated into Kellan's head as he stared at the board. His team was next. Brenner had made that clear.

I need to discuss this with Xiang.

Kellan turned on his heel and almost ran straight into Jace. The man with the mechanical eye disturbed him, but only for half a second. Rage immediately dominated his actions. Kellan grabbed Jace by the collar of his leather biker jacket.

"*You think this is funny?*" Kellan asked, trying to keep his voice down, but ultimately failing. "My whole team could've died out there!"

Jace didn't react with much surprise. He lifted the eyebrow over his human eye and smirked. "You should learn to rein in these outbursts, you know. They're going to get you in more trouble, Alex Kellan the Rulebreaker."

Their conversation garnered the attention of everyone in the room. All side conversations stopped as everyone glanced over to see what was happening. Kellan didn't care. His new title was on the board for everyone to see, and he the was certain news of their exploits in the game was going to spread like wildfire.

All Kellan cared about was getting answers from Jace.

"What's with you?" Kellan demanded as he released Jace's jacket and shoved the man away. "First you help me out, then you give me my dog tags—and now you're stealing from my team and acting like it's all a joke?"

Jace straightened his clothing and then smoothed back his dark hair. "I'm just curious about you, that's all. And what're you getting so worked up for? I knew you'd find another key. There's no way Xiang would let a key slip through her grasp in the first game."

Whispers filled the corners of the room as the cliques began their commentary. Kellan ignored them all.

"Are you going to keep doing this?" Kellan wasn't sure what he would do if Jace said *yes*, but he just wanted to be prepared.

"Probably," Jace replied. "I mean… You're an easy mark, you know that? So focused on completing the game. So trusting. So ignorant of how magic works."

Kellan clenched his hands into fists. "It's not going to be that way forever."

"And maybe then I'll leave you alone. But until then…" Jace shrouded himself in invisibility, disappearing completely from view. His disembodied voice rang out with, "I might as well get some use out of you, right? That's what the smart player would do."

Kellan cracked his knuckles by lacing his fingers together and clenching. The Oasis would prevent him from taking any violent actions, but that didn't stop him from fantasizing. Jace obviously thought this was amusing.

"How did you find us?" Kellan asked. He knew Jace was still around—lingering like a dirty pigeon hoping for more crumbs.

Still invisible, Jace replied, "What're you talking about? I followed you around the game arena." His voice came from a spot behind Kellan.

Kellan didn't turn to face the man. He just stood in the middle of the room, his gaze focused on the far wall. "*Bullshit.* You didn't just follow us. You tracked us. Somehow. Probably with magic, but maybe tech. Tell me how you did it."

"What makes you think I'm tracking you through some means?"

Kellan didn't reply. He couldn't.

He had given Jace's theft a lot of thought, and Kellan had realized something startling. Jace couldn't have followed them because… Xiang had teleported them twice. Once to Pan Town, and once out of it. How had Jace found them in the park, then? Obviously, he had to have some way to find them—and it hadn't been with his eyeballs.

But Kellan couldn't say that. He couldn't say Xiang teleported, therefore he knew Jace had some sort of magical way to follow them.

So Kellan just waited.

Jace laughed, his voice coming from Kellan's left. "Like I said—you're an easy mark, Kellan. It's amusing to get the better of you through simple means, especially because you've done this to me a hundred times. *Learn by doing*, that's what you always said."

"Oh, I get it," Kellan said with a dark chuckle. "This is about the *other* Kellan."

"Something like that." Jace patted Kellan on the shoulder. "Just think of it like this—when I was younger, you used to torment me with all sorts of magical powers I didn't understand. And now that I'm older, I think it's funny to do it to you. Well, a *version* of you. The version I can still mess with."

"I asked if you knew me—if you knew Alex Kellan—and you said no."

"I don't really know you, or the other Kellan. I told you… This happened a long time ago."

Kellan ground his teeth, his frustration building. "I don't find any of this funny."

"That's not really the point." Jace moved away from Kellan, his steps as silent as the grave, but his footfalls leaving impressions on the rug. "Don't worry. I'm not going to do anything too serious. I'm not a psychopath."

"Taking the key was more than just messing with me. You're messing with my whole team."

"Heh. Don't get high and mighty. I already spoke with the members of Team 80. You *gave* a key away just to save someone. You've clearly got a screw loose." Jace snapped a finger. "Think of it this way—I really needed your help, and you totally came through for me. That make you feel better?"

Kellan was actively starting to regret his actions. Hank had gone around telling everyone he gave the key away? Now everyone would be expecting that. Or they'd be like Jace—ready to follow him around and take advantage of his actions.

"And there's no way to get you to stop?" Kellan asked.

But Jace never replied. He left the room, his steps visible until he reached the door. The door never opened, and Kellan knew the man must've stepped into the darkness and slithered underneath.

The whispering never stopped. Some people pointed, and others giggled as they pointed to the team boards. Kellan didn't care. They could concoct all sorts of rumors about him, it didn't matter.

He strode out of the room, intent on returning to Xiang's suite.

—Chapter 42—
—The End of the First Game—

Kellan dwelled on everything that had happened over the last day. His thoughts spiraled downward like quicksand, stealing his focus. The first game—out of ten—had taken its toll. Monsters. Deadly environments. Crazy competitors.

He wanted more of a game plan. A strategy. When he had run operations in the Delta Force, he had intel on the location, the target, and the potential nearby threats. Kellan disliked running blind on every mission, practically playing catch-up with every step of the process. Everyone else seemed to know what was going on.

I've just got to up my game. No excuses. The game will be rough if I don't get my shit together.

He lightly slapped himself on the side of the face, trying to focus.

After a long exhale, Kellan climbed a set of elegant stairs and made his way to Xiang's suite. He pushed open the door, intent on speaking with her about travel magic. To his surprise, the rest of Team 101 was gathered in the central sitting area. Husker and Mavis sat on the couch, while Xiang and Sen stood in front of the TV.

Kellan held his breath as he shut the door and walked inside.

"There you are," Sen said, pointing. "What happened? What rule did you break? *Did the Arbiter punish you with a hex*?"

"Let the man gather his thoughts," Husker growled.

"We've been waiting! He had time to think on the way over here."

Xiang held up a hand. Both her brother and Husker quieted themselves.

While Kellan was away, Xiang had changed her clothes. She now wore a giant yellow sweatshirt and slimming black jeans. Some hanzi was printed on the back, and the outfit gave her a youthful urban look—something straight out of a modern fashion magazine.

Another illusion? Kellan was starting to think *all* her clothing was fake.

"The Arbiter told me that our team would have to participate in a PvP match for the upcoming game," she said matter-of-factly. "Is that because of you?"

Sen whipped around and held his hands to his mouth in a silent gasp. Even Mavis seemed concerned—she turned her attention to Kellan, her eyebrows knitted. She silently mouthed, *That means we'll be fighting the other teams, right?*

"I attacked Jace during the first game," Kellan muttered. He ran a hand through his hair. "So we have to do a PvP game as punishment. I… I'm sorry about that. I wasn't thinking when I lashed out, and this is my fault."

The others didn't respond.

Xiang and Husker exchanged knowing looks. No words, but their intense gazes were worth a whole novel's worth of text. Then Xiang combed her silky hair with her long fingers.

"In the future, please restrain yourself," she said. "We don't need pointless complications. Things are already going to be rough."

Kellan nodded once. "Really… I'm sorry about this."

"You needn't be so apologetic." She sighed and then waved away her own comment. "I knew this would happen eventually. We have to face Brenner at some point, and it should probably be *sooner* rather than *later*. If that man takes any more hexes, we might be in for a rough time."

"You want us to do a PvP match?"

"I would've preferred to wait one more game, but honestly, this isn't as bad as it could be. If the Arbiter had killed you, we would've been down a member, and all the arcana you gathered during the game would've been wasted."

Husker stood up from the couch. Sometimes Kellan forgot how tall the werewolf man was—he towered over everyone else, his ears giving him an extra few inches that added to his imposing stature.

"It's a relief to know the Arbiter isn't imposing a harsher punishment," Husker said. He tightened his coat around his large body and walked for the door. "Now that I'm not as worried, I'll gather us something to eat." He headed out of the suite without another word.

The others glanced between each other.

Xiang turned and headed for the door of her room. Kellan leapt to her side. He didn't want to waste any more time.

"Wait. Can you teach me that magic now?" He had the arcana. It would be simple, wouldn't it?

"Not now," Xiang said, a slight strain to her voice. "Later tonight. After I've… rested."

Until that moment, Kellan hadn't realized she was tired. But now that he was close to her, he could see the fatigue and the stress. Was she hurting? She stood like someone in pain but trying hard not to show it.

Why was she so secretive?

"Do you need something?" Kellan asked, his voice a whisper.

Sen hurried to his sister's side. He pushed Kellan aside. "I'll take care of my sister. You and the others just make sure you're prepared for the next game." Sen motioned Kellan away. "Just sit in this room and *don't get into any more trouble.* I doubt the Arbiter will be as forgiving if you break the rules a third time."

Without another word, both Xiang and Sen disappeared into one of the far rooms. Kellan watched as they went, his attention on Xiang's shaky gait. Something was wrong. Why would she hide it from the rest of her team?

Mavis stood up from the couch. She brushed off her pants and then made her way to Kellan's side. With a smile, she said, "I'm so glad you're not getting flayed or something. You should've heard Sen and Husker talking before you got back. They were both really worried you were going to be gutted."

"Oh, yeah?" Kellan lifted an eyebrow. "You sure Sen wasn't hoping for it?"

"No. He seemed genuinely concerned." But before Kellan could comment further, Mavis grabbed his arm, her excitement unable to be contained. She smiled as she said, "You're not going to believe this, but I got a *focus*. I'm D rank in magma magic. It happened during the games."

"I believe it." Kellan motioned to the room. "Show me. What did you get?"

Mavis took a step back, rolled the sleeve of her T-shirt up, and then motioned to her skin. Her pale complexion wasn't much to look at, but in the next moment, she glowed with inner heat and then hardened. A black crust, similar to the top of cooling lava, formed on her arm all the way down to her knuckles, creating a protective layer over her body.

The heat and blackening spread to the rest of her. In a matter of seconds, she had a new second layer over her body—including her face, but not her hair—and although it looked stiff, it moved with her, never hindering her actions.

"Awesome, right?" When Mavis spoke, her mouth glowed with the same type of intense heat her skin had demonstrated. Her insides were ablaze with inner fire. "It's called *Stone Colossus*. I get plus four armor rating, touch damage that's fire, and my stamina is counted as double for checks. Husker was excited." She held out her arms and stared at the black crust. "I feel like a superhero," Mavis whispered.

Kellan snorted and crossed his arms. "You look like a superhero."

"Really?"

He nodded and half shrugged. "Yeah. I like it. Impressive."

"You mean it?"

The magma-hardened crust disappeared from her body, turning to ash in an instant. Mavis rubbed at her forehead and chuckled, her cheeks pink.

"You okay?" he asked.

"Yeah." Mavis motioned to the room. "We made it back, right? That's the best feeling in the world. And we have more magical powers. I think we might actually win this."

"We're only ten percent of the way through." Kellan didn't want to become lax. They needed to stay focused until the last game was over. "What else did you learn?"

"Husker and I fought a yami. It wasn't large, but the thing was some sort of nightmarish horse. It was black and at least the size of a truck." Mavis held her arms out as she pantomimed everything she said. "We were walking along the road when some fighting broke out. Another team started fighting this giant monster, and Husker and I fought the horse while trying to dodge chunks of falling building. It was something. More intense than my deployment, let me tell you."

"Next time you get hit with a grenade, you're gonna have the armor to take it."

Mavis sarcastically laughed as she stepped close and hit Kellan on the shoulder. "There won't be a next time. Apparently, magma mages can cause things to combust, even from afar. If an enemy has an explosive, they're the ones who'll explode."

Something about her excitement made Kellan smile. Although the Nexus seemed bleak and unforgiving, it had completely changed Mavis—for the better. She had seemed alone and distant when they met in the bar not just two days ago. Now she seemed enthusiastic about everything, even a creepy adventure through an unforgiving hellscape.

Kellan's kind of woman.

The door to the suite swung open. Husker stomped in, his breathing rough. He carried a large box in one hand—it had a metal hand on the top, similar to a lantern.

But the box…

It looked like a miniature dresser, complete with three drawers. Was Husker bringing them more clothes? The outside of the box was painted a bright red with pink and white flowers decorating the corners.

Husker set the box on top of the large coffee table in the middle of the sitting room. "It's time to eat."

Kellan took a seat on the couch and eyed the strange chest of drawers. "What is that?"

"A lunch box. Don't you have them in your dimension?"

Mavis sat next to Kellan, so close her leg touched his. She leaned forward and squinted at the dresser. "A lunch box, huh?"

Husker snorted and then carefully—with the tips of his claws—opened the top drawer. Inside was a whole host of steamed rice and vegetables. Apparently, the dresser had been keeping it fresh, because Kellan hadn't been able to smell it until Husker set it on the coffee table.

Then he opened the second drawer. Meat and flat pieces of bread. Small jars of sauce were tucked into the corners.

The last drawer had finger-sized dessert cakes with fresh fruit. The smell of sugar was almost as strong as the meat from the second drawer, enough to give Kellan cavities even just looking at the desserts.

"I didn't know what you were accustomed to," Husker muttered. He spread out the drawers and then revealed the underside of each had thin plates tucked beneath. Each plate had its own set of flat utensils. "So I grabbed something from the most popular categories. Humans eat many things, yes?"

Mavis nodded. "Yeah. This looks delicious. Where did you get it?"

"The kitchens in the AVU Palace are run by androids who serve the Arbiter. He provides food to all contestants, no matter the time of day. You may eat there whenever you need."

Kellan grabbed a plate, some rice, vegetables, and meat. He wasn't entirely sure what kind of meat it was—brown and red—and he wasn't about to ask, either. Some part of him knew the answer would disgust him, and he just wanted to eat without thinking about it.

It tasted good, whatever it was. Sliced thin, yet still juicy. Definitely not beef or goat.

Mavis grabbed several dessert cakes and some bread.

But Husker… He piled half the meat onto his plate and took a seat on one of the many chairs. Then he removed his coat, relaxed back, and slowly plucked the meat from the plate and nibbled on it, obviously enjoying the moment.

Once Kellan had gotten halfway through his meal, he realized a single point of mana had returned to his reserves.

He swallowed his rice quickly and turned to Husker. "Wait, eating restores mana?"

"A little bit each day, yes," Husker muttered between bites. "About four mana can be restored through eating. Unless you're a body mage… Then you can benefit more from food."

"No one told me this."

"You've been informed now." Husker then pointed to the balcony at the back of the suite. "Besides, we have a mana spring here. You can restore everything once you bathe."

Yet again, Kellan felt he was being left out of vital information. He poked around his food, remembering his fight with the man in the dark alleyway—the one who had tried to kill Twi and Hua. If Kellan had kept some food with him, he might not have been so close to death.

I'll need to pack a Snickers or something when we head out to the second game.

Xiang's door opened. Sen shuffled out into the common room, his legs heavy. He wasn't wearing robes—he wore a kid's outfit. A T-shirt with a happy-face skull and a pair of small jeans.

Kellan was about to make a quip about how he was finally dressing his age, but he held back once he noticed Sen's sullen expression. The kid ambled over to the TV and then stared at the black screen, straight into the eyes of his own reflection.

No one said anything as Sen touched his face.

Had he gotten younger again?

There wasn't too much difference, but Kellan could've sworn Sen didn't look right.

What had happened with Xiang?

Kellan knew Sen wasn't going to discuss it, though. The kid never wanted to talk about anything that would make him seem weak. So, instead, Kellan grabbed one of the many plates and scooped some rice and vegetables.

"Sen," he said, holding up the plate. "You should come eat with us."

The man-child continued to stare at his reflection. A full minute went by before he turned around and shuffled over to the couch. To Kellan's surprise, Sen took a seat on Kellan's other side. Sen grabbed his plate and held it close.

With a look of *not giving a shit,* Sen ate his food without bothering with the utensils. He used his pudgy little hands and shoved some rice into his mouth as though he were an actual child.

Again, Kellan was tempted to make a joke about table manners, but he decided against it.

No one else commented either. They returned to their food, slowly eating everything from the bizarre lunch box chest of drawers. Although it was mostly quiet, Kellan found it pleasant.

No chaos. No yami. Just peaceful eating.

Kellan savored the moment.

When Sen held out his plate and pointed to the desserts, Kellan handed over half a dozen. Sen slowly ate them, one at a time, his eyes watery.

Then the TV flickered to life.

The pleasantness died as fast as a flame hitting water.

The news came on. Everyone's favorite creepy news anchor, Bitso, sat behind a different steel desk, this one with etchings across the surface. Writing? Kellan couldn't tell from the camera's angle on the room.

"And that's the end, gentle souls," Bitso said with a sweep of his arms. He wasn't chained down this time, but instead, free to swing around in his chair. "The last key in the PvP Seek and Destroy has been claimed! That means… *the first game is officially over!*"

Screens behind Bitso played footage of fireworks, birthday cakes with candles, and a piñata being exploded by an RPG.

"Are we ready to hear some numbers?" Bitso slammed his hands on the desk and laughed as though he had just made the best quip of all time. "Of course you are! Numbers are everything! And get this—seven hundred and ninety-six people registered for the Nexus Games this time around. Intense, right? Not the most ever, but pretty damn high."

"That's almost an average of eight people per team," Sen said, some cake in his little mouth. He rubbed fruit juice from his lips and added, "Outrageously high. Who would want a team that large? Risky, that's what it is."

"Of those seven hundred and ninety-six, four hundred and two died." Bitso yanked at the collar of his suit. "Oof. That's rough. More than *half* of you chumps couldn't make it through the first round. That does not bode well for the rest of the games. We might not have a winning team this year…"

No one said anything. Everyone just watched the TV, the tension in the room building. Kellan hadn't thought about the possibility of *everyone* losing.

Bitso placed his elbows on the desk. The screens behind him played scenes from throughout the games. Kellan recognized a few, including the bird yami who had given birth to several chicks, and the centipede with the bunny clutched in its pincers.

But most of the scenes were unfamiliar to Kellan. People fighting monsters. People fighting each other. At one point, there looked to be a storm raging through the city, complete with rain and hail. Kellan hadn't seen a storm. Had that been in the PvP match?

"One hundred and one teams registered for the Nexus Games, but thirty-eight of them are completely out of the running." Bitso motioned to the screens. His blindfold darkened with blood, and he had to take a moment to fix it tight around his head. Then he returned his attention to the playbacks. "That leaves only sixty-three teams. And of those teams, only *twenty-seven* of them earned keys! I've never seen a Nexus Games start off that rough. Is anyone even *trying*?"

Sen scooted forward on the couch and used his small fingers to help him count. He mumbled a few words and then said, "Five PvE keys were found… and four Lucky Door keys were found… which means only eighteen teams in the PvP match managed to get keys."

"Brenner took twenty-three keys for his entire team," Kellan stated.

Everyone turned their attention to him, as if to see if he was joking. Kellan offered them a serious glower. Why would he josh around when it came to Brenner? The man was clearly a sociopath.

"Why would he do that?" Mavis asked. She set her plate down. "I thought he couldn't use those extra keys? He has to gather the keys from different games."

"He did it to prevent *other* teams from getting them." Sen huffed and threw down his own plate. Then he crossed his little arms. "And he's likely trying to intimidate us. Brenner likes to get inside people's heads."

Husker nodded once. "Yes… I think you're right."

"Are we ready for the more amusing numbers?" Bitso chuckled as he stood up from his chair. The desk was yanked away by something offscreen, as though being cleared for a larger stage. "We have so many highlights to go over, so everyone pay close attention! You might need to know some of this for later…"

—Chapter 43—
—The Rule Book—

Kellan watched the TV, his attention on the screens behind Bitso. While the lunatic news anchor spoke about the games, footage of people playing in the Nexus Games continued in the background. Kellan recognized some of the other teams, and he studied their actions in the brief scenes he was shown.

Team 80… Hank and Fern.

Video showed them running around the city as a pair. They avoided yami, used some minor powers, and then fled to the underground. Fern's hand was marked with the sign of the Straggler, and although there wasn't any sound for the video, Kellan saw the two of them pointing to her hand several times.

And then footage played of Kellan meeting them in the sewer…

He turned away from that screen and watched another. He didn't want to see the Kuji a second time. And he *definitely* didn't want to see Fern die.

Another screen displayed a Nexus resident… The leader of Team 5. What was his name? *Nosferatu*. Kellan thought the name was somewhat cruel, but he suspected it was a moniker.

And while the man was misshapen, he didn't conduct himself like a monster from an old-timey novel. He wore a suit—black and white, crisp and clean—and walked through the game with such confidence and ease that he seemed as though he owned the place.

Nosferatu strode through a city—not the city Kellan had been in. It was a place of museums, amusement parks, and zoos. Gates, signs, cages, and maps were everywhere, a mishmash of entertainment Frankensteined together, and not in a coherent manner, either. Pathways led to walls, food shops were inside tiger pens, and a single skyscraper seemed to be in the center of it all.

The Net surrounded the massive creepy Disney World, keeping all the players inside while the games commenced. Nosferatu didn't seem interested in the rest of the game. He walked from one location to another, stopping only for a few seconds to glance around, as if searching with his nose rather than his eyes.

Kellan paid close attention as Nosferatu walked to a carnival game stand, stared for a short moment, and then climbed over the counter. He walked straight to a stuffed bunny hanging on the backboard—one of two dozen—and then ripped it open and removed one of the USB drive keys from the animal.

He just…

Knew where it was.

And because he was in the PvP Seek and Destroy, he wasn't instantly teleported away. He had to hold on to his key for at least an hour.

And to make matters worse, the key glowed a sinister red, bright and vibrant—enough to see from hundreds of feet away. Even when Nosferatu tucked it into the pocket of his slacks, the glowing key was quite noticeable.

Then Nosferatu headed to the next location—a pen for bears in the middle of a zoo. The yami bears in the pen were bizarre amalgamations of several animals. The bears had several heads—a goat's head, a snake's head—all stitched together with crude white string stained with blood. They were much larger than normal bears, practically the size of a truck, their mouths weeping spittle and mucus.

Kellan had no idea why such yami existed, but there they were, spitting in the eye of nature.

And when Nosferatu approached, the two multiheaded bears lumbered over, their many mouths open, their fangs ready. Nosferatu threw out bits of metal—too tiny on the screen in the background of Bitso's show to see the details—but Kellan could see the bits of metal fly through the air as if caught in an invisible storm.

With bullet-intensity, the bits of metal shot throughout the bear pen, cutting into the bears and ripping them apart from the inside. The bears didn't seem to notice, however. They still rushed for Nosferatu, and when the first one drew close, it tried to bite the misshapen man.

But then a shimmer of pink and gray appeared around Nosferatu, built with tiny hexagons, flashing into existence as the bear was about to connect. The shield blocked the monster, deflecting its many heads.

Nosferatu waved a hand, and the metal bits sped up, ripping the monsters to shreds. Some sort of telekinetic attack? Or were the metal bits just magical items? Kellan was impressed when both the bears died, but he didn't know why.

Bitso had said Nosferatu was an M-rank metal mage. Did he have other magics?

Once finished with the monsters, Nosferatu scooped up the arcana—he didn't absorb it—and strode to the back of the pen. Again, he just seemed to know where the key was. He picked it up and left the pen, no other business to perform.

Both keys glowed bright crimson.

Kellan kept his attention on Nosferatu, even as Bitso rattled off bizarre numbers.

"Forty players were killed by the Kuji," Bitso said, pointing at a back screen. "Low, given the number of deaths, but we can all thank Brenner Hawke for the bloodbath." With a laugh, Bitso continued, "The dead ones are the lucky ones, if you ask me, but the Arbiter wants *someone* to win, so some of you might want to consider acquiring a bit more arcana in the next game."

Again, Kellan tuned it out. He wanted to focus on Nosferatu, and the man's game plan. Was he like Brenner? Was he hoarding keys to prevent others from winning?

No. That wasn't it.

As Kellan watched, he saw Nosferatu head to a group of mages. The mages started to scatter—obviously spooked by Nosferatu's presence—but the misshapen man held up a hand and then underhand-threw one of the keys to the group.

He had… given them a key.

Bitso's laughing cut into Kellan's thoughts.

"These Nexus Games are going to be some of the craziest," Bitso said, his smile so wide it seemed painful. "Twenty-seven teams have keys, but half of them came through unconventional means." He pointed to a screen with Kellan on it. The Kuji was dragging away Hank, and right before he was killed, he grabbed the key out of the stuffed animal. "See this? Team 101 gave one of their keys to Team 80."

Kellan crossed his arms. The eyes of Sen, Husker, and Mavis were upon him. He didn't regret helping Hank, but he knew it probably wasn't the best play for surviving the games.

He didn't want to discuss it.

"And Team 5 gave away *ten keys.*" Bitso motioned to the screen with Nosferatu. With a chuckle, he added, "Apparently, Nosferatu wanted to balance out Brenner's complications. Team 42, led by Brenner Hawke himself, hoarded twenty-three keys, killing several other teams in the process, but Nosferatu actually *protected* people from the madman's rampage. I thought Xiang would be Brenner's rival, but it seems the Nexus resident has different plans…"

The information gave Kellan hope. He thought *everyone* would be a murder-happy lunatic during the games. He hadn't imagined Nosferatu would be like him.

"Speaking of Xiang…" Bitso leaned over and smiled at another screen. "It seems she's too busy grappling with past complications to be bothered fighting with Brenner."

One of Bitso's many TV screens showed a montage of Xiang and Kellan. The moments they stood close. The few times she had touched him. Even a short video of her smiling while they spoke. The footage had been edited together so quickly, and so tightly, that it *looked* like Kellan and Xiang were having the greatest of times together.

Kellan held his breath, shocked Bitso would even cover that.

"The gods have truly cursed us," Husker muttered, his ears flattening out.

Sen ran both his hands down his face but said nothing.

Why? Kellan still couldn't believe it. *Why show that?* Somehow, Xiang had known it would be shown. She had made a point about "posing for the cameras." Why?

Everyone else's silence added to the tension. Kellan knew this would cause problems. They *all* knew it would cause problems. Brenner was clearly the jealous type. Well, the psychotic type with jealous tendencies, but close enough.

What did Xiang hope to gain from this? *More* animosity?

Bitso chuckled as the montage looped again. "I guess Alex Kellan has the best meat in all the known universes, because Xiang couldn't go without him. She got herself a knock-off brand to cuddle with at night, it seems."

If Kellan knew how, he would've turned off the TV. He placed his face in his hand, unable to look at the others in the room, his face hot.

"It's not true," he said, his gaze drilling a hole into the floor.

"Of course it's not true," Sen said with a huff. "My sister isn't about to settle!" He threw an arm into the air. "This is purely for drama! Bitso is instigating something. I wouldn't be surprised if someone put him up to this! Someone who wants Brenner and my sister to fight each other as soon as possible."

Just to change the subject, Kellan exhaled and then waved at the TV. "How did Nosferatu find the keys? Did any of you see that? He just knew where they were. Why?"

Husker, who probably wanted to change the subject himself, scooted to the edge of his lounge chair. "Metal mages have abilities to locate magical items. Metal magic encompasses the use and enhancement of tech and equipment."

"So, he can find all the keys without trouble?"

Sen huffed and shook his head. "Eclipse magic hides things. Magical items—even tech—can be concealed with eclipse."

Kellan ran a hand over his eyebrow. He had been relying on his Blitzkrieg Analysis to tell him all about magical items, but some of them were concealed? Would he know when? Or would he just never get a notification?

"Mind magic involves a lot of trickery," Husker muttered. "Mind mages can easily conceal tech and items as well."

Sen nodded once. "And a mind *and* eclipse mage can create combination powers that conceal things to ridiculous levels. They are the sneakiest of mages—and if their magic is used to hide something, it'll never be found, even those keys."

So magical items could be hidden, just like a mage's basic information. Kellan hated that. He *wanted* to know everything he could. He was trying to gather intel just so he could—

He stopped himself and stood up from the couch. Bitso was still breaking down odd numbers, including how many steps some of the teams had taken while on their hunt for a key, but Kellan wasn't interested in those types of facts. He strode from the main room, his mind elsewhere.

Mavis stood. "Kellan?"

"I'll be right back."

He went to his bedroom—the one he had shared with Mavis the night before—and threw open the door.

The bed had been made, as though they had been visited by maids. Kellan walked over and stared at the sheets. He got no information—they were just normal bedding. But when he turned his attention to his pillow, he caught his breath.

A large booklet with spiral binding sat at the head of the bed.

Kellan scooped it up. The cover was written in a language he didn't understand. With narrowed eyes, he flipped through the hundreds of pages, his eyes scanning for something familiar. To his surprise, he found an English section halfway through. The first page read:

The Nexus Games Official Rule Book
English Edition

With a smile, Kellan sat on the edge of the bed and went to the second page, eager to learn all the rules of the competition. To his dismay, the "English" of the book was rougher than he would've liked, as though the entire thing had been translated by someone who knew English as their seventh language.

The first few lines read:

The Nexus Games is created and sustained by the Arbiter.
He is the only judge of all judgment controversies.

Fantastic, Kellan thought. He flipped through the next few pages, trying to find the meat of the rules. He managed to find a couple. They read:

1. Each game will be different.
2. Each game will have its own type of keys.
3. Each team must acquire a number of different keys to match its members.
4. The rules of the games will be announced before the season.
5. Any broken rule will be judged by the Arbiter.
6. Each team must register before the first game.
7. After the fifth game, a selection will be held.
8. The winners of the Nexus Games enter Zenith using their keys.
9. Teams can lose their keys in games three, six, and nine.
10. Players cannot leave the gameplay arena.
11. The Stragglers must perform in games two, four, six, eight, and ten outside their lines.
12. No extra help is allowed while games are in progress.

Kellan stared at the page, baffled by some of the wording. Rule eleven didn't make much sense to him. With little understanding, he flipped the pages and only stopped when he came upon a section regarding the magics.

All twelve of them were listed.

Elemental Magics:
Eclipse
Magma
Storm

Being Magics:
Mind
Body
Soul

Destiny Magics:
Wyld
Metal
Entropy

Ascendancy Magics:
Fate
Travel
Meta

Two lines under the magics read:

Ascendancy magics are restricted.
The Arbiter alone can determine who can learn them.

When Kellan turned the page, he noticed descriptions of all the magics. Types of powers, famous mages who had mastered the magics—even weird information, like the types of personalities that best fit into each type.

Eclipse mages were listed as loners who worked well by themselves. Kellan touched the page, his fingers gliding over the ink that made up the words. Then he glanced over travel magic. It said:

Those who learn travel magic separate themselves from all society and are released from all others.
They care too little.

Xiang had separated herself from the group the moment they returned to the suite. Even now, the only people away from the common room were the eclipse mage, and the travel mage. Kellan stared at the paper, wondering if learning travel magic would change him…

The rule book said *yes, it would.*

With a sigh, he turned his attention to fate magic. It read:

Those who learn fate magic let out a look at the future.
They see many events, but rarely the truth.

The awkward writing made it hard to understand, but Kellan could see why Bitso had warned him away. Seeing the future? Seeing potential possibilities? It could drive a man insane.

Out of curiosity, Kellan read the description for personality change regarding meta magic, the last of the ascendancy trio:

Those who learn meta magic think outside the box.
They have many tricks and sway magic at their will.

Sway magic at their will? What does that even mean?

Kellan touched the part of the page that said, *They have many tricks*.

Who else had meta magic? The Arbiter… and Brenner. Kellan hadn't seen anyone else with it. Of course, he hadn't seen all the contestants, and some of them concealed *all* their magics, but it had to be rare.

When Kellan turned to the next page, he was surprised to see a list of potential rooms. Apparently, the rooms were spawned at random, and in difficult to find places, often within buildings. Kellan examined the list.

Potential Rooms:
Prize Room
Puzzle Room
Trap Room
Shadow Room
Chance Room

A prize room consisted of a single question and then a prize awarded upon a successful answer. The questions were always something the player knew, never a question that the player couldn't answer.

Puzzle rooms consisted of deadly obstacles that could be disarmed by correctly solving riddles and physical games. A prize was hidden in each puzzle room, but they were harder to find than the exit. If the mage didn't leave the room within a set amount of time, they died.

Trap rooms were just that—traps. Mages caught in a trap room would have to escape, but at the end, they were awarded arcana.

Shadow rooms…

Kellan stared at the awkwardly worded description for a long moment.

The shadow rooms are filled with doppelgängers and wizards.
It is to be fought or consumed by its demons.

He didn't know what that meant, but a prize was listed for beating the room, so he moved on to the last.

Chance rooms seemed to involve some sort of lottery problem. The mage could risk arcana to play, or they could simply leave the room. If they played the game, they could win multiple prizes, but if they lost, they didn't recover the arcana.

The door to the room opened, and Kellan immediately stood up from the bed.

"Kellan?"

Mavis stepped inside, one eyebrow raised.

"Yeah," he said. "What is it?"

"You never came back."

He nodded and then walked over. He pointed to the rule book. "Sorry. I was reading. I'll do it out there."

Mavis motioned her head to the front door. "Also, apparently something came for you. A package."

"For me?"

She replied with a shrug.

Keeping the rule book close, Kellan walked over to the front door. He expected the package to be inside, but he found nothing. Instead, he opened the door and glanced out into the hall.

An image of the dead children haunted his thoughts for a moment. He hadn't seen their blood in his mind's eye when he arrived at the suite, but glancing into the hall brought it all back.

Brenner…

It took Kellan a moment to remember why he had glanced out.

A package was on the ground in front of him. It was wrapped in brown paper and tied with a string. A handwritten note topped it all off. Kellan plucked the note off the package and glared at it.

His name had been poorly written across the top, with a message scrawled out beneath it. The note read:

Alex Kellan the Rulebreaker,

You do not know me, but I am the leader of Team 80. Thank you for helping our team during the first game. As a token of my gratitude, I have enclosed a gift.

As a token of appreciation, Hank Gardener has also enclosed a gift.

I look forward to meeting you in person,
The Leader of Team 80

Kellan thought it strange that the leader didn't leave their name, but he knew he could figure it out if he wanted. He grabbed the package and backed up into the suite. No part of him wanted to speak to the other players at the moment.

"What is it?" Husker asked.

"I don't know." Kellan headed over to the couch and sat down. He placed the package on his lap. It didn't weigh much. "Should I open this? I feel like it's going to be a poison dart or a terrible hex or something."

He just assumed everything would be negative, given his experience with the Nexus, but a small part of him hoped they were pleasant gifts. Perhaps Kellan had made allies.

"Who is it from?" Sen asked.

"Team 80."

"The team you saved." Sen motioned with his arm. "Open it. I doubt it'll be deadly."

—Chapter 44—
—The Rewards of Self-Sacrifice—

Kellan pulled on the strings of the box.

The others watched with bated breath. Kellan unwrapped everything and then opened the top, his muscles tense, his teeth gritted. If the box turned out to be a monster itself, he wouldn't be surprised.

But…

When Kellan glanced inside, he found an egg.

Not a normal tiny egg, but a large ostrich-sized egg. It was longer than Kellan's hand, and practically spherical. The shell was speckled with orange, blue, and black dots—a bizarre design that reminded Kellan of cupcakes.

His eyes gave him information on the egg.

Magical Item [Animal of Pure Magic Egg]—Astra Egg

This egg contains an Animal of Pure Magic of *astra* quality. It seems close to hatching…

Husker practically leapt from his chair. He walked over and stared into the box, his tail half-wagging. Then he sniffed at the egg, and Kellan wondered if the man wanted to eat it.

"Oh," Husker muttered. His tail stopped wagging. "It's not divine quality… A shame. This is just astra quality—still powerful, but not the *best* familiar a mage could have."

"Wait, so this is like that divine egg you were talking about?" Kellan asked. He offered Husker the box. "If you want a familiar, you can have it."

Husker snorted and moved away from the box. He rubbed at his long snout and shook his head. "It was a gift. A token of thanks. You saved Team 80, and this was their show of gratitude. It would be an insult to take the gift from you. Especially since you don't have a familiar."

"Do I want one?" Kellan asked as he carefully pulled the egg from the box. It was light. And warm. And Kellan felt something… moving inside. "I don't know if I want some sort of freakish owl hanging around me all the time."

"Owl?" Sen asked, his brow scrunched in confusion. "Why would you assume it's an *owl*?"

"Isn't that what a familiar is? Or a black cat? Or, uh, a rat or something?"

Kellan hadn't paid much attention to witches and wizards from old tales, but he could've sworn most of them had owls or cats as familiars. How would that help him in a death match? How would it help with *anything*? He didn't have letters he needed delivered.

"Listen, *fool*, an Animal of Pure Magic can be *anything*." Sen clapped his palms together, laced his fingers, and then stared up at Kellan. "Familiars have their own magics, amplify your abilities, and are loyal beyond doubt. They elevate their mage and give them more options. You want one, of course."

Mavis leaned close to Kellan and stared at the large egg. With a hesitant hand, she touched the shell and then jerked her fingers away. "It's warm."

"And moving," Kellan muttered. The animal inside the egg twitched with lively energy. "Wait, this can be *anything*?"

Sen nodded once.

"So… that means it *could* be an owl?"

With a huff and a dramatic roll of his eyes, Sen waved a hand through the air. "Sure. Yes. It could be an owl. But if it was, it would be the most impressive magical owl you've ever seen in your life, I guarantee."

"I've seen sword familiars," Husker muttered as he returned to his seat. After he relaxed onto the cushion, he offered a shrug.

"A sword?" Kellan shook his head and chuckled to himself. "The egg could hatch and a reveal a sword?"

"Yes. Well, sort of." Husker stared at him, no amusement in his wolf-like face. "You didn't have familiars where you came from? None at all? Animals of Pure Magic start off small, and they only grow once they've bonded to a mage. A dagger could appear from the egg, and if you bond with it, you'd eventually have a very powerful sword."

"What about a pistol? I'm fond of firearms."

Husker shrugged. "It's possible. A pistol familiar might become a rifle or something larger."

After a short moment, Kellan asked, "What about… a blender? Could a baby blender come out of the egg? Grow into a food processor?"

Mavis snorted and coughed, unable to stop herself from laughing. She ran a hand over her mouth, biting back her mirth.

"Everything is a joke to you," Sen sardonically commented. He dismissively waved his hand. "Husker, don't bother answering these inane questions. If our warrior doesn't want to take this seriously, why should we?"

"Most of the time, Animals of Pure Magic are, in fact, animals," Husker drawled. He sighed as he picked at his claws. "You'll likely get a dog, and if you're bonded long enough, it'll grow to become a gargantuan wolf—a warg, as some call them."

The TV continued with Bitso's report, including video footage of other teams fighting yami. Husker turned his ears toward the screen the moment Bitso uttered, "The Arbiter is proud of everyone who managed to pass the first round of games. He will be awarding each team that successfully found a key. In the morning, before the second games begin, the leader of those teams will have an advantage they can distribute amongst their teammates."

Kellan returned his attention to the box. Something else was at the bottom.

It was a handwritten note. The English and handwriting were perfect—Kellan suspected it came from Hank himself.

Alex,

Thank you for your help during the first game. My team leader said I should reach out to you and offer something of value.

I don't have much. I accidentally ended up in the Nexus during the Conflux, and I barely understand my surroundings. I wish I had your confidence and skills.

I found this thing. Maybe you can find a use for it.

Merry Christmas,

Hank

Kellan found something else under the note. A gold coin. On one side, there was a picture of a snake. On the other side, there was a picture of a city. He stared long enough to get the extra bit of information.

Magical Item [Device]—Andratome Coin

This coin shines with inner power. The snake side glows whenever deceptive mind magics (such as illusions and subtle mind control) are being used nearby (ten feet times the mage's wisdom score).

If the Andratome Coin is placed on another magical item, the city side will glow if there are concealed abilities within the other item (such as tracking, disruption, bad luck, and mind reading). The mage can spend 5 mana to temporarily negate either the deceptive mind magic or concealed item abilities (negation lasts thirty seconds) if the powers are considered S rank or lower.

Kellan turned the coin over multiple times in his hand. His wisdom score was considered low, thanks to his flaw. It was still a useful item, however. Kellan was surprised Hank would part with it. Then again, perhaps Hank didn't know what it was. Not everyone had Kellan's sight.

"You should keep your egg warm," Husker said, drawing Kellan's attention.

"Right..."

With his box, coin, rule book, and egg held tightly in his arms, Kellan stood and headed back to his room. While he wanted to see more of Bitso's broadcast, he also wanted to do more reading.

Mavis watched him go, and Kellan hesitated right as he reached the door. "You want to join?" he asked her.

She smirked and then pointed to the balcony with the mana spring. "I'm going to take a dip, and then I'll join you."

He gave her a reverse nod and then entered his bedroom. His egg continued to jostle around. Kellan didn't like that. He carried the giant ball of proto life over to the bed, sat down, and quickly dragged a bunch of blankets over. With little finesse, he made a nest and placed the egg in the middle.

"There," he said. "Now you'll be safe, my little blender."

The egg didn't respond.

Kellan sat close to it and covered the top with another blanket. He wasn't excited for an animal, but a dog would be pleasant. Kellan had always enjoyed dogs. But then his thoughts went back to the golden retriever he had first seen when he arrived in the Nexus. She had been… ripped apart by the Pestbyters. Would his familiar just be a liability?

He shook away the thought.

One problem at a time.

Kellan cracked open his rule book and immediately tried to find something on familiars. It wasn't difficult, but the bizarre translations left him a little baffled.

Each mage can have one family member, familiar.

He had to read that rule several times.

With a laugh, Kellan flipped through a couple other pages, hoping to find something interesting. When he came to the section about arcana, he stopped. Arcana…

Arcana is the secrets from the souls of others.
The Arbiter uses the secrets of the world's deceitful monsters.

Kellan ran his fingers along the words. It had to be a translation error. What was it even saying? Kellan already knew arcana was just people's souls. But why did the Arbiter need it? He was powerful enough. He ruled the Nexus.

The more Kellan read, the more he became intrigued. The last page on arcana read:

Gold reveals the apex of magic.
Great secrets come from gold.
Mighty is the power.

"It's like I'm reading someone's terrible poetry," he muttered to himself. Kellan chuckled as he set the rule book down on the bed. "This wasn't as useful as I had hoped…"

The sound of water splashing filtered into Kellan's room. Mavis, Sen, and Husker had gone into the mana spring, their voices loud enough for Kellan to hear their tones, but not loud enough for him to make out their specific words.

He listened for a short while as they maintained a lengthy conversation.

Fatigue clawed at him. Kellan rubbed his chest, desperate to spend his arcana on travel magic and go to bed.

Although… meta magic did seem more useful. Since Xiang already had travel magic, it probably wasn't good to double up. That was what Sen had been screeching about—since Sen could heal and fleshcraft, why did they need another person who could do the same things?

And the rule book had said meta magic was for people who thought outside the box.

But who would teach him? Kellan didn't know any meta mages. Well, besides Brenner.

Kellan laughed to himself just thinking about asking Brenner for a short lesson.

With a sigh, Kellan rested back on the bed. He decided to stay close to the egg, just in case it needed his body heat. Then he closed his eyes. He'd rest… just for a short while. Just enough to regain some of his energy. Not too long.

Just enough…

To sleep for a bit.

***

When Kellan opened his eyes again, the room was dark.

Thankfully, his eclipse magic prevented that from being a problem. He could see no matter the darkness. He forced himself to sit upright and glance around, his eyelids heavy. The sheets weren't magical—they hadn't forced him into slumber—he had just been exhausted. After a long yawn, Kellan checked on the egg.

It was fine. Still speckled. Still shaking.

Kellan patted it gently and then stood.

He didn't hear any sounds. Not from the mana spring. Not from the rest of the suite.

With his breath held, Kellan exited his room into the common area. The TV was off, the couches were cold, and all the lights were off. No one was here—or perhaps everyone was sleeping. Kellan crept into the room, his eyes on the glass doors to the balcony.

The night sky sparkled with red and white stars. Kellan stood still for a moment to admire them.

Music and shouting—friendly shouts of jovial delight—echoed up from around the AVU Palace. Obviously, people were celebrating and having a good time.

Kellan rubbed his face. He headed for the front door, intent on finding Mavis, but when he passed by Xiang's door, he noticed a flicker of light coming from underneath. He stopped, and then carefully knocked on her door.

No reply.

"Xiang?" Kellan asked, his voice rusty with sleep.

But there was no answer.

Was she awake? Was she gone? Perhaps she was in trouble? Kellan had no idea. He didn't know what to expect.

Kellan tried knocking once more. When he still didn't get an answer, he glanced around and then stepped into the darkness. With his shadow-stepping, he slid under the crack of the door and into Xiang's room.

He exited the void and found himself in a gigantic bedroom complete with a boat-sized bed. Xiang's room came with its own balcony, sitting area, table, desk, and humongous bathroom. It was its own small house—a place away from everyone. Kellan would've loved to have it over his apartment.

After a short moment of glancing around, Kellan eventually spotted Xiang.

She stood out on the large balcony, her attention on the city in the distance. The glass door to the balcony was so clean, Kellan almost hadn't seen it at all.

Someone stood with Xiang. A man.

The moment Kellan saw the other man's information, he almost choked on his own breath.

Name: Alex Kellan the Defector
Race: Concealed
Magics: Concealed
Rank: Concealed
Armor Rating: Concealed
Health: Concealed
Stats: Concealed
Abilities: Concealed

Although the man's basic information was concealed, all Kellan cared about was his name.

It's the alternate me.

The man wore combat tactical gear—heavy cargo pants, chest armor, a tactical turtleneck that went to his chin, thick boots, and armguards. Something on the other Kellan's arm blinked blue, an obvious piece of electronic equipment strapped to his limb. When he moved, it was with purpose and precision. Even from within Xiang's room, a good twenty feet away, Kellan could tell his alternate-self was a man of physical prowess.

Alternate-Kellan stood with his back to the balcony door, almost right behind Xiang. He placed a hand on her shoulder. Xiang leaned into him, her head gradually resting on his chest.

Kellan watched the scene with ever-growing hesitation. Should he leave? Announce himself? A part of him was rapt with fascination. He… hadn't met himself before. Did they even know he was here?

Xiang and the Alternate-Kellan said nothing. Their gazes remained on the distant horizon. After a silent thirty seconds, Kellan shifted his footing back toward the exit.

Then Xiang turned around, wrapped her arms around Alternate-Kellan's neck and pressed her lips against his. Her eyes remained closed as the man pulled her into a tight embrace.

Kellan wasn't sure if he should be proud or jealous. On the one hand—his alternate-self was clearly on top of things. On the other hand—what did his alternate-self have that *he* didn't?

I can't be jealous, Kellan thought, smirking to himself at his outlandish musings. *He's not me. He's just someone else who sort of looks like me. And I barely know Xiang. This doesn't involve me.* Kellan practically chanted the same phrases over and over in his head, trying hard to dispel any sort of negative feelings.

Before Kellan could leave Xiang's room, his alternate-self broke away from Xiang. He turned on his heel, threw open the glass door, and strode into the room.

Kellan held his breath.

Alternate-Kellan…

The right side of his face was gnarled with scars. His right eye was mechanical—similar to Jace's—but instead of a blue light in the center, Alternate-Kellan had gold. His face had been so slashed that his right ear was ripped and fragmented.

Kellan had seen similar wounds before—on animals. They were the type of combat scars someone got from claws, talons, and fangs, not bullets, knives, or knuckles. Had his alternate-self been wrestling with bears? The scars were old—healed and white—and it gave Alternate-Kellan a more *serious* expression than Kellan usually wore.

Tense and unsure of what to do, Kellan didn't move. He had been caught. Surely, Alternate-Kellan would have words for him.

But his alternate-self didn't say anything. He slowed his stride as he approached the door, his gaze narrowing on Kellan. Then he stopped. He gave Kellan the once-over, his half-mechanical gaze homing in on Kellan's dog tags for the briefest of seconds.

They were similar in many ways. The same height, same dark-brown hair and eyes… But Alternate-Kellan was more muscular, much to Kellan's irritation.

"Sorry," Kellan said as he ran a hand through his hair. "I was looking for Xiang. I didn't expect to see you here. I wasn't trying to disturb anything."

Alternate-Kellan said nothing. He just narrowed his eyes into a glower.

He didn't seem to have any weapons on him. No visible rifle or knives.

But Kellan wasn't fooled. The other man carried himself like he could kill half the people in the AVU Palace. But why remain silent? Just an intimidation tactic?

He wore small colored bars on the shoulder of his chest armor. Six bars, all colored silver. He was an S-rank eclipse mage. At least, that was one of his magics and ranks. Which explained why his information was concealed—Husker had said it was the magic of hiding.

"I'm the other Alex Kellan," Kellan said as he held out a hand. "It's nice to meet you."

Alternate-Kellan didn't move.

Since his other-self wasn't cooperating, Kellan opted for sardonic. He tucked his hands into his pockets. "Really? Well, I guess it's good to know that in some dimensions I become a delta-bravo. Really puts things into perspective. If I hang out with men like Brenner, I'll become just like him."

With gritted teeth, Alternate-Kellan grabbed the high neck of his shirt and pulled it down. The scars on his face traveled the length of his neck, all the way to his collarbones. His throat looked mangled—a large chunk was missing down the middle.

Kellan had never seen anyone survive an injury that horrendous. He stared for a few moments, realization dawning on him.

"You can't speak?" he asked.

Alternate-Kellan tugged the neck of his shirt up and offered half a nod. Then he walked past Kellan, grabbed the door handle, and threw it open. He left without a single glance back, or even an indication that he cared about Kellan at all.

To Kellan's surprise, he didn't hear his alternate-self open any other doors. Did he slip into the shadows? Or just go invisible, like Jace? He wasn't sure.

When Kellan turned back around, he tensed again.

Xiang stood a few feet away from him. Her large yellow sweatshirt, skintight pants, and socks were smeared with spots of crimson. Had someone been bleeding? But Kellan didn't see the evidence for long. Once he blinked his eyes, all the red was gone—most likely concealed behind illusions.

Kellan motioned to the door. "I'm sorry. I didn't mean to come in here and see anything. I just woke up, and I wanted to speak with you about magic, and the lights were—"

"It's fine," Xiang said, curt. Her eyes never lifted to meet his. She stared at the floor, her gaze practically drilling a hole in the carpet.

After a short exhale, Kellan asked, "Are you okay?"

Xiang fidgeted with the sleeve of her baggy sweatshirt. Her new outfit wasn't as elegant or powerful as her suit or robes. She almost looked like she was cosplaying a pile of laundry…

She was more down to earth. Kellan preferred it.

"Did he just break into your room or something?" Kellan asked. "Was he bothering you?"

Xiang finally glanced up. With a cold smirk, she said, "I knew he'd come. It's exactly his and Brenner's style to do something like this. I just… I didn't expect him to be so soft. Not after the last time we saw each other."

"Maybe he wants to make things right. He seemed pretty happy to see you."

Xiang brushed back some of her black hair, her expression shifting to amusement. "Oh, I sincerely doubt it. I suspect he came here hoping to hurt me. Or trying to manipulate me with false promises."

Wow. I really am a delta-bravo.

But Kellan didn't know what else to say. "Sorry," he muttered. "Exes can be… difficult." He almost added, *At least you'll get a chance to kill yours*, but he held back. Xiang probably wasn't in the mood for humor.

Her gaze remained distant, her posture weak. Something had happened, yet she refused to talk about it. Instead, she said, "Once upon a time, Alex wasn't like that at all. And I think… if I hadn't gotten together with Brenner, maybe all our futures would've been different…"

"How?"

But she didn't reply. Xiang seemed lost in her whirlpool of thoughts. Was she drowning in doubt? Kellan knew the look.

He cracked his knuckles together.

"So, about travel magic," he said. "Are you still willing to teach me?" Any excuse to change the subject was preferable.

Xiang stepped closer to him, her movements slow. "Alex," she said under her breath. "Would you do me a favor? Just for a moment."

"What is it?"

"Forgive me, but… just for a moment." Xiang placed her hands on his chest and leaned against him. "I'd like to pretend."

Kellan remained stiff and unmoving as Xiang rested her cheek on his shoulder. He didn't know what to say and pushing her away seemed callous. Could he let her pretend? What did that entail? Using him like a stand-in for someone else?

Xiang said nothing. She didn't try to embrace him, or kiss, or touch him in any way other than her hands on his chest. Kellan eventually relaxed, though it required effort. He placed a hand on her shoulder, letting her know it was okay, but nothing more.

Several minutes went by in silence.

She smelled good. Kellan tried not to think about it.

The moment Xiang moved away, Kellan took a step backward, feeling a bit more awkward than he liked.

"So, that travel magic," he said with a forced chuckle. "It would be great to learn."

Xiang rubbed her eyes. "Yes. It would be a boon." Then she turned on her heel and faced away from him. "And thank you. I needed that."

"Sure," Kellan said. He was about to add *anytime*, but he held back.

"Travel magic is complicated, but once I've revealed its secrets, you'll be able to advance your ranks without me."

He nodded once. "Thank you. Uh, can we learn now?"

Xiang glanced over her shoulder and smiled. "Of course."

—Chapter 45—
—My Blender Hatched—

Kellan wasn't sure what time it was. The night sky outside and beyond the balcony told him it was evening, but wasn't the next game starting in the morning? How long would it take Xiang to teach him?

"Magic is born from your soul," Xiang said.

"Okay." Kellan crossed his arms and mulled over the statement. "What does that even mean?"

"It means you can't learn new magic like you would learn a new language. Think of new magics as a tattoo you'll mark your soul with—something that alters you forever. Since I have travel magic, I can mark your soul with the same type of energy, allowing you to gain access to travel."

Kellan hadn't wanted to think of it like that. He had a tattoo—a single mark on his shoulder blade—that he had gotten when he joined the Delta Force, but that was it. The thought of changing his soul didn't sit right.

"Before I get this tattoo… What do you think about meta magic?"

"It's not an actual tattoo. It's metaphorical." Xiang walked over to the edge of her bed and then turned around, her eyes narrowed. "You know someone who will teach you meta magic?"

"No. I was just asking. I've been giving this a lot of thought." Kellan rubbed at the side of his head. His sleep had been irregular, and he felt off. "Just tell me—what do you think about it?"

"Meta magic is the magic of magics. A powerful tool for any mage."

Kellan still liked the sound of that. Versatility had been his gimmick so far, even if Bitso scolded him for it. But since he couldn't plan for specific encounters, he wanted options to get himself out of trouble.

"What if I found someone in the AVU Palace to teach me meta? Do you think meta would be better than travel?"

Xiang's skeptical expression never waned. She crossed her arms. "I don't think you'll find anyone willing to teach you. Other teams will consider you an enemy. We should just stick with this plan and move on. Travel magic will give you powers that other mages will find impossible to deal with."

Any sort of edge would be advantageous.

Kellan nodded once. "All right. I'll stick with my original plan. Teach me."

Xiang held out a single hand. "Here. Close your eyes and place your palm on mine. You'll feel energy, but don't be afraid. Use your arcana and allow your soul to be altered."

Although the situation felt off to him, Kellan exhaled, stepped forward, and placed his hand on her palm. Her touch… reminded Kellan of the first time he saw her. Something about her magic was off.

Was it her hex? Kellan didn't know.

He closed his eyes. The arcana cost…

Cost to Learn E Rank Travel Magic: 5 arcana

Something clawed at his chest, deep beyond his ribcage. In his mind's eye, he could see the magic, just like he had with eclipse, metal, and body. He *knew* travel magic was about escaping everything—even his current reality. It was about distance, space, evasion, breaking things apart…

And Kellan could see the first couple E-rank powers.

Travel—E-Rank Powers

Teleport, rank I [1 arcana]

Teleporting is the signature ability of the travel mage. It is the ability to fold space so that "here" and "there" are one and the same. At E rank, the mage's ability to do so is extremely limited, but can be crucially useful in a few situations.

The mage spends a mana, and teleports one foot per point of wisdom.

Store Object [1 arcana]

One of the travel mage's key abilities is the ability to master the extra-dimensional space formed from the connection between the mage and the Sea of Chaos. At this early level, the travel mage may store things in a pocket dimension housed in the mage's very shadow.

While the mage is holding an object, they may spend a mana and store an object up to person sized in their shadow. The mage may later withdraw the object from his shadow without spending mana. The mage can store up to travel rank number of objects (E = 1, D = 2, C = 3, etc.).

Collect [1 arcana]

The mage gains the ability to teleport an object straight into their hand.

The mage may spend mana and teleport any object, up to a pound per point of wisdom, to their hand from up to twenty feet away.

Blink, rank I [5 arcana]

The mage's understanding of teleportation and their spatial awareness means that they can dodge incoming attacks by shifting away from them, even if the attack would otherwise hit. The mage "blinks" out of existence for a single second, allowing the attack to pass harmlessly through the area they once occupied.

The mage has a static 10% chance to avoid all aggressive, non-AOE (area of effect), actions, including beams of magic, bullets, swords, arrows, and strikes.

And while these powers seemed amazing, Kellan still felt off. It wasn't the travel magic, per se—it was Xiang. Something about *her* magic made Kellan uneasy whenever he felt it. And since she was "teaching" him the magic, it was like whatever she had would come to him, like a sickness or disease.

Kellan yanked his hand away before he could learn travel magic.

He opened his eyes and rubbed at his wrist, the feeling of connection leaving him.

"What happened?" Xiang asked, curt.

"Something is wrong," Kellan said. "I don't know enough about *magic* to articulate what, exactly, I'm feeling. I just know it's not right."

"You're being difficult. It's unbecoming."

Kellan narrowed his eyes. "If you know what's going on, I'd love to hear it."

Xiang waited for a moment, silence growing between them. "I assume you're just nervous," she finally said. "There's no other explanation for your hesitation."

That wasn't the answer. Kellan didn't know what was going on, but he knew when people were bullshitting him. He turned for the door. "Never mind. I need time to think about this."

Instead of opening the door, Kellan slipped into the shadows and left under the crack, just like how he had entered.

When he stepped out of the darkness, he found himself in the common room of the suite. His stomach twisted, and he felt grimy from his awkward sleep, like sweat had crusted over his skin.

Kellan scratched at his arms and went straight for one of the many bathrooms in the suite. The shower, tub, and two sinks offered enough in terms of water, but the containers of "soap" disturbed him. They looked like wooden frogs, carved in such a way as to appear gutted. They were just bowls, and the insides were filled with creams and soap, like someone had a sick sense of humor.

Without dwelling on it, Kellan closed the door, locked it, and quickly set to the task of bathing. The sick feeling he had gotten when he had touched Xiang hadn't left him, and as Kellan stood under the showerhead, he closed his eyes and scratched at his arm, trying to get the sensation to leave.

After several minutes, he felt normal again.

Kellan sighed, finished with his frog-gut soap, and then dried himself with a towel the size of a blanket. He had no idea which dimension everything here came from, but it was bizarre.

As he got dressed, Kellan hesitated over the dog tags. Did they belong to Alternate-Kellan? Obviously. Jace and he had some history together. They both had the mechanical eye. *Why did Jace have the dog tags?*

Kellan threw them around his neck and then finished with the remainder.

Boots. Cargo pants. Shirt. A bizarre coin. He had armor… When Kellan reached back and felt his spine, he remembered that the piece of futuristic tech was somehow part of his body, giving him armor whenever he activated it.

Satisfied he had everything, Kellan exited the bathroom.

To his surprise, Mavis stood in the middle of the common room, her attention on the black screen of the TV. She glanced over as Kellan walked into the room. For a long moment, she just stared.

"You were with Xiang earlier," Mavis said, her attention drifting to the bathroom. "You two have a good time?"

Kellan fought the urge to laugh. "As fun as a car accident."

"You don't have to hide anything from me. I get it. She's very beautiful." Mavis crossed her arms and leaned away. "I can handle the truth."

Kellan tapped his side with a balled fist. He mulled over how he would word everything and decided instead on frank honesty. "Look, I'm not very good with relationships. You know that. You saw my apartment. The only women I've been with are mostly one-night stands."

She lifted an eyebrow.

"I'm not the type of guy who gets involved in whatever Xiang is doing. I went into her room to learn magic, she was with… the other me… and I tried to talk to her afterward about it, but I had all the charm of a lamp, and basically just stood there while she fantasized about another man." He sarcastically gave her a single finger-gun. "Nothing is going on between us."

Mavis couldn't seem to stop herself from smiling. She rubbed at her chin, trying to hide her mirth, but it just wouldn't work. "The way you phrase things… Did you take classes on being that self-deprecating and sardonic?"

Kellan walked over to one of the long couches and leaned against the back. "You're the only one that seems to laugh at all my jokes. I just assumed you had a terrible sense of humor."

With a single chuckle, Mavis walked over to the opposite side of the couch and smiled. "Never had a long-term relationship, huh?"

"Longest was six months." Kellan rubbed at the back of his neck. "But then work demanded too much of my time. She left. I don't blame her." He stared at Mavis for a brief moment before asking, "You?"

Mavis glanced away. "I had someone."

"And?"

"That was when I was hit with that homebrew grenade. I was hospitalized, and the doctors said I might have to use a wheelchair or cane for the rest of my life." Mavis's voice grew softer and slower. "A few days later… My fiancé left. He didn't even wait to see if I'd make a full recovery."

Kellan absorbed the information and nodded. "Joke's on him. Now you're a superhero."

Mavis blushed. As if to hide it, she turned away from him, her hands on her hips. "Yeah, well, I'm starting to like Sen, even though he seemed weird at first. He gave me the ability to walk right again. Now, if I ever do see my ex, I can't wait to show him."

"I'd like to see the look on his face, too."

"Oh, yeah?" Mavis walked around the couch and stood next to him. "I don't know. You come with a lot of baggage. You have a giant egg you need to take care of."

Kellan smirked as he stood straight. "What? You don't want to help me raise a baby blender?"

Again, Mavis couldn't seem to stop herself from smiling and laughing.

Out of all the women Kellan had been flirtatious with, Mavis was different. She had the pragmatic sensibilities of a soldier, while retaining the good nature of a comedy club audience. It made it easy to speak with her, even if Kellan had all the charm of a lamp.

But thinking about the egg reminded Kellan…

"I should probably have food on hand for when it hatches," he said.

Mavis calmed herself and rubbed her eyes. "I'm impressed. Maybe raising an egg wouldn't be so challenging with you."

Although he'd love to spend another hour joking, Kellan walked back to his bedroom and went straight for the egg. It was exactly where he had left it, curled up in the blankets, jostling around.

"I know where the food is," Mavis said from the common room. "I'll be right back with something."

Kellan voiced an acknowledgement and patted the top of the egg. His thoughts went straight to his eclipse powers. He could make his shadow its own *thing*, but the description had said it would cut down on his familiar's growth. At the time, he hadn't understood, but now he knew.

With careful motions, Kellan picked up the egg and held it. Then he sat on the bed and relaxed.

The next game would begin soon.

The TV mounted to the far wall was blank. A subtle reflection of the room was all Kellan had to watch. When would Bitso announce the rules? And what was Kellan going to do with his seventeen arcana in the meantime?

Perhaps I should just return to Xiang and learn travel magic. Maybe I was overthinking things, like she said.

Before Kellan came to a decision, Mavis walked into the room holding a handful of jerky. It was dark brown and curled, almost like bacon. What was it? The mystery meat confused Kellan. He didn't ask—he just took it from Mavis and placed it next to the egg.

And incentive for hatching.

"We should probably get some sleep soon," Mavis muttered. She sat on the edge of the large mattress and turned back to Kellan. "If you don't mind… Can I stay in here again?"

"You gonna help me raise this?" Kellan quipped, holding his egg close.

Mavis smiled. "Only if I get to name it."

"I suppose." Kellan patted the bed next to him. "But now you're stuck with me and all my terrible or dark jokes."

Mavis scooted up on the bed until she was right next to Kellan's side. "I can think of worse punishments."

***

Although Kellan had already napped previously, exhaustion still claimed him. His dreamless sleep had instead been filled with vague feelings of unease. The partying around the AVU Palace had offered random noises throughout the night, but most of it was ignored and forgotten.

Kellan hadn't felt the need to celebrate.

And once he was asleep, nothing seemed important enough to wake for.

"Good morning, Fayetteville!"

The announcement almost didn't pull Kellan from his slumber. He rolled over, caught in the blankets of the bed, his head foggy. Mavis was there, tucked in his arm. Kellan blinked several times and then sat up.

"This is the morning news!"

Bitso's overly exuberant voice was a calm reminder of everything that had happened.

No, the first game hadn't been a nightmare.

Yes, he was stuck in a death game, fighting in some alternate dimension with mages and high-tech weaponry.

None of this would go away until he handled it.

After reaffirming his situation in his head, Kellan felt more awake. He had to get up. He had to do this. The games wouldn't wait for him.

"Wasn't last night refreshing?" Bitso asked with a laugh. "The Arbiter's parties are the best in the Nexus. The glitter potions will help everyone stay focused in today's game. Be careful, though… The recipe for those is rather frightening." He punctuated his statement with another wild round of laughter—more so than most.

Kellan had no idea what he was talking about. Parties? Glitter potions?

He shook his head and kicked his feet off the bed.

Eggshells fell onto the floor. Kellan held his breath as he stared at them all. He stood, and then threw off the blankets. More eggshells.

But the jerky was gone.

Mavis got onto her elbows. "It's morning?" Sun streamed in from the far window. She glared at it. "What're you doing, Kellan?"

"I lost my blender," he muttered as he glanced under the bed.

"But onto more important things," Bitso said once he calmed his lunacy. This morning, his suit was crisp, and his blindfold clean. He looked better than he had in days. "I'm your designated host, here to deliver you information straight from the Arbiter. It's 8:30, and it's time for the rules of the second games."

Mavis jumped off the bed, her eyes wide. "Holy shit. It's already time for the games?" She rubbed at her purple hair, half of it squished to one side, pasted in place with sweat. "Husker said he would train me in the morning, before we heard the rules. I should've gotten a wake-up call or something."

Although Kellan had the same amount of panic as Mavis, he still couldn't find the creature that hatched from the egg. He stood up and ran a hand through his hair. Then he noticed the blankets moving.

Something was crawling around through the sheets.

Something the size of a house cat.

—Chapter 46—
—The Rules of the Second Game—

Kellan yanked the blankets off the bed.

A monster tensed and stared up at him, frozen with wide eyes. It was… some sort of lizard. Its back legs had large talons, and its front legs doubled as wings, leathery and folded in on themselves, like scrunched umbrellas.

And its scales…

They were a pale, sickly white.

Its eyes…

They were a disgusting mix of pink and red, and its pupil were slits, like a snake.

The monster swished its tail, and that was when Kellan noticed the scorpion stinger at the tip. It was a bizarre creature, both in coloration and physical appearance. Nothing Kellan imagined. He would've been happier with a blender.

"I'll be right back." Mavis grabbed her pants off the floor, and then smoothed her shirt in place. "I need to speak with Husker."

Before Kellan could gather his thoughts, she ran from the room. He tried to motion to the beast on the bed, but Mavis didn't have the focus for anything else. Alone with the monster—and Bitso on the TV—Kellan sighed and just stared at the animal on the bed.

"I hope everyone got enough rest," Bitso said with a smile. "I know I did. One sip of lani rum, and it's four to six hours of nightmare-filled sleep. Really makes you appreciate your wakefulness, let me tell you. This is probably the first day I've appreciated the light of our godforsaken sun."

Although Kellan wasn't looking at the TV, he could see the broadcast in his mind's eye. Bitso with his distinct appearance, the creepy backgrounds, the bizarre setting. Kellan imagined it while he kept his eye on the monster.

It shifted two feet toward the headboard, as fast as a lizard across hot rock.

Kellan tensed and then glanced over at his rifle. Would he have enough time to grab it and then shoot the white-scaled lizard?

"I can't wait to announce this round of games. They're some of my favorites."

Kellan inched toward his weapon as the monster slithered itself under his pillow. Then it poked its nose out and frantically sniffed, as though frightened. Kellan exhaled and forced himself to relax.

It was a newborn, even if it was a newborn monster.

"Hey, little guy," Kellan said as he moved closer to the bed. He held his hand out, his fingers grazing the edge of the mattress. "I'm not going to hurt you."

The lizard pulled its nose under the pillow, out of view.

"As just a reminder, each team leader will have three game types to choose from." Bitso's enthusiasm couldn't be understated. He chortled with a hint of lunacy. "A lot of strategy goes into the decision. Whatever the team leader decides, the entire team will have to abide by it."

Kellan stared at the pillow, wondering if the animal would move.

"The PvE game this time around will be *Yami's Horde*. That's right! Everyone's favorite game as a child, right? Only, instead of the ugly kid playing the yami, the Arbiter has graciously provided several of his own. All dragons. All fearsome. One of them is even undead. What a hideous sight—nothing is worse than undeath, let me tell you."

Yami's Horde? Kellan had never heard of it, but he barely paid attention. Due to the fact that he had attacked Jace, his team wouldn't be participating in the PvE competition. Whatever happened in that game wasn't his concern.

"Players will have to find the three dragons and raid their treasure without getting caught. And trust me, you definitely don't want to get caught. The Arbiter has created each of these yami with eyes that can kill—their stone gaze will stop your heart and render you a statue. Such a fast and painless death. Only a lucky few will experience it, since the dragons will be hidden behind traps. Wonderful, agonizing traps."

With a sigh, Kellan used his thumbnail to slice open the tip of his ring finger. Blood beaded out of the wound, but then a single Tyranny Worm wriggled out of his skin and healed the slice in an instant.

The one droplet of blood was all Kellan needed. He held his finger close to the pillow.

"C'mon," he muttered. "Come out here. Nothing will happen."

The lizard monster poked its nose back out from under the pillow. Then its black tongue flicked out of its mouth. After a short moment, the creature yanked itself out from under the pillow and hurried forward to Kellan's finger.

It bit his finger trying to grab the droplet of blood.

Kellan grimaced, but he didn't yank his hand away. The worms would heal him. What did it matter if the lizard took a few more slurps of blood?

The lizard gnawed on Kellan's finger, its teeth like little needles. The pain was surprisingly harsh, and the longer the monster chewed, the more Kellan's arm was bombarded with shooting agony.

Kellan spent a point of his mana and activated *Ignore Pain*.

It was a quick dose of soothing relief. No more agony. No more pain.

He felt the lizard gnawing, but Kellan didn't get any of the suffering.

Kellan had six mana remaining—but he knew he could visit the mana spring before the game started.

The lizard made a cute clicking noise as it slowed its teeth and gradually just drank Kellan's blood. The worms in Kellan's body constantly repaired the teeth wounds, and the lizard chewed to break open the skin another time.

While the monster was distracted, Kellan carefully reached over with his other hand and petted the beast. Its cold scales were smooth, and its leathery wings were soft to the touch. The monster stared up at him, its pupils slowly growing larger, until they were circular, and almost as big as the entire eye.

Kellan couldn't help but smile.

"You're adorable," he muttered. "Don't tell anyone I said that, though."

More clicking noises.

Was it happy? Kellan had no idea. He wasn't good with animals. They had never interested him much.

"The second game is a PvP classic."

Kellan turned to the TV, giving Bitso his full attention. There was less than thirty minutes until the start of the game. Whatever rules Bitso laid out, Kellan would have to form some sort of strategy and discuss it with the rest of the team.

The TV screens behind Bitso in the newsroom had been replaced with crude drawings, all of which were done with crayons. The dragons behind Bitso were rather amusing—one was a skeleton, but drawn with all the expert skill of a six-year-old.

The wall behind Bitso was wheeled away, and a new one was brought in by off-screen helpers. This new wall had equally terrible drawings, some of which were comically over-the-top, including one with a picture of a man exploding outward, his eyes giant Xs.

"The PvP match for game two is none other than *Infection*," Bitso said as he motioned to the pictures. First, he pointed to one at the top—a picture of stick figures all standing together and smiling. "Once all the teams have entered the game arena, ten *lucky* individuals will start with the infection. If they touch someone, the infection will leave them, and transfer to their target."

Bitso's finger lowered to the second drawing.

Some of the stick figures were frowning.

"Each infection has a strict time limit." Bitso waggled his finger. "Three hours. And that timer doesn't start when you get the infection—it starts from the beginning of the game. At the end of the three hours, whoever has the infection…"

Bitso pointed to the next picture—the one of the exploding man, and his Xs for eyes.

"They die." Bitso smiled so wide his sharp back teeth became blatantly noticeable. "And then the key will appear. It'll be in the pile of their useless organs."

Kellan held his breath, unsure of what to make of this.

"Oh, but I can already hear some of you asking questions." Bitso dramatically frowned and laid his head down on his desk. "I hate questions. Why can't people just be satisfied?" He sighed and held up a hand, his thumb and fingers pressed together like a sock-puppet mouth. "*What happens if I kill someone who is infected?*" Bitso said the whole sentence in a mock-child's voice, his hand opening and closing along with the words.

Then Bitso lifted his head and smiled.

"Good question." He slammed a fist on the desk. "If you kill someone who is infected, the key is lost forever. The keys will only appear at the end of the three hours, and only from the exploded remains of the poor sad sacks who couldn't tag anyone else before the timer runs out. So, I suppose if you want to limit the number of keys... The infected could make for nice targets."

He slammed his head back on the desk and lifted his hand up a second time. Blood wept out from under his blindfold, staining the metal of the desk.

"*What if I have a magical ability or item that prevents instant death effects?*" The child-like tone grated Kellan's ears.

Bitso lifted his head. Apparently, he had slammed his forehead so hard, his skin had busted open, causing a waterfall of crimson to run straight into the blindfold and then over his left cheek.

"Good question," Bitso said, completely ignoring his self-inflicted injury. "When the infection triggers, your ability will activate, and the key will be nullified, reducing the number available."

Without warning, Bitso slammed his head down again, a sickening *thwap* sound echoing throughout the newsroom, like raw meat thrown onto a counter. The puddle of blood on the desk had been large enough that splatters went everywhere. Some even landed on the crayon drawings.

He lifted his hand again. "*What if someone with an infection touches another person with an infection?*"

Bitso raised his bruised and raw head. "What an interesting question. Where do you chumps come up with this stuff?"

Slam. His hand puppet returned.

"*I just want to know if one person can have multiple infections!*"

With a deranged laugh, Bitso lifted his head. "As much as I'd *love* to see someone *extra explode*, you cannot infect someone who is already infected. I apologize."

Kellan could hardly believe that he was watching a man have imaginary arguments with himself. Then again, he could hardly believe most of what was going on—a man having a conversation with himself was the least insane thing happening in the Nexus.

"The last game is another quick and dirty spectacle," Bitso said, though with less enthusiasm. "Each team who signs up for *Death Pit* will send their Straggler into a large pit. Technically, there's a way out—but it's hidden. The Stragglers will have five minutes to escape or be killed when the pit collapses in on itself."

Bitso slapped his hands together for dramatic effect.

Then he leaned on the edge of the desk and sighed. "There's a key at the end of the secret passage for anyone who makes it out. Or—to make things interesting—if only two Stragglers are alive in the pit when the five minutes is up, they'll both be rewarded with keys. How generous of the Arbiter."

A part of Kellan thought the five minutes of stress would be enough to kill people already. Finding a secret passage or killing everyone around him? That "game" would be nothing but madness.

"During the first game, several teams went out of their way to cull others." Bitso pointed to a few drawings off to the side. They were covered with red crayon marks and nothing else. "The Arbiter thinks this is a smart move. The weak don't deserve to win the Nexus Games, after all. Only the strongest and the best should have access to Zenith."

Kellan had almost forgotten he was allowing the little white lizard to chew on his finger. He picked up the monster and held it in his arms, cradling it like a cat. The beast clicked and swished its tail, but it didn't fight back or protest.

Bitso snapped his fingers. "And this is round two—which means it's an even-numbered game. That's right, folks. You know what I'm talking about." He leaned his head back, his face so covered in blood, some of it had smeared across his teeth. "This is a *Straggler round.* That means that the Stragglers will not only have to contend with the Kuji, but they'll also have to contend with other players. *No matter the game, Stragglers can be targeted.* And anyone who kills a Straggler will be rewarded with twenty arcana from the Arbiter himself."

Kellan lifted an eyebrow, intrigued by the incentive.

"Keep in mind that every even-number round will become increasingly difficult for the Stragglers… The Kuji will gain extra stats, and some will even multiply… So you might want to watch yourself, weaklings."

Before Kellan could process that added information, Bitso sat up straight.

"Speaking of extra stats! I almost forgot… Players might *want* to be the infected during the PvP match. At least, for a little while. Each infected will gain five to all physicals—strength, dexterity, and fortitude—and their health will count as double. It'll make tagging someone a little easier."

The lizard monster curled up in Kellan's arms and closed its eyes.

Kellan petted its head, his focus shifting from the TV and falling to the floor. What strategy would be best for a game of *Infection*? Hiding? Seeking out someone who was infected and trapping them somewhere?

The latter option seemed… darker than Kellan would've liked.

He turned for the door, but before he reached the handle, it burst inward. Kellan leapt back, his lizard held close.

Mavis stepped into the room. "Kellan?"

He nodded. "What is it?"

Her eyes fell upon the monster, and she frowned. "What is *that*?"

"It's my blender," Kellan quipped.

"*That's* what came out of the egg? It's… disgusting."

Kellan placed a hand gently over the creature's head, shielding its little ears. "Not so loud. He'll hear you."

"This isn't the time to be sarcastic."

"What? He's fine. Look—he's cute. Hold him." Kellan held out the lizard for Mavis to see.

The moment it got close, the creature hissed, and its scales flared. Mavis cringed and backed away. Kellan stepped forward, and then the lizard lifted its scorpion tail and tried to sting her.

Mavis frowned deeply. "I hate this thing."

The lizard hissed louder.

Kellan turned it away from her and patted its head. "Don't say that. You were going to name it, right? It's friendly. So long as you let it eat one of your fingers."

None of his arguments changed Mavis's expression.

"Stop messing around with the animal," she said. "Come with me. Everyone is waiting out in the main room." Mavis turned for the door, only offering one last glance over her shoulder as she sneered at the lizard.

Then she left.

Kellan exhaled and stared down at his monster. It stopped hissing and stared back at him, its pink-red eyes practically glowing.

"Don't worry," he whispered, feeling a little insane himself. "I'm sure she'll change her mind." *It's not like the creature can understand me. Why am I even talking to it?*

But the lizard wagged its tail slightly as Kellan headed for the door.

He needed to focus. They had a game to win.

—Chapter 47—
—Extra Arcana—

The other members of Team 101 were waiting in the common room of the suite.

Sen and Husker stood next to the coffee table. A pile of supplies sat on top, neatly stacked and organized. Both Sen and Husker wore new clothing—more tactical and sleeker, though oddly fitting. Sen clearly had taken some sort of young-teen shirt and pants and secured them with a leather belt. The ends of his pants were rolled up several times. Husker sported a hunting jacket and cargo pants. His didn't fit to his wrists or ankles, however, revealing some of his hex-chains.

Husker looked like a deranged experiment who had escaped from an evil science lab. His red fox fur was matted, and he stood with a slight hunch.

Xiang waited by the front door, her clothing a mix of antiquated and sophisticated. She wore old-world white robes with a giant red cloth belt around her waist and shoulders. It looked complicated, but Kellan suspected illusions were easy to pull on and yank off.

The TV on the far wall continued to play Bitso's broadcast. More odd drawings and statistics were brought up in the background. A pair of dirty hands could be seen at the edge of the screen, drawing Kellan's attention. Who was helping Bitso run the broadcast? It clearly wasn't the Arbiter. Some filthy street urchin?

Mavis walked over to Husker and then glanced at the supplies. "This seems like a lot. We need to move with purpose out there if we're going to participate in the PvP game."

Husker snorted and then motioned to the supplies with a clawed hand. "I'm not entirely familiar with the types of items you and Kellan would prefer. I gathered what I thought was useful, and now the two of you can decide for yourselves."

"Or I can decide for you," Sen interjected. He crossed his little arms. "We don't know what the game arena will be yet, so just in case, we should take some survival staples."

"What do you mean?" Mavis asked.

Then Husker glanced over at Kellan and practically gasped. His ears stood straight as he stomped across the room. Kellan leaned back as the werewolf man got up close, his dog-breath hot.

The lizard in Kellan's arms hissed and flared its scales.

"Your astra egg hatched," Husker said, his tail wagging. "And it's an albino wyvern."

"A wyvern?" Kellan asked, an eyebrow raised.

The *wyverns* Kellan was familiar with were the Westland Wyvern, a single-seat strike aircraft for the Royal Navy, and Wyvern Safety, the airplane data survey group. Neither were a bizarre animal that hatched from giant eggs.

Husker made a clicking noise with his tongue, and the white lizard stopped its hissing. Then Husker petted the creature, slow and gentle, his claws scratching the underside of the lizard's chin.

"Wyverns are relatives to dragons," he muttered. "They have two wings, and two legs, whereas dragons have two wings and four legs. See your albino wyvern's front wings? They look like legs when the wings are folded, but they're much weaker and don't have much muscle, except for the shoulders."

"What if I had a lizard with *no* legs and two wings?" Kellan sarcastically asked, not expecting any real answer.

"Those are called *coatls*," Husker replied with an instructional tone. "Their snake-like body can grow to giant sizes, and their wings are typically feathers."

Sen rolled his eyes. "We don't have time to educate our warrior on the basic concepts of wyverns. They're very common Animals of Pure Magic. He can read about them on his own time."

"Albino wyverns are much rarer than standard wyverns. They're rather venomous."

"Fantastic. He'll at least have an interesting familiar for all our whimsical romps through death traps. Hurray."

Mavis stared at the wyvern with a deep frown. She offered nothing to the conversation other than her blatant disapproval.

"How do I bond with it?" Kellan asked. He held the wyvern up and it clicked it at him. "I want a magical half-dragon if I'm about to run through another post-apocalyptic wasteland of skyscrapers and bird monsters."

Although Kellan wasn't sure how to train or use a wyvern, he liked the idea of increasing his magical options. Surely he would be able to use this beast for something? Even if it was just an escape device or scout or messenger pigeon. Having some options was better than having no options.

"Try to push your mana into the creature," Husker stated. "Similar to how you would use a magical ability." Then he took a step back and waited, his ears still straight and his tail still wagging.

Xiang glanced over, her keen eyes focused on the wyvern.

Not wanting to waste time, Kellan tried to do as Husker instructed. He "pushed" his mana from his hands into the wyvern, visualizing the process as best he could. He liked to think of his mana as a second bloodstream. It made it easy to picture in his mind's eye.

A feeling of acceptance and warmth soaked into Kellan's palms and went through his arms, shoulders, and chest. The sensation caused him to breathe deep, and afterward, the wyvern was no longer a mystery to him.

[Alex Kellan] bonded with an Animal of Pure Magic (rank 1).

His analytical sight even gave him more information.

Name: Vlaze
Race: Animal of Pure Magic [Albino Wyvern]
Magics: Eclipse, Body
Rank: —
Armor Rating: 1 [Scales]
Health: 4/4

Stats:
Strength—1 [Baby]
Dexterity—1 [Baby]
Fortitude—1 [Baby]
Charisma—1
Manipulation—3 [Scary]
Intelligence—1 [Baby]
Perception—3
Wisdom—1
Willpower—2

Abilities:
Hidden—This Animal of Pure Magic hides its magical nature from divination abilities (or A rank or lower). It does not appear magical until it chooses to reveal its nature.

The wyvern stared at him for a long moment, its red eyes a little unsettling, but somehow more friendly than when Kellan had first seen them. And for some reason, Kellan could swear he felt the creature's heart beating, even though he hadn't been able to before.

Kellan smirked. "Its name is Vlaze?"

"He's a boy," Husker stated. "You can tell by the spine on the tail. Females are slightly smaller."

"*His* name is Vlaze?" Kellan said again. "Interesting."

"I'm glad the blender named itself," Mavis muttered.

Kellan examined his wyvern all over. The creature was surprisingly docile as he turned it up and around. "And this thing gets bigger?"

"Yes, it gets bigger," Sen practically shouted, disturbing the whole room. He waved his hands around, and then continued, "We don't have time for this! Do you see the TV?"

Bitso pointed to a paper on the back wall with various numbers. "Last game, mages betting on the outcomes gained five hundred and thirty-seven arcana." He chuckled and scratched at his chin. "Apparently, the biggest winners were those betting on who would and wouldn't die. Which means the second game will be even more entertaining, given that we're playing Infection. Most players try to avoid each other—but some teams make a concentrated effort to cull the infected, limiting the number of keys gained. And who starts as an infected person is completely random chance."

"We need to discuss our plan," Sen said.

Kellan nodded once. "I agree."

Sen opened his mouth like he would protest, but then he quickly shut it. After a short moment, he lifted a finger. "Good. I'm glad to see you're practical."

"Brenner's team will be in the PvP match," Xiang said from the door, no emotion in her voice—no worry, anxiety or fear.

"To nobody's surprise," Kellan muttered.

"My plan is to ignore him, but if we get a chance, to kill him when he's least expecting it." She leaned against the wall and then turned her gaze to the ceiling. "I don't know what game arena we'll be given, but it doesn't matter. Once we're in the game, I'm going to give us all illusions—my most powerful, especially."

"What kind of illusions?" Mavis asked, her eyes narrowing.

"I'm going to disguise our identities. Instead of Team 101, we're all going to look like Team 42."

It took Kellan only a second to piece together her plan. He half-laughed as he said, "Wait, you're going to make us look like Brenner's team?"

Xiang glanced over. "Correct. I'll play the part of Brenner, Mavis will play the part of Ysa, Sen will play the part of HR-8, Husker will be Viniss, and you'll… You'll be yourself."

"Why?" Mavis asked before anyone could add any commentary.

"Team 42 has already made a name for themselves. They're killing the competition, which means most other teams will avoid them at all costs. If the other teams think *we're* them, then they'll avoid us as well. We can focus on finding someone who is infected and leave the rest to slaughter each other."

Kellan nodded along with her words. It made sense. Xiang had made a lot of enemies—many of the contestants didn't seem to like her, and if they found Xiang in the middle of a PvP match, Kellan was certain Team 101 would be dragged into a fight. But if they looked like Brenner and his team of goons, then their fighting would be limited.

Then again…

"If someone does fight us, we're going to have a *rough* time," Kellan stated. "They'll be pulling out tricks meant for high-ranking mages. Stuff we can't handle."

His wyvern made a clicking noise as if agreeing.

"That's why my plan involves avoiding the other competitors, even disguised as Team 42." Xiang brushed back her black hair. "I didn't want to have to use this tactic this early in the games… I wanted to save it for a competition later… but I don't think we'll make it to later games unless we use this now." Xiang turned her attention to the door. "Which is why I need you all to focus on gathering arcana. Our low magical ranks will hinder us in the long run."

"How will people figure out we're illusioned?" Mavis asked with a shrug. "It seems to me like we'll get away with it so long as we're not caught red-handed."

"Bitso will be more than happy to point out our tactics in the recounts," Xiang stated. "The Arbiter wants competitors to know the tactics of other teams—it prevents the same strategies being used over and over for every game."

That made sense, and Kellan was almost sad that Xiang would have to use such an intriguing tactic. It did seem like more of a trump card maneuver… Or did she have other strategies up her sleeve?

Xiang stepped into her bedroom. She returned moments later holding a wooden box with a picture of a mechanical dragon burned onto the top. Without a word, she walked over to Sen, unlatched the box, and then opened it for him.

A red glow emanated from the inside of the container.

"Take three," Xiang said.

Arcana.

Sen took three crimson crystals and absorbed them through his hand.

Then Xiang walked over to Husker. "Take two."

Husker nodded as he reached into the box and absorbed two arcana.

When it came time for Mavis, Xiang held the box out a little further. "Take five," she commanded. "You need to grow a lot more than the others. You're behind—a liability."

Mavis clenched her jaw as she reached into the box. Once she had absorbed her arcana, Xiang pulled the container away and then turned on her heel.

She walked over to Kellan and offered the entire box to him. "Take the remaining. Perhaps you'll use it for travel magic if you ever find the courage to develop it." The instant Kellan took the box, Xiang strode back to the front door, leaving him with an icy silence.

Obviously, she was upset with his decision to leave the other night. Kellan didn't care. He wasn't about to be pressured into learning the magic when it was obviously going to mess with him. Perhaps, if he had long enough with the rule book, he could find something about the unknowable magics that would explain what he had felt.

Or perhaps he could find someone to teach him meta magic.

Either way, he wasn't questioning his previous decision.

After a short exhale, Kellan reached into the box and picked up the arcana.

[Alex Kellan] absorbed 5 arcana.

That brought his total up to twenty-two.

Sitting on it seemed like a waste, however. Wouldn't he need powerful abilities for the next game? *Perhaps I should just learn something to help me get around. There are so many abilities in body and metal I could take…*

Kellan shook his head and decided to wait until the game started. What if the new game arena was filled with specific hazards he had no current way to deal with? He could learn a magical ability to help then.

"The second game is about to begin," Bitso said, drawing everyone's attention.

They only had five more minutes before 9am.

Kellan's wyvern wiggled in his arms. He released the creature and the wyvern dragged himself up onto Kellan's shoulder. The beast sat there like a parrot on a pirate's shoulder, his tail wrapped around the back of Kellan's neck to better steady himself.

Kellan dashed into his bedroom. He quickly grabbed his rifle and backpack. Before he slung everything onto his shoulder, he examined the contents of his pack. He still had the Perfume of the Damned and a bunch of hane cigarettes. Would those be useful? He didn't know. And Kellan no longer had magical blankets in order to barter with.

He ran out of the room and then went straight to the coffee table. Husker's supplies were definitely varied. They had rope, duct tape, a lighter, a few knives—and some feminine products. *How considerate of the wolf-man.*

There were also a few bottles of water, and some snack bars, the names and list of ingredients in a language Kellan didn't know. He packed away at least one of everything, though he ignored the extra sets of clothing, blankets, and flashlights. If he needed clothing, he could likely find it among the abandoned buildings, right? And his ability to cause things to light up—along with his ability to see in the dark—negated his need for a flashlight.

Mavis grabbed a duffle bag and filled it with supplies. Husker pocketed a few more items, but for the most part, his tactical coat was always filled.

Sen and Xiang didn't seem to care about the items. They carried nothing, and waited in silence.

"Are we going to split up to look for keys this time?" Kellan asked. "I guess we'll be looking for someone infected this time around…"

"We'll stay together until we find the person," Xiang said, her tone all business. "Then we'll incapacitate them, hide them away, and wait until the key emerges from their corpse. During the wait, we'll gather arcana for ourselves—perhaps in smaller groups."

Mavis placed a hand on her hip. "What if we run into someone from Team 42?"

Xiang turned to Husker. "You'll deal with it."

He nodded.

"What if the Kuji finds us?" Kellan asked, a shiver running up his spine. He still couldn't believe what it looked like. The monster would plague his nightmares for the rest of his life.

"Husker will *also* deal with it."

It seemed a lot to demand of someone who had a hex that killed members of his family, but Kellan wasn't going to argue. It seemed Husker had decided on this path and was willing to follow it. Plus, what other choices did they have?

"It's time!" shouted Bitso from the TV.

Kellan's insides felt like they were being tugged as he teleported out of the suite.

—Chapter 48—
—Infected—

Kellan stumbled forward, his wyvern familiar clinging to his shoulder. His *Ignore Pain* was still active, so even though the creature dug his talons into Kellan's scapula, the agony didn't register, just the wetness of his warm blood.

Husker, Sen, Mavis, and Xiang appeared around him, but Kellan didn't bother paying much attention to them. His focus was immediately glued to his surroundings. He held his breath, shocked by the environment.

They were standing in a room, next to a giant window. The floors were steel grating, the walls were sleek gray metal, the panels so smoothly interwoven, Kellan couldn't tell where one ended, and the other began.

And the window…

It wasn't glass. It was some sort of thick, transparent metal.

And it had to be metal, because they were in space.

Out beyond the room, Kellan saw the stars, the distant sun, and the planet Earth. He walked over to the window—the glass stretched from the floor to the ceiling—and he stared into the black tide that surrounded each twinkling star.

When he turned his focus onto Earth, he spent a long while admiring the bright greens and vibrant blues, all of which were tainted by the red hue of the Net which was placed between him and the planet. The clouds that swirled through the atmosphere were so beautiful, it was like he was staring at a glorious oil painting, everything perfectly arranged.

Kellan's eyes focused on the continent of Africa. Several large bodies of water were in the middle of the giant landmass. That wasn't right. It was like the continent had an inland sea.

This isn't my Earth, Kellan reasoned. *This is the Nexus. A mirror of Earth… but different.*

He glanced around, still amazed by the beautiful construction of the room around them. How was Kellan standing upright? Where was the gravity coming from? Or the oxygen? Where were they?

"This is Overseer Station," Xiang said, her voice distant and laced with awe.

Sen spun in a tight circle, his eyes on the walls and ceiling. "*Overseer Station?* That weird building *above the clouds*? That can't be right. The Arbiter wouldn't want us fighting here, would he?" Sen ran both his hands down the sides of his face. "This must be a mistake."

"What is *Overseer Station*?" Mavis asked. She, too, went to the window. Then she pressed her hand on the transparent metal. "Are we actually in orbit around the planet?"

Husker's legs shook. He bent down and then scratched his clawed hands on the floor, almost like he was a literal dog. "I have no idea what this location is." He sniffed at the floor, and then rested all the way down. "I don't like it. This environment doesn't seem right."

Xiang sighed as she smoothed her old-fashioned robes. "Yes, we're in space. Overseer Station is a facility built on the side of a giant asteroid orbiting approximately 0.003 AU around the planet."

Mavis lifted both eyebrows and turned around. "AU? What measurement is that?"

"Astronomical unit," Xiang answered matter-of-factly. "A single AU is the exact distance between the Earth and the sun. It's used to measure the distance between some celestial bodies in space."

Husker remained on the floor, his ears laid back. If he were human, Kellan would've guessed he was seasick. Did rennic get nauseous easily? Kellan had no idea, but he kept the information in mind as he turned his attention to the vastness of space.

He'd never thought he would ever leave his planet's atmosphere.

"Life is nuckin' futs sometimes," Kellan whispered to himself.

Vlaze, his wyvern, poked his nose in Kellan's ear and made a quiet clicking noise. It almost seemed like he was whispering something, but his tongue tickled, and Kellan pushed the creature away.

"*The Arbiter welcomes you all to Overseer Station,*" a regal and feminine voice said, her voice coming from the walls of the room, no doubt from hidden speakers. "*I am the Control and Security Index—you may refer to me as Cari. For all intents and purposes, I am the AI who controls the systems of Overseer Station.*"

Kellan held his breath as the computer gave her speech.

"*The Arbiter has forbidden me from helping any of the competitors during this Infection Game. Additionally, the Arbiter has disabled my security droids, so while I would ask that you leave the workers, residents, and prisoners unmolested, I have no way to enforce that request.*"

Prisoners? Kellan mulled over the word. Was there a prison on the space station?

"*Finally, the security code for all nonrestricted doors is 1-7-8-2. The codes for all restricted doors are scattered throughout Overseer Station.*" Cari spoke every word with a false cheeriness.

Husker lifted his head and snorted. "I hate these soulless machine people. They have the words of concern, but their cold logic knows no loyalties. The Arbiter has done us a favor by preventing the machine from interfering."

"*Competitors, if you touch any of the computer terminals, the Arbiter has given me permission to answer basic questions about the station.*"

Sen let out a long sigh. He gave the window a brief glance, obviously unimpressed with the sight. He rubbed at his arms, waiting with jittery energy.

"*The starting infected competitors will now be chosen at random. If you are infected, you have a visual manifestation on your neck that will shine even through clothing.*"

Silence followed her statement.

Kellan wondered how many teams had signed up for the PvP match. He also wondered where Brenner was—the man had killed children in an attempt to threaten them, yet he hadn't done anything after the first game. Had he given up on pursuing Xiang?

Then Kellan's neck tingled with bizarre sensations.

Cursed!— Magical Item [Armor]—Shadow of a Dying Star

The curse on your armor has taken its toll. The curse has been broken, and the armor recognizes you as its one true owner.

You have been infected!

At the end of three hours, you will instantly die. In order to transfer this infection, you must touch the bare skin of another competitor. Once you've transferred the infection, the target of your transfer cannot "tag" you back. You can still be infected, but it must come from another player.

Infection Buff

While you are infected, you gain +5 to all physical stats (strength, dexterity, fortitude) and your health is doubled.

The "buff" that applied to Kellan gave him a jolt of energy. In a single second, he felt powerful and fast and unbreakable. It was intense—Kellan liked to imagine it was what taking cocaine felt like.

He ran a hand over his face and closed his eyes.

Alex Kellan the Rulebreaker
Magics: Eclipse, Body, Metal
Rank: D, E, E
Mana: 6/10
Health: 14/14 [Infected]
Unspent Arcana: 22
Strength—9 [Infected]
Dexterity—9 [Infected, Accurate]
Fortitude—8 [Infected, Tough]
Charisma—3
Manipulation—1
Intelligence—2
Perception—5 [Keen-Eyed]
Wisdom—1 [Broken]

Willpower—10 [Defiant] (Halved)

Kellan grabbed at his neck, his heart beating harder than before.

The others all stared at him, their eyes wide. No one said anything, their attention on the glowing red mark on Kellan's neck. He couldn't see the design, but he knew it would be recognizable to everyone in the game. They would avoid him at all costs.

Or worse… they'd try to incapacitate and imprison him, and then wait for the infection to run its course.

Kellan scratched at his chin, smirking out of sheer nervousness. He didn't appreciate starting as one of the infected, and the fact that no one spoke meant they hadn't expected this would happen.

"What does this mean?" Mavis asked as she slowly turned her head to Xiang.

"It means nothing," Xiang stated, cold and precise. She walked over to Kellan, her expression aggressively neutral. "Our plan will actually be easier to execute. Since we have someone with an infection, we can find a weak player, trick them, and then infect them ourselves."

Mavis confidently strode over to Kellan's other side and stood directly next to him, a mere whisper away. She narrowed her eyes at Xiang. "You want us to *trick* someone?"

Xiang forced a smile. "That's right."

"Why?"

"Obviously, so we can win. I didn't think it was a difficult concept. Or would you rather Alex dies in order to provide us the key?"

"Why don't we just fight someone outright?" Mavis asked as she crossed her arms. "We're in a competition. This is a *Player Versus Player* game, apparently, which means everyone knows we'll be fighting one another. Why not just fight? Why hide and do trickery?"

Husker huffed as he wandered over. He pushed Mavis away from Xiang, his fur standing on end. "*Enough.* Fighting should be avoided. *I won't kill more of my family so we can pretend at being honorable.* The other teams won't provide us the same courtesy."

Xiang didn't even reply. She allowed Husker to impart all the passion in the decision.

No one else protested. Even Kellan didn't know what else to say. They didn't have many options. They would utilize their abilities—which involved a lot of illusions—or they could struggle to fight the other mages of the Nexus Games who were armed to the teeth with magic meant to cause mass genocides.

Always play to your strengths, Kellan thought as he remembered the words of his CO.

Xiang lifted her hand and waved it over at Sen. In an instant, an illusion wrapped itself around Sen's small body.

The little boy was suddenly taller, muscled, and armed to the teeth. His head was shaved, and some sort of black mark was branded into the flesh of his skull—literally, *branded,* as if someone had pressed red-hot steel against his flesh.

His black tactical gear was as military as it was practical. A thin vest, heavy cargo pants, and tight gloves. Sen also had a thin metal collar around his neck—something with bizarre writing on the side.

His new face was one marked with stress and scowl lines, his skin a healthy tan, almost burnt. His eyes were as dark as his clothing, almost devoid of emotion.

"You're HR-8," Xiang stated. "Act like him."

Sen—in his new illusioned body—scoffed. "It won't be difficult. The man only ever speaks in grunts." Even Sen's voice had changed. He sounded gruff and raspy, almost like it pained him to utter words.

"You can make people taller?" Mavis asked. She stepped a few paces closer and examined Sen's athletic physique. "Could you have made him shorter? Or invisible?"

"That isn't how it works," Xiang said. She tossed back some of her black hair and then faced Mavis completely. "My illusions are like paints. I can put more on a canvas, but I can't remove the canvas itself. I've just painted a frame around Sen's body—the illusion will move to hide him without any direct thought from Sen itself."

"Oh..."

When Xiang waved her hand a second time, Mavis shimmered and shifted until she looked like someone else entirely. Unlike HR-8, who Kellan didn't know at all, Mavis became Ysa, the insane girl Kellan had met briefly in the AVU Palace.

Mavis now sported a black Mohawk and a sleek suit of skintight armor. Little hexagonal plates lined the outside, giving the armor flexibility.

With a nervous laugh and a smirk, Mavis held out her arms and stared at herself. The shadow around her feet moved a bit—growing bigger and then shrinking smaller.

"You're Ysa," Xiang stated firmly. "She's hyper, insane, and thinks the world is a joke. If in doubt, start screaming at people. And if you must get into conflict, bite someone. Ysa has always been on the feral side."

Mavis touched her lip, nose, and eyebrows, her fingers grazing the dozens of piercings. "Why do these feel real?" she whispered, obviously impressed.

Xiang smiled. "My illusions are quite difficult to detect. Don't worry. If anyone tries to rip one out, you won't feel any phantom pain."

The group admired Sen and Mavis for a few moments, examining the many details Xiang had managed to create in mere seconds. But Kellan wasn't that impressed—he had seen what Xiang was capable of. Instead, he turned his attention to the room. There was a single door out.

And nothing else.

He didn't know his way around Overseer Station. It was a completely different environment compared to a wasteland city. They would be trapped in corridors and fighting in narrow spaces. And there was only so much space. They wouldn't be able to run and hide whenever they wanted.

It worried Kellan, and he wondered if there were any maps of the station nearby.

Perhaps Cari can provide me with that…

"Alex."

Kellan almost didn't recognize his first name. He slowly turned to Xiang. "Yeah?"

"Your turn next. But you need to listen to me." She stepped close, but not close enough to touch him. "Alex Kellan the Defector is mute. If you speak to anyone while you're wearing this illusion, it'll be easy for them to figure you out."

—Chapter 49—

—Brenner Hawke and the Flestiss Dominion—

Although Kellan didn't like the idea of remaining silent, he understood the necessity. He could pretend to be mute, but he suspected it would cause problems if he ever had to interact with anyone for an extended period of time.

"Does the other me know sign language?" Kellan asked, trying to hold back his sarcasm, but failing.

Xiang narrowed her eyes in a glare. "He wasn't born mute." But then her face reddened a bit. "But yes… He does know how to communicate with several visual languages, including ASL."

"Yeah, well, unless your illusions can teach me *that*, I think I'm going to make a poor impersonator."

"He doesn't use it often," Xiang stated. "Brenner and the other members of his team never communicate with him in that fashion. And none of the other teams will ever bother trying to strike up a conversation. You needn't worry."

"What about Vlaze?" Kellan asked. He placed a hand on top of his albino wyvern's head. "Should I just leave him here?"

Xiang shook her head. "All mages may store their familiar in their shadow."

Momentarily taken aback, Kellan mulled over the statement several times. "*Inside* the shadow? Like how I dive into the darkness and move around?"

"No. Familiars may use your shadow as a gateway to a quasi-plane of existence that all mages have. This plane stores their familiars or other soul-bonded items. Think of it as a pocket for a soul." Xiang spoke the words almost like she was explaining something to a child, but Kellan didn't care. He just wanted to know what was going on.

Kellan glanced over at his familiar. "Vlaze? You know what's going on, buddy?"

His wyvern made a clicking noise and then lifted his front arms, unfurling his wings. The wyvern struggled for a few seconds, but then managed to awkwardly fly off Kellan's shoulder, his wings flapping out of sync. Then he dove for the floor. The moment Vlaze hit the shadows, he disappeared into them, like someone diving into a lake.

Then Vlaze was gone.

Kellan knelt and felt the cold metal plates and grating of the space station. Vlaze was nowhere to be seen.

"Why did he fly so weird?" Ysa-Mavis whispered, her strange voice more high-pitched than normal. The Mohawk gave her a punk-rock vibe, even when she was just speaking.

Husker shook his head. "Vlaze is a baby wyvern. That was probably his first time flying."

Obviously tired of the discussion, Xiang waved her hand. An illusion settled over Kellan in an instant. He carried the same scars he had seen on his alternate-self, and his clothing resembled the outfit the man had been wearing last night. Kellan appeared geared up for combat—even his backpack had transformed to be blacker and sleeker.

When he ran a hand over his face, his fingers grazed the gnarly scars and he shivered.

"I can feel them?" he asked, his voice almost identical to his original.

"Don't speak," Xiang stated. "And of course. My illusions are among the best." She turned away, anger in her actions. Then she went to Husker and stood before him.

Ysa-Mavis gave Kellan the once over. Then she smirked. "You look like a helicopter blade hit you in the face."

"Flattery will get you everywhere," Kellan quipped.

"I think it's sexy."

Kellan held up a hand. "Whoa, whoa. Let's not get any more complicated here. Too many people may, or may not, be pining after the other, and if my *other self* finds himself in a love hexagon, I'm going to be very disappointed."

Ysa-Mavis couldn't stop herself from chuckling. When she smiled, her expression took on a lunatic vibe, but Kellan knew that was from the illusions. Ysa was just… insane.

The joke didn't seem to go over well with everyone else, however. Both Xiang and HR-8-Sen shot Kellan glares. Husker didn't seem amused at all. He laid back his ears, almost worried.

"*Mute*," Xiang said, her voice icy.

Kellan replied with a sarcastic salute.

"Better." Then she turned back to Husker. "Viniss Tarkin the Vanguard Queen will be the most difficult to impersonate. The flestiss are a putrid race with alien thoughts. I apologize, but I must ask that you let us speak for you in most instances. I doubt you can convincingly pull off Viniss."

With a slow nod, Husker said, "I understand."

Xiang waved her hand. The illusion she created was the largest one of all, giving Husker—who was already over eight feet tall—another foot of height, along with a few inches on either side of him.

Ysa-Mavis and Kellan both caught their breath. Mavis moved away, practically backing into the steel wall, her eyes wide.

Husker had become… a monster. Or perhaps an alien.

He wasn't human.

His new illusioned body was black and shiny—like it was wet—with no hair or fur at all. He had four legs that ended in points, like a spider, but with sharp limbs. Husker also had four arms—two large and muscled, practically dominating the shoulders, and two small and thin. All four arms ended in hands, but the muscled arms had claws, and the smaller arms had fine, delicate fingers.

The head was the most disturbing. Husker's face had been replaced with some sort of insect or crustacean. He had feelers and movable mandibles, with spines on the chin and head. He looked like some sort of black-skinned spider-crab hybrid, his body giant, his abdomen thick and heavy.

"What is *that*?" Kellan asked.

Xiang placed a finger on her chin as she examined her work. "This is a female flestiss. They're a matriarchal race of mages who jump from one dimension to the other, conquering planets with mages so they can feed their creator."

For a prolonged moment, Kellan just stared at the alien beast. It had to weigh at least 700 pounds. Maybe more. It was huge, and the appendages in front of its mouth—moving and rubbing each other, like deformed hands—disturbed him most of all.

"Why is Brenner on a team with an alien?" Kellan just couldn't understand how it even came to be.

The question silenced the room.

HR-8-Sen, Xiang, and Viniss-Husker all exchanged glances, like they didn't want to have to be the one to answer. Kellan waited, his attention still on the alien. It was part of a race that jumped from dimension to dimension? What other mind-blowing concepts were they going to throw at him?

HR-8-Sen cleared his throat. His masculine and gruff tone was completely different from Sen's child voice, but his word choice and condescension were right on-point for Sen. "Listen. It's a complicated story. You probably wouldn't understand."

Before Kellan could protest, Xiang immediately said, "Brenner and the other Alex Kellan originate from the same dimension. On their world, the United Earth Defense Force built Overseer Station in an attempt to find magical nodes on other planets."

The few statements almost made Kellan laugh. Magic space stations. That was a concept he never thought he'd hear about. *Yet here I am.*

HR-8-Sen didn't protest her explanation. He just waited, silent and glaring.

"Wait," Kellan said, holding up a hand. "Their Earth had magic? And enough technology to build space stations? My Earth doesn't have those things." Well, his Earth technically had the International Space Station, but it was a closet compared to Overseer Station.

"Not every dimension follows the same timeline. They're different. Magic helps people advance technologies faster, since magic can be used as a clean fuel source, among many other useful purposes."

HR-8-Sen waved a hand around—his exaggerated mannerisms giving away his identity for Kellan in a heartbeat. "Brenner and the other Alex Kellan are probably a good twenty years older than you. Their dimension is further along."

Kellan hadn't been expecting that. "They don't look twenty years older."

"Mages age slower than non-mages," Xiang said. "The higher your rank, the longer your lifespan. And since they come from a dimension with magic, I'm sure they also have body mages who alter and elongate lives even beyond that."

The sheer amount that magic was capable of was starting to shock Kellan. He had only seen a tiny fraction of the possibilities, and he wanted to know more, but he knew they didn't have time. They were probably down a good ten minutes of their three-hour time limit, but he didn't want to stop asking questions.

There was an alien in the room. Kellan had to know about the alien. And now he wanted to know how Brenner got in league with one.

Xiang continued, "Now, if you'll stop interrupting… The Flestiss Dominion invaded Brenner's dimension. They arrived in order to harvest the planet Earth and consume the mages there. The United Earth Defense Force tried to fight them off, but Brenner—an admiral at the time—betrayed humanity. He gave the flestiss control of Overseer Station, along with the orbital defenses of the planet."

"And that's why he has the title *Traitor to Humanity*," Ysa-Mavis muttered. She exhaled and crossed her arms. "That's insane."

"Brenner's lunacy didn't end there," Xiang stated. "He aided the Flestiss Dominion in destroying the planet's atmosphere, killing all life on Earth." She shook her head and then turned her attention to the large window overlooking Nexus-Earth. "It's because of Brenner that his home dimension is basically controlled by the flestiss now."

"He helped kill *billions* of people for an alien race of murderers?" Ysa-Mavis forced herself to chuckle, her anxiety bleeding into her tone. "Why?"

"Brenner is a true autocrat—someone who wants power over others. I've no doubt in my mind that the Flestiss Dominion offered him more authority and magic than humanity ever could. And then he took the offer."

"And you were with that guy?"

Xiang tensed and didn't reply.

"You must have terrible taste in men."

"If that's the case, you might want to watch yourself," Xiang stated as she shot Kellan a glower. "The men I've dealt with have always turned traitor."

"What's that supposed to mean?" Kellan asked, balling his hands into fists.

Ysa-Mavis smirked. "Look, my Kellan isn't like the other Kellan, and he's especially not like *Hitler 2.0*. He's different."

Once again, Xiang didn't bother to answer.

HR-8-Sen stepped forward. "He has been different," he muttered in a small voice. "I can attest to that fact. Perhaps we should leave the name calling and accusations off the table. Or at least until our Kellan gives us a reason to use them."

Kellan glared at the man and held up both hands. "Really?"

"I'm just being realistic."

With a sigh, Kellan decided to steer the conversation away from hypothetical betrayals. "So Brenner is playing the Nexus Games with one of the flestiss on his team? Why? I mean, I get he wanted power, so he betrayed the United Earth Defense Force, but… I just… I don't understand why he would *keep* working with them."

"I don't know," Xiang whispered. "It was around that time that… things between us became strained. In more ways than one."

When Kellan glanced around, he noticed that no one met his gaze. They were either staring at the floor, or their attention was on the window. No one knew why Brenner was associating with dimension-jumping genocidal aliens? It seemed… insane. Even for Brenner. What were the aliens going to give him? Or maybe he joined a team with one to help him win the games?

But if they hated humanity so much, wouldn't they hate Brenner as well?

Kellan wished he had answers, but clearly everyone here was ignorant or they just weren't going to say anything.

Viniss-Husker lifted his four arms. "I feel like a lobster." His half-hiss of a voice disturbed Kellan almost as much as Husker's bizarre new form.

"You look like a nightmare," Ysa-Mavis said. "No offense."

"None taken. The flestiss are a plague across all dimensions. I'm loathe disguising myself as one. It's a disgrace. My family would be so disappointed."

The grate of the flestiss voice didn't sit well with Kellan. He lifted his hands and half-covered his ears, trying to block out most of the sound.

"Wait, have the flestiss ever tried to take over the Nexus?" Kellan asked with a chuckle. *What would the Arbiter think of that?*

HR-8-Sen shook his head and snorted. "No. The Arbiter's magic is too strong. His influence over this dimension is nearly absolute. None of the flestiss can deal with a primordial dragon. Instead, they focus on dimensions with weaker levels of magic—where the strongest magics stand little chance against their queens."

Mavis caught her breath. "What about my and Kellan's Earth? Will they come there?"

"No. Your Earth has *no* magic. The flestiss wouldn't want it—unless they just wanted to capture more humans for their pens. But that's highly unlikely."

Again, silence settled between them.

Kellan stared at his "new" body, his thoughts wandering for just a moment. Why was the alternate Kellan helping Brenner? The number of unanswered questions left him baffled. And his other self was almost twenty years older? *I look amazing for being in my mid-forties.*

Without a word to the group, Xiang waved her hand and stitched together an illusion of Brenner Hawke to shroud herself in. Her disguise was just as Kellan remembered the man. Military. Muscled. Almost plain—but confident. Brenner-Xiang wore a suit of armor that was snug to the body and mostly mechanical. It reminded Kellan of Iron Man, except the metal plating was smaller, more flexible, and mostly black.

She kept the helmet open, revealing Brenner's smug face.

A useful mask.

Kellan remembered how the members of Team 77 had fled at the mere presence of Brenner.

"This isn't right," Kellan stated. "Brenner has an aura of *cold* around him. It's from his many hexes, apparently."

Brenner-Xiang lifted an eyebrow. "Is that right?"

The way she said it…

Brenner had used the same phrase, with the same tone. Kellan tensed, a little spooked by how well Xiang could impersonate the man, apparently.

A slight aura of chill filled the space station room. Kellan shivered and rubbed at his arms. Then he glanced down at his bare hands. He was infected. If he touched someone, he would pass it over to them. *I should have gloves, just so I don't accidentally touch someone I don't want to infect, like Mavis or the others.*

"Everyone satisfied with their disguises?" Brenner-Xiang asked.

Kellan had another thought.

He reached into his pocket and withdrew the coin given to him by Hank of Team 80.

It was glowing on one side—which meant it detected illusions nearby.

"Wait," Kellan said. "What about our basic information and stats and all that?" He motioned to his glowing coin. "This apparently detects illusions, and I just get this feeling that the other higher-ranked mages will be able to see our real names, even if we're disguised."

Brenner-Xiang smirked and laughed. Then she motioned for everyone to get close. "You needn't fret. Once I finalize everything, you won't be detected. Trust me. Now get close. I'm only going to do this once."

Once everyone was within a few feet, Xiang snapped her fingers.

[Alex Kellan] is hidden by [Sun Xiang]'s *Grand Illusion*. His basic stats are concealed, and false information will now be shown.

Kellan blinked a few times, and then rubbed at his eyes. When he glanced at everyone, he saw their basic information as though they were the people Xiang had created.

Viniss-Husker was the most intriguing.

Name: Viniss Tarkin the Vanguard Queen
Race: Flestiss
Magics: Mind, Metal, Travel
Rank: Concealed
Armor Rating: 4
Health: 16/16
Stats: Concealed
Abilities: Concealed

The real Viniss knows travel magic as well?

Kellan cursed under his breath. A part of him still wanted Xiang to teach him travel magic, but he knew the odd feeling would deter him. He had twenty-two arcana. What was he going to do with it?

He shook his head and glanced down at the coin.

It wasn't glowing.

Her illusions have tricked the magical item… Sen said mind and eclipse magic could do that.

Kellan was momentarily impressed. Now they really were Team 42, and no one would know the difference unless they revealed themselves.

"Come," Brenner-Xiang said. She strode toward the lone door out of the room. Then she stopped next to it and placed her hand on the wall. A screen—that had been hidden to look like the wall—appeared under her hand. "One, seven, eight, two."

The door opened with a soft *whoosh*, so fast it was almost startling.

"We're to stick together until I say otherwise," Brenner-Xiang stated. Then she stepped out into the massive corridor. "This way."

Ysa-Mavis, HR-8-Sen, Viniss-Husker, and Kellan all went out with her, each walking with a stiff gait. Kellan suspected the disguises were awkward for everybody. The thought of getting caught haunted him, but not as much as his desire for gloves, or a way to rid himself of the infection.

Once they all entered the hall, the door slammed itself shut.

The corridor of the space station reminded Kellan of an Apple Store. The observation room had been gray and plain, with a single window and nothing else. The corridor was white and sleek, and the bulbs overhead were a faint blue. Everything felt calm and cold, like there was no rush to do anything, even though the countdown on his life had already begun.

"Wait," Ysa-Mavis said. She held out her left hand. The number *42* was right where it needed to be. "Who is Team 42's Straggler?"

None of them had the skull mark.

Brenner-Xiang glanced between them and then pointed to HR-8-Sen. "You. HR-8 would definitely be the one they picked to be made the Straggler."

"I agree," her brother said. "Viniss no doubt considers him disposable."

The statement didn't sit well with Kellan. It only reminded him that the flestiss had apparently killed all of humanity in some other dimension. Clearly, they weren't to be trusted.

Brenner-Xiang waved her hand, and a skull appeared on the back of her brother's illusionary hand. Now that they were finally ready, they hurried forward, toward the end of the corridor, and three other doors that led deeper into the space station.

—Chapter 50—
—Trap Room—

When Team 101 reached the end of the corridor, Brenner-Xiang glanced between the three available doors. Each had a computer screen next to it, but nothing was displayed. The screens just glowed a faint blue, pulsing with power, as if waiting for input.

She stared at the doors, quietly contemplating something.

The space station rumbled. Everyone kept their footing, but Kellan already knew what this meant. The game had begun—other teams were already blowing their way through the Arbiter's obstacles, no doubt leaving a wake of destruction and blood in their path.

Kellan glanced around, taking note of the pristine corridor and how it was different from their original room. Was the space station an amalgamation of the same space station from multiple different dimensions? Just as Nexus-Fayetteville had been a mix of several Fayettevilles, some more twisted than the others?

It had to be.

Kellan glanced over at Husker's hideous alien body. The multi-arms were segmented, like an insect. The legs clicked on the ground as he walked, similar to a crab. The illusionary disguise reminded Kellan of a sci-fi horror movie.

He had seen multiple races during his time in the Nexus, but they had all been humanoid. The flestiss were clearly… not. They appeared more like insect lobsters, and Kellan wondered why. How were all the other races so similar, but these beasts were closer in appearance to yami?

Viniss-Husker met his gaze, his eyes shiny and black, like pools of oil.

"Yes?" Husker asked, his illusioned voice grating.

"I was going to ask about Vlaze. What do you think he can do for us?"

A moment later, Kellan's shadow-stepped out across the beautiful white floor. He wheeled on his heel, shocked by the event. Then Vlaze leapt out of the darkness and landed near his feet. Vlaze stared up with his pinkish-red eyes.

Vlaze flicked his tongue out and nuzzled Kellan's boot.

"Hey, buddy," Kellan said as he knelt down to pet his familiar. "What're you doing? How did you get out of the shadow?"

Viniss-Husker snorted. "Your familiar can hear things from his shadow pocket. When you call his name, he'll come to you."

"Interesting. Good to know."

"What did I say about *speaking*?" Brenner-Xiang turned and glared. "Please. Other teams could be nearby. For the sake of everyone here, I would be forever grateful if you stuck to the plan."

After a long exhale, Kellan picked up his wyvern and then glanced at his shadow. "Back in the hole, buddy." He gently tossed his familiar, and it disappeared into the darkness. Kellan almost felt bad. It seemed like Vlaze had been frowning. But lizards couldn't frown.

Could they?

Brenner-Xiang strode up to the door on the right. She placed her hand—Brenner's hand—on the computer terminal. "One, seven, eight, two."

The door slid open without a second's delay. Then Brenner-Xiang walked inside, followed by the rest of her team. Kellan bit his tongue, trying hard to deter himself from saying anything whatsoever. He took a deep breath, grabbed the strap of his backpack, and walked after the others.

The room they had entered…

It was perfectly square, with a sleek ivory desk and a slim computer monitor. A TV on the far wall—seemingly made from a thin sheet of translucent paper, projected Bitso's broadcast.

"Those in the PvP match have already begun crawling around their new environment." He rubbed at his blindfold, smiling widely. "Some of you might be thinking… What kind of environment? How big is it? But I can't answer that until after the game. All you need to know is that the Net will be an amusing obstacle this time around… Since most players won't be able to actively see it."

Kellan's heart skipped a beat.

He hadn't even thought about the Net.

It was encasing the space station, likely growing smaller with each moment. How much time did they have, though? Surely longer than three hours. The Arbiter wanted them to collect the keys, didn't he?

As if answering Kellan's unspoken question, Bitso continued with, "The Net will fully close in on the environment at the end of five hours. *However*, if all the keys have been found, the game will instantly end… So kill infected people, or make sure you know where they are when they explode, and everything will be fine."

The others didn't seem concerned with Bitso's broadcast. They crossed the sterile room all the way to the opposite side. Two other doors awaited them.

Kellan glanced over at the desk in the room. One of the drawers was open. Tools—tiny tools—rolled around inside, almost like someone had *just* been here. Had they fled?

Where had they gone?

Bitso leaned forward, closer to the camera, still smiling. "Ladies, gentlemen, and everything in between… If you're into long, drawn-out moments, you're going to *love* what comes next." He slapped a hand on his metal desk. "It's time to watch some Stragglers struggle to get out of a deadly pit. It's both hilarious and wildly bloody. There's no better way to spend your next five minutes."

But Kellan was too curious about the desk. When he walked around behind it, he found crimson stains on the seat and floor. Someone had been dragged under the desk? Or out of the room?

He held his breath, moving closer to the futuristic furniture, wondering how he was going to announce this to the group when Xiang was insistent that he not speak.

"Come, Alex," Brenner-Xiang said.

Brenner's voice really irritated Kellan, but he thanked whatever gods were listening that Sen wasn't using the Tyranny Worms anymore. He stepped away from the desk, hesitant and still concerned.

Brenner-Xiang opened the right-most door. It slid open in a quick *whoosh*, but Kellan hadn't been prepared for what was on the other side.

A machine yami stood mere inches behind the other side of the door. Its body was so massive, the beast almost didn't fit in the room. It was humanoid in shape, with two legs and arms, though it was crouched down, so that its head wasn't slammed against the ceiling. Flesh was stretched over the machines of its body, like someone had wanted to graft biomaterial to a mechanized man and see what happened.

A face was stretched over the chrome head, like a crude mask over a flashy bumper. Metal teeth showed through the mouth hole, and small lenses through the two eyeholes. The monster roared—but its mouth didn't open—and then it thrust an arm at Brenner-Xiang, its fingers ending in knives that slashed right through her illusions and flesh.

Kellan's analytical eyes gave him some information.

Name: Mr. Andy #3
Race: Lesser Yami
Magics: Body, Metal
Rank: Impossible
Armor Rating: 5
Health: 25/25

Stats:
Strength—7 [Cyborg-Enhanced]
Dexterity—5 [Cyborg-Enhanced]
Fortitude—5 [Cyborg-Enhanced]
Intelligence—1 [Insane]
Perception—2
Willpower—1 [Insane]

Abilities:
Flesh Eater—The yami regains health whenever it consumes raw flesh. One point of health per point of health taken from the target.
Undead Machine—The yami is immune to poison, gas, and phantasmal attacks. The yami does not need to breathe or eat to survive. Additionally,

the yami feels no pain.

"Mr. Andy" was so frenzied and flesh-hungry that it clawed and dragged its way into the study, its first action was to lean down to the splatter of Xiang's blood on the floor. When its mouth opened, a three-foot-long tongue stretched out and lapped up the vital fluid, foamy pink saliva sliding off its undead lips.

Kellan aimed and rapidly fired on it. Damage notifications flared across his eyes, most of which were reduced by the yami's armor rating. He managed to deal a grand total of four damage after a solid couple seconds of firing.

He also spent a mana and activated his armor.

Kellan went down to five mana. *I should've spent time in the mana spring. Dammit!*

Shadows leapt around him, providing armor under his illusions.

Then Kellan placed his boot on the side of the desk and kicked forward. He had intended to move the furniture a slight distance—to provide cover while he fired—but instead, the desk flew across the room, almost hitting Ysa-Mavis in the process.

The desk crashed into Mr. Andy like it was a speeding car. The crunch and twist of metal even made it sound like two vehicles had collided.

"What the?" Kellan muttered aloud, shocked he had flung the desk so far.

Everyone glanced in Kellan's direction, their faces twisted in confusion.

Kellan took a long moment to realize his stats had changed. He once had a four strength—and now he had a nine. Sen had said that five was human maximum, and that anything over that was superhuman levels. Kellan hadn't expected to effortlessly toss the desk. He almost laughed. The feeling of power was exhilarating.

Mr. Andy didn't share everyone's bewilderment. It slammed the desk aside and then hurried toward Kellan, practically walking on all fours since it was too large to stand straight on its feet and walk.

The yami swung its claws in a wide arc.

Kellan easily ducked under the monster's slash. Again, Kellan was shocked at how well he could move his body. The moment he thought of an action, his muscles jolted to comply. Was that his heightened dexterity?

Then Kellan lifted his rifle and fired again. He thanked whatever Nexus-gods were watching that he didn't need to carry ammo, but he always felt an urge to reach for another magazine at his belt.

[Alex Kellan] shot [Mr. Andy #3] for 9 damage. (5 +50% Sharpshooter Modifier + Sevriss Bonus)
[Mr. Andy #3] reduces damage of each hit equal to its armor rating of 5.
[Mr. Andy #3] takes a total of 4 damage.

The monster had a total of 25 health, now down to 17. Kellan knew this would be a slog if he didn't do something more.

Mr. Andy glared at him with mechanical eyes through the holes of its flesh mask. The yami flexed its fingers, extending its claws, and then swung again. Kellan dodged and backed away, but then his back hit the wall.

Every move the monster made sounded like gears grinding. It didn't breathe or scream in frustration, and Kellan suspected it could go forever. When Mr. Andy slashed a third time, Kellan braced himself against the wall and grabbed the monster's arm while avoiding the knife-like claws.

Kellan wasn't tall enough—or large enough—to wrestle the beast, despite being stronger. So instead of throwing the yami to the floor, Kellan twisted the arm in one quick and brutal action. Mr. Andy's arm dislocated and broke apart, some of the gear crashing into the shoulder, and wire snapped out of the sockets.

[Alex Kellan] torqued [Mr. Andy #3]'s arm for 10 damage. [Mr. Andy #3] suffers a -1 dexterity until repaired.
[Mr. Andy #3] reduces damage of each hit equal to its armor rating of 5.
[Mr. Andy #3] takes a total of 5 damage.

Kellan chuckled under his breath, still amazed at how strong and fast he had become due to the infection buffs. He was confident in his victory, but then Mr. Andy's chest opened, like Legos separating and rebuilding themselves so that there was an opening in the armor. A red crystal pulsed within, and Kellan recognized it.

That was the same type of crystal inside the Pestbyters.

It flashed quickly, and Kellan remembered the laser beams the Pestbyter's crystal had created. Kellan rolled to the side just as Mr. Andy blasted light beams into the wall, scorching part of the white metal.

Viniss-Husker and Ysa-Mavis joined the fray. Although Husker appeared like a freakish alien, the illusion moved with him as he ran over and clawed at Mr. Andy's back. Husker didn't use his hex—Kellan understood why—but that meant Mr. Andy could claw at the werewolf man.

Ysa-Mavis aimed with her own rifle and fired, damaging the yami.

"*Sen!*" Kellan shouted. "Use your *Shield Ally* ability!" He jumped to his feet and shot the monster in the fleshy-mask face, drawing its attention.

HR-8-Sen shivered and then forced himself to nod. He had just been *watching* the fight, his eyes wide. Bitso had been right—Sen sometimes panicked, but Kellan couldn't tolerate that right now.

When the yami targeted Kellan with its laser, Kellan rushed forward, his rifle held up. The laser struck him.

[HR-8] used *Shield Ally* on [Alex Kellan], reducing the next attack's damage by 90%.
[Mr. Andy #3] used *Dragon's Breath* on [Alex Kellan], dealing an automatic 20 damage.
[Alex Kellan] suffers 2 damage.

[Alex Kellan] reduces damage of each hit equal to his armor rating of 2.
[Alex Kellan] suffers a total of 0 damage.

There was no injury, but Kellan was more surprised at the fact that *HR-8* appeared within the combat information. Xiang's illusions fooled even the ambient magic.

Shaking away the thought, Kellan plowed forward and struck the butt of his rifle straight into the yami's chest. With his enhanced strength, he smashed the crystal. Mr. Andy shuddered, and its gears screeched. Kellan leapt away.

Husker and Mavis continued their onslaught. While the werewolf was ripping wires from its back, Mr. Andy slowly collapsed to the floor, brown fluid leaking from busted tubes in his chest.

Five arcana sprouted from the oil, glittering with inner power.

Kellan glanced around.

In the corner of the room, far from the fighting, Brenner-Xiang had her arms crossed and her eyes narrowed. She met Kellan's gaze, obviously unconcerned with the entire ordeal.

"Why didn't you use your mind blast?" Kellan asked. "You could've ignored its armor rating, right?"

"The yami was immune to phantasmal damage," Xiang replied matter-of-factly. "And instead of wasting my mana with other forms of weaker attacks, I figured I could leave this task to our team's warriors."

HR-8-Sen walked over to the arcana. His whole illusion bent over to scoop up a crystal, but Kellan knew it wasn't necessary for a kid his size. What amused Kellan the most was how the illusion moved around—it took every step with a short gait, never allowing its legs to fully separate. It was a bit awkward, but that way Sen's body was always covered by illusions.

"Each of us should get one arcana," HR-8-Sen said.

Ysa-Mavis huffed and then laughed once. "Xiang didn't do anything. I think she's SOL."

"SOL?" Viniss-Husker asked, his insect face displaying emotion as well as a potato.

"Shit outta luck."

"Ah. Another odd human phrase."

"Wait, Xiang provided us with the illusions," Kellan said, holding up a hand. "She's a member of the team, and without her we wouldn't even be here doing this. I agree with Sen. She should get one of the arcana."

His argument was met with silence. HR-8-Sen offered him a slight smile, however. Kellan didn't return the gesture. He hadn't sided with Sen—he had just stated his opinion.

Brenner-Xiang lifted an eyebrow. In a gruff and masculine tone that bordered on pompous, she responded, "Everyone here needs the arcana more than I do. You're still low-ranking mages. Until that's fixed, it's better that you all share everything we acquire."

"Very selfless of you, sister," HR-8-Sen replied, his new adult voice clashing with his statements. The way he said *sister* didn't sound right to Kellan.

Ysa-Mavis leaned down and picked up an arcana.

Although he still hadn't decided what he would spend his arcana on, Kellan knelt and absorbed a single arcana, bringing his unspent total up to twenty-three. *Perhaps I should focus on the ranks of magic I already have… I only have one power from metal and body.*

"You were quite strong," Viniss-Husker stated. When he walked, his illusionary feet clicked across the floor. "Are you enjoying the added strength?" He knelt and absorbed two arcana.

"Definitely." Kellan ran his hands over his chest. "I didn't realize it made such a difference."

"Once you leave the realm of standard non-magical limits, you will start to think of things in different terms. Horses are no longer heavy. Running four miles straight no longer impacts your stamina. You might even become more precise."

Kellan stared at his feet for a long moment. Body magic offered several stat-increasing powers… *Perhaps that should be the route I take while I wait for someone to teach me meta magic.*

Brenner-Xiang motioned to the two new doors in the room. One was open—the one Mr. Andy had powered its way out of. And the other was still closed. The Mr. Andy room was dark and empty, but he noticed another door on the far wall.

"I can't see in there," HR-8-Sen muttered.

"I can." Kellan walked over to the doorway. "It's empty."

"Well, *now* it is, since the monster left it."

After a short sigh, Brenner-Xiang glanced over at the closed door. "My brother and I will search this room. You three, thoroughly search the other. I doubt this space station would just have empty rooms."

Again, the whole place rumbled.

"*Warning,*" the station's AI said in a cheery feminine voice. "*Deck 18 has been flooded with deadly gas. Please wait until it can be drained before entering.*"

Kellan glanced around, his heart leaping into his throat. What deck were *they* on? Deadly gas was one of the worst ways to go.

"We needn't worry," Brenner-Xiang stated. "We're on Deck 11." Then she turned and headed for the sealed door. She had to step over the busted yami in order to make it. "Search the room and then return. We shouldn't go too far from each other."

"Why search the room?" Kellan asked.

"This station is likely filled with useful items. High-tech armor and magic should be in abundance. Focus."

Kellan nodded along with her words. That was a good point. If they could get new—and advanced gear—it would be helpful. Perhaps they could loot most of the station before teleporting back to the AVU Palace.

Once the three of them were grouped up, Kellan, Ysa-Mavis, and Viniss-

Husker walked into the dark room. They made it all the way to the center when the door slammed shut and a variety of colored spotlights flashed into existence. Kellan shielded his eyes, but he also smiled.

Confetti went everywhere, raining down around them like a waterfall of rainbows. Small horns tooted for their arrival.

And an imp wearing a tiny suit sat at a doll-sized desk at the far end of the room. Its clawed fingers were laced together in front of it.

"Congratulations," the imp said with a smile that dominated the tiny creature's face. "You've found a prize room! Come over here and claim your *amazing* item!"

"Oh, really?" Ysa-Mavis laughed and turned to Kellan. "Are we lucky or what?"

Viniss-Husker nodded. With a smile in his voice, he said, "Now we can ask for something game-changing."

"I can't believe we found one. I know exactly what I'm going to ask for."

Kellan wanted to celebrate along with them, but something was wrong. Ysa-Mavis and the werewolf went forward, but Kellan just stared at the two-foot-tall imp. Its red skin and little horns were familiar, but…

The information Kellan received from his analysis told a different story.

Name: Trap Imp #22
Race: Semi-Sentient Construct
Magics: Mind, Meta
Rank: Impossible
Armor Rating: —
Health: 2/2
Stats: Concealed
Abilities: Concealed

Trap Imp?

Before Ysa-Mavis and Viniss-Husker could reach the imp's desk, Kellan shouted. "*Wait!* It's a trap!"

Viniss-Husker was the first to react. He immediately leapt backward and growled, his voice still altered by the illusions so that he sounded like he was hissing. Ysa-Mavis, on the other hand, wasn't as fast, but she did stop and glance over her shoulder.

"What is it?" she asked.

A wall jutted out of the floor with all the speed of a reverse-guillotine. It slammed into the ceiling, creating a barrier between the team and the imp—a barrier made of transparent metal. When Kellan turned to the door, he noticed another wall had slammed upward, blocking their escape.

The trap imp laughed with all the unhinged energy of a lunatic. It flapped its little bat wings and took to the sky, spiraling upward as it wiped laugh-tears from the corners of its beady eyes.

It pointed at the transparent wall—a small wrist-sized hole was in the middle.

When the creature spoke, its voice filtered through the narrow opening. "You spoiled my fun! I didn't get to see anyone sliced in half!"

Ysa-Mavis took several steps backward until she was next to Kellan.

"But you're still *fools*," the imp shrieked in delight. "You're going to die here in my trap, and then I'll consume your arcana, and become a demon the likes of which none of you have ever seen!" The creature threw its small head back and laughed, its tiny lungs creating an impressive amount of noise.

—Chapter 51—
—Overseer Station—

Kellan glanced around. They were surrounded by metal walls, the room cut in half by the transparent metal wall that had sprung up from the floor. The fist-sized hole seemed odd, but Kellan thanked his luck. His ability to shadow-step would allow him to slip right through the hole, even though it was normally too small for a fully grown adult.

But when Kellan attempted to dive into the shadows, his foot met with solid ground. Then he received terrible information.

> **[Trap Imp #22]'s *Aura of Anti-Magic* prevents all enemy C-rank activatable powers. Passive magic, innate capabilities, personal abilities, and enhancements are unaffected.**

"Anti-magic?" Viniss-Husker growled as he stepped back. "The imp is using meta magic on us… We won't be able to use our powers."

The little imp, still wearing its tiny suit, flew around on the other side of the transparent wall, its smile so wide, it gave the Cheshire Cat a run for his money. "Just you wait! The fun has yet to begin! Arcana tastes so much more delicious if the mages suffer ahead of time…"

The little monster laughed, its thin tail twitching around behind it.

The floor underneath the imp opened up and two objects rose upward. First, was a computer panel, complete with a glowing blue screen, just like at all the doors. The other object…

Kellan caught his breath, uncertain of why a buzzsaw would be in a space station.

The saw was on the end of an arm-like contraption. The machine flared to life with the intensity needed to cut through steel. The metal on the arm and the blade were stained blackish-red, and Kellan knew it was crusted blood from past victims.

Both the computer terminal and the saw were next to the hole in the transparent wall. Kellan suspected he could reach the computer terminal if he stuck his own arm through the hole and stretched out fully.

And he quickly understood why that was the case.

The imp snickered and pointed. "The computer will free you from the room, but if you're cut up by the saw, you'll die in an instant!" The imp laughed and flew around its side of the room, its eyes watery from mirth.

Kellan glanced between Ysa-Mavis and Viniss-Husker.

The buzzsaw was clearly positioned between them and the computer terminal so that it could cut whoever reached their arm through the hole. What kind of twisted trap was this?

"Will we really die?" Ysa-Mavis asked.

Viniss-Husker snorted. Then he shook his head. "I'm not certain. Perhaps we should look for a trick—a hidden release button, or a panel in the floor we can crawl through. These trap rooms usually have some way to get out that doesn't involve instant death."

Kellan glanced at the buzzsaw and focused on it. His Blitzkrieg Analysis still worked…

Magical Item [Semi-Sentient]—Trap Saw

This sawblade is made from the bones of a dead Oom. Mages who take damage will suffer the *Wreck the Mage* entropic attack. The mage makes a fortitude check (difficulty unknown). Those who fail, and are below B rank, die instantly.

The imp slammed into the transparent metal and smooshed its face like a pancake. With a freakish grin, it spoke into the wall. "Oh, how foolish! *I'm Trap Imp #22*! The higher the number, the more powerful the imp! My trap rooms are always deadly! *Always!*"

A soft hiss filled Kellan's side of the room. He held his breath and glanced toward the ceiling. A tiny hole—smaller than a penny—had opened up. And although he couldn't smell anything, he already knew what was happening.

"Deadly gas," he whispered.

Ysa-Mavis and Viniss-Husker stared at the ceiling as well.

"*Oh, no,*" the imp sarcastically said as it flew away from the transparent wall. "You won't last longer than a few minutes! Whatever will you do!" The little monster sped up its flying. It zoomed around its side of the room, laughing so hard it almost couldn't breathe.

Again, Kellan turned his attention to the others. What were they supposed to do? They held their hands over their mouths as the hissing increased in intensity. Several deadly gases had no odor or visual component, and Kellan knew that if they didn't escape soon, they could easily pass out or be damaged in other ways…

Kellan hurried to the hole in the wall. He clenched his jaw as he slowly lifted his hand and brought it to the opening. The buzzsaw on the other side moved around—the machine arm capable of 360-degree movement. The saw was too large to fit through the hole, however.

With his insides knotted and his heart beating loudly, Kellan briefly stuck some of his fingers through the hole. The buzzsaw whipped around with the speed of a viper. The *buzz* of deadly steel whirled by the hole in the wall, nearly catching Kellan's fingertips mere milliseconds after he withdrew his hand.

There's no way I can touch the computer without getting cut.

When he glanced over his shoulder, he found his teammates just watching him, their stances stiff and their attention on his hand.

It was unreasonable to ask anyone to kill themselves to release the trap—someone could probably touch the computer terminal a second before dying—but what other choices did they have?

As if realizing the same thing, Viniss-Husker searched around the floor, grabbing at the panels on the ground, trying to force something open. Ysa-Mavis leapt to the nearby walls and felt around, touching every inch, and sometimes slamming her fist. The metal wouldn't break, and Kellan had no way to activate his *Mold Metal* ability.

The hissing of the gas grew louder. Although Kellan had been holding his breath, his vision grew blurry. The chemicals in the gas were seeping into his body, likely through his eyes, nose, and mouth. If he was already being affected, Kellan suspected they only had a few seconds left.

"That's it!" the imp shouted. "*Ta-ta! You're dead!*" And then it chortled, this time salivating.

Kellan's vision tunneled.

He ran a hand through his hair, slightly distracted by the scars he felt on his scalp. Illusions. But he didn't care. That didn't matter. He needed to find a way out of the room, and he had no time.

Ysa-Mavis slammed her hand on the transparent wall, but then she coughed, wheezed, and then hit the floor on her knees, her body trembling.

Without the use of magic, Kellan decided he would resort to his default problem-solving method—his rifle. He unslung it from his shoulder and fired through the hole, attempting to strike the imp. The creature screeched as it bobbed through the air, its wings flapping as the echo of gunfire filled the small room.

Unfortunately, the damn imp managed to dodge away. It hit the floor and hid near the base of the transparent wall, out of Kellan's range.

Unless Kellan wanted to stick his arm and rifle through the narrow hole.

Which he didn't.

Dammit. Think, Kellan! Think!

The imp chuckled. "You missed me! *You missed me*!"

"Vlaze!" Kellan shouted and then coughed.

His shadow-stepped across the floor, and Kellan silently thanked magic itself that his familiar wasn't something blocked by anti-magic. His albino wyvern appeared by his feet, and Kellan quickly scooped him up.

Vlaze was small.

The perfect size.

"*Kill the imp.*" Kellan carefully, but quickly, tossed his snake-like familiar through the hole in the transparent metal, praying that the saw wouldn't catch him before he was out of range.

Fortunately, the little wyvern flew over the deadly obstacle and hit the floor with a small *whamp*. At first, Kellan wasn't sure if the creature would understand the order, so he walked over to the portion of the see-through wall that the imp was hiding next to and pointed to the beast.

Vlaze scrambled to his feet, flared his scales, and then rushed for the imp. The tiny demon was about to take to the air, but Kellan readied himself with his rifle, prepared to shoot the bastard if it got within range.

The imp's hesitation was its downfall.

Vlaze leapt on it and immediately sank his fangs deep into the imp's neck. Then he stabbed the imp repeatedly with his scorpion tail. Nothing the wyvern did required any magic—the imp's anti-magic aura did nothing to hinder Vlaze's onslaught.

"No!" the imp screamed. "*Get off!* Help! Ehg—"

It only took a few seconds for the imp to die.

Kellan was about to order Vlaze over to the computer, but that wasn't necessary. The moment the imp perished, the computer, buzzsaw, and walls lowered back into the floor, returning the room to a plain square again.

Vlaze ripped off a wing of the imp and then scurried across the pristine white floor, leaving a trail of blood in his wake. He dropped the wing at Kellan's feet and then stared up at him, his pupils giant. Kellan leaned down and patted his familiar.

The gas still lingered, however. Kellan pressed a hand over his mouth and then picked up Vlaze. Viniss-Husker grabbed Ysa-Mavis, taking her in his alien arms, and the group exited through the door they had entered.

A small pile of arcana awaited them on the other side of the door. Kellan almost stepped on it all and tripped. He stared, bewildered, but then remembered the rule book had mentioned there was a reward for escaping trap rooms.

Once the door had closed behind them, and they were safe in the room with the dead Mr. Andy, Kellan gasped for breath. He gulped down air and then shook his head, trying to rid himself of his tunnel vision. Ysa-Mavis coughed for a minute straight before Viniss-Husker set her down on her feet.

"Are you okay?" he asked.

Ysa-Mavis nodded, though she was still struggling to breathe.

Kellan knelt and counted the arcana.

Six.

Which meant two for everyone who had dealt with the trap.

Kellan grabbed his two, which brought his total up to twenty-five.

Viniss-Husker and Ysa-Mavis eventually absorbed their arcana. Then they took one more moment to rest. While they took deep breaths, Kellan petted Vlaze on the head. His wyvern, still in his arms, nuzzled himself into the crux of Kellan's arm.

He wanted to say *good job*, but Kellan thought better of it. Instead, he knelt on one knee and placed Vlaze back in his shadow, thankful he'd had a tiny little assistant to help with the bizarre trap room.

I need more ways to deal with the unexpected. Kellan rubbed at his temple. *A grenade would've been a lifesaver in that moment. Maybe there's an armory somewhere on this station... Maybe we can get a few more supplies.*

Kellan stood and glanced around.

Mr. Andy was still dead, and the desk was still twisted.

But he didn't spot Xiang or Sen.

Tense and anxious, Kellan went to the door they had gone through. He placed his hand on the computer terminal and the screen lit up. It asked for the security code. Kellan narrowed his eyes, wondering if he had to speak the code, like Xiang had. Instead, he moved his fingers around and a keyboard appeared.

The keys...

They were in English.

With a smile, Kellan typed in the code.

The door slid open with a powerful whoosh. He stepped inside, but to his surprise, it was another corridor. This one was... nothing like he had been expecting. Light flashed from the ceiling in strobe-like patterns, and a soft *bunz-bunz-bunz* style music reverberated through the station's speakers.

It felt like Kellan had stepped into a nightclub, not a hallway.

He turned his attention to the left and right. More lights. More music. But no Xiang or Sen. Where had they gone? The corridor went for some ways in both directions, and then turned. Had they gone left or right? Why hadn't they come back?

Kellan glanced over his shoulder at Ysa-Mavis. She looked at him, and Kellan motioned with a tilt of his head. Not needing any other communication, Ysa-Mavis hurried to his side. Viniss-Husker followed suit, his insect-style claws clicking along the floor.

Together, the three of them headed into the corridor, but without any indication of which way Xiang or Sen had gone, Kellan opted to turn right. They headed forward, the lights blinking so fast, and with such a powerful shine, that it seemed like everything was moving in stop-motion.

Kellan almost didn't notice the hatch open above them, but the instant he did, he brought his rifle up, ready to waste whatever monster had the courage to attack them.

But it wasn't a monster.

Two people leapt down from a vent in the ceiling. The first was an older man—perhaps in his forties?—with a rugged outdoorsman vibe to his entire look. He wore a vest with ammo, carried a hunting rifle, and sported thick cargo pants. His boots could probably protect him through a deep swamp, and his beard had been trimmed close, but not shaved off completely.

Name: Nasbit Wayne
Race: Human
Magics: Soul, Wyld
Rank: D, C
Armor Rating: —
Health: 7/7
Stats: Concealed

Abilities: Concealed

The other man was in his late twenties, and he looked more like an average kid who wandered around a college campus during the day. He even wore a sweatshirt with an odd logo on the chest. His jeans were stained with blood, and his sneakers seemed scorched. His longer hair, disheveled and half in his eyes, had stolen its black hue from coal.

Name: Ryan Macias
Race: Human
Magics: Mind, Soul, Metal
Rank: C, D, C
Armor Rating: —
Health: 7/7
Stats: Concealed
Abilities: Concealed

They both had the number *10* on the backs of their left hands.

Team 10—neither of them were the Straggler.

The younger man, Ryan, stopped breathing the moment he caught sight of Kellan and the others. He locked up, as still as the dead, his eyes wide.

Nasbit—who had the name *Nasbit?*—shoved Ryan behind him, and then lifted his hunting rifle. "Stay behind me," he commanded, his voice shaky and his hands unsteady. "Let me handle this."

"*Don't do anything reckless.*" Ryan grabbed Nasbit's shoulder, his fingers twisting the fabric of the other man's vest.

Nasbit held his ground. Kellan could tell the man had military experience. It was in the way he stood, the way he kept his feet slightly apart. And the way he kept his hands on his weapon.

Normally, Kellan would've been happy to see other humans, but at the moment, he wasn't sure what to do. He couldn't speak, and if they got into combat, he wasn't sure they'd win. Both Nasbit and Ryan were C-rank mages, but Kellan and his teammates had the element of surprise, and a few tricks up their sleeve.

If things got too rough, Husker could kill them both with his hex…

Nasbit swallowed hard. Then he said, "We got your message."

Now it was Kellan's turn to be confused. He waited—in silence—and just narrowed his eyes, attempting to portray the intimidating aura that everyone seemed to think Alex Kellan the Defector had.

"We're looking for Team 101," Nasbit stated. "And we haven't found anyone infected. I swear. Our leader said he'd stay in contact with yours."

Ah. Kellan already knew what was going on. Brenner had likely convinced the other teams to help him sniff out Xiang. He probably threatened them. *Do as I say, and I won't murder everyone.* What a delta-bravo tactic.

Which meant all the teams were, in fact, against them. Xiang's illusions were the only things keeping them from getting run down.

Wait.

Kellan went over the conversation in his mind. He ran a hand over his neck. The mark that distinguished him as one of the infected… It wasn't visible. Xiang had hidden it from sight with her *Grand Illusion*.

Viniss-Husker stepped forward and stood tall, his black chitinous body shining in the strobe lights. Nasbit shook and scooted his feet back, inching away from Husker while protectively shielding Ryan.

"*Humans*," Viniss-Husker hissed, his tone different, like he was acting out the role. The illusion made his voice perfect. "You dishonor me with your lack of information. If you show yourself in my presence without something to offer, I'll gut you where you stand."

Ryan gripped Nasbit's vest even harder, his breathing shallow. "Let's go," he whispered. "Please. Tell them we'll keep searching."

"We're on it," Nasbit said. Then he scooted away farther, more confident in his movements. "Sorry for disturbing you."

Once Nasbit and Ryan were ten feet away, they turned and hurried down the corridor.

Viniss-Husker leaned in close to both Ysa-Mavis and Kellan. "The younger one is weak," he whispered. "Shoot the older one, and while he's staggering, I'll kill him. Then knock out the other one, and we can infect him for the key."

The plan… wasn't bad. Nasbit had his back to them. One well-placed rifle shot would probably do significant amounts of damage. And Husker had proven that he could kill someone in an instant.

And Ryan *did* look like a weaker competitor…

Ysa-Mavis lifted her rifle and took aim. Then she glanced over at Kellan and lifted an eyebrow.

Although he felt conflicted, Kellan lifted his rifle as well.

Forty feet away, and almost to the end of the corridor, Mavis fired. Kellan held his breath and fired half a second afterward. He knew it was too late. The first bullet struck Nasbit in the base of the neck, and his bullet slammed into the wall.

But still…

Nasbit hit the floor face-first, blood exploding out of the injury upon impact.

For a brief second, Kellan feared that Ryan would just turn the corner down the strobe-filled corridor and disappear from sight. But to Kellan's surprise, Ryan leapt to Nasbit's side, his panic so apparent, and all color drained from his face.

Kellan and Viniss-Husker hurried forward. Ysa-Mavis kept her rifle up and aimed at Team 10. She would fire if anything went wrong, and she moved to the wall of the corridor to get a better angle on the situation—trying her best not to put Kellan or Husker in the crossfire.

When Kellan approached, Ryan leapt between him and Nasbit. "No! No, don't!"

Nasbit struggled to get to his feet, his arms shaky. The bullet wound healed slowly, no doubt through the use of mana. Would Nasbit have enough to use his magical abilities afterward?

"We were doing what you wanted," Ryan said, confusion lacing his words. "*Please.* Just let us go. I'm begging you."

Viniss-Husker stepped forward, and Kellan let him. This was what they had to do, wasn't it? It just… It made his stomach hurt.

Nasbit grabbed his rifle, but Kellan couldn't allow that. In one quick shadow-step, Kellan leapt into the darkness and then emerged during a half-blink of strobe right next to Nasbit and on the other side of Ryan. He kicked the older man's weapon away from his hands.

Then Kellan pointed his weapon at the man's head.

Ryan whipped around and then threw himself over Nasbit. "No! Not Naz! Anyone but him."

"Get off me, Ryan," the other man shouted, his voice strained. "I can—"

"*I can't do this without you!*" Ryan clung to him. "I won't."

"Just *run.*"

"*I won't.* I won't! I told you I won't."

When Viniss-Husker approached Team 10, Kellan's guilt intensified. He glanced up at Husker, and he could see in the alien expression that Husker wasn't pleased with the situation. Kellan lowered his weapon and then motioned Husker away.

For a long moment, Viniss-Husker didn't move. Was the werewolf going to just kill the man anyway?

Ysa-Mavis waited down the corridor, obviously confused by everyone's hesitation.

Kellan subtly shook his head.

There were other teams in the Nexus Games—teams that were filled with bastards and assholes who deserved to get turned into a key. People like Brenner Hawke. But these two… Kellan didn't want to do this to them.

"Consider this a warning, humans," Viniss-Husker said as he backed off. "Team 42 means business."

Kellan exhaled and then stepped away from the others.

The two members of Team 10 conferred in quiet murmurs. Ryan then helped Nasbit to his feet, but by the time the man was on his feet, the wound was completely healed.

Nasbit shot Kellan a cold glare before hurrying off with Ryan. The two didn't say anything else. No offer of thanks, or even a glance over their shoulders. They just hustled until they came to a door and entered the room.

Viniss-Husker stomped close to Kellan and growled. "You're soft." The hands of his four arms clenched and unclenched. "That isn't going to help us win. We could've been done with this whole damn thing."

Ysa-Mavis ran to Husker's side. She lowered her weapon and shook her head. "We let them go?"

"Kellan didn't want to kill them."

"Why?"

"One of them was rather emotional. Clearly, the two men are family." Viniss-

Husker sighed. "I can understand their plight… I just didn't want to keep playing this game."

Kellan sighed. He wished he had a better solution, but there weren't any he could articulate. Surely they would find someone to trap and kill.

Just not people like Nasbit and Ryan.

Ysa-Mavis turned her attention to him. "It's okay. We'll find someone else. Let's just keep searching."

Kellan exhaled and then nodded.

"We don't have much time," Viniss-Husker stated. "Come. There's another door down there. We should continue searching, especially for the others."

—Chapter 52—
—The Final Gold Arcana—

Kellan, Ysa-Mavis, and Viniss-Husker went in the opposite direction of Ryan and Nasbit, heading down the other side of the corridor. Kellan allowed the other two to get ahead of him as he mulled over their current situation. If they didn't find *someone* to turn into a key, Kellan would die.

Husker is right. I should harden myself to the reality of the situation.

The short, bright flashes of light irritated Kellan's eyes. He could technically see the corridor between flashes, but it still messed with his sight. And the constant *dunz-dunz-dunz* drove him insane. Could Xiang and Sen really stand the atmosphere here? Only people high as a kite could stand the hyperactive pulse of the music.

Ysa-Mavis ran to the nearest door and stopped. With her hand hovering over the computer terminal, the blue glow of the screen shining across her palm, she turned to the others. "Hus—I mean, *Viniss*—is there any way to leave a message for, uh, the other members of our team? Writing on the floor or wall? Or a note? Something so that they know we went this way?"

"The problem is our team leader has many ways of *moving around*." Viniss-Husker emphasized the words with an odd quality. "I'm beginning to believe our teammates aren't even around here… We might have to find a way to another deck."

Damn.

Kellan had almost forgotten Xiang had teleported around the last game. Had she done that here? But why? Had she done it to escape something? Or had she found the location of someone infected? Kellan wished they hadn't separated.

"Okay," Ysa-Mavis muttered. She opened the door and then all three of them stepped inside the new room.

The door closed behind them, and they were left with a dilapidated bathroom. Rust covered most surfaces, including the walls and sinks. The mirrors were cracked and clouded, barely reflecting the environment. The drain in the middle of the floor, as well as the showerheads on the far wall, made Kellan think this was some sort of military facility. It was a bathroom with ten toilets and twenty urinals—industrial and impersonal.

He was about to voice his observations, but he decided not to speak. *I'm mute.*

Stay quiet.

The station shook again, the metal groaning in protest.

Viniss-Husker huffed and then shook his head. "This game is shorter than the previous one… We won't have as much time."

"We need to hurry," Ysa-Mavis muttered. She glanced over at Kellan. "Let's just move on. I doubt the bathroom has anything useful."

While Kellan wanted to agree, he thought back to where he had found his cursed rifle. They had dug it out of a swamp next to a trailer park. And Nosferatu had found a key at a carnie game booth in the last PvP game. Just because they were in a bathroom didn't mean it would be devoid of useful items.

"We should still search it." Viniss-Husker motioned to the room. "Quickly."

With a nod, Kellan complied. He glanced around the rusty areas, trying to spot anything of worth. The place smelled like stale urine. Or maybe something worse. Kellan tried to push it from his mind.

When he came across a toilet bowl filled with murky yellow liquid, he hesitated. Would something useful be hidden in the… water? He wanted to assume it was water.

Ysa-Mavis walked over, her nose wrinkled in disgust. "I once lived in the barracks in Baghdad, and the bathrooms there remind me of this, but even then… We never had puke-bowl toilets. This is straight from the Hell dimension or something."

Viniss-Husker joined them near the toilet bowl. All three of them stared for a good ten seconds, silence lingering between them.

"You don't think anything is in there, right?" Ysa-Mavis asked. "I mean, it's crazy. There's no way. Why would anyone hide something here? Right?"

Kellan shrugged. He had already seen weirder.

"There could be something." Viniss-Husker exhaled. "Knowing the Arbiter… There probably *is* something." He glanced over, and Kellan gave him a *seriously?* with his eyes alone. Viniss-Husker shook his head. "Fine. I'll do it."

He knelt near the toilet and shoved one of his hands into the foul liquid.

"I can't believe this," Mavis muttered.

The werewolf grumbled. "Humans don't have fur, you know. It would've been *easier* for one of you to clean your arm afterward. And my nose is sensitive… *Arg*. I'll be detecting this for weeks."

Kellan hadn't thought about it like that. He sometimes forgot Husker was so different—with his own unique problems and irritations. *I bet fur really is difficult to deal with.*

Viniss-Husker rummaged through the toilet water with a thoroughness that Kellan admired. When the man withdrew his hand, his insect-lobster claws were clenched around a plastic baggie. Inside the bag was a piece of paper.

There was also a wad of hair wrapped around Viniss-Husker's fingers. Coarse, black hair, like something fished out of a shower drain after years of neglect. It was almost worse than the smell. Almost.

"What is that?" Ysa-Mavis asked, pointing to the baggie.

When Viniss-Husker handed it over, Ysa-Mavis begrudgingly took it, her lips curled down in a sneer. She opened the bag and withdrew the small scrap of paper. It read: CENTRAL CODE 6223.

They had a new set of numbers for the doors.

Ysa-Mavis showed it off as Viniss-Husker went straight for a sink and washed his hand. The entire time, he muttered things about the stickiness of the toilet bowl water, and how human hair was different when compared to his fur.

"I can't believe there was something there." Ysa-Mavis glared at the toilet. "Everyone in the Nexus has a sick sense of humor."

Kellan chuckled to himself, but he didn't offer any commentary. Had Mavis forgotten about Bitso or the many wacky things they had seen throughout the competition? Insanity. The whole thing was pure insanity.

"We need to investigate faster," Viniss-Husker muttered. He glanced over his alien shoulder and the feelers over his mouth wiggled as he added, "Do quick glances around. There probably aren't any other special rooms nearby. They're rarely clumped up. If you spot a yami, just meet in the corridor. We just don't have time to waste."

Kellan and Ysa-Mavis both nodded. They headed out of the bathroom together, entering the nightclub corridor once again.

Dunz-dunz-dunz.

Ysa-Mavis went to the next door, opened it up, and then went inside. She seemed fine—no monsters, no other teams. Once he was certain she was okay, Kellan went to the next door on the opposite side of the corridor. He glanced around the entire time, but there wasn't much to see.

No one around, no yami lurking in the corners. Kellan still didn't feel safe, however. The Nexus Games always seemed to be filled with surprises, and not the good kind.

Kellan approached the door. He placed his hand on the terminal and typed in the access code. Then the door slid open with the same pleasant whoosh and revealed a perfectly square room with mirrors on two walls. Kellan entered and caught sight of himself in the leftmost mirror, his appearance almost startling.

He ambled over and touched the scars on his face.

The mechanical eye disturbed him a bit. Although he didn't like touching his eyeball directly, he gently placed one finger on the mechanical orb. He *felt* the metal and machinery, just like he could feel the fake scars. Xiang's illusions continued to impress him.

Then the room shook.

At first, Kellan thought it was part of the games—the quaking that resulted from dead yami and time passing. But then the computer, Cari, spoke over the speakers.

"*Heading to Deck 13,*" Cari said with a pleasant tone.

Kellan tensed and whirled around. He rushed for the door, but it was sealed shut. The shudder of the room bothered him, but then he realized it wasn't a room at all. It was an elevator of some sort.

Right as Kellan was contemplating using his shadow-stepping to exit the elevator prematurely, the shaking stopped.

"Arrived at Deck 13."

That was fast.

The door opened. A rennic, one of the werewolf people, stood on the other side, her black fur and icy blue eyes a striking combination. She wore thick body armor and pants clearly tailored for her unique body type, including having a hole for her wolf-like tail.

Name: Quint Nuns
Race: Rennic
Magics: Wyld, Metal
Rank: C, C
Armor Rating: —
Health: 9/9
Stats: Concealed
Abilities: Concealed

The rennic, Quint, went to enter the elevator, but she stopped mid-step, her fur on end. She was the Straggler of Team 90, according to the number and skull on her hand.

Kellan met her striking gaze. His natural urge to utter a greeting almost got the better of him, but he remained silent. The two stared at each other for only half a second.

Without a word, Quint slowly backed out of the elevator. After a hard swallow, she shook her head. "Uh, you're from *Team 42*… Look, there's arcana just right over there. It's being made from the prisoners. I was, uh, gonna get my team, but you can have it." She pointed out of the elevator and down another corridor. "I'm gonna go. I won't tell anyone I saw you."

Quint took off in the opposite direction.

Kellan hesitated. Arcana was being made from the prisoners? What did that even mean?

The computer system spoke over speakers hidden in the ceiling. "*Prisoner 554, sentenced to death for being an Outsider and failing to report himself to the Arbiter, has been eliminated. His belongings can be claimed at the processing counter.*" It was Cari's voice, but it sounded harsher and uncaring.

Outsiders… That means they're killing people for stumbling into the Nexus.

The thought disturbed him, and curiosity fueled his steps forward. The new corridor of Deck 13 was more practical and military than the dance deck above. Thick steel beams created arches overhead, which reminded Kellan of a ribcage. He ran through the hall, stepping into the darkness to increase his speed as he made his way to the far door.

Above the computer terminal were the words: PRISON BLOCK.

Kellan placed his hand on the terminal. It asked for the code, but when Kellan input the standard one-seven-eight-two, it didn't work. The prison was restricted and required a higher authority code.

He tried the new code they had obtained. Six-two-two-three.

Nothing. It didn't work.

Kellan spent a mana—reducing him to four—and activated his *Mold Metal.* He grabbed the door and attempted to force his way through. Unfortunately, only a small part of the door bent to his will, like he was leaving his handprint on the metal, and going no further. Large sections of the door—and the corridor wall, as well—were made of *something else*. It was like… a non-metal material had been woven into the metal, creating a hybrid substance that resisted Kellan's magic.

Was it because the space station had been built on a dimension rich in magic? Was it meant to be a security measure because everyone knew of the low-ranking *Mold Metal* ability? To prevent mages from breaking in?

Or maybe the material had been created because it was simply stronger than standard metals. Either way, Kellan couldn't seem to mold his way in.

When he tried to shadow-step under the door, he found he couldn't. Unlike normal doors, which had a small opening at the bottom, the space station seemed airtight and sealed, preventing airflow and shadows from creeping through.

Kellan cursed under his breath. Another muffled scream, barely audible, came from deep within the prison block. It sent shivers down his spine. Desperate to get to the source, Kellan mulled over all his magical options. His mind filled with a list of available powers, and then things he could purchase with arcana.

In D rank of metal, he found a power he could purchase…

Intuitive Tech [2 arcana]

The metal mage quickly understands how machines, vehicles, and foreign computers work…

The mage spends a mana, and for thirty minutes, he has a "phantom" understanding of machines. He can temporarily pick locks and use most vehicles, firearms, planes, and computer terminals as though he has trained with them before.

Would that work? Would it give Kellan the information he needed? It said it allowed him to "pick locks" and use most computer terminals…

It required Kellan to rank to D in metal, however. After a short sigh, he decided to do it. He spent five arcana to unlock D-rank metal, and then he spent the two arcana to purchase the power.

He still had eighteen arcana remaining.

A rush of energy flooded him, tingling his muscles and invigorating his thoughts. He gritted his teeth as information filled his mind.

His mana increased. It went from four out of ten, to five out of eleven. Which meant his maximum pool increased by one from ranking up secondary magics. His first D rank in a magic had increased it to ten mana, but his second was only eleven. Diminishing returns.

But Kellan didn't dwell on it. Now he had his new power—*Intuitive Tech.*

Kellan exhaled, spent another mana, bringing him down to four again, and then touched the computer terminal. At first, nothing happened, but then Kellan felt the processes of the computer deep within. The coding, the processes, the purpose… The computer terminal was simple in design and spoke to a central system. Its functionality was limited, and Kellan could sense the code needed to open the door, like the computer was speaking to him.

He could also feel Cari, the AI in control of the station. It was like the computer was aware of what he was doing, and just allowed him to continue without interruption. Was Cari normally supposed to prevent people from breaking in, but because of the Arbiter's orders, she refrained?

Whatever the reason, Kellan liked this new power. He half-laughed as he typed in the new code. Seven-seven-three-five.

The door to the prison ward opened.

The computer terminal hadn't blocked his metal magic—was that because the Arbiter had told Cari not to interfere? Kellan didn't stop to investigate.

When Kellan stepped inside, he caught his breath. It was a front room, complete with a waiting area, a desk, several "self-service" computer terminals, and one large door at the back. The walls, floor, and ceiling were black in coloration, and everything looked more *organic* than machine. There were no hard edges. No glass. No shiny surfaces. Everything was matte and the wall had wrinkles or veins, Kellan wasn't entirely sure.

A single person stood by one of the self-service computers. A man. Not a normal man—or a competitor in the games—but a misshapen man with a hunchback and an underdeveloped arm, so tiny and thin, it could've been mistaken for a loose string hanging off a shirt.

One of the inbred residents of the Nexus.

Kellan didn't get any info for him, which meant he was a non-mage.

Cari spoke over the speaker again. "*Prisoner 555, sentenced to death for being an Outsider and failing to report himself to the Arbiter, has been eliminated. His belongings can be claimed at the processing counter.*"

Another one dead. Kellan felt like time was constantly his enemy.

The Nexus resident glanced up and looked around, like he was trying to find where the voice had come from. He wore a T-shirt with moth-bite holes in the gray fabric, and a pair of faded blue jeans, the hems stained brown and red.

When the man finally turned around, Kellan realized his eyes were two different shapes—one a golf ball, the other a dime.

"Oh," the hunchback said, his voice much more articulate than Kellan had suspected. "You're a competitor."

Kellan wanted to speak, but again, he held back. He held up both hands, trying to say he wouldn't hurt the man, and then pointed to the ceiling. The hunchback raised a misshapen eyebrow. Kellan pointed to the computer and then shrugged.

Would the man understand? Kellan just wanted to find the prisoners.

"They're through that door," the resident said as he pointed to the large door at the back of the room. "In the factory. They're being processed."

Factory?

Kellan wanted to ask, *Isn't this a prison?* but he held back. Instead, he offered a smile and then strode toward the back door.

The hunchback grimaced and cringed away, his one good arm up and shielding his face. Kellan ignored the man. He wasn't about to kill him to get cheap arcana.

Once Kellan reached the door, he touched the computer terminal and entered the same code from before. It worked. With a smile, Kellan watched as the door slid open with a slow whoosh. Before he left the front room, Kellan glanced over his shoulder, hoping to offer the hunchback a nod of appreciation.

But the man was gone.

Kellan turned all the way around and gave the room a thorough once-over.

Empty.

Do the residents also live on the space station? He stepped away from the door and gave the room another hard look. Did they have illusions here as well? Kellan reached into his pocket and withdrew his bizarre coin. It was glowing, but just faintly.

Illusions nearby.

The residents lived on the space station as well, it seemed.

But Kellan knew he didn't have all the time in the world. If he didn't finish this—and save some Outsiders quickly—he would likely lose Mavis and Husker to the maze-like quality of Overseer Station.

Determined and focused, Kellan went back to the door, opened it, and stepped forward. The next room wasn't what he had been expecting. Prisons normally had cells, bars, and inmates… This really was a factory.

Kellan stood on a mezzanine floor above storage units, cranes, and crates. The cranes grabbed crates, lifted them high above the catwalk mezzanine, and then dropped them onto platforms that shifted the contents into a vat.

There weren't many lights, nor were there any workers. It was entirely automated. Where were the prisoners?

What's going on?

Kellan craned his head back and stared at the massive warehouse-shaped room. The catwalk and mezzanine went on forever. With an exhale, he shadow-stepped away from the door and down the walkway. When he exited the darkness, he was halfway across the room.

From his new angle, he saw that the crates had bars on one side. He stared at the contents of one crate as it was lowered onto a platform and brought over to the vat.

People.

Humans, rennic, some of the weird birds… All people. Just unconscious.

Were they the prisoners?

Kellan couldn't seem to reach them, though. They were so far, and he wasn't sure if his shadow-stepping would reach them in the limited distance he had. The crates were dumped into vats with dark, boiling liquid. The unconscious people were… just drowned in the water.

And their arcana floated out of the crates, through the bars, and went to the surface of the water, for some reason. Kellan hadn't thought they were buoyant, but perhaps the magic contained within made them lighter.

Was this a factory to… farm arcana?

Kellan was tempted to reach one of the vats, but judging by the roiling bubbles and copious amounts of steam, they were much too hot to swim through. He'd become a pile of arcana himself if he tried.

Who was doing this?

Kellan spotted a door labeled: INTERROGATION AND FINAL CREATION.

With his breath held, Kellan went straight to the door. He opened it and stepped inside.

This looked more like a classic prison.

There was a guard station with several monitors, each displaying the inside of a cell. The prisoners within wore brown jumpsuits and cuffs. Most were curled up on the floor, some were twitching, but all of them appeared docile and emaciated.

The hallway with the cells was just beyond Kellan's current room, at least according to the computer readouts that displayed a localized map.

Unfortunately, the room had more than just the guard station. A hospital bed was in the middle of the open space—the kind of bed reserved for patients who needed to be strapped down. A single man was there, his stomach open wide, like a deviled egg without any filling.

A small table was next to the bed—covered in vials and twinkling with two arcana.

What kind of messed-up room was this?

The man on the hospital bed had a blanket over his lower waist and legs, and a single IV stuck in his arm, but otherwise nothing else. His graying beard and pepper hair told Kellan he was older, but not yet out of his prime.

Somehow, beyond all reason or Kellan's understanding of medicine, the man was still alive. His bloodshot eyes shifted to get a better view of Kellan, and the man slowly turned his head to face in Kellan's direction.

"Help," the man whispered, his voice raspy.

Kellan carefully made his way to the side of the hospital bed. He stared at the arcana, and the obvious vials of blood. What was going on? Who was doing this?

"Help," the man repeated.

Kellan stared at the man's empty abdomen and wondered how he was even speaking. The man's diaphragm had to still be intact… but his stomach and intestines seemed to be missing.

No pools of blood or pus or stray membranes. It was clean and hollow.

The man's red eyes grew wide. "Wait," he rasped. "You're Alex… Kellan… Defector…"

Kellan leaned down close. The man wasn't a mage or a competitor—Kellan's analysis gave him no information. "I'm not who you think I am," he whispered to the man. "This is an illusion. I'm not the defector. I'm here to help you."

The man seemed to relax. His shoulders eased into a casual position, and his head rested easy against the thin hospital pillow. His gaze seemed more vacant than before…

Again, Kellan found himself scrambling to think of something. He glanced around the bizarre room. The black walls, ceiling, and floor gave everything a claustrophobic feeling. No one else was here. There was no medicine—just two arcana on the table. And as far as Kellan knew, only mages benefited from the arcana.

What did he have? He had food, but would that help a man without any insides?

Kellan chuckled to himself at his own crazy rhetorical question.

What magic did he have?

He hadn't wanted to spend a bunch of his arcana—because he wanted to save it for something special or advantageous—but he didn't know what else to do. Body magic apparently had healing. Kellan had body magic. He could save this man.

So he purchased C rank in body magic.

His max mana went from eleven, to twelve, and his mana pool went from four to five.

Then Kellan purchased a D-rank power.

Heal the Body [2 arcana]

This power is the simplest manifestation of the body mage's well-known ability to heal others.

The mage may spend a point of mana to heal another of three points of damage.

He had eleven remaining arcana.

With his healing purchased, Kellan spent one mana—going back down to four—and touched the dying man on the hospital bed. The man couldn't be infected, since he wasn't a competitor in the games, but Kellan still hesitated before making contact. The man took in a deep breath, and right before Kellan's eyes, his body filled out. Color returned to his cheeks, to his hair, and even to his beard. The man's insides…

They remained missing.

But blood began to pool in the empty cavity, as if his body were producing more and didn't know what to do with it.

Kellan had no idea what to do about that.

If only Sen were here… He would know. The damn kid knows everything about the human body. Dammit!

The man on the medical bed fought against his restraints. Kellan released one arm, and then the man grabbed Kellan's sleeve, his grip surprisingly tight.

"You're not… you're not Alex Kellan?" the man asked, his voice stronger, but his tone laced with agony. "*Tell me.* Alex can't… he can't speak… You can't be…"

"I'm not the Alex Kellan you're thinking of," Kellan replied as honestly as he could without going into details.

"Then… listen. I don't have much time." The man shuddered and groaned. He scrunched his eyes shut and forced himself to continue with, "It's the flestiss… I came to the Nexus because the Flestiss Dominion has plans…"

Kellan shook his head, his brow furrowed. He spent another point of mana and tried to heal the man again. More blood spilled from the man's gaping injury. It was almost as if… now that the man was healed, he could now fully feel the agony his body was in.

"The Dominion has plans to… gain access to Zenith…" The man gulped down breath and spoke through clenched teeth. "They only want to win… the games… to steal the magic of Zenith… To help them destroy the primordial dragons…"

The information seemed important. Kellan glanced around, suspecting the info was intended for someone other than him. Had this man—a soldier, clearly—traveled a fair distance just to get gutted and left to die on a table?

"How do you know this?" Kellan asked.

"I was with the United Earth Defense Force…"

A soldier. Kellan had known. He could always spot another veteran.

The man coughed and then gritted his teeth. "Brenner betrayed us… We were captured…"

"What is this place? It's like a prison was merged with a factory. What's going on?"

"It *was* a prison… But this is a flestiss facility from my dimension… meant to turn lesser races into… magical resources…" The man held Kellan's sleeve even tighter, his breathing now ragged. "*Listen.* You must inform the Arbiter. No one from the Dominion should be allowed to compete… They can't reach Zenith or… or they'll use that magic to conquer and control everything."

Kellan had bad news for the guy, but he wasn't sure how to inform him.

There was already a flestiss in the games. Maybe more than one, Kellan wasn't entirely sure. And they wanted to use the magic of Zenith for their own bizarre dragon-hunting conquest? At least Kellan had answered one question. Brenner was with Viniss to help her win the games. That was why he was really here—power from Zenith for him and the Dominion.

Kellan wasn't sure what to do with his newfound information. Maybe the Arbiter would kick the flestiss out of the games? He had to inform everyone.

"I'll tell the Arbiter," Kellan said. "Don't worry. You did good, soldier. You got your message through, no matter the cost."

The man breathed a little easier, despite his obvious pain. He loosened his grip on Kellan, a slight smile on his agony-wracked face.

"I'm not going to make it," the man managed to murmur. "My wife… is she still alive? In cell seven?"

Kellan glanced over at the monitors near the guard station. The monitor labeled with the number seven showed a young woman writhing on the floor.

"She's alive," Kellan said as he returned his attention to the man.

"Please… save her. I can't… I won't be able to… She doesn't deserve this…"

The man became too choked up to continue. Kellan hated the strain in his voice more than anything else. He nodded along with the man's request, unable to deny it.

"Of course," he said. "I'll go get her right now."

Kellan left the hospital bed and headed over to the guard station. There was no keyboard, and he wasn't sure how to operate the futuristic computer, but he didn't need to. His *Intuitive Tech* ability would allow him to use the computer without much effort.

He touched the side of the terminal, and the information filled his mind. He had control over the cell doors, and even control over the information in the system. Kellan marked the woman—whose name was Lily Meyers—as dead, and then opened the cell door. Perhaps this would prevent anyone from looking for her.

Then he opened all the doors.

He couldn't carry the twenty people here—but at least this way they could have a chance of escaping.

Without another word, Kellan ran to the door and then entered the cell block. He passed the many people in brown jumpsuits until he came to Lily's cell. She had chin-length auburn hair and bright-green eyes, but they were half-lidded, like someone under the influence of a truckload of drugs.

Kellan scooped up Lily, who was surprisingly light, and carried her out of the shabby prison. He took note of the walls and floors—pristine white, like the first corridor. Not the music area, and not the black organic-tech from the flestiss portion of the station.

He ran out of the prison.

Ran.

Kellan almost couldn't believe how effortless everything was. He had picked up people before—they had never been *this* lightweight. Then he remembered… His infection gave him increased physical capabilities. *No wonder this is so easy.*

Lily twitched and convulsed in his arms. Kellan spent another mana—bringing him down to two—and healed her with his body magic. It didn't seem to bring her out of her drug-induced state, but she did stop twitching. Lily closed her eyes, her head limp. Kellan had to support it.

When Kellan returned to the guard room, he went straight to the man's bed.

Mr. Meyers, the soldier from the United Earth Defense Force.

He was bleeding… but he still managed to tilt his head and get a look at Kellan and Lily. He managed a small smile, his eyes never leaving his wife. Then they dulled, and to Kellan's surprise, the arcana on the table next to him shifted in color. They changed from red to gold—sparkling with brilliant magical power.

Two more arcana appeared on the man's chest.

Four arcana? It seemed high for someone without magic.

Kellan didn't know why, and it wasn't like he had anyone to ask. Instead, he just reached out and touched the arcana, all four of them, and absorbed them. Now he had fifteen arcana in total.

He was prepared to leave and bid the terrible factory and prison a *forever farewell*, but then something strange happened. His chest twisted, and his heart beat out of rhythm. Something was wrong. Kellan closed his eyes and stood still for a moment.

When Kellan managed to open his eyes again, a pulse of power brought him down to one knee. He refused to let Lily fall to the floor, so he held her tight.

The Essence of Pure Magic

The mage who has collected at least ten gold arcana has cleansed their soul of stains. They have helped, saved, or aided others, sometimes to the detriment of themselves—and their sacrifices are now rewarded. They are now capable of wielding the strongest abilities in their primary magic…

Any curses the mage possesses are nullified, and the mage is now capable of learning *Apex Magical Abilities* (of E rank). With more gold arcana, the rank can be increased.

Kellan took a deep breath and struggled to comprehend the abilities that soaked into his thoughts.

—Chapter 53—
—Jace—

Kellan exhaled. For his primary magic, there were options… Apex magic. They were the peak abilities at each rank. Although Kellan had never been trained on magic, he just *knew* that these abilities were far stronger than anything equivalent on the same rank. It was like the arcana itself was speaking to him, whispering to him the secrets no one else would utter.

Something about the arcana was… brilliant and shining.

Eclipse—E-Rank Apex Powers

Void Knight [10 arcana]

The mage understands that light is tiny and insignificant when compared to the darkness that spans the infinite universe. While shrouded in shadows and void, the mage becomes more powerful.

Whenever the mage is in darkness (less than 1,000 lumens per 100 square feet) they are empowered, gaining +5 to all physical stats (strength, dexterity, fortitude), +2 to their armor rating, and immunity to all shadow-tendril attacks or grapples from other eclipse mages. Gain the title "the Void Knight."

Once taken, the mage may never acquire "Solar Scion."

Solar Scion [10 arcana]

The mage revels in the sheer destructive force of the light. While in the light, the mage becomes more powerful.

Whenever the mage is in light (more than 4,000 lumens per 100 square feet) they are empowered, gaining immunity to laser damage, one mana regen every six seconds, and +25% damage to all laser-type beam attacks. Gain the title "the Solar Scion."

Once taken, the mage may never acquire "Void Knight."

Light and shadow…

Measured by lumens?

Sen's right. Everything can be broken down into numbers, including the brightness of light sources. Kellan almost laughed. *When I think about it like that, having number-based magic doesn't seem so farfetched...*

He shook away the random thought and focused on eclipse magic. It was his primary, after all. But Kellan hadn't done much with the light side of it yet. He could make an object, glow, sure—but his focus had been on the shadows. A *solar scion*, he was not. And now that Kellan had experienced the benefits of increasing his personal numbers—the strength and speed that came from superhuman physical capabilities—Kellan knew he wanted more of that, especially once he rid himself of the infection.

There was no real choice in Kellan's mind. He decided to take *Void Knight*, immediately purchasing it with his arcana.

His other magical powers had given him a sense of energy, but nothing was as intense as the apex power. Kellan felt as though he had touched infinite possibility—but only for a second. It was gone a moment later. That was it. A brief glimpse of raw magical power.

Kellan inhaled and then exhaled, almost forgetting he was in the hybrid factory-prison. When he focused on himself, he realized he was no longer *Alex Kellan the Rulebreaker*. Now he was *Alex Kellan the Void Knight*.

It was definitely better than the other names people were giving him.

Kellan got to his feet. With Lily Meyers in his arms, he exited the guard room, and went straight for the mezzanine over the factory floor. The crates were lifted and dumped into the vats, slowly and steadily.

The computer made another announcement as Kellan reached the end of the catwalk.

"*Prisoner 556, an Outsider who hasn't presented themselves to the Arbiter, has escaped. The Arbiter will reward any and all who help capture Prisoner 556.*"

Kellan didn't care. He continued out of the factory, into the corridor, and then straight for the elevator. He ran the entire time, never growing tired. Now that he was a *void* knight, Kellan paid more attention to the light all around him. The hallway was dim—only some lights above, embedded in the arched ceiling.

With even breaths, Kellan stopped at the elevator door and then placed a hand on the computer terminal. He input the code, but the door didn't immediately open. The elevator was on its way. It would be here in seconds.

"Oh, that's a surprise."

The voice startled Kellan. He whirled around and spotted Jace standing a few feet away from him. He wore the same biker's jacket, but he no longer had a neutral or friend expression. For the first time since Kellan had known the man, he looked rather angry.

Jace's mechanical eye glowed a harsher blue.

"Let me guess," Jace drawled as he crossed his arms. "You found your alternate-dimension counterpart and you took your dog tags back, didn't you?"

Kellan held his breath. He didn't know what was happening. It took him a full thirty seconds to remember he was disguised as his own alternate-dimension self. Jace wasn't talking to *him*, Jace was talking to Alex Kellan the Defector.

"I like your alternate." Jace stepped close, limiting the distance between them to only a foot. "Or should I say *liked*? You killed him, didn't you? Is that what happened? Or is Brenner going to do that?"

Kellan said nothing. He had to maintain his disguise.

Jace's attention slid down to Lily. "Who is she?"

Again, Kellan remained silent. What did Jace want him to do? Tap out Morse code?

"It doesn't matter." With a huff, Jace ran a hand through his darker hair. It reminded Kellan of himself. "But I think you should set her down. We need to discuss something, and I need your full attention."

The elevator door opened. Kellan opted not to put Lily inside—he didn't want her getting out of his sight. Instead, he set her down on the floor near the wall, careful to tuck one of her arms under her head, so she wouldn't wake with a crick in her neck. Once Kellan was confident she was okay, he turned back to Jace.

Still, Kellan remained silent.

"I brought your dog tags to give them back to you," Jace muttered, his attention on the ceiling. "But then I ran into the other Alex, and I thought… No. It doesn't matter what I thought. He took me by surprise, that's all. I almost wish I didn't have to kill you, because… what if you were more like him, ya know what I mean?"

Kellan tensed. So, this was going to turn into a fight? How was he going to handle it? By smashing the lights and hoping his new *Void Knight* ability won the day? Kellan wasn't even sure what Jace's rank was.

Jace sighed. He brought his gaze down to meet Kellan's. "I didn't think you'd be alone until way later in the games. I'm glad you took those tags—it's the only reason I was able to find you."

The tags…

Kellan cursed himself under his breath. Jace had been following him because of the *dog tags*. That was how he had found him so quickly in the first game.

Dammit.

"I'm sorry, Father," Jace said, his tone flat and harsh. "But the only reason I joined the Nexus Games was so that I'd get a chance to kill you." His gaze hardened into an icy glare. "The time for redemption is long over."

Wait, what?

Kellan thought he had misheard. Had Jace just called him *Father*?

Jace's mechanical eye glowed with a harsh blue.

[Jace Kellan] used *Nightmare World* on [Alex Kellan].
[Jace Kellan]'s *Blue Dragon Eye* increases the difficulty of magical powers.
[Alex Kellan] succumbs to *Nightmare World*.

In an instant, the space station melted away from Kellan, like wet paints on a canvas, mixing together until they were jumbled. For a short moment, Kellan couldn't breathe. His head pounded, and he stumbled backward until his back hit a wall. What was going on? He closed his eyes and tried to focus, unsure of how he would handle the situation.

Kellan figured he had two options. He could either fight Jace, and attempt to kill him, or he could tell Jace the truth—he wasn't Alex Kellan the Defector. He wasn't his father.

But that would mean giving up his disguise to someone who wasn't trustworthy. Jace had already robbed their team of a key in the past, just because he could. Jace wouldn't keep his secret—Jace might even try to exploit it.

So, what was it?

Fight him?

Kellan opened his eyes, determined to try out his new ability.

And then his heart stopped. He really wasn't in Overseer Station anymore. He was… in Syria. He knew it like a parent knew their child. The heat, the spice, the dryness, and the stones… Kellan had dreamed of the capital, Damascus, for months after returning home. The Arabic writing on the far flags in the distance…

Kellan shuddered.

When he glanced over his shoulder, he saw no wall. No elevator. No Lily.

Kellan took breaths, but they were shallow, and they didn't give him any comfort. The sand… He had forgotten how much he hated the sand in the air.

This is a nightmare, Kellan reasoned. He had seen it in the logs of the combat. Jace had put him in a *Nightmare World.* But what did that mean? Was it an illusion? A trap? Teleportation? Had Jace somehow brought Kellan back to Earth? *His* Earth?

Kellan shivered as he glanced around.

What was going on?

The sky darkened, a rush of chill wind blew by. Kellan watched as the sand and ground shifted, and fingers clawed their way up from the depths. Bodies rose—undead monsters—like something straight from fiction. And while most of them were people Kellan didn't recognize, two of them were individuals he *knew.*

Jones and Greer, the two men Kellan had been with in Syria. They had died—Kellan had dragged their bodies all the way to safety. The guilt of surviving, when Jones and Greer hadn't, had lingered with Kellan, and now here they were…

It had to be a nightmare.

Kellan lifted his rifle, ready to destroy zombies.

But then the undead bodies, half-clothed and with skin rotting off their arms and faces, shambled together. They gathered as a tight group, and their disgusting flesh melted together, forming a blob of decay. One by one, the bodies piled on, making a larger and larger blob, the faces of the undead on the outside, all staring in Kellan's direction, their eyes milky, yet moving with life and attention.

Kellan lifted his rifle to shoot, but he couldn't bring himself to pull the trigger.

Jones and Greer became the two main heads on top of the creature, their bodies fusing into a centaur-style beast on top of the blob.

"What is *this*?" came Jace's voice on the cold wind.

Kellan couldn't look away. His chest twisted and tightened, and the horror of the monster was all he could focus on.

"This isn't right! This isn't your nightmare… I've seen what you fear. This isn't… This isn't right…"

Claws formed out of the undead monster, formed with bones and sinew weaving together in a hideous fashion. The claw was large enough to crush a car, and the beast swiped at Kellan.

The jagged bone claws ripped through Kellan's clothes, illusions, and armor, slicing up his chest and legs. He hit the ground, his blood everywhere.

Six damage in a single hit, even after reductions. Kellan rolled to his side, the searing pain of the attack filling his thoughts.

It wasn't real—but it *felt* like it was real.

A small part of Kellan thought it might be real… He *might* be in some sort of twisted pocket dimension, away from the others. What was he going to do? If he hadn't been infected, he feared he would've died.

The many faces of the flesh blob made gurgling words, as if trying to speak. Their haunting babbling drilled into Kellan worse than the pain of the attack. It sounded like they were trying to say his name.

But Kellan had seen worse in the Nexus.

This wouldn't stop him.

No. No—he refused. He hadn't gone through therapy, traveled dimensions, and fought in the Nexus Games to be brought down by guilt. Jones and Greer wouldn't want this. *They never would've wanted me to suffer.* Kellan had tried to promise them he would live for them, but instead of enjoying life to its fullest, Kellan had hidden away in a barren apartment, never finding anyone to start a family with, or to build a future…

That was Kellan's greatest regret. Squandering the life he had, when his friends and brothers-in-arms hadn't gotten the opportunity.

He had to live. He had to get out of here. It was the least he could do.

Kellan spent a mana and activated his *Ignore Pain.* Unable to feel the agony of the injury, Kellan cursed to himself. He brought his rifle up, intent on shooting at the monster, but then he remembered his coin.

If this *was* an illusion, couldn't he briefly cancel it? He grabbed it from his pocket and saw the glow—this was an illusion.

But then he remembered the cost of using the coin.

Five mana.

Which he didn't have.

The undead blob lumbered forward, the susurrations of Kellan's name like a field of crickets at night. One after another, after another. Kellan shivered and used the last of his mana to heal his injuries. Once his mana was depleted, he managed to get onto one knee.

When the undead creature swiped with its scythe-like claws, Kellan hit the ground and dodged, but just barely.

"*Jace*!" Kellan shouted. He rolled away from the monster and dragged himself behind the crumbled remnants of a stone wall. "Goddammit, Jace—*I'm not Alex*

Kellan! Well, *I am*, just not the one you're thinking about!"

When the monster attacked again, Kellan stepped into the darkness and avoided the swipe. The beast destroyed the crumbled wall, sending debris across the sand.

Kellan emerged from the shadows away from the monstrosity. Whenever Kellan looked over, he shuddered, disgusted by the faces, but also furious that Jace would attempt to use his old comrades against him.

But then… the colors bled away again, swirling and melting into a single dark color.

Kellan closed his eyes, rubbed at his eyelids, and then opened them. He was back in the space station, but now he was halfway down the corridor, stumbling around like he was injured. But he wasn't. His health was intact—it had all been an illusion. No slice to his stomach, just bruises on his knees and side from when he had been rolling around.

Unfortunately, he had spent his mana. He had none left.

Jace stood near the elevator, his expression incredulous.

"You… You've disguised yourself as the other Alex?" Jace then sarcastically chuckled. "Oh… This is all Xiang's doing. I should've known… I can't believe this."

Kellan ran a shaky hand down his face. "What was that?"

"A figment," Jace muttered. He narrowed his eyes, all mirth gone. "A trap of the mind to make mages easier to kill. I should've known it was *you* the moment I saw your deeper fears. My father isn't afraid of the past—he never would've seen his fallen brothers. He's afraid of the future. Always running from everything, including his family. He left me, my sister, my mother… He left Xiang when she wasn't just following along with the plan. The man flits from place to place, going with whoever is stronger in the moment, just to make sure he's always on *the winning side*."

Jace spoke the words with venom.

Kellan didn't know what to say to the man. This was more complicated than a couple of pick-me-ups could cure.

"He left you?" Kellan asked.

"He left *us*. Me, my sister, and mother. And we were taken by the Flestiss Dominion. He didn't care. He… never came for us." Jace's gaze turned to the floor, his mechanical eye glowing bright.

Fantastic. I'm a loser in another dimension. Just what I've always wanted.

"Look," Kellan said with half a smile. "I'm way behind on the social, interpersonal, and economic situation of the contests in the games, and if you wouldn't mind giving me a rundown of—"

Echoes traveled down the corridor.

Followed by a chill, like the temperature had lowered a few degrees, very suddenly.

Kellan stopped all talking and movement, his blood pressure high. It was either Xiang, or the actual Brenner. The chill of the man's multiple hexes was unmistakable, and since Xiang had copied it, there was likely no other explanation.

"We need to disappear," Jace said as he shrouded himself in invisibility.

But Kellan had no way to become invisible. And his attention immediately went to Lily. He couldn't step into the shadows if he was holding her.

"*Jace, I can't take her*," Kellan said in a harsh whisper.

The echoes grew louder. Kellan turned to the far end of the corridor and watched as Brenner stepped around the corner. His sleek armor, damn near skintight and scaled, was hard to miss. The man walked with confidence, and although Kellan just stood in the middle of the corridor, unhidden, Brenner didn't seem shocked or bothered.

But where was HR-8? If this were Xiang, wouldn't she have her brother nearby?

Kellan glanced over his shoulder.

Lily was gone. Jace must've taken her, much to Kellan's relief.

"There you are," Brenner said. Or was it Xiang? Kellan still couldn't tell. Brenner had spoken in a calm and collected manner, no hints as to his identity. He approached Kellan and then stopped next to him. "I thought I had lost you."

—Chapter 54—
—Team 42—

Kellan said nothing. He just stood stiff and silent, waiting for some sort of indication this was either the *actual* Brenner, or just Xiang, the leader of Team 101.

"Well?" Brenner asked, his dark eyes shifting to meet Kellan's gaze directly. "Have you found anything?"

That was it. All Kellan needed.

Xiang wouldn't have asked him a question like that. She wouldn't have invited him to speak, not when she had been so adamant about his silence.

This was the actual Brenner Hawke, Traitor to Humanity.

Kellan slowly shook his head. In his mind, he cursed his luck. The moment he could, he needed to get out of this man's presence. He would try to find an excuse—anything would do—to shadow-shift away.

"If you haven't found anything, then we should meet the others at the central control room." Brenner's sandy blond hair was slicked back, held in place with some sort of product. Xiang hadn't done that. Another confirmation that this wasn't her. "Come. Let's go."

This was the worst possible outcome.

Brenner turned and headed down the corridor, but he stopped just a few feet away and glanced over at Kellan. "What're you waiting for?"

There has to be some way to get out of this.

Kellan pointed in the opposite direction and then shrugged. He tried to convey a sense of curiosity. Perhaps Brenner would allow him to search more, and then Kellan could escape.

"*We don't have time,*" Brenner said, his jaw clenched. "Searching the entire station within five hours is impossible. We need to just move forward with the plan."

If I act suspiciously, then he'll know something is up. Kellan balled his hands into fists, trying to think of anything to escape the situation, but failing to concoct an exit strategy. He walked over to Brenner and followed him down the archway corridor, their footfalls echoing together.

Since he was unable to speak, Kellan couldn't really probe for useful information. He wanted to know—at the very least—why Brenner was helping the flestiss, especially after everything Kellan had learned from Meyers.

Then again, *did it matter*? Kellan already knew what he needed to do and that involved killing everyone in Team 42. Or perhaps just Brenner.

When Brenner turned down another corridor, Kellan shadowed his steps, but he kept his eyes open for somewhere to duck and hide. Unfortunately, most of the doors were closed, and Kellan didn't want to take the time to input the access code, for fear Brenner would instantly discover his farce.

"None of the other teams have been useful," Brenner muttered, more to himself than to Kellan. "And only twelve of them are here. It seems the other competitors are mostly cowards… To no one's surprise, really."

Kellan nodded once, hoping he was acting in character for his alternate-self.

After rotating his shoulders, Brenner gave Kellan a sidelong glance. "Did you manage to see Xiang last night? I'm telling you—she'll break if we just continue like we have been. Eventually, she'll stop hiding, especially when she thinks she's strong enough to fight us. The real key is to make her think we're weaker than we are."

Xiang was right, Kellan realized. *They really were just messing with her.* Kellan held back a snort and a laugh. *Damn, Brenner is petty. No wonder he turned traitor and helped a bunch of aliens. He's the kind of soldier who would grenade his own CO just because the man said something mean to him one time.*

The lights in the corridor were dim, and a few flickered.

To Kellan's surprise, he felt… faster and stronger and more in control. Was it his *Void Knight* power? Was it kicking in now? He didn't really have a way to measure lumens…

Brenner sighed. "Well? *Alex*? Did you?"

With another nod, Kellan continued to keep Brenner's pace.

"I have something for you," Brenner said, cutting off Kellan's train of thought. "*This* Overseer Station has anti-magic woven into some of the doors and walls. I managed to find a few tools with the substance as well. That will help us with the upcoming yami. Anti-magic goes straight through shielding."

The doors and walls had anti-magic?

Kellan nodded along with the other man's words, his thoughts on the door he had tried to mold in the prison. Had it been anti-magic that prevented Kellan from clawing his way inside?

"The tool I found is a blade of some sort. Small, but effective." Brenner didn't have a backpack or any sort of gear outside of his armor. Kellan wasn't sure where he was going to pull the tool from. Brenner must have seen him giving him the once over, because he shot Kellan a smirk. "I don't have it with me. It's by the central door. The anti-magic prevents me from storing it with my magic."

They turned down another corridor, and then another, the ribcage aesthetic continuing for the whole deck. Kellan wondered why, or where it came from, but since he couldn't ask, he focused on remembering their route. He just had to get back to the others.

The corridor was empty—for most of the trek, at least.

A lone door at the end of a long stretch opened as Brenner and Kellan walked by. A misshapen boy, someone in his late teens, stepped out of a small room with a large computer screen. His pockmarked skin and swollen elephant-like leg betrayed his inbred heritage. He was yet another Nexus local.

Kellan only had a fraction of a second to comprehend the other man's presence before Brenner leapt into action. With all the agility and power of an action star, Brenner roundhouse kicked the Nexus resident. Brenner's leg hit the resident with all the force of a steel beam. The man's face broke open even before he hit the far wall, teeth and blood splattering everywhere.

Brenner held out his hand, his palm opened to the floor. A sword—the blade a glowing laser—flew out of the darkness, hilt-first into Brenner's grasp.

With his weapon in hand, Brenner lunged for the wounded resident. The laser blade effortlessly cut the pockmarked man in half. All the blade was missing was a *buzz* and *swish* noise whenever it swung through the air, and Kellan would've sworn it was a lightsaber straight out of Star Wars.

Instead, the sword hummed with an inner power, and the pulse of the laser blade matched that of a heart beating.

Once the Nexus local was dead, Brenner knelt and scooped up the two arcana that sprouted from the pool of blood. He returned to Kellan a second later, no change in his expression. Brenner dropped his sword back into his shadow, like it was a familiar, and then continued down the corridor as though nothing had happened.

Kellan was almost impressed Brenner could be so nonchalant about murder.

"You're getting slow," Brenner commented, cracking his knuckles. "Next time, at least *try* to get the arcana. This is why you're falling behind."

Without any words, Kellan could only offer a nod.

Finally, after what seemed like a week of torturous company, Brenner brought them to a large door labeled: CENTRAL CONTROL. Kellan perked up, curious as to why Brenner had brought them here. *Isn't this the area Husker found that access code for?* Kellan crossed his arms and stared at the door. It was far larger than the others—big enough for a truck to drive through, if someone managed to get it into a space station.

To Kellan's surprise, and mild horror, three people appeared around them, their invisibility melting away.

They were the other members of Team 42—Ysa, HR-8, and Viniss.

Only these were the *real* ones.

Ysa and her punk-rock look stood out differently. She wore thin skin-tight armor, one sleeve pink, and her boots up to her knees. Her face had so many piercings, Kellan almost didn't have time to count them all. She carried an honest-to-god body bag over her shoulder. The limp body of the poor unfortunate soul within didn't seem large or heavy. Ysa's shadow flickered around—it even occasionally lifted off the ground and reached for the bag.

"Don't worry," she said with a smile. "He's still alive. Just drugged to the gills."

Then there was HR-8...

He looked exactly like Xiang's illusion, right down to the type of generic battle armor. The scar on the side of his head—a brand of some sort—was the man's most distinguishing feature. He had all the cheer of a dead clown at a kid's birthday party, his face hardened into a permanent frown.

And Viniss was just as disgusting as before, but unlike Xiang's illusion, the alien was wearing armor fitted for her insect-lobster abdomen. Her four arms were tucked close to her body, fitted into the groves of her chitin exoskeleton. Her nine feet of height gave her an imposing presence, even among a group of thugs.

"Where were you two?" Ysa asked with a laugh. She licked her lips, her tongue stopping on each piercing along the way.

"We couldn't find any of the codes." Brenner glanced between the rest of his team. "Any of you have any luck?"

In a gruff and almost pained voice, HR-8 nodded once. "We have the central code, but we couldn't find anything to access the master controls… I suspect our metal magic isn't going to help either. That's where the AI is housed, and from our tests, it's more powerful than we suspected."

Brenner cursed under his breath. Then he shook his head. "It doesn't matter. I'll get us the code when we get there."

HR-8 lifted an eyebrow, his forehead so wrinkled from stress that the skin didn't move much. "You're going to use your meta magic? *For this*?"

"I suspect I'll be fine."

"You gamble far too often."

Brenner smirked. "You only win big if you risk big."

For a short moment, Kellan wasn't entirely sure what they were arguing about, but then he examined Brenner using his analysis ability. One of Brenner's hexes seemingly made his meta and travel magic dangerous…

It read:

> **Hex—[Connected to the Sea of Chaos]—**The mage's mana pool is doubled, and they gain access to the unknowable magics, capable of ranking them as any other. As punishment, the mage's soul cracks each time they use a C rank or higher power (and after an unspecified number of cracks, the mage's soul shatters, killing them).

So, Brenner could use his magic, but there was a chance he could die? Kellan also thought that was a terrible risk. What was so important about the master controls that Brenner absolutely needed them?

Ysa tossed the body bag to the floor and kicked the side of it. "Well, we have our key for the round, at least. If we manage to pull off everything else, this will be pretty entertaining."

Kellan stared at the bag for a long moment. Who was inside? Did he even want to know?

Maybe I can steal it.

"Good." Brenner walked over to the massive truck-sized door. "But first we need to deal with the yami. Are you ready?" He glanced between his teammates.

"How is everyone on mana?"

The others—including Viniss—replied with quick nods and affirmations of their readiness. But Kellan couldn't. He had no mana whatsoever, and he wasn't sure he could deal with a yami in his current state.

With a short sigh, Kellan held up a hand and shook it back and forth, trying to indicate he wasn't completely ready to handle anything.

Ysa poked at an eyebrow piercing and turned to him, her eyes narrowed. "You're out of mana? What have you been doing?" Then her sharp eyes went straight to Kellan's rifle. "And what is *that*?" She walked over, frowning slightly. "Are you carrying around Sevriss? Isn't that the cursed weapon that, like, *every* dimension has?"

The rest of Team 42 stopped what they were doing and turned to face Kellan.

What was he going to do? Laugh this off and tell them he was just an illusion? He couldn't do that—he had to maintain this ruse no matter what.

"It's not cursed," HR-8 muttered. "I don't think… I've ever seen a Sevriss that wasn't riddled with a death curse of some sort."

Viniss's oil-black eyes stared long and hard at Kellan. For a short moment, Kellan thought the alien could see right through Xiang's illusion—that she knew his real identity and was just messing with him by not saying anything.

Then, in a raspy voice far worse than Husker's illusion tone, she said, "*The maggot reeks of sweat and conflict. I suspect it earned the favor of the rifle whenever it killed its previous owner. Such occurrences are not uncommon.*"

HR-8 bowed his head. "It's likely as you say, my queen."

"Where's your *normal* weapon?" Ysa asked, her lip curled in disgust. She couldn't seem to leave Kellan alone—her gaze stayed fixed on him. "This garbage isn't better than what you had."

"*Enough*," Brenner growled. "I don't care. We'll be using the anti-magic tools anyway." He held out his hand, and a small vial zipped out of his shadow, lifting upward as though the gravity had been reversed. The vial hit his palm with a soft *smack*, and then Brenner tossed it over to Kellan.

Without even thinking, Kellan caught the vial and then brought it close to his eyes.

Magical Item [Consumable]—Greater Glintberry Potion

Once consumed, the mage gains 3 mana every five seconds for the next minute, for a grand total of 40 mana.

Both Kellan's eyebrows went for his hairline. Brenner just *had* potions like this? Why didn't Xiang have anything as useful? They needed things like this on their team.

Without waiting another moment, Kellan drank the tiny vial—barely a mouthful of liquid—and then shoved the empty glass container into his pocket. Sure enough, his mana increased by three. And then three more. And then three more.

And then he was full.

He suspected the other Alex Kellan had much more than twelve mana as his maximum capacity, but Kellan wasn't about to dwell on it.

Then Brenner picked up a black tool propped up by the door and tossed it to Kellan as well. With an effortless motion, Kellan caught the arm-length "weapon" and examined it. Unlike the potion, his analysis gave him no details on the item.

It was shaped like an asparagus knife—a small handle with a long metal shaft and a sharp spade at the tip. Asparagus knives were used for cutting into the plant with one quick motion. Why was something like this on a space station?

Kellan turned the tool around in his hand. His *Mold Metal* was still active, and when he tried to bend the shaft, nothing happened.

Anti-magic. Just like Brenner had said.

"Focus," Brenner commanded. He motioned everyone close. "Once we kill the yami, we head straight into the central computer area. Remember—speed is the key. Don't let the monster touch you."

Kellan grew stiff and anxious. It seemed as though the other members of the team had already heard the plan to defeat the yami. Had the plans included Kellan? *Hopefully I'm not the linchpin to this, or else I might be the downfall of Team 42, just not like I had been hoping for.*

After placing his hand on the computer terminal, Brenner opened the massive door. It slowly slid open, revealing a dark corridor roughly fifty feet in length. It was straight and perfectly square, with polished metal surfaces so clean and pristine, they were practically all mirrors.

But then something emerged from the depths of the reflections, rippling the surface of the walls and ceiling. A mechanical person, like Mr. Andy, showed its head, chest, and hands... Only it wasn't person-sized at all. The monster was a giant. Its mouth could fit three people inside, and its hands were the size of small cars. Its cyborg body was covered in flesh, but half of it remained in the mirrors around the corridor.

More hands emerged—a dozen more—some with claws, some with syringes, some with blades. And when the monster's chest was half out of the wall, Kellan spotted several smaller mouths around the ribcage. Skin and sinew were stretched over everything, like someone had attempted to disguise the beast as a human and gave up partway through.

The monster's gargantuan body was blocking the way to the door at the far end of the fifty-foot corridor.

The eyes in its chrome skull were intact and fleshy, but without eyelids.

Name: Dr. Davies, Scourge of Overseer Station
Race: Master Yami
Magics: Body, Mind, Metal
Rank: Impossible
Armor Rating: 20 + 20 Shielding
Health: 150/150

Stats:
Strength—25 [Cyborg-Enhanced]
Dexterity—25 [Cyborg-Enhanced]
Fortitude—25 [Cyborg-Enhanced]
Intelligence—2 [Insane]
Perception—3
Willpower—2 [Insane]

Abilities:
Undead Machine—The yami is immune to poison, gas, and phantasmal attacks. The yami does not need to breathe or eat to survive. Additionally, the yami feels no pain.
Mirror World—The yami is immune to laser damage and blinding effects. Additionally, the yami's laser attacks bounce off reflective surfaces, the damage halved after each bounce until the attack would deal less than 5.
Tied to the Arbiter—If the Arbiter is alive, this yami cannot be fully killed. If its health is reduced to 0, it stops functioning, but does not drop arcana. After a short recovery period, the yami is revived at full health. If the Arbiter is dead, this ability doesn't activate, and the yami drops arcana as usual and then ceases to exist.

"*Another* master yami?" Ysa shouted. "I swear the Arbiter doesn't want to give us *any* arcana."

"Quiet," Brenner snapped. "Let's kill this as quickly as possible." He lifted his own anti-magic tool and then stepped into the mirror corridor. He touched the neck of his armor, and it lifted up over his face, becoming a fully functional helmet, complete with a visor. He was now covered completely from head to toe.

Although Kellan wanted to leave, Ysa and HR-8 walked into the corridor with him, Viniss close behind, like they were surrounding him. More and more, Kellan had a terrible feeling as though they all knew his secret.

Once they were inside, the massive door slammed shut behind them, practically rumbling the whole station. The tall ceiling—at least twenty feet up—shimmered with movement. Kellan glanced upward, but all he saw was his illusioned reflection. What was that?

Three overhead lights kept the corridor well lit, but otherwise there was nothing else on the ceiling.

Then the fight began.

Dr. Davies opened its skull mouth, its chrome teeth just as reflective as the walls. It wailed and screamed, the piercing noise enough to go straight to Kellan's eardrums. While everyone grimaced and cringed, Kellan ignored the pain thanks to his ongoing ability.

"Oh, this bitch has to *go*," Ysa said with a laugh. She waved her hand through the air.

[Ysa Voight] casted *Corrosive Aura* on all allies. Attacks now ignore

half of the enemy's armor rating.

Brenner lunged forward at frightening speeds. In less than six seconds, he attacked Dr. Davies a grand total of six times, effortlessly slashing at the many arms of the monster. Brenner was so physically strong that he managed to slam his anti-magic tool straight into the rotting flesh of the creature. And the tool—surprisingly—didn't break. It was just as tough as the doors and walls of the space station, capable of withstanding great amounts of pressure and force.

The many smaller mouths on Dr. Davies's chest opened and closed, clacking their metal teeth together and creating a *chittering* noise that drilled into Kellan's thoughts.

[Dr. Davies] used *Madness Requiem*. All damage dealt will come from the enemy's willpower score rather than health pool. If a mage drops to 0 willpower, it will be the same as if they dropped to 0 health. Lastly, all enemy mages' perception is halved, and if below 5, they are deafened and dizzy.
[Brenner Hawke] succumbs to *Madness Requiem*.
[Ysa Voight] succumbs to *Madness Requiem*.
[HR-8] succumbs to *Madness Requiem*.
[Alex Kellan] succumbs to *Madness Requiem*.
[Viniss Tarkin] resists *Madness Requiem*.

Kellan's hearing instantly cut out, and his balance nearly left him. Dr. Davies swung with six of its arms, attempting to stab Brenner with syringes and knives. Despite his befuddled state, Brenner dodged the many attacks, sometimes with the grace of a dancer, his eighteen dexterity plain to see.

Then the alien lifted two of her arms.

[Viniss Tarkin] cast *Fortress of the Mind* on all allies, granting them +20 defensive willpower for the purposes of resisting mind-altering magical abilities.
[Brenner Hawke] resists *Madness Requiem*.
[Ysa Voight] resists *Madness Requiem*.
[HR-8] resists *Madness Requiem*.
[Alex Kellan] resists *Madness Requiem*.

Kellan's deafness left him as quickly as it had come.

HR-8, no longer stumbling around, lifted two handguns and fired as fast as the weapons would allow, damaging Dr. Davies across the face and chest. When the yami swung for him with its other six arms, HR-8 leapt backward, narrowly avoiding the attacks—though nowhere near as gracefully as Brenner.

The shadows around Ysa flared to life and created tentacles and tendrils. With the ferocity of a kraken, the darkness lashed out at Dr. Davies, grabbing some of its rotted-skin arms and holding them in place. Some of the shadows even shattered two of the three lights in the corridor, creating a dim atmosphere. Was Ysa also empowered by the darkness?

Then she shot Kellan a smile. "You gonna just watch us do all the work, big boy? *Get in there.*"

Holding his anti-magic tool tightly in his hand, Kellan moved forward and slashed at one of the arms restrained by Ysa's shadows. It was easy to strike—the thing couldn't move—but Kellan was more surprised by the amount of damage he managed.

[Alex Kellan] struck [Dr. Davies] with a mining cutter for 16 damage.
[Dr. Davies] reduces damage of each hit equal to its armor rating of 10. (Halved due to Corrosive Aura)
[Alex Kellan]'s mining cutter ignores [Dr. Davies]'s 20 shielding.
[Dr. Davies] takes a total of 6 damage.

Kellan had been certain he wouldn't be able to deal any damage at all—the monster was just too far out of his league. But due to the buffs given to him by Team 42, he actually had the ability to cut into the yami's health.

And having a nine strength had been a wakeup call, but having a fourteen made him feel like he could rip apart a sheet of steel if he wanted.

As if frustrated by the tide of battle, Dr. Davies screamed again. Then its many hands opened, their palms flat and each facing at least one member of the team. Before anyone could use any more magical abilities, twelve laser beams shot through the corridor, each erupting out of the hands of the monster. The beams ricocheted off the mirrors, blasting around the room and creating a spiderweb of damage—a deadly laser light show that Kellan wasn't sure he would live through.

Dr. Davies moved its hands around, and the lasers danced throughout the corridor, hitting everyone at least once.

Several beams struck Kellan, but the shadows jumped to protect him, both from his armor and his *Void Knight* ability. He took ten damage from the heat of the lasers, but before he took another hit, Kellan focused and lunged out of the way. When two more beams moved toward him, he rolled in another direction, keeping an eye on his surroundings.

The worms in his body went to repairing the damage.

He had a fourteen dexterity thanks to his infection, and the five extra to his physical stats from *Void Knight*—even with the lasers in the room, the light wasn't enough to deactivate his ability. Or perhaps it was because of Ysa. Her shadows shielded him just as much as they shielded her, shrouding him in blackness more than before.

Kellan felt… weightless. He moved around the lasers with more ease than he thought possible, his only limitation his perception. He almost wanted to laugh, but he kept it to himself.

Brenner rushed at the yami and attacked six more times, striking the monster like a helicopter blade cutting down a butter sculpture.

HR-8 continued his bullet barrage. A shimmer of magic seemed to lessen his damage. Was that the shielding in effect? The bullets clearly weren't anti-magic.

Ysa lashed out with shadows, the tendrils corrosive on their own, even damaging the mirrors whenever they touched.

And Viniss… She seemed to be doing something, but it had no visual manifestation. And Kellan couldn't see most of the information when he wasn't directly involved with the magical powers.

Again, something shimmered on the ceiling, catching Kellan's attention. When he stared, he saw nothing. Was it invisible? Was it Jace? No. Jace didn't walk on the ceiling.

Then was it… a Kuji? Even though the lasers were everywhere?

The yami screeched a third time, blood weeping from its mouth by the bucketful. The beast collapsed out of the mirror wall, its many arms dangling from the walls. Its eyes popped like ruptured water balloons as it went motionless and stiff.

They had defeated it already?

Kellan was speechless. The monster had well over a hundred health—the most he had ever seen. And Team 42 had dismantled the monster with minimal damage.

And if their Alex Kellan had been here, I'm sure they would've been a well-oiled machine.

Dr. Davies didn't have any arcana. It just sat in a lake of its own blood, the mirrors reflecting the crimson. It was an eerie sight no matter the direction Kellan glanced.

The Tyranny Worms healed the last of Kellan's damage, and thanks to Xiang's illusions, he couldn't see them. That was the worst part—the sight of their writhing bodies, and knowing they dwelled within his veins and organs.

Thankfully, Kellan was back to full health. The other members of Team 42 seemed scorched, however. Even Brenner had taken one or two lasers straight from the palms of the monster—he seemed rough around the edges, his blond hair singed. With a shaky hand, Brenner pressed the side of his helmet, unsnapping it. Then he cleaned his face of any sweat.

When Kellan used his analysis, he saw Brenner was fairly wounded. The man was down to only fourteen health out of fifty-five.

"Let's go," Brenner growled, pointing to the far door. "Before this beast picks itself back up."

—Chapter 55—
—Central Control—

The large door beyond Dr. Davies slid open and revealed the central control room for all of Overseer Station. The circular room was empty except for a single power cell directly in the center. It was a futuristic device that reminded Kellan of a large server. Lights on the side blinked with power, and blue crystals were woven into the metal and the controls. It was mounted to the floor and went all the way to the twenty-foot-tall ceiling.

It pulsed with constant power, and Kellan almost felt like he had walked onto the set of a knock-off Star Trek episode. The computer terminal in front of the power cell reminded him of the other terminals by the door. Cari was here too?

This has to be the location they don't have an access code for.

Kellan took a deep breath and glanced at his anti-magic tool—the mining cutter. He wanted to keep it for the rest of the games. So long as he found a way out of this situation, he knew he would need anti-magic in the future.

Team 42 strode into the central control room. Each of them had been so focused on the fight, that they had to take a few moments to recover themselves. They healed—likely with mana—and then brushed themselves off. Even Viniss took a moment to scrape her many lobster legs, but she mostly waited for HR-8, who shuffled over to Viniss's side and did the cleaning for her.

Kellan shivered and rubbed his arms. The entire central control room was freezing. It was kept dark—which he now preferred—and the temperature was low. His breath became visible, steaming out of his mouth with each exhale.

With a confident gait, Brenner went straight to the central control power cell. He placed his hand on the computer terminal and stared down at it as if he was prepared to punish it for existing.

"You sure this'll work?" Ysa asked, playing with a pointed part of her Mohawk. "I mean, if we shut down the life support, some mages will have ways around it, won't they? Some entropy mages are undead, ya know. They don't need to breathe."

"Don't explain things to me," Brenner snapped. He glared at her over his shoulder. "We don't need to kill them *all,* we just need to kill most of them."

They were preparing to shut off the life support for the whole station? Kellan was taken aback, stunned they'd want to do something so drastic.

Brenner returned his attention to the computer. "And it'll work. On my dimension, Overseer Station had the capability to do anything, even self-destruct. I'll set it for a timer—three hours, two minutes. Any of the teams who don't have an infected won't have long to search. They'll die searching the station—either by freezing to death or asphyxiating. Either way, we'll be down opponents."

As Kellan stared, he realized Brenner's health was recovering. Slowly—one point of a health every six seconds—but still.

And the thought of just *killing everyone* who didn't have their hands on a body seemed insane. Brenner and his team wouldn't even get the arcana for it. Why were they doing this? Just to make sure they *absolutely won*?

Brenner glowered at the terminal, his fingers unmoving.

"Are you afraid?" Ysa snorted and placed a hand on her hip. "Don't want to use your power, huh?"

Brenner didn't reply. He just narrowed his eyes further.

What ability was he using? He had meta and travel magic, both of which had a chance to kill him if he used abilities C rank or higher. It had to be meta. Hadn't someone said meta was the magic of magics? Perhaps Brenner was planning on manipulating the magic in the computer terminal to get it to do what he wanted.

Kellan could only guess—he had yet to get meta magic for himself.

"Are you seriously still stalling?" Ysa rolled her eyes. "*Big Bad Brenner* getting cold feet gets me drier than the Mojave Desert."

Brenner turned to face her, and Ysa immediately grimaced and backed away.

"It was a joke," she said, waving a hand.

He didn't move.

"R-Really. C'mon. I was just playin' around. Aren't you happy we got here so quickly? Everything is going according to plan. Let's have some fun."

Brenner didn't seem amused. He returned his attention to the computer and then said, "Ysa, where is the body we need for our key?" His voice was too calm and cold for Kellan's comfort.

"I didn't bring it into the fight with me." She half-shrugged. "So I left it outside."

"Go. *Get it.* Before someone takes it from us."

"You want me to drag it in here?" Ysa glanced around the empty space.

Brenner tapped his fingers on the computer. "Yes. We'll stay here. No one will venture into the corridor guarded by a master yami. And if they do… They'll be weak when they enter the room, and that's when we'll strike."

With an exaggerated sigh, Ysa turned on her heel. She stopped for a moment and gave Kellan a playful grin. Then she practically danced to his location, whimsical to the point of mental illness. Kellan didn't like it. He grew tenser the closer she drew near.

When Ysa reached him, she placed her hands on his chest and then went to her tiptoes. "Come with me," she whispered, leaning closer to him, her breath practically on his chin. "It's always funner when we're alone."

The moment she tried to bring her lips to his, Kellan panicked.

If he touched her bare skin, his infection would transfer—and Team 42 would know something was terribly wrong.

Kellan shoved Ysa away before they touched. But he had forgotten how strong he was. Ysa flew backward and slammed onto the ground, back-first, a good twenty feet away. She slid across the smooth metal floor, so winded she couldn't breathe.

Clearly, Ysa wasn't operating with a fourteen strength.

Everyone else on the team turned their attention to Kellan. At first, Kellan thought he had revealed himself as an imposter, but the others just stared for a moment and then chuckled. Brenner especially—he returned his attention to the computer, as though nothing had happened.

HR-8 returned to cleaning the alien, and Viniss didn't even glance in Ysa's direction.

Kellan almost walked over and helped Ysa up, but it wasn't necessary. She slipped into the darkness and then slithered across the floor until she reached the far door. Then she stepped out of the shadows and huffed. Without a glance backward, she exited the central control room.

"*Warning,*" Cari said over the station's speakers. "*Tampering with Overseer Station's life support systems could result in loss of life.*"

Brenner typed at the computer terminal, his attention tunneling.

The warning message had chilled Kellan's thoughts. After a deep breath, he walked over to the terminal and placed his hand at the top, drawing Brenner's gaze.

"What is it?" Brenner whispered, slow and deliberate.

Kellan shook his head. He knew it was a risky move, but he couldn't sit by and do nothing. What if his team died due to the life support loss? There were more than twelve teams here, which meant there was a minimum of sixty competitors—maybe more. What if they all died because Kellan had been too afraid to talk Brenner down?

Brenner just stared at him for a long moment. Then he relaxed a bit and forced a tight smile. "Feeling guilty? You don't like doing this a second time, huh?" He chuckled and then shrugged. "I thought it would get easier for you, but I guess you're just too wishy-washy."

Although Kellan didn't know exactly what the man was talking about, he didn't care. Whatever got Brenner to stop.

"How many times do I have to tell you? There are duplicates of people. They live in alternate dimensions, living peaceful and happy lives. Who cares if some carbon copy of them dies here? You need to stop taking it so personal." Brenner motioned to their surroundings. "Look at this place. It's almost like ours, remember? There are hundreds of Overseer Stations, too. No one's life is special—they're just arcana, waiting to be absorbed by a tougher, stronger, more ambitious mage. Let this go, Alex. I can't talk you out of every existential crisis."

Kellan hated every word.

Even if Brenner were correct, it was obvious that the other *Alex Kellans* weren't *him*. They were different enough, even if they shared the same name and face. And Brenner's speech didn't account for the Nexus locals who lived on the station. *They* didn't have alternate dimension counterparts. They were… unique.

Kellan hadn't thought about that before.

He shook away the tangent and kept his hand on the computer terminal.

If he could voice his objects, he would, but for now, Kellan hoped Brenner would just be reasonable.

A scratching on the ceiling interrupted their conversation, however.

Everyone glanced upward. There wasn't anything to see—even though they had dim lighting, it was still possible to see the smooth metal of the ceiling. It didn't appear as though anything was there…

Kellan's heart pounded hard and fast as a bizarre thought crossed his mind. He slowly turned to HR-8. The man had a skull on his left hand, just above the numbers *42*. He was the team's Straggler, but…

He wasn't as injured as Brenner.

With unsteady movement, Kellan removed his hand from the computer terminal and unslung his backpack from his shoulders. Brenner glanced away from the ceiling and—upon seeing Kellan had moved—went right back to his work to alter the space station.

Kellan removed the *Perfume of the Damned* from his backpack.

Magical Item [Consumable]—Perfume of the Damned

Perfume that makes the wearer smell like a Straggler. All effects that say "only target the Straggler" also target those who wear this perfume. Lasts for six hours.

The tiny vial was sturdy and pristine, and he twirled it between his fingers before uncorking the stopper. He knew this was a risky plan, but he also knew he needed to act quickly. It was now or never.

While Brenner was distracted with the computer, Kellan gently splashed him with the perfume. It was just barely a teaspoon of liquid, and it all went onto Brenner's armor.

In slow and sarcastic disgust, Brenner stopped typing and then glanced at the stain on his clothing. He narrowed his eyes as the odor wafted up for all to smell. It was a sour aroma that reminded Kellan of an unwashed gym.

"What the fuck was that?" Brenner asked, an edge of amusement in his harsh words.

Kellan pointed upward, and he made sure not to glance up himself. The moment Brenner turned his gaze to the ceiling, he was paralyzed.

The haunting sight of the Kuji would do that… Kellan hadn't forgotten.

The next few seconds were the tensest of Kellan's life. The Kuji slashed downward with its disgusting hand, catching Brenner across the face, marking his forehead, cheek, and chin with several disgusting claw gouges.

Still, Kellan didn't look up. Instead, he lifted the mining cutter, and with all the strength he could muster, he slammed it into Brenner's exposed neck. Kellan's anti-magic weapon went through Brenner's shielding, and Ysa's Corrosive Aura halved Brenner's armor rating.

But it wasn't enough—the sixteen damage didn't bring Brenner to zero, but maybe there was still a chance. When Kellan pulled the weapon from Brenner's neck, it was obvious he was no longer paralyzed. He snapped his gaze up to Kellan's, rage in Brenner's eyes.

[Alex Kellan] struck [Brenner Hawke] with a surprise attack using a mining cutter for 16 damage.
[Brenner Hawke] reduces damage of each hit equal to his armor rating of 7. (Halved due to Corrosive Aura)
[Alex Kellan]'s mining cutter ignores [Brenner Hawke]'s 15 shielding.
[Brenner Hawke] takes a total of 9 damage.
[Brenner Hawke]'s personal ability, *Overconfident*, activates, doubling his physical stats.
[Tyranny Worms] restore [Brenner Hawke] for 1 damage every 6 seconds.

Kellan had been afraid of Brenner's personal ability activating, but he hadn't expected the worms *at all.* It almost startled Kellan into inaction, but his combat training kicked in hard.

Before Brenner could rip him in half with his bare hands, the Kuji latched five of its hook-clawed hands into Brenner's body. The spider-monster lifted Brenner off the floor and dragged him toward the ceiling.

This was an even-numbered round of the Nexus Games, which according to the rule book, meant the Kuji were more powerful…

But Kellan knew the Kuji was no match for Brenner. With mere seconds to act, Kellan slipped into the darkness and shifted to the door of the room—his mining cutter couldn't go in the shadow with him, so it dropped to the floor near Brenner's feet.

Kellan then lifted his rifle and fired at the computer terminal, riddling it with bullet holes.

HR-8 and Viniss whirled on Kellan, both tensing for a fight. All buffs—the *Corrosive Aura* and the *Fortress of the Mind*—seemed to disappear from everyone on the team. Clearly, they wanted to rest for another combat.

Kellan wasn't about to stick around for that, though. He opened the door, ran into the mirror corridor, and shadow-stepped again, trying his damnedest to get as far as possible as fast as possible. When he emerged from the darkness, he was in front of the opposite door. He slammed his hand on the computer terminal.

And then Dr. Davies—already revived from its fight—reached a syringe-claw over and sliced up Kellan's back for seven damage. Kellan stumbled forward as the door opened, his mind spinning.

Goddammit.

The yami screamed as Kellan stumbled out of the corridor, his vision blurring. What were in the syringes?

Ysa, standing outside and smoking a bane cigarette, glanced over. She had one boot on the body bag, but otherwise wasn't doing anything. When she caught sight of Kellan, she frowned.

"What happened to you?" Ysa snorted and laughed. "Tried to fight the yami yourself?" She huffed and turned away. "Serves you right for being a dick."

Kellan hurried over, and after a deep breath, kicked her as hard as he could in the stomach. Ysa slammed into the space station wall, her head cracking on the metal support arch.

Although he felt conflicted about attacking her without warning, Kellan didn't have time to dwell on it. He grabbed the body bag, effortlessly threw it over his shoulder, and ran down the corridor as fast as his superpowered body would allow.

Ysa lifted her arm and the shadows in the corridor sprang to life. The tendrils grabbed at Kellan, but then they all slipped off, negated by Kellan's *Void Knight* ability. Ysa shouted an incoherent scream of frustration as Kellan rounded a corner.

A few seconds later, Kellan heard shouting in the corridor.

"*I'll fucking kill you*!" Brenner yelled, his voice already growing louder.

Kellan turned down one hall, and then another, never stopping to glance backwards. Laser beams lit up the corridors behind him, the light show so intense, it could be the coming of a second sun. Fortunately, the space station had been constructed with anti-magic… Brenner could rage all he wanted, but he wouldn't blow the walls apart.

But Brenner was faster. He gained on Kellan, zipping down the corridor with more fortitude, strength, and dexterity.

And Kellan couldn't step into the shadows if he was carrying the body bag…

His thoughts twisted together as dread set in. Kellan knew he couldn't outrun Brenner, so what was there? Abandon the body and just shadow-step away? He could, but he didn't want to give Team 42 the opportunity to make it out of the game with a key. And he definitely needed a key for his own team.

Desperate, Kellan reached into his pocket and withdrew his bizarre coin.

The residents of the Nexus…

They hid nearby.

Kellan ran at superhuman speeds, and the moment the coin glowed, he leapt from one wall to the other, feeling around for a hidden door or passageway. Sure enough, he slammed a hand on one wall and nearly tumbled to the floor as he passed through an illusion.

He stood in a new corridor, one far smaller than the ribcage corridor he had come from.

Brenner shot past him—his speed on par with a superhero from a comic book.

Kellan could barely breathe, his chest had been so twisted in doubt and dread.

No… Wait.

Kellan struggled to breathe. He grabbed at his clothing, his lungs burning slightly, but he hadn't felt the agony thanks to his ongoing *Ignore Pain* ability. What was wrong? Had it been Dr. Davies's attack? What had been in the syringes?

Then Kellan heard the distinct cock of a shotgun.

"If it isn't our lucky day," someone muttered. "A member of Team 42… And he looks pretty injured."

—Chapter 56—

—End of the Second Game—

Unable to breathe, Kellan turned around and held a hand up in the air. When he tried to speak, it only came out as a hoarse wheeze. His lungs practically caught fire in an attempt to burn a hole in his body to receive oxygen.

Two people stood before him. Kellan recognized both. It was Nasbit and Ryan—the two men from Team 10. Nasbit held a shotgun a few feet from Kellan's face, his finger on the trigger.

"Think they'll be able to figure out it was us?" Nasbit muttered, taking careful aim.

Ryan stood behind him, his eyes narrowed as he glared at Kellan. "I think it's reasonable to assume that some sort of magic will allow them to identify a killer. But if we hide the body… We might be able to circumvent that."

"Good enough for me."

Nasbit fired.

Although Kellan thought it impossible, he managed to move slightly out of the way—his fourteen dexterity really giving him superhuman speed and precision that was just unheard of. Unfortunately, the buckshot from the shotgun caught him down the arm, damaging his side as he rolled away. Thankfully, his armor had absorbed some as well.

And the harsh sound of the gun was probably the worst part. It echoed in the tiny space, ringing in Kellan's ears.

Dammit. I should've killed them when I had the chance!

Kellan struggled to see straight. With what energy he had left, Kellan leapt out of the illusioned corridor and back into the main area. He still remembered the way to the elevator. He hurried there, carrying his body bag. Nasbit and Ryan leapt out after him, but Kellan turned a corner before they could fire again.

Halfway to the elevator, Kellan's vision darkened around the edges. He gritted his teeth and pressed forward, unwilling to drop the body.

He had carried dead bodies before… for longer than this… he wasn't going to let go. He refused.

And then Jace appeared out of thin air, his invisibility shimmering away. For half a second, he seemed amused, almost delighted.

Kellan coughed and strangled out, "It's me."

All of Jace's amusement instantly dropped. His mechanical eye, glowing blue, homed in on the body bag. After a prolonged moment, he asked, "Brenner is searching for *you*, isn't he?"

Kellan managed a nod.

"If I help you—what's in it for me?"

Now wasn't the best time for negotiation. Kellan's thoughts drained from his head faster than water through a colander. He glanced at the body bag, his chest throbbing. Should he give up the key? No. Never.

With a shaky hand, Kellan reached into his pocket and threw his coin to the floor. It clattered and spun, stopping between them. The coin had been useful, but Kellan didn't have anything else to offer. He just… he needed someone to get him out of the corridor.

"I could just kill you, and then take the coin and the body." Jace snorted and then tucked his hands into his jean pockets.

Kellan grabbed at his shirt, and with the last of his breath, he said, "*Let's see you try.*" He was done playing games. If Jace wanted this to be a fight, Kellan was just going to have to fight without any air.

During his extreme circumstances training, Kellan had trained himself to hold his breath for up to two minutes, but he remembered what the instructors had said. The dizziness and lack of oxygen to the brain could mean he could pass out at any second—and no one wanted to pass out in the middle of combat.

After mulling it over for what felt like decades, Jace eventually smiled. "Fine. I'll take the coin. Let's go." He held out a hand.

Kellan shook his head. He couldn't touch him.

Although Jace didn't know what was going on, he lowered his hand and then turned to head for the elevator. When Kellan attempted to follow, he stumbled around. Jace stopped, ran back, and then pulled a small vial from his pocket.

"Drink it."

Kellan's *Blitzkrieg Analysis* gave him information, but he couldn't see it. His vision blurred. He drank whatever Jace handed him, and a moment later, he felt better. Kellan's vision came back, his body felt limber, and he hefted the bag further up onto his shoulder.

With some breath, Kellan said, "I'm infected."

Jace nervously chuckled. "Oh. I see."

Before Jace and Kellan could continue on their way, Brenner appeared at the far end of the corridor. He dashed around a corner, not moving quite as fast as he had been before, but still with enough speed to be classified as a deadly weapon.

Kellan was certain this would end in death, but Jace held up a hand. Kellan couldn't see the combat information. He just watched as Brenner stumbled to a halt and then grabbed at his head. The injuries to Brenner's face were gone, but the blood remained, matting his hair, and giving him a look of lunacy.

"*Jace*," Brenner hissed. "*I swear I'll kill you, too*!" He dug his fingernails into his scalp, drawing even more blood before the worms in his body healed the minor injuries. "End the Nightmare World, you sick bastard…"

"Where's your flestiss?" Jace taunted with a laugh. "Not here to save you from mind magic effects? Tsk tsk. What a shame."

Brenner—his eyes closed and barely acting rationally—lunged forward, his hand outstretched. He was trying to fight through the illusion, and Kellan just barely moved out of the way. Jace ran around Brenner and then went straight for the elevator door.

Kellan followed him. Once, he glanced over his shoulder, surprised to see Brenner pulling his laser sword out and slashing at the wall like it owed him money. The Nightmare World illusions really did a number on people, even S-rank mages like Brenner.

But if Brenner even slashed them once—by accident—they would be done.

The elevator door opened, and they jumped inside. Kellan's vision darkened a second time as the ill effects of the yami returned. Whatever Jace had given him, it wasn't enough.

"I need to see Sen," Kellan rasped.

Jace nodded, his blue eye glowing brighter. "He's close. Don't worry."

The elevator door opened, and they exited on another deck. The computer said the name of the deck, but Kellan hadn't been paying attention. He put all his focus onto holding the body bag, and that was it.

Jace led him to a set of escalators and carefully went up with Kellan, making sure the other man didn't fall. Kellan struggled, but he eventually made it.

"There they are."

With blurry vision, Kellan made out the shapes of Team 42. They rushed over, took the body bag, and spoke to him as though concerned. Kellan strained his ears, trying to figure out what they were saying.

"He brought back a body bag with an unconscious person inside."

"It must be a key."

"He said he needed to see Sen."

"Me? Why? Is he sick? Is that why he's acting like this?"

"I don't know. Brenner must've done something to him."

"Brenner?"

Murmurs and huffs flew around Kellan like ghosts. He could barely hear it all.

Then someone guided him over to a bench. Wait, a bench? Kellan didn't remember seeing one of those in the space station. But here it was. He rested back on it, his consciousness fading.

"Are you still infected?"

It sounded like Ysa, but Kellan recognized her tone and word choice.

Mavis.

He slowly nodded.

"Don't worry, Kellan. We've got you. Everything is going to be okay. You brought us the key, Sen is going to help you feel better, and I'm going to take care of this infection, okay?"

Kellan couldn't muster the strength to respond. He closed his eyes and tried to think of the words, but the yami venom made it impossible. No wonder everyone had avoided the claws in the fight…

Soft lips touched his, and Kellan didn't know if he was dreaming, or this was reality.

> **You've tagged another player!**
>
> You are no longer infected. You lose your Infection Buff and cannot be "tagged back" by the same player.

Mavis had taken the infection?

Once Kellan lost his increase to fortitude, he closed his eyes and drifted into a deep sleep.

***

Warm sunshine streamed onto Kellan's face, waking him from his deep sleep. At first, the heat felt nice. He had missed the sun. But then his senses returned, and panic gripped him. Kellan shot up into a sitting position, his breathing ragged.

Why was there sunshine? That was impossible, wasn't it?

He glanced around, his heart hammering.

This was his apartment. His tiny little home in Fayetteville. Not Overseer Station.

For a short moment, his thoughts were nothing more than white static. *This isn't real. Someone has a sick sense of humor.*

"Look at that—sad sack is awake."

Bitso's voice sent a shiver down Kellan's spine. He turned and found the news anchor leaning against the doorframe of his bedroom. Bitso crossed his arms and smiled, then he hooked one foot behind the ankle of the other, like this was a casual social call and not the disturbing nightmare it actually was.

"What's going on?" Kellan asked as he slid off the side of his bed and slowly stood. "Where are we? I know this isn't my apartment."

Bitso sarcastically rubbed at his chin. "No fooling you, huh? That's no fun." He chuckled and then offered a shrug. "Most people wake up and start screaming, *it was all a dream! Thank goodness!*" He flailed his arms a little and then laughed again. "Priceless."

Kellan remained stiff and quiet, waiting for a proper explanation.

"I just wanted to see where you lived." Bitso motioned to the tiny bedroom. "Apparently, your dimension stores most of its humans inside dull boxes. Its drab and plain—the Arbiter would disapprove." Bitso rubbed at this blindfold. "*I* almost fell asleep looking around the place, and this is just illusion inside your thoughts. You need to spice up your life, sad sack."

"I'm in the Nexus Games," Kellan quipped. "Doesn't get any spicier than that."

Bitso clapped his hands together once and pushed off the wall. "That's the spirit! I knew I liked you—you're still my second-favorite competitor."

"So, why are we in an illusion in my thoughts?" Kellan asked. He didn't want to stay here any longer than necessary. Weren't the others waiting for him in Overseer Station?

Bitso sauntered around the room, "glancing" at the simple furniture as he went, despite the fact that he was blindfolded. He touched everything, including the edges of the nightstand. "I told you… The Arbiter *really* likes that you're collecting gold arcana. Apex magic already? Wonderful. He wants to reward your efforts."

"Really?" Kellan readied himself for the catch. "What kind of reward?"

"What do you want?"

The question seemed odd—Bitso's voice was laced with an odd tone, like this were a trick. Kellan mulled it over for a good thirty seconds while Bitso picked up a pillow and fluffed it repeatedly in his hands.

"This is filled with so much oil and dead skin cells." Bitso smiled as he turned it over several times. "And a little of something else… Tsk tsk. What would your mother think?"

"*Meta magic*," Kellan snapped, trying to bring the conversation back to the realm of serious. "I want to learn meta magic."

"Oh? That's it?"

"Well, yes, but… I wanted to ask you something first."

Bitso set the pillow back on the bed. "I literally can't wait. Ask me anything."

"You once told me there was black blood I could consume in order to learn eclipse magic at a reduced cost. Is there something like that for meta magic?" Kellan had thought it over for some time, and he knew *this* was what he wanted. Eclipse magic was already his primary magic—he couldn't change that. But if he could learn meta fast…

"I suppose the Arbiter has something like that." Bitso smiled wide enough to show off his sharp teeth. "But you'll need to be awake to drink it. So, whenever you get up, it'll be by your bed in the AVU Palace."

"Really?"

Bitso's smile disappeared. He seemed a little more serious than Kellan had ever seen him. "The Arbiter *really* wants you to collect more gold arcana." He said each word with a harsh edge—uncharacteristic for the news anchor. "Use the meta magic to gather more—to learn additional apex abilities. *Capisce?*"

"Why does the Arbiter want me to do that? Why does he care? It seems… odd."

Bitso groaned and then scratched at his blindfold. "So many *questions*. Do you know how much mana it takes to keep this illusion going? Of course not, or else you wouldn't be chatty."

A part of Kellan wanted to make a sarcastic comment about Bitso's need to speak at length about everything, but he kept the jab to himself. Something about the Arbiter's insistence with gold arcana bothered Kellan. It didn't seem right…

But then Kellan remembered Meyers.

"Wait, Bitso. Before you go—I have to tell you something. The flestiss are competing in the Nexus Games so they can use the magic in Zenith to kill the Arbiter."

Bitso waited for a silent moment. Then he smiled and asked, "And?"

"And..." Kellan exhaled. "That doesn't disturb you? The Flestiss Dominion plans on attacking all other dimensions."

With a snort and surprised chuckle, Bitso shrugged. "Did you forget that the Arbiter sees *everything* that happens in the Nexus? Even on that tin can of a space station. He knows all about the Flestiss Dominion and their human-devouring queens." Bitso ran a hand through his dark hair. "So, who *cares*? The Arbiter literally made a giant undead machine monster just to mess with players trying to reach the control center of Overseer Station. He has little fucks to give."

"But—"

"Look at you! All tense and fearful because you thought you might not get to deliver the message." Bitso laughed again, louder than before, even slapping his knee in delight. "Oh, that's cute. Very adorable. You've surprised me yet again. Good for you. Ten points to Team 101."

Kellan gritted his teeth, irritated by Bitso's insanity and lack of concern for life. Then again, Bitso didn't seem to like or respect the Arbiter—or anything, for that matter. Perhaps madness had claimed the man so thoroughly, it didn't matter to him what happened to the rest of life in all the known universes.

Kellan might as well have been speaking to a brick for all the good it was doing him.

"It's not against the rules to use the magic of Zenith to harm the Arbiter?" Kellan asked.

Bitso half-chortled and then shook his head. "Nobody cares why someone enters the Nexus Games. Their intentions could be noble or selfish—or straight evil—but that doesn't matter. The Arbiter only judges by the number of keys a team brings him."

"What if... What if I wanted to stop the flestiss from getting to Zenith?"

"Kill them," Bitso replied, no hesitation in his voice. "I mean, I thought that was obvious, sad sack. If you want them to fail the Nexus Games, make it happen. What did you think I was going to say? *Take them to court and appeal the decision?*"

Kellan stepped closer to the man, hoping to appeal to his humanity. "You don't care? *Really*? About anything?"

Silence stretched between them. Bitso tapped his jawline, uttering a soft *hmmmm* as though he was a cartoon mulling over an obvious joke. Finally, he said, "I think... that enough mana has been used on this dream sequence, and that I need to get back to announcing all the death and mayhem." He shrugged. "But I'll give your question serious thought. If I think of anything I really care about, you'll be the first person I tell."

"Thanks," Kellan sarcastically replied.

"And congrats on living through the second game, by the way." Bitso slapped him on the upper shoulder. "Good job. I really enjoyed that, too. Next time, kill some members of Team 42 while you're impersonating them. The best deaths are the ones that happen by surprise. Trust me."

Before Kellan could reply, the colors of the room melted and swirled, and his consciousness faded.

***

When Kellan managed to open his eyes again, he wasn't in the space station. He stared at a ceiling. One he was familiar with.

He was back in the AVU Palace.

END Book I

The Nexus Knight

—Chapter 1—
—The Nexus Games Continue—

Alex Kellan wasn't the type of person who thought himself insane. Even though the last few days had been an *Alice in Wonderland* drug trip worth of crazy, Kellan was still convinced he had his wits about him. Everything had felt like a terrible nightmare. No—worse than a nightmare, if that were even possible.

But he was still here.

"Good morning, Fayetteville!"

Kellan sat on an unreasonably large bed in the middle of a strange room. Rain beat the windows and the glass door leading to the balcony, creating a dreary atmosphere. Fluorescent lamps and overhead lights kept the gloom at bay, but the chill of the frigid weather crept inside regardless. Kellan took deep breaths, his attention on the waterfall of liquid washing across the otherwise clear glass.

"Another day in the Nexus. Another list of bodies."

Kellan ran a hand through his short hair. The room had an 80-inch flat-screen TV mounted to the far wall, opposite the bed. And that was it. No other furniture. The TV screen flickered in and out, as though the wires were faulty. A bizarre news anchor sat at a rusty metal desk. He was the only person on the screen.

"Don't worry, ladies, gentlemen, and everything in between," the news anchor said with a smile. "The Nexus Games are just getting into full swing. Only two games down! *Eight to go*! We have plenty more to see. The Arbiter is full of surprises."

The man on the screen wore a crisp, black suit and a white blindfold. His dark-red hair, matted with dried blood, was slicked back in a semi-professional manner.

Kellan rubbed at his forehead, applying pressure to his eyebrows. A fog lingered on his thoughts, but he didn't care. He forced himself to get off the bed. *On your feet, soldier,* he thought with a chuckle. *People are depending on you.*

As per his training, he went through a list of known facts.

It was sometime just after Christmas. There were worms in his body. He was a participant in the Nexus Games, an interdimensional sadistic event made up of teams fighting to gain keys. His team had…

Maybe two? Out of five?

Kellan wasn't sure. He had lost consciousness during the last game.

The news anchor slapped the desk and smiled widely, exposing his perfectly white teeth. The molars in the back were sharpened into frightening points. "Do we need a few instant replays? I think so! Look at this chump here. The one who accidentally stumbled across Dr. Davies."

The TV flicked and then showed a scene of a man walking into a mirror-covered hallway. The floor, walls, and ceiling were reflective—the man stared at his own haggard expression for a long moment, pointing at the blood splatters on his face, T-shirt, and jeans. The sweat under his armpits and along the back of his shirt betrayed his anxiety.

A monster emerged from the mirrors, a scene straight out of a horror movie. It was a humanoid machine, large enough to eat someone whole. Its human-skull was chrome and just as reflective as the hallway, with bits of flesh stretched over its body like it was trying to wear clothing that was four sizes too small.

The beast—a mechanical giant straight out of a sci-fi version of *Jack and the Beanstalk*—reached a clawed hand for the sweaty man.

The man screamed and crumpled to the reflective floor, his arms up and shaking. The monster, Dr. Davies, slowly pressed its car-sized hand down on the man, the metal of its android body unforgiving. The man squished like a fat tick.

The TV switched back to the news anchor. The blindfolded man chuckled. "Yikes. That chump had all the confidence and skill of a popped balloon. Doesn't really make for great television, but it'll make for one hell of a viral video!"

Kellan shivered. He had fought the mechanical monster during the last game. It had been easy, but only because he'd had the help of Team 42.

Which reminded him…

I need to tell everyone about Team 42's plans.

Kellan stumbled forward, his body a bit weak. He recognized the sensation. Drugs. Something in his system. He took a deep breath and forced his legs to carry him to the TV.

The news anchor cackled with laughter as another clip played, but Kellan couldn't bring himself to watch. He slammed his hand along the side of the TV until it flicked off. The patter of rain on the windows was the only sound that remained.

Kellan patted himself down, concerned with his well-being. He stared at his white T-shirt and black sweatpants. He rarely wore sweats, and he definitely wouldn't opt for them in a strange environment. Even when he went to the gym, Kellan tended to wear shorts.

He also didn't have any socks or boots.

I need my damn equipment. Kellan glanced around and felt the dog tags around his neck. They weren't really his, but his name was on them—they had belonged to an Alex Kellan from an alternate dimension. After a short sigh, he ran a hand through his dark hair.

Ice filled his veins as he stared at his own reflection in the smooth black screen of the TV. When he glanced down to stare at his left hand and saw the number

101 inked into his skin. That was the mark of his team—prominent for the world to see.

Team 101.

Sun Xiang was the leader.

Husker Linis was the Straggler.

Mavis Cartwright, Sun Sen, and Kellan were all members.

Where were they? Kellan turned full circle. The room remained barren—a single bed, one TV. Nothing else. He was alone with the rain.

A cold sense of urgency took hold of him. Kellan reached for his waist and then shoulders, looking for any kind of weapon. He hated the fact that he found nothing. Where was his rifle? His handgun? Kellan walked over to the bed and felt around, hoping to find a KA-BAR knife or *something*. But he came up emptyhanded.

Mistakes were written in blood, and Kellan couldn't afford to slip up during this deadly competition. Kellan rotated his shoulders, dwelling on his current location. Fortunately, he was inside the AVU Palace—an Oasis zone that prevented players in the Nexus Games from attacking one another.

Priorities. Kellan inhaled and made a list in his head of all the things he needed to accomplish, in descending order of priority.

"I need to find the others," Kellan muttered.

What had happened to them? Was Mavis still alive?

"Hopefully they made it," he said aloud as he walked toward the door in his room.

Kellan placed his hand on the cold doorknob and hesitated. *Wait,* he thought. *Something else happened.* He closed his eyes and thought back. The news anchor had visited him in his dreams. *Bitso.* The news anchor was Bitso. A mysterious and deranged individual who served the Arbiter, the primordial dragon in charge of running the Nexus Games.

Bitso had come to see him.

With a sigh, Kellan backed away from the door. The rain intensified, battering the glass like it wanted to break into the room. Kellan ignored the storm just beyond the windows and instead walked back to the bed.

In his dreams, Kellan had spoken to Bitso. The lunatic news anchor had said the Arbiter wanted to reward him for gathering gold arcana. It was strange—Kellan didn't understand why he was being rewarded—but it seemed that no one else even really knew what gold arcana was, and Kellan was the only one collecting it. Everyone else gathered *red arcana*, a crystal-like material that emerged from the bodies of the dead.

But gold arcana...

It came from people who gave their arcana willingly.

And the gold arcana had unlocked some sort of hidden magical abilities.

"Goddammit," Kellan murmured.

He didn't understand the ramifications of the situation, and it bothered him. Back on Earth—*his* Earth, not the Nexus-version of Earth—he had been a member of a Special Forces unit known as Delta Force. They always had intel on their targets, and the exact parameters for their missions. The Nexus Games didn't offer Kellan that luxury. He was constantly playing catch-up. He didn't know the rules, he didn't understand magic, and he wasn't sure if he was making the right decisions.

But he also couldn't sit around and do *nothing*.

During the dream with Bitso, Kellan had asked for a reward—something to help him develop magic easier and cheaper.

"And everyone loves cheap and easy," Kellan said as he searched around the mattress.

Bitso had said he would leave him his reward close by.

It had to be in the room.

The moment Kellan lifted his pillow, he found what he was looking for. It was a glass vial with a metal stopper. The insides were a glittering purple.

Words flashed over Kellan's eyes. Normally, that would be irritating, but Kellan had grown used to it. Whenever he stared at magical people or items, his *Blitzkrieg Analysis* offered him information that only he could see. The info had always been helpful, and Kellan was thankful that he at least had some ability to know what was going on.

His eyes gave him more information on the vial.

Magical Item [Consumable]—Rare Hydra Corp. Serum

A strange potion developed by the Immortal Megadonis, owner of Hydra Corp. The mage who drinks this gains access to meta magic and has a 20% reduction to the cost of ranking.

Kellan picked up the vial. It was smaller than his pinky finger, and the liquid inside probably wouldn't fill a tablespoon. Was that it? That was all that was needed? Kellan thought it bizarre, but he also wasn't about to question it.

The Nexus was a mysterious dimension too strange for him to fully comprehend.

Who was Megadonis? What was Hydra Corp.? Why did they make serums? Normally, Kellan would demand the answers to all those questions before he did anything with an odd liquid, but in this circumstance, he knew he wouldn't get another chance like this.

He either drank the serum now, or he would likely lose it.

Kellan undid the metal stopper and then threw back the small amount of liquid, swallowing everything without tasting it. The glittering fluid tingled as it went down Kellan's throat. He blinked back the odd sensation and then shivered once it had reached his gut.

Something had changed.

Kellan closed his eyes. In the Nexus, everything was measured in numbers, right down to a person's physical capabilities. If he focused hard enough, he could see his physical and mental attributes.

Alex Kellan

Magics: Eclipse, Body, Metal, Meta
Rank: D, D, D, E
Mana: 12/12
Health: 7/7
Unspent Arcana: 5
Strength—4
Dexterity—4 [Accurate]
Fortitude—3 [Tough]
Charisma—3
Manipulation—1
Intelligence—2
Perception—5 [Keen-Eyed]
Wisdom—1 [Broken]
Willpower—10 [Defiant] (Halved)

Abilities:
Personal—[Descended from Zenith]—The mage has the raw magic of Zenith in their blood and has no rank maximum. The mage can also develop one "unknowable" magic.
Personal—[Blitzkrieg Analysis]—The mage can see *basic* details of other magical beings and objects upon first glance without the need to spend mana.
Training—[Sharpshooter]—The mage adds a 50% bonus to gun damage.

Flaws:
[Greater Attachment]—The mage suffers greater from personal loss than normal. Whenever the mage loses someone close, the mage's wisdom is reduced to 1 and their willpower is temporarily halved.

Kellan wasn't sure why the Nexus operated like this, but he had an educated guess. Since the Nexus had people arriving from multiple dimensions—some with magic, some with limited magic—the numbers were a simple way to convey information that almost everyone could understand. They weren't vague or up for interpretation.

It was the difference between saying *this room has a few chairs*, and *this room has three chairs.* They were both conveying information about the room and its chairs, but one sentence was definite and left nothing to the imagination.

Kellan still didn't like the numbers. Not because he hated numerical systems—quite the opposite. He just hated being left in the dark. So much about the Nexus, and the magic, was a mystery to him. While it was easier to see who was stronger based on a single number, or who had more health, or mana, Kellan wasn't sure how personal skills or flaws were allocated.

"One damn mystery at a time," he muttered to himself as he rubbed at his eyes.

Then he headed for the door. Without another thought on the situation, Kellan left the barren bedroom, intent on finding the rest of his team.

Especially Mavis.

—Chapter 2—
—The Power of Zenith—

Kellan entered a massive sitting room.

Every team staying at the AVU Palace had their own personal area, it seemed. Team 101 had been graced with a suite, though Kellan had never seen anything like it. The sitting room had a giant couch and a massive TV hanging on the wall. Four doors led to individual bedrooms and bathrooms. And the balcony had a spa built into it. Well, not a normal spa, but a *mana spring*, a place for mages to quickly recover their mana.

The suite wasn't built for beauty, though. Most of the décor was black and dark red, like it had once been the set of a *Dracula* movie. It wasn't Kellan's favorite and didn't instill within him a sense of *home* or *comfort*.

When Kellan glanced around, he noticed the ambient magic. Information showed up across his eyes, explaining the aura around the building.

The AVU Palace Oasis

You have entered an Oasis. While inside this non-conflict area, all mages are forbidden from initiating direct violence. Offensive magical abilities are limited. Any who attempt to circumvent this rule will answer to the Arbiter himself.

He rubbed away the message. While he appreciated the fact that he was in an Oasis—especially since half the other teams wanted him dead—Kellan was already well aware that the AVU Palace was a safe sanctuary.

Kellan's Blitzkrieg Analysis didn't seem to care, however. It provided information on anything magical whenever his gaze fell upon it, or whenever he seemed to actively contemplate the object. Kellan could dismiss the info, and sometimes he could ignore it, but the readout often interjected.

Kellan went straight for the door out of the suite and stepped into the massive hallway. He rubbed his temple, trying to remember the layout of the palace. It was a bizarre place that gave Escher a run for his money, especially since so many architecture styles were used in the construction.

As Kellan made his way down the hall, he had to shield his eyes from the bright lights. Rock-style techno music pulsed through the floor, the bass disturbing the Gothic paintings hanging on the walls. When Kellan passed by an open door, he took note of a bar and dance floor. Neon-colored lights blinked with the intensity of a strobe.

No one was inside.

The bar was empty, with no one manning the joint.

No one danced on the empty floor.

Yet the music and lights continued going, seemingly with a life all their own. Kellan didn't understand, but then again, he figured this was another mystery best left unsolved. He quickened his steps as he made his way to a staircase leading down.

When Kellan reached the bottom steps, he found himself face-to-face with two Pestbyters—machine servants to the Arbiter himself. Every Pestbyter seemed to be a floating ball of machinery with wires that hung limply from the underside. Antennae and odd radio receivers poked out of the top of the sphere, and the Pestbyters hovered in the air with powerful engines that hummed in a pulse-like rhythm.

Kellan glanced at the first. The machine's information was given to him in an instant.

Name: Pestbyter #36
Race: Semi-Sentient Construct
Magics: Metal, Eclipse
Rank: Impossible to Rank
Armor Rating: 5
Health: 20/20
Stats: Concealed
Abilities: Concealed

When Kellan stared at the second, he received an identical readout, except the other was named *Pestbyter #37*. The two machines hovered near the foot of the staircase, their wires dragging along the red carpets of the palace as they moved a few feet back and forth. Were they pacing? Could semi-sentient constructs even get bored?

Kellan walked past them, tense and unable to relax.

The Pestbyters turned in his direction, each of them with camera eyes on the front of their spheres. The camera zoomed and focused, but Kellan ignored it. He hated the Pestbyters with a tiny passion.

"*Good morning*," one Pestbyter said in a sickeningly-cute girl's voice. "*Remember to follow the rules of the games.*" It ended the statement with an artificial giggle.

A shiver ran down Kellan's spine. The machine was anything but innocent and pure.

Kellan said nothing as he continued, opting not to engage the bizarre machines. The Pestbyter didn't follow up its statement with anything else, or even pursue. It just resumed its pacing, its camera eye swiveling back and forth.

The front double doors of the AVU Palace caught Kellan's attention as he jogged by. They were comprised of two sets of double doors, each made of thick wood with designs of dragons carved into the center. The dragons themselves were made of cogs, gears, and pistons, amalgamations of myth and machine.

Grand, sweeping archways dominated the ceiling, reminding Kellan just how large the AVU Palace was. Several football stadiums could fit within the many wings and ballrooms, and with each hallway Kellan hurried down, he found himself more lost than before.

He had expected to see more people around as well, but to his bewilderment, he spotted very few. Mages milled about in some of the quiet rooms, and Kellan even spotted a pair in a room with soft jazz music playing from speakers mounted into the walls, but that was it.

"Where the hell is everybody?" he murmured to himself.

Normally, the AVU Palace was filled with mages.

The absence of people put Kellan on high alert.

Becoming increasingly anxious, he rushed into the next hallway and slammed open doors as he came to them, looking for anyone on his team. What if they had all died during the last game?

No, Kellan thought. *That can't be right. If Xiang had died, the team would have lost, and I wouldn't be alive.*

Which meant, at the bare minimum, Xiang was still around. Somewhere.

Kellan slammed open a large, wooden door, the handle crashing into the wall. To his surprise, the room was occupied, but not by partygoers or individuals trying to relax.

This was an operating room. The sterile tile floor and white counters reeked of disinfectant. The lights overhead shone brighter than any fluorescent bulb had the right to. The chair in the middle of the room was tilted all the way back, practically becoming a flat surface. A man sat within, but he was covered by operating sheets, including his face. Only a small hole in the sheets showed the man's stomach.

He was open and bleeding, his organs clearly on display.

Standing on a step stool next to the chair was a little kid. The moment Kellan met the child's gaze, Kellan was given information he already knew.

Name: Sun Sen the Puppetmaster
Race: Human
Magics: Mind, Body, Soul
Rank: Concealed
Armor Rating: —
Health: 6/6
Stats: Concealed
Abilities: Concealed

Sen stood over the unnamed man, a bored expression on his child-like face. Sen's hands were coated in a thin layer of blood—the man's blood.

"Ah, you finally woke," Sen said. He spoke with the cadence and vocabulary of a man in his thirties, but he had the voice, and height, of a seven-year-old boy.

With slow and careful movements, Sen stepped down from the stool. Then he walked over to the nearest counter, dragged over another step stool, and climbed up to use the sink. He washed the fresh blood from his hands.

Sen wore an outfit that suited his childish body, including kid's jeans and a sweatshirt with the Power Rangers across the front—five multi-colored sci-fi sentai, each with a little helmet. It seemed comically childish for a series of magical death games, but Kellan wasn't about to comment.

"I've been meaning to speak with you." Sen finished wiping his hands together before switching off the water. "But clearly, you needed to rest first."

Kellan strode into the room, his nose burned by the cleaning chemicals hanging in the air. With a sneer, he went straight to Sen's side.

The kid had the honeyed skin and narrowed eyes associated with Asian features, but Kellan had come to learn that Sen wasn't from *Earth*, he was from some sort of alternate dimension with an Earth-like world. A bizarre dimension. One where people practiced *flesh-crafting*, though Kellan didn't completely understand what that entailed.

Sen's long, black hair had been tied back in a ponytail, likely to prevent it from hanging in his face while he had operated.

Kellan grabbed Sen's upper arms and jerked him close, practically pulling the kid to the edge of the step stool. Sen stared at him with wide eyes, obviously startled by the rough manhandling.

"I need to tell you something, and then I need to ask a few questions," Kellan growled, barely restraining his urge to yell. "*And I don't want any weird interruptions or sarcastic comments until I'm finished.* Understood?"

Sen's shoulders bunched at the base of his neck, his eyes still wide, but his eyebrows lowered into angry slants. "What're you—"

Kellan tightened his grip on Sen's upper arms. "Did we get the key from the second game?"

Sen stopped his words and swallowed. Then he finally said, "Yes."

"And did Mavis live?"

"Of course," Sen said matter-of-factly.

While that provided Kellan some relief, it wasn't the only thing weighing on his mind. "Okay. Listen. I met with Team 42 during the second game. Since I was illusioned, they didn't know it was me."

Sen lifted an eyebrow, but otherwise said nothing.

"They discussed things in front of me," Kellan stated. "I know their plans. They're intending to win the Nexus Games so that they can use the magic of Zenith to kill the primordial dragons and conquer the other dimensions."

For a brief moment, Kellan wanted to chuckle. A sarcastic, *I'm obviously insane*, type of chuckle. Never in his life had he uttered a more nonsensical and preposterous string of words. If this had been Earth—his dimension—he would've been locked away in an asylum.

Sen said nothing.

Kellan, who had expected more of a reaction, shook Sen once. "*Can they do that*? Is that possible? Or are they just crazy?"

"Do what?" Sen asked. "Use the magic of Zenith to kill primordial dragons?"

"Yes."

Sen pursed his lips as he mulled over the question.

Zenith, as Kellan understood it, was another alternate dimension where people and mages dwelled. Unlike all other dimensions, however, Zenith was supposedly *perfect*. It was the most magical, most technologically advanced—and everyone wanted to go there but couldn't.

The only way to get to Zenith was by winning the Nexus Games. Victory in the games meant getting a one-way ticket to the perfect land of magic. Only the Arbiter could grant such passage, apparently.

And according to Sen, the magic in the dimension was so powerful and amazing that nothing compared.

"Primordial dragons are creatures of immense power," Sen murmured, his gaze on the floor. "But the magic in Zenith is said to be absolute."

"Is this a *Can God microwave a burrito so hot that he himself can't touch it* situation?" Kellan quipped.

Sen frowned as he slowly lifted his gaze to meet Kellan's. "The primordial dragons are strong, but Zenith is *all strength*. Therefore, I would have to say *yes*, it's possible to kill the dragons with the magic acquired from Zenith."

"You're not worried by this information?"

"If that really is their plan, you should tell the Arbiter." Sen smirked. "Perhaps they'll be removed from the Nexus Games."

"I tried telling the Arbiter." Kellan gritted his teeth, struggling to recollect everything. "I spoke with Bitso and told him all about Team 42's plans. He said the Arbiter already knew, and that he didn't care."

"When did you speak with that madman Bitso?"

"While I was sleeping. He was in my dreams."

Again, Kellan reflected on the nature of his statement. He had never thought he would be having such a discussion. *This is my life now*, Kellan thought, half-smiling to himself, his own inner tone sardonic.

Sen huffed. "Well, there's your problem. Clearly, you should speak to the Arbiter himself and not one of his crazed minions. I'm sure the Arbiter would love to hear about how some of the Nexus Games players are plotting his death."

"There's also a flestiss on Team 42, remember? One of those weird alien people." The second game was a blur in Kellan's mind, but the hideous crustacean-like body of the alien flestiss remained clear in his thoughts. "I think I saw flestiss machines during the second game. On the space station. They were harvesting arcana from dead bodies."

"You *saw* this?" Sen asked.

"Yes. They were drowning people in cages." Kellan tightly closed his eyes, remembering the arcana in the tubs, and then the jail cells where he had met the dying soldier. Then he opened his eyes again, his memories hazy. "I need to know—do you think it's likely that the flestiss in the games will really follow through with invading other dimensions?"

"I'm not an expert on the matter," Sen said. "But yes. I think they would. The number of dimensions they've invaded is rather high, according to my sister."

The man on the medical chair groaned.

Sen squirmed and pointed. "Have I answered enough questions?" he demanded. "Because I was in the middle of an operation."

Kellan released the kid and stepped away. With prim little steps, Sen got down from the stool and walked over to the one by the chair, ascending as though to a throne. The man groaned again. Sen touched the man on the shoulder, and the pained noises stopped.

"What're you doing?" Kellan asked. "Harvesting arcana from sad sacks who stumbled into the Nexus?"

Kellan was well aware that arcana crystals came from dead bodies. Everyone was. The number of deaths during the games—simply to take the arcana—had been shockingly high. Was Kellan's own teammate torturing people to take their arcana as well? It brought a disgusting taste to his mouth.

Team 42 had practically made a sport of hunting down innocent people.

Sen scoffed. "I'm not harvesting arcana, *fool.*" He slid his small hands into the bloody guts of the man, his fingers curling around a small portion of intestines. "First off, we're in an Oasis. I can't take actions to attack people here. This surgery—while painful and bloody—is meant to strengthen. Secondly, I'm helping our team by procuring us resources, thank you very much."

"How so?"

"This mage is paying me in magical items." Sen glanced over his shoulder and smiled. "I thought it was an appropriate use of my time and valuable skills."

Kellan stared at the bloody insides. Sen returned his focus to his work, his child-hand fidgeting with the soft organs. With careful movements, Sen molded the flesh of the man as if it were clay. He wove some membranes together and even reached deep enough to fiddle with the muscles. Chunk by chunk, Sen took bits from one area of the man and folded them into another, creating sturdier parts afterward.

Everything seemed thicker afterward—corded and reinforced.

It was like taking Play-Doh and kneading it together to make something new. Or perhaps like a surgery to remove fat from one area and stick it in another.

Kellan glanced between Sen and the man covered by the medical sheets. "Aren't you worried about anything I just told you? Team 42 is going to help the flestiss invade all remaining dimensions."

"*If* they win the Nexus Games," Sen stated. He glared at the organs in front of him, rearranging them like mushy Tetris pieces until they were fitted back into place. "And I already told you the solution. Inform the Arbiter directly. You have plenty of time to do so."

"What do you mean?"

"The games aren't even halfway over. You need *five different keys* in order to access Zenith. Well, a number of keys equal to players in the team… but still.

You get the picture. Team 42 needs five keys."

Kellan crossed his arms. "How many do they currently have?"

"They have two keys. They gathered one from the *Seek and Destroy* game, and then one from the *Infection* game. That means they need three more. We have plenty of time to stop them or think of another plan."

After a long exhale, Kellan glared at the tile floor. He walked over to the medical chair and frowned, trying not to look at the spaghetti that was another man's insides.

"And we also have two?" Kellan asked, trying to make sure he knew all the facts and had them straight.

Sen nodded once. "That's correct. We also just need three more, and *we'll* get access to Zenith."

"What if Team 42 tries to cheat?" Kellan turned his attention to the far door. The squish and slap of blood and organs was etched into Kellan's mind forever. "What if they use *travel magic* to somehow teleport to Zenith? I mean, didn't you take me from my dimension and bring me to the Nexus? You and Xiang?"

Kellan wasn't an expert on magic, but he at least understood the concept of jumping between alternate dimensions. That was how he had arrived in the Nexus. That was how *everyone* arrived—except for the inbred residents. Everyone else was from some other alternate reality.

Sen shot Kellan a glare. "*Don't mention my sister's travel magic in front of people.*" Then he returned to his work. "We don't want anyone to hear."

Kellan slapped the bare foot of the man on the medical chair. "I'm sure Corpse-Face here will keep our secret."

"There are others here who can shroud themselves in invisibility or shift their shape. It's best to *keep quiet* about these matters." Sen stopped his disgusting work. "And clearly, you still lack understanding of certain magical elements, so let me set something straight."

"I'm listening," Kellan stated.

He *wanted* to know more about magic, and it frustrated him whenever people tended to give him the CliffsNotes version of what was going on.

"Traveling between dimensions is difficult. High ranks of travel magic can do it, but only in a limited capacity. It's currently the *Season of the Conflux,* which means travel between dimensions is easier—think of it like weather. Right now, there are fewer clouds between dimensions, so it's clearer sailing."

"Okay. Sure. I understand."

"*In theory*, a magical item could be used to gather people to the Nexus because that's where the Conflux originates, thus making it easy to travel here. Some people come here *accidentally* because that's how weak the barrier is between this dimension and others."

Although Sen hadn't said it, Kellan now understood. Xiang had made an item that Sen had used to transport Kellan and Mavis into the Nexus. The Season of the Conflux made it easy, so high ranks in travel magic weren't necessary.

"No one can travel to Zenith," Sen concluded. He resumed his work on the helpless man. "Zenith has the most powerful barriers around it. *Perfect* barriers, if you will. No one gets through, except for the Arbiter, who controls the gates. End of story."

Kellan turned on his heel and headed for the door. He had heard enough. Now he wanted to find the others and warn them about the same things he told Sen, and perhaps even speak with the Arbiter.

"Where are you going?" Sen asked.

"To find Mavis and the others," Kellan muttered as he grabbed the door handle.

"W-Wait! I wanted to speak with you!"

Kellan glanced back.

Sen, still bloodied and elbows-deep in another man's guts, just frowned. "Give me a moment to finish this, and then I'll travel the palace grounds with you."

—Chapter 3—
—Should We Risk It?—

The operating room smelled of copper and sweat.

Kellan licked his lips as he paced along the wall, his eyes drawn to the white countertops. Syringes and scalpels were laid out on crisp towels, each clean and ready for use. Kellan gave serious thought to picking up a needle and taking it with him—perhaps it would come in handy—but he didn't have his backpack, and his sweatpants weren't suitable for carrying around anything sharp.

"Where's my gear?" Kellan asked.

Sen glared down at the insides of the bloody man. "Husker likely has everything. My sister asked him to handle that."

Frustrated, but still antsy, Kellan slowly paced around the chair, watching Sen as he worked. The child placed the body parts back inside the man and then reconnected membranes so that the organs would stay where they were supposed to. Then Sen grabbed the man's stomach and sealed it closed with his bare fingers. Every time Sen pinched the flesh, it was like closing raw pasta—it reminded Kellan of an uncooked ravioli.

But moments later, the skin melted into itself and healed. The man's stomach returned to normal. Kellan couldn't detect any evidence the man had just been open and bleeding—other than the blood splashed around on the medical sheets.

"What did you do?" Kellan asked.

"I just rearranged the man's physical nature," Sen said as he carefully descended the step stool. "You see, the man was rather strong, but he had suffered the effects of a curse that lowered his overall wellbeing."

"You mean, his stats? Like, his stat for *health*?"

"Correct. But also, not correct. Because I'm not talking about his *health*. I meant his physical stats." Once Sen was on the floor, he walked around the chair and stood next to Kellan. "Shall we go?"

Together, they made their way to the door. Kellan stopped when he touched the handle. "Aren't you going to wake the guy?"

"No. He'll be fine in just a few minutes. He's not a particularly interesting conversationalist, and I've already received payment."

Still, Kellan hesitated. He glanced over his shoulder and stared at the sheet draped over the man's body. Nothing moved.

"Well?" Sen said, motioning to the door. "Weren't you in a hurry?" He shook his head. "You baffle me sometimes with your nonsensical demands."

"*Hurry up and wait* was the motto I learned in boot camp," Kellan muttered. "How did you rearrange the man's stats? And why isn't health one of them? I want to know more about… everything."

Sen grabbed at his Power Ranger sweatshirt and tugged the collar around his neck down a bit. "Health is just a measurement of how much damage you can take before you die. Normally, a human has about seven or eight. Sometimes more, if they're bigger, and sometimes less, if—"

"They're a child?" Kellan said with a smirk, staring down at Sen.

The smaller man frowned deeply. "*Moving on.*" He cleared his throat and then continued, "Obviously, the more health someone has, the more damage they can take before dying. Altering health is different from other stats… Our fine fellow over here wanted to make sure he could live through more of the games, so I moved some of strength over to fortitude. You see, *fortitude* is a measurement of your endurance, both at running and taking a beating. The more fortitude, the less damage you take from a punch or a bullet."

"Uh-huh." Kellan opened the door and stepped out into the hall.

Learning about *how much someone could take a beating* sounded amusing. He hadn't thought it would be quantified into a number, yet here it was.

"Since I'm a master at fleshcrafting—" Sen smiled to himself as he held his head high, "—I offered my services for a price."

Kellan walked the massive hallways of the AVU Palace. "Can you do that with anyone? What if I wanted you to move some points of my charisma and put them into health?"

With a stutter start, Sen struggled through his words, his anger a barrier to communication. "*Are you insane*?" he finally managed. "Do you really think putting chunks of your brain in your chest will help absorb damage?"

Large windows with iron bars lined the halls. Rain streamed down the glass, distorting the view of the gardens outside.

"You said you can rearrange stats," Kellan replied, calm and unbothered by Sen's child-like flailing. "Charisma is a stat. I have a number for it. *Three.*"

"Physical stats! Physical!" Sen huffed and snorted and scoffed, as though he couldn't think of another way of expressing his indignation. "Strength, dexterity, fortitude—they're physical. Charisma, manipulation—those are social. The last few stats—intelligence, perception, and wisdom—are mental. I can't rearrange *everything*. Well, that's not true. I *can*. You'll just become a vegetable. Which isn't our desired outcome."

"What about willpower and health?"

"Ah, well, those are more reflections of defenses, not really stats. Mind magic can use willpower offensively, but otherwise, willpower is a measurement of your will to resist. And health measures resistances to cutting, bruising, and breaking. I just told you that. Weren't you listening?"

"Yeah, yeah."

Sen had to walk faster than Kellan, his stride much shorter. Kellan could've slowed to accommodate the man-child, but he opted to continue forward at a fast walk. He wanted to speak with the others as soon as possible. He didn't know when the third game would start, but he knew it could be at any moment.

The Nexus loved its surprises.

"What we need is more arcana for you," Sen said matter-of-factly. "Body magic can increase your physical stats, as well as your health. And since your perception is at non-magical human maximum, it would behoove us to up it as well. As soon as possible, really. You're too weak at your current state."

Apparently, from what Kellan had learned, people from non-magical dimensions couldn't have higher than a five in any stat. Two was average. One was terrible. Zero was either death or paralysis.

Kellan did have a five in perception.

"What happens when I get a six?" he asked.

"You'll have superhuman levels of perception," Sen replied. He gulped down air as he hurried forward, obviously running out of breath. "You'll be able to sense *magic*, and your ability to notice subtle changes in your environment will be heightened."

Kellan opened a door to a closet. Then a door that led to another hall. Then a third door to an empty sitting area. When he arrived at a tall wooden door with techno music thumping from the other side, constant and rhythmic, he decided to stop and investigate a little further.

"W-Wait," Sen said. He stepped close to the door, half-blocking the way. "I said I needed to speak with you, and I meant it."

Kellan lifted an eyebrow. "What is it?"

"I…"

But Sen ended his sentence prematurely. He turned his eyes to the floor, his jaw clenched. Kellan waited, but he was inches from just shoving the man to the side. *I wonder what my patience would look like as a stat,* Kellan sardonically thought.

Sen took in a deep breath and then forced a smile. "I wanted to thank you for helping us acquire the second key. You basically did it on your own, and it was very much appreciated."

For a long second afterward, both Kellan and Sen were quiet.

Sen then clapped his hands together once. "There. I said it. I hope you're satisfied with your acknowledgement."

"That's it?" Kellan asked with a snort. "You made it sound like it was a *big deal* we speak alone. You couldn't have said that back in the other room? In front of the unconscious body?"

Sen's face grew red as he stammered, "W-Well, it was personal. Where I come from, mages of my status don't just offer praise to their subordinates."

"Wow. I feel really privileged." Kellan grabbed Sen's shoulder and moved him to the side, trying desperately to keep all his sarcastic commentary to himself. Then he placed his hand on the door handle.

Sen practically stumbled. He flailed his arms a bit to regain his balance. With a glare, Sen brushed off his clothing. "Listen, I'm *trying* to be agreeable. We got off on the wrong foot, and well, you did a good job, and you had a point about trusting you, so…"

"So?"

"So perhaps I've given thought to removing the Tyranny Worms in your body."

The mere mention of the worms made Kellan's skin crawl. Technically, the worms infested his entire being, preventing him from dying. Whenever he was injured, the worms killed themselves and used their bodies to stitch his flesh back together—one health every six seconds.

If that was *all* they did, Kellan wouldn't mind them, but the queen worm was somehow inside of Sen, giving the man-child a bit of control over Kellan in a way that Kellan found insufferable.

"Really?" Kellan asked with a cold and serious tone. No joking. This wasn't a joking matter. "When? Right now?"

"Once I have the tools." Sen glared up at him, his little kid face screwed up into something serious, but it was difficult for Kellan to see anything other than a pouty kindergartener. "Soon. Very soon. If you continue to help us."

Kellan replied with a slow and sarcastic salute.

Sen crossed his arms. "You're not as funny as you think you are."

"Says the man who needs a highchair to eat at the big boy table."

"Need I remind you that I started this conversation by thanking you?"

"And it ended with you reminding me that you control people with horror-show worms." Kellan knelt, patted the man on the shoulder, and then stood with a smirk. "This is probably our best conversation yet."

Sen threw back some of his long, black hair, his eye half-lidded in a sardonic glare. "You're *strange*. Work on that."

With no more words for the conversation, Kellan shoved the door and then stepped inside. A wall of smoke greeted him with open arms. Kellan coughed and waved a hand, trying to fan away the haze, but with little luck.

Neon lights flickered from the ceiling, catching on the smoke particles in the air, creating visions of pink and blue clouds. Kellan squinted and glanced around. Fortunately, Husker was an easy man to find—the werewolf creature was nearly nine feet tall and wore a heavy trench coat.

Kellan waded through the smoke. Husker stood next to a pool table, a black cigarette in his canine mouth. Husker's hands were a mix of a human's and a fox's. Black pads covered his palm and five fingers, and red fur covered everything else. He held the pool cue awkwardly, his hands too large for the human-sized pool equipment.

Didn't seem to bother Husker, though. He leaned down onto the table, his fox ears laid back as he lined up his shot.

The smoke-filled room reminded Kellan of a Moose Lodge—a type of old-school bar meant to cater to families of smokers and drinkers. There were tables, couches, darts, a drinking area, and even several TVs mounted to the walls. The room was the size of an apartment, but the thick wall of smoke obscured everything.

Kellan didn't spot other people. Husker was playing pool alone.

Where was everyone? Judging by the thickness of the haze, dozens of people had been smoking in the room just minutes prior.

"Husker," Kellan said as he approached the pool table. "I'm glad I found you. We need to talk."

The giant of a man straightened his posture. After a long drag on his black cigarette, Husker exhaled a line of smoke. "Warrior Kellan, I'm pleased to see you conscious." His gruff voice had the deep rumble of a growl. Then he glanced down to Sen. "You're done with your fleshcrafting?"

"Of course." Sen walked around the table, but he was too short to really see over.

The moment Kellan glanced at the smoke in Husker's hand, his Blitzkrieg Analysis told him everything he needed to know.

Magical Item [Consumable]—Hane Cigarette

The mage gains +2 perception and mana recovery while the hane remains in the mage's system. Highly addictive.

Although Kellan wanted to comment on Husker's decision to use hane, he decided against it. Instead, Kellan went straight to his main point. "I met with Team 42 during the last game."

Husker's ears stood erect. "Oh?"

"They're planning to win the Nexus Games so they can kill the primordial dragons and help the Flestiss Dominion conquer all other dimensions."

"Primordial dragons? Like the Arbiter?"

"Exactly."

"Oh, shit, man," someone else said between a short series of coughs. "That's crazy, man."

Kellan turned on his heel. He reached for his sidearm, but that was just muscle memory. He still wore only a T-shirt and a pair of sweatpants. He didn't have a weapon outside of his magic.

Through the haze of smoke, Kellan spotted the mysterious speaker.

An older teen reclined on a couch, his feet kicked up on one of the armrests, his head on the other. He, too, had a stick of hane on his lips, smoke streaming out his nostrils. The teen rubbed at his bloodshot eyes, though it seemed difficult for him to keep them open.

"Who are you?" Kellan demanded.

The teenager wore a purple baseball cap with the words *Taco King* across the front. He also had a white T-shirt and a button-up shirt over it, an odd style choice that wasn't Kellan's favorite. His jeans had holes over the knees.

Technically, Kellan didn't need the boy to answer. He already got his information.

Name: Robert Jameson the Friendly

Race: Human
Magics: Soul
Rank: C
Health: 7/7
Strength—2
Dexterity—2
Fortitude—1 [Tired]
Charisma—2 [Friendly]
Manipulation—1
Intelligence—2
Perception—2
Wisdom—1
Willpower—2

Abilities:
Personal—[Friends in High Places]—The mage has two additional familiar slots and 500% familiar growth.

Kellan was unimpressed.

The kid didn't have anything over human average, even if he was a C-rank mage. The only high number was the percentage increase to familiar growth. And the man was a soul mage? Kellan wasn't familiar enough with the magics to know what it entailed. All he knew was that Sen also had soul magic.

After fixing his cap right, the teen replied, "I'm Robbie. Who're *you*?"

"Alex Kellan."

"Oh, shit, man. *The* Alex Kellan?" Robbie took a quick drag of his hane and then exhaled, coughing the entire time. He smacked his chest, his left hand marked with the number of his team: 79. "I've heard of you. I thought you were mute? Or something."

Kellan sighed. "No. I'm the *other* Alex Kellan."

The alternate-dimension Alex Kellan on Team 42 was mute, but not him, obviously. And how had Kellan missed the fact that *Robbie the Taco King Worker* was in the room? He had a five perception—they had just talked about this. The thick smoke bothered Kellan. With a wave of his hand, he tried to clear it away, but there didn't seem to be much ventilation. The low beat of techno music wasn't helping his ability to concentrate, either.

Robbie wheezed, took another drag on his hane, and then said, "If the Arbiter is in danger, you should, like, do something about that. Sounds really important." But he didn't get up or encourage anything. He just continued to relax on his couch, practically mimicking the cushions.

"We won't take orders from the likes of *you*," Sen stated. "What're you? Some sort of lowborn food worker?" He squinted his eyes. "Or maybe… the janitor of a food establishment?"

"Whoa, man." Robbie lifted his baseball cap and widened his eyes. "I didn't know babies were allowed to participate in the Nexus Games."

"I'm thirty years old, you buffoon."

"Oh, right on. You look amazing for thirty, bro."

Husker threw his hane down and stomped on it with his bare foot, the pads of his soles calloused. Then the claws of his toes scraped across the wooden floor. He pulled out a new stick and placed it in his mouth, his fangs holding it in place while he spoke. "Robert the Friendly is correct. We should warn the Arbiter and do something about Team 42."

Robert the Friendly. Kellan couldn't stop himself from smiling. *What a preposterous name.*

"Do you know where Mavis and Xiang are?" Kellan asked. Then he glanced at the mostly empty smoke-filled room. "Or where everyone else is, for that matter?"

Husker tilted his hand back and forth. "Mavis and Xiang are at the Exchange. And I believe most teams have entered themselves into the challenge round."

"Challenge round? What's that?"

Robbie held his hand up with the enthusiasm of an elementary school student. "Oh, it's this game that's, like, optional, and people compete in it."

"Don't listen to this idiot," Sen said, waving his arms. "He's as useful as a chocolate teapot. *I'll* tell you everything you need to know about challenge rounds."

"I'm listening," Kellan said. He coughed and waved away more smoke. "I don't care who tells me what's going on—I just want to know."

"Occasionally, the Arbiter will offer a challenge round in between games." Sen held up a finger. "No keys are awarded, but arcana and powerful magical items are often the rewards. No teams are made to participate, but it's advantageous to do so."

Robbie smirked. "So, an optional game? People compete in? I said that, man."

Ignoring their couch-companion, Husker walked around the pool table and went to the one of the TVs mounted to the wall. The 80-inch flat screen was caked in a thin layer of hane smoke. Husker used his large hands to dust the electronics.

"Bitso is always relaying information about the games." Husker snorted as he searched for the button to switch on the TV. "The Arbiter forces him to announce every detail and mechanic, and to show highlights of the games… He'll provide all the details if I can just get this… this *thing* to function."

Kellan stepped close to poke the power button and the TV flickered to life.

The TV was set to a channel with a children's show. Kellan watched for a few seconds as some deformed kids ran across a green field chasing someone in a sun costume. The face of the sun—buttons for eyes, and a mouth stitched into place—seemed to be twisted in agony. Kellan wanted to know the context for such a show, and what the children were doing, but he quickly switched the channel to Bitso's news program.

Bitso sat behind a metal desk, a small screen behind him playing a cartoon of a maze. Not a paper maze, but a large, stone maze with walls as tall as a two-story house. The footage looped over and over again, showcasing someone entering the maze and a metal door shutting behind them.

The news anchor poked at his blindfold—jabbing hard straight into the socket. Blood bloomed across the white cloth, making it seem like he had a red eye painted in place.

"That's right, ladies, gentlemen and everything in between. The challenge round is about to begin, but there are a few limitations. No team leaders or Stragglers allowed. The only ones who can play are the sad sacks who make up the hard-working backbone of the team. You know the people. The ones who never get the recognition they deserve."

Robbie sat up on his couch and stretched, his hane cigarette dangling from his lower lip as though glued there. "He's right, man. Hard-working blokes never get their due."

Kellan ran a hand down his face.

If he was going to survive the Nexus Games, he needed more arcana and magical items, there was no way around that fact. If the challenge round would give Kellan those things, he would have to join, wouldn't he?

But I should still attempt to speak with the Arbiter at some point, Kellan reasoned. *In person. So I can explain the severity of the situation.*

"This challenge round is a bit of *risk versus reward,*" Bitso said, smiling. His white teeth seemed frighteningly sharp in the back. "You see, the deeper you go into the Catacomb Maze, the more arcana you'll find. That's right. The catacombs are filled with *dead bodies.* Beautiful, rotting corpses. Their arcana is just sitting there…"

Kellan glanced over to Husker. With the eyes of a dog who was confused, Husker met Kellan's gaze.

"Yes?" Husker asked.

"Arcana emerges from a body after a person dies… And then it just stays there? Forever?"

"Not quite. Arcana eventually rots. That's where yami come from. The rotted arcana is a form of corrupted magic."

Yami—foul monsters of twisted designs—were creatures Kellan despised. Vile cats, undead machines, robotic crocodiles… The list of yami beasts that Kellan had seen was quite interesting, if a bit unsettling.

"I thought the Arbiter controlled all those yami monsters?" Kellan asked while Bitso continued on the TV, spouting off statements about arcana and corpses.

Husker nodded once. "You seem surprised, but primordial dragons have a tremendous amount of control over their dimension. They're connected to the raw magic—the Sea of Chaos—and that gives them some control over the yami."

Kellan rubbed at his chin, mulling over the information. No wonder the primordial dragons could prevent people from taking over their dimensions. If they were *that* in control of the situation, to the point they had influence over all monsters and magic, they were basically undefeatable.

"And some of these alternate dimensions don't have dragons?" Kellan asked, continuing to ignore the TV.

Husker snorted. "They died. The old-fashioned way. Or fighting each other.

Who knows anymore? Most of them died long before you or I existed. Those dimensions… the magic is less prevalent. Or gone. Like your world. A terrible fate."

It seemed weird to Kellan that the dimensions were similar yet so different. Not all of them, apparently, but enough that someone with his same name and general skill set could exist in one dimension while he existed in another.

But all this information just reinforced Kellan's desire to speak with the Arbiter. If the Arbiter controlled the Gates to Zenith, would that mean *anyone* could enter the "perfect dimension" once he was dead? Would the Flestiss Dominion attempt to invade that dimension as well?

Kellan wasn't sure of the limitations of aliens—or the magic, for that matter.

He needed more information.

It was a constant problem he couldn't seem to shake.

"But listen to this," Bitso said with a laugh, drawing Kellan's attention back to the TV. Bitso slammed his hand on his desk. "At the center of this maze is a *Summoning Chime.*"

"A Summoning Chime?" Sen asked through a gasp.

"Trust me, you want this item. Normally, it's outlawed during *the early parts* of the Nexus Games because of the unfair advantage it grants… But the Arbiter is feeling generous. There's one Summoning Chime for each team who makes it to the center."

—Chapter 4—
—Risk and Reward—

"Sweet, man," Robbie said as he slid off the couch and stood. He threw his stick of hane on the floor and stomped it out. "A Summoning Chime is definitely worth gettin' involved for."

Husker snorted. "Stragglers can't participate." He returned his attention to the pool table. "And I don't want to watch the death circus the Arbiter has planned for anyone who risks themselves in a challenge round."

Without glancing at anyone, Sen hurried away from the pool table, muttering something excitedly under his breath. He went all the way to the door and then stopped. He counted things on his fingers, hesitating before reaching for the doorknob.

"What's a Summoning Chime?" Kellan asked.

"You get to call a mage to help you." Robbie slid his hands into the pockets of his ripped jeans. "Ya know. For the games. And that person can be *anyone*. And they are *forced* to help you, controlled by, like, the magic of the Chime. That's my favorite kind of help."

"Compulsory?" Kellan quipped.

"Yeah, man. The kind of help where you know the person can't betray you. Because *reasons*." He fluttered his fingers around, jazz hands style, as he said the last word.

Kellan glanced over to Husker, hoping for a thorough explanation.

The werewolf man snorted, his long snout wrinkled as though disgusted. "The Summoning Chime does, in fact, compel someone to help you. It lasts for a mere fifteen minutes, but if you summon the correct person, it could turn the tide of an entire game. The previous Nexus Games gave out Chimes once, and Xiang's mother used hers to win the final game."

Although Kellan wasn't entirely sure who he would summon, he found it interesting that the Chime was so powerful that it had allowed Xiang's mother to win. It sounded like the Chime was normally banned early in the games. For what reason? What mage could possibly be so strong that fifteen minutes of their support would be considered overpowered?

Perhaps I should get one. Since Kellan wasn't his team's Straggler or leader, he could participate in the challenge round. But…

The TV flickered as Bitso slammed his hand down on the desk. Then he pointed to the smaller screen behind him, the one playing the cartoon animation of the maze. Bitso practically leaned onto the screen and stroked at the lines of the walls. He put so much of his weight on the smaller TV that it cracked and tilted.

Bitso pressed his face against it. "Listen to this. The Catacomb Maze is one of my favorite places ever. The coffins either have prizes or traps. The traps not only try to kill you, but they also lower the total time *everyone* has in the maze. Nothing gets everyone's blood boiling like the incompetence of others!"

The cartoon played childish animations of people falling into a pit or outrunning a gigantic, spherical boulder. Bitso chuckled the entire time, watching with crazed glee.

"Everyone will have eight hours to dive into the maze and then turn around and make it out," Bitso said through his laughter. "The Summoning Chimes will be located at the very center of the catacomb—but each time one Chime is taken, an hour will be subtracted from *everyone's* allotted time."

"Whoa, man," Robbie said, though there was no shock in his voice whatsoever.

Husker clicked his tongue. "Tsk. This is what I'm talking about. The Arbiter has sick games in mind."

"This won't be a PvP match," Bitso said with an exaggerated pout. He rubbed the screen again, stroking the little cartoon image of a man in the maze. "No one is allowed to attack any other teams during the challenge round, which is disappointing, I know, but you'll be racing against the clock in this one."

Robbie snapped his fingers. Then he nudged Kellan with his elbow. "I bet ya that whoever doesn't make it out of the maze dies, dude."

"You're probably right," Kellan muttered. He was very familiar with the dangers of the Nexus Games at this point.

"Whoever is inside the maze when the time ends will be crushed!" Bitso grabbed the TV mounted on the wall and then threw it to the ground, smashing the glass and cracking the plastic frame. Bits of electronics flew across the newsroom as the man cackled with delight.

The lunatic-level laughter lasted a solid thirty seconds.

"I love that man's enthusiasm for his job," Robbie said with a smile.

Kellan walked over and switched off the TV. He had heard enough. The challenge round was about gathering arcana from the catacombs, all while making one's way to the center to grab the Chime. It didn't sound too difficult, but he knew that once a couple of people had Chimes, the possibility of exiting the maze would decrease.

"How large is the maze?" Kellan asked, hoping someone in the room would be familiar with it.

No one answered.

Damn. Kellan gritted his teeth, hating how difficult it was to gather information at times. *I need to find a library… or a Nexus version of the internet. Anything to get the Wikipedia page on all these locations.*

"What did you say about the death rates of challenge rounds?" Kellan asked.

Husker extended black claws from his fingers and scratched at his furry neck. "The challenge rounds always have difficult puzzles, monsters, and traps. And there's no chance of winning a key. Never worth it, in my opinion. Those challenge rounds are a trap meant to ensnare the greedy."

"That's the talk of a loser, man." Robbie turned for the door. "Ya gotta believe in yourself once in a while. That's how you get great."

The low beat of the ambient techno music covered Robbie's steps as he headed out. He tipped his purple fast food baseball cap to Sen as he stepped around and exited, smiling the entire time. Kellan glanced over his shoulder, still bothered by the copious amount of smoke, but intrigued that *Taco King* had the gumption to take on the difficult challenge round.

How was Robbie even still alive? Two rounds deep into the Nexus Games, with the stats and demeanor of a dull sandwich…

"Quickly, quickly," Sen shouted. "We must find my sister before entry into the challenge round ends. We should participate."

Husker huffed, smoke streaming through his fangs. He adjusted his hane with his tongue. "You shouldn't bother with this. It's too early in the competition."

"Our warrior managed to gather the second key for us all on his lonesome. I think you underestimate him." Sen dismissively waved his hand. "This will be easy."

"You forget that everyone has seen the extent of Xiang's illusionary skills." Husker leaned down onto the pool table, his tone casual. "Now that it's common knowledge that her illusions fool lower-rank divination, other teams are going to start gaining abilities, forming tactics, or acquiring items to combat that."

"We don't need to worry about that *just yet*. Xiang can't even participate in the challenge round, anyway." Sen huffed, opened the door, and then stepped into the hallway. "We need every advantage we can get!" He left without another word, flouncing as he went.

Once alone with Husker, Kellan walked over to his side of the pool table. "Do you have any of my gear, werewolf?"

Husker shot him a glare. "Werewolf? You know I'm a *rennic*. There's nothing *were* about me."

"It's an affectionate nickname."

"I hate it. Call me that again, and I'll assume that you want our relationship to be antagonistic."

"Very well. Do you have any of my gear, *rennic*?"

Husker twitched his pointed ears. Then he resumed his solo game at the pool table. "Of course. It's over there. By the circular table."

Despite the smoke, Kellan spotted the table to which Husker referred. Sure enough, his backpack sat near one of the legs. Kellan jogged over, picked up his bag, and slung it over his shoulders. His rifle sat on a chair nearby. When he picked it up, and grabbed the strap, he discovered the weapon had a distinct… feeling.

Kellan shivered as he hoisted it onto his shoulder.

It was as if the rifle had emotions that transmitted themselves to Kellan's being.

Magical Item [Semi-Sentient Weapon]—Sevriss [Mk-17 SCAR-H Mode]

A mythical weapon that is said to appear once in every dimension. Powerful and versatile, it transforms to match the preferred weapon-type of its wielder. It's also cursed. Weapon damage varies depending on the weapon [SCAR, (7 + dexterity – target's dexterity) and doubles the bonus from firearms-enhancing abilities and magical skills]. Has a 10% chance to double arcana when used to make the finishing strike.

Sevriss…

It had once been cursed, but after Kellan had gathered enough gold arcana, the negative effects had disappeared. Kellan patted the gun, and again, he was met with a bizarre feeling, like the rifle had missed him.

Which was more than a little disturbing, but at least it wasn't actively out to kill him. Kellan chalked it up as a win.

"Husker," Kellan said.

The rennic lifted his head and stared with the intensity of a wolf. "Yes?"

"Do you really think joining the challenge round is a terrible idea?"

"Heh. Absolutely."

Kellan waited for a follow-up, but none came. Husker returned to his game, his attention on the pool balls.

"I thought it was a bad idea bringing you here, though," Husker eventually muttered. "Sen doesn't bother listening to my advice. But maybe I'm not always correct."

Although that wasn't the answer Kellan had been hoping for, he mulled over the information and decided to leave. Once free of the smoke, he coughed to clear his lungs. The long hallway was empty. Sen had disappeared.

Irritated that he had somehow lost a small child, Kellan jogged farther into the AVU Palace, his attention on his surroundings. He passed three more doors, each open to reveal a small study. When he came to the fourth, Kellan threw it open, shocked to find a meat freezer. Carcasses of cows hung from hooks in the ceiling.

The red muscle and white marbling of fat startled Kellan, but only for a moment. A mist of cold air rushed into the hall. Kellan slowly shut the door, shaken. He had almost forgotten how jumbled the Nexus could be. Every dimension apparently collided with this one, combining to make bizarre buildings and places.

Shaking the thought from his mind, Kellan jogged down the hall. When he made a turn, he recognized a set of stairs. They led to the Arbiter. The stairs would lead him to the field where the giant hole was. Part of Kellan wanted to run there and tell the Arbiter, but…

Two Pestbyters hovered near the base of the stairs. Their camera eyes turned to face Kellan, the wire tentacles hanging from their bodies jiggling with anticipation.

Kellan stepped back.

"*You aren't allowed to be here,*" one of the Pestbyters said in a sweet, but mechanical, voice. "*Please return to your quarters.*"

Movement near the ceiling caught Kellan's attention. He glanced up and caught his breath. A single eye protruded from the ceiling. It had an organic cover over the lens of the camera. Kellan's own eyes gave him all the information he needed.

Magical Item [Semi-Sentient]—Eyes of the Arbiter

An observation tool used by the Arbiter to keep tabs on the citizens of the Nexus. They appear across surfaces with electronic components. Can see through moderate levels of obfuscation. It's rather creepy.

Kellan stepped away from the Pestbyters.

The Eyes of the Arbiter watched his every move. They watched *everyone's* movements, no matter where they were, basically. Which meant Bitso was correct—the Arbiter already knew about Team 42's plan to win the games.

So why hadn't the Arbiter acted?

"I'm leaving," Kellan said to the eye. "Don't worry. I'm not going to break any more rules."

The eye blinked, much like a lizard. A transparent flap of flesh slid over the half-sphere of the eye, cleaning away all dirt.

Kellan turned and left the hall, disturbed, but not as much as he had been when he had first arrived in the Nexus. The Eyes of the Arbiter had been everywhere during the games. Apparently, the Arbiter had blinded himself just to gain that ability—to watch over the games like a god.

Satisfied that he had at least *thought* about the correct thing to do, Kellan hurried down a different hallway. He opened the first door, and more smoke wafted over him. Less than before, but more than he liked. Then Kellan spotted someone.

Sun Xiang.

The leader of Team 101.

—Chapter 5—
—The Challenge Round—

Xiang was a woman with enough emotional baggage to wreck the Denver airport.

Two of her ex-lovers were in the games and wanted her dead, her mother had disappeared after the last games, her brother was trapped in the body of a child, and she was apparently under the effects of a terrible hex. Any one of those things would've justified alcoholism in a normal individual.

Despite that, Xiang stood in a room that reminded Kellan of a casino, confidence in her stiff stance. The lights were dim and large screens hung from the ceiling, displaying odds and probabilities. To his surprise, most were in English, but occasionally the words switched to other languages—alphabets he didn't recognize.

The blue hue of the screens tainted the smoke in the air, creating a turquoise fog. Xiang strode through the haze, her long, black hair fluttering behind her, her heels tall enough that they added six inches to her already statuesque height. She wore a tight dress, form-fitting to the point that, if she had any flaws, they would all be on display.

But Xiang had no flaws.

Her smooth skin, her supple lips, her inky hair, the noticeable curves—all perfect. When her stats came up for display, Kellan ignored the notification and instead kept his gaze on her. Xiang's stats were hidden regardless.

When she made her way to his side, Kellan smirked. "What is this place?"

He motioned to the screens, and then the counters and bookie boxes. Robots—or maybe androids?—ran the place from behind the counters, each with screens for faces. They dealt in red, glowing crystals. Arcana. The magical material used for learning and improving magics.

"It's an Exchange," Xiang said, her voice as beautiful as she was.

Kellan knew it was all a lie, however. Xiang's illusions fooled everyone, even Kellan's Blitzkrieg Analysis. She could be anybody—or anything. Even her voice could be completely different, for all he knew.

"What do people exchange here?" Kellan glanced over at the counters. The place was empty, though. No teams or players.

"Magical items found in the games." Xiang combed her silky hair with her fingers. She had the same Asian-style facial features as her brother, but just like Sen, she wasn't from Kellan's Earth. She was from somewhere very different. "Or sometimes individuals exchange familiars, or other people. It just depends. The Arbiter likes to purchase back anything not in use. The Exchange opens for everyone once the second game has concluded."

"Why are *you* here? Did our team find a bunch of magical items that I'm unaware of?"

"No. But perhaps there is an item *we* can use."

"*Time is running out to join the challenge round,*" a polite, feminine voice said over the speakers. "*All teams who wish to participate must register within the next five minutes.*"

Xiang smiled, but it was brief and devoid of real emotion. "I'm pleased that you're awake. That means Team 101 can participate in the challenge round. And while I'm still upset that my brother chose an alternate-dimension version of my ex-lover to join us, I'm glad that you're at least competent enough to brave these games and win."

Kellan wasn't sure if that was a compliment. He didn't care.

Then she touched Kellan's shoulder—just as briefly as she had smiled. Xiang jerked her hand away, as though shocked by static. Then she rubbed at her knuckles, her eyebrows knitted.

"You have *meta* magic now?" she whispered.

Kellan turned his attention to their surroundings. Wouldn't Sen and the others be upset if he suddenly started telling everyone about his rare magic? But again—he saw no one. "Yeah. I just acquired it."

"How?"

"Bitso… gave me a potion. For doing what he had wanted."

Kellan found it difficult to describe the circumstances of the potion. Bitso had wanted Kellan to gather gold arcana, and Kellan had. End of story. Why had Bitso wanted this? Why did Bitso want *anything*? Kellan found it difficult to explain to himself.

"What potion?" Xiang demanded, her voice edged. "What was its specific name?"

"It was an experimental potion made by some guy named Megadonis. It was called *Hydra Corp Serum*."

Xiang crossed her arms and forced an exhale. Then she turned her attention away, her shoulders tense, her fingers gripping hard on her forearms. "Megadonis—that filthy ritual mage. Bitso must've had one of his potions…" She cursed under her breath and then glared at Kellan. "Well. I'm happy for you. Congratulations."

There was no happiness in her tone.

"Really heartfelt," Kellan quipped.

"I still think you would've been better served learning travel magic. But since you *refused* to allow me to teach you, I suppose you should do everything in your power to master meta magic."

She said every word as though it were venom leaving her mouth. Kellan refrained from making another sarcastic comment.

"*Last call for the challenge round*," the woman over the speakers chimed again. "*All teams who wish to participate must register within the next four minutes.*"

The urgency in the robotic voice unnerved Kellan a bit. He didn't like the constant pressure of evaporating time.

"Xiang," he said. "Do you think the Summoning Chime is worth braving the dangers of the challenge round?"

"I think it's worth having, but I do believe this is a trap." Xiang rested her chin on the top of her hand. "The Arbiter intentionally put the Chime in the first challenge round to lure out rubes. Since the Chime was so crucial in the last games, naturally, mages now would want to get their hands on one."

"And the Arbiter just wants to kill as many people as possible?" Kellan asked, his tone dry.

"Yes. I think this challenge round will be a bloodbath."

"And you still want me to participate?" Kellan scoffed, almost indignant, but what had he expected? Of course she would want him to risk himself.

"You've proven yourself resourceful," Xiang stated matter-of-factly. "You gained multiple keys in the first game, and then single-handedly brought our team the key in the second game. Despite your unorthodox methods, you're doing something right. It's early enough in the game that now is the time to push our luck. I have faith you'll avoid the worst of the round."

Kellan wasn't a fan of running headfirst into dangerous situations. All it would take was a bout of bad luck, and he could find himself dead. The Nexus Games had too many perilous situations—by design, obviously.

"Just pushing our luck because we can… That's a terrible strategy," Kellan said.

Xiang smirked. "You don't understand. You've never seen the Nexus Games play out. We should—"

But Kellan caught his breath, his attention drawn to a person walking through the smoke-filled Exchange. He recognized her immediately. Mavis. Her freckled skin, athletic form, and confident stride were everything Kellan had been hoping to see. She had a certain stride that betrayed her military training.

When she spotted Kellan, her eyes went wide, and she smiled.

Mavis jogged over—something she seemed to love doing now that her leg wasn't giving her trouble, thanks to Sen's fleshcrafting. Her purple-tinted hair was tied back in a ponytail, but it still fluttered as she moved. She wore a heavy jacket, a T-shirt, and jeans, all brand new, as if taken straight off a store rack.

Xiang stopped speaking and turned to follow Kellan's gaze. The moment she spotted Mavis, she stiffened. "Oh. Our *other* warrior."

"Kellan!" Mavis picked up her pace, ran straight at Kellan for the last few feet, and threw her arms around his neck. "You're awake."

He embraced her back, holding her tightly against his body.

Xiang watched with narrowed eyes, never bothering to return to her explanation. She merely watched with the passion and movement of a statue.

"Where have you been?" Kellan asked Mavis, keeping his arms around her.

"I've been trying to find things for our team." Mavis didn't move away, either. She kept her arms around Kellan's neck, tightening her grip. "Sen and Xiang taught me about magical items, and curses, and other things we should look out for."

As if summoned by his name being spoken, Sen jogged around the corner and headed over to the group. His childlike appearance made it seem like Xiang was an irresponsible parent who allowed her kid to run through a gambling hall. Sen's Power Rangers sweatshirt made everything more childish.

"W-Wait for me," Sen said through labored breaths. "Mavis!"

Finally releasing Kellan, Mavis turned with an even wider smile. "Oh, sorry. Our team is assembled. It's time to go."

The man-child reached the group, and then stopped and huffed. "Thank goodness… We need… to get that Summoning Chime…"

"You'll need to be quick," Xiang muttered. She pointed to a far door. "And keep in mind that you can head for the exit at any point during the challenge round. If you're running low on time, just turn around and leave."

"We need to leave enough time to get to the exit?" Kellan asked.

"That's right."

Sen formally bowed to his sister, bending so far that his long hair touched the carpeted floor near his feet. "Consider it done, my honorable sister." Then he straightened his posture and headed for the far door.

"We need to go," Mavis said. She flashed Kellan a smirk. "You were sleeping for a while. I have new magic abilities to show you."

The constraints of time irritated Kellan. He wanted more gear and supplies—and especially information—but the clock ticked down, stealing his ability to properly prepare. Rolling with the punches was a strategy that only worked so long.

Kellan followed Mavis to the far door, passing the many screens flickering with numbers. The androids behind the counters looked like old-fashioned silver robots, their arms tubes, their heads square and bulbous, like retro computer monitors. The bizarre androids waved their hands as Kellan rushed by.

Once Kellan had pushed himself into the next room, the smoke cleared. It was a singular space with a counter and one of the old-school androids. Its monitor head flickered. A happy face appeared on the screen.

"*You're just in time to register*," it said with the inhuman voice of a machine trying to mimic a child. "*Please show me your team number.*"

Sen walked over to the counter and then struggled to get his left arm up high enough for the android to see. He showed the robot the 101 on the back of his left hand. Then he vanished from the room in a *pop* of displaced air.

Mavis went to do the same, but Kellan grabbed her shoulder.

"Are you okay?" he asked.

She shot him a glare. "Of course. Why wouldn't I be?" She jerked her shoulder out of his grip. "We have to hurry, Kellan."

"Last I saw you… you were infected."

"Oh. That."

"*Only thirty seconds remaining,*" the android said sweetly.

Mavis placed her left hand down on the counter, showing off her 101 mark. "This can wait. We'll discuss it during the challenge round."

After the android had scanned her number, Mavis disappeared just as suddenly as Sen. A quiet *pop* and then she was gone. Kellan was the only human left in the tiny room with a counter.

He walked over and showed his team marking.

The android scanned it, the face on the computer screen flickering to something sad. "*Oh,*" it said, still upbeat in tone, even with the weird facial expression. "*You're that rule breaker. Please make sure to adhere to all the rules this time. Or else.*"

Kellan forced a smile. "I'll do my best."

As soon as he spoke the words, a power gripped Kellan from deep within. His insides twisted as he was ripped out of the room in an instant. His lungs hurt as he was jerked from one location to a new one.

This wasn't the first time he had teleported, but this time felt more… painful. Kellan didn't have an explanation for it, other than the Arbiter's apparent love of torture.

Kellan stumbled forward, breathing heavily.

To his surprise, the room he had appeared in—the room he had been *teleported into*—was a tiny five-by-five square with no windows or doors. There was no carpet. No chairs or furniture. No ledges or bricks. Smooth cement walls. A plain, gray ceiling. A featureless floor.

And no light.

While Mavis and Sen glanced around, their eyes wide, their sight stolen, Kellan wasn't in the same boat. He could see. All the horror-movie details were easy for him to spot, his magically-enhanced eyes telling him everything.

"Kellan?" Mavis asked, her voice panicked.

"It's okay," he said. "We're not in any immediate danger. Except for, well, we might run out of air at some point."

Sen huffed. And then took a deep breath. Then he shot a glare in Kellan's direction. "You can see? Everything?" Then he waved a child-like hand. "Of course. You're an eclipse mage. You can see in darkness, can't you?"

"That's right."

Kellan moved until his back was against the wall. He slung his backpack around and sifted through the inside. There wasn't much. He had black cigarettes—hane—and a rule book for the Nexus Games. And that was it.

"I can make fire," Mavis said. She ran a hand through her purplish hair. "I keep forgetting I have magical abilities." She shook her head. "Should I create light for us?"

"Not *fire,*" Sen said matter-of-factly. "We'll run out of air faster. Fire also needs to breathe. We should let our warrior handle everything." He slowly shifted over to Mavis's location. "Don't worry, Mavis. As soon as the challenge round starts, we'll be let out of this room."

Kellan briefly took note of Sen's willingness to say Mavis's name. For the most part, Sen never referred to Kellan as anything other than *our warrior*.

"What if the Arbiter doesn't let us out?" Mavis asked. "What if part of the challenge is getting out of this room?"

Sen tugged on the bottom of his sweatshirt. "Yes… Well… That's a possibility."

"Do you have any magical abilities that can get us out of the room?"

"I… I don't think so. Soul and body magic are about the soul and the physical being."

Mavis reached out with a shaky hand and touched the nearby wall. Then she vaguely turned in Kellan's direction. Without focusing her eyes, she asked, "Kellan? Do you have anything?"

Kellan closed his eyes and thought about his magical abilities. He *was* an eclipse mage. And a metal mage. And a body mage. He had powers. *I should refresh myself before we get into the thick of it.*

"My eclipse abilities," Kellan muttered.

They flashed in his mind.

Primary Magic—Eclipse—Focus [Void Agent]

The mage gains the C-rank power "Shadow Step" for free (the ability to step into the shadows, move their full distance, and then exit the shadows). Diving into the "void" of darkness only lasts 6 seconds, but the mage may travel anywhere that a shadow could fit through.

Illuminate [E-Rank Eclipse]

An extremely early light-based power, this allows the mage to make an object give off illumination; it leads to far more powerful things later…

The mage spends a mana, and an object is made to glow with light equal to a torch for thirty minutes.

Pierce the Darkness [E-Rank Eclipse]

Mastery over light and dark includes the ability to pierce the shadows…

The mage can always see in the dark.

Void Knight [APEX, E-Rank Eclipse]

The mage understands that light is tiny and insignificant when compared to the darkness that spans the infinite universe. While shrouded in shadows and void, the mage becomes more powerful.

Whenever the mage is in darkness (less than 1,000 lumens per 100 square feet) they are empowered, gaining +5 to all physical stats (strength, dexterity, fortitude), +2 to their armor rating, and immunity to all shadow-tendril attacks or grapples from other eclipse mages. Gain the title "the Void Knight."

Once taken, the mage may never acquire "Solar Scion."

"I can step into the shadows and manipulate them." Kellan ran a hand down his face. "And I can make light."

"And see in the dark?" Mavis asked.

"Yeah."

"Make us some light."

Kellan thought for a long moment. His power, *Illuminate*, required an object to turn bright. What did he have? A T-shirt. Sweatpants. A backpack. Some cigarettes. A book. A rifle.

No shoes.

No handheld objects.

With a sigh, Kellan reached into his bag and spent a mana. He illuminated a small hane stick. It glowed brightly, with an intensity that almost hurt his eyes. He held it high, and it lit up the small room.

Mavis squinted and then glanced around. "No windows? No door?" She turned her attention to him, her brow furrowed. "What other magical abilities do you have?"

After a second of shallow breathing, Kellan thought about his metal abilities. They showed in his mind.

Mold Metal [E-Rank Metal]

The most basic metal mage power, and one that is quite useful. This power represents control over metal in its most limited form; the mage can shape it.

The mage spends a mana, and for thirty minutes, they can mold metal as though it were clay.

Intuitive Tech [D-Rank Metal]

The metal mage quickly understands how machines, vehicles, and foreign computers work...

The mage spends a mana, and for thirty minutes, he has a "phantom" understanding of machines. He can temporarily pick locks and use most vehicles, firearms, planes, and computer terminals as though he has trained with them before.

"I can mold metal and learn how to operate or use foreign or strange technologies." Once Kellan spoke, he realized that sounded less than impressive. And it wasn't going to help them.

"You're a metal and eclipse mage and you haven't learned to use *lasers*?" Sen snapped. He used a hand to shield his eyes from the intense glow of the hane stick. "Eclipse mages can shoot beams out of their hands—*laser beams*. Metal mages can do the same. *These powers stack*. In case you don't know what I'm talking about, imagine simple addition. One plus one is better than just *one*, right?"

Kellan forced a quick sigh. "I'm sorry. I was focused on survival, and blasting everything with a laser didn't seem like the best solution at the time. As soon as

I get some more arcana, I'll try to build that up."

"Good." Sen turned his back to the light. "I'm glad you're finally listening."

"Do you have anything else?" Mavis asked. She stepped closer, her eyes squinted so much, they were almost closed. "Anything at all?"

"I have body magic, same as Sen," Kellan muttered. Then he offered a shrug. "I think I have some minor abilities…"

They flashed in his mind.

Ignore Pain [E-Rank Body]

Body mages learn to control the autonomous functions of their body, one of the simplest of which is pain.

The mage spends a mana to ignore agony for thirty minutes. This power ceases if the wound itself disappears.

Heal the Body [D-Rank Body]

This power is the simplest manifestation of the body mage's well-known ability to heal others.

The mage may spend a point of mana to heal another of three points of damage.

"I can ignore pain and heal people," Kellan finally stated.

The other two were silent, like they were waiting for more. But that was it. Kellan had nothing else.

"You can *heal* people?" Sen turned on his heel, his eyebrows knitted in obvious frustration. "*I told you specifically not to do that!* I can heal people! We don't need *two* mages who can do the same thing! That's a waste. We shouldn't have overlaps."

"I needed the ability to heal," Kellan stated. "So I learned it. End of story."

"None of that is going to get us out of this room," Mavis said, motioning to the cement. "What're we going to—"

Before she could finish, the far wall shimmered like a desert mirage. A metal door, built with heavy rivets, appeared as though hidden behind a blanket of invisibility that had fallen to the floor. An electronic speaker was mounted to the top of the doorframe. It shook as someone shouted into the room.

"*The challenge round has begun! You may now enter the Catacomb Maze.*"

—Chapter 6—
—The Catacomb Maze—

Sen turned to Kellan, a slight frown on his face. "Well? You go first."

Before Kellan could head over to the door, Mavis reached into her jacket and withdrew a Desert Eagle, a semi-automatic pistol. Kellan was familiar with their design, though he wondered where Mavis had gotten it.

"Didn't you have a rifle?" he asked.

Mavis nodded once. "Yeah, but some crazy shit happened during the second game. I had to fight someone, and I lost it down a vent." She motioned to the door. "You want me to go first? I have shoes."

With a smirk, Kellan shook his head. "By the way, you should know what I found out during the second game. It's about Team 42."

"Sen told me." Mavis held her handgun close. "Team 42 is working with aliens to kill primordial dragons so they can invade other dimensions. Right? And they're going to use the super-powered magic of Zenith to do it?"

"That's right." Kellan glanced over at Sen and then back to Mavis, the light in the room irritating his eyes. He closed one and said, "We should talk about it at some point."

There was only one other person who Kellan trusted in the Nexus Games, and that was Mavis. She had come from his dimension, and they had started this journey together. Kellan wanted to ensure they were on the same page with what needed to be done.

Team 42 could *not* be allowed to win the games.

Kellan had come to that decision when he had seen glimpses of the aliens—the Flestiss Dominion. He needed to discuss it with Mavis, to make sure she knew the horrors, and to confirm that he could rely on her to help with this self-imposed mission.

No team would emerge successful unless all the members were on the same page and working toward the same goals.

"Does Xiang know?" Kellan asked, glancing down at Sen.

The child crossed his arms. "I told them both at the same time, thank you very much. My sister said she suspected they were up to no good when they registered with one of the flestiss on their team." Then he pointed to the door. "Now we need to go!"

With a huff, Kellan walked over to the door. The cold metal handle practically burned his palm. He held his rifle close before shoving the door open and stepping into the maze.

His right forearm burned, and Kellan glanced down at his skin to see a new number emerge.

It read…

07:59

Their remaining time. Seven hours and five-nine minutes. Kellan wished they had been provided seconds, but apparently the Arbiter wasn't *that* precise.

The speaker in the room shook again as it spoke. "*Whenever you're ready to leave the Catacomb Maze, enter your designated room before your time runs out. You will be returned to the AVU Palace, along with all your prizes. If you fail to return to your room with remaining time on the clock, you will die. Thank you and enjoy!*"

Fantastic.

Kellan glanced around at the maze. A long hallway stretched before him, one of stone bricks, and decorated with cobwebs and dust. A chill ran down Kellan's spine when he spotted one of the tiny spiders. He didn't have arachnophobia, but the Nexus Games had given him a whole new healthy respect for avoiding *spiders.*

"The Kuji aren't in the maze, right?" Kellan asked.

Sen, who remained in the safety of the room, shook his head. "Of course not. Stragglers aren't allowed to join, remember? *Get your head in the game.*" He shooed Kellan into the hall with a wave of both his hands. "Check for traps."

Kellan returned his attention to the hall. They were underground, obviously—all catacombs were—but he didn't understand how a straight hallway could be considered *a maze.* With a slow step, where he kept his attention on his surroundings, Kellan walked forward.

The metal door behind them was etched with the number *101.* Obviously, it was their escape room. They'd have to remember where it was in order to return to the palace.

Sen crept out of the room and followed a good ten feet behind, his hands clenched together in front of his chest. Mavis walked behind him, her weapon up and ready. She, too, remained vigilant, checking behind them occasionally, even if there was no place for an enemy to come from.

They had left an empty room, into an empty hall.

Kellan's bright hane was their only source of light, and it illuminated their path for a few feet. They continued at a steady pace, the stone bricks uneven and rough, as though the walls and floor had been assembled by amateur architects.

Two minutes of walking, and Kellan hadn't seen a single door or turn. They just walked forward, at a steady pace, never encountering anything but the spiders on their webs. Then Kellan's right forearm burned. He gritted his teeth and glanced down.

07:47

"Our time went down?" Mavis asked, staring at her own arm. "Why?"

"Someone triggered a trap," Kellan muttered, thinking back to Bitso's explanation of the game. "The time goes down whenever that happens."

"Seriously?"

Kellan nodded, and as the sting of the numbers slowly faded, he was struck with *another* burning sensation on his right arm. When he glanced down a second time, he was shocked to find the numbers had changed.

07:37

"*Another* person triggered a trap?" Kellan balked. "What're these delta-bravos doing?"

"Delta-bravos?" Sen asked, frowning. "You've said that before…"

"It's code for *D-B,* which means *douchebag.*" Mavis glared at the number on her arm.

"Seems needlessly complicated for insulting someone."

"This maze seems needlessly complicated for killing people," Kellan sarcastically muttered. "I'm just sticking to the Nexus theme."

"Keep walking! We're running out of time!"

Sen's shouts echoed throughout the hallway. Kellan took in a deep breath, asking for whatever gods were listening to grant him the patience needed to find his way through a death maze. He moved forward at a quicker pace, trying to find *something* that indicated it was a door or another pathway.

He didn't see anything.

The hall seemingly went on *forever*. In one direction. No turns. No escape.

There weren't any enemies, thankfully. No monster yami, or traps with buzz saws, or bizarre imps out to kill people.

Kellan's arm burned a third time. The numbers had decreased *again*, more than with just the normal passage of time.

07:25

"We lose ten minutes every time?" Kellan shook his head and tried to think of how often it would occur. How many people were in the maze?

Mavis touched the stone brick walls, running her fingers through some of the cobwebs. "*How* are they triggering traps? We haven't found anything yet. We can't even add to the incompetence."

"There must be illusions over the walls," Sen said. He walked over and felt the hall walls, never sullying his hands by rubbing the dust or webs. "If we all work together, we're bound to find something."

Kellan was familiar with illusions. Xiang had created them repeatedly in the last game. That didn't help much, however. All he had learned about illusions was that he couldn't see through them or detect them. Well, he had also learned they weren't tangible. They only *seemed* tangible.

Which gave Kellan an idea.

"How do we see through illusions?" Mavis asked, her volume increasing with her obvious frustration.

Sen stopped his searching. "Mind magic and soul magic have abilities to see through invisibility and deception."

"*You're* the soul mage," Kellan stated. Then he waved his hand around the maze. "See the way."

"Y-Yes, well, I'm too low rank. You see, you must be equal rank or higher to see through such abilities. Whoever made the maze—likely the Arbiter himself—is high rank. Perhaps A, S, or M. Which is, unfortunately, outside my capability to handle."

"Then why did you even bring any of that up, ya piece of toast?"

Sen's face reddened, then his ears. He pursed his lips, his eyebrows knitting downward into a glare. "How dare you. I'm using our *valuable time* to instruct you on the rules of the Nexus, so that you can use your two functioning brain cells to hopefully live through the *rest of the games* and *this* is how you repay me? *Insults*?"

Sen's shouting was legendary. It filled the hallway, bouncing off the walls.

But that was exactly what Kellan wanted.

Ignoring Sen's tirade, Kellan moved forward. He closed his eyes, listening to the echoes.

"You're *leaving*? Disgraceful!"

"Kellan!" Mavis added, her own voice echoing down the halls.

As Kellan ran down the straight hall, he paid careful attention to the sounds. A few feet forward, he heard it—the sounds echoing in a different direction. Off to his right. Kellan, without opening his eyes, turned to face the faint sounds disappearing down another tunnel.

When he opened his eyes, Kellan saw a stone brick wall, just as he had thought he would.

"You will return or else!" Sen shouted, his tone harsher than before.

Kellan tensed. When he turned to face Sen, he fought the urge to end this once and for all.

With gritted teeth, Kellan said, "I found the illusions."

Sen opened his mouth, as though ready for another tirade, but Mavis grabbed his Power Rangers sweatshirt and twisted her fist, practically yanking Sen off his feet. "*Stop*. No more threats. We're in the middle of an operation. We don't need this."

Sen huffed and then sharply turned his head to the side. "All right, all right." He dismissively waved his hand and then tugged his way out of Mavis's grip. "But next time, articulate your plans, lest you risk angering me."

Kellan balled his free hand into a fist several times, willing himself not to succumb to rage. A feeling of bloodlust and revenge emanated from his rifle, of all places. He glanced down at the black metal; he occasionally forgot that the weapon was semi-sentient. Did it *want* to kill Sen?

In a perfect world, Kellan sarcastically thought.

"*Yes...*" a haunting voice filled Kellan's mind. "*In a perfect world...*"

He flinched, surprised by the dark voice, wondering if it had actually come from his rifle.

Sen sucked in air through his teeth and grabbed at his shoulder. He whined as he hit the ground on his knees, his eyes scrunched closed. Mavis touched his back, her brow furrowed in confusion.

"Sen? What's wrong?"

He shoved the sleeve of his Power Rangers sweatshirt up past his elbow. With deep breaths, he touched at his arm, his small fingers sliding down to his wrist. A bulge writhed around, something snake-like under his skin.

The Queen Tyranny Worm.

"Jesus," Mavis said as she leapt away, her eyes wide.

Kellan held the glowing cigarette up a bit higher, staring at the wriggling worm moving around Sen's arm. "Maybe next time you'll use protection," he quipped.

"Enough of your *pathetic jokes*," Sen hissed, his voice strained. He gripped his arm, closing his fingers around the wiggling worm, and the disgusting creature eventually calmed down. "This wouldn't have happened if it weren't for you. Whenever I… think about them… the queen gets agitated. She hates that I haven't used her children…"

"Yeah, it's *my* fault you puppet people. Airtight logic."

Mavis walked over to his side. In a low whisper, she said, "Kellan, please. I think Sen can be reasonable. He fixed my leg, remember? Let's just… try not to antagonize each other. Not here. In the middle of a death game."

Kellan exhaled. "He's testing my patience."

"I understand. Let's just try to solve this civilly."

Kellan wanted to point out that Mavis had just yanked the kid around by his sweatshirt but opted not to say anything. Mavis had leapt to his side when it had seemed Sen might have been trying to start something. She just didn't want Kellan to act in the same manner as the child.

"Fine. I'll try."

Mavis returned to Sen's side. "Are you okay?"

With a huff, Sen shoved the sleeve of his sweatshirt down. "I can control it."

A hint of hesitation laced Sen's child-like voice. Kellan recognized it, and he wondered if he should be worried. But Mavis was right. Now wasn't the time to deal with the problem. Their time was quickly dwindling away.

Mavis glanced at the wall. "Kellan, you said you discovered the illusions?"

Still disturbed by the rifle, and the argument with Sen over the worms, Kellan ran a shaky hand down his face. They had a new way forward. He shouldn't waste it.

"That's right." Kellan walked over to the wall—the place where he had heard the echoes. "This is it. But…"

He knew if he touched the wall, the illusions would mess with his mind. Sure enough, when Kellan lifted his hand, his knuckles grazed the rough bricks. It felt real, even though he knew it wasn't. He would act as though he were touching something physical, which would prevent him from just walking through.

"How do we get through now that we know it's an illusion?" Kellan asked.

Sen swallowed and then managed to get back to his feet. He pushed his sleeve down to his wrist. "Just run through. Or have somebody shove you through. The illusions will stop you if you're hesitant and unsure, but if you're confident or merely thrown into one by accident, the illusions will crumble."

There was a long moment of silence. Then Kellan's right arm burned *yet again.*

The numbers…

07:10

They only had a little over seven hours remaining, despite the fact that they had only been in the maze for a handful of minutes. *At this rate, we're just going to die in the maze,* Kellan thought.

"Should we head back?" Mavis asked.

Sen waved his arms. "No! People are just being brazen because this is the beginning of the maze. We haven't even gathered any arcana. We need to keep going. Come. Shove me into the wall. Let's continue."

"This seems risky," Kellan muttered.

Was the Chime worth it?

"We can't return to my sister empty-handed." Sen clenched his jaw and said nothing else.

Kellan hesitated. Then he glanced back at the wall. They still had plenty of time…

"All right. Let's go. *But quickly.*"

—Chapter 7—
—Coffins—

Kellan, with force and confidence, walked forward into the wall. He basically threw himself through it, the illusion incapable of offering any resistance. He stumbled into a new hallway, this one with a four-way intersection a few hundred feet from his location.

And holes in the walls. Holes filled with coffins.

Kellan stopped and glanced around, taking in as much information as possible. Twenty coffins from here to the four-way intersection. He glanced at the coffins, his rifle at the ready. They didn't have names—neither on the coffins nor engraved into the bricks of the stone shelves.

But there were words.

Percentages.

Kellan stepped close to the first coffin, his eyes narrowed. Burned onto the redwood were the words:

Arcana 80%

Trap 19%

Other 1%

For a long moment, Kellan just stared. Was the coffin… randomized? Was that percentage the likelihood of the contents? The majority percentage indicated arcana. If he opened the coffin, would the contents most likely be arcana?

Sen and Mavis stumbled into the hallway a moment later. It seemed as though Mavis had thrown Sen forward and then charged forward herself. The two almost tripped over each other as they entered the coffin-lined hallway. In an attempt to stop himself from falling, Sen grabbed hold of Mavis's upper leg.

With the speed of a reflexive action, Mavis smacked Sen off and then stumbled into the nearest wall. "*Watch it,*" she hissed.

Sen hit the ground, unable to steady himself in time. Then he rubbed at his face as he got to his feet. "I assure you that wasn't a tasteless attempt at human contact." He brushed himself off with a huff. "For your information, my *child-like* body comes with *child-like* limitations. Such as the inability to be intimate."

"You can't get it up?" Kellan snorted and half-laughed. "This is the first time I've legitimately felt bad for you."

The cold breeze of the coffin-filled hall slowly wafted by. A chill ran down

Kellan's spine. He glanced back, trying to keep his attention on everything around.

"For your information," Sen said matter-of-factly, "men are capable of erections as soon as they're born. However, the ability to consummate a relationship isn't possible until the testes swells during the early stages of puberty. And since my body has—"

"Stop," Kellan interjected. He pinched the bridge of his nose. "I can't believe we're having this conversation."

"Really?" Mavis smirked. "I thought men *always* wanted to talk about their junk?"

He returned the smirk. "Speaking of junk, I've already gone through puberty, and everything works just fine for me."

With a blush, Mavis nodded once. "I'll keep that in mind."

Sen sighed loud enough for his voice to carry down the hall. "Yes, *rub it in.* The shame of my situation doesn't hurt enough."

The thought that Sen had somehow lost *that much* of his physical capability did bother Kellan. He glanced over at the child-like man and half-shrugged. "Sorry. I'll keep the jokes to a minimum."

"I'm so fortunate." Sen crossed his arms.

Then Kellan motioned to the nearest coffin. "I think these contain arcana. Mavis, why don't you open it?"

She walked to the nearest coffin and frowned. Then she grazed her fingertips over the words etched into the wood. "Percentages?"

As if to answer the question, the timer on Kellan's right arm burned. He glanced down and stared at the remaining time.

06:58

Goddammit, he thought. *All the other teams are triggering traps constantly.* When Kellan glanced back at the coffin, he took note of the nineteen percent associated with the trap. How many coffins were the others opening?

Kellan turned his attention to the other coffins in the hallway. If he opened all twenty, he would, most likely, trigger four traps, which would subtract forty minutes from the overall time. But if they were going to acquire arcana… They had to open a few coffins at the very least.

"Are you sure?" Mavis asked. She grabbed the side of the coffin's lid. "What if it's a trap?"

Kellan hefted his rifle. "If it's a yami, I'll handle it. If it's poison darts or something similar, we have two healers, right?" He motioned to himself and then Sen.

Before Mavis opened the coffin, she stared for a long moment. Then she inhaled and closed her eyes. Her exposed skin shimmered for a second. Pebble-like formations appeared across her skin, hardening like armor. They shifted with the pale tone of her complexion, becoming nearly invisible. Kellan still noticed the scale-like texture across Mavis's body, but it was subtle.

"I have this ability," she muttered. "Magma magic apparently lets me create natural armor."

Her statement reminded Kellan of his own armor. He touched the back of his neck and slid his fingers down his spine until he grazed a small object injected straight into his skin. While he was still wearing a T-shirt and sweatpants, the armor he had discovered had been connected straight into his body.

The armor had once been cursed, but not anymore…

Magical Item [Armor]—Shadow of a Dying Star

Uniform armor worn by the stealth gunners of the Flestiss Dominion. Sturdy and reliable, this piece of armor attaches to the mage's spine and requires a mana to activate. Once activated, the armor covers the mage completely and grants +2 "living shadow shell" armor defense, and +2 armor rating. The mage can deactivate the armor at will.

The armor rating reduced damage off the top, and the living shell was some sort of shadowy health source beyond his own. Kellan would've surely died in the last game if he hadn't been wearing his armor.

"Ready?" Mavis asked, drawing him back to the present.

"Do it, soldier," Kellan said, readjusting his focus to the coffin.

Since it cost a mana to use his armor—and since he only had twelve mana in total and had already lost one—he decided to hold off on using it. There would come a time he needed it later.

She shoved, and then grunted and finally—with considerable effort—managed to push the coffin lid off and reveal the contents. The inside glowed with a sinister red, the hue enough to briefly light up the hall. Kellan's glowing hane stick almost didn't compare.

But the red glow faded just as quickly as it had appeared.

Mavis held her breath for a long moment. Then she glanced down at Sen. "Was that a good sign or a bad one?"

"Look in the coffin," he said with a wave of his hand. "Since you weren't attacked by anything, I would say it was good."

Kellan didn't typically associate *red* with *good*, but this was the Nexus.

After a hesitant moment, Mavis leaned forward and stared at the contents of the coffin. Kellan moved forward as well, curious as to what was inside. He leapt back as soon as he caught a brief glimpse of the corpse inside.

The dead body was half-preserved. The skin was wan and sunken, the eyes nothing more than pools of jelly, and the clothes stiff with dried fluids. Thin hairs were everywhere, and the scratches on the inside of the wooden prison told Kellan the man had been alive before the coffin had been stuck into the Catacomb Maze.

Kellan didn't get many more details. He turned away too quickly to really know who the man had been.

"There's arcana in here," Mavis muttered. She had to push the corpse to the side—her face twisted in a grimace the entire time—but she managed to gather up a single glowing red crystal.

She held it up for a brief second.

Arcana…

It sparkled with inner power, crimson and mystic.

But then it melted into the palm of Mavis's hand. She shook out her arm and then wiped her hands onto her jeans. "That was disgusting." She flapped her hand in front of her nose. "And that corpse reeks."

"Most bodies decompose into a set of gases," Sen said, holding up a finger. "Cadaverine and putrescine smell like rot, whereas the gas, *skatole*, often smells of feces."

"I don't think that knowledge is gonna help us in this situation," Kellan muttered. He glanced over at the next coffin. "We're only getting *one* arcana from these? Some of the magical abilities we can obtain require *a lot* more. In order for me to rank my magic, I need at least ten. I only have five, currently. At this rate, we'll trigger several traps before we'll gather enough."

"That's because this is the early portion of the maze." Sen pointed to the four-way intersection. "This is a *risk versus reward* challenge round. That means the more we risk, the greater the gains. The center of the maze has the ultimate prize, and all the coffins around it will likely have *plenty* of arcana."

Both Mavis and Sen turned their attention to Kellan. He glanced back at them before turning his attention to the four-way intersection. They had to go deeper? The time was the biggest factor. He couldn't account for what everyone else was doing. Would they continue to trigger traps until they *all* died?

No. The other competitors had already lived through two games themselves. That meant they were clever enough to make it through some of the Arbiter's tricks. They were probably just taking risks because their time was so high.

Once the time was lower…

Would they stop risking themselves?

Or perhaps the other competitors would leave the maze before the time became an issue.

"Let's go deeper," Kellan said. "Forget these coffins. One arcana isn't enough incentive to trigger traps and decrease our time. Let's head straight for the center, and on the way out, we'll check these death boxes."

"Sounds like a plan," Mavis said. She readied her handgun and motioned for Kellan to take point. "I'll cover the rear."

He nodded in acknowledgement.

As a group, they ran to the four-way intersection. The whole catacomb was just as Kellan had imagined it would be. The dark halls, stone archways, and many coffins were the things of nightmares. Instead of running down a random hallway, Kellan stopped in the middle of the intersection and glanced around.

"What're you waiting for?" Sen asked. "We don't have a map. Any pathway is as good as the next!"

"Shh."

Kellan rummaged around in his backpack. He pulled out a stick of hane and then threw it down. He stomped on the black cigarette and smeared the contents on the stone floor.

"What're you doing?" Mavis asked.

Kellan motioned to the hall they had come from. "I've marked it. Now we know how to get back."

Her eyes went wide for a moment. "Oh. That's a good idea."

"Now can we go?" Sen asked.

Kellan held a hand up, silencing his teammate. He glanced down each hallway, trying to decide which path to take. Some paths had spiderwebs… and others did not. Had someone been through here already?

Then Kellan turned his attention to the coffins in the holes in the wall. Some of them had been opened on the route with no spiderwebs. People had been down that way. *But should we follow them?* Kellan narrowed his eyes. *Or should we take our own way?*

This wasn't a PvP game, which meant the players weren't allowed to fight each other. If Kellan ran into others, they wouldn't be struggling for their lives, but that didn't mean strange things couldn't happen. Kellan had had his key taken from him in the first game…

We should avoid everyone else if we can.

Kellan pointed down a hall that hadn't been traveled. "This way."

He jogged forward, keeping his attention focused on the way ahead. Sen and Mavis followed without saying a word, agreeing through their actions. The stomp of Mavis's shoes was the loudest sound they made as they hurried into the dark and gloomy hall.

The spiderwebs grew more numerous as they went. Kellan had to wave his arm to clear them away, the gentle tickle of their presence more of an irritation than anything else. When Kellan stopped to glance at the coffins, he was surprised by the numbers. One coffin read:

Arcana 60%

Trap 39%

Other 1%

The percentage for the traps went up?

Mavis stared at the coffin as well. "What is *other*?" She pointed to the last category.

"I'm sure that's for magical items or other useful objects," Sen stated. "Sometimes the Arbiter likes to put in random gifts for the participants in the Nexus Games."

"Will these coffins have more than one arcana?" Kellan asked. "Why else would the percentage shift so drastically like that?"

Sen had to stand on his tiptoes to even look at the percentages etched into the coffin. "That would be my guess." He stood back on his feet and crossed his arms. "I say we test this theory. The other teams have already stolen time—it wouldn't hurt if we did it once."

Kellan motioned to the coffin. Mavis stepped close, tucked her handgun away, and then grabbed the edge of the coffin.

"Ready?" she asked.

Kellan lifted his weapon. "Let's see."

After another grunt, as well as some effort, Mavis shoved the lid of the coffin off. But instead of crimson light and a corpse, Mavis stared down at a dark hole that seemingly led into the ground, like a hole that just went straight down.

Before they could discuss what they had found, Kellan's right arm burned. The numbers changed.

06:43

And then a scream echoed up from the hole in the coffin. It wasn't a cry for help, but a wail that chilled Kellan's blood. Mavis flinched away and drew her gun.

A mass of hands—human hands—like a centipede had been stitched into existence out of human corpses, jutted out of the coffin and scrambled around. The fleshy centipede screamed again as it dragged most of its body out of the coffin and slinked into the hall, its movements fast enough to rival a viper.

"Kill it!" Sen commanded. "And don't let it touch you!"

—Chapter 8—

—I Thought There Was a Problem—

The disgusting corpse-centipede was made exclusively of human body parts. The arms and hands writhed in formation, and the body of the creature was several spines woven together, like a rope. Three human heads made up its face, and the tail was complete with a stinger formed from broken and sharpened bones.

Kellan's Blitzkrieg Analysis gave him basic information on the horrific monster clawing its way into the maze.

Name: Carrion Centipede
Race: Lesser Yami
Magics: Body, Entropy
Rank: Impossible to Rank
Armor Rating: —
Health: 20/20

Stats:
Strength—4
Dexterity—8 [Fast]
Fortitude—2
Intelligence—1
Perception—2
Willpower—1

Abilities:
Diseased—The yami infects everything it wounds with *Shaken Sickness*. This disease can be resisted with 6 or higher fortitude.
Undead—The yami is immune to poison and gas. The yami does not need to breathe or eat to survive. Additionally, the yami feels no pain.

The monster had snaked its way out of the coffin with lightning speed, but Kellan was ready. He fired on it. The Nexus—a world with rules and exact dealings—gave him information on his attacks. The notifications came quickly and were somewhat distracting, but Kellan put up with them.

[Alex Kellan] shot [Carrion Centipede] for 6 damage. (3 + 100% (50% Sharpshooter Modifier x 2 Sevriss Bonus))

The entire string of information was like an equation done for him. On his Earth, there weren't quantified numbers for what happened. Kellan just shot and whether he hit or missed depended on factors he couldn't really describe outside of his own aim. The Nexus took into account the speed of his target, the power of his gun, his own training, and even Kellan's dexterity—all to calculate an exact amount of damage dealt to the target.

Kellan understood that if he shot at specific points on the body, different numbers would be added to the equation—a weak spot was always more vulnerable. But outside of that, his bullets did a near fixed amount of damage.

They ripped through the corpse centipede, but the undead monstrosity was barely affected. Its "health" seemed derived from the fact that it had multiple body parts worth of flesh.

Kellan continued to fire, no need to worry about ammo.

He dealt out another chunk of damage before the beast whipped around its tail. Kellan rolled out of the way. When the yami attempted to hit him a second time, Kellan threw his light source and then ducked into the shadows.

He could move a short distance while protected by the darkness. He "dove" into the shadows like they were water only he could enter and then emerged a good ten feet away, resurfacing in the hallway. Kellan took a deep breath when he stepped out of the void. He couldn't breathe while under.

Mavis shot the creature with her handgun.

There were no notifications for Kellan.

He suspected it was because he wasn't involved in any way. The Nexus only provided information when it applied to Kellan, somehow.

Perhaps a magical ability would allow him to know everything happening in combat? If there was one, Kellan didn't have it.

Sen clapped his hands, and a pinkish rose barrier shimmered into existence around Mavis.

The carrion centipede lashed out with its stinger tail. The broken bones broke through the barrier and struck Mavis across the shoulder. She cried out and fired again.

Kellan unloaded with his rifle. His many bullets ripped the creature apart from behind. It tried to turn—tried to hurry over to Kellan—but it had already taken too much damage. The beast screamed and then collapsed to the floor, its corpse body decomposing faster than Kellan had ever seen before.

Soon, it was just a mass of bones and liquid body parts. Blood bubbled, and the skulls of its three heads were scarlet from the mucus.

One arcana appeared out of the gore. Its red shimmer lit up the hall a bit.

"I see now," Sen muttered. During the fight, he had pressed his back up against the wall. Now that the danger was gone, he pushed himself away and walked over to the edge of the pooled blood. "The yami in these catacombs… They're likely traps all their own."

"What do you mean?" Kellan asked as he approached the open coffin.

He glanced inside. There was a hole leading down, with a ladder mounted to the bricks. The creature clearly hadn't used the ladder. What was it for? Other people? Were they supposed to go inside the coffin?

Kellan mulled over the situation and backed away from the bizarre container.

"*Shaken Sickness* is a disease that limits your movement," Sen said. He turned his attention to Mavis. "It usually causes shivers, and gradually lowers your dexterity. Which would prevent people from easily escaping once the time was low…"

Mavis tucked her Desert Eagle into the waistband of her pants. She exhaled, her hands shaky, just as Sen had said. When she turned to Kellan, she frowned. "You said you can heal people?"

He nodded and then walked over. When Kellan touched her, he used his *Heal the Body* ability.

Kellan spent one mana, and healed Mavis of three damage. The power felt warm and inviting, and the scratch on Mavis's shoulder stitched itself up. The blood on her T-shirt didn't disappear, though.

And Mavis's shaking didn't stop, either.

She stared down at her unsteady hands. "Wait… I'm going to get shakier as we go along?"

Sen stepped close to her side. "That's correct. I suspect most of the creatures will have that unfortunate disease…"

After a long moment of just staring, Mavis slowly wrapped her arms tightly around her own body. Her fingers gripped her upper arms as she glared at the floor.

"And healing won't make it go away?" she whispered.

"*His* healing won't," Sen stated. With a scoff, he added, "I told him not to pick up healing abilities. It requires *investment.* Healing damage is fine—perhaps even useful in the right situations—but the ability to heal poison, disease, genetic defects, and permanent magical injuries requires a lot of body magic, which requires a lot of arcana. Our warrior should focus on *combat* abilities, rather than trying to pick up all the healing abilities there are out there."

"Body mages can heal genetic defects?" Kellan asked, almost in awe. "Like… what?"

Sen shot him a glower. "What did I just say? Don't think about those abilities! You don't have enough time, or arcana, to properly invest in becoming a legendary healer. *I'm already there!*" He pulled back his volume to add, "Well, not *all the way* there. I'm very good."

Mavis's fingers twisted into the sleeves of her shirt as she tightened her grip. "Wait, can *you* heal me of the disease?"

"Yes. Of course."

"Well?" Mavis knitted her eyebrows and frowned. "What're you waiting for?"

"We should wait until after we've made it a little deeper," Sen said matter-of-factly. "The ability requires that I spend mana, so if you're going to get struck by the enemy a few times, I should wait to use my healing until we absolutely need it. Understand? Your shaking shouldn't be too bad right now. It's a disease that gradually takes effect. In a few minutes, it'll take another point of dexterity, and then a few more minutes, another."

Kellan examined Mavis for a moment. She wasn't shaking too bad, but it was obvious enough. She could probably continue without any healing, and they would be okay.

"Just heal me right now," Mavis said, her tone cold.

"I told you. That's a waste of mana." Sen sighed and rubbed at his temple. "I go to great lengths to explain things, and I swear no one listens..."

"I heard what you said. Heal me anyway."

"We shouldn't—"

"*I don't care about that,*" Mavis snapped, her voice bordering on a shout.

The echo of her anger traveled the hall in both directions. Kellan glanced around, hoping nothing was around to mess with them. Fortunately, he saw and heard no movement. He returned his attention to the conversation, confused by Mavis's sudden outburst.

"What's wrong?" Kellan asked. "Is something happening?"

Mavis inhaled, obviously calming herself. Then she just stared at the floor as she replied, "I just don't want to be weak again, okay? Please. Heal me now. I'll avoid the monsters better in the future."

Not weak again...

Sen had been the one to fix her leg. Before then, she had walked with a notable limp. Mavis had hated it, but Kellan hadn't realized how much.

"Very well," Sen finally stated. He stepped close to Mavis and placed his hand on her side. "There. You should feel better any moment."

The use of his magic seemingly had no visible component. Sen had just touched Mavis, and a few seconds later, her shaking stopped. She stood still for a long while, as if making sure the shiver of weakness wouldn't return.

Once she was convinced that she was cured, Mavis smiled widely. "Thank you."

"So much drama," Sen said, rolling his eyes. "No one thought you were *weak*. We all knew it was the work of the disease, not your lack of courage or willpower."

"That's what you say." Mavis stepped away from him and readied her handgun again. "But after I was injured while on active duty, a lot of people who I thought were my friends just abandoned me. Even..."

Her significant other, Kellan thought, recalling their conversation on the matter.

It seemed her scars hadn't healed completely. At least, not the ones on the inside.

In order to change the subject, Kellan motioned to the coffin. "There's a ladder down."

"Oh?" Sen glanced over. "Well, go down there."

"Alone?"

"Of course *alone.*" Sen sneered. "You're an eclipse mage, aren't you? The darkness is your kingdom. Slip in there, search around, and then come back to us." He clapped his hands. "Chop chop."

After a long exhale, during which Kellan gave serious thought to just continuing their trek, he turned his attention to the coffin with the ladder that led deeper underground. He hoisted himself up on the brick ledge of the hole in the wall, and then crouched over the coffin in order to get an even better view. He stared down into the pit, thankful he noticed the floor. It wasn't too far down.

After a deep breath, Kellan dove into the darkness and quickly traveled as a shadow along the wall and then to the floor. When he emerged, he was greeted by the stench of rot and decay. He covered his nose and glanced around, his eyes watering.

There wasn't much. No glowing arcana, no obviously magical objects. The room wasn't even large—it was the size of a household pantry at most.

But he *did* see a lump of flesh. Not just a rotting bit of decayed human, but a pulsating lump—something akin to a mole on someone's skin. It writhed around, reminding Kellan of a hamster. It was no larger than his fist, and when he knelt to pick it up, the little lump practically leaned away from him, as though sentient.

His ability gave him information, though he almost wished it hadn't.

Magical Item [Raw Material, Permanent]—Crafting Clay

A rare material dropped from primordial dragons when they molt and slough their old scales for newer ones.

A body mage with the ability "Fleshcrafting, Rank II" may use this clay to add +2 permanent physical stats to their being (increasing different categories, not adding both points in one stat) OR may correct penalties resulting from "Gift Grafting" OR may add a bizarre physical feature (wings, tail, additional arm, horns, claws, etc.) to their person. This feature isn't genetic and will not pass to offspring.

Dropped from primordial dragons, huh?

Kellan was surprised he had found anything at all. Hadn't the centipede been a trap? Or had the ladder and the room below the coffin been a secret hideaway that most would miss because they wouldn't have bothered to investigate the resting spot of a monster? Kellan was convinced it was the latter.

The Arbiter seemed to enjoy hiding special rooms around the game arenas.

It took most of Kellan's willpower not to just leave the disgusting tumor-chunk alone, but he knew he had to show it to Sen. But the thought of touching it…

This is the Nexus. The thing could be secretly diseased. Kellan mulled over the situation for a few seconds. *Then again, the description didn't indicate it was negative. Still…*

Kellan removed his T-shirt and used it to scoop up the jiggling lump. Then he used the ladder to leave the hole, just in case diving into the shadows would cause him to lose the bizarre flesh. He emerged from the coffin, the odor of death following him as he went.

"You somehow lost your shirt down there?" Sen frowned. "Unbelievable."

Kellan handed over his impromptu sack of flesh by just dropping it on the ground. "I found something. Probably for you. This looks like a thing you'd get excited over."

With an eyebrow raised, Sen knelt and unwrapped the flesh. Then he gasped—both hands on his cheeks.

"By the might of Hakael! Do you know what this is?" Sen reached for the flesh with hands shakier than Mavis's had ever been. "It's so beautiful…"

Mavis stared at the disgusting tumor, her eyes narrowed. "Why did you bring this up the ladder?" She turned to Kellan. "Was this supposed to be a joke?"

Without the Blitzkrieg Analysis ability, Kellan suspected that Mavis couldn't tell the flesh was actually magical. He considered that a moment before answering.

"Are you seeing Sen's reaction?" Kellan motioned to the kid, who was now petting the blob. "I figured he'd be excited. That man goes on about being a fleshcrafter more than a room of attorneys go on about practicing law."

"This is *Crafting Clay!*" Sen declared as he held the flesh above his head. He might as well have been holding Simba. He smiled widely and then hugged it close to his chest, the gooey flesh sticking to the Power Rangers on his sweatshirt. "This isn't as good as Langarren Clay, but it's just one step below! With this…. I can repair some of my body."

He practically rubbed the tumor against his cheek, as though caressing it.

Kellan couldn't stop himself from frowning. "I'm so… happy for you." He didn't know what else to say. "But we should probably keep moving." He pulled his shirt back on and brushed off the front.

He glanced at his arm.

06:32

"We've already lost an hour and half."

"I agree, we should go," Mavis said.

Sen, clutching the lump of jiggling pale flesh as though it were his own baby, hurried over to grab the lit hane stick off the floor. He held it in one hand and the flesh in the other. "Fine. Let's hurry along. The sooner we can get out of here, the better."

—Chapter 9—
—Crypt Widows—

Kellan ran down the length of a hall until they came to another four-way intersection.

Shouts and screams echoed around them, traveling down the narrow corridors from every direction. They were the other teams—Kellan was certain. Phrases like *Stop* and *This can't be real* reached him like faint whispers. This time, every pathway was cleared of cobwebs. The other teams had been through here—even some of the coffin lids were shoved to the side, exposing empty insides.

I need more of a strategy here, Kellan thought.

He closed his eyes and went back to his basic training. His field manual had stressed the importance of methodical testing to gain intelligence on the enemy. He needed a plan—one that he could stick to until they found their way out. Or in case they were separated.

How could they find a way out of a maze?

In theory, if someone placed their hand on a wall and followed it through all the twists and turns and dead ends, they would always find their way out of a maze. The only exception was if the maze had an "island" of walls, meaning the wall cluster didn't connect to anything else in the maze. But even then, if Kellan marked the floor, went along the entire wall, and found it to be an island, he could just switch to an outside wall and follow that.

Eventually, by keeping a hand on the walls, he would find a way out. It worked every time to escape a maze.

But that would take too long.

We're going about this the wrong way. Kellan gritted his teeth. *If there were illusions in the beginning, there are likely illusions in other places. But how will we find them if we don't have any abilities that see through their tricks?*

"Which way?" Mavis asked, her handgun at the ready. Her eyebrows knitted as she glanced down the other three directions. "We shouldn't just stand here."

Struck with an idea, Kellan jogged forward and grabbed the lid off a coffin. He threw it to the ground and fired at it with quick bursts from his rifle, making sure to angle his shots so that the bullets ricocheted down an empty hall, away from the teams. The redwood lid shattered into hundreds of pieces, the splinters twirling through the air.

His gunshots added to the noise of the maze, mixing with the shouts from other teams.

Once the cacophony had ended, Sen stepped forward, hugging the lump of flesh close. "What're you doing? The coffins won't have arcana! There's no reason to destroy them."

Kellan knelt and gathered up bits of wood. Then he passed out pieces to Mavis and Sen. The occasional splinters irritated him, but to his fascination, the slivers of wood were pushed out of his fingers by the Tyranny Worms. He spotted their wriggling, yellow bodies as the wood slipped out of his body, as though even *they* were irritated by the splinters.

Sen and Mavis examined their bits of wood.

"Why?" was all Mavis asked.

"Throw them at the walls as we go along," Kellan said. "If there's an illusion, the wood will pass through. If the wood bounces off the bricks, obviously, it's real."

Sen slowly smiled—almost a smirk, but not quite. "Clever. I wasn't expecting that from our warrior. No wonder my sister is enamored of your alternate-dimension self."

Kellan held back a sarcastic remark as he walked into the first corridor and threw a bit of wood at the wall. The coffin fragment bounced off the rough bricks. Then Kellan did the same for the other side. Again, the wood clattered against the wall and then tumbled to the ground.

This might take too long. We'll have to run and throw if we want to keep a decent pace.

"Mavis," he said. "You throw at the right wall, and Sen, you throw at the left. I'll carry extras. Just tell me when you need more."

"We're not going to pick them up?" Mavis knelt and gathered up the two bits Kellan had thrown. "We won't need more if we just collect what we've thrown."

"It'll take too long. Let's just focus on moving forward."

"Are we going to open up any other coffins along the way?"

"No."

"Why not?" Sen interjected. "We need the arcana. And what if we find more clay? I need more. At least one more. Maybe two."

Kellan shook his head. "The coffins are a trap."

"*Some* are."

"No, you don't understand. They're meant to slow us, and they're not even worth it. Remember? We're here for the Summoning Chime. We need to get that first and then come back here and check coffins. If we search these halls looking for coffins with good percentages, we're just wasting time."

The *Risk Versus Reward* game became clear in his mind. They needed to prioritize getting the Chime, and only then could they risk fighting monsters or triggering the timer to hit zero.

"Let's go down this hall." Kellan threw another stick of hane on the floor and crushed it. The mark remained—both on the bottom of his bare foot and the bricks. "This is so we know what way we came."

He hurried forward, his weapon ready, his attention on the darkness within the hall. The shadows didn't obscure his vision, and if he was ahead of the light, he could take advantage of his eclipse magic.

Mavis and Sen followed after him, each tossing bits of wood at the walls.

As they ran, Kellan glanced at the coffins. The percentage numbers on each were slightly different, and he could see how he could waste an inordinate amount of time checking the lids of each and every one.

One coffin had:

Arcana 30%

Trap 50%

Other 20%

That was the highest he had seen for an "Other" category.

Another coffin read:

Arcana 80%

Trap 19%

Other 1%

Kellan almost stopped for that coffin, but he didn't want to deviate from his plan. All of his field training told him that he shouldn't alter the articulated plan unless absolutely necessary, and he was determined to stick to that.

"Kellan!"

He stopped and whirled around on his heel, his rifle up.

Mavis and Sen stood by a wall. She pointed at the bricks and then tossed another piece of the coffin lid. The chunk of wood sailed right through the wall—as though it didn't exist. Kellan had been right. There *were* more illusions, and the pathway to the center was likely filled with them.

"Good work." He ran back over and then went headfirst into the wall. When he stumbled through, and found yet another corridor of bricks, webs, and coffins, he smiled. "C'mon. It's clear."

Kellan ran forward, but he slowed, his attention on his surroundings. The bricks, the shadows—the very walls—seemed to be moving. Subtly. Slowly. It was hard to describe. It felt like small pieces were shifting around, not whole bricks at a time.

When Kellan stepped forward, something squished between his toes. The slimy sensation reminded Kellan of a peeled grape. He glanced down and his chest tightened.

Spiders.

Hundreds of spiders.

Not normal spiders—with normal black bodies and eight legs—but spiders with an eyeball on their abdomens. A human eye, open and staring, unable to blink. The eyeball protruded from the spider's body, practically jiggling.

Kellan had stepped on one, the juices of the eye gushing between his toes and across his foot. He swallowed hard as he took a step back.

All the movement on the walls and the floor was nothing more than spiders. Each arachnid had a human eye on its back, but also a pair of giant fangs that hung from its mouth, so swollen with venom, it seemed as though the creatures couldn't tuck them in.

This was some sort of hallway decorated in nightmares.

Mavis and Sen entered the hall.

Then Sen lifted the little light. Its bright shine cast away the darkness, and with it, the confidence of the spiders. They scurried away, to the edge of the illumination, their pupils constricted into tiny black dots.

Some of the eyes were blue. Some were green. Some brown.

"What is that?" Mavis asked, her voice breathless. "Was that… were those… Were those spiders?"

"Yes," Kellan muttered.

Although his gun had infinite ammo and didn't need to be reloaded, he didn't have enough bullets for all the disgusting creatures that lined the corridor.

"Are they magical?" Mavis asked.

"I can't see anything magical about them." Kellan narrowed his eyes, hoping they'd provide some information, but nothing happened. But they *had* to be magical. A spider couldn't possibly have an eye in its abdomen.

"They're *Crypt Widows*," Sen said matter-of-factly. "They're quite magical, but easily killed. Their venom causes paralysis, and once you're immobile, they steal body parts."

"Like eyeballs?" Kellan asked with a sardonic edge.

"Precisely."

"Why can't I tell they're magical? My Blitzkrieg Analysis usually provides me with *something*."

"Creatures with eclipse or mind magic can sometimes hide their basic information." Sen stepped closer to Mavis, his eyes locked on the distant spiders that writhed around in the darkness. "Crypt Widows use eclipse magic to remain quiet and hidden and sometimes use the shadows to travel to their victims at frightening speeds."

Mavis shuddered. "Well, I vote we go back and find another way."

"No." Kellan shook his head, trying to undo the knot of anxiety in his chest. "This is definitely the way. The spiders are meant to scare us—or actually paralyze us. Slow us down. I say we run through here and keep going."

After shaking her hands out, Mavis glanced down at Sen. "You can heal disease… Can you heal poison and venom as well?"

"Of course." Sen huffed and then petted his flesh lump. "I'm a skilled healer, thank you very much."

"Will the paralysis happen immediately if we're bitten?"

"It'll take hold of your whole person after thirty seconds, roughly. For a child, however… Much sooner."

Some of the eyeball spiders ventured into the light, growing bolder the longer Kellan and the others stood in the hallway. The eyes stared at them, the pupils constricting and dilating as they watched.

Kellan suspected a few would grow daring enough to attack.

He knelt and then motioned to Sen. "Here. Get on my back. Mavis and I will run, and you just make sure we don't collapse."

Sen's eyebrows shot to his hairline. "*Run down the hall?* I wouldn't trust you to run a bath, why would I trust you to run with me down the hall?"

"I carried you through the last bit of the first game," Kellan stated.

The statement almost acted as a slap. Sen gripped his flesh lump tighter, his lips pursed. But he gradually relaxed, his distant gaze on the floor. "Yes. You're right. You did… carry me through most of it."

"And I'll carry you here. Get on."

The statement seemed to change Sen's demeanor. He glanced up, his brow furrowed. Then he slowly walked over to Kellan. Before Sen climbed onto his back, he carefully tucked the Crafting Clay into the front pocket of his sweatshirt, while also holding the brightly lit hane. Sen wrapped his arms around Kellan's neck and pressed himself against Kellan's backpack. He held on tightly, his fingers lacing together in front of Kellan, like an odd bowtie.

Kellan hefted Sen up higher as he stood. "See? I got you."

"Let's not speak of this."

With a chuckle, Kellan nodded. "Fine by me."

"And don't let any of the Crypt Widows touch me."

"Spoiler alert: That's the plan."

When Kellan was carrying someone, he wouldn't be able to dive into the darkness and travel as a shadow. But this way, he could protect Sen. If he was bitten, Sen would have the capability of healing him before anything could be stolen by the spiders…

"Are you sure about this?" Mavis whispered.

"I'm confident." Kellan offered a smile. "Are you with me, soldier?"

That got her smiling. "Well, if you're *that* confident. Yeah. I've got your back."

The Crypt Widows leapt into the light, three and four at a time. They scurried closer and closer, their fangs prominent. Before they could reach Kellan's bare feet, he grabbed Sen's legs and then rushed forward.

Their light, made by Kellan's eclipse magic, seemed to frighten most of the spiders in the stone corridor. But there were *hundreds* of spiders, and some of them had more courage than others. Kellan stepped on several as he ran, the squish of their fleshy bodies—especially the eyeballs, which popped like bags of water—sent shivers up and down his spine.

But one leapt from the ceiling and landed on his face. Kellan acted out of instinct and smacked it away, but not before the disgusting monster could sink its fangs into his cheek.

Kellan grunted, his jaw clenched. The sting of the venom was immediate—the stuff burned through his face, straight to his sinuses, and then to his ear.

Sen touched his fingers to the front of Kellan's neck. Warmth spread outward from his touch.

[Sun Sen] used *Purge* to heal [Alex Kellan] of all poisons and venoms of B-rank and lower.

The relaxing sensation allowed Kellan to breathe easy. He smiled to himself as he picked up the pace, the *splat* of spider bodies under his feet almost a delightful reminder that he was taking his revenge.

Mavis kept close, and when a spider leapt for her arm, she stumbled. But when the tiny beast tried to bite her, its fangs couldn't seem to pierce through her magically pebbled skin. Mavis swatted the spider away before it could find a soft spot.

Then Kellan saw the end of the corridor—a flat wall.

A dead end.

The Crypt Widows clustered over everything, their swarming bodies making it difficult to see. But they weren't on the far wall at the end of the corridor. Why? Because they didn't want to climb across the dead end?

Or because they can't. Because it's another illusion.

"Hang on," Kellan shouted.

And then he ran at the wall full tilt.

—Chapter 10—

—The Center of the Catacomb Maze—

Sen gripped the collar of Kellan's T-shirt and yanked back, practically choking him. "*What're you doing?*"

But Kellan didn't slow. He closed his eyes right as he was about to go face-first into the stone bricks. Instead of giving himself a concussion, Kellan flew through the wall, just as he had expected to. Sen, physically shaking, obviously hadn't expected that result.

Kellan forced himself to come to a halt. He wasn't sure where he was running anymore, and he wanted to make sure Mavis kept up with him.

Slight movement caught his attention. He turned, but he was too slow.

A muscled man lumbered forward, at least seven feet tall, his fist cocked. Kellan's first thought was to dive into the darkness to avoid the incoming strike—but Sen's presence prevented that. Kellan only managed to take one step backward before the man slammed his fist into Kellan's noggin.

Kellan was hit so hard, he forgot cursive.

His vision went black for a split second, and when he regained consciousness, he was leaning against the rough stone wall, his breathing ragged. The warmth of healing magic spread from his neck through his busted lip and nose.

Kellan didn't even remember seeing a damage notification after getting struck. But when the second swing came, the haze over his mind was sufficiently cleared enough that he managed to leap out of the way.

The muscled man—so buff that his neck had disappeared into the mountain of his shoulders—moved with the speed and force of a steamroller. He slowly turned, his T-shirt straining to keep itself together, practically ripping at the seams. Kellan didn't know why, but the man also wore bicycle shorts, a bizarre and unsettling combination that left little to the imagination.

When the man lifted his fist again, Kellan ripped Sen off his neck and threw him to the ground. The man-child hit the stone bricks with a grunt.

Their attacker swung, and Kellan dodged under. Then he jumped to Sen's side, grabbed the glowing stick of hane, and crushed it in his palm. Kellan's eclipse magic responded to the sudden darkness. He felt as though it were strengthening him—without any light, the shadows reigned supreme.

Kellan's *Void Knight* ability increased his physical stats by five each, elevating him to superhuman levels. Like some sort of fucked-up vampire high on coke-laced blood, Kellan jumped, kicked off the wall, and then roundhouse kicked his attacker.

> **[Alex Kellan] struck [Gero] for 6 bashing damage.**
> **[Gero] reduces damage of each hit equal to his natural armor rating of 2.**
> **[Gero] takes a total of 4 damage.**

The muscled man—Gero—slammed into the wall. In one clean motion, Kellan unslung his rifle and struck the man across the face. Blood exploded from his nose and mouth. The man crumpled to the floor, crashing like a tree. He gargled down air and then lifted an arm to shield his face.

The man only had one eye.

The other had been… dug out.

That wasn't the worst part. The man only had four fingers per hand, each digit awkwardly shaped and of varying lengths. They weren't injured or scarred—the man was just deformed. Even his neck—thick as a trunk—wasn't *just* from muscle.

How much health did the man have? After the two strikes, Kellan was certain he had done more than seven points of damage, which meant Gero had more than seven health. But probably not much more. He was at death's door.

"It's one of those *inbred* Nexus residents," Sen shouted. He felt around on the floor, his gaze unfocused. "Kill him! We need to continue on our way."

Kellan hesitated.

The residents of the Nexus were distant, inbred children of the Arbiter. Their misshapen bodies were just as twisted as their dimension. Kellan had met a couple of residents during the first few games, and each had seemed frightened, at a disadvantage, just looking to avoid death at the hands of the Nexus Games participants.

And since Kellan's eyes didn't offer him any information on Gero, it was likely he wasn't a mage—just a mortal who loved lifting weights, apparently.

Mavis stumbled through the illusion wall, finally joining them. She shivered and patted at her arms, several Crypt Widows scuttling over her pebbled skin. When the arachnids fell to the floor, Kellan jumped close and crushed them with his bare feet, trying not to picture the eyeballs exploding, but unable to block out the squishing noise they made.

"You okay?" Kellan asked.

"Yeah." Mavis reached out and grabbed his shoulder. "Why is it dark? What's going on?"

"I need to handle something. Just stand here."

Kellan turned and found the inbred resident getting to his feet. Kellan aimed his rifle but waited with his finger on the trigger.

"Don't move," Kellan commanded.

Then his arm burned. Kellan sucked in air through his teeth and glanced down at the timer. The numbers read:

05:19

His heart sank, his whole body tensing with realization. *Someone picked up a Summoning Chime.* An hour had disappeared from their collective time.

Goddammit, Kellan thought, glaring at the numbers. *We shouldn't be wasting time.*

"If you let me go, I'll tell you the way to the center of the maze," Gero said, his voice gurgling, as if he had cobblestones in his throat. "Please. I have a family."

"Do you live here?" Kellan asked.

"I… No. I came here looking for information."

Information? Kellan wanted to inquire about that, but the sting on his forearm remained—reminding him that other teams were already collecting their chimes and heading out. Did he have enough time to interrogate a Nexus resident *and* make it to the center of the maze?

After slowly lowering his weapon, Kellan sighed. "Gero, right? That's your name?"

The question took a long moment to sink in. Gero's one eye was wide, his mouth slightly open as though the words wouldn't come. Had he heard? Why was he so stunned?

"Who cares what his name is?" Sen asked. "Let's just get the information and hurry on!"

"My name *is* Gero," the Nexus resident said.

The darkness was too thick for anyone but Kellan to see. He wanted to point to the illusion wall and tell Gero to get out, but that was pointless. Instead, Kellan just said, "Look, if there are other residents in this maze, gather them all up and leave. Once the time on this challenge round is over, the Arbiter intends to kill everyone here."

The statement didn't meet with an immediate reaction. Gero stared with his one eye—his empty socket swollen, puffy, and red.

"At least have him tell us the way," Sen shouted. "He offered! What's wrong with you? You spurn all our advantages!"

Gero stood to his full height. His impressive seven feet brought his head close to the stone ceiling. He used his four-fingered hand to smooth his shirt. "You… I've seen you on the TV. You spoke before the Arbiter. You're… Alex Kellan the Void Knight."

Kellan smiled to himself. *At least it's not Alex Kellan the Rulebreaker anymore.* "That's me."

With a sigh, Gero said, "Merry Christmas."

"Wait, what?" It only took Kellan a second to remember all the things he had said to the Arbiter. He *had* said Merry Christmas on TV, and then later Bitso had explained it was a phrase that meant: *Thank goodness I'm alive.*

"Right," Kellan stated. "Merry Christmas."

The man didn't move. He swayed on his feet, likely dizzy from the many strikes to the head. Then he waved a large hand and pointed.

Kellan glanced around. They stood in a long hallway. Down one end was another four-way intersection. Down the other end was a T intersection. The illusion wall that led to the spiders blended perfectly with everything around them. Kellan marked the floor with a smear of blood from the spiders on the bottom of his feet.

Gero continued to point, but his arm shook.

Knowing that everyone else needed to see, Kellan reached into his backpack and withdrew another stick of hane—the black cigarette was thin, and when he spent another mana to activate his eclipse power, the hane glowed brightly, illuminating the area.

Everyone squinted against the light.

Kellan lost his improved strength, dexterity, and fortitude. He felt weaker—like he hadn't slept in weeks—and regretted brightening the area for everyone else.

Gero waved his arm forward, more confident. "I'll take you to the center of the maze. This way."

"I just told you everyone is going to die." Kellan glanced down at the timer on his arm. "You should just tell us the way and then leave."

"It'll be faster if I show you."

Although Kellan didn't like this outcome, he turned to Mavis and Sen to see if they would agree. Mavis brushed back her purplish hair and nodded once. Sen, still upset and brushing himself off, was more concerned about the lumpy tumor in his sweatshirt than anything else. He pulled out the Crafting Clay, whispered things to it as he patted it off, and then returned it to his pocket.

"Carry me," Sen said, his arms up. "I don't trust inbred lunatics, but since you seem *so determined* to make friends with these genetic defects, I guess I'll go along with it. *However*, if we start rapidly running out of time, we need to head back to our room."

Kellan sighed, knelt, grabbed Sen, and then headed over to Gero. "Lead the way."

Gero lumbered forward, walking with an odd gait. He favored his right leg—which was slightly longer than the other. Kellan took note of that as he stayed a short distance behind the man. Mavis stayed close as well, but she kept grabbing at parts of her clothes, itching and patting, as though looking for more spiders.

Without hesitating, Gero led them to the T intersection, and then took a right. A few feet down the new corridor, he turned straight into the wall. The illusions didn't seem to bother him. Kellan followed, trying not to get too far behind as he cautiously watched Mavis over his shoulder.

"You helped us before," Gero said through huffs of breath.

"*Us?*" Kellan asked.

"The residents of the Nexus."

"Ah." Kellan thought back to the children he had helped. The ones who had died. "I wouldn't say I was that much help."

"You didn't kill me for arcana."

"Hm."

Gero turned into another wall, seemingly at random. He passed through another illusion, and Kellan dashed after him. Mavis stayed close, but her attention was on her surroundings and less on Gero. Whenever Kellan glanced back, he wasn't so sure what Mavis was staring at.

Another illusion wall.

And then another.

Kellan stepped into a third hallway and found more Crypt Widows. Gero covered his face, and Mavis crushed them at every opportunity, either with her shoes, or her fist. When she struck one, it exploded like a blood-filled water balloon.

The moment they ran through another illusion, Kellan found himself in a large, stone room. The rot of dead bodies hung on the stagnant air, stinking the place up worse than a morgue. He coughed back the noxious smell.

The room wasn't large—a mere ten feet by ten feet—and Kellan noticed something lingering in the corner like a hobo lingered in an alleyway near a dumpster. What was it? At first, Kellan thought it was some sort of monstrous yami, but before he could throw Sen off his back, he managed to make out all the details.

It was… two people.

Two people melted together, their bodies seemingly twisted into one being. The thing had two heads—one looking forward, the other looking behind. Its chest was giant compared to its three thin arms and two stumpy legs. It wore clothing only through the liberal application of belts and strings to keep everything up and in place.

Was it a man? Both heads seemed masculine, and there were no feminine features, but the skin was twisted and shiny, as though it had been melted for a few moments like a partially used candle.

Kellan hefted his rifle.

His gun seemed eager to kill the beast.

"*What're you doing, Gero*?" the two-man shrieked as he held a hand up over one set of eyes. He squinted and pressed himself into the corner of the room, the second head trying to crane around enough to see what was happening. "Why have you brought players here?"

"Alvo, Juan—this is the man from the TV. The one who helped."

Gero lumbered over to the two-man fusion. Then he pointed at Kellan.

"The Merry Christmas fellow?" one head asked.

"Yes. He let me live. I'm taking him to the center of the maze." Then Gero turned back around, his one eye large. "This is Alvo and Juan." He gestured to each head. "They're twins."

"They're an omelet," Sen quipped.

Mavis shot him a glare. Then she placed a finger over her lips. "*Shh.*"

"This isn't the center of the maze," Kellan said, his rifle still at the ready. "Why did you bring us here?"

"Alvo and Juan need help escaping the Catacomb Maze. They have important information." Gero stomped over to Kellan and then placed a massive hand on Kellan's shoulder. "Please. If Alvo and Juan try to leave by themselves, one of the other players will find them. I… I was out trying to find a clear path, but everywhere I looked, there were either traps or Nexus Games players."

And the players would definitely kill them for easy arcana…

Kellan sighed. Then he lowered his weapon.

"Are you insane?" Sen hissed into Kellan's ear. "These defenseless boobs are worth a single arcana each. At least. The blob-man might be worth two, I'm not sure…" Sen tightened his grip around Kellan's neck. "We don't have time to help them."

"What kind of help do you need?" Mavis asked.

Gero slapped his hands together. "Alvo and Juan must make it to the AVU Palace. They must speak with Nosferatu. He's another player in the Nexus Games. Please."

Nosferatu? Kellan knew the name. Some high-ranked mage—a resident of the Nexus. He was the leader of another team.

Before Kellan could answer, Gero pointed to the far wall. "There's an illusion. Walk through, enter the main corridor, and head to the left. The center of the maze is right there." Then he turned back to Kellan, his one eye screwed into half a glare. "But please. Return here afterward and take Alvo and Juan with you to the exit."

"Xiang would hate this idea," Sen said matter-of-factly.

That made Kellan want to do it now even more than before. Although he didn't know Gero, or the *twins*, he knew that helping the residents of the Nexus had been beneficial for him in the past. And murdering a bunch of defenseless individuals never sat right with him.

"I'll help," Kellan stated.

Mavis turned to him with a smile. She said nothing, but the brief look got Kellan smiling in return. It was only Sen's loud groan of irritation that ruined the moment.

And then Kellan's arm burned *again*. Even Mavis sucked in breath this time as they all glanced at their forearms.

04:01

The challenge round was halfway over, and they hadn't yet found a Summoning Chime, yet two other teams *had*.

Goddammit.

Kellan gritted his teeth and ran for the illusionary wall. "I'll be back. Get ready to run."

The residents said nothing. Kellan ran by them, dove through the stone wall, and then tumbled out into a large corridor—one larger than all the others. The ceiling was at least twenty feet up, and the walls were lined with holes containing coffins. But the stench of rot was far worse in the corridor than anywhere else.

Kellan held a hand up to his nose as he glanced at the coffins.

One coffin read:

Arcana 90%

Trap 5%

Other 5%

While another read:

Arcana 5%

Trap 90%

Other 5%

This is the corridor with all the highest reward, no doubt, Kellan thought, his heart beating harder than he liked. But his musings came to an end when he stared down the hall. He caught his breath, the mystery of the foul odor finally solved.

A mountain of bodies blocked their path.

Not *recently* dead bodies. Flesh fell off the bodies in gooey chunks. The skulls were sunken in, the hair was mostly missing, each body stiff with rigor mortis.

Kellan glanced away, his breathing becoming shallower with each second the image remained in his mind's eye. The pile of bodies had been disturbed—corpses littered the ground, and there was a path through.

The wall of bodies blocked the way to the center of the maze, and some teams had just dug their way through, no care for the decomposing flesh.

"What're you waiting for?" Sen asked. "Go! There's a way through."

Kellan had to force himself to find the words. He glanced at Mavis, careful not to look at the bodies. "Can you… clear more of a way? And then can you carry Sen through? I'll go after through the darkness."

"Is everything okay?" she asked. "You look pale."

But Kellan found it difficult to articulate the problem. He just motioned to the wall between them and their goal. "Please. I just need you to do this." Then he knelt and allowed Sen off.

The man-child glared up at him. "Why are you hesitating? This isn't like you *at all.* You're a man of action and quick decision. This isn't even a monster—it's just fleshy debris."

"I don't want to touch the bodies," Kellan muttered.

"Why not? I'll cure you of any diseases."

"I'm not worried about diseases." He pointed ahead, keeping his gaze down. "Just *go*. I'll catch up."

Sen frowned. Then he crossed his arms. "I told you about my inability to be intimate, and you can't explain why a few rotting husks have you spooked?"

Kellan ran a hand down his face, clearing away the sweat. It hadn't been so long ago that he had carried corpses home after a botched Delta Force operation. Since then, bodies left him a little shaky.

Although he didn't want to talk about the experience, even Mavis stepped a bit closer, her attention fixed on him rather than their grim environment. The chill of the catacombs added to Kellan's unease. They didn't have time to recollect, either—but Sen had made a fair point.

"Listen, two Special Forces soldiers died on one of our assignments," Kellan said, his words forced. "I carried them home. Like a good soldier should. But… it took days. I just… I don't want to handle dead bodies."

For some reason, the undead monstrosities of the Nexus hadn't rattled him as much as the inanimate ones. Perhaps it was because the undead monsters were moving—Greer and Jones hadn't moved after their deaths—and that made things easier.

"I understand," Mavis said. "I… watched a few of my friends get torn apart by homemade grenades." She stepped close to Kellan and hugged him briefly. It was quick—almost cold—but she seemed stiff herself. "I'll take Sen, and you go across however you need."

"Wait, *that's it*?" Sen asked. He huffed and shook his head. "You carried a couple dead bodies? Pfft. I was expecting something more… horrific."

It hadn't just been the dead bodies.

But Kellan found it hard to describe the terrible, suffocating weight of the *guilt.*

He had been the only one to survive the operation. And for days, all he could do was stare into the blank faces of men who had depended on him. Men who wouldn't make it home.

How could Kellan articulate the twisted barb of anguish he felt when he thought of it in those terms? A barb lodged in his mind, threatening to poison his thoughts.

Sen sighed. "Never mind." He dismissively waved away his own comment. "I know the perfect solution. We'll fiddle with your head, perhaps remove the memories, and you'll be fine."

"No, thanks," Kellan sardonically replied. "I'll keep my head how it is."

"You clearly have a flaw. Everyone does, but yours is an easy fix."

"I said, *no*."

The putrid odor caused Kellan to gag. He motioned them away, hoping to end this as soon as possible. Then he handed Sen the little light.

But Sen stepped forward, like he wanted to continue protesting. Mavis knelt and scooped him up. Then the pair ran toward the barrier of bodies. Mavis hurried over the corpses, her feet finding unsteady ground when she tried to climb the pile. Kellan didn't watch much. He heard her gag a couple times before finally disappearing over the cadavers.

Kellan closed his eyes and then sank into the darkness. With the cold protection of the shadows—and no odor to irritate his stomach—he slid across the ground, then through the cracks between rotting bodies, and hurried down the corridor. Once on the other side, Kellan emerged from the darkness as though stepping out of a pond.

He stood in the center of the Catacomb Maze.

It was a massive burial chamber, complete with statues of kings, pharaohs, and dragons—a gigantic, circular stone room dedicated to all things great, whether they be fantasy or reality.

And then Kellan saw members of the other teams.

—Chapter 11—
—Race Against the Clock—

There were four other players in the burial chamber.

Kellan didn't recognize three of them. One was a rennic, the werewolf-like individuals who stood around ten feet. Another was a *rezrah*, which Kellan associated with dragons. They had scales on their arms and legs, and even had thin, scaly tails. This one wore a biker jacket and jeans, but he left his clawed feet exposed.

It was easy to see the fur and scales—the whole room was brightly lit.

Futuristic chandeliers hung from the high ceilings, offering light to an otherwise ancient tomb. It was an odd juxtaposition, but Kellan even saw computer monitors mounted to the bases of the statues.

The last two enemy players in the room were humans.

Kellan recognized one, and he almost couldn't believe it.

Robert the Friendly. The man who had been as a high as a kite back in the AVU Palace. Somehow, despite the tricks, the spiders, and the traps, *Robert the Space Case* had managed to make his way to the center of the maze. Kellan never would've bet on that horse.

Then again, he's still somehow in the games, Kellan reasoned. *Maybe he has an extremely competent team.*

Mavis and Sen stood off to the side, eyeing one of the many dragon statues. The decoration was as tall as the ceiling was high—a good twenty feet—and the beast was half made of machines. The attention to detail impressed Kellan, if only because he could see the circuit board wiring in some places on the statue itself.

His first thought was to join them, but Robbie spotted him first. The man sauntered over, his *Taco King* baseball cap hard to forget. Its purple clashed with the rough gray stone and gloom of the catacombs.

"Hey, bro," Robbie called out. He jutted his chin up in a reverse nod. "I see you made it. Right on."

Kellan remained tense. He didn't particularly trust the man. "I'm surprised to see you here."

"Oh? Why's that?" Robbie reached into his pocket and withdrew a silver tin case. He opened it, popped out a stick of hane, and then lit it with a tiny lighter he had plucked out of the opposite pocket. After a deep inhale on the black cigarette, Robbie exhaled smoke and said, "Want one?"

"No, thank you."

"They really help me focus."

"I somehow doubt that."

Robbie shrugged. "Suit yourself, man." He tucked the rest of the smokes away. "How'd you get here? You seem a little weak."

"What does that mean?" Kellan growled.

"You're only D-rank, right? I mean, that's pretty low. There's like, seven ranks in total, and D is the second from the bottom. I'm at least C-rank, ya get me? I'm the weakest one here. Well, I *was*. I guess you're here now."

Kellan didn't know what to make of the conversation. Where was it going? He knew of the ranks. E, D, C, B, A—and then the last two were special. Specialist rank and master rank—S and M. Apparently, magical abilities increased in power with the ranks, so Kellan understood that the higher the rank, the better the mage's ability and mana, but what good did it do anyone to discuss it? And in the middle of a challenge?

"Do you have a point?" Kellan asked, curt.

Robbie exhaled another line of smoke. "Point? Nah. Just talkin'." He allowed his hane to rest on his lip as he spoke. "You have any familiars? That's how I got here. They helped me. Wanna see mine?"

Familiars?

Kellan had almost forgotten about his familiar. He glanced down at his shadow—the lights from above made it harsh and circular around his feet. "Vlaze?"

Despite the lighting, his shadow stretched out, becoming a hole, and out popped an arm-sized lizard. Well, not a normal lizard. It was an albino wyvern—a creature with wings for arms, two back legs, a long tail, and a dragon head.

Vlaze, as small as he was, leapt from the shadow and then scampered to Kellan's feet, his red eyes wide.

"Aww," Robbie said, placing a hand over his heart. "It's a *lil baby*. I love him, man. A scale-baby, am I right?"

Kellan wasn't ever certain how to reply to Robbie. Were these rhetorical questions? Or was Robbie just so high, and so California, that he couldn't handle a conversation without thirty *mans*, *bros*, and *likes*?

Vlaze, once settled, rested on Kellan's bare feet. He was cold, like any reptile, and his bat-style wings were as soft as leather.

"I've got three familiars," Robbie said, smiling. "But let me show ya this guy. Come out, Kenzo."

Then Robbie's shadow stretched from his feet—much farther than Kellan's. The void of darkness hollowed, and out stepped a fully grown chimpanzee. It wasn't normal, though. Its fingers were tipped with bone claws, and the beast wore half a human skull as a mask over its face. Its dark, black eyes stared out from the eye sockets as it turned to face Kellan.

"Kenzo, you're adorable." Robbie patted the back of the massive chimp.

The beast had to weigh close to two hundred pounds. Kellan's magical gaze gave him additional info.

Name: Kenzo
Race: Animal of Pure Magic [Chimpanzee]
Magics: Metal, Entropy
Armor Rating: —
Health: 12/12

Stats:
Strength—5
Dexterity—6
Fortitude—5
Charisma—1
Manipulation—3 [Scary]
Intelligence—4
Perception—4
Wisdom—3
Willpower—2

Abilities:
Entropic Damage—This Animal of Pure Magic's attacks are considered entropic and rot the injured. Entropic damage can only be healed one point per day.

Kellan had read about how violent chimps could be. But this seemed different. Dark energy shimmered over the bone claws, which matched the description of its sinister ability. This was some sort of death creature—a magical beast from the darkest jungles of myth.

"Did yours hatch out of an egg, too?" Kellan quipped.

"Yeah. Of course. They all do."

"Really?"

Robbie slapped his knee and then pointed. "Oh, man. Let me show you my other one. You'll laugh. I was shocked when this little guy came out of an egg." He glanced back down at the ground and whistled. "Come out, Klink."

Robbie's shadow opened a second time, but instead of an animal floating out, a single key with a keychain rose into the room. The key itself was the length of Kellan's finger. It didn't have a face—no eyes, no mouth, nothing—it was just a silver key, as if to a car, and a gold keychain, simple yet beautiful.

The key twirled in the air, seemingly dancing.

Kellan was surprised when he got information.

Name: Klink
Race: Animal of Pure Magic [Mythic Key]
Magics: Eclipse, Mind, Metal
Armor Rating: 3 [Metal]

Health: 4/4

Stats:
Strength—1 [Tiny]
Dexterity—5
Fortitude—1 [Tiny]
Charisma—4 [Likeable]
Manipulation—2
Intelligence—3
Perception—4 [Mystic]
Wisdom—1
Willpower—2

Abilities:
Lockpick—This Animal of Pure Magic may open or lock any non-magically locked door, and any magically locked door of A-rank or lower.
Guide for the Lost—This Animal of Pure Magic can sense nearby nodes, hubs of magic, or dragons (range is one mile per perception).

"Klink is a lifesaver," Robbie said as he petted the floating key. He used only a single finger. "Isn't he cute?"

"A *sentient key* hatched out of an egg?" Kellan asked, just to make sure he hadn't heard incorrectly.

"Yeah, man. Back where I come from, we didn't have magic and stuff, so this was all new to me. Never expected the key to be all covered in yolk or whatever that slime is."

The chimpanzee glowered at Kellan the entire time, its dark eyes narrowed. Kellan didn't appreciate the look and took a step back, wondering if this would somehow turn violent. The game was a non-PvP event, which meant players couldn't attack each other, but did that extend to their familiars? Kellan hoped so. He was pretty certain his baby wyvern would be ripped to shreds if he had to send it after a fully grown chimpanzee.

"Your familiar is about to get bigger," Robbie stated. "They, uh, grow as you grow. All the arcana you gather. It helps them, too. They get real dangerous."

"Uh-huh."

Robbie slapped his hands together a couple of times and then motioned to the wall of bodies—the only exit from the burial chamber. He flashed a smile at Kellan, his teeth yellowed, and smoke leaked out from between them. "Whelp, I gotta get goin'. I got my Chime, so, uh, sorry about this, bro. You seem nice, but this is a game, ya know? I gotta kill ya at some point. Now is as good a time as any."

The way he had said it—Kellan almost laughed.

Did Robbie think he was going to do something?

"Kellan!" Mavis called out. Her voice echoed in the burial chamber, and the other members of different teams glanced in her direction. She lowered her voice as she called out again. "Come over here. We found something."

Kellan gave Robbie a forced wave before turning and jogging away. Vlaze scurried after him, the little wyvern keeping pace and staring up at him with all the affection of a puppy.

"See ya later," Robbie called out.

But Kellan didn't answer.

When Kellan neared his team, he found Mavis and Sen staring at a computer screen mounted to the base of the dragon statue. The massive decoration was actually filled with electronics, and Kellan briefly grazed his fingers over the cold, gray stone when he examined the clawed foot of the carving.

"What is this?" Kellan asked, glancing at the screen.

It glowed dark green, similar to old-school computer monitors from the 60s. There were only words on the screen, blocky and typing themselves. Several languages appeared, each being typed out in a slow manner—English showed up as the seventh language on the screen.

"We think it's a puzzle," Mavis muttered as she stared at the words. "The sentences appear over and over again, and I think it wants us to rearrange things on the statue." She pointed to five holes located between the dragon's feet, and then to three metal rods sticking out of the side of the dragon's leg.

Just as Kellan was about to ask questions, his arm burned again.

02:57

"Got it!" someone shouted.

Kellan, Mavis, and Sen turned. The rennic roared as he flashed his teeth. He held something in his massive, werewolf-like hands.

"The Chime is mine," he said with a growl and laugh.

Without waiting for any other statements or questions, the man lumbered for the wall of bodies, hurrying out of the burial chamber with the Chime clutched in both hands.

"We need to get out of here," Sen muttered. He turned to the screen. "Quickly! Help us solve this."

Mavis grabbed the three metal rods and handed them to Kellan. Confused but determined to make this work, Kellan examined them. His eyes didn't provide any additional information. Instead, he noticed each silver rod was etched with an image.

One rod had the picture of a raven.

The second had the picture of two lovers intertwined.

And the last had the picture of a… misshapen whale. The deformed whale had four fins and a bulbous head, its tail much longer than normal.

The rods clearly fit into the five holes at the base of the statue—but was Kellan supposed to have two more?

"Read the puzzle," Mavis said, pointing at the words. "I think we just have to place the rods in a specific order."

Kellan's arm burned again. He glanced down, wondering if someone else in the chamber had gotten a Chime.

No.

02:46

Someone had activated a trap.

He returned his attention to the puzzle.

The English on the ancient computer screen read:

The dragon collects silver, three to behold
He orders them to keep track, his conquests are told
At the far end, a herald of death
At other, there is no breath
Two are forever one,
Next to an alien they are spun
They cannot stand the sounds of flight
In the distance, quite a fright

"What is this?" Mavis asked, almost breathless.

Sen pointed to the five holes in the statue, then to the first two lines of the puzzle. "It clearly wants us to order these. Three is enough. Two of the holes will be empty. See? The first clue—which of these rods is a herald of death?"

"The raven," Kellan muttered. He held up the silver rod. "And it's at the far end." He placed it in the hole without hesitating.

"*What're you doing*?" Sen barked. "We didn't agree on that!"

"There's nothing to figure out. The puzzle clearly says it's at the far end." The five holes were in a perfect line. "But if you're concerned, I'll just take it out."

But when Kellan tried to remove the rod, it was stuck in the hole. He tugged on it, but the rod was fixed in place, unmovable.

Each rod they inserted wouldn't come out.

Which meant… they only had one chance at solving the riddle.

"You can't remove it?" Mavis whispered.

Kellan slowly shook his head. "It's fine. I'm certain that's correct. We just have two others." He glanced down at the lovers and the odd whale. "If *Robbie the Taco King* got a Chime, we can do this."

His arm—it burned again.

02:35

Who is triggering all these traps? Kellan thought, glaring at the black numbers stained into his flesh. *What's happening?*

"Well, if the last one is the raven, then the first hole will remain empty," Sen stated. "*At the other end is no breath*, which probably means *nothing*."

"I agree," Mavis muttered. "So, first is empty, last is the raven… what are the three between?"

"Is the second spot the *couple*?" Kellan asked.

He moved the silver rod over the hole.

Sen waved his arms in frantic panic. "No! Not that one."

"Why not? The next clue is about the lovers, obviously. *Two forever one*."

"They're next to an alien," Mavis said, her brow furrowed.

"The alien is the Oom!" Sen grabbed at his long, black hair, his teeth gritted, his patience clearly gone.

Kellan just frowned. "What the fuck is an *Oom*?"

Sen pointed at the whale rod with the frustrated energy of a child. His face was even slightly red. "It's an Oom on the rod! It's clear as day! Now will you pay attention? The lovers are next to the Oom, but they're also close to the raven, but distant, which means the solutions is, *empty, Oom, lovers, empty, raven*. Simple!"

"How can you be so sure?"

"Because the lovers are next to the alien—their rods are touching. But they hear the sound of distant flight, which means they aren't *next to* the bird, they're just close. See! There're only three rods and five holes! And since context clues were given in relation to the lovers, the Oom has to be on one side, and the bird has to be on the other!"

He yelled so loud, the chamber was filled with his barking.

Kellan grabbed Sen by the collar of his Power Rangers sweatshirt. "*Keep it down.* You want the other assholes to hear you? You want them to get a Chime, too?"

The other two individuals in the chamber worked hard with their own silver rods. Was it all the same puzzle? Kellan hoped not.

Then pain flared through Kellan's arm.

It was getting old at this point.

02:24

"Do it!" Sen said through gritted teeth. "The Oom is in the second hole. The lovers are in the third. We don't have time to debate this any longer!"

Despite his uncertainty, Kellan decided to trust Sen's assessment. He shoved the whale rod into the second hole, and then the lovers rod into the third. They fit easily—no fuss or confusion.

And then Kellan took a step back, his albino wyvern clinging to his sweatpants.

The green monitor flickered. Then it cracked down the middle and opened up as if broken from the other side. The glass of the screen shattered, and shards fell to the floor. But inside… Kellan spotted it in an instant.

A gold chime, practically a bell. It was spherical and marked with lettering Kellan didn't recognize. Fortunately, his Blitzkrieg Analysis knew what it was.

Legendary Magical Item [One-Time Use]—Summoning Chime

The mage thinks of the name of an individual and then rings the Chime, summoning the person to the mage's dimension. For the next fifteen minutes, the summoned individual will answer the commands of the mage, following instructions to the best of their ability. If the mage attacks the summoned or commands the summoned to harm themselves, the power of the Chime fades.

The following sentient races may not be summoned:

- Primordial dragons
- Oom

- Starkin

The following individuals may not be summoned:
- Anyone dwelling in Zenith
- Those participating in the Nexus Games
- Those locked in a Grand Duel
- Those currently serving another user of a Summoning Chime
- Alternate-dimension selves of the Chime's owner

Kellan glanced at Mavis and Sen. For some reason, they both hesitated. No one reached for the Chime. Since they wouldn't, Kellan reached into the broken computer screen and yanked the Summoning Chime from its bizarre hiding spot.

The letters on the Chime rearranged themselves. They became English, and they read:

Alex Kellan the Void Knight

That baffled him for a moment, but he didn't have time to question it. Agony lanced up his arm. The pain… it was getting more severe as the time ticked down.

The clock read:

01:22

Then his arm pulsed with another round of aching.

01:12

"Dammit!" the rezrah in the burial chamber shouted.

He slammed his fists on the base of the statue and then took off toward the door, running as fast as he could. There wasn't any more time to get a Chime—and if anyone picked one up, they would reduce the time by another hour, and would certainly kill themselves.

The last human also ran for the pile of bodies, obviously abandoning the puzzle in favor of their life.

"We need to go," Mavis said, glaring at the time on her arm.

Sen was practically running for the wall of corpses. "We don't have time to search anything else! Quickly, quickly! I can't die here."

Kellan tucked the Chime into his backpack, scooped Vlaze up into his arms, and then hurried after Sen.

To his horror, however, the time ticked down *yet again.*

Now they only had…

01:01

Their remaining time to escape was dwindling faster than ever.

—Chapter 12—
—The Collapse of the Maze—

Mavis helped Sen make it over the decomposing bodies. They slipped as their footing caught on odd parts of the corpses. Mavis's foot sank into a stomach as though she had stepped on a rotten jack-o-lantern.

Unable to watch for long, Kellan took a deep breath, and then tossed Vlaze back into the shadows. After the knots in his chest untangled, Kellan dove into the shadows and slid across the floor at impressive speed. He zipped through the bodies and emerged from the liquid void on the other side of the cadaver barrier.

Get it together, Kellan, he thought to himself. *People are counting on you.*

When he glanced up, he caught his breath.

The main corridor—the largest in the maze—was covered with arcana.

Glittering red crystals littered the brick floor. Dozens of coffins were opened, their lids sprawled out on the walkway. Several yami—more centipedes, some much larger than the one Kellan had fought—crawled out of open coffins.

The yami centipedes screeched so loud, their terrifying cries echoed throughout the entire Catacomb Maze.

There were at least ten monsters—multiple were emerging from the same coffin.

Who had opened them all?

Kellan answered his own question.

Kenzo, the bizarre death chimp, was running around the hall, flinging the lids of the coffins off one at a time. He leapt from one hole in the wall to the other, his strength great enough that he effortlessly yanked the lids off and then jumped to the next location.

Arcana spilled from some of the opened coffins—like candy showering out of a broken piñata. The coffins had been so stuffed, Kellan suspected they had tons more arcana within.

But they didn't have time.

Kenzo the chimp opened another trap coffin, and Kellan's arm burned as another monster shot out into the corridor, its fangs large.

Their time…

00:50

It was *Kenzo* who was intentionally cutting their time down. Now that his master, Robbie, had a Summoning Chime, the ape was busy cutting the time down for everyone else. Robbie's cryptic message about having to kill Kellan was because he had intended to harm everyone as soon as he left.

But Kellan couldn't fight the chimpanzee.

There was no PvP allowed in the challenge round.

"Mavis, take Sen and go meet up with Gero," Kellan commanded. Then he tossed her his backpack but kept his rifle.

"Do you see all this arcana?" Sen asked, breathless. But when the yami started heading their way, he gritted his teeth and grabbed on to Mavis. "On second thought…"

Mavis didn't hesitate or gawk at the arcana like Sen. She grabbed the kid's hand and then rushed for the illusionary wall. In order to distract the monsters and make sure they didn't rush after Mavis, Kellan opened fire on the corpse-centipedes in the corridor.

While most of the beasts had an entire grocery stores' worth of health, that didn't matter. The moment bullets started cutting through their stitched-corpse bodies, they turned their hate and hunger in Kellan's direction. All twelve monsters rushed for him, the legs of their centipede bodies nothing more than human arms pulling them across the stone bricks.

Thankfully, the burial chamber was the only place in the maze with lights. And once Mavis and Sen took the glowing stick of hane, the corridor was mostly shrouded in darkness. The last light remaining came from the crimson glitter of the arcana, haunting the corridor with its red hue.

Empowered by the shadows—heightening his physical prowess to fun new levels—Kellan leapt away from the beasts, dove into the darkness, and then emerged near Kenzo.

The chimp, who had his hands on the lid of a coffin, flinched. His eyes under the skull mask grew wide.

Kellan slammed his hand down on the lid of the coffin, preventing the chimp from opening it. "No more of this."

The primate went to open his mouth, but he only strangled back a bark when the yami rushed in their direction. Both Kellan and Kenzo leapt away, but the chimpanzee was slower than Kellan.

Kenzo slashed at the undead centipedes with his deadly claws, his rotting ability seemingly having little effect on the corpses, who were already rotting. The chimp slashed and dodged and then continued running down the corridor. When he stopped and headed for another set of coffins, Kellan dove back into the shadows and emerged near the creature.

The chimp grimaced and backed away.

Kellan was considerably stronger now. The beast wouldn't be able to open the lids of the coffins without a fight, and since that wasn't allowed…

The monsters rushed toward them, all still angry about the cuts and bullet wounds.

Satisfied that he had kept them distracted, and angry at the chimp, Kellan shifted through the darkness and stepped out into the corridor near the arcana.

He scooped up multiple pieces, the crimson glow of the crystals warm and inviting.

[Alex Kellan] absorbed 10 arcana.

But he knew he couldn't root around for more. Time was ticking. As long as the ape was preoccupied, he wouldn't trigger any more traps.

Kellan headed for the illusion wall and dashed through it.

He entered the square room, expecting to find his teammates, as well as Gero, Alvo, and Juan. But instead, he found no one. His heart rattled around in his chest, and Kellan ran a hand down his face, clearing his thoughts. He rushed to the other end of the room, back into the hallways with the Crypt Widows, and kept hurrying down the path he had taken before.

They're just heading to the exit, he reasoned with himself. *I'll find them along this path.*

Then Kellan made the mistake of glancing at his arm.

00:46

It had taken them several minutes of running to actually make it through some portions of the maze. Did they have enough time? Kellan picked up his pace.

Thankfully, he heard footfalls ahead of him. Kellan controlled his breathing, trying to hide his presence as much as possible as he ran through the darkness of a catacomb with no light. The glow of the illuminated hane was a welcome sight. Although the light drained Kellan of some of his strength, it was enough to know that he had reconnected with his group.

Alvo and Juan traveled with them, but not Gero.

When Kellan reached the group, he realized they were traveling slower because of the merged twins. Their fused body was… awkward. They limped and waddled, almost without balance. Rushing wasn't helping matters, either. Both heads panted as they went, clearly strained from the effort.

At this rate, they'll collapse halfway to the exit.

Mavis was busy carrying Sen.

Kellan ran to Alvo and Juan, offered his shoulder, and basically carried half the men's weight on his own. The Nexus resident tried to protest, their stuttered words killed by their inability to breathe properly.

"Just run," Kellan stated.

His arm stung.

He didn't even look this time. Kellan knew. They had about thirty minutes to escape. He didn't need to be reminded by the black stained numbers on his skin.

And that was when the maze started to crack.

The walls, the floor, the ceiling—tiny chips formed in the bricks. Each small crack spiderwebbed out, creating jagged lines across all the stonework. Bits of debris and dust rained on them at a steady rate, and more than once, Kellan almost tripped over a brick that jutted upward from the pressures all around it.

"Keep your eyes on the floor," Kellan shouted. "I marked the locations where we need to turn!"

Mavis nodded. Sen just continued to clutch her tightly.

Alvo and Juan pointed a few times—seemingly to walls—and Kellan suspected they were trying to direct them to a different location. Was there an exit to the Catacomb Maze that didn't involve the rooms the Arbiter had made? Most certainly. Gero, Alvo, and Juan had to have gotten into the maze *somehow.*

But they couldn't go that way.

"We have it," Kellan said.

The twins didn't like that answer, though. They grunted and pointed again, but Kellan ran by each location they tried to steer him. Kellan had no interest in deviating from the path. They had to escape, and he wasn't going to risk getting lost.

His arm burned again.

Twenty minutes.

His lungs ached, desperate to get enough oxygen. Kellan hadn't thought about it, but he suspected the maze was filled with thin air—not to mention poor ventilation and odd bodily gases. When his head grew light, he knew they shouldn't have been exerting themselves so much, but there was no choice.

Mavis turned and ran into an illusion wall. Kellan just followed. His mind dwelled on their surroundings, trying to stay vigilant, just in case a monster emerged from a nearby coffin.

The cracks grew larger, and the maze shook.

At one point, Mavis slowed and searched the ground, her eyes squinted. The harsh shadows and bizarre lighting made it near impossible to see a smear on the bricks when they were actively crumbling apart.

Kellan grabbed the bright hane, crushed it in his hand, and then allowed the darkness to settle over them. Not only did he get the physical boost from the shadows, but his ability to see in the dark made everything easier. The others were blind, but Kellan didn't care.

"Hold on to my shirt," he said.

Mavis grabbed his sleeve.

Without another word, Kellan spotted his own marking and dashed forward. He almost toppled over Mavis, and he had to force himself to slow his pace. With nine strength and nine dexterity, he felt like Superman, capable of zipping through the crumbling corridors. But none of the others could keep up with that, so Kellan did his best to shoulder most of Alvo and Juan's weight and also keep Mavis close enough that she could follow without problem.

When they made it back to the never-ending first hallway, Kellan wanted to reassure them.

"Almost there," he muttered.

Then a searing pain lanced through his arm.

Less than ten minutes.

Kellan couldn't bring himself to look at the numbers—he just flew forward, running as fast as the others would allow. Their heavy breathing mixed with the destruction of the maze, creating a cacophony of panic. The dust clung to his lungs, and Kellan coughed the entire way, his throat hurting as much as his lungs.

Then he stepped on a jagged rock on the floor. The arch of his foot hurt so badly, he almost went face-first into the wall.

Mavis wheezed and grabbed at her throat. The thin air, and debris raining from the ceiling, was becoming too much.

Kellan spent a mana and activated his *Ignore Pain* ability. The fire in his chest and throat, as well as the lightning strike of agony in his foot, were all a thing of the past. He hefted most of the twins onto his shoulder, grabbed Mavis and Sen, and with his increased abilities, ran the rest of the length of the hall.

The *instant* he saw the mark he had left on the ground, he turned and hurled himself through the wall. If it *hadn't* been an illusion, he probably would've broken his neck. Fortunately, it was an illusion, and they all stumbled back into Room 101.

"Time's up!" a voice from an old set of speakers rang out, the tone filled with static.

A boom and crash echoed beyond the door of the room. Metal doors slammed shut, protecting everyone inside the room from any more dust, debris, and foul odors.

"What an intense challenge round."

Whoever had spoken was way too happy for Kellan's taste. He set the others down and gulped in air, trying to regain his composure.

"It's time to bring all our players back! And *four people* managed to get Summoning Chimes? Impressive! We'll have to teleport them straight here for an interview. Everyone loves to see a chump get his fifteen seconds of fame, am I right?"

"Will I go as well?" Alvo asked, breathless. His twin brother, Juan, mouthed the question as well. "You didn't take us to the exit. I don't know if… if the Arbiter will remove us from here. We're not part of Team 101."

And before anyone could comment, a feeling of pressure grabbed at Kellan's insides and tugged him forward.

He was teleported out of the room and back to the AVU Palace.

—Chapter 13—
—The Interview—

Kellan thought he'd be transported back to his team's room in the AVU Palace. Or at the very least, the registration room next to the Exchange, since that was where he had disappeared from.

But that wasn't the case.

Kellan teleported onto a football field, one under the dome of a massive stadium. And not just any football field, but one that had been repurposed for late-night television. A desk, several couches, and a coffee table were in the middle of the gigantic stadium, clustered together on the green field, the dead center of the halfway line.

The stands…

Shadows lingered over the bleachers. Bright spotlights illuminated the field, creating a fishbowl effect where the audience was supposed to be obscured. Kellan's magical sight allowed him to make out the forms of individuals in the stands, most of them clumped close together. They watched with opera binoculars, pointing and speaking, but were just too far away for Kellan to get specific details.

Who were they?

He wasn't sure.

His eyes tried to give him information, but there were hundreds of people, and everything became jumbled. He rubbed at his temples, dispelling the words and numbers. He focused on the here and now. The cheering from the stands made it difficult.

What were those people celebrating for?

Kellan stood in front of a red couch.

The scarlet fabric was bright under the harsh lights of the stadium. He ran a shaky hand down his face, realizing he was still wearing a T-shirt and sweatpants, but he didn't have his rifle.

Several gigantic televisions lowered from the dome ceiling above. They were stadium screens, larger than most movie theaters, and the black surface reflected the bizarre late-night television scenario all around Kellan.

Four other people were with him on the field.

Kellan recognized the man behind the talk show desk. It was the bizarre news anchor, Bitso. The man wore a crisp, black suit, complete with a black vest, shirt, and tie. He wore white gloves, though—gloves stained with blood. That particular item of apparel matched his blindfold, which was also a beautiful shade of white, smeared with red.

This information… Kellan focused on the words.

Name: Bitso, Unwilling Servant to the Arbiter
Race: Human
Magics: Storm, Fate
Rank: A, A
Armor Rating: —
Health: 7/7
Stats: Concealed
Abilities: Concealed

Bitso sat at the desk, one elbow up, his chin propped in his hand. He had an amused expression, but the way he leaned on the desk made Kellan think the man was bored.

"Sit down," Bitso said into a microphone mounted to the metal frame of his desk. His voice boomed out over the stadium, as though this were a grand performance. "The interviews are about to begin."

Bitso motioned to the couch, his smile perfect, his teeth so ivory, they were almost reflective.

The moment was surreal. Kellan took a seat on the couch and then stared down at the emerald grass beneath his feet. The coffee table had four cups on it, but each was filled with a different liquid. One was coffee, one was tea, another looked like syrup, and the last was a strange shade of dark green that Kellan couldn't identify.

Electric excitement pulsed through the crowd. Their cheers grew into applause, and some people chanted names, though Kellan had a difficult time understanding who they were all calling for. The rumble of their enthusiasm shook the whole damn stadium, and Kellan gripped the armrest with his left hand, trying to remain calm and collected.

There was also a giant pit next to the late-night show area.

A pit so wide, someone could easily drive multiple semitrucks into it at once. And the pit was so deep, it was impossible to see the bottom.

A constant stream of hot air gushed up out of the pit, the distant sounds of pistons wafting up into the cheers.

The stadium TVs played footage from inside the Catacomb Maze. The dark corridors, the coffins, even the Crypt Widows were on full display. But Kellan couldn't watch, his attention still on his strange surroundings.

Besides Bitso, there were three others.

Robbie the Friendly.

The man adjusted his purple *Taco King* hat and took a seat on another couch. A stick of hane hung from his lips, and he exhaled smoke into the bright lights of the stadium.

The second person was a rennic. And not just *any* rennic—the one who had acquired a Summoning Chime during the challenge round. His fur was black, except for his snout and the tips of his clawed fingers. His ears stood erect, and he reminded Kellan of a wolf in more ways than one. His fangs were larger than most, and he lifted his lips in disgust more than once as he glanced around.

Kellan saw the rennic's information, but he immediately dismissed the words, trying not to take his attention off his surroundings.

The rennic wore an outfit that Indiana Jones would have died for. Leather jacket. Tan pants. A whip hanging from his belt.

He was a mage. Kellan saw that much. B-rank. Wyld, magma.

The last individual…

Kellan knew him well.

Bitso laughed into the microphone, his voice thundering across the stadium. "Oh, I was wondering when we were going to see *both* Alex Kellans in one place. Look at them! They could be twins. The perfect selfie moment."

Kellan wasn't pleased to see his alternate-dimension self.

The man was tall, imposing—just like Kellan—but his chin was covered in stubble, his face lined with scars, and his expression more haunted than any man's should have been. One eye was dark brown, and the other was mechanical. The pupil of the machine eye glowed gold, and when Alternate-Kellan glanced over, the light of the eye caused Kellan to flinch.

At least Alternate-Kellan had proper clothing. He wore tactical cargo pants, an armored vest, a thick black shirt, and armored gloves. He stood with a stiff readiness that betrayed military training.

Of course, Alternate-Kellan appeared a bit older. Apparently, the dimension he had come from was one filled with magic, mayhem, and an alien invasion. Alternate-Kellan was over forty years old and had been a mage for a long time.

Kellan didn't like being so far behind.

It felt like looking at his father, rather than a different version of *him*.

"Would you look at that, ladies and gentle things? We have *Combat Kellan,* and *Just Got Home from the Gym Kellan.* A rare edition." Bitso laughed at his own joke. "What kind of sad sack participates in a challenge round while wearing his pajamas?"

Someone who had zero prep before the round, Kellan sardonically thought to himself.

Alternate-Kellan took a seat on the red couch next to Kellan. He sat slow and tense, as though prepared to leap into action at any moment.

Other Kellan said nothing.

Obviously. He was mute.

Indiana Jones Werewolf took a seat next to Robbie on the opposite couch.

The cheering grew more intense.

Kellan wasn't sure what to do. The Nexus had all the predictability of a cat in a minefield.

Should he take a drink? Should he pretend this *was* a late-night talk show and just roll with Bitso's insanity? Should he stay quiet and wait for the bizarre scenario to end? It *would* eventually end. That had been Kellan's experience with such events.

"It's a great time to be alive and in front of a television," Bitso said with a chuckle. The crowds calmed a bit as he added, "This challenge round saw some fan favorites. And *four* Summoning Chimes for this Nexus Games? The last game was *won* with a Chime, and there was only *one*. This is gonna be a crazy series of events, let me tell you."

The TVs above them played scenes from what Kellan assumed was the previous Nexus Games. The red sky, the broken buildings—a woman stood among them, her black hair and honeyed skin the same as Xiang's and Sen's. She had a mechanical eye, just like Alternate-Kellan, the gold glow easy to recognize.

Then she lifted the spherical bell above her head.

Her clothing seemed post-apocalyptic in nature, like she had scavenged it off corpses after fighting her way through zombies. Her armor consisted of metal plates bolted together, and her pants were sized for someone with twice her bulk.

"The winner of the last Nexus Games, in the final game, decided to summon the legendary, and rather infamous, *Ygg'Exos Vain*." Bitso chuckled as he pointed to the screens. "She ordered him to murder the last survivor of the opposing team. It was—" he made a chef's kiss motion, "—hilariously violent."

The screens played footage of the Summoning Chime breaking in Xiang's mother's hand.

Then a beam of light broke through the crimson of the sky. Someone descended from on high—an individual with white-feather wings and a physique so perfect it looked photoshopped. Kellan would've said it was like an *old-world vengeance angel*, but it was difficult to tell. Whoever was filming the event was far away.

The angel descended to the wasteland, his feather wings shimmering with magic and power.

Then Ygg'Exos Vain seemingly lifted his hand and proceeded to unleash another beam of light, this one so powerful, it decimated the nearby skyscraper, blowing a hole through it as though it were a wet napkin.

The camera filming jostled with static, and then part of the building toppled over on top of it. The destruction had been thorough.

What kind of magical ability was that?

The crowd went wild. People in the stands cheered, and a few threw food. It was wild, and Kellan felt their jubilation through the rumble across the ground.

The TV screen returned to its black state.

The cheering quieted again—at least enough so that everyone could hear Bitso.

"The Tyrant King Ygg'Exos Vain was the deciding factor in the last game." Bitso tapped his finger on the microphone, dragging all attention back to him. "So, I have to ask—who will our four lucky individuals be summoning?" Although Bitso was blindfolded, he turned to Alternate-Kellan. "*You* were the first to retrieve your Chime."

The TV flickered back to life and played footage of the Catacomb Maze. It was dark, but everything was clearly visible, as though through night-vision goggles. Other Kellan slipped through the maze with little problem, rushing forward with a single-minded purpose. He never touched the coffins. He just used the shadows as pools of water he dove into and out of.

He didn't even have anyone else from his team with him.

Team 42 couldn't be bothered to risk more than one person, apparently. Kellan knew their tactics. They weren't subtle or forgiving.

Alternate-Kellan was the first to make it to the burial chamber. He shoved the dead bodies out of the way—clearly not bothered by corpses—and strode into the gigantic room. His gold eye glowed brightly as he approached a statue and then proceeded to stare at the puzzle.

"Well?" Bitso asked, snapping his fingers. "Who do you intend to summon?"

Alternate-Kellan tapped at his throat. He wore a turtleneck, the cloth covering his skin. Then he shook his head, his eyes narrowed in a glare.

"Ah. That's right. You're broken." Bitso leaned forward on his desk. "I guess whoever you'll summon will be a *surprise.*" With a manic laugh—which only lasted a few seconds—Bitso turned his attention to Robbie. "If it isn't everyone's favorite fast-food worker. Robert Jameson. Welcome to the show."

Robbie scooted to the edge of the couch. Unlike in the maze, where he had seemed cool and confident, Robbie rubbed his sweaty palms on the tops of his legs. "I, uh…"

His voice boomed across the stadium, even though he didn't have a mic in front of him.

The screens above showed Robbie's arrival at the burial chamber. He wandered around, glancing at everything like he was in a museum. Once he had found a screen on the statue, he snapped his fingers and went to work.

His key familiar floated out of his shadow…

It pointed to something on the screen.

The sentient key didn't solve the puzzle… Did they? Kellan watched the TV with baffled curiosity. *The fucking key was intelligent enough to solve a complex poem riddle and then tell Robbie the Friend Biscuit how to complete it?*

"I'm just a player for Team 79, man," Robbie managed to mutter. "They said, uh, I'd get to go home if I helped them win the Nexus Games, ya know? So, I, uh, got the Summoning Chime for them."

"Only the person who first touched the Chime can use it," Bitso said matter-of-factly, his smile still fixed in place. With a sweet tone, he continued, "You'll have to think of a name at some point. And hopefully a good one."

"Well, uh, Ygg'Exos seems good." Robbie pointed to the screens above. "A real bombastic personality, am I right?"

He chuckled.

Bitso didn't. The news anchor kept the same wide smile, but didn't say a word or react to the joke in any way.

It was off-putting.

After a prolonged moment of strained silence, Bitso finally replied, "Oh, yes.

Summoning him again is a viable option, if you want to be completely *unoriginal.*" Bitso shrugged. "I mean, Ygg'Exos is a master of killing. A perfect pick if you need someone dead in a jiffy."

"R-Right on."

"But just out of curiosity, if you *had* to summon someone from your dimension, who would you pick?"

Robbie fiddled with his *Taco King* hat. Then he frowned. "Uh, I dunno. Chuck Norris?"

"Oh? I've never heard of that mage. Let me guess—you come from one of the *chump dimensions*, don't you? No mages whatsoever?"

"Well, yeah. That's right. No magic like you all have."

"It's no wonder you're *so unimpressive.*" Bitso motioned to the screens again. "Is that why you commanded your familiar to die?"

The screens played images of Kenzo opening the coffins. The familiar was doing that until the maze collapsed around him.

Robbie didn't answer. He stared at the TVs, his brow furrowed. The crowds didn't seem to like the reveal. They booed and threw objects onto the field. It was only after the footage stopped that they quieted down.

Bitso snickered as he turned his smile to the rennic. "And *you*. What's your name? Wast Finn?"

The wannabe Indiana Jones sat a little closer to the edge of the couch. His ears twitched as he seemed to harden himself to the situation. The crowds cheered for him, enough to actually drown out the interview.

Wast shook his head, his long, canine nose scrunching a bit as he spoke. "Team 5 is going to win the Nexus Games, and now that I have the Summoning Chime, nothing will stop us." Just like with Robbie, his voice carried.

And that statement got the crowds going.

Another quake of excitement rocked the whole stadium. Everyone loved a showboat, and claiming that Team 5 would win made him the showiest of them all.

Bitso lifted his hands. It took the people in the stands a while to quiet themselves, but once the cheering had dulled, he spoke into the microphone. "Aren't you worried about *Taco Champ* over here summoning Ygg'Exos?"

"Nosferatu has thought of all possible situations and has a plan," Wast stated with a growl. "No fifteen-minute fighter—not even a tyrant king—will hinder us."

Nosferatu? Kellan paid a little more attention now. He needed to take Alvo and Juan to Nosferatu. Well, if they were still alive. Kellan wasn't sure about that.

Bitso slid a finger across his desk. "Hm. So you don't know who you'll be summoning?"

"Not yet. That's for Nosferatu to decide."

"How dull." Bitso finally turned his "gaze" to Kellan. The bloodied blindfold seemed extra crimson, as though the man had been bleeding the entire interview, and the cloth was almost completely soaked. "Ah. If it isn't my second-favorite player. Alex Kellan. It's so good to have you with us tonight."

The crowds got quieter.

Anxiety tainted Kellan's thoughts for a fraction of a moment. It seemed as though everyone wanted to hear what he had to say. He gripped the armrest of the couch, his heart pounding.

Perhaps it would just be best if he played along.

"It's great to be back," Kellan said, forcing a smile, his words booming over the stadium. "It's been a while since I've seen you and *the pit*." He sarcastically waved at the hole in the ground. His words echoed over the stands.

Bitso sat up straighter, his expression never changing, but his mannerisms became more energetic. "Oh, *someone* is in a good mood."

He slid down the desk, getting closer to Kellan. He drew so close that Kellan could see that all his white teeth in the back—all of which were *supposed* to be molars—were sharpened and canine-like.

"I like it when you're in a good mood," Bitso whispered.

When Bitso leaned away from the microphone, his words remained quiet. No one in the crowds heard.

Kellan already regretted playing along. When he glanced over to his alternate-dimension self, the man glared in Kellan's direction, his one gold, mechanical eye fixed on everything unfolding.

"Bitso." Kellan turned back to face the news anchor. After a deep breath, he said, "Team 42 is planning to kill the Arbiter once they win the Nexus Games. They're going to use the magical power they gather from Zenith to invade other dimensions and kill all the primordial dragons."

The statement hadn't been made for Bitso's sake. Kellan had already told the man, after all. No—Kellan was saying it so that *everyone* knew. He didn't want to keep it hidden or pretend he hadn't heard. In his mind, Team 42 *had* to be stopped.

The crowds didn't like the information. Again, there was more booing, but not as much as before. A general confusion seemed to spread through the audience.

Bitso waved his hands and once again spoke into the mic. "Calm down. The Arbiter is already aware. There's no need to get dramatic." He turned to Alternate-Kellan—a member of Team 42. "Do you have anything to say about that?" With a laugh, Bitso continued, "Oh, wait. *Broken*. I had almost forgotten."

Other Kellan ran a hand over the stubble on his chin.

Before Kellan could insist that this was a problem that others should be concerned with, Bitso slammed his hands on the metal desk. The sound echoed across the stadium like a gunshot over the speakers.

"*No*." Bitso then ran a hand through his dark-red hair. "If I'm going to be forced to do these interviews, I don't want to rehash old news." He pointed at the screen. "We need to review the tapes."

The screens flickered to life.

Bitso tried to stand, but when he got up from his chair, some sort of chain—a manacle attached to his ankle—kept him in place. He struggled with the restraints, growing visibly irritated, muttering dark curses under his breath.

The more Bitso fought, the more bloodied his ankle, hands, and eyes became. The blindfold became so soaked, a small rivulet of blood ran down his face.

While the TVs played footage, Kellan asked, "Are you okay?" His words were drowned out by the excitement from the crowds.

But Bitso had heard.

The deranged news anchor "glanced up," and then touched his blindfold, his hand shaky when he pulled it away and "stared" at the blood.

Was he actually blind? Could he see through the crimson rag over his eyes? Kellan really wasn't sure.

"Don't worry, this *moment of clarity* will soon pass." Bitso gestured to the screens above. "Just watch the damn footage, and maybe we'll be treated with visions of the lucky few who got to die."

His odd statements always bothered Kellan.

When he turned his attention to the massive TVs, he expected to see footage of him and his team completing the puzzle, but that wasn't the case. Instead, the footage playing was of the corpse wall before players could make it into the burial chamber. He held his breath while it was on screen, watching as Mavis and Sen went over the bodies, and he had to go afterward.

Laughter from the crowds drifted across the stadium.

"Do you want to explain to everyone in the Nexus Games why you putzed around the bodies?" Bitso asked as he adjusted his blindfold.

"No," Kellan stated. He turned away from the screen, unable to watch any further.

"Oh, really? That's not how this show works. I ask questions, and you answer them."

"You asked if I wanted to explain. I don't. It was a simple answer."

Bitso grabbed the microphone on his desk and pressed it closer to his mouth, his smile never waning. "Very well, *smartass*. Tell the audience your greatest strength and greatest weakness."

There was no way Kellan was going to do that. The other teams were watching—he knew—and this wasn't the time. But he knew he should answer with *something*.

"My greatest strength is whooping ass," he said, deadpan. "And my weakness is enjoying it."

The crowds in the stadium broke into applause. The cheering and the clapping became a music of their own. Kellan didn't mind the attention—it was much better than the kind he usually received.

While the audience continued cheering, Bitso once again moved the microphone to the side. He leaned on the edge of the desk closest to Kellan, his smile gone, all mirth missing.

More blood streamed down his face, like crimson tears.

"Listen," Bitso said, his tone so serious, it was almost unsettling. "A part of you will always be trapped in your past trauma. That's true for everyone. A piece of you is stuck in the worst moment you've ever had. Don't let that be the piece that controls your actions."

The words of advice hit Kellan hard. He hadn't thought of it like that. He knew the trauma was hindering him, but the analogy of being trapped resonated with him. Why would Bitso go out of his way to give him that advice? Was this another *moment of clarity*? A brief few seconds in which Bitso wasn't completely ruled by insanity?

Was Bitso *trying* to help him?

Kellan wasn't sure. He didn't even know how to ask.

But then Bitso's manic side returned in full force. He grabbed the microphone and pulled it close to his bloodied mouth. Then he laughed, splashing pink spittle on the equipment.

"Who will *you* be summoning, Alex Kellan?"

"I don't know yet," he managed to say.

"Really?" With a snort and a chuckle, Bitso shrugged. "I guess the fast-food worker is the only one who has a plan. Everyone else is a patsy or just confused. Sorry, ladies and gentle folk. Nothing extra exciting for you today."

Hot air streamed up from the massive pit. Steam went with it, gushing into the stadium in a frightening amount. Kellan tensed as the hot air washed over everyone on the couches.

"That concludes our interviews," Bitso announced. "But don't worry. We'll continue bringing you footage of the games. *Especially* given what's happening in the next one."

—Chapter 14—
—Nosferatu—

As the crowds continued to cheer, Bitso waved his hand at the four sitting on the couches. Kellan wasn't sure if he should get up—or even where he'd go to get off the field and back into the palace.

"You four were some of the worst guests I've ever had," Bitso said with a sigh. "*Mute*? *Stuttering*? Where am I supposed to go with that? And where are all the women? You all need to make more progressive choices and put more ladies into those death mazes, understand?"

His voice wasn't projected to the crowds. The show was over.

"There weren't even that many deaths." Bitso rubbed at his temples. "The one highlight in my pathetic existence is watching you all die. And you all couldn't even provide me much of *that*..."

The ground shook.

Not from the audience or from intense cheering—but from the movement of something large beneath their feet. Kellan stood from the couch, his heart hammering. He already knew what it was.

The Arbiter.

The massive pit spewed steam into the stadium.

Robbie, Wast, and Alternate-Kellan all got up from the couch. Wast flashed his canine fangs, his black fur standing on end. Robbie kept rubbing his sweaty palms over his shirt and pants, as though he just couldn't keep them dry.

Only Alternate-Kellan stood his ground. He watched the pit with an intense gaze.

"The Arbiter wants to wish you luck," Bitso said as the hot air washed over the field. "Consider yourselves honored by his presence."

The whole stadium shook with the movement of the Arbiter. Kellan almost lost his footing. He held on to the side of the couch, ready for his second encounter with the primordial dragon.

A mechanical claw reached out of the pit and grabbed onto the edge of the field. The tips of the claws were blades that sank into the ground, cutting deep into the dirt and creating grooves.

The Arbiter pulled himself into the stadium, his massive body almost too large to fit under the dome. His machine body, laced with flesh from within and without, hissed and groaned as he moved. Gears, cogs, and pistons worked overtime throughout his massive form, steam gushing out of the Arbiter's body at several locations.

When the Arbiter opened his mouth, rows of serrated fangs glittered under the spotlights. His throat glowed neon green, as though radioactive. The dragon roared, his voice a mix of screeching metal and fearsome force.

Kellan took a step back as he stared at the beast.

Name: Lord of the Nexus, The Arbiter, Keeper of the Gates to Zenith
Race: Primordial Dragon
Magics: Mind, Metal, Entropy, Travel, Meta, Fate
Rank: Concealed
Armor Rating: Concealed
Health: Concealed
Stats: Concealed
Abilities: Concealed

The Arbiter lowered his gargantuan head, bringing his fangs close to the late-night setup. With each breath, the dragon threatened to topple the coffee table. The four mugs spilled onto the grass.

The dragon had no eyes. His mechanical head had scaled flesh covering some of the metal components, but otherwise, there were no eyeballs, not even eye sockets or cameras in the places eyes should have been.

The Arbiter's breath knocked Robbie's hane from his mouth.

"Oh, man!" he shouted. Robbie covered his face with his arms, but his legs just trembled as he attempted to stay upright. "I'm n-not cut out for this!"

Kellan shuddered as another round of heat washed over him. The smell of copper and iron irritated his nose. When the Arbiter shifted his weight between his deadly claws, the whole stadium quaked again.

The Arbiter wasn't even all the way out of his pit. Half his body remained underground, while the top half was above ground, like someone hanging on to the side of a swimming pool.

"The Arbiter congratulates you," Bitso said, his voice half swept away by the winds. "And now he'll send you to any location you want. Keep in mind you need to stay close for the third game—wouldn't want to miss that, would you?"

"I wanna go home, man."

"Sorry. *This* dimension only."

Robbie exhaled and then inhaled. "My room."

The stadium… Kellan felt a suffocating presence, as though the air pressure had doubled. Then the Arbiter exhaled, and thick steam rushed over everyone. The mist smelled of smoke and industry, and Kellan had to shield his eyes. This was magical. He somehow knew, in his gut, the Arbiter had done something. A second later, when the mist had cleared, Kellan glanced over to see that Robbie had vanished, spirited away by the breath of fog.

"I can walk," Wast growled. "Our team is here in the AVU Palace."

Bitso shook his head. "Either name a place or the Arbiter will pick for you."

"I… want to see Nosferatu."

The intense pressure pulsed through the stadium again. The Arbiter inhaled and then exhaled another massive cloud of hot mist and smoke. Wast disappeared within the steam, just as Robbie had. Kellan rubbed his arms as he thought over the Arbiter's magic. The dragon had *travel* magic, the one used for teleporting. How powerful was he? Xiang had needed to touch someone to teleport them, but the Arbiter wasn't constrained by the same limitations.

Before Kellan could voice his destination, Other-Kellan grabbed his shoulder and jerked him close. Kellan wasn't sure what the man wanted. He tensed, his jaw clenched. Alternate-Kellan grabbed the chain around Kellan's neck—the one holding the dog tags.

They were technically Other-Kellan's tags, but…

Kellan jerked out of his grip, keeping the dog tags around his neck. "They're mine. Jace gave them to me. Back off."

But his other self couldn't voice a response. Instead, Alternate-Kellan just stared, his eyes searching Kellan's. The mechanical eye glowed a darker gold than before.

Kellan had no idea what the other man was trying to say.

"Stop playing with yourself," Bitso called out with a laugh. "The Arbiter's time is precious, after all."

"I…"

He had several things to do, including speaking with Xiang. But what had happened to Alvo and Juan? Kellan's thoughts went to Nosferatu, the strange man of Team 5.

Before he could voice a location, Bitso leaned further forward. "You take *forever* to do anything." He tapped his fingers on the bloody desk. "I wish I could die of boredom. You'd be the perfect poison." Then, with a cackle, he added, "I wish I could die at all!"

The madman laughed and slammed his hand down over and over again, as though it were the joke of a lifetime. Kellan didn't find it amusing. Bitso *had* asked Kellan to kill him in exchange for sixty arcana. Kellan would just have to find him outside of an Oasis to grant his wish…

But that was for a different time.

When Kellan turned to face the Arbiter, he said, "I want to see Alvo and Juan."

He wasn't sure if the dragon would take him anywhere, but he hoped the conjoined twins were okay. The Arbiter turned to face him, the dragon's deadly teeth mere feet from Kellan. There was a prolonged moment where the primordial dragon did nothing. Kellan had an urge to reach out and touch the dragon's metal teeth—the sharp bits of serrated steel, no doubt used to shred bodies—but Kellan held back.

He didn't know how the Arbiter would take being touched.

Then the massive dragon exhaled smoke and steam, blanking Kellan in a hazy, white mist.

Kellan felt the pull of the teleportation. He closed his eyes, and he was jerked through space in an instant. Then he stumbled forward and opened his eyes to find he was standing in the middle of a room in the AVU Palace.

It was a quiet location. Classical music played from the walls. Rows and rows of bookshelves filled the room. Kellan counted ten of them, each at least eight feet tall and stuffed with massive tomes.

The whole room smelled of mold and paper. Kellan glanced around, caught off guard by the seemingly normal library. It couldn't just be *normal*, could it?

"Hello?" Kellan called out.

Something thumped around between the bookshelves.

After a deep breath, Kellan carefully made his way around the shelf next to him. The overhead lights flickered once, but otherwise remained bright enough to keep the shadows at bay.

Kellan glanced between the shelves and spotted Alvo and Juan. The deformed twins, merged together and sharing most of a body, stumbled around the library, both heads glancing around.

When they spotted Kellan, they stopped and stared.

"Are you okay?" Kellan asked. He walked over, his head spinning. "You… You were teleported here after the challenge round?"

"Where are we?" Alvo asked. He reached for the books, his hands shaking.

"The AVU Palace."

Both heads gasped. Then Alvo and Juan fell to the ground, unable to stay on their feet. Both of them muttered quiet words, their eyes wide. The whites of their eyes were red with broken blood vessels.

"What's wrong?" Kellan walked over and helped the twisted twins back to their feet. "This is an Oasis. It means no one can kill you here."

"Nexus residents shouldn't be here," Alvo whispered. One eye didn't quite stare in the same direction as the other. "We… We don't want to get too close to our progenitor."

"Your *progenitor*?" Kellan repeated. "Is that what you call the Arbiter?"

"Sometimes, yes. He is our first father. The one who created all of us."

Kellan tried to stop himself from imagining the Arbiter mounting anything. The thought of the Arbiter impregnating a skyscraper was too much. What the hell had the dragon done to have so many children?

"How are you all human?" Kellan fumbled with the words. "Well, *human-shaped*. How are you all human shaped?"

Alvo and Juan glanced down at their mutated, twisted form, both faces scrunched in mild disbelief. Then they returned their gazes to Kellan.

But they understood the question. Alvo replied, "The Arbiter controls the Nexus. It's his will that made reality. He took scales from his primordial flesh and shaped them into people to dwell in his realm."

"The Nexus is the dimension that converges with all others," Juan whispered, his bloodshot eyes widening further. "Other primordial dragons made their children untainted by outside influences, but the Arbiter has twisted flesh, as warped as his dimension."

"Or so they say. Such myths are just that—legends told to children."

"The Arbiter claims us as his own," Juan muttered, his expression shifting back to something neutral. "So it must be true."

Alvo nodded once.

"Why are you afraid of him, then?" Kellan asked. "Most children don't fear their parents."

"What if he sees us?" Alvo asked as they motioned to their body with their three thin arms. "What if the Arbiter is disgusted with how twisted his children have become? He allows the players of the Nexus Games to kill us for arcana. He must hate us. He must despise the shape of us."

Kellan disliked the turn of the conversation. He wasn't sure what to say. He wasn't familiar with this cold world, and he didn't know what to think of the Arbiter's bizarre actions.

"That's why Nosferatu has to win," Juan said, smiles creeping across both their wax-like faces. The muscles didn't quite work. Their smiles reminded Kellan of a stroke victim's.

"What will happen when Nosferatu wins?" Kellan asked.

"The winners of the Nexus Games are granted access to the perfect dimension, *Zenith*, where there's infinite arcana and mages have the most powerful of magics."

Alvo nodded three times. "Yes. Yes! Nosferatu will use his magic to fix us. To make us beautiful again. Then the Arbiter will care—he'll protect us from the outsiders again."

Kellan said nothing.

The more he heard about *Zenith the Land of Gold-Brick Roads and Infinite Magic*, the more he wondered if it could actually do the things that everyone claimed it could. But he also couldn't bring himself to voice the skepticism with the twins. Not when they desperately wanted it to be reality.

"Listen," Kellan said. "That's a lot to unpack. How about I just take you to Nosferatu, like I promised? I need to get back to my team."

Perhaps Xiang will be in the mood to discuss Zenith further. Kellan exhaled. *It would be fantastic to get some sort of proof or explanation of how this all works.*

"Please take us there," Alvo said. "But don't take us anywhere near the Arbiter."

"Do you know where Nosferatu is?"

The twins glanced at one another, their hands awkwardly craning to the side. Then Alvo said, "Wast was supposed to find the Chime and then find us in the Catacomb Maze, but he never did. Just bring us to Wast. He will know where Nosferatu is."

"Yeah, well, Wast was *teleported* to the man, so we're shit out of luck." Kellan glanced around the library as he cracked his knuckles. But then he remembered Wast's interactions with the Arbiter. "Wast said his team was staying here at the AVU Palace… So, come with me. We'll find Nosferatu."

Alvo and Juan nodded their heads, their eyes shaky and blinking less than normal. With quick steps, Kellan guided them around the bookshelves. Then he found a door out and stepped into a gigantic hallway. The gothic architecture clashed with the simple design of the library. Gargoyle statues perched on top of stone pillars. Tapestries hung on the walls, each depicting dragons attacking each other.

Kellan jogged by the odd decorations and continued through the AVU Palace. The large structure was practically a megamall in terms of size and varying interiors. When Kellan ran by a window, he spotted the dome of the Arbiter's stadium across the palace's courtyard.

"This way," Kellan said, opting to turn down a hall that went in the opposite direction of the stadium.

The beat of intense music rang throughout the palace.

Kellan stopped in the middle of the hall, Alvo and Juan behind him.

Dread twisted in his chest. The palace was once again full of the Nexus Games players. The last time Kellan had associated with any of the Nexus residents, another player had killed them to make a point. Kellan knew that if he wandered the palace with Alvo and Juan, they would become the target of a malicious attack.

"We should go the long way," Kellan muttered, backing away from the sounds of partying.

The misshapen twins stumbled around him.

Kellan turned around, went down a different hall, and headed in the direction of the stadium. He wanted to get away from the other people as fast as possible. Alvo and Juan kept pace, but they lumbered and breathed with heavy huffs, creating more noise than Kellan wanted them to.

"Oh, look, it's Xiang's boy toy," a sweet and sinister voice said from the shadows.

—Chapter 15—

—Team 5—

A striking woman stepped out of the darkness in the corner of the hallway. If this wasn't the Nexus, Kellan would've assumed she was a mugger. A dozen piercings marked her face with metal, from her lower lip, to her eyebrow, to her nose. She had a Mohawk—not too large, but spiked—and the dark rings around her eyes were either makeup or a complete lack of sleep, Kellan wasn't sure which.

She had an athletic build and wore a skintight outfit that looked like a futuristic sci-fi bodysuit. Besides her heeled boots, Kellan was pretty sure she wasn't wearing anything else. Her suit was black, except for one sleeve, which was a bright neon pink. Kellan likened the coloration to a poisonous frog.

He knew this woman.

The number on the back of her left hand told him everything.

Team 42.

Name: Ysa Voight the Wraith
Race: Human
Magics: Entropy, Eclipse
Rank: Concealed
Armor Rating: Concealed
Health: Concealed
Stats: Concealed
Abilities: Concealed

Ysa sauntered over, her gaze flicking from Kellan to Alvo and Juan. She smirked, her teeth visible.

"Wow, you've let yourself go," Ysa said as she motioned to Kellan's sweatpants and T-shirt. "I've met Ziploc bags with more sexual energy."

She circled around like a shark, getting closer as she did, even grazing her fingertips over Kellan's shoulder as she went behind him. He tensed but didn't lash out. He couldn't—the magic around the AVU prevented hostile actions.

"Good to see you again, Ysa," Kellan said, terse. "But I have to get somewhere."

Alvo and Juan shuddered as Ysa drew near. Both heads tried to crane around at the same time, their three arms folded tightly against their giant chest. When she smiled, Alvo and Juan cringed away, frowning.

"You're *still* associating with these inbred freaks?" Ysa asked.

When Kellan went to walk forward, she stepped in the way.

"Are you insane, or do you just want to start a fight?" Ysa met Kellan's gaze, her eyes intense, almost crazed. "You think the *Arbiter* is going to help you? Is that why you went crying to him? That piece of shit trash dragon isn't going to get involved. *He never gets involved in the games.*"

Alvo and Juan stepped closer to Kellan, their expressions ones of disgust and shock. Kellan could practically *feel* Ysa's rage. She shook, but kept her smirk, like the Oasis was preventing her from acting.

Her shadow moved around the floor—like Peter Pan's fucked-up cousin. It made clawing motions at the darkness around Kellan's feet.

"I really need to get going," Kellan said, never betraying his own frustration.

From what he could remember, Ysa had magics that eroded people's defenses. And her shadows acted on their own to attack and hold people in place. She had been deadly during the second game, and angering her wasn't worth it.

She needed to die, but Kellan couldn't do anything about that yet.

When Kellan tried to step around her again, Ysa posted her arm on the nearby wall, blocking his path. They stood inches apart, and if they *hadn't been* in an Oasis, Kellan would've been tempted to punch her square in the face.

"Xiang's illusions aren't going to save you in the next game," Ysa said sweetly. "Now that Brenner knows how powerful they are, he already has a way to deal with them."

Why would Ysa tell him that? It was good information—but Xiang already feared that outcome. She had known the moment she had used her illusions in the second game that it would give away her capabilities.

"What do you want from me?" Kellan asked, defiant. "We can't fight in this hallway, so unless you have something to say, this is all a waste of time."

Ysa lifted a pierced eyebrow. After a prolonged moment of strained silence, she removed her posted arm. "What do I want? To win this goddamn game. Brenner said he offered you a chance to join us, but you refused, probably because you're Xiang's bitch, but maybe for some other stupid reason."

Kellan was done with the conversation. Ysa wasn't the sharpest tool in the shed, and he really did have better things to do.

"Anyone ever tell you that you're a delight?" he sarcastically asked.

Ysa offered Alvo and Juan a sneer. "*What's your deal?* You… You're some hobo-loving vagabond. I thought it was funny at first, but now it just makes me sick."

"Is that a quote from your mother? I think I recall hearing her say that once."

Ysa's lip twitched—a tic that betrayed her itching need for violence. "The moment Quasimodo steps outside this palace, he's dead. Along with everyone else you've ever associated with." She pressed a single finger against his chest. "*Our* Kellan is a trained killer. And I'm going to help him rip you apart."

Kellan brushed her hand aside. "Anyone ever tell you that your voice is shrill? You're speaking at frequencies only dogs should hear."

With her teeth gritted, Ysa stepped away. Then she ripped out the piercing on her lip, tearing her flesh in one quick action. She did it so fast, and so aggressively, that blood splattered forward. Kellan flinched as some of it hit his shirt.

A dozen red spots now marked his clothing.

"Oopsie-doopsie," Ysa said. Then, with a manic giggle, she turned and headed for a darkened part of the hall. "Sorry about that! Guess I'll see you later, then, *Alex*. Stay out of trouble until then."

Kellan glanced down at his clothes. They were already dirty from his time in the challenge round. With a sigh, he just motioned to the path ahead of him. "Let's go."

Alvo and Juan stared, their whole body shaking. "Outsiders revile us."

"I think she reviles everyone."

"Thank you for speaking to her." Alvo and Juan stepped closer. Then they patted down their body, their deformed hands small and shaky. With a sigh, Alvo said, "Merry Christmas."

"Yeah, I'm happy to be alive, too. But we should get going." Kellan grabbed their shoulder and pushed them forward. "You're not going to die until you leave the palace. So, just stay here for a bit. I'm sure it'll be fine."

"The rules of the Oasis don't apply to the Arbiter. If he wanted to kill us, he could."

"I've got good news. He's living in a pit in the middle of a football stadium. I think you'll be fine. C'mon."

Together, they continued down the hallway. And although Kellan had been blasé about the encounter with Ysa, inside he regretted the fact that he had run into her. Ysa—and all of Team 42—was a lunatic. She *would* kill Alvo and Juan, simply to spite Kellan.

Kellan didn't want that on his conscience.

As Kellan went, he opened doors, checking all the bizarre rooms in the palace.

One was a pinball arcade. One was an indoor swimming pool.

The only theme for the AVU Palace seemed to be recreation and luxury. Every place, area, and section of the palace was designed for games, relaxation, gambling or drinking. And also, debauchery. With the music picking up and the lights of the hall dimming, Kellan wouldn't have been surprised if he ran across people engaged in more scandalous activities.

His suite wasn't in this kind of hall, however. It was upstairs.

Kellan motioned for Alvo and Juan to follow him up to the next floor. The partying in the palace grew loud enough for him to hear even as he ascended the steps. The dying light outside made Kellan nervous. He didn't fear the night—quite the opposite—but time was a precious commodity, and here he was just wandering around.

He opened three more doors, growing more impatient with each empty room.

Alvo and Juan followed close behind, lumbering as quickly as their stumpy legs would allow.

Then Kellan spotted someone leaving a room—a rennic dressed like Indiana Jones.

Wast.

"There," Kellan said. "We found Team 5."

He jogged forward, and Wast turned in his direction. The giant werewolf man laid his ears back against his skull and flashed his fangs. But the moment he spotted Alvo and Juan, his whole demeanor changed. His ears perked back up, and his haggard, black tail actually wagged a bit.

"You made it?" Wast asked, not even glancing in Kellan's direction. "Do you have the information for Nosferatu?"

Alvo and Juan both nodded. They headed for the door, no more words for anyone. Once they'd entered, and the door had snapped shut, Kellan turned on his heel, ready to leave.

"Wait," Wast growled.

Kellan stopped and glanced over his shoulder. No one else was around.

"You should see him, too," Wast said. "He'll want to thank you."

"It's fine. I can just pretend I heard the thanks."

Wast's ears flattened again. "What's with you? Some random *human* lurkin' about, makin' friends with the Nexus residents, only to turn down an invitation from their leader?"

"You know about me?"

"I've seen footage of you in the games. Everyone is talkin' about the Alex Kellan impersonator. The one makin' all the strange decisions. Even Nosferatu finds your actions questionable."

Questionable?

Kellan wanted to sigh—to let out his building frustration on *something*—but he swallowed his anger yet again and turned to face the rennic. With a sardonic gesture of his hand, he motioned to the door. "After you, then. Lead the way to this *legendary* Nosferatu."

Wast snorted. He grabbed the door to the suite and opened it. "Get in."

What grace and ceremony, Kellan thought as he stepped into the room.

Then the door shut. Wast hadn't entered—he had simply left.

Kellan stood still for a moment. He glanced around, taking in his surroundings. While Team 101's suite was expansive, spacious, and contained multiple sub-rooms, *this* suite felt small, but in a posh way. Large curtains hung from the ceiling, draped across most of the walls, hanging for decoration.

An incense burner sat in the corner of the main room. The smoke wafted through the air, clinging to the wall drapes, filling the cozy space with the smell of lilac.

There were no windows. No balcony. No mana spring.

Even the lights were dimmed, creating an underground effect that unnerved Kellan.

He spotted several doors, and he suspected they must have led to sub-rooms, but he wasn't sure. Each door was shut tightly, and one even had a metal grating across it. As Kellan crept inside, he had to avoid the cushions on the floor, as well as a short coffee table.

A large TV was in the central area, but it, too, had drapes on either side, like the curtains could be closed over the screen. Was it a theater TV? Why would anyone design a room in this fashion?

Alvo and Juan stood near the back of the room, beside the TV. Another man was there—one wearing a three-piece suit.

Name: Nosferatu the Iron-Willed
Race: Human
Magics: Metal
Rank: M
Armor Rating: 20 + 10 Shielding [Metallic]
Health: 30/30 [Cyborg-Enhanced]

Stats:
Strength—7 [Cyborg-Enhanced]
Dexterity—5 [Cyborg-Enhanced]
Fortitude—10 [Cyborg-Enhanced, Tough]
Charisma—5
Manipulation—3
Intelligence—10 [Analytical]
Perception—9 [Cyborg-Enhanced]
Wisdom—15 [Mystic Sense]
Willpower—15 [Determined]

Abilities:
Personal—[Resolute]—The mage is not easily deterred from his path. The mage's willpower counts as double for the purposes of resisting enemy magics. Additionally, the mage cannot be dominated or enslaved.

Nosferatu.

The number 5 was on the back of his left hand, clear as day for all to see.

And since he was one of the Nexus residents, Nosferatu had a wide variety of deformities. Boils, lumps, and lesions marked every visible portion of his skin, including his face. Some wept fluids, but whenever it became too much, Nosferatu grabbed a handkerchief from his suit pocket and dabbed away the gunk.

If it weren't for his leprosy-style appearance, Nosferatu wouldn't have been horrible to look at. He stood straight, he seemed fit, and his charcoal-gray suit was pressed beautifully. In all ways, Nosferatu stood like a tall, dark, and handsome man.

But he wasn't. Nosferatu's thinning hair reminded Kellan of a cactus. The man was basically bald, except for the white wisps over his misshapen scalp. Nosferatu was like a diseased corpse wrapped in a suit, pretending to be handsome.

"Ah, Alex Kellan," Nosferatu said, slowly turning to face him.

The collar of his suit had seven metal pins snapped onto the fabric. They were gold, and they glittered, even in the dim lighting.

Those pins symbolized his highest rank of magic. Gold stood for metal, the magic of civilization and technology, and seven meant the man had achieved M-rank. If Kellan hadn't had his magical sight, the metal pins would've at least given him some clue as to the other man's strength.

Nosferatu placed a hand on Alvo and Juan's shoulder. "Thank you for the information. Please take a seat and rest here. It isn't safe for you to leave."

The conjoined twins nodded their heads and then lumbered over to the pillow seating. They carefully sat near the coffee table, both heads turned so they could watch everything unfold.

"Thank you for helping Alvo and Juan out of the Catacomb Maze," Nosferatu said.

His voice was rich, thick, and lyrical. He could make reading the back of a cereal box sound poetic.

Kellan nodded once. "Don't mention it."

"I'm pleased you came to see me."

"Oh? Why's that?"

Nosferatu stared at him with discerning eyes. "I wanted to ask you why you're here. Why you want to win the Nexus Games." He moved slowly to the TV and then placed a lumpy hand on the side of the screen.

"I was forced into the Nexus Games. Technically, if my team wins, they'll let me return home."

"Hm." Nosferatu frowned. Even his lips were marked with disease lines. "A pity. Well, then, you can go. There's nothing more for us to discuss."

"Wait, that's it?" Kellan scoffed. "Your teammate made it seem like you wanted to speak with me about something important."

Nosferatu turned and waved his other hand. "If you have no passion for what's going on, there's little to speak about. An employee clocking in for a paycheck isn't the same as someone building a business. If you have no reason to win, I doubt you ever will." Nosferatu motioned to the door. "You may leave, Alex Kellan."

"I have a reason to win," Kellan stated, getting defensive. "Didn't you see me on that bizarre late-night talk show? Team 42 is planning on killing the Arbiter so that they can invade Zenith, get superpowered through *ultimate magic*, and then take over every *other* dimension, which includes my home. So, *yeah*, I have a reason to win—it's to stop Team 42 from carrying out their twisted plot."

Kellan hadn't realized how worked up he had gotten until he forced himself to take a breath. It irritated him that no one seemed to care or listen. He wasn't spouting off words just to hear his own voice. Why wouldn't anyone get behind his cause?

When Nosferatu faced him this time, it was with a smirk. "Ah! There it is. Your passion." He took a single step away from the TV, his gait stiff. "I've seen it from you a few times whenever you've been filmed by the Arbiter."

"What're you talking about?"

"You have a passion to save and protect people. The rezrah girl, Nexus residents, even members of other teams… Time and time again, the Arbiter has filmed your desperate struggle to save those around you."

"Well… Innocent people."

"And *my* people. You're selfless, even in a world as dark as this. That's rare."

Kellan crossed his arms. The wet blood on his body disturbed him. He rubbed at his shirt and then opted to keep his arms at his side. "What does it matter?"

Nosferatu's gaze drifted down to Kellan's shirt. He stared for a long moment. "The blood on your clothing is fresh."

Kellan touched the crimson drops. "Yeah, I ran into Ysa in the hall, and she threw a little tantrum. This is her blood, not mine."

"Then you should remove the shirt at once."

With a chuckle, Kellan tugged at his clothing. When Nosferatu didn't join in the laughing, Kellan stopped. "Are you serious?"

"Ysa Voight is an entropy mage. They have powers over death—some powers include the ability to use their blood in devious ways. I'm not saying she's spying on us, but I wouldn't put it past her. Remove your shirt. Then burn it, I say."

Kellan tugged the garment off, dwelling on the information. Entropy magic involved death and blood—but he didn't know many of the specifics of the magic. This was good information, even if it was coming to him a week too late.

He wasn't sure if what Nosferatu said was correct, but he got a feeling he could trust the misshapen man. "All right."

Alvo and Juan stood, walked over, and took the shirt from Kellan. Then they walked over to a door and entered a bathroom. Perhaps they could flush the shirt away?

Once the door had shut again, Nosferatu touched the tips of his fingers together. "There. Now we are alone." He forced a smile, but the lesions on his cheeks made it difficult. "What I was trying to say is that I judge people by their commitment."

"What?" Kellan asked.

"Only those with deep convictions are worth allying with," Nosferatu said matter-of-factly. "I want to propose our teams help each other win the Nexus Games. Obviously, not every game will work out that way, but if we *can* aid each other, we *should* aid each other."

Kellan lifted an eyebrow.

This was the first time another team had tried to form an official alliance.

Alvo and Juan returned from the bathroom, no shirt in hand. Then they walked to Kellan's side, both sets of eyes on him. Kellan said nothing as he mulled over the situation.

"Why aren't you speaking to Xiang about this?" Kellan asked. "She's our team leader."

Nosferatu stifled a laugh. "She's disgusted by Nexus residents, like myself. Our inbred visages aren't worthy of being in her presence." He waved away the comment as he returned to the side of the TV. "But that doesn't matter. Xiang isn't special in this regard. *No one* trusts or cares for Nexus residents. You are a rare exception. I assume whatever dimension you come from, there's more emphasis on empathy."

Kellan wouldn't have said that. But it didn't matter. "Well, okay. I'd like to form an alliance."

Nosferatu's eyes lit up, and he smiled genuinely. "Brilliant."

"You're going to help Nosferatu?" Alvo asked.

Kellan nodded. "Seems that way."

"Then… I want to give you something for helping me and my brother."

The way Alvo said everything made Kellan think he was about to die. Kellan turned, his arms crossed. He wanted to tell the twins he didn't need anything, but then Alvo held out one of his three hands.

It was empty.

But then… a crystal emerged from his palm, lifting out of the flesh as though pulled upward by an invisible string.

The sparkling crystal that emerged was no larger than a thumb. It wasn't red, like most arcana—it was *gold*. It glittered with inner power, bright and vibrant.

"Take it," Alvo said, pushing his hand forward. "I want… to help you succeed in the games…"

Kellan, taken aback, hesitated for a moment. "I thought arcana was the essence of someone's soul? I can't just… I can't just take this."

Nosferatu laced his fingers together. "You came from a world with no magic?"

"That's right."

"Then fear not. Arcana is, indeed, fragments of someone's soul, but Alvo and Juan can continue, even if they give you a piece of themselves."

With that statement, Kellan breathed easier. He reached out, took the gold arcana, and marveled at the warmth that spread through his arm and then to his chest and body. Gold arcana… it just felt different.

[Alex Kellan] absorbed 1 gold arcana.

"Wait," Kellan muttered. He turned to Nosferatu. "You know about gold arcana? Half the people I speak to deny it exists."

"Oh, yes. All Nexus residents know of gold arcana. It's freely given, whereas red arcana is taken by force." Nosferatu straightened his vest and then recited, "*Gold arcana cleans the soul, red arcana takes its toll.* We learn about it at a young age, you see."

"Why?" Kellan asked. He turned to Alvo and Juan, and then back to Nosferatu. "Why do you all know what's going on, but no one else does? And how did you give me the gold arcana so easily?"

Kellan hoped these people would just give him answers. He hated not knowing. Clarity would help him so much.

"The Arbiter told us all about the differences between red and gold arcana." Nosferatu stared at Kellan for a long time. "You don't know much about magic?"

"No."

"Then let me explain something simple. When light passes through a prism, it emerges as colors on the other side. Think of a mage as the prism, and light as raw magic straight from the Sea of Chaos. But… people aren't perfect prisms. When the light filters through their bodies, only *certain* colors shine through."

Nosferatu's rich voice made it easy to listen. Kellan absorbed every word.

"Those colors are specific magics," Nosferatu said. "Your colors are…" He touched Kellan's bare shoulder. A moment later, he jerked his hand away, his brow furrowed. Despite that, Nosferatu continued, "Your colors are silver, tan, gold, and… *dark blue.* They represent eclipse, body, metal, and meta."

Kellan tensed. He probably shouldn't have revealed his ascendancy magic—meta was rare, after all—but it couldn't be helped now.

"Okay," he said. "Go on."

"Every time you absorb red arcana, it's like you're smudging the outside of the prism. The light won't shine as clearly, and your magics will be muddled and weaker. But—" Nosferatu held up a finger, "—every time you absorb *gold* arcana, it's like taking a cloth to your prism and wiping it clean. A beautiful thing. It makes your magic stronger. Breaks curses. Weakens the hold of outside magics on your mind."

"So my prism is cleaner thanks to Alvo and Juan?"

"In a way, yes."

Kellan wanted to thank the twins, but it was getting redundant. He had saved them from the maze, and they were just thanking him for going out of his way.

"Are there any drawbacks to handing over your arcana to others?" Kellan asked.

Nosferatu frowned. "If you give *all* of your arcana, you die."

"Alvo and Juan gave me *some* of their arcana?"

"That's right. And they will feel a loss in energy, drive, and will to live because of it." Nosferatu held up a pox-marked hand. "Think of your arcana like blood. You can live without all your blood, but the more you donate, the more sluggish and weaker you are for a time."

"How much arcana does an individual have?"

Kellan almost felt bad for bombarding Nosferatu with so many questions, but since he was one of the few people who would answer, Kellan had to take advantage of the situation. He knew next to nothing about arcana. If Nosferatu was an expert, why not get a few things straight?

"The arcana a person has is dependent on many factors," Nosferatu said with a shrug. "How old you are. If you're magical. How many trying experiences you've lived through. A theory among my people is that the higher quality you are as a person, the more arcana you have at any one time. The Arbiter has implied as much."

"And why does the Arbiter tell you all this?" Kellan asked, still fascinated.

"He is our progenitor. He instructed us on all things magic. There is no greater teacher than a primordial dragon. He was born from the raw magics of the Sea of Chaos—he and his brothers and sisters were the first beings in all the many universes."

"That doesn't explain *why.*"

Nosferatu paused. When pus wept from an active lesion on his hand, he wiped it away with his handkerchief. "The Arbiter taught us long ago, when he wanted us to control the Nexus. He no longer teaches us. Unfortunately, the Arbiter seems to care very little about us now. I assume it's because the inbreeding has led to our degeneration, but I don't know that for certain."

Kellan took a deep breath, the smoke from the incense burner too thick for his liking.

"What should we do about helping each other in the next game?" Kellan asked.

"We'll have to wait to see what type of game it is. Once we know, I'll send you a message, and we can coordinate."

"Thank you." Kellan tightened his hands into fists and then relaxed. "I really appreciate you answering my questions, by the way. Very few people do that."

Nosferatu bowed at the waist, deep enough that Kellan was momentarily surprised. When Nosferatu stood straight, he said, "Thank you for agreeing to help us. Whenever you have need of knowledge, you may speak to me at any time."

—Chapter 16—
—The Perfect Build—

Kellan liked Nosferatu.

Sure, he looked like a leper, but that didn't take away from his etiquette, nobility, and charismatic demeanor. Kellan appreciated that. Being an officer and a gentleman was about more than just appearance and power. It was a mentality—holding yourself to a higher standard, even when that meant hardship or struggle.

When Kellan left Team 5's suite, he headed for the middle part of the AVU Palace. The sun had set, blanketing Nexus-Fayetteville in darkness, and filling the palace with feverish partying. The music played nonstop from every corner of every room. And most of the genres weren't the same. Techno, classical, jazz—Kellan walked by several distinct musical eras.

Smoke, booze, and lust stank up the place.

Kellan remembered his first night in the AVU Palace, and how the partying had been intense, even back then. This time seemed worse. Groups of people stumbled their way into the halls, each carrying drinks in their hands.

The TVs played clips of the games.

Unpleasant clips.

Kellan glanced at one briefly and locked up, surprised by the gore. A woman was torn apart by two alligator creatures. She and her group had been hiding in a shallow puddle of mud, and when the woman tried to cross—it looked like to gather a bunny keychain—the monsters had leapt from the mud and grabbed her before she had known what was happening.

Another clip…

It showed an older teenaged boy fighting with a rennic man. They had magical powers—the boy flung fire like an old-school wizard, and the werewolf had dark energy crackling across his claws. They fought atop a skyscraper. The teen tossed fire around, obviously trying to get the rennic to fall off the edge.

But the rennic powered through the flames, burning off most of his brown fur as he charged. When he caught the teen, he cut through his stomach and then threw him from the top of the building. It was a twenty-story drop.

Kellan glanced away before the screen could show the finale.

A smart man would watch, he reasoned with himself. *To study the abilities of the competition. Especially since there are a wide variety of magics and powers… This would be the best way for me to learn.*

Kellan slid his hands into the pockets of his sweats. He stared at the floor as he walked, mulling over his plans for the evening. The thump of dance music made it difficult.

I'll head to my room and watch the clips from my bedroom. If I do that for a few hours, and take notes, I can study everything and learn on my own. Kellan also thought back to the rule book for the games. *I can cross reference everything.*

He pulled one hand out of his pocket and stared at his palm, remembering the gold arcana.

I should spend all this arcana I have and improve my own magics. Everyone else seems to have better health, stats, and abilities than I do. Even Robbie the Taco King commented that my rank is lower than others.

And now that he had meta magic, Kellan wanted to take the time to review the powers available to him.

Kellan glanced up just as a woman stumbled into his path.

She wore barely anything, just a half-open shirt and skintight pants. Well, she also wore a single flipflop. The other was nowhere to be seen.

The woman had wings—raven black, feathers so large that they almost touched the floor—and her darker skin had a healthy sheen. She smiled, her lips shiny, her dark eyes alight with interest as she looked him up and down. Then she stared through her eyelashes, batting them playfully.

"I love that you ditched your shirt." She leaned closer to him, her breath smelling of powerful whiskey. "You're cute for a human. Ever been with a niav?"

Kellan stared at her for a long moment.

Name: Nirah Enst
Race: Niav
Magics: Storm, Wyld
Rank: C, C
Armor Rating: —
Health: 10/10
Stats: Concealed
Abilities: Concealed

Although Kellan knew it was extremely simplistic, he thought of the niav as *bird people.* Every one he had met had some sort of feathered wings, though it seemed as though they had trouble moving around. The palace was built wide, but not in such a way as to accommodate birds.

The back of her left hand had a number: 76.

Kellan pushed Nirah to the side. "I'm busy. Maybe some other time."

She clicked her tongue in disappointment and then frowned. "We might not have *another time.*"

"What does that mean?" Kellan asked, turning back to face her.

Nirah opened her wings slightly and fluttered them. "Look around, asshole.

Half the people who were here a few days ago are dead. Might as well have fun now, while you still can."

Ah. That's why they're partying like delta-bravos.

But partying the stress away wouldn't help him prepare for the inevitable fight ahead.

Kellan resumed his path back to his suite. "I'll take my chances."

There were too many things Kellan had to do. He couldn't waste his time partying with the lunatics in the AVU Palace. Nosferatu wasn't partying. He had met with Alvo and Juan and…

Kellan rubbed at his jaw.

He hadn't asked about one specific bit of information. What had Alvo and Juan discovered in the Catacomb Maze that had interested Nosferatu so much?

I'll ask him next I see him.

The dim lighting fueled some of Kellan's magic. He dwelled on the fact that when he first acquired powers, they hadn't done much. Now he had several abilities and powers. They didn't overlap, though. They were separate. Everyone seemed to criticize the decision to diversify, and from what Kellan could see, most other mages seemed to have one or two powerful tricks they relied on.

Best to focus. Have a niche. Be the best at it.

Which made sense. Operative teams were typically made up of a few elite individuals. They all had common skills, but some were skilled at disarming explosives, or speaking a certain language, or handling high-risk individuals. Kellan had gone through several sharpshooting courses.

I should focus. I have sixteen arcana now.

Kellan avoided most people as he continued through the halls. Most were drunk, or in a partial state of undress, and he didn't want to find any more members of teams who hated him.

Once he had gone up a set of stairs, Kellan found himself in front of Team 101's suite. He opened the door, surprised to find the lights off. Was *his* team out partying? That didn't seem like something Sen would have done.

Maybe Husker and Mavis.

Kellan weighed the chances Xiang would be out and mingling, only to stop dead in his tracks. Their suite's balcony was actually a spa that overlooked the palace's courtyard gardens. The soothing pink waters regenerated mana for any mage bathing within.

Xiang was there.

Her flowing, black hair swirled around the still waters. Her gaze was fixed on something in the distance, far from the suite. Her back was to Kellan, her slender—and bare—shoulders just slightly out of the water. She rested her chin on her folded forearms.

The door to the balcony was wide open. A chilly night breeze wafted into the suite.

Kellan coughed loudly, announcing his presence, since he was pretty sure she wasn't wearing anything.

Xiang glanced over her shoulder, her smooth and beautiful face marked with curiosity, rather than shock or concern. Unbothered by Kellan's presence, she returned her attention to the distance. "Welcome back."

For a long moment, Kellan didn't move. He wanted to speak with her, but Xiang made no move to get out of the spa, or even to initiate further conversation. Her aloof and distant demeanor made it difficult to even tell what she was thinking.

"Do you have a moment?" Kellan asked from the middle of the room. He didn't head for the door. "Once you're done, I mean."

Xiang ran her fingers through her wet hair and then tossed it all over one shoulder. "We can speak now."

"I spoke with Nosferatu, and I've been thinking about my magics. I wanted to know if you would help me decide what I should do."

"Nosferatu? That inbred resident?" Xiang glanced back at Kellan, her eyes narrowed. "Why?"

"He proposed we make an alliance. I thought it was a good idea."

Xiang smirked. "It's a terrible idea."

"Because he's a Nexus local?"

"Because trusting mages from other teams is the fastest way to lose the Nexus Games. We don't need his help. He's simply hoping to leech from us." Xiang lifted herself a bit out of the water, exposing more of her bare back. "His team is *weak*. He might be powerful, but once he's gone, all of Team 5 will fall. He desperately needs allies, and there's little he can offer in return."

"I don't think he'll betray us."

Xiang chuckled, though it was cold and short. "No. You don't understand. Risking ourselves for him will never be worth it. And trust me—people may look trustworthy, but they're not. If Nosferatu had the chance to throw us in a blender in order to win, he would."

Kellan wasn't a fan of pessimistic speeches, but he understood. So far, the Nexus Games had been filled with a lot of people out for themselves.

After he rubbed his arms, Kellan stepped closer to the balcony door. "All right. Everyone is destined to betray us. Good talk." He exhaled and then added, "So, how about we discuss magic?"

"Very well. Come, join me in the mana spring."

Kellan hesitated.

Xiang sighed and then waved a hand through the air. A white swimsuit and robe appeared across her body. An illusion. But it was so real, the robes swirled around in the water, acting as any normal fabric, easily able to fool the most discerning eye.

"Better?" she asked.

Without answering, Kellan walked to the edge of the spring. He just had sweatpants—and dog tags—nothing else. That was fine. He stepped into the pink waters, the warm and soothing sensation spreading through his body in an instant. It recovered his mana. He hadn't been out, but now he had his full reserves, just in case.

He walked into the spa until the water was up to his waist. Then he rested against the side, close to Xiang.

She remained on the edge of the spring, her arms on the side. "I'm impressed," Xiang whispered. "You managed to get a Summoning Chime. And Sen praised your planning and reflexes."

"I gathered ten arcana from the maze, and one gold arcana from one of the residents."

"Hmm." Xiang glanced over. "Have you developed any of your meta magic?"

"Not yet."

"Then we should start with that. All of the ascendancy magics—meta, travel, fate—are typically restricted. They're too powerful, and primordial dragons find mages with those magics to be a threat. It's your secret weapon."

Kellan nodded. "All right."

"Fortunately, you have a rare trait—*Descended from Zenith*. It means someone who is related to you, no matter how distant, dwells in Zenith. It gives you a connection to the deep and endless springs of magic there."

Kellan thought about his stats and abilities. He had known he had the Descended from Zenith trait, he had just never understood why. Until now.

> **Personal—[Descended from Zenith]**—The mage has the raw magic of Zenith in their blood and has no rank maximum. The mage can also develop one "unknowable" magic.

"How do people get these traits?"

"Every sentient being has a personal trait," Xiang said. She scooted closer, until they were a mere foot apart. "Yours is the Blitzkrieg Analysis. Rare traits, like your bloodline, are innate abilities some are born with. And sometimes, through certain intense training, you can develop technical traits, like your sharpshooter ability."

"So, you have a personal ability?"

"That's right." Xiang held out her hand. "Normally, I conceal it. But I'll show you."

Kellan slowly touched his fingers to the palm of her hand. Then he received information—not her stats or ranks of magic, just her abilities.

> **Personal—[Descended from Zenith]**—The mage has the raw magic of Zenith in their blood and has no rank maximum. The mage can also develop one "unknowable" magic.
> **Personal—[Master Manipulator]**—The mage is a master of manipulation and trickery. Their illusions are always considered 5 ranks higher (even beyond maximums) in order to avoid detection and divination.

"I've seen this before," he said as he dismissed the information from his sight. "You're just a very talented illusionist. And someone related to you is in Zenith."

"My mother."

"Right," Kellan muttered. "After she won the last Nexus Games."

Xiang smiled. "Most people pick magical abilities that complement their personal trait." She closed her fingers around Kellan's hand, her skin soft, her grip gentle. "Since yours doesn't synergize well, why don't we look at your meta magic abilities? You should be able to see a list of some E-rank powers."

Kellan thought about meta magic. He hadn't yet looked at the E-rank powers.

Analyze Magic [2 arcana]

Meta magic is fundamentally the alteration of one magic into another, but to alter, you must first understand.

The mage spends a mana, and for the next fifteen minutes, he can see through B-rank and lower concealing abilities on mages and magical items.

Lock Power, rank I [2 arcana]

Meta mages are the trolliest of mages, able to alter, distort, and shut down the effects of other mages, "taking away" their magic.

Whenever an enemy mage uses an E-rank or D-rank magical ability, the mage may spend an equal amount of mana to "lock" the ability from use. This lock happens instantly, negating magic before it can fully form.

If the opponent has 5 more wisdom than the mage, the opponent may spend double the mana to activate the locked power, ignoring the meta mage's lock.

Shell, rank I [2 arcana]

Meta mages use raw magic itself to negate damage.

The mage develops +2 shielding, which reduces damage from all attacks (except for anti-magic or other meta magic attacks).

Empower, rank I [3 arcana]

Meta mages can empower another power.

By spending an additional mana when activating a power, the mage may add +10% damage to the attack or effect (if numerated, round up).

"Meta magic is the *trolliest*?" Kellan repeated. "What does that mean?"

"It means you mess with your opponents," Xiang said with a slight chuckle.

"Right. Well, these are all interesting facts. Do you have a recommendation?"

"Yes." Xiang tightened her grip on Kellan's hand. "*Empower* and *Shell*. You're a warrior. You should act like it."

Kellan stared at her hand, mulling over his options. "But you said we should take powers based on our personal abilities. *Analyze Magic* would allow me to see people's concealed abilities."

"It's a waste of arcana," Xiang said matter-of-factly. "You can guess at people's abilities based on their magics. Body mages are fast and strong and can heal. Metal mages are great with technology. Mind mages create illusions, read minds, use telepathy—you get the picture. A body mage can't make illusions. A mind mage can't heal. Why bother taking the time to analyze when a well-studied individual already knows?"

"Are personal traits standardized?" Kellan asked. "Obviously we both have the Zenith one."

"There are almost as many personal traits as there are people. Some are powerful, but most are just interesting spins on magics or skills."

"*Yours* seems very powerful." Kellan narrowed his eyes. "Why?"

Xiang pulled her hand out of his. Then she turned away, glaring at the far horizon. The sounds of partying carried up to the suite on the cold winds. Steam lifted off the mana spring waters.

She didn't speak. Kellan decided to press the issue.

"Brenner and all of Team 42 were surprised by the strength of your illusions in the last game. But… why? Brenner and *Other Me* apparently knew you well before the games. You were lovers, or some shit. I'm not sure. But what I do know is that they would probably know your capabilities. They would've seen your personal trait—or you would've told them about it, right? So why were they surprised? My guess would be… you've changed it somehow."

Kellan paused, allowing his words to sink in. The mana spring was comfortable, and he didn't mind just waiting for her to answer.

With a smirk, Xiang said, "Oh, so you're getting used to this world of magic, I see."

"Slowly and painfully," Kellan quipped.

"Well, pat yourself on the back, detective—you caught me. I *did* augment my personal trait. I needed to. I knew that if I joined the Nexus Games, I would require an advantage to win. So…" She glanced down at her hand. "I did what I had to."

"How did you do that? Some sort of magical power?"

Xiang shivered. She slowly dunked herself into the water until she was fully submerged. Then she rose up and turned to face Kellan. Her swimsuit was some sort of bikini, and her robes were practically transparent.

"I took several hexes before I came to the Nexus Games," Xiang said, curt and cold.

"*Hexes*? Multiple? Not just one?

"Yes."

Kellan sarcastically added, "Those incurable curses that affect you *forever*? The ones that people warn you against? You took *multiple*?"

"Exactly. Hexes have benefits… but the costs are typically too high. And deadly." Xiang held out her hand again. "Let me show you one of mine."

Kellan touched her wet palm.

Hex—[Corrupted Personal Ability]—The mage increases the power of their personal trait. As punishment, the mage loses a single mana from their pool every day, though it can be restored. If the mage ever uses all of their mana pool down to zero, they die.

"You *die* if you run out of mana?" Kellan balked.

He had run out of mana several times while playing in the Nexus Games. He couldn't imagine taking this hex.

Xiang jerked her hand out of his and frowned. "That's right. But my personal ability is beyond powerful now."

"Wait. This is exactly what Brenner did to improve himself. He has *four* hexes that all give him bizarre abilities, but all of them have weird instant-death side effects."

"Once we get to Zenith, my hexes will be broken. I'll be free." Xiang combed her black hair with her fingers. "It'll be a flawless victory, so long as we win."

"You told me that you joined the Nexus Games because there was a hex you needed to break. A hex that affects your people and kingdom. Is that true? Or was that just a lie to get me to agree?"

Kellan was honestly questioning everything. Xiang *hadn't* told him that she had *multiple* hexes, and she was obviously hiding most of her traits and powers. She had mentioned one—a hex that affected her and her kingdom—but not this.

"It's true," Xiang said. "But we don't need to dwell on that. Just know that I *must* win the Nexus Games, and this hex will help me."

"Right."

Silence settled over them. The lap of the spa water against the edge of the balcony was soft and calming. The beat of high-tempo music added to Kellan's growing frustration.

"So," he said. "*Empower* and *Shell*—those are the meta abilities I should take. What about my other magics?"

"Your primary magic is eclipse, correct? Rank to C. You'll get more mana—you get that every time you rank magic, even if it's not your primary—but C-rank allows you to purchase some universal abilities. A few are crucial to survival. Then you should focus on lasers. Eclipse and metal magic both have the ability to use the light to their advantage."

Light?

Kellan thought about that.

Laser, rank I [3 arcana]

Eclipse mages rely on light, or "laser," energy in their attack. This power is, weirdly, shared by metal mages.

The eclipse mage gains "laser" as an energy type and may spend a mana to shoot a destructive beam from their hand. The damage dealt is equal to eclipse magic rank (E = 1, D = 2, C = 3, etc.) + half the mage's dexterity score. This stacks at half rate (round up) when added to any other light power.

Spending a mana to shoot a beam? Since it was a numerical damaging ability, *Empower* would work to strengthen it.

Kellan thought about the second rank of the laser ability in metal magic.

Laser, rank II [3 arcana]

Metal mages rely on "laser" energy in their attacks. This power is, weirdly, shared by eclipse mages.

The metal mage gains "laser" as an energy type and may spend a mana to shoot a destructive beam from their hand. The damage dealt is equal to metal magic rank (E = 1, D = 2, C = 3, etc.) + the mage's dexterity score. This stacks at half rate (round up) when added to any other light power.

"Ranking to C requires ten arcana," Kellan muttered. "But if I pick up *Laser, rank I* from eclipse, then *Laser, rank I* and *rank II* from metal, and then *Empower*… I'll have spent twelve arcana out of my sixteen. I'll only have four left."

Xiang lifted a perfect eyebrow. "That means you'll spend a mana to shoot a beam of laser-type magic. You'll deal damage equal to your dexterity, plus your rank of metal… and then your eclipse rank and dexterity. Plus, the ten percent from *Empower*. You have four dexterity, don't you? Ten damage isn't amazing, but it'll instantly kill a non-mage in most situations."

"But my *Void Knight* ability gives me five more dexterity… Do you know what *Laser, rank III* does? I can't seem to see the C-rank abilities."

Xiang waved her hand through the air and created illusions of the information for him to view.

Laser, rank III [4 arcana]

Metal mages rely on "laser" energy in their attacks. This power is, weirdly, shared by eclipse mages.

The metal mage gains "laser" as an energy type and may spend a mana to shoot a destructive beam from their hand. The damage dealt is equal to double the metal magic rank (E = 2, D = 4, C = 6, etc.) + the mage's dexterity score. This stacks at half rate (round up) when added to any other light power.

The first rank of *Laser* used half his dexterity, and his rank for damage.

The second level used his full dexterity, and his rank for damage.

The third level used his full dexterity, but also double his rank, as damage.

"That means if I have C-rank of eclipse, plus my *Void Knight*, plus the metal powers, I'll… spend one mana to deal twenty-one damage. Much more than my rifle. Which seems like it'll kill a lot of lower-ranked mages who aren't defensive. Is that right?"

Xiang touched her lower lip with her finger. "Yes. And for a single mana, it's quite effective."

"I think I understand now." Kellan exhaled. "This would've been much easier if I just leveled up or something. Skill trees are confusing."

"You should be careful, though." Xiang ignored his complaint and added, "Some mages and yami will be immune to laser damage."

"But they won't be immune to bullets—even if it's weaker, I can still shoot them."

"I suppose you should also be aware that certain people and monsters will take *extra* damage from your lasers. Everyone has a personal trait, and they also have a personal *flaw*. You would be surprised to know how many of those flaws basically equate to additional damage from certain sources."

"Flaw?"

"You have one. Everyone does. You just can't see other people's flaws without stronger analysis magics."

"Wait," Kellan said, his thoughts drifting to his magics. "Body magic has an ability that increases my dexterity. And so does metal."

The body power was cheaper.

Increased Dexterity, rank I [4 arcana]

As the body mage increases in rank, magic comes to permanently infuse their musculature, granting them increased speed and control.

This increases the mage's dexterity by +1.

But the metal ability sounded more thorough.

Servos [Cyborg] [1 mana drawdown/5 arcana]

Metal mages who have taken "Cyborg" abilities gain multiple options, including servos, in which the mage generates a system throughout their body that instantly controls muscles with feedback to more closely mirror the mage's intent, increasing precision of force applied, and increasing the rate at which they react to minute changes in the physical environment.

The mage gains +1 dexterity.

"What's *drawdown*?" Kellan asked. "I have to pay that *and* arcana?"

"Your permanent mana pool will be reduced. The cyborg enhancements are typically worth it, though. If you manage to build up your dexterity, your beams will become devastating."

"If I purchase all the lasers and empowering, and then the body magic for dexterity…" Kellan mulled over everything. "As long as the target isn't immune to laser damage, I'll be blasting a goddamn hole through their body every time."

Xiang genuinely smiled. Then she turned her gaze down to the pinkish waters. "It amuses me how similar you are to your alternate-self. I had the exact same conversation with him at one point."

"Were you both swimming around a spa?" Kellan quipped.

"Rolling around a bed, actually." Xiang splashed a handful of water onto Kellan. "It was only after we were lovers that I started helping him with his magic. He, like you, favored eclipse magic. He *didn't* take my advice to focus on lasers."

"He also didn't gather any gold arcana."

Xiang stared at him for a moment. Then she waded through the warm waters, drawing closer. Kellan didn't move. He just waited until she stopped an inch from him.

"Your gold arcana… Your *Void Knight* ability is special. I've never heard of it before. I assume they're connected."

"That's right. Nosferatu said the gold arcana was strengthening my magic. I'm a prism. Or something. And the gold arcana allows my magic from the Sea of Chaos to shine bright." He half-shrugged. "I'm not entirely sure what that all means, but that's about what he said."

She held a hand over her mouth and chuckled. Then her mirth disappeared as she said, "You really shouldn't trust Nosferatu. It'll be a mistake that will cost you."

"You're extremely distrusting. I think not having allies will hurt us more in the long run."

"Forgive me," Xiang said with a sneer. "But when your lover turns on you, who can you trust?" She splashed him again and then stormed out of the spa.

Kellan ran a hand down his face, clearing away the warm water. He found it frustrating that it was somehow *his* fault that his alternate-self was a delta-bravo, but he didn't comment. Clearly, he had to suffer in silence.

Before he went into the suite to finish his talk with Xiang—and maybe learn why she and Team 42 were enemies—Kellan decided to spend his arcana.

He purchased *Laser, rank I* in both metal and eclipse, and then purchased *Laser, rank II*, and then *Improved Dexterity, rank I* and lastly, *Empower, rank I.*

All sixteen arcana used.

Now he had zero.

Damn. I really need to get my hands on a lot more.

Kellan's insides twisted for a moment. He grabbed at his dog tags. After a long exhale, the pain faded. He had increased his dexterity to human max—and he felt it. He moved a little quicker, even around the spa. It wasn't as significant as his shadowy empowerment, but it was noticeable enough.

"And now I can shoot lasers from my hands," he muttered to himself.

Kellan wanted to try it out, but when he attempted it, the power of the Oasis stilled his ability. He couldn't seem to fight against the influence. Activating the laser beam just wasn't an option.

After a quick smirk, Kellan dragged himself out of the spa. He'd speak with Xiang, thank her for the advice, and—

But then he spotted someone in the suite. He caught his breath.

It was a teenager.

A mage.

Why were they here?

—Chapter 17—
—Why Are You Wet?—

Soaking wet, Kellan walked into the suite. If he could've attacked, he would've, but as things stood, he just strode forward, tense and ready to talk a punk down.

The lights switched on, and Kellan blinked for a moment.

The teen… was a boy.

He wore a simple hoodie and jeans, but it was his long black hair, sandy-toned skin, and pinched look of irritation that gave away his identity.

"*Sen?*" Kellan asked. "Is that you?"

The teenager shoved his hands into the large pocket of his hoodie, his eyes narrowing into a genuine glare. "Of course it's me, you buffoon. Who else would it be?"

His voice cracked a bit as he spoke.

Sen was taller now—five and a half feet—with lean muscle and a slight slouch to his shoulders. And he wore facial hair like he had glued black sprinkles to his chin and called it a day. It was an odd combination.

Kellan snorted. "Oh, your testes finally swelled, huh? Congrats."

"Get all your quips out now," Sen said, his teeth gritted. "Because I won't tolerate it later."

"Don't be that way. You're a real boy now."

Sen rolled his eyes so hard, he almost hit his eyebrows. "*Anything else?*"

"One more, one more." Kellan smirked as he said, "Is that a thread hanging from your shirt? Oh, wait. My bad. It's just your left arm."

"Really? A masturbation joke? You're an infant."

Kellan walked over and slapped Sen on the shoulder. "At least you're not wearing Power Ranger pajamas anymore. You're moving up in the world."

With a deep frown, Sen glanced down at the damp spot on the sleeve of his hoodie. Then he dramatically brushed it off with the indignant huff of a debutante. "Would you mind telling me what you were doing with my sister out in the mana spring?" he asked, his voice strained. "Do you have something to tell me?"

He was watching that?

Kellan didn't reply. He headed for his room, water dripping from his wet sweatpants. With a quick twist of the handle, he entered his portion of the suite. When he went to shut the door, Sen was already there, his arm posted against the frame.

"Well?" Sen demanded. "What were the two of you doing?"

Kellan slipped his hands into his wet pants. "Why did you bring me to the Nexus? I know you needed a warrior for your ragtag team. I mean—*why me*? If I'm some alternate-dimension version of your sister's ex, why would you pick *me* of all people to bring with you to the Nexus?"

"It was easy to find you." Sen held up a single finger. "Your Zenith trait is useful." He lifted a second finger. "I know your general capabilities." He put up a third finger. "And if you died…"

Sen put all his fingers down. And didn't answer. Kellan waited for a prolonged moment, hoping something would happen, but Sen just shrugged.

"Well?" Kellan asked.

"Well, I thought it would make my sister happy," Sen finally stated. "I mean, she was rather upset when you left. Not *you*. The other you. And since one of the past games was *Guillotine*, I thought it would make everything easy for us."

"Guillotine?"

Sen sighed. "In the last Nexus Games there was a game that required each team to kill someone from their ranks in order to acquire a key. It wasn't used in the Nexus Games *beforehand*, so it might not be used this time, but just in case… We would have someone whom my sister would love to see beheaded."

There wasn't much to say about any of that, so Kellan headed over to the TV mounted on his bedroom wall. He switched it on, and then turned down the volume. *I need to find a notebook or a phone or something to take notes with.* The rule book for the games was much too thick to just hold in his hands as he explored the next game arena.

Sen didn't leave his room. He stood by the door, his arms folded.

"Is there something you need?" Kellan asked.

"You never answered my question."

"What does it matter what I did with your sister? Are you her chastity belt?"

Sen clenched his jaw. He seemed to fumble with his words for a moment as he said, "I-I just want to know. So that I'm not surprised by anything in the future. Your actions have surprised me a bit. You're not *exactly* like your alternate-self."

"Yeah, you never know what I might do." Kellan walked over to Sen, grabbed his shoulder, and then shoved him toward the door of his room. Sen feebly fought back, but it was clear he was gangly and awkward, like he wasn't used to his new, teen body. Sarcastically, Kellan added, "You never know. You're handsome now. I might be after you."

Sen's face shifted to a bright red, his ears practically strawberries. Kellan shoved him out of the room before he could find any more words. Then he shut the door with a slam, hoping to make his point.

After waiting a few moments—to make sure Sen wouldn't return—Kellan headed over to his bed. He glanced down at the sheets, hoping they were magical.

Unfortunately, they weren't. Just plain sheets. No strange sleep properties, no abilities he could exploit.

After a short exhale, Kellan sat down on the edge of the mattress.

He felt… worked up, after having his conversation with Xiang. He didn't like the way she conducted herself. It was as if she had read the playbook for being a *honeypot* and decided to make that her entire personality.

Something about her was off.

Her abilities, her attitude, her distant demeanor.

Kellan glared at the far wall, his thoughts drifting.

There are apparently games that require someone to die. Sen just admitted that. And the games get more difficult as we go along, with even-numbered rounds being extra difficult for the hell of it.

He rested his elbows on his knees, leaning forward and exhaling.

Xiang's mother was the sole victor for her team. Coincidence? Or is Xiang treating her whole team as though she expects we're all going to die eventually? That would explain why she keeps herself at a distance and wants everyone else to do the dirty work. But Husker and Sen both seem to think highly of her—neither think they're going to die.

Kellan glanced over at the TV.

The Nexus had other programming, but Kellan didn't care. He watched as Bitso slammed his hand on his desk and reported on the games. The sound was still muted, but Kellan could see the other players fighting for their lives in the background.

Kellan positioned himself at the foot of the bed and decided to watch in silence.

He took note of individuals with numbers on the backs of their hands.

Players from Team 16. And Team 90. And Team 62.

It seemed that the majority of players were human. The second most common were rennic. Then rezrah—the lizard people with the scaled tails—and then niav, the bird people. Kellan paid special attention to the magics they used as they fought twisted monsters in the game.

Patterns…

He had been trained to spot patterns.

The human players didn't seem to have a preference for a certain magic. They were as varied with their abilities as they were with their clothing choices. Kellan couldn't get a beat on them.

But the rennic had a pattern. Most of them seemed to have abilities revolving around earth, fire, and plants. Some grew things. Others molded stone, or had armored skin, like Mavis. Which meant they tended to favor wyld and magma magics.

What did that mean?

Kellan rubbed at his chin as he watched the lizard people.

The rezrah were similar-looking to humans. They had the same human faces, heads, and chests, but their arms and legs were covered in scales. They had claws, both on their feet and hands. And then, of course, they had tails.

Kellan recognized a rezrah player on one of the screens.

Levvy.

From Team 89.

She had been with Kellan when he had first met the Arbiter. She had destroyed a Pestbyter, and had been set to be executed, but the Arbiter had allowed Kellan to decide her fate. He had spared her, and the rezrah girl had seemed smitten with him ever since.

Kellan paid close attention as he watched her on the screen.

She was lithe, and short, and she moved around with surprising agility. Her scales were copper and shimmered under the light, similar to polished metal. Several times, she almost died—a monster caught her foot, the wall collapsed around her—but each time, she narrowly avoided death, sometimes in comical manners. The monster was eaten by a larger monster. The wall collapsed all *around* Levvy, but not on top of her.

Lucky.

I can't believe she's still alive. Kellan observed her through the second round. *I thought she probably wasn't going to make it. Isn't she Team 89's Straggler?*

All the rezrah he observed, except for Levvy, seemed to have similar abilities. They rotted the things they touched and molded metal, similar to Kellan. Most of them also had a laser blast ability, and a few jumped through the shadows.

It seemed the rezrah favored metal, eclipse, and entropy magics.

Kellan decided to turn up the volume. He walked to the TV, fumbled with the buttons on the side, and upped the sound until it was prominent throughout the room. Then he took a seat again.

He didn't have a notebook, but that didn't matter. He could remember the information he was observing, and if it was important, he could write it down later.

Some magical abilities were clearly better than others.

Kellan saw a rennic place his clawed hands on the ground and cause an earthquake that demolished a five-story building.

A magma magic ability?

A rezrah in one round exhaled a black cloud of rotting dust. It killed several people who appeared to choke on it, and it eroded part of a sewer system to the point that the street above it crumbled.

Entropy magic.

The more advanced the ability, the more devastation it could do.

Kellan's gold arcana had allowed him to develop better magical abilities than most. If he gathered enough, would he have abilities like his enemies, just at lower ranks and lower costs to himself?

"And look at this chump," Bitso said with a cruel laugh. "He tried to get greedy, but we all know what happens then."

The TV flashed a scene from the Catacomb Maze. A man was running from coffin to coffin, gathering red arcana. He was in the main hallway when the timer was counting down at a rapid rate. Kenzo the chimp opened several coffins, spilling arcana everywhere. Once Kellan and Kenzo ran off, this third man stayed behind to gather up all the excess crystals…

He smiled as he scooped up the arcana.

Bitso smiled wide, pointing to the screen behind his desk. "Avarice is a hilarious thing." He rested on his desk, his arms stretched out. "If that sad sack had made it out of the maze, he would've walked away with seventy-four arcana. Too bad, so sad."

The maze collapsed on the man, killing him instantly.

Seventy-four arcana would help me a lot. Kellan rubbed at his chin. *But unless I'm going to mow down an entire village of Nexus residents, I don't see how I'm going to get that much.*

An odd thought struck Kellan as he watched Bitso just lie on top of his desk.

Bitso had said he wanted to die. He had offered Kellan sixty arcana to do the deed.

Before Kellan could think out the plan any further, the door opened. He turned, ready to shout at Sen and tell him to leave, but he caught his breath when he realized it was Mavis. She smiled at him and then half-laughed.

She's sloshed.

Kellan knew immediately. Her unfocused gaze and slight wobble gave it away.

"Did you have fun?" he asked.

Mavis brushed back some of her dyed purple hair. Then she shrugged. "Husker said we should celebrate. I just went with him. To make sure he didn't get into trouble."

"You've been drinking?"

"Just a little bit. I only drank the things that, uh, I knew what they were." She slowly made her way over to the bed. "There were *so many* drinks that I'd never heard of before. I was a fucking bartender."

Kellan ignored Bitso's reporting to give Mavis his full attention. "I think we should talk. It seems some of the games in the future will require us to kill teammates. I know we haven't talked about the games much, but I think we need to strategize between ourselves."

Mavis took a seat on the mattress right next to him. "Okay. That sounds serious."

"We should also talk about your magics. Xiang and I just went over synergizing abilities with our personal traits. We should look at what you have."

Kellan already knew what she had. His eyes gave him all the information he needed.

Name: Mavis Cartwright
Race: Human
Magics: Magma, Metal
Rank: D, D
Armor Rating: —
Health: 7/7

Stats:

Strength—2
Dexterity—3 [Accurate]
Fortitude—2
Charisma—2
Manipulation—2
Intelligence—3
Perception—4 [Mystic]
Wisdom—2
Willpower—4 [Tough]

Abilities:
Personal—[Rebuilt]—The mage can develop their physical stats (strength, dexterity, fortitude) for half the arcana cost.

"You have metal magic, so all the cyborg enhancements should cost you less arcana," Kellan said. "Which means we should—"

Mavis placed a finger on his lips. Kellan stopped speaking, a little baffled by her action.

"I'm not in the right mind space to talk life and death and magic," she muttered. "My thoughts are a little fuzzy." Mavis removed her finger. "We can talk about it in the morning."

"Don't you remember the last two games? They announce the new rounds in the morning. When we wake up, we'll barely have any time to prep for whatever crazy game we'll be assigned."

Mavis rubbed at her face. Then she combed back her hair and gave Kellan an odd glance. "Why aren't you wearing a shirt?"

"It got blood on it."

"Uh-huh. Why are you wet?"

He snorted and smirked. "That sounds like *my* line."

It took Mavis a long moment to get the joke. When she finally grasped the punchline, she chuckled. "I forgot how corny you are sometimes."

"I warned you. To quote my therapist… *Kellan, these constant jokes are a metaphorical barrier that prevents you from forming meaningful relationships.*"

That had Mavis laughing more. After a few moments, she calmed down, still smiling, her face slightly red. "I think… I'm going to vomit."

Kellan blinked once. Then he motioned to the bathroom door. "You want me to hold your hair back for you?"

"No." Mavis got off the bed, shaky at first, but then she steadied herself. "I'm a good soldier. I've done this rodeo before." She wandered into the bathroom, closed the door, and then turned on the sink water. It didn't cover the sound of her retching.

When Mavis was done, she exited the bathroom with a towel in one hand. She seemed paler than before, her eyes narrowed into a glare. "Fuckin' worms," she whispered.

Kellan lifted an eyebrow. Mavis showed him the towel. It was stained with vomit, and several yellow Tyranny Worms writhed around the cloth.

"I'll get rid of them," Kellan stated. "One way or another."

Mavis stumbled over to the bed. She threw the towel into the corner of the room before flopping down on the mattress. After a long exhale, she glanced at Kellan. "I met my ex one night after I had been drinking. I woke up in his bed the next morning, and we started dating after that." She sighed. "You don't seem interested."

Kellan scooted back on the mattress and lay down next to her. "You're putting me in an awkward position. They forced me to watch *Sexual Harassment and You: How NOT to Get Charged with Assault* on fourteen different occasions, and I'm pretty sure there's an entire section dedicated to girls who are slightly tipsy."

Mavis giggled as she slid over and placed her face against his shoulder. She mumbled into his arm, "Oh, my God, you *do* use jokes as barriers."

"Well, let's be real—your ex left you because you were scarred and in the hospital for a while. Sounds like a delta-bravo if I ever heard of one. It's a safe bet to do everything the exact opposite of him."

Mavis laughed some more as she wrapped her arms around Kellan's chest. "Fine. Let's… just take a nap for a little bit. And when we wake up… we can discuss the games."

Although Kellan was awake and wanted to review the video footage of the previous games, he nodded. "All right."

Mavis kissed his shoulder and closed her eyes. Kellan didn't complain. He snuggled close to her, hating the fact that they hadn't gotten under the blankets.

He closed his eyes and listened to the sounds of celebration all throughout the AVU Palace. Just a quick nap wouldn't hurt.

Would it?

—Chapter 18—
—The Third Game—

When Kellan opened his eyes, it was raining.

The beat of the water thumped across the windows and the roof of the palace. Mavis was tangled around his arm, so fast asleep, she didn't even move when Kellan sat up. He ran a hand down his face and exhaled, unsure what time it was.

The TV was still on.

Bitso was in his typical newsroom, but the TVs behind his desk flickered with silent static. He lay across his desk, his blindfold once again stained red with blood. His hair—which was its own dark shade of crimson—was matted and clumped to one side. He looked more drunk than an entire football team after the winning game.

With his head on the desk, Bitso spoke with little enthusiasm. "It's 8am. Today's forecast… It will be rainy."

The beating of water on the windows reminded Kellan that the weather in Nexus-Fayetteville was just bizarre compared to his home dimension. He scooted to the edge of the bed, sore from the awkward night's sleep next to Mavis. She had refused to allow him to move around.

"Rain is just the death of the clouds," Bitso muttered onto his desk. "Their blood cascading onto the world, only to be brought to the sky a second time, reborn as another nimbus, probably far weaker and more disgusting than before."

Kellan had absolutely no idea what Bitso was going on about. The dark atmosphere outside obstructed his view of the sun. Was it morning? Or still the middle of the night?

The lack of music disturbed him.

Probably morning.

Kellan stood and headed to the bathroom. As quickly as he could, he washed and readied himself. Where were his clothes? His backpack? *My bag has the Summoning Chime in it…* Kellan gritted his teeth, frustrated he hadn't been able to spend more time last night discussing strategies with the others. *Why do I always do this?*

He wondered if the AVU Palace had some sort of magical presence that made it easier to sleep. He wouldn't have been surprised if that were the case.

Once Kellan had exited the bathroom, he noticed Bitso was still on his desk on TV, no life in his movements. Corpses had more charisma.

"The third games are about to begin," Bitso said, a pool of drool forming around the corner of his mouth. "Aren't you all excited? The third round is special… During this game, teams can *lose* their keys. What a shame."

Kellan held his breath as he approached the television.

"There are three games to choose from. The first is *Escort*."

Bitso didn't move from his spot. He spoke into the metal desk as though he were just speaking to himself. The static TVs in the background flashed with images, however. Footage of the games played on a loop, displaying what Bitso discussed.

"Escort is a fan favorite. Not for the teams playing it—but for the people watching." Bitso smiled, his squished cheek disturbing the drool puddle. "Each team will have to make their way to the center of the play arena. There, they'll find their doll. They must escort the doll out of the arena. *Safely*, mind you. Any doll that's destroyed means the team automatically loses."

Kellan didn't like the sound of this game at all.

Bitso laughed. With each new breath, he seemed to gain renewed interest and energy. He sat up, straightened his white tie, and then leaned back in his swivel chair. "Oh, yes. The dolls… So fragile. The real charm of this game is watching the teams try to smash each other's precious, precious dolls. You see, if a team loses their doll, they lose a key. If a team keeps the doll intact but fails to bring the doll to safety in the time limit, nothing happens. *But*—if they manage to safely transport their doll, the team gains a brand-new shiny key, and then they're one step closer to winning the Nexus Games."

The thought of escorting a fragile doll to any location had Kellan's imagination running wild with all sorts of terrible scenarios. *Escort* sounded like one of the worst games to play.

"*Escort* is also a PvP game," Bitso said, tapping the tips of his fingers together. "Which, for the slow ones in the audience, means that the players can fight each other without consequences."

Kellan kept his attention on the TVs in the background of the news show. Teams were huddled around each other, forming circles as they rushed through an island setting. The many beaches and trees were an odd juxtaposition to the death in the background. Gunfire, magic use, and explosions were frequent enough to ruin the peaceful atmosphere of the island setting.

The dolls…

They weren't dolls at all.

The teams were all carrying puppies. Actual, live, *puppies*. And they were defending them from an onslaught of attacks. The environment seemed out to get them. Yami seagulls, traps in the water—Kellan could already see the game was going to be a shitshow.

But Kellan agreed with Bitso. It would be hilarious to watch people running from one side of an island to another while protecting a small puppy from a horde of killer opponents. Great TV.

"The next option for *round three* will be a simple game of *Davie's Gauntlet.*" Bitso circled his chair around, smiling wider than before. "*Everyone* loves Davie's Gauntlet. Each team that picks this option will have to run down five floors of deadly obstacles. This game of physical prowess demands focus. The teams will only have ten minutes to complete everything. And for every teammate they lose, they will lose a key. A thrilling and wild ten minutes that'll be sure to give anyone gray hairs!"

Sweet Baby Jesus.

Kellan watched the TVs in the background play footage of obstacle courses straight out of a horror movie. Large rooms with rusty saws and blades. Machine spiders clung to the walls and ceiling, attacking teams who tried to make their way from one door to the next. They were the size of adult men, their needle-legs stabbing into people as they tried to avoid the traps.

It was a nightmare scenario.

But…

Kellan was confident he could make it through *most* of an obstacle course without much problem. His magics were suited for it. He could mold metal, dive into the shadows… He wouldn't even need ten minutes.

But the others weren't as lucky. Could Sen, the awkward, gangly teenager, run through a room of sawblades and monsters? Probably not.

Bitso shrugged. "At least it's a PvE game, am I right? No one fights each other then—you'll be too busy fighting the clock. What an intense game! Definitely one of my favorites." Bitso turned to face the TV behind him. He rubbed at his blindfold as he watched someone's arm get cut clean from their body. "Oh, what I wouldn't give to be part of a team…"

Then he quickly swiveled back around.

Kellan flinched when Bitso slammed his hand on the desk.

"The last game offered this time around will be *Spin and Win.* You know the game. You spin the wheel, and whatever you land on, you win."

Bitso snapped his fingers. The screens played short clips of individuals spinning a terrible wooden wheel. It was a rickety device that squeaked as it went round and round. The clicking of a little dial indicated the prize.

Click-click-click-click-click… click… click…

The prizes on the wheel weren't written in English. The lettering was strange—similar to Chinese hanzi, but clearly more complex and woven together. When the wheel stopped and the player gasped, Kellan had no idea what they had won.

"Oh, what a shame," Bitso said with a frown. "They won a key."

The person on the screen screamed and flailed their arms as a Pestbyter floated into the camera's range and handed them a key.

It appeared to be a USB device.

Kellan chuckled to himself.

That was an awful game of chance. No doubt several places on the wheel were things like *Instant Death* and *Lose All Your Keys.*

"That's it," Bitso said with a smirk. "Those three options. Remember that the team leaders will pick the game they want to participate in, and that you need to make your decision within the next hour." He twirled around in his seat again. "The Stragglers will have to deal with Kuji no matter the game you play! Even *Spin and Win*. And trust me, the Kuji are very hungry. They can't wait to be let loose into the game arenas."

Kellan really didn't like the Kuji. He had only seen them twice, and both had been horrifying experiences. They were the ultimate nightmare fuel—the monster that every child imagined when they pictured the thing under their bed.

But out of all the games listed as options…

The best one for them was likely the *Escort* game.

It's such a terrible game. Kellan rubbed at his chin as he paced around the room. *But Xiang's illusions could help us. Then again, Ysa said that Team 42 had a way to deal with the illusions.*

Kellan stopped walking and stared at the rain.

Maybe Team 42 will pick a different game.

A soft knock on the door caught Kellan's attention. He jogged over, his heart beating faster than he liked. When he opened it, Husker stood on the other side, looming over Kellan with his considerable height. Husker's fox ears twitched as he shoved Kellan's backpack, rifle, and a set of clothing toward him.

"You humans sleep in too late," Husker growled.

Kellan took his gear and the new clothing and held them close. With a smirk, he asked, "Rennic don't sleep much?"

"We wake up when there's work to be done."

"I normally wake up just fine, but ever since I've gotten to this place… I don't know how to describe it." Kellan rubbed at his head. "Before, I would have nightmares or wake at the sound of a spider moving across its web. Now there's nothing."

Husker relaxed a bit. He scratched at his canine snout with his claws. "It's because you're a new mage. Your magic is like a new muscle. You're just getting used to it." He snorted and motioned to the main room. "Come. We should discuss the games and our tactics. Wake Mavis."

Once Husker had left, Kellan shut the door. He threw the backpack down on the bed and examined his clothing. A new shirt, a jacket, cargo pants, and boots. No socks—Kellan wondered if the rennic had a dislike for socks—but he could make do.

As Mavis slept, Kellan stripped off his sweatpants and quickly dressed in his new attire. It fit, which was all he needed. Then he checked the backpack, pleased to find the Summoning Chime still within. He touched the curious little bell sphere, making sure it was real.

But who to summon?

Kellan knew he needed to discuss it with the others.

His backpack also contained some hane cigarettes, a pack of jerky, a KA-BAR knife, a lighter, the Nexus Games Rule Book, and some rope. Husker had clearly gone out of his way to make sure Kellan would have everything he needed for the next game.

I need to thank the man at some point.

Kellan then walked over to Mavis's side of the bed and gently shook her shoulder. She was a new mage, too. Perhaps Husker was right. They just needed more rest to acclimate to their new magical powers.

Mavis fluttered her eyes open and then glanced up at Kellan. The soft patter of rain sounded through the room, occasionally interrupted by Bitso's news report.

"Is it time already?" Mavis asked.

Kellan nodded. "On your feet, soldier."

Without even a stretch, Mavis got to her feet and stood straight, the years of active duty plain to see in her movements. Kellan smirked and gave an approving nod. Mavis replied with a quiet once-over, admiring his black jacket and cargo pants.

"You got dressed without me," she said.

Kellan snorted. "I didn't know it was a team activity."

She stepped close, leaned onto his chest, and then got to her tiptoes. "Well, let me thank you for being a gentleman last night."

"I don't think we have time for—"

Mavis gently pressed her lips on the side of his neck, offering a brief kiss. He smiled, but she ended the show of affection as quickly as she had started it.

"I understand," she said as she jogged to the bathroom. "We have the games to get ready for." Mavis stopped at the bathroom door. "I'll be out in a second."

Bitso slammed his hand on his desk, distracting Kellan for a moment.

"Remember that each game has the chance for great rewards." He rubbed two of his fingers together. "Hidden rooms throughout the game arena have been placed to spice things up. The Arbiter loves a good surprise."

Kellan headed out of his room. Bitso continued with his presentation to his empty newsroom.

"And remember, folks, you want to make sure you get your keys before the fifth game. After that, everything will become so much more difficult..."

—Chapter 19—
—A Friendly Offer—

Kellan walked out to the main room of their suite. He had his backpack over one shoulder and held his rifle on the other. His fellow mages weren't as geared out for combat as he was. They waited around the center room, standing near different corners.

It was bizarre seeing Sen as a teenager. Kellan had almost forgotten it was him.

"Why are you staring?" Sen asked, his voice raspy and awkward.

"How did you make yourself older?"

"With the Crafting Clay." Sen rolled his eyes and crossed his arms. "I thought you would've put one and two together."

"You slapped on a foot of height and some extra muscle with a glob of cancer?"

Sen threw back his long black hair and huffed. "I'm a fleshcrafter. I wouldn't expect someone like *you* to understand, but it's not the physical proportion of the flesh that matters. Crafting Clay is a representation of the raw body magic. The clay can be used to reverse some of my de-aging."

Kellan wasn't about to argue with the man. If he could somehow turn a tumor lump into ten years of growth, more power to him. Kellan didn't care.

Throughout the conversation, Husker carefully packed away some supplies of his own. He stuffed the large pockets of his trench coat with food, hane, and a couple of small vials, and he even packed a small bag and set it on the coffee table. The entire time, the rattle of chains accompanied his movements. The weird restraints—iron manacles and bindings—were hidden under his coat. They still had room to clack against each other.

Despite Husker's large, clawed hands, he was careful with the smaller items. The vials were the size of one of his claws, but he gently placed them in the inner pocket of his coat.

"Thank you for doing this," Kellan said, motioning to the supplies. "Where are you getting everything?"

"I got the food from the kitchens," Husker said. "But since the Exchange is open, I gathered together a few potions. Mana restoration, and one for healing. I didn't have much to trade, but I got us things."

The Exchange...

Kellan hadn't thought to return, but it wasn't a bad idea. Did he have time before the start of the next game? Probably not. He would have to visit it after the fact.

"We must win the games," Husker muttered as he stood straight, his coat all packed. "There are no other options for us. It's either go hard or go straight to the grave."

Xiang casually paced the length of the balcony door. Water streamed down the glass as the rain continued unabated. She didn't glance at the others or even add to the conversation. She stared out into the distance—in the same direction she had last night.

Unlike last night, she wore an ankle-length leather jacket, heels, and a black dress. Kellan would've considered it clubbing attire, nothing appropriate for a *death game*, but it all could have been illusion. There was a chance she was wearing nothing.

That wouldn't be useful, either, but Kellan couldn't get the thought out of his head.

Xiang's long, black hair was tied up, several strands flaring out in a semicircle, like a sun crest. Her striking appearance distracted Kellan more than he liked to admit. So far, he hadn't met anyone in the Nexus Games who even came close to her elegant beauty.

A soft knock at the door drew everyone's attention.

Kellan walked to the front door of the suite. Everyone else tensed and waited, no words between them. When Kellan glanced out into the hall, he found Alvo and Juan standing before him. The misshapen set of conjoined twins waved one of their tiny hands. Then they handed Kellan a letter in a dyed yellow envelope.

"Good morning," Alvo whispered. "Nosferatu wanted me to give you this."

Kellan took the envelope and turned it over in his hand. On one side, written in perfect English, were the words:

For Alex Kellan, of Team 101

"Thank you," Kellan said.

"I hope you do well in the games today."

"So do I."

Alvo and Juan lingered, their two heads and mismatched gazes glancing around the hall. But they didn't offer anything else, not even words.

Kellan stepped back into the suite and then closed the door. He wasn't sure what to say to Alvo and Juan, other than the simple statements. Anxiety gripped him as he tore open the envelope. The letter inside was just as neatly written as the text on the outside.

Alex Kellan,

Have your team join the Davie's Gauntlet this round. It's PvE, which means we can cooperate without interference, and most obstacles are technological in nature. My mastery of metal magic makes this a simple game for me to complete. I can ensure Team 101 victory as well.

N

Only signed "N," huh?

Kellan turned the paper over and found nothing on the back.

"Well?" Sen demanded. "What is it?"

"It's a letter from Nosferatu, of Team 5. He wants us to join the Davie's Gauntlet. He says he'll help us."

Husker walked over and took the letter. Then he strode across the massive room and handed the piece of paper to Xiang. With a delicate touch, she took the note and examined it. A half second of contemplation, and she tossed it back at Husker.

"No," she said. "It's a ruse."

"How can you be so certain?" Kellan asked.

"Nosferatu is a Nexus resident. They hate outsiders—haven't you listened to their radio announcements? Or seen their programs on TV? If they can, the residents torture outsiders." Xiang resumed her steady pacing. She grazed her fingers across the glass doors to the balcony. "And Nosferatu asked for nothing in return. All he wants is our compliance. All the hallmarks of a poorly laid trap. If we agreed, we would deserve the fate he has planned for us."

Kellan walked over to the side of the couch and crossed his arms. "He told me he appreciated the fact that I was helping the Nexus locals. He might want to trust us. Legitimately. And he probably didn't require anything on our part as a show of that trust."

"You're a fool if you think a few random instances of kindness would change his mind." Xiang stopped and turned, her eyes narrowed in a glower. "Outsiders kill the residents for arcana. It's been happening since the very first Nexus Games. Millions of Nexus locals dead at the hands of dimension travelers. That kind of blood, hate, and fear won't disappear so easily."

Killing the residents since the first games?

Kellan held his breath for a moment, wondering if the Arbiter was so cruel as to create a race of people *meant* to be slaughtered for arcana. Would the dragon do that? Kellan wasn't sure. It sounded fucked up, but everything in the Nexus seemed along those lines.

"I spoke with him," Kellan said, trying to think of an argument.

"My mother killed hundreds of his kind," Xiang stated matter-of-factly. "I assure you, Nosferatu wants me dead, and he's trying to bring our whole team down by getting to me through you. Don't be a fool."

There weren't any more arguments Kellan could cobble together. He didn't know Nosferatu *that* well, and it was true—outsiders killed the residents at an alarming rate.

"We shouldn't entangle ourselves with that leper," Sen stated.

Husker nodded. "I agree. He's not to be trusted."

"The Davie's Gauntlet game is PvE," Kellan offered, his last argument for the matter. "He can't attack us during the game. What's the harm of trying?"

Sen held up a finger. "He can't attack us, but he can certainly trick us. All it would take is for him to say, *stand over here, you'll be safe.* Only then—" Sen slapped his hands together in a dramatic smack, "—*boom*! The ceiling crushes us. Or a Kuji gets lucky."

Although Kellan would've preferred to make allies, he said nothing. Technically, any number of teams could win the Nexus Games, so why not ally? But if Nosferatu was looking for arcana, tricking the team into certain death would be an easy way to empower himself.

"We'll be playing the *Escort* game," Xiang stated. Then she returned her attention to the world beyond the balcony door. "We have the greatest chance of victory then. And even if we fail, as long as we don't have our doll broken, we'll maintain the number of keys we have."

"I thought you didn't want to play beyond round five?" Sen asked, his brow furrowed.

"I don't. But game five will likely have several ways to win keys we've missed—completing sub-games within the game. So as long as we live through these rounds, I'm confident we can still complete the game as quickly as I had hoped."

A door opened, and Mavis stepped out into the main room. She wore a pair of ripped jeans, a T-shirt, and a heavy coat. Her boots had been scuffed—probably during the challenge round—but they were still durable. She glanced between everyone and then walked to Kellan's side.

"What's going on?" Mavis whispered. "Why is everyone so tense?"

"We'll be playing *Escort* for our next game," Kellan replied.

Mavis grimaced and stared at him with wide eyes. "S-Seriously?"

He snorted and laughed. "Not *that* kind of escort. I mean we'll be taking a doll from one location to another. If it gets broken, we fail *and* lose a key. If we fail to deliver it, we get nothing."

"A doll?"

"The *doll* was a live puppy last time, so who knows what we'll get this go-around. I suspect something breathing, but helpless. Makes the escorting part of the game all the more difficult."

Husker's ears twitched. Then he smiled, his fangs visible. "That's right. Makes it easy to tell if the doll is *broken*, too. If it's still alive, we're fine, but the moment it stops breathing, we've lost."

"So, what will be our strategy?" Sen asked. He glanced around the room and frowned. "We have enough time to at least discuss it. Obviously, illusions will help. We can pick up a rock and make it look like our doll, whatever it happens to be. If we hide the real doll in a backpack, enemy teams won't be able to get a surprise attack."

"Our enemies know about Xiang's illusions," Kellan stated. "Team 42 is ready, apparently."

"But not *every* team will be ready!" Sen huffed and shook his head. "Most other teams are varied in skill and competence. They were formed because they were *outsiders caught in the Conflux*—people teleported to the Nexus against their will. They may be playing the games now, but they probably aren't strategizing as much as Team 42."

Kellan shrugged. "Then what's our strategy if we run into a competent team? What will we do if we're facing Team 42?"

The silence that followed his question unnerved Kellan. They didn't have any other options? No other tactics or tricks up their sleeves?

"I'll handle any problems that come our way," Husker finally stated. He rattled his chains as if to make the point. "That's why I'm here. I'll use my hex to kill the powerful mages who might target us."

"So, our plan is to stick together during this game?" Kellan asked. "All five of us?"

Everyone glanced over at Xiang. She was the team leader, after all. She had been calling the shots the entire time. Her hesitance to answer wasn't reassuring, however.

"The five of us will travel together to the center of the game arena." Xiang paused for a moment, her gaze on the floor. "Once we've gathered the real doll, we'll split up. Two of us will hide the doll and quietly take it to the goal. The other three of you will draw attention with the fake doll. When other teams come to attack, you'll kill them. But if ever you're in trouble, drop the decoy and run. I suspect most teams will attempt to break the doll before pursuing, to ensure we, as a team, lose a key."

It wasn't a bad plan, but Kellan had a feeling the Arbiter was going to throw in a few curve balls before the event was over. However, without any other information, he was at a loss for what to add to the strategy.

"Who will be the team with the fake doll?" he asked.

"You, Husker, and Sen," Xiang stated. "Myself and…" She glanced over at Mavis and frowned. "… our *other* warrior, will take the real doll to safety."

"You wouldn't want to stay with us and use your illusions to trick enemy teams?"

"If I die, our whole team fails."

The last statement left a powerful impact. It meant she thought there was a chance the other team might run into deadly complications. But that was fine—Kellan agreed with her statement. If Xiang died, they would fail, so it was best to keep her out of harm's way.

"I think we're ready, then," Husker stated.

"I've finalized my decision," Xiang said. "The Arbiter knows where we need to go."

Which was perfect timing, as Kellan felt the terrible pull of teleportation take hold of his insides. In a flash, he was removed from the AVU Palace and transported to the game arena.

—Chapter 20—
—Escort Mission—

Kellan stumbled forward and immediately shivered back the rush of cold wind.

He glanced around, hefted his rifle, and took deep breaths. His surroundings were a shock at first, but he quickly calmed a bit. He stood in the middle of a residential street, on the broken yellow lines of a US road. But the darkness and clean skies told him he wasn't anywhere near Nexus-Fayetteville. This was someplace different—far from the East Coast, perhaps all the way on the other side of the continent.

Or perhaps not.

It was an alternate-dimension, and Kellan wasn't entirely sure of the properties. He knew for a fact the time was different. It had been 8am back at the AVU Palace, but in this new location, the sun was far from rising.

Despite the darkness, Kellan examined his surroundings. His eclipse magic made it so that the darkness no longer obscured his vision. And it empowered him, adding to his physical strength, dexterity, and fortitude. He preferred himself with the empowerments.

This was… a wealthy residential area. The McMansions lined both sides of the street, each with their own fence and privacy hedges. Perfectly cut grass and trimmed shrubbery decorated the vast lawns. Most houses were two stories, and those that weren't took up more space than any normal house would have.

The streetlights occasionally flickered to life, but for the most part, they remained dead and useless.

As Kellan glanced around, a red shimmer streaked across the sky.

The Net.

A deadly barrier that kept all the players *inside* the play arena until the game was done.

It was a dome that stretched from one side of the massive unknown city, all the way to the other. Kellan couldn't even see where the edges of the Net touched down, but he knew he was close to one end. If he touched the Net, even just slightly, he would die. Or at least, that was what he had been told.

A bird shot out of a tree in the distance. Just for good measure, it confirmed all of Kellan's musing. It flew straight into the shimmering, wicked red and then exploded into a puff of feathers and gore.

Convenient.

Kellan glanced up at the street sign. The words were written in Sanskrit. The writing was rather distinct, and Kellan had seen it multiple times when studying historical languages. It wasn't really used anymore… Yet here it was.

When he turned around, he spotted the other members of his team. Husker, Xiang, Sen, and Mavis stood around on different points on the road, dazed for a moment as they regained their balance.

The darkness hindered all of them, however. Their eyes were unfocused as they glanced around.

Kellan walked over to Mavis and placed a hand on her shoulder. She jumped and pulled her handgun out of its holster all in one motion.

"It's me," Kellan stated. "We're in the game."

"Where are we?" Mavis lowered her weapon. "It's not raining."

"We're in some sort of city."

Their conversation drew the others closer. The click of Xiang's heels echoed down the empty road. Kellan took a moment to inspect the nearby driveways. No cars. Not a single one. Had the Arbiter made sure there would be no functioning vehicles in the game arena, or were they just hidden?

Much to the surprise of everyone, a TV flickered to life, its bright-white static screen cutting through the darkness of the early morning. It was mounted to the side of a mailbox, wires and cords tangled around the wooden post and leading straight to a hole in the cement of the sidewalk.

Why was there a TV in the middle of nowhere?

It was crooked, slanted to one side, but it eventually showed a crisp and clear picture.

Bitso and his newsroom were nowhere to be seen. Instead, it was the set of a children's show. A few of the Nexus residents were there in a semicircle, facing a man in clown makeup. It was obvious they were residents from the boils across their faces. One boy didn't have any ears. Another girl had a giant forehead and swollen head.

"During this game, the players will only have *ten hours* to get their doll and make it to the designated safety area," the clown-man said.

Was he a resident? Kellan couldn't tell. He wore a mask over his entire head, and the rest of his body was covered in frilled clothing. The rubber mask had eyeholes, but they were too dark, and Kellan couldn't see within. The permanent smile on the mask drooped a bit. It was clear the mask was intended for someone larger, and it barely fit the man correctly.

A child raised their hand. The clown pointed to them.

"Where is the safety area?"

"Good question! The doll museum will have the answer. Every team has to pay close attention, or else they won't figure it out!"

The children clapped and nodded, like this was exciting news tantamount to being served freshly made ice cream. Kellan didn't understand why any of the residents would want to watch the Nexus Games. Was it to see the players die?

Because most of the time, they were just slaughtering Nexus residents.

Not really a kid's show, Kellan thought with a sarcastic laugh.

Then the TV flickered off, casting the whole street back into darkness.

"We should get moving," Xiang said. Then she turned to Kellan and frowned. "You don't have the ability to travel in the shadows with other people, do you?"

"I haven't even seen that ability as an option," Kellan muttered.

"At higher ranks in eclipse magic, you'll see options to modify your shadow-step ability."

"Well, I'm still D-rank."

Sen groaned. "All that arcana, and what have you done with it? I keep telling you to focus!"

Kellan unslung his backpack and rummaged through the contents. He withdrew the Summoning Chime and held the small item in the palm of his hand. It pulsed with inner power, like a slow heartbeat. It was too dark for the others to see, but Husker wrinkled his canine nose.

"What do you have the Chime for?" he asked.

"I can summon Bitso with it." Kellan returned the bag to his shoulder, keeping the Chime close. "He *wants* to die. He said he'd give whoever killed him a good sixty arcana. I thought… maybe it'll be worth it."

The others were silent. Xiang finally crossed her arms. "I think it'll be a waste to use it for sixty arcana… But killing Bitso might have other benefits as well."

"Like what?"

"The man is carrying several magical items on him. I've seen them before, when I've had private conversations with him. They must be powerful. Sixty arcana, *plus* the magic he carries, could be worth giving up our Chime… But we must never tell anyone we used it."

Mavis smirked and chuckled. "Oh. I get it. The good 'ol *unloaded gun still scares people* trick. You want everyone to think we can use the Chime."

"Exactly."

"So…" Kellan turned the Chime over in his palm. "Should I use it?"

Sen fidgeted with his hoodie. He didn't say anything, however. He just stared with an ever-increasing discomfort.

Finally, Xiang nodded. "Do it. The rest of us should be prepared, though. I think it'll take more than one strike to kill him."

The excitement got to Kellan. He smiled to himself as he lifted the Chime, his hand shaking with anticipation. Why was he so anxious? The thought of using a powerful magical item to gain quick rewards almost seemed like cheating. And the thought of helping Bitso—even if Kellan would've preferred to just help him escape—made everything seem worth doing.

"Bitso," he said, thinking the man's name while calling it out.

The Summoning Chime *dinged* with a sound and pressure like a gong. It was small, yet somehow, the sound reverberated off the nearby McMansions and even shook the TV screen. The *ding* that followed was harsh and sharp, a musical note that seemed to pierce every frequency.

Then the sound and vibrations suddenly stopped.

Kellan's palm burned slightly. He tightened his grip on the Chime and pulled it close to examine it.

The words across the top were a message…

Invalid Target

Invalid target? Kellan almost scoffed. Why was Bitso an invalid target?

"What happened?" Sen demanded.

"I can't summon him," Kellan replied. "The Chime said Bitso can't be called."

Was Bitso a participant in the Nexus Games? It was the most logical conclusion—the Chime couldn't summon other Nexus Games participants, after all. That bummed Kellan out, though. He had thought this was a clever idea, and now he was just disappointed.

"Well, we still have the Chime for the game," Husker said with a snort. "It's not wasted, right?"

"Yeah. We still have it."

Xiang held out a delicate hand. "Give it to me."

Kellan tightened his grip on the object. "I'm the only one who can use it."

"I know, but I don't want you to have it while you're distracting other teams with your fake doll. It can still be *taken* from you, and if it's with me, I can disguise it."

There was a long moment of silence. Those were all good points, but Kellan still didn't feel right about parting with the Chime. What if he needed it? After all, if he died, no one could use it anymore, so he might as well have it just in case of an emergency.

The scratch of claws on a nearby rooftop got everyone tense. Kellan wheeled on his heel and glanced over to the nearest house. Someone was scrabbling over the tiles, barely clinging to the slanted surface.

A woman.

Kellan recognized the lucky rezrah. Levvy. His eyes filled in the rest of the information.

Name: Levvy Torrin
Race: Rezrah
Magics: —
Rank: —
Armor Rating: —
Health: 7/7

Stats:
Strength—2
Dexterity—2
Fortitude—2 [Scaled]
Charisma—2

Manipulation—2
Intelligence—2
Perception—3 [Keen-eyed]
Wisdom—2
Willpower—2

Abilities:
Personal—[Vampiric Fangs]—The rezrah can drain mana from a target whenever making a bite attack that deals damage.
Half-Mage Power—[Lucky]—The half-mage has fortunate events happen to them (once per fifteen minutes) in minor and major ways.

She ran to the chimney and then glanced around. Her eyes went wide when she spotted Kellan and the others. Levvy didn't call out, though. She went still and quiet, like a cat who didn't want to be caught.

"What's going on?" Mavis whispered.

Kellan reluctantly handed Xiang the Chime. "I'll go check it out. I'll be back in a moment." Then he jogged over to the fence, hopped over, and strode across the perfect lawn.

Levvy watched the entire time, her eyes wide. Her clawed hands clung to the bricks of the chimney, and she didn't move a muscle.

Without giving away that he could see her just fine in the dark, Kellan made his way around the side of the house, as though investigating. Levvy remained quiet, the shadows her friend. But they were also Kellan's ally, and the moment he was out of her sight, he dove into the darkness and slithered his way onto the roof. A few seconds later, Kellan emerged on the tiles, just on the other side of the chimney.

His sudden appearance caused her to flinch. Her clawed feet scratched the roof as she steadied herself. With quick breaths, she dug her claws into the bricks of the chimney.

Kellan placed a finger to his lips.

Levvy quieted down. Her copper scales matched her tanned skin, and her short, black hair defied gravity. She stared with amber eyes.

"Alex Kellan," she whispered.

"What're you doing here?" he asked.

"I heard… the sound of a Summoning Chime. My team told me to investigate and report back."

Kellan caught his breath, stunned that the sound of the Chime had apparently carried a few streets over. Had the whole game arena heard? Did they all think that Kellan had used his Chime?

"Did you… Did you summon someone?" Levvy asked.

"No. I tried, but it didn't work."

"Ah. I see." She exhaled and placed a hand on her chest. The number 89 was emblazoned on her skin—along with the picture of a skull. "I was worried. I saw you on the screens in the AVU Palace. I thought the men there would try to convince you to summon the Tyrant King."

Kellan half-shrugged. "Well, I don't know many names. If Xiang's mother used the guy to win, I'm sure he could do the same for me."

With her eyes wide, Levvy shook her head. "You shouldn't. That man is disgusting. You should summon someone noble and just and beyond powerful."

The statement had Kellan intrigued. Although his team waited for him on the dark road, obviously confused by what was happening, Kellan decided to investigate just a little more. The rest of his team could wait a few minutes.

"You come from a dimension with mages, right?" Kellan whispered.

Levvy nodded.

"Which mage would you summon?"

"Councilor Zero." She moved closer to the chimney and smiled. She had vampire-style fangs that stood out to Kellan, even at night. "He's powerful and cunning, and much better than the Tyrant King, Ygg'Exos."

Kellan recognized the name *Councilor Zero*. "Bitso said he was an *edgelord* who infused his blood with the void of black stars or some shit."

"What?" Levvy's scales practically stood on end as her voice increased in volume. "Councilor Zero is a legend. H-He fought with Ygg'Exos! They used to be friends, but that bastard king tricked Councilor Zero and threw him from their nation! Ygg'Exos had Zarr Mantis's name removed from every book and public document and claimed he had never been a councilor of Psi, and that's why Mantis changed his name. He wanted to remind everyone that *he* was the first councilor, not Ygg'Exos!"

Her actual yelling was loud enough that Husker on the road started walking toward the house. Kellan held up a hand and shushed her.

"*Quiet*," Kellan hissed. "I got it. Those two don't like each other. They had a big beef. It resulted in weird names. Glory to the old country." He was sarcastic through all his statements, but Levvy didn't seem to catch on. She nodded along with every word.

"Yes," she muttered. "Glory to the old country! That's a good phrase."

Husker walked across the lawn, heading straight for the front porch.

Kellan motioned to the back yard. "Maybe you should leave. I don't think the rest of my team is going to be keen on letting you live."

"Oh?" Levvy slinked down and slid across a portion of the roof, heading toward the back yard. "Thank you, Alex Kellan. Merry Christmas! I hope to see you at the end of the game."

"Yeah. Maybe we can talk more then."

Levvy used her scaled tail to help keep her balance as she leapt off the roof and landed on the grass. Then she quietly made her way across the property, leaving Kellan alone atop the McMansion.

"Kellan?" Husker called up. "Are you there? I heard voices."

"I'm here." Kellan stepped into the darkness, traveled through the shadows, and stepped out close to Husker. He was still empowered, and he rotated his arms, reveling in the power that coursed through him. "We can go."

"Did you find someone?" Husker asked.

"I chased them off. Don't worry about it."

The rennic snorted, his ears half-back. "Very well. Xiang says we should hurry. We want to be one of the first teams to discover the center of the game arena."

"All right." Kellan pointed to the street. "I'll lead the way."

—Chapter 21—
—Laser Beams—

Kellan met with the others on the street. Since he was the only one capable of seeing through the darkness, he led the way. Husker stayed close to him, his ears and nose occasionally twitching. Sen and Xiang stuck together like only siblings could. Mavis brought up the rear, not able to see much, her skin already hardened with pebbles from her magma magic.

As they walked down the residential road, Kellan noticed several TVs, computers, wires, and other electronics in the strangest of places. A tree in the front yard of a large home had a tire swing with a radio hanging from it. Another home had a computer system mounted into the wall. One place had a set of speakers jutting out of the perfectly mowed lawn.

The Nexus was a bizarre amalgamation of multiple dimensions, all squished together. It reminded Kellan of an *everything sandwich*. Peanut butter, jelly, salami, potato chips—even a knife—all crammed together between two different types of bread.

The group remained as quiet as they could.

Xiang was the loudest, her heels always clicking.

While they walked, Kellan mulled over his encounter with Levvy. He hadn't met anyone else from Team 89, and he didn't know if he wanted to. When Kellan glanced over at Husker, he took note of the skull marking on the back of his hand.

The skull marked people as the team's Straggler. The Kuji would hunt the Straggler throughout the game until they were dead. Then the skull marking would move to another member of the team, and the cycle would start all over again.

"What's wrong?" Husker whispered. His breath came out as a fine mist.

"Can rezrah see in the dark?" Kellan asked. He didn't want to discuss the grim reality of eventual death. "The person I chased away was a rezrah. It seemed as though she could see."

"Yeah, they can. Their kind likes to live in dark places. Far northern places, where the sun rarely shines."

"Aren't they lizard people? They're not cold-blooded?"

Husker snorted and laughed. Then he glanced over, smiling a toothy smile.

"*Lizard-people*. Yeah, they kinda look that way, don't they? A disgusting lot. I don't think they're cold-blooded, though."

"Not a fan of rezrah?"

Husker tightened his trench coat. "They're aggressive warriors. Territorial. Fierce. They tend to stick to themselves and kill anyone who gets in their way. The few times I've fought rezrah armies, it was brutal. I have unpleasant memories."

"In your dimension… you fought in the military?"

"That's right. I fought under the Immortal Rarn's banner. Gruesome affairs, wars. We didn't fight long, which I thank the good stars for."

Although Kellan knew very little about Husker's world and history, he had a little more respect for the man now that he knew he had served time in the military. It wasn't quite the same, though. Kellan could tell by the way Husker spoke—his dimension was a war-torn world of conflict and aggression, like Earth before WWI.

Husker lived in a time of conquest.

"You're a warrior," Husker said, his tone curving upward like it was half a question. "You fought for…?"

"My nation."

"Not a person? Not a set of ideals?"

"My nation stands for a set of ideals." Kellan rubbed at his arm. "We don't have mages who live forever. And we got rid of all our kings and queens. So now we just serve governments." He laughed to himself. "Makes me sound like a tool when I say it like that, but… I've never been much good at anything else."

Husker exhaled, his breath thicker than before. The chill in the air seemed more intense in general. Even Kellan pulled the collar of his coat higher.

"There's something odd ahead. Smells off." Husker flashed his fangs. "Like rot."

Kellan stared down the road only to discover the street abruptly ended at a golf course. Not a normal golf course with green grass and sand traps—a minigolf course, complete with a windmill and a giant T-rex. It had been plopped down in the middle of the suburbs with no rhyme or reason.

The shapes of people wandering through the minigolf attractions caught Kellan's attention. He held out an arm, stopping Husker in his tracks. "There's another team ahead."

"Oh? Who?"

"I don't know."

The people were too far away for Kellan to make out any details. They seemed human in appearance, though. No rennic or rezrah or niav.

Mavis, Sen, and Xiang made their way to Husker and Kellan. When they approached, they slowed their movements. Sen shivered, constantly rubbing at his arms.

"Shouldn't we have illusion disguises?" Mavis asked, her handgun up. "We pretended to be Team 42 last time. Why not do that now?"

"It's a possibility." Xiang ran her fingers along the edge of her chin. "But we'll potentially run into the same problem as last time. And our enemies know this tactic."

"Why don't we pretend to be Nexus residents?"

Sen scoffed and offered Mavis a glare. "Because then people will target us. They'll think they can get a quick bit of arcana and move on. We *definitely* don't want that."

"Can you make us look like horses or something?" Kellan asked.

Xiang laughed, the sound of mirth velvety and perfect. A moment later, she calmed, but she had to cover her mouth with a hand as she said, "Five *horses* sticking together and wandering around the game area? Searching through buildings? Yes. The perfect disguise. Why hadn't I thought of something like that."

"Pestbyters, then," Kellan snapped. "Or yami. Something that the other players would hesitate to approach. We'd just have to keep our talking to a minimum."

The suggestion seemed plausible to Kellan. Why not make themselves look inhuman? Then they could get away with a lot more before the other teams took note of them.

"For now, we'll make our way to the dolls," Xiang said matter-of-factly. "My mana isn't a plaything we can all use to test out theories."

"Are you really worried about your mana?" Mavis asked with a frown. "It's not that big a deal."

But Mavis didn't know about Xiang's hex. If Xiang ran out of mana—hit zero in her total—she would instantly die. Kellan understood why she would be hesitant to just use a bunch of illusions and see which one would stick.

Mavis waved at Xiang. "You illusion your clothes all the time. If you can do *that,* you should be able to help us."

With a sigh, Xiang folded her arms across her chest and stared straight ahead. "For your information, I took an illusion focus for mind magic. Here. Let me show you." She held out her hand. Mavis took it, but curiosity got the better of Kellan.

"May I?" he asked.

Xiang nodded once.

Kellan placed his hand on her forearm. Xiang allowed them to see her primary magic and focus.

> **Primary Magic—Mind—Focus [Illusionist Extraordinaire]**
> The mage only needs to spend one mana to activate their illusion-based powers. Additionally, the mage is given a phantom ten additional drawdown for permanent illusions only (illusions that maintain until the mage destroys them or the mage dies). Lastly, the mage may shift their personal appearance (and clothing) at will for no mana cost.

It seemed to Kellan that most focuses a mage could take reduced the mana cost for a single type of ability. It made sense to then specialize in it.

Mavis frowned. "So, you really doubled down on illusions, huh?"

"That's the smart way to do things," Sen interjected. "When you pick magical abilities, they should complement your natural skills and predilections. Especially your personal trait and any skills or training you might have. That's how you become a powerful mage—how you *master* your magic. My sister is quite talented."

Kellan wanted to tell the kid to calm down, and remind him that this wasn't *Incest Hour*, but his quip was cut short. The people in the minigolf course screamed and ran from the attractions. Something along the course was slithering across the holes and decorations—a giant worm or snake, Kellan wasn't sure which.

"Quiet," he commanded the others. "We have a yami coming our way."

"A large one," Husker said with a snort. "It has an odd odor. And doesn't make much noise."

"It looks like a serpent."

Husker growled, his fur standing on end. "Careful. Its breath stinks. It's what I've been smelling… It's what reeks of rot."

The speed of the snake-like beast was frightening. The monster clambered over a tiny minigolf castle, crushing the little drawbridge as it shot around the course and headed in his direction.

With a steady hand, Kellan hefted his rifle. "I think we have company." He took aim, prepared to shoot it square in its reptilian face.

The monster wasn't a snake—it had a dozen legs. It reminded Kellan of a skink. The yami also had six eyes, each large and unblinking, and gold as an old coin. The skink's gaze covered all directions as it rushed for them. Once it got close enough, Kellan saw more of its information flash before his eyes.

Name: Vizer #3
Race: Lesser Yami
Magics: Body, Entropy
Rank: Impossible to Rank
Armor Rating: —
Health: 15/15

Stats:
Strength—10
Dexterity—9
Fortitude—2
Intelligence—1
Perception—4 [Vigilant]
Willpower—1 [Animal]

Abilities:
Escape Route—The yami can teleport ten feet.
Camouflage—The yami can shroud itself in invisibility. This shroud

breaks if the yami makes a violent action.

And the yami was large, too. At least the length of a bus, with the thickness of an inner tube.

Within a few seconds, the vizer was already close. Kellan decided to fire.

[Alex Kellan] shot [Vizer #3] for 6 damage. (3 + 100% (50% Sharpshooter Modifier x 2 Sevriss Bonus))

His attack shattered one of the beast's shoulders, but also the silence. The other team across the minigolf course glanced in their direction. They had probably seen the flare of light from Kellan's weapon.

Kellan didn't care. He held down the trigger, hoping to rip the yami to shreds with bullets, but that was when the beast disappeared. The yami popped out of existence and then reappeared elsewhere. Kellan heard the displacement of air. But the creature was invisible, and it moved at such a fearsome speed, he wasn't even entirely sure if it was still on the golf course.

"Everyone needs to stay on high alert," he said.

Kellan also remembered his armor.

He spent one mana, reducing him to eleven remaining.

The armor slid over his skin, forming a tight suit of shadowy protection. It felt like a wetsuit under his clothes, the armor thin and nonintrusive, while being firm enough to block damage.

As if the monster had a sense of comedic timing, it appeared and lunged at Mavis, clamping down on her arm with its fangs. She screamed and shot at its face with her handgun, the bullet exploding one of its six eyes.

Then the beast teleported again, just as Kellan whipped around to fire.

Husker crouched and readied his massive claws and fangs.

When the deadly yami appeared again, it went straight for Sen. He froze, panicked, his eyes wide. Kellan managed to leap in the way. The monster sank its fangs into Kellan's arm. A shimmer of magic seemed to dull the attack, the fangs never really making it through Kellan's magical skintight armor.

[Sun Sen] used *Shield Ally* on [Alex Kellan], reducing the next attack's damage by 90%.
[Vizer #3] bit [Alex Kellan], dealing 7 damage.
[Alex Kellan] reduces damage of each hit equal to his armor rating of 4 (armor + *Void Knight* darkness bonus).
[Alex Kellan] suffers a total of 0 damage.

But the vizer suddenly bit again, faster than Kellan could react.

[Vizer #3] bit [Alex Kellan], dealing 7 damage.
[Alex Kellan] reduces damage of each hit equal to his armor rating of 4 (armor + *Void Knight* darkness bonus).

[Alex Kellan]'s shadow shell absorbs 2 damage.
[Alex Kellan] suffers a total of 1 damage.
[Tyranny Worms] restore [Alex Kellan] for 1 damage every 6 seconds.

The large fangs of the yami excreted some sort of ooze. Kellan gritted his teeth as he jerked his arm away. Blood and yellow worms splattered onto the street. Fueled with a desire to rid the world of the fucking monster, Kellan held out his hand and used his newest ability.

He spent a mana for the laser, and a mana to empower, reducing him to nine.

A beam of bright, hot light shot from his palm. It streaked through the air and struck the skink.

[Alex Kellan] blasted [Vizer #3] for 15 damage.

The monster's head practically melted, the hole through its skull precise. It collapsed to the street, twitching. The flash of light had been bright enough that everyone had seen. Kellan was just glad he hadn't hit anyone *behind* the creature. His laser blast had traveled off and struck the house across the road.

Husker laughed and then slapped Kellan on the back. "There's no kill like *overkill.*"

Five glittering red arcana popped out of the yami's body and rolled onto the asphalt, clinking as they went. All five glowed with an inner power, illuminating the street with a sinister crimson hue.

Kellan's body knitted back together thanks to the disgusting worms.

"Well, I should probably be doing this differently," Kellan muttered as he stared at the palm of his hand. "Apparently, my rifle can sometimes double the amount of arcana dropped if I manage to kill the target with it. So… in the future… I should *start* with the laser, and end with the bullets."

Sen hurried to Mavis's side. He grabbed her arm and examined the injury. Tyranny Worms were already working to stitch her flesh together, but that wasn't acceptable to Sen, apparently. He used his body magic to heal her the rest of the way, and even stared at her skin for a long moment after he was finished.

"Everything okay?" she asked.

"I just want to make sure there's no venom or ill effects," Sen said matter-of-factly. He brushed his fingers over her uninjured skin. "Nothing hurts, does it?"

Mavis smirked and half-laughed. "It's weird seeing you older like this."

Sen stopped and glanced up at her, his eyes narrowed. "Weird?"

"I mean, you look like this one kid I used to know in high school. He was so awkward. It wasn't until college that he finally finished with puberty."

Sen ripped his hand away from Mavis, his face a soft red. He ran his hand over his speckly beard, his lips pursed. "*I'm an adult.* I've already gone through puberty. I've just used my flesh in ways to… well… *do things.*"

"Don't worry. It's adorable. Really." Mavis gently brushed some of his black hair to the side. "You have a cute nerdy look."

With an exaggerated huff and scoff combo, Sen flounced away from Mavis. He went straight to his sister's side, his words never fully forming. His face and ears shifted from pale red to deep scarlet, like this was the first time anyone had ever touched his hair or paid him a compliment.

"Th-This never would've happened back home," Sen muttered under his breath as he crossed his arms.

Mavis turned to Xiang. She glanced the other woman up and down. "Was there a reason you just stood there and did nothing?"

With a perfectly lifted eyebrow, Xiang forced a smirk. "That's why we have two warriors, isn't it? To handle the trash."

Before anything could turn into an unnecessary argument, Kellan stepped between them. He took Mavis by the shoulder and motioned to the arcana on the ground. "You take three, and I'll take the other two, all right?"

Mavis grumbled something under his breath. Instead of arguing, she knelt, absorbed her arcana, and then stood. Kellan did the same.

[Alex Kellan] absorbed 2 arcana.

"Everyone knows we're here," Kellan said. "Our gunshots and my laser made sure of that. I think we should head out. If we stick to the minigolf course, maybe we can avoid some of the other teams while we look for the doll area."

"Lead the way," Xiang commanded.

The others nodded in approval, but no one else said a word. Silence descended upon them again as they headed forward, over the fake green grass and gnome decorations scattered over the minigolf course.

—Chapter 22—
—Dead or Alive—

The sun rose overhead, the rays of sunshine filtering through the Net and becoming a crimson glow. It reminded Kellan of the smog-covered skies that haunted places like LA and Beijing.

As they traveled over the minigolf course, Kellan stopped at a fake castle and motioned for the others to wait. Across the fake grass, he spotted the movement of other skinks, Vizer #1 and Vizer #2. The yami patrolled the area, as if searching for things to consume.

"Yami are just mindless animals?" Kellan whispered, his eyebrows knitted.

"They're corrupted beasts that look only to consume," Husker replied in an equally quiet voice. "They'll target mages first, in most cases. Some yami are controlled by the Arbiter himself or placed in these games for the specific purpose of guarding areas."

Once the yami turned and headed in a different direction, Kellan led his team away from the brightly colored castle. He stepped over several tiny signs that indicated the par for each course. One even said the par was nineteen. Did the par ever go up that high? *Ever*? He wasn't sure. Just another twisted detail in the Nexus.

On the other side of the golf course, Kellan found a small go-kart track. He hurried across, motioned the others to follow him, and then scouted a bit ahead. He found another residential street, this one ten times dirtier than the last. Broken glass littered the road, the buildings were stained urine yellow, and the stink of waste wafted over the area.

Every building looked like a group home for recovering drug addicts.

The noises from inside one building got Kellan nervous.

Then he remembered his familiar…

"Vlaze," Kellan said.

His shadow stretched out, and the albino wyvern leapt up out of the darkness. With baby-like fascination, Vlaze turned to Kellan and tilted his head, his red eyes wide.

"Check out that building for me, buddy."

With surprisingly high levels of understanding, Vlaze turned and scuttled toward one of the group homes. His front arms doubled as his legs but were clearly weaker. He waddled as he went. Kellan even considered it cute.

The white wyvern jumped into the air and flew for a broken window. Then Vlaze disappeared inside, rather stealthy for a little lizard.

"It's a shame you're not a soul mage," Husker said. He had watched Vlaze hurry off with intent fascination.

"Why's that?"

"Soul mages have abilities to make their familiars grow faster."

"Huh." Kellan glanced over at Sen. The teenager just offered him a glare. "You don't have a familiar?"

"They're rare, thank you very much," Sen muttered. "And I don't have those abilities, regardless. Unlike you, I focus my skills. I heal, protect, and alter my allies."

"A familiar is an ally."

Sen held up a finger, as though he was ready to rebut that statement, but then lowered his hand with a frown. He had nothing. A familiar *was* an ally, but he clearly didn't want to participate in the conversation.

A minute later, Vlaze reappeared. He flew out of the broken window and went straight for Kellan. With surprising grace, Vlaze landed on Kellan's shoulder. He had a piece of paper gripped tightly in his mouth.

Kellan took the paper and unfolded it. There weren't any words on the inside—just a drawing.

It was a picture of a meth lab, complete with jars, beakers, and heating sources. The drawing was flimsy, and done with a thin pencil, but detailed enough that Kellan didn't have to guess at what it was.

Vlaze shoved his snout into Kellan's ear and hissed—his noise sounded more like a whisper.

"Hey now," Kellan muttered as he pushed his familiar away. "Where did you get this?"

Vlaze glanced at the building, and then back to Kellan.

"There was just a drawing inside?"

The wyvern shook his head. Then he made grasping motions with his little front claws.

"You did this?" Kellan asked.

He… couldn't believe it. Wasn't Vlaze an animal? The wyvern had made a little drawing of the inside to convey the contents of the building?

Kellan turned to the others on his team. "Are you all seeing this? Look what Vlaze made."

Sen dismissively waved away the drawing. "Yes, yes. You have a familiar. Congratulations. Now stop rubbing it in our faces."

"But—"

"It's not *that* amazing. The drawing is rather amateurish."

Vlaze's head shot up. Then he flashed his fangs. Kellan still couldn't believe it, but everyone else seemed completely uninterested in Vlaze's apparent skill and intelligence.

"Look." Sen pointed to something in the distance. "I think we found where the dolls are being kept."

Although the others turned to see what Sen was pointing at, Kellan couldn't help but glance back at the group home. It was three stories tall, like a run-down apartment complex, and figures seemed to move around inside. If this had been a normal operation—one with the Delta Force—Kellan would've felt uneasy running around a neighborhood that contained so many hazardous areas. Especially now that he knew the building was filled with prohibited substances.

Monster-filled golf courses, and now a highly explosive meth lab?

Kellan had a terrible feeling about the game arena. That they weren't going to see the *real* fun until they had their fragile doll in hand.

The crack of a gunshot snapped Kellan out of his musings. He wheeled around on his heel and spotted a man on a different nearby group home, a sniper rifle mounted on the edge of the roof. He was too far away for Kellan to see his information with his Blitzkrieg Analysis, but he didn't need it to know the man was out to kill them.

"*Sister!*"

Kellan glanced over to find Xiang bleeding from a massive bullet wound through the leg. She was slouched on the ground, breathing deeply. Sen leapt to her side, his hands shaky.

The sniper had targeted Xiang first.

Then the shooter fired again. A bullet slammed into the road next to Xiang, blasting a hole into the asphalt.

Two more mages appeared seemingly from nowhere. They had been cloaked in invisibility, and when they dove from the sky, Kellan had only fractions of a second to process what was happening.

Both mages flew at them with wings, one with hawk wings, one with raven wings. They swooped near the group, rushing by with impressive speed. The hawk mage waved his hand and unleashed a torrent of fire near Xiang. The other pulled the pin out of a grenade.

"*Team 56 sends its regards!*" the raven mage said with a cackling laugh.

He threw the grenade dead center into the group and flapped his wings hard enough to lift back into the sky.

Husker leapt at the grenade. He threw most of his giant body over the device right before it exploded outward, spraying everything with deadly shrapnel. Kellan shielded his eyes and sucked in a breath when he felt the burning sting of metal rip through an arm and one leg.

[Sammis Blain] threw a grenade.
[Husker Linis] takes the brunt of the damage, but remaining AOE splash strikes [Alex Kellan] for 7 damage.
[Alex Kellan] reduces damage of each hit equal to his armor rating of 2.
[Alex Kellan]'s shadow shell absorbs 2 damage.
[Alex Kellan] suffers a total of 3 damage.
[Tyranny Worms] restore [Alex Kellan] for 1 damage every 6

seconds.

Kellan lifted his hand and shot a laser blast at the raven mage.

The deadly beam of magic ripped through the wing of the man in an instant, and he plummeted to the ground, screaming. Kellan didn't bother to read any more of the notifications. He focused his attention on the fight in front of him—he had to deal with multiple targets at once.

Mavis shot at the raven mage once he had hit the ground, her aim true. The man had tried to get up, but her bullets tore through his back and kept him down permanently. Mavis's skin had been hardened, and while the shrapnel had ripped apart some of her shirt and jeans, her body remained unscathed.

The sniper didn't waste any time.

He fired again—this time at Husker.

A magical barrier shimmered between Husker and the shooter. Sen's protection lessened the sniper bullet's speed, but it still struck Husker in the side of the head, splattering his blood across the street in a wide arc.

Kellan ran toward the building, intent on shadow-stepping his way to the roof to deal with the mage directly. But the sniper took aim at him as he headed over. *At this rate, he'll get several more shots off before—*

Then the sniper's head exploded from the inside out.

Kellan jerked to a stop, his eyes wide. He immediately glanced back at Xiang. She stood in the middle of the street, no longer bloodied, her hand up, her fingers flared. Then she turned her hateful gaze to the other hawk in the sky. When she waved her hand, *his* head exploded from the inside out as well, as though his brains had become a volatile explosive.

The body of the hawk mage twirled as it sailed to the ground.

With a disgusting *thwack*, the body splattered, organs scattering across the road, feathers coating everything afterward.

But the sniper hadn't fallen off the roof—even after his head had ruptured. The man was somehow *healing* after that. How was it even possible?

Kellan resumed his route to the building, inches from stepping into the darkness. The sniper shrouded himself in invisibility and seemingly disappeared, his weapon and all.

Was he gone?

Kellan held his breath, ready to act. But nothing ever happened.

Did he flee?

"What was that?" Mavis asked.

Sen circled his sister, examining her without actually touching her in any way. "Are you still hurt? Do you need any healing?"

"I'm fine," Xiang stated, curt. She smoothed her clothing—no rips, no injuries, no blood—and then straightened her styled hair. "But we should avoid the open roads."

Mavis ran to Husker's side. She helped the man up, and even offered her shoulder if he needed it. Husker was nearly three and a half feet taller than her, and darkly chuckled at the assistance. He shook his head and grunted as he pressed a clawed hand over the gaping hole in his belly.

Without a word, Sen hustled over and grabbed at Husker's wound. His fingers swam through Husker's fur, muscles, and organs like they were malleable clay. Sen wove everything back into place, stitching Husker a new stomach as though he were a statue and Sen were an artist.

The healing body magic did the rest.

Husker had been struggling to breathe, but after a few moments, he was whole again. He smiled, his canine fangs flashing in the red light.

"That was close," he muttered. "Too close."

"It was Team 42." Sen stepped back and admired his work. "They've made deals with the other teams. Whoever kills us gets lots of arcana and magical items. That's why Team 56 just *attacked us out of nowhere* like that."

"I thought Team 42 wanted Xiang for themselves," Kellan interjected. "Why would Team 56 shoot Xiang first?"

"They were probably hoping to incapacitate her. While she was broken and bleeding, they would kill us, and then bring Xiang back with them. A simplistic plan, but one that might have worked if we weren't paying attention."

Mavis waved her hands around, obviously still shaken. "Did you see how their heads *exploded*? What was that?" She glanced over at Xiang. "Was that you? What kind of magic does that?"

"Mind magic." Xiang offered a smirk. "Alex has lasers, and I attack people's willpower. If it's low, their heads rupture. If it's high, I don't deal so much damage. Fortunately, these halfwits were simple targets."

Kellan motioned for everyone to get off the street. "The sniper fled, even after you exploded his noggin. We shouldn't stick around here. If he comes back, we could be in trouble."

"He won't return this game," Xiang said with confidence.

"We can't know that. Clearly, he wasn't the most tactically minded individual I've seen."

"If he does, it'll just be more arcana for us."

The mention of arcana got Kellan glancing around. The two niav mages were dead on the streets, their blood everywhere. Six arcana had sprouted from the body of one, and seven arcana from the body of another.

"I want some of it this time," Husker stated. His clothing had been shredded by the grenade, and he held up the tatters as proof of his assistance. "I think I've earned it."

The others exchanged glances and then motioned to the crystals. Husker lumbered over, scooped five up, and left the rest. Xiang took the two remaining arcana from the one body, and then gestured to the last six.

"Alex, you take those."

"I also helped," Mavis stated.

"But less."

Kellan wasn't entirely sure why they were so tense with each other, but he quickly realized it was a problem. He held up a hand and shook his head. "Look, Mavis can have it all, okay? I want to focus on gold arcana, anyway."

The mention of the gold arcana got everyone quiet. Kellan had been the only one of them to get any, and they exchanged hesitant glances, as though it were a terrible idea. Kellan didn't care. He had seen the benefits for himself. Mavis strode over and absorbed the six arcana.

Kellan still only had two arcana. If he could get eight more—preferably gold arcana—he could rank up his eclipse magic.

Together, they moved off the bloody road and made their way into an alley. They hurried between group homes, covered by the shadows of the tall three-story buildings. Kellan directed them around, and Sen pointed to the sky.

A spotlight streaked across the Net from a place on the ground. They were close.

Kellan took the team around a series of dumpsters, careful not to disturb even the garbage bags. He didn't want to draw any more attention to him or his team.

Was the sniper from Team 56 following them? It was the only thought that repeatedly came to mind.

Once they finally made it around the building, Kellan stopped.

He stood at the edge of a gigantic parking lot, the kind only found at amusement parks and grand stadiums. Unfortunately, there weren't any of those nearby. Instead, all Kellan found was a shopping mall—a three-story megastructure designed as a shrine to capitalism. It had thirty "FOR SALE" signs hanging on poles out front, like they were the flags of a bargain bin nation.

Two Pestbyters floated around the parking lot. Their machine bodies, perfectly spherical, hovered over the asphalt, their wire tentacles dragging across the ground. Several antennas jutted up from their backs and into the air, each vibrating with the odd movement of the machines. They were large, and loud, and impossible to miss.

"What're you waiting for?" Husker asked.

Kellan stared at the spheres as they hovered back and forth.

"Those are servants of the Arbiter. They won't hurt you."

"I still don't like them," Kellan muttered.

"Heh. I agree. But that doesn't mean we need to fear them."

After a few seconds to contemplate the situation, Kellan headed out across the massive parking lot. The Pestbyters turned, stared at him with camera-eyes, and then resumed their patrol. Kellan breathed easier when the hideous machines weren't staring at him. He hated those soulless bots with a tiny passion.

"I think this building is where we'll find the dolls," Sen said.

A mall.

It seemed a fitting location.

As soon as Kellan made it halfway across the lot, a new notification flashed in his vision.

The Heavenly Shopping Mall Oasis

You have entered an Oasis. While inside this non-conflict area, all mages are forbidden from initiating direct violence. Offensive magical abilities are limited. Any who attempt to circumvent this rule will answer to the Arbiter himself.

An Oasis? The mall?

Kellan cracked a smile.

It made sense to place the dolls in an Oasis. This way, no team could "camp" on the location and attack people who arrived. And no team could destroy all the dolls since they were in a safety zone. By placing the dolls in an Oasis, most of those complications were removed.

People could camp outside the mall, and wait for enemy mages, but the mall was too large to keep covered with a small team. And since the dolls were inside the Oasis, teams could rest before collecting their precious cargo.

Kellan thought it clever, but at the same time, he knew the mall would attract all sorts of mages. And if one team had already attacked them because Team 42 was incentivizing them…

We'll just have to be careful.

—Chapter 23—
—The Heavenly Shopping Mall—

Kellan strode up to the large glass doors of the shopping mall.

The sterile entrance, perfectly immaculate floors, and glittering glass of the gigantic windows made the place seem like a dreamscape. No mall was this clean. Not one used by hundreds of thousands of people a day, at least.

Kellan walked in and took some time to thoroughly glance around. It was an Oasis, so he knew he wouldn't be attacked, but an odd feeling crept up his spine. Was he being watched? The Oasis wouldn't prevent people from being invisible.

Maybe the sniper?

Mavis stopped next to him and let out a long exhale. "This game hasn't seemed as crazy as the others."

"Don't say that. You're going to jinx us."

"Well, I was trying to be optimistic. We made it here without getting hurt *too* bad, and it was basically a straight path." Mavis glanced down at her torn and bloody clothing. "I hated the grenade, though. If Husker hadn't jumped in the way…"

Sen, Xiang, and Husker walked into the mall. Only Husker seemed surprised by the surroundings. He stared at everything—from the fake plants to the map kiosk, even the signs for the bathrooms.

"Humans and their indoor cities," Husker muttered. "I swear you all hate the sky."

Massive advertisements flashed across screens mounted to the second-story balcony. They blinked and moved with vibrant colors, but there were no sounds. Some of the ads promoted brands Kellan had never heard of.

Glint Water! Refresh your body AND soul! Nothing helps your mana like Glint Water!

Buy Kuku Soap! Do it, you chump!

Hydra Corp. needs new researchers TODAY! Help advance our understanding of magic and empower the future!

The last one caused Kellan to stare for a long moment. Hydra Corp. had been the company to make the meta magic potion. The one that had granted Kellan access to the rare magic.

They were some alternate-dimension company that clearly loved magic.

Kellan wasn't sure what he would do with the information, but he tucked it away, just in case it could help in the future.

Husker stared at a lingerie ad, one ear twitching. The woman on the ad wore nothing but skimpy underwear, black and lacy. She winked and rolled around on a perfectly white bed. Kellan thought it amusing how long Husker stared, but after a few more seconds, it became awkward.

"You like what you see?" Kellan quipped.

"The scene out the window…" Husker pointed to the ad. In the background, beyond the bed and out a window, there was a tower in the middle of a green field. "I think I've been there. I wonder what dimension this ad is from… The Nexus has so many places converging with it."

"You're not looking at the woman?"

Husker wrinkled his nose and snorted. He glanced over at Kellan, his eyes narrowed. "Humans are disgusting. You're like a sad patch of dirt with occasional sprouts of tough grass. Fleshy. Soft. Wrinkly in all the wrong places."

"When you put it like that…" Kellan smirked. "Nope. I still prefer humans. They're my favorite."

"Ha. That's because you've never been with anything else. Rennic are loyal, affectionate, and covered in glorious, silky fur."

Kellan would've made another quip, but his nerves wouldn't let him. He turned his attention to a nearby shop. A sporting goods store. Then he glanced at another. A place with fresh baked cinnamon rolls.

A giant mechanical-eye stuck out off the wall above the cinnamon roll shop. The half-flesh, half-machine organ observed Team 101. It was an Eye of the Arbiter, filming their every movement.

It sank into the wall and disappeared after a short while, though. The eyes wanted to keep themselves hidden, it seemed.

"Shouldn't we have illusions now?" Mavis asked as she walked over to the map kiosk. "Then again, do we really need them? If our enemies can see through them…"

Xiang glared. "They *can't* see through them. Perhaps they have a way to detect them, but my illusions will hold. And we need it so that no one goes out of their way to target us."

"Why is everyone killing each other? It's not really needed in this game. We could be helping each other instead."

"Because future games *will* require us to face off. The faster stronger teams are eliminated, the better. If there are no teams to fight, all the games would be easier—that's why *we* should be killing everyone as well."

"Let's just avoid the other teams," Husker muttered. "I don't want to have to use the power of hex, and if we get into needless fights, I might not be able to avoid it."

Xiang nodded. Then she motioned for the team to approach her. "Very well. We'll have illusions, and we'll pretend to be a different team—one that has yet to distinguish itself."

Everyone gathered around her, near the entrance to the sporting goods store.

The advertisements blinked overhead as Xiang waved her hand. The illusions she made covered each person from their head to their feet, practically painting on a new appearance.

Which was appreciated, considering their shabby appearance after the two fights. Kellan looked like a character from a zombie flick.

The illusions over Sen gave him the physique of a biker, and the clothing to match. Husker was still a rennic—the illusions couldn't take away from his imposing height or body—but now his fur was black, his eyes a striking blue, and his coat more a military jacket.

Mavis became a bulkier, notably uglier, woman in her late forties. Her skin wrinkled, and cracked, and her face seemed distorted, leaning to one side. It was amusing, but in a petty way that Kellan couldn't help but take note of.

Had something happened between them?

When it came time for Xiang to mask herself, she still decided on a beautiful woman, only this time she was one of the niav. She gave herself swan wings. Then her hair changed to a bright chestnut, practically glittering with beauty.

Mavis just sighed.

When Kellan glanced at himself in the reflection of a nearby glass door, he noticed he had the same biker-appearance as Sen. Black jacket. Dark jeans. Gloves. And a large beard. It was the perfect disguise—for some reason, several of the other teams picked this style as their preferred clothing choice.

"Good," Husker said, his voice slightly different. Xiang's illusions masked everything, apparently—even people's stats and names in the notifications. "Hopefully we won't be harassed while we gather our doll."

Kellan stared at his left hand. Their new number was: 33.

He hadn't seen anyone from the real Team 33, and he hoped he wouldn't while they played this game.

Now disguised, the team stuck close as they wandered the mall. More TV screens were littered around the area in bizarre locations, including a screen in a water fountain. It showed the same disturbing children's programming with the clown. The kids discussed the Nexus Games as though it were a Saturday morning cartoon.

Kellan didn't pay much attention. He remained vigilant, wondering when their stalker would finally reveal himself.

When they made it to the food court, Kellan caught his breath.

It stank of unwashed bodies, and he could see why. Massive cages—the kind found in zoo loading docks—were stacked in the middle of the food court. People were trapped within, most of them teenaged or just a little older. The metal bars, made of blackish-blue rock, were thick and sturdy.

At first, Kellan had the urge to rush forward and see if the people needed help, but he stopped himself.

The people in the cages were malformed and lumpy, each one more hideous than the last. They were the inbred residents of the Nexus. Why were they in cages?

Other players of the Nexus Games stood around the food court. They visited the counters, getting food from the various shops, though Kellan didn't recognize any of the franchises. Fortunately, everything was written in both English and Sanskrit.

What the hell was *Moss Burger?* Kellan didn't like the sound of that at all.

The other players from various teams grabbed their food and then went to the cages. They opened a barred door, dragged a Nexus resident out, and then half-carried them to the nearest exit. The resident was handcuffed, and their feet bound. They couldn't move much.

What was going on?

A voice boomed across the food court, more playful and exuberant than the scene demanded.

"Welcome! *Welcome!* We have another team. How pleasant. Oh, I like this one, too."

Kellan recognized Bitso's over-the-top inflections and showman-style speech. To his surprise, Bitso stepped out from between two of the larger cages, his crisp suit perfectly pressed. He wore a black blazer, vest, and pants, his shirt and gloves glaringly white.

His blindfold, light blue this time, was free of blood or stains.

Bitso strode over, smiling wide, his freakishly sharp teeth a little disturbing. "Who do we have here?" Bitso snorted and laughed. "Oh? Team 33? That's a good one."

He said nothing else on the matter, though. He just smiled and chortled to himself, in a joke no one else seemed to get.

Kellan and the others walked around him, no one engaging with the bizarre news anchor. Determined to figure out what the cages were about, Kellan went straight for one.

The Nexus residents…

They trembled inside their zoo confinements. Kellan was half-tempted to let them all out, but he stopped once he saw they were wearing necklaces. A pendant hung on the chain, each one marked with a word and a number.

Team 77.

Team 95.

Team 52.

Realization struck Kellan like a truck to the side of the head. *These* were the dolls. The Nexus residents were the "object" they were supposed to transport across the game arena. They were supposed to find *their* doll, take it out of the cage, and leave the mall.

"I'm going to investigate the food," Mavis said, her elderly voice raspy. "Something makes me think we might need whatever is around here."

"I'll go with her," Sen said. He chased after Mavis as she jogged over to Moss Burger.

Husker and Xiang stepped to the side, whispering and pointing at the cages.

While they all gathered information and discussed the current situation, Kellan walked between the cages, searching for the resident with the 101 pendant. The deformed Nexus inhabitants gave him wide-eyed and frightened glances. Then moved away from the edges of their cages, trying to stay as far away as possible.

"Well, well, well," Bitso said as he stepped around a cage to face Kellan. "You look like you're having fun."

Kellan hesitated for a moment. He opted to ignore the man and keep searching.

"You tried to summon me with your Summoning Chime." Bitso's smile remained as wide, and manic, as ever. "I heard you call my name. What an odd choice."

"I was trying to kill you," Kellan whispered. He glanced around, hoping no one else would hear. "I figured, if I summoned you outside of an Oasis, you'd be vulnerable."

Bitso placed both of his gloved hands over his heart. "D'aww! You were trying to kill me? That's literally the nicest thing anyone has ever done."

"You promised me sixty arcana if I managed to do it."

"And you were motivated by *greed*?" Bitso wiped an imaginary tear from his eye. "You all grow up so fast. I couldn't be prouder."

"Yeah," Kellan said with a forced chuckle. "Sorry it didn't work out."

"Don't worry. You're not the first person to disappoint me. I've long since given up hope."

Conflicted, Kellan returned his attention to the cages. The residents refused to look at him or even make the task easy. He shifted around the metal bars, glancing at the pendants, but only when the residents moved enough to show them off.

Why were they being so difficult?

Kellan gritted his teeth, irritated that they weren't immediately showing themselves.

"Over here," a woman said. She scooted to the bars, her feet and hands cuffed. "I'm your team's doll."

With a smile, Kellan jogged over. He stopped when he saw the number on her pendant, though.

Team 33.

He cursed under his breath.

"Do you know where Team 101's pendant is?" Kellan asked.

The woman held her breath. Her thinning hair, a mix of blonde and black, hung mostly across her face. Her skin sagged in odd places, and one of her hands was missing three fingers. Other than that, she seemed mostly normal. No humpback or extra limbs. She wore mall clothing, which was slightly amusing—designer jeans, a shimmery gold blouse, and glittering jewelry.

"I don't want to betray the others," the woman whispered. "Please don't hurt my family."

"What?" Kellan asked, baffled.

Bitso slid over, seemingly amused by the interaction. "What's that? You're going to take Team's 101 doll out of this Oasis and murder it? That won't work. The dolls control whether the cage opens or not." Bitso banged his knuckles against the blackish-blue metal. "And the cages are made of anti-magic."

"But…"

Kellan cursed again, growing increasingly frustrated.

Other teams ran into the mall. Over a dozen new mages rushed around the cages, each searching for their number. A few tried to open the barred doors, but none of them budged. Was this a preventative measure to make sure the wrong dolls weren't taken?

The real Team 33 never showed, much to Kellan's relief.

He leaned in close to the cage with the deformed woman. "Listen. I'm not really from Team 33. This is an illusion. I'm from Team 101, and I need to find my doll."

The woman's saggy face twisted with her visible confusion. Her two-fingered hand—just a thumb and her pointer—tapped nervously on her cuff. "You… W-Wait, are you on the same team as *Alex Kellan?* The man who helps my kind?"

"I *am* Alex Kellan."

"R-Really?"

Kellan motioned for her to keep her voice low. "That's right. Can you help me?"

"Of course." The woman pointed to a cage two over. "The woman with the Team 101 pendant is right there."

"Thank you."

Kellan turned to leave, but the woman grabbed the leg of his cargo pants. Kellan jerked to a halt and turned around. She stared up at him with wide eyes.

"Take me with you," the woman whispered.

For a long second, Kellan didn't know how to reply. He glanced around. The other teams hurried with their tasks, each grabbing a doll before rushing toward the exit. No one from Team 33 was here.

"I think your team will be here shortly," Kellan said.

"I'd rather go with you. I don't know the mages of Team 33… But you… You're different."

"You'll be safer if you just stay here."

The woman tightened her grip on his pants. "*No.* Please. If our team never shows up… we'll be killed."

Disgusted by the bit of information, Kellan turned to Bitso. The news anchor leaned against a nearby cage, just "watching" the other teams run about, as though he had nothing better to do.

"Is that true?" Kellan asked.

Bitso picked at one of his sharpened molars and then licked his teeth. "Huh? What? Them dying if no one shows up for them?" He tilted his head back and chuckled. "Of course! The Arbiter likes his kids, but not *all* his kids, if you catch my drift. Sometimes you must thin the herd. And some of these residents are more *overly ambitious tumors* than they are *people.*"

Kellan already knew what he was going to do, but he hated himself sometimes for his inability to deviate course. Taking on a *second* liability wouldn't help their chances of winning.

But he couldn't leave the woman—not when she was pleading for him to take her.

"Fine," Kellan said, curt. He grabbed her cage door. "Let's go. Quickly."

The woman's eyes went even wider. She sat up straight, her whole body trembling. "R-Really? You'll take me?"

"That's what I said, lady. Now open the cage."

"You, but, I thought…" She steadied herself with a shallow breath. "I thought you would demand something in return."

"Look, we don't have time for this. Pretend it's your birthday. *Happy birthday. Your present is getting rescued.* Let's go."

Before the cage door could open, Bitso stepped over and placed his hand on the cage. His blindfold covered most of his face, and Kellan had no idea what the man was thinking. He retained the same damn smile he had for nearly everything.

"You're making a terrible mistake," Bitso said, sweetness in his tone. "The more you show off your bleeding heart, the more likely it'll be used against you. One of these games, the Arbiter is going to wrap the key in a ball of helpless women and children, and he's going to expect you to cut your way through."

"Why?" Kellan balked.

"Because he knows it'll disturb you."

The statement caught Kellan off guard. Was that why the Arbiter did so many creepy things? To disturb the players?

Kellan grabbed Bitso's shoulder and guided him a few feet from the cage. In a low voice, he said, "I thought the Arbiter wanted me to get more gold arcana?"

Bitso rubbed at his blue blindfold. "He does."

"Then, obviously, I should take the girl, right? She'll reward me for helping her."

Kellan didn't like the spin he gave the story. It made him feel dirty, like sewer scum, but he didn't care. He just wanted Bitso—and the uncaring Arbiter—off his back.

"Oh, that's low." Bitso snorted and laughed. "I approve. Go out there and get your gold arcana. I'll try to convince the Arbiter this is all for the greater good. Maybe he'll look the other way with you."

—Chapter 24—
—Team 42 in the Flesh—

Kellan returned to the woman's cage. He grabbed the door and pulled. It opened without a problem, like it hadn't been locked at all.

The saggy-skinned woman waited, the cuffs around her ankles and wrists preventing her from standing. She fidgeted with her two-toned hair, pulling some of the thin strands so that they blocked most of her face. Was she avoiding eye contact? Kellan didn't have time to dwell.

He walked over and effortlessly scooped her up into his arms. She was thin—like she was half-human, half-coat rack. The woman pressed her face against Kellan's chest, her breathing quick and ragged.

"Everything's going to be okay," Kellan stated. "I'll get you out of this."

She said nothing.

Kellan hurried out of the cage and made his way over to the one with Team 101's doll. The woman inside wore designer clothing, just like the others, but she was smaller, hunched over, and her head leaned to one side because her neck was too weak to support it.

Her pendant did, in fact, have the number 101.

The woman in Kellan's arms glanced over at the new cage. "Look over here, Kay," she whispered. "This man here is actually the one from the TV. The one who spoke with the Arbiter and lived."

The girl in the cage, Kay, scrunched her forehead. "What?" Her head basically rested on her shoulder, that was how poorly supported it was.

"He's wearing illusions, Kay. He's tricking people. You're his doll. Hurry and unlock the door."

"Are you sure, Millie?"

"Yes. Quickly."

The girl in Kellan's arms—Millie, he assumed—went back to pressing her face into his chest. He wasn't sure how he was going to carry both of them, so he turned in Mavis's direction. Mavis stood next to the counter of Moss Burger, glaring down at a tray of food. The worker behind the register was nothing more than a dummy mannequin. It seemed to move using robotic mechanisms, but Kellan wasn't close enough to really get any details.

When Mavis caught him staring, he motioned her over with a quick jerk of his head.

It was odd seeing her in the illusion of an old woman, but he didn't give a shit. They had bigger problems to worry about. Several other teams had taken their dolls and gone. That meant the enemy players were *ahead* of them. If at any point they decided to lie in wait, they could prepare an ambush.

Kellan didn't want to deal with that. He wanted the entire Escort game over.

Mavis jogged over. She stared at the inbred resident in his arms, and then the one in the cage. The confusion was thorough.

"That one there is our doll," Kellan said, motioning to Kay. "This one—" he glanced at the woman in his arms, "—is the decoy. She's actually Team 33's doll. Her name is Millie."

"What happens if you return a different team's doll for them?" Mavis asked.

"Just in case anyone is wondering," Bitso said, his voice booming over the food court. "If you *somehow* deliver another team's doll to the finish, they'll receive the key for your efforts! So strange, to help them out, but what do I know?"

His manic, cackling laugh punctuated his statement. The other mages in the room didn't seem concerned with the message. Kellan found it off-putting that Bitso somehow knew what they were discussing, even though he was several cages away.

Perhaps the Arbiter just tells him everything.

"Do we really want to help Team 33?" Mavis asked.

Kellan half-shrugged. "Who cares? If they get a key, it doesn't affect us, and we needed a decoy anyway."

"All right. I just… I hope you know what you're doing."

"What's with the food?" Kellan glanced back at the odd burgers. Sen grabbed up five of them and awkwardly carried them over to Husker and his sister. "Why eat any of it?"

"Apparently, the food around here gives you *immunities*." Mavis pointed to Moss Burger. "That one makes you immune to rot." She jutted her thumb at a shop called *Kitten Corn Dogs*. "That food makes it so you can't drown." Then she motioned to a counter with the words *Internal Lemonade*. "That drink makes it so you can't be burned."

"Why?"

Mavis shook her head. "Sen said it's probably part of the game. Apparently, we can only take one of the foods."

"And you picked the moss-covered burger?" Kellan glanced between the three options. Immunity to rot?

"The other two sounded… questionable. And much worse, in my opinion."

"I suppose it doesn't matter anymore since you've already picked. We should go."

Mavis knelt and picked up Kay, the Nexus resident. Fortunately, Kay was small. She, too, was like a skeleton, thin and practically rattling. Mavis held the woman tight, but it was clear she wasn't used to the strain.

When Kellan lifted an eyebrow, Mavis shook her head. "It's like boot camp all over again," she quipped.

With a snort and laugh, Kellan nodded. "All right. Let's go."

Kellan and Mavis hurried to the others, their dolls in their arms, both silent. Xiang, Sen, and Husker had their burgers, each wrapped in a strange white wax paper. Once Kellan got close, his analysis gave him further information.

Magical Item [Consumable]—Moss Burger

The mage becomes immune to entropic rot effects for the next 15 minutes. Tastes like fresh moss.

What freakish dimension thought moss would make for a great burger topping? Kellan shook his head, hoping to Baby Jesus that the corndogs and lemonade weren't also named literally.

"Why do you have two residents?" Husker asked as he glanced between the two misshapen women. "I thought we only needed one."

Kellan held Millie close. "We needed a decoy anyway, right? Well, now we have one."

"But it's alive. We don't want that. We can just illusion a rock."

"*She* will be fine," Kellan stated.

Husker flashed his fangs. "*Don't.* If you go making things personal, this will be a lot harder than it needs to be. Don't ask the dolls their names. Don't go thinking they're people."

"I already did."

Husker ran a clawed hand over his long, canine face. "Ephrath help us… We're gonna suffer through this one."

Sen rolled his eyes as he passed out the burgers, but he didn't add any commentary to the discussion. One burger went to his sister, another went to Husker, a third went to Mavis, the fourth went to Kellan, and the last one Sen tucked into his hoodie pocket. They smelled of BBQ sauce and beef, which Kellan appreciated, but he dreaded having to eat it.

"Shouldn't we get two more?" Mavis asked. She struggled to hold her Nexus resident, but after hefting her up a bit, managed to get a good hold. "These *dolls* will need protection, right?"

"The worker robot would only provide me an equal number of burgers to the members of our team." Sen motioned back to the android behind the counter. "We're not allowed to have any more."

Which worried Kellan. He already had a bad feeling about this.

Then Sen handed his sister a paper map. He held a second map, and he walked over to Kellan to show it off. Although everything was written in Sanskrit, the pictures and lines were easy enough to decipher.

The mall was in the center of the city. The minigolf course was on the west side of the massive shopping center, giving Kellan enough perspective about the layout of the city, and rough distances. The end goal was far to the east, at the very edge of the business district, but the map made it seem as though getting there would be difficult. The main roads were marked with solid lines. Were they blocked off? It seemed that way.

And some roads were labeled with a skull. Others had terrible stick drawings of monsters.

Flame and water symbols were also placed on certain buildings and in parks. Mass fires and flooding? The food items seemed to make more sense.

Everywhere on the map was some sort of hazard.

Technically, Kellan saw a completely safe route—no lines or bizarre warning pictures—but it required them going back to the golf course, going far north around most of the city, and then down to the goals.

"How much time do we have left?" he asked.

Sen turned his attention to a massive clock built in the center of the food court. "Eight hours."

Could they walk across an entire city in eight hours? Seemed like they would be pushing their luck. Would other teams be there?

Kellan pointed to the route. "Listen up. If Xiang and Mavis go north and take this path without any hazards—and while staying safe under illusions—I think they won't be harassed. Sen, Husker, and I will take this path here." He ran a finger along a line toward the goal. "It… requires us to go through the skulls, which I'm going to assume means *rot*."

"Why?" Mavis asked.

"Because of the burgers, obviously. That's our one immunity." Kellan glanced up and met Xiang's gaze. She tensed under his gaze, like she wasn't expecting him to address her. "Since you and Mavis won't need a burger, I'd like one of them."

"For what?" Xiang asked.

"For the doll," Kellan drawled. He tightened his hold on Millie. The Nexus resident made no comment about their plan. But Kellan knew, if he was going to run through the area on the map marked with a fucking skull, he was going to need every advantage he could get.

"Very well," Xiang said.

"*What*?" Sen snapped. "My sister shouldn't give up her advantage for this trash."

Millie flinched at the term.

"What we need to do is—"

Xiang held up a hand, and her brother swallowed his tirade. She shook her head. "It wouldn't look convincing if we didn't try to keep our doll alive. Alex is correct. We should do what's required to protect it."

"I don't think this is a good idea," Husker muttered. "We need our key as well."

Mavis shook her head. "Listen, *I'll* give up my burger. Our fearless leader can keep hers, and we'll just make do, all right? Everyone, calm down."

She handed over her burger wrapped in wax paper. Kellan—with one arm holding Millie—awkwardly packed it away in his backpack, along with his own burger. Since they only lasted fifteen minutes, he knew he couldn't just eat them now.

"We'll meet up at the goal," Xiang said.

Mavis gave Kellan a sideways glance. "You better not get into too much trouble."

"Oh, I'll try," Kellan quipped.

With that, Mavis and Xiang headed back through the food court, and toward the minigolf course. Hopefully, by turning around, no other teams would see them leave. And with their disguises, no one would bother them anyway.

Kellan, Sen, and Husker headed for the front of the mall. The other dolls watched them go from deep in their anti-magic cages, their eyes wide. Bitso stood among them, greeting new teams who ran into the mall from various locations.

"Greetings!" Bitso's voice boomed over the food court. "You've made it to the doll selection phase. I guess you aren't all the chumps I thought you were."

Before they left the mall, Kellan glanced around for a quick and easy shop. He found a knickknack place near the front door, and he slid inside. He went straight for the register and grabbed an assortment of items. Pens, paper, measuring tape, keychains, and even a jacket. He threw it into his backpack, all with one hand, while Millie watched, her eyes wide, though she never questioned anything.

"What're you doing?" Sen hissed from the front of the shop. "We need to go!"

Kellan nodded. Once his pack was full, they headed for the front of the mall. Husker held out a clawed hand.

"Do you want me to carry it?" the rennic asked.

Millie twisted her fingers into Kellan's shirt.

"I'm fine," Kellan stated. "Just focus on keeping us safe, all right?"

"As you wish."

They exited the Heavenly Shopping Mall and headed out into the gigantic parking lot. Halfway across, and beyond two more Pestbyters, they exited the Oasis. Kellan breathed a bit easier without the odd restraining magic over his thoughts.

The sun rose in the sky, illuminating the whole city. The red Net still tainted everything in a horror show vibe, but Kellan felt a little more confident that their team could make it. He thought back to the map, and which roads they needed to take to avoid the fires and flooding. Kellan turned toward a road with multiple office buildings, his bootsteps echoing as he picked up the pace. Controlled breathing helped him maintain his pace, but he quickly realized that only Husker was managing to stay close.

Sen had fallen behind. The teen gulped down breath after breath, like he hadn't ever run in his life.

Kellan slowed. The shadows of the tall five-story buildings shaded him and Husker as they waited for Sen to catch up. The nearby trees rustled with the breeze, and Millie shivered.

Kellan was about to ask Husker to just carry Sen so that they continue, but a terrible chill washed over him. A slimy feeling ran down his spine. Kellan had felt this before, but only with people who had taken multiple hexes… The corrupted magic of the hexes seemed to alter their magic in a way he could *feel.*

With his breath held, Kellan turned around.

Someone stood in the middle of the road just a few hundred feet away. The man wore a sturdy suit of futuristic armor, the type that completely covered the individual. The black shine of the metal, and the reflective mirror of the visor on the helmet, would've prevented most people from identifying the individual.

But Kellan wasn't like most people.

His eyes gave away everything—but even then, Kellan knew who this was.

Brenner Hawke, of Team 42.

Name: Brenner Hawke, Traitor to Humanity
Race: Human
Magics: Body, Metal, Entropy, Travel, Meta
Rank: A, S, S, A, D
Armor Rating: 15 + 10 Shielding [Metallic]
Health: 55/55 [Cyborg-Enhanced]

Stats:
Strength—20 [Cyborg-Enhanced, Iron Grip]
Dexterity—18 [Cyborg-Enhanced, Pinpoint Accuracy]
Fortitude—20 [Cyborg-Enhanced, Tireless]
Charisma—5 [Controlling]
Manipulation—11 [Dark, Occult]
Intelligence—8
Perception—14 [Cyborg-Enhanced, Keen-Sighted]
Wisdom—6
Willpower—6 [Ambitious, Nightmares]

Abilities:
Personal—[Overconfident]—The mage can never hide their basic information, but if they are ever in combat with an enemy mage who does, this mage's physical stats (strength, dexterity, fortitude) are doubled.
Hex—[Wielder of Arondight]—The mage is capable of wielding the legendary laser sword, Arondight. As punishment, the mage must kill one member of a sentient race every seven days (the counter starting after each death), or the wielder dies.
Hex—[Apex Growth]—The mage gains double the arcana from all his kills. As punishment, the mage suffers from *mana burn* (mana use burns them, dealing damage equal to mana spent).
Hex—[Exarch's Power]—The mage gains an immunity to a magical energy type (fire, ice, lightning, laser, phantasmal, entropy, or phase) and becomes immune to all *mana burn* effects. As punishment, the mage's permanent mana pool is cut in half every time they rank to S in a magic. If the mage ever drops below 20 permanent mana, they die.
Hex—[Connected to the Sea of Chaos]—The mage's mana pool is

doubled, and they gain access to the unknowable magics, capable of ranking them as any other. As punishment, the mage's soul cracks each time they use a C rank or higher power (and after an unspecified number of cracks, the mage's soul shatters, killing them).

Hex—[Trickster's Bane]—The mage is aware whenever there's an illusion or invisibility in use within 250 feet of him. This detection is always in effect, acting as a "sixth sense" and always triggers no matter the rank of the obfuscation, including beyond M. As punishment, the mage suffers from nightmares and only sleeps half the normal amount, losing natural mana regeneration, and halving their willpower.

Hex—[Infinite Use]—The mage may pick a single power or ability that has a mana activation cost. That power or ability no longer costs the mage mana. As punishment, the mage picks an energy type (fire, ice, lightning, laser, phantasmal, entropy, or phase) and becomes weak to it, taking double damage from all sources.

Just my goddamn luck.

The last two hexes were new, and Kellan suddenly understood what Ysa had been alluding to. Brenner Hawke, the madman of Team 42, would now know whenever they were illusioned. Even if he wasn't seeing through the illusion, or spotting someone who was invisible, he would know that it was nearby.

Brenner held out his hand. His shadow stretched out, just like when someone summoned their familiar, and his laser sword flew up from the depths and went straight into his hand. He gripped the hilt, turned the blade, and the edge crackled to life, like hot plasma.

"These ones are illusioned, too," Brenner said, his voice machine-like as it filtered through the helmet of his power armor. "I don't know who they are, but let's just be safe."

"What if one of them is Xiang?" a disembodied voice called out.

"If she's here, she'll reveal herself. Otherwise, kill the lot of them."

Kellan wasn't sure who Brenner had given orders to, but he already knew it was too late.

Glints of stars appeared overhead. A whole night sky's worth of twinkling dots.

They grew larger and larger, and pulsed with an inner power. The swell of magic in the area grew intense.

Then the "stars" fell straight down to the ground, each a powerful laser blast that practically demolished everything in its path. The lasers rained down on the street with the intensity of a meteor shower.

A second later, the whole street was covered in an orb of darkness—a bubble of pitch black, to steal everyone's sight.

The falling lasers flashed through the void, creating a strobe effect while simultaneously destroying the sidewalk, the nearby trees, the front of multiple buildings, and even the streetlights and manhole covers. It was a combination of *light show* and *carpet bombing* the likes of which Kellan had never experienced.

A shimmering pinkish barrier went up around Kellan.

He managed to spend a mana to activate his armor right before he was struck with the lasers, the beam of light cutting through his clothing and flesh.

[Sun Sen] used *Shield Coterie* on [Alex Kellan], reducing the next AOE attack's damage by 90%.
[Alex Kellan] used *Hammer of God Barrage* and AOE strikes [Alex Kellan], dealing 30 damage to everything in range.
[Alex Kellan] reduces damage of each hit equal to his armor rating of 4 (armor + *Void Knight* darkness bonus).
[Alex Kellan]'s shadow shell cannot absorb laser damage.
[Alex Kellan] suffers a total of 0 damage.

The notifications that Kellan received told him that Alternate-Kellan was here—the one raining down destruction all around them. The orb of darkness had likely come from Ysa, who was a master of the shadows.

And while Kellan hadn't taken any damage from the massive storm of laser beams, he knew that wouldn't always be the case. If Sen ever *failed* to shield Kellan from the hail of lasers, Kellan was sure he would probably die from the attack…

Which meant they had to take cover.

The orb of darkness robbed everyone of their sight but Kellan. As a matter of fact, it activated his *Void Knight* power, granting him additional physical strength. Between the blasts of lasers, Kellan leapt to the side with enough power and speed that he effortlessly flew through a window, shattering through glass and landing inside an office building.

Millie, who had been hurt in the attack, and slashed by some of the glass, trembled in his arms.

Kellan used one mana and healed her of three damage. She was still injured, despite that. Then he set her down behind a desk, leapt back out into the street, and grabbed Sen. He moved at such speed, he surprised himself. His thoughts almost couldn't keep up with the ridiculous movements his body was now capable of.

But Brenner Hawke also had those capabilities—and more.

The lunatic man blasted forward into the orb of darkness. He swung his sword as he went, slashing everything he touched, including a devastated tree and streetlamp.

"Look out!" Sen shouted.

Brenner was on top of them before Kellan could bend his knees to jump again. He slashed with his sword, cutting through part of Kellan's arm, the laser blade burning flesh as it went.

With gritted teeth, Kellan managed to slightly pivot on his heel, moving just enough to save his arm from being cut clean off. Sen's magical barrier shimmered to life as well.

[Sun Sen] used *Shield Ally* on [Alex Kellan], reducing the next attack's damage by 90%.
[Brenner Hawke] slashed [Alex Kellan], dealing 25 damage.
[Alex Kellan] reduces damage of each hit equal to his armor rating of 4 (armor + *Void Knight* darkness bonus), but *Arondight* ignores 10 points of armor rating.
[Alex Kellan]'s shadow shell cannot absorb laser damage.
[Alex Kellan] suffers a total of 3 damage.
[Tyranny Worms] restore [Alex Kellan] for 1 damage every 6 seconds.

Kellan only had seven health. The writhing worms in his body did everything in their power to stitch his flesh together, healing him of the damage, but they weren't enough to combat Brenner's insane speeds and Alternate-Kellan's *Area of Effect* attack.

His low health was rapidly becoming the worst problem Kellan had to deal with.

He dove for the office building, leaping through the same shattered window and rolling across the office floor, his heightened dexterity making the landing easy. Sen clung to him—even as a teen—like Kellan was his personal safety vest.

Kellan wasn't sure what he was going to do about Husker. The rennic threw off his coat, howled, and then lunged for Brenner. Xiang had illusioned him, but the clink of his chains could still be heard through the devastation of the street.

"*We need to get out of here,*" Sen shouted, his tone bordering on hysterical.

The lasers slammed through part of the office building, destroying the roof, front of the building, and multiple desks. The lasers didn't have much impact—they were just light—but everything crumbled, and some things caught fire. The lasers came straight down from the sky, as though from a satellite, though Kellan knew nothing could come through the Net.

This was just a high-rank eclipse or metal ability, the only two magics with lasers.

Kellan staggered away from the front of the building, but more and more laser blasts continued to hail down around them.

Alternate-Kellan's attack radius was so huge, Kellan would have to book a flight just to get out of it. Thankfully, the laser blasts came in waves. They had a few moments to deal with the situation.

The shadows in the building moved and twisted. Physical tentacles made of darkness rose up all around them. The tendrils lashed out, knocking over desks, crushing chairs, and shattering windows. The manic laugh of Ysa bounced off the walls all around them.

"Come out, whoever you are! *Time's up for you and your pathetic team.*"

Her delight soaked every word.

Dust and debris hung in the air from the vast amount of devastation. Husker fought for his life in the street. Without much time to dwell on the situation, Kellan knew if they were going to live, it came down to his next couple actions.

—Chapter 25—
—Hunted like Dogs—

Although Kellan hated the thought of leaving Husker to deal with most of Team 42 on his own, that *was* Husker's designated role. He had his own hex—perhaps he could win against Brenner.

But Kellan couldn't worry about that. With his enhanced strength and speed, he rushed over to Millie, shoved the desk out of the way, threw her over his shoulder and ran deeper into the office building.

Kellan didn't know where he was going. He didn't care. He needed to get out of the *Hammer of God Barrage*, and he needed to get as far away from Brenner as he possibly could.

Unfortunately, he couldn't move through the darkness while holding others—a fact he loathed—so he kept to the hallways of the building, running as fast as his body would allow. Sen and Millie both held on to his body and clothes, their fingernails digging into his flesh, causing him to bleed for a moment before the Tyranny Worms patched everything up.

The second he exited the orb of darkness—and the lights of the office building washed down around him—Kellan lost access to his physical enhancements. He slowed, his chest burning from the lack of oxygen, and his legs stiff from the overexertion.

Kellan spent a single mana—he was down to nine—and activated his *Ignore Pain* to fight through any sort of ache that would attempt to slow him. Pushing forward, he ran at a slower pace, but still managed a good clip.

Dark tentacles rose from the shadows in the corners. They attempted to grab him—to hold him down and bind him—but once again, his *Void Knight* ability came in handy. It prevented the shadows from taking hold.

But his eclipse powers didn't extend to Sen and Millie. The darkness snatched the deformed woman, the shadow tentacles grabbing around her thin waist and yanking hard.

Kellan wheeled on his heel and held out his hand. A blast of laser erupted from his palm and disintegrated the shadowy tentacle, reducing his mana to eight. Millie collapsed to the floor, shaking.

"Oh, Arbiter, please have mercy," she frantically whispered to herself. "What have I done to anger you?" She kept her eyes tightly closed, unwilling or unable to watch the fight happening around her.

Ysa leapt out of the shadows.

Kellan hadn't been prepared.

She slashed with a dagger, the blade extending as she struck—the darkness literally coalescing onto the edge of the weapon and striking on its own. The blade sliced into his gut. After the reduction of his armor and shadow shell, he still took *five* damage, his blood splattering across the hall walls and on the floor.

Worms infested all his vital fluids. Yellow and spaghetti-like, they writhed around, looking for flesh and finding none.

"*Goddammit, I need your help,*" Kellan said through gritted teeth, frustrated Sen hadn't used his *Shield Ally* ability for the strike.

Then he shoved Sen off his shoulder and blasted another beam of light. Ysa leapt into the darkness, dodging his attack.

Kellan had seven mana remaining.

Confused—and *certain* Ysa would return for another strike with her shadow dagger—Kellan glanced around. He activated his *Mold Metal* power, grabbed the handle of a nearby office door, and tore it off. The metal acted like putty in his hand, but the moment he let go of it, the metal would return to its stiff and durable consistency.

Six mana remaining.

Ysa had targeted Millie first. She had been trying to destroy the doll.

Kellan jumped to stand over Millie. When the shadows moved, he was ready. Ysa leapt out of the darkness, her blade in hand. Kellan stepped into her attack. Sen's magical barrier shimmered into existence just before the blade went into Kellan's flesh. And then, while Kellan was close, he took the metal of the door handle and slammed it across Ysa's eyes.

The twisted bits of brass dug into the soft bits of her eyes, and then hooked into the eye sockets. When Kellan removed his hand, the metal was fixed there, blinding her, and sending her into a panic.

Ysa screamed and leapt away. She dove back into the shadows and exited a few feet away, clawing at her face. She couldn't rip the metal off, though. Not without dealing more damage to herself.

While she was distracted, Kellan grabbed Millie and then ran back to Sen. He grabbed the teenager's arm and kept running, desperate to find an exit and escape these lunatics.

The building shook from a powerful tremor, but then things went still. Kellan swallowed air as he pushed himself to run. He slammed through a door, and then another. He molded the handles of doors that were locked and just raced through the office building, barely paying attention to his route, simply searching for an exit sign.

Sen grabbed him, and the warmth of healing flooded Kellan's injured body. The Tyranny Worms had been slowly mending everything, but Sen's body magic made the process instant.

"Your blood," Sen said between huffs. "It would… lead them to us…"

When Kellan glanced back, he realized Sen had a point. He had left a small trail of blood splatters as he ran. Now that he was healed, it wasn't as much of an issue, but Team 42 would still follow them halfway through the building.

Finally, he found an exit.

Kellan slammed out the door and into the street of the bizarre town. TVs mounted into the sidewalk and the sides of the building were all on and playing the clown show. Without much time to analyze every possible answer, Kellan dashed forward and went for another alleyway.

An explosion of glass caused him to duck behind a dumpster. Shards of window clattered into the alleyway. The dumpster shielded Kellan, Millie, and Sen from the devastation.

"Oh, Arbiter, p-please have mercy," Millie repeatedly whispered, her face buried in Kellan's shoulder. "What have I done to anger you?"

Sen gulped down his breath, his eyes wide. He sat on the ground, his back to the dumpster, his gaze unfocused. "What're we going to do? What're we—"

Kellan slammed a hand over Sen's mouth. Then he tightened his grip on Millie and whispered, "Quiet. All of you."

More shattered glass. Another explosion. Something was happening in the building.

"*Come back here!*" Ysa screeched. She stomped into the street, her boots crushing glass as she went. "*You fuckers are dead once I find you!*"

One of Kellan's survival courses had involved a segment on tracking down individuals. The number one way someone messed up their chances of escape was deciding to hide. Most hiding places weren't ingenious—the dumpster was far from a *good spot*—and if Ysa did search, she'd likely find them.

Kellan tapped Sen on the shoulder. Then he placed a finger to his mouth. Together, they quietly made their way down the alleyway. At one point, Sen almost stepped on a pile of glass shards, but Kellan yanked him back and pointed to the ground. Sen nodded. His clothes had been burned by the laser attack, and his body carried several injuries, mostly burns. And unlike Kellan, Sen's wounds weren't slowly healing on their own.

The queen worm doesn't keep him alive like the others?

Kellan shook his head. He stayed focused on the alleyway, and jerked Sen to the side the moment they were out. Making his way through the shadows, he dragged Sen and Millie across the street, and then ducked into another building.

A hotel.

The front entrance room was massive and open—everything Kellan hated. He ran for the receptionist's desk and ducked behind it. As he headed for a door, the glass of the front windows blew inward from a massive release of pressure.

Kellan's ears practically exploded. He clenched his jaw, unable to hear anything other than a constant ringing. He fell to the floor on one knee, a rivulet of blood trailing from his ear down his neck.

Goddammit.

Sen placed a hand on Kellan's neck. The warmth of Sen's healing repaired everything. Kellan could hear, his thoughts weren't buzzing, and he managed to get back to his feet.

Millie, on the other hand, sobbed a bit, blood now staining her odd hair and designer clothing.

Kellan touched the side of her face and used his *Heal the Body* ability. He repaired what damage had been done by the concussion blast. She glanced up at him, tears in her eyes. Kellan hated seeing civilians caught up in war zones, and everything about Millie reminded him of that.

"Everything will be okay," he said, forceful and confident. "Just close your eyes. It'll all be over soon."

Millie replied by simply tightening her grip on his ruined shirt.

Kellan had five mana remaining.

Sen shot him a dark glower, but it didn't last long. He shook, clearly disturbed by the events unfolding, but he didn't object to Kellan's statements.

Debris and dust washed through the hotel. Kellan shielded his eyes. The stomp of boots on glass caught his attention, and he ducked low to the ground, dragging Sen along with him.

"They're somewhere here," Ysa said, her shrill voice hard to mistake.

A growl answered her. No words, just a guttural noise.

"Blast this area," she shouted. "Blast it like you did all the others!"

She was far enough away that the sound of her voice wasn't as clear. Was she just outside the hotel? Kellan suspected so.

Another growl answered her, this one shorter and angrier.

Other-Kellan didn't respond with words—it had to be him. The tone of his growl was raspy and broken, like it was painful to even voice that much. Kellan wondered if he was also signing something. Xiang had said Other-Kellan knew how—but did Ysa? Kellan suspected the woman barely knew how to read.

"You're out of mana already?" Ysa scoffed. "That *Hammer of God Barrage* isn't useful against, like, three assholes. We should've saved that for multiple teams at once! If you don't have any mana left, what good are you to me? Go get a glintberry potion from Brenner!"

Kellan glanced around the receptionist's desk.

The nearby shadows, outside and inside the hotel, shifted and flickered. Were they searching for Kellan? It seemed as if they were semi-sentient, checking under coffee tables and chairs, and sifting through the wreckage of the buildings.

Knowing he had to move, Kellan crouch-walked forward. He managed to open a door and slide through, but he wasn't sure if Ysa would see something so blatant. As soon as he was on the other side of the door, he stood and ran. Sen tried to keep up, but his shaky legs weren't up to the task.

Kellan stopped in an employee's lounge and waited. After a few deep breaths, Sen caught up to him.

"Is she following?" Kellan quickly asked.

"I don't know," Sen whispered.

"Do you know if Husker is all right?"

Sen shook his head.

Frustrated, and out of options, Kellan decided to keep moving. He turned for a door he thought would lead to an exit. Without much thought, he opened it and ran through.

Only to find himself in a bizarre room.

He froze, stunned by the white walls, ivory carpet, and stark black furniture. It felt like he had walked into a black-and-white movie, as the whole room was devoid of color.

"What the?"

Sen ran in after, and the door slammed shut.

A single desk in the middle of the room—just as black as the chairs, bookshelf, and couch—had a single sheet of white paper on top of it. A tiny creature sat in the swivel chair behind the desk. It was no more than a foot tall, humanoid in shape, and had black skin and tiny bat-like wings.

The little horns on its head were curved in a semicircle, similar to a goat's.

It was an imp.

And it wore a tiny suit the same shade of white as the walls.

Name: Puzzle Imp #10
Race: Semi-Sentient Construct
Magics: Mind, Travel
Rank: Impossible to Rank
Armor Rating: —
Health: 2/2
Stats: Concealed
Abilities: Concealed

"Hello, there," the imp said, its voice a chipmunk parody. "Congratulations, you found a *Puzzle Room!* The Arbiter hides these around the game zones and—"

Sen whirled around and grabbed at the door handle. He shook the door and pulled, but the door refused to open. With ever-increasing panic, Sen jiggled the handle. "We're trapped."

Kellan turned around, pushed Sen aside, and grabbed the handle. His *Mold Metal* should've allowed him to effortlessly escape, but the bluish-black handle was made out of the same anti-magic the doll cages had been.

The puzzle imp frowned. "You can't leave."

"Can other people come in?" Kellan asked as he turned back around.

"Wow. You guys are weird. Most people have *other* questions." The imp tapped its little fingers on the desk. "Yes. Other people can come in here."

"And you said *we can't leave*?"

"Not until you solve the puzzle or give up."

"We give up," Kellan immediately stated. "Now let us out of the room."

They couldn't afford to be *stuck* in a room when Ysa, Other-Kellan, and Brenner were actively searching for them. What if those lunatics entered the Puzzle Room with them? It would turn into a bloodbath. The room was only twelve feet by twelve feet. It would be like having a gun fight in a phone booth.

The imp smiled wide, all its teeth pointed and needle-like. "Oh, well, if you give up, the price of failure is exactly one death. So, which of you will die as punishment for failing to solve the puzzle?"

"What?" Kellan balked.

"Uh, I don't think I can be any clearer." The imp sighed. "If you give up, someone has to die. If you win, you get a prize. Easy-peazy-lemon-squeezy."

Goddammit.

"Okay, fine—what's the puzzle?" Kellan asked.

Sen didn't even bother engaging. He shook the door handle again, and even tugged on it harder, like he might be able to break it down if he strained hard enough. Kellan knew that wasn't going to work. The Arbiter always had weird restrictions in rooms like these—Kellan had already been in a Prize Room *and* a Trap Room. If they wanted to leave, they just had to deal with the puzzle.

"*Quickly,*" Kellan growled. "What is it?"

The imp pushed the single piece of paper forward. With a wicked grin, it said, "It's a simple puzzle. Turn this paper into gold. Once you've done that, I'll reward you with a prize."

—Chapter 26—
—Puzzle Room—

Kellan had been expecting a *Lord of the Rings* style puzzle, or something similar to the riddle in the Catacomb Maze. How was he supposed to transform a piece of paper into *gold*? Was that even fair?

With quick movements, Kellan set Millie down on the floor. She watched as Kellan approached the black desk and grabbed the single sheet of paper. It was thin and flimsy.

Kellan turned it over.

Blank on both sides.

"Can I… have a pen?" Kellan asked.

The little imp scrunched its face in disgust. "Are you touched in the head? What will a *pen* do for you?"

"I… I don't know. I just figured it was part of the puzzle."

"I can assure you, it's not."

Kellan scratched at the side of his head. His first thought, since it was a riddle, was to fold the paper into something. But how could he fold it into gold? A bird, sure. A star, definitely. But gold?

"Is there a magical ability in one of the spheres of magics that turns objects into gold?" Kellan asked. He didn't know all the magics well enough. Could *metal* magic somehow be linked to alchemy?

"There's no ability like that," the imp said matter-of-factly. "There's a travel magic power that allows mages to pull something into this dimension from another dimension—and maybe that can be gold—but it doesn't transform anything." With a tiny, clawed hand, the imp motioned to the paper. "You need to change that paper into gold, not just make gold appear."

Sen shook the door handle harder. "This is inane!" he finally shouted. He turned around, his breaths shallow. "We don't have time for this."

"Team 42 might not come looking in this room," Kellan stated. "Calm down."

"You don't understand. Puzzle Rooms will kill you if you take too long. They, themselves, are traps. You might not see it now, but that's how Xiang's mother lost the first member of her team."

Xiang's mother?

It took Kellan a moment to remember they were half-siblings. Different mothers, same father.

He shook the thought from his head. "I don't care. Just help me solve this."

Sen glanced over at the imp. "You said a death is payment enough for leaving?"

"That's right," the imp replied in a cheery, chipmunk tone.

"It doesn't have to be a mage? It doesn't have to be someone on our team?"

"Nope."

Sen motioned over to Millie. "Good. Let's get rid of the doll and get out of here."

Before Kellan could open his mouth and voice a complaint, the room rumbled. He tensed and whirled around, his rifle in his hands through reflex. But there weren't any enemies.

The walls…

And the ceiling…

Kellan's eyes widened as he realized they were slowly collapsing in on themselves. The room *had* been twelve feet by twelve feet, but now it was smaller, and shrinking at a noticeable rate. By Kellan's calculations, they had less than two minutes to solve the puzzle, or else they'd all be crushed.

"Once the door vanishes, you're gonna lose the option to surrender," the imp said, pointing to the door on the far wall. It slid down, slowly lowering into the floor as the ceiling came down by itself. They had less than a minute before the door would disappear.

"We can't turn paper into gold," Sen stated. "Just kill the doll."

Millie trembled, her saggy and deformed skin pale with fright. She clasped her hands together, shaking so bad, Kellan suspected she'd fall over.

"Why are you hesitating?" Sen waved his arm around. "*This* is why we never should've learned its name! We have to do whatever it takes to win! You've grown too attached. Kill it, or else—"

Kellan grabbed Sen by the front of his illusioned hoodie. Fueled by rage, but tempered by years of training, Kellan jerked Sen closer and twisted his grip, constricting the collar around Sen's neck.

"I'm not going to kill an innocent civilian just because it's convenient." As Sen tried to grunt out an answer, Kellan slammed the teen back against the wall. "And if you try to force me, I promise I'll burn this whole goddamn team to the ground." Then Kellan released him.

Sen rubbed his shoulders.

Millie watched the entire confrontation with wide eyes.

The imp leaned its chin into one hand, his eyes half-lidded in obvious boredom.

The low-volume scrape of the walls and ceiling sliding closer and closer was the only sound in the room.

Sen glared up at Kellan. "You're willing to die for things like… *honor* and *compassion*?"

"Those are some of the few things *worth* dying for," Kellan stated. "And I don't care how crazy this shitshow gets, I refuse to believe anything else."

"What an idiot," the imp said with a snicker.

Kellan snapped his glare over to the tiny imp. "What did you say about surrendering? We have to pay with a death? Doesn't matter which of us?"

The imp yawned and stretched its little wings. "That's right."

"Then we surrender."

"Oh? And who will—"

Kellan lifted his rifle and shot the imp square in its tiny face. The creature had two health, and Kellan did way more than two damage. Its brains splattered over the chair, the floor, and the back wall, the blood a mix of black and red.

Millie gasped and flinched.

"You shot it," Sen said, breathless.

The walls and ceiling stopped their death march. Kellan lowered his weapon, thankful that hadn't backfired on him. *He said any death would do,* Kellan mused to himself. *I guess the Nexus Games really doesn't give a shit about the people who work it.*

"You just gave me an impassioned speech about not killing people!" Sen scoffed and flailed his arm at the dead body of the imp. "You blew that creature's brains out, and you didn't even care!"

"It wasn't an innocent person." Kellan turned to Millie and scooped the woman up in his arms. She leaned into him, her hands gently gripping his shirt. "That imp was going to kill us, and he probably would've laughed about it the entire way, too."

Sen grabbed the door and shoved it open. He sighed in relief as he stepped outside. "It was a servant of the Arbiter, though… We could get in trouble."

"Look, something trying to kill me is an enemy. That's the fucking line. I think it's a reasonable one."

Kellan dove out of the puzzle room and ran across the employee lounge of the hotel. The shadows weren't moving, but distant explosions told him that Ysa was still nearby. He went in the opposite direction of the noise and headed for a long hallway. Sen kept pace, still muttering statements of baffled disbelief.

When Kellan reached an emergency exit, he kicked it outward and then jogged out into a service alleyway. Damaged trucks clogged the space between two buildings, like they had all piled up and crashed trying to deliver goods. The twisted trucks were smashed together from wall to wall, piled ten feet high.

Sen examined the wreckage with a long exhale.

Another explosion—this one closer than the last—told Kellan that Ysa was systematically destroying the area.

That twisted bitch.

The hotel shook, and bits of the trucks and buildings rained down around them. Kellan shielded Millie as best he could while dodging the debris. Coughing back the dust, Kellan tried to think of some sort of magical way to solve their problem, but he couldn't think of anything. He didn't have *that* many powers.

Sen wheezed and then shook his head. "This way." He motioned to the alleyway behind them. He jogged a few feet and then turned around. "What're you waiting for?"

"You're heading toward the destruction," Kellan stated.

"I know. But I have a soul ability that allows me to sense magic. There's a swell of it near here. And also, a knot of corrupted magic—I suspect from Brenner and Husker, since both of them carry hexes."

Determined to live through the godforsaken game, Kellan exhaled as he turned around. He ran through the clouds of dust and followed Sen. Xiang's illusions maintained, giving them the façade of bikers, but Kellan could only see the scrawny teen version of Sen in his mind. Could Sen be trusted to lead them away from danger?

Once out of the alleyway, Sen took a hard left. He kept his head down as he sprinted forward, clearly trying to keep a low profile while running. Kellan also turned left, but he glanced around, taking stock of their surroundings.

Ysa stood in the middle of a four-way intersection, her attention on a nearby building, her back to Kellan. She glanced around, which meant the metal was likely out of her eyes. There were other people in the building—another team? She waved her hand, and shadows leapt to answer her bidding.

Unfortunately, the shadows around Sen and Kellan also sprang to life. Kellan dodged out of the way, careful not to touch any of the dark tentacles, but Sen wasn't as dexterous. The shadow tendrils slammed into him, and he collapsed to the road.

Ysa could obviously sense whatever her shadows touched, because the moment she struck Sen, she whirled around on her heel. With a smile, she shouted, "*Alex!* I found them!"

Kellan set Millie down and readied himself for an attack, his heart hammering around in his insides. What was he supposed to do? He was halfway out of mana and running out of tricks. Ysa and Other-Kellan could obviously deal an insane amount of damage.

But as Ysa ran in their direction, snickering to herself, someone leapt out of the nearby building. They crashed through a window, sending glass cascading down to the street in a hail of deadly shards. The person who landed did so with a superhero's grace.

Kellan recognized the new man. He was about Kellan's height, with short crew-cut dark hair. And he, too, wore an outfit suited for a biker. Leather jacket, jeans, white T-shirt—like he had just exited a biker bar for motorcycle enthusiasts.

The man's right eye…

It was a machine. Like a high-definition camera but glowing in the center with a soft blue light.

Name: Concealed
Race: Concealed
Magics: Concealed
Rank: Concealed
Armor Rating: Concealed

Health: Concealed
Stats: Concealed
Abilities: Concealed

Kellan shook away the useless information.

That was *Jace Kellan*, of Team 77, the son of Other-Kellan, and an enigmatic player in the Nexus Games who had both helped and hindered Kellan's games. He had also given Kellan his dog tags…

Jace stood and brushed himself off. He flashed Ysa a smile. "Where are you going? I thought you said you wanted to duke this out?"

Ysa glanced between Kellan and Jace, her lips twisted in a snarl. In the distance, a battle raged. The ground shook, and more explosions could be heard. Was it Brenner and Husker? Kellan couldn't see beyond the many office buildings and hotels.

Ysa must've felt the electric urgency in the air as well. She shifted her weight from one foot to the other before finally smiling. "You better be careful, *boy*. Your father is due to come back any minute."

"I'm counting on it," Jace said, his machine eye glowing a brighter blue. "After all the mana he's been using, and all the mages your team has been fighting, I think this'll be an easy kill."

"That's what they all say," Ysa replied with a laugh. Then dark energy pulsed off her arm, like a snake forming out of pure magic and wrapping around her limb. "*But you haven't seen anything yet!*"

She waved her arm, and the deadly energies slithered off her body and washed out into the surrounding area. Everything her magic touched rotted and wilted, as though rapidly advancing in age. The sidewalks crumbled to dust, the wrecked cars rusted and twisted inward, and the asphalt cracked and decayed.

When it hit Jace, he gritted his teeth and cursed. His clothing slowly paled and unraveled, and his skin withered and aged.

The pulse of rotting magic headed in Kellan's direction.

Sen staggered to his feet. "*Run!* Don't let it touch you!"

Not wanting to argue, Kellan dashed over to Millie, scooped her back up, and then ran down the road. All three of them managed to shove their way into the front door of a local restaurant before the rotting magic could take hold. Safe inside the building as the wave of corrosive magic washed across the street, Kellan took a deep breath.

Once again, he set Millie down, not wanting to be encumbered by her weight if a fight broke loose.

"That was rot?" he asked.

Sen nodded. "Ysa is a powerful entropy mage."

Kellan turned his attention to the window. It slowly decayed into a pile of sand. Once it had aged away, the rotting stopped. The destruction wouldn't continue to spread forever, it seemed.

But Kellan's thoughts went immediately to Jace. Although the man wasn't really related to Kellan—since Jace hailed from a different dimension entirely—

there was still a slight connection Kellan couldn't deny. Jace could be his brother, they looked so similar.

With a sigh, Kellan reached into his backpack and withdrew one of their three moss burgers.

He glanced over the sand-covered windowsill. Jace fought Ysa in the street, her rot causing him to boil and bleed. His magic clearly fought against the decay. His clothing mostly lost the war—his jacket, boots, and belt became moth-eaten rags. His shirt and pants weren't really affected, however. Kellan wasn't sure why.

"I'll be right back," Kellan muttered.

Sen turned to him and frowned. "You're not going to help that man, are you?"

"I think I owe it to him."

"He's…" Sen ran a hand down his face and shook his head. "You know what? Never mind. Just get this out of your system and tell me when you're ready to keep moving. I'll watch our doll."

Kellan patted the other man on the back and chuckled. "Good. I'll be right back. Get ready to run."

—Chapter 27—
—Rest and Restoration—

As Kellan was about to jump over the windowsill, Millie the deformed girl held up a hand. He paused mid-step, confused and worried she needed help. She fumbled with her words for a moment, and then averted her gaze.

"Uh, please stay safe," Millie whispered.

Kellan forced a smile. "I'll be right back. Don't worry, Sen isn't going to do anything." Then he leapt over the windowsill and landed on the street.

Finally unencumbered, Kellan dove into the darkness and shadow-stepped down the street, avoiding the dust, rubble, and debris. When he emerged a few feet down, he just dove back again, using the shadows like a dolphin used waves.

Ysa and Jace fought in the middle of the road. Ysa used her shadow blade, lashing out with surprising ferocity. She, too, leapt into the shadows and exited in strategic locations, trying to get Jace from behind.

But Jace seemed a few steps ahead of her. Every time she attempted to outmaneuver him, he turned to meet her blade with one of his own. Then he went invisible and struck her from the side. The rot on his body caused him to bleed, but his personal healing seemed to stave it off. That required a lot of mana, though.

Kellan leapt out of the shadows.

Ysa dove away and exited the darkness on top of a nearby bus bench. She glared at Kellan and lifted her blade, as if preparing to fight him as well.

"Here," Kellan said. He threw the burger at Jace, underhanded and gentle.

Jace caught the burger and then turned it over in his hand. Then he gave Kellan a puzzled glance.

"Who are you?" Jace called out.

It occurred to Kellan that he still wore Xiang's perfect illusions. While Brenner could sense it was a disguise, most people were incapable of seeing through her mind magic. Kellan still appeared to be a member of Team 33.

"I'm just helping you out," Kellan shouted back. "So keep this in mind next time you try to steal my key."

The last statement was cryptic on purpose. Jace would understand, but Ysa probably wouldn't. Which was exactly how it played out.

Ysa stood on the bench, her blade close in hand, her eyes narrowed. "Would you two stop making out and face me? I can take you both. And I need the arcana."

Jace just smiled as he unwrapped his moss burger. After a couple bites, the wounds on his body slowly faded. The immunity to rot would make the whole fight easier for him.

"I didn't think you'd be here," Jace said between bites. "You're braver than my father, that's for sure." He held up the half-eaten burger. "Cheers, mate. See you on the other side."

"Oh? Your boyfriend thinks he's leaving?" Ysa snorted as she smirked. "That's not gonna happen." She waved her arm, and the shadows sprang to life all around the road.

The shadows of the streetlamps, fire hydrants, and ruined trees all formed into tendrils that shot for Kellan. Fortunately, his *Void Knight* ability made him immune to the shadow-control of others. His gold arcana, and apex magic, was just more potent than Ysa's. When the tendrils attempted to grab him, Kellan simply slid out of their grasp and shadow-stepped away, diving into the darkness again and appearing farther down the road.

Ysa gritted her teeth, her hands shaking. "*What the hell?* Why can't I grab him? *What the fuck is this?*"

"You're making me jealous," Jace said with a dark laugh. He waved his hand and telekinetically threw debris at Ysa—a whole wave of rubble went shooting her way. She dodged and slipped into the shadows, cursing the entire way. "Stop talking to other people and face me!"

Although Kellan couldn't see Jace's stats or magics, it was obvious that Jace had eclipse and mind, at the bare minimum. Eclipse mages could become invisible, and mind mages had the power of telekinesis. What else did Jace have? Kellan didn't have time to deduce *everything*.

While they were engaged in combat, Kellan took the opportunity to flee. He jumped through the darkness, but halfway back to Millie and Sen, a bullet grazed his chest.

[Hank Gardener] shot [Alex Kellan] for 6 damage.
[Alex Kellan] reduces damage of each hit equal to his armor rating of 2.
[Alex Kellan]'s shadow shell absorbs 2 damage.
[Alex Kellan] suffers a total of 2 damage.

Dammit.

Kellan entered the darkness and then exited in the restaurant, reuniting with Sen and Millie. His Tyranny Worms did their best to heal him, one point of damage at a time, but that wasn't what concerned Kellan.

The streets were littered with enemy teams.

Hank Gardener was a man from Team 80. If Kellan hadn't been illusioned, he was certain that Hank wouldn't have fired on him, but here they were.

All this meant was that there were several teams just lying in wait, some obviously with snipers. They were going to kill him, or his doll, and they were going to do it from the safety of range. A smart plan. But Kellan couldn't linger here, and he couldn't risk running in the open.

"Are you okay?" Sen asked.

Kellan nodded. "I'll be fine."

"Merry Christmas," Millie said with a sigh of relief.

Sen stood and pointed to the back of the restaurant. "The source of magic is this way. And the corruption feels weaker now… Which means Husker is probably done with this fight."

As Kellan scooped Millie into his arms, he hardened his gaze. "Is Husker still alive?"

"I'm not sure. But since my sister picked him *specifically* to deal with Brenner, I would guess that Husker was victorious."

"That would be a boon." Which was why Kellan was certain it hadn't happened. Nothing in the Nexus ever came easy, it seemed.

Together, the three of them ran to the back of the restaurant. While they went, Kellan took note of the bizarre decorations. Bull heads, Japanese kanji, and pictures of lions adorned the walls. And the place smelled of so much urine it gave the New York subway a run for its money. What kind of establishment was this?

The Nexus seemed to twist together four different themes, each one more bizarre than the last.

Sen slammed through the kitchen doors and dashed by the many cooking stations. Kellan stayed close, constantly glancing around for yami or other teams. They could be attacked at any moment, and Kellan hated that he was unfamiliar with their surroundings.

Once they plowed through the exit door, Kellan had expected to land outside. Instead, they were in a second restaurant, this one with a blue, fish, and butterfly theme. It felt like running into a child's birthday party, only the kid had a fascination with salmon and caterpillars.

But once inside, Kellan breathed easy.

The Blue Bayou Oasis

You have entered an Oasis. While inside this non-conflict area, all mages are forbidden from initiating direct violence. Offensive magical abilities are limited. Any who attempt to circumvent this rule will answer to the Arbiter himself.

The Blue Bayou?

"This is it," Sen said. He closed his eyes and held up a hand. "Something about this place is deeply magical. It's an Oasis, yes… but something more. I'm not sure what."

"Your soul magic brought you here?" Kellan asked. "It has some sort of detection?"

"Divination, yes. For souls and magic, specifically. The ability to recognize and understand magic, as well as sense its potential."

Kellan set Millie down. As long as they were in an Oasis, she wouldn't come to any harm. When he tried to walk away, she held up a hand again. He glanced over, and she immediately set her gaze to the floor.

"Um, may we sit?" she asked, her voice barely audible.

"Sure," Kellan said.

He helped her over to a booth, waited until she sat, and then took a seat next to her. His legs protested the rest. Adrenaline coursed through his body, keeping him limber, but as soon as it was gone…

"Do you still have that map?" Kellan asked.

Sen reached into his pants pocket and withdrew the paper map. He placed it on the table. Then he turned his attention to a nearby door. "I'm going to check nearby. That feeling of corruption is near… Wait here. I won't be long." He strode off, not even bothering to wait for Kellan's response.

Kellan preferred that. He stared at the map and ran a finger from the shopping mall over the route he thought they had taken. Then he found what he was looking for—a restaurant named *The Blue Bayou.*

They were a fourth of the way to their destination, and just beyond the restaurant was a whole host of streets marked with a skull. Kellan sighed. If it wasn't one problem, it was another.

"Get your act together, soldier," he muttered to himself.

Millie sat with a stiff posture while Kellan studied the map. After a few minutes, she relaxed a bit, her gaze on the rest of the room. Her bloodied clothes, and misshapen body, made it seem like she had just crawled out of a blender. Fortunately, she wasn't actively bleeding. Left to her own devices, she took a napkin off the restaurant table and brushed her clothes down until they were slightly cleaner.

"Alex Kellan," she whispered as she returned her attention to him. "Um…"

Kellan stared at the map, wondering if there was a trick he had missed. At first, he considered the sewers. Going under the streets could be helpful.

"Hm?" he said when he realized Millie hadn't finished her statement.

"Most outsiders, uh, think I'm disgusting." She touched the odd parts of her skin that hung down from her chin. Then she caressed her own thin hair, some of which had fallen out during all the fighting and destruction. She had bald spots. "Even if they don't say it with words, I can tell by… their looks and gestures."

"Hm."

They obviously couldn't go through the sewers. There were flooding icons on the map—over the parks and stamped across large buildings. The sewers were likely flooded as well. How were *other* streets not flooded? Kellan had seen barricades, but he suspected it had something to do with elevation. The parks could be lower, or the buildings could have a basement level.

Flooded sewers would've been perfect. If only we had taken some of the water-breathing foods…

Millie ran her fingers across the tablecloth. "I, uh, wanted to thank you."

"Hm-mm."

"You're the first outsider who doesn't make me *feel* disgusting." She brought both her cuffed hands up to her cheeks. Slightly red, she finished, "This is silly to say, but, uh, the way you protect me… and go out of your way for me… You make me feel beautiful."

Kellan slowly nodded in acknowledgment. "I'm glad."

He ran a finger over the lines of the map, barely registering her words. He understood—she had felt unwanted, he was different, that made her feel good—but none of that would help him get out of the city in time. Kellan had to focus. What was he missing? Were they just destined to run through the rot?

They were down a hamburger.

Could he think of an alternate route? Or would he just have to suffer through it?

Sen walked back into the room, and Millie's posture became tense, and she just stared at the top of the table. When Sen took a seat across from her, she scooted closer to Kellan.

"What're you looking for?" Sen asked.

"A new route," Kellan muttered.

"Why? If we manage to get away from Team 42, we'll have an easier time of everything. We should stick to the plan."

"I gave away one of our burgers, and it's obvious that the other teams are going for some quick arcana." Kellan ran a hand down his chest. The hole in his shirt reminded him of the quick sniper shot. "I was just weighing our options…"

Sen stared for a moment, then sighed. He stood from the booth, walked around to Kellan, and then held out a hand. "Here. Let me help you with the rot."

"I don't have any on me," Kellan stated.

"Of course not, *you rube*." Sen glared. "The amount of damage you take from entropic rot depends on your fortitude. The more you have, the less it takes effect—fortitude is a measurement of your resilience, after all. And since you also have *Tyranny Worms* in your system, a combination of high fortitude and their healing effects should be good enough to get you through a few streets."

"You think so?"

Sen huffed. "I wouldn't have wasted my time and breath on a plan that I wasn't serious about." He shoved his hand forward. "Come. Get up. And…" Sen glanced at the booth. "Just lie on this table, actually."

The plan sounded risky, but it was better than *no* plan. And Sen was a talented fleshcrafter, even if Kellan didn't appreciate the art.

And although Kellan hated the thought of going under the knife, he removed his backpack, rifle, and jacket, and then got onto the table. Sen motioned him to lie down. With an exhale, Kellan lay on his back and stared up at the blue ceiling. The table wasn't quite large enough, and Kellan braced his feet on the booth seats.

Sen grabbed at Kellan's shirt and rolled it up. Kellan's futuristic armor remained in place. It was skintight, and he forgot he even had it on most of the time.

Kellan willed the armor to retract. The armor slid off his body and coiled into a small pocket on Kellan's spine. With his stomach and chest exposed, Kellan glanced down to look at himself. The Tyranny Worms had done their work—no injuries remained.

Millie covered her eyes with her hands, her face red. "I think that, uh…"

"Nudity is the natural state of all life," Sen said matter-of-factly. "There's no need to be ashamed of gazing upon it."

"You're going to fully undress him?" Millie pressed her blistering crimson face into her hands even harder.

"N-No!" Sen placed a hand on Kellan's bare chest. "I don't need to alter his *whole being* for my magic to take effect. I simply need to move around some of his physical structure, and then rewire the ley lines of his soul."

"What does that even mean?" Kellan whispered, already hating everything about the encounter.

"Ley lines of the soul are pathways for spiritual and magical power."

"Like chakra or something?"

"*Just listen.* If I alter your physical form, and then tie my intended changes with the ley lines, your body will be able to maintain the changes and adapt to everything naturally. If I *didn't* alter your ley lines, everything I did would ultimately revert, or your body would fall apart, attacking my changes as though they were an infection."

"Are those the worst things that can happen if you mess up? Or is there something you're not telling me?"

"*I won't mess up,*" Sen snapped. "I've *never* made a mistake on this level. Fleshcrafting is my life's work! Have you seen my title? I didn't earn that by slouching!"

He yelled so loud that his voice echoed around the dining room of the restaurant.

Kellan didn't know how to reply. He had seen Sen work on people multiple times. Sen had even corrected Mavis's limp. This would work. At least, he hoped it would.

"Just get it over with," Kellan said as he pinched the bridge of his nose.

"Excellent. Hold still while I rearrange your insides."

—Chapter 28—
—Spider, Spider on the Wall—

Sen pressed his hand down into Kellan's chest. Sen's fingers slowly sank into the skin, and then beyond the rib cage. Kellan tensed. He couldn't breathe. His body shook as he tried to move. A pressure came over his thoughts, like he needed to decide something, but panic made everything difficult.

"I can't do this if you fight me," Sen stated. "My magic only works on willing targets."

That knowledge eased some of Kellan's worries. Although he still couldn't breathe, he forced himself to remain calm. He stared at the ceiling, and ultimately accepted that Sen, the lunatic fleshcrafting teenager, would alter his body.

It was almost a nightmare come true, but Kellan tried not to dwell on it.

Kellan closed his eyes, the odd atmosphere of the amalgamation restaurant adding to his stress. The Blue Bayou was a metaphor for cramming things together. Sen wasn't doing that to Kellan's body, but Kellan's imagination made it seem that way.

Sen pressed his other hand into Kellan's chest.

"You needn't worry," Sen said, an attempt at a soothing bedside manner. "I've never failed to alter someone."

Still unable to breathe, Kellan just clenched his jaw.

Sen stopped working. "Oh, shit."

Kellan snapped his eyes open, his heart wild with panic. But Sen just snorted and smirked.

"I jest," Sen said. "Everything is perfectly normal. You're a healthy man, and this will be a simple procedure. I just wanted to see your reaction."

If Kellan could've moved, he would've punched the other man in the face. Sen was one of the few people who loved what little amount of power they got their hands on. Kellan closed his eyes again, his heart refusing to calm.

Sen moved his hands slowly through Kellan's chest. The flesh acted as clay, and Sen was the sculptor. Everything that Sen touched seemed to freeze, as though Kellan's body was waiting in stasis for all the changes to be made. For a few seconds, it even felt as though Sen was touching Kellan's spine, his fingernails scratching against the bone.

Kellan wanted to shiver and push the teen away. Thankfully, he still couldn't move.

The disturbing sensation of being unable to breathe bothered Kellan. His insides burned. While he wanted Sen to hurry, he didn't want him to make mistakes, either. Finally, after only a few short and strained minutes, Sen withdrew his hands from Kellan's insides.

After a deep breath, Kellan sat upright. He grabbed at his chest, fearing he would feel a hole in his body. But nothing. He felt fine. Better than fine. Sturdier. Healthier. Kellan closed his eyes and received additional notifications.

[Sun Sen] grafted +1 fortitude into [Alex Kellan].

Kellan went from a three in his fortitude, to having four.

"Can you do that for anyone?" Kellan asked, breathless. He rubbed at his chest and collarbones, a little uneasy and stiff. Something about his muscles seemed… different. Words failed him. He just felt *tougher*.

Sen stumbled backward and ran into another booth. He trembled slightly as he shook his head. After a few seconds to catch his breath, he said, "N-No… This isn't something I can keep replicating." Then Sen crossed his arms tightly over his chest. "I just figured, since you've done so much this round, that I should make sure you live through the upcoming hazards."

The quiet restaurant allowed Kellan to quickly gather his thoughts. He slid off the table and exhaled. "What did this cost you?"

At first, Sen said nothing. Then he held out his hand. "Here. Just look at my personal trait yourself. Then you'll understand."

Kellan stepped closer and grabbed the man's hand. Just like with Xiang, he somehow sensed the information that Sen was imparting to him.

Personal—[World Weaver]—The mage may substitute parts of their soul for all magical abilities that require additional components, arcana, or outside requirements (this substitution works for rare or unique requirements as well). The more of their soul the mage loses, the younger they appear, imposing penalties on their physical stats (strength, dexterity, fortitude), as well as the mage's wisdom stat. If the mages de-ages too far, they die. Can be reversed through magical means only.
Training—[Student of Norticum]—The mage reduces the arcana cost of all alteration, buffing, and debuffing magical powers by 50%.

"Your soul?" Kellan asked. "Like your arcana?"

"Something like that," Sen muttered. He leaned against the nearest table, breathing deep. Xiang's illusions prevented Kellan from seeing the *real* him.

Kellan was reminded of Alvo and Juan, and what Nosferatu had said about people who gave away pieces of themselves. This wasn't the same. Sen was using bits of his own soul to power magical abilities. It was as Xiang had said—Sen was twisting himself in order to make things easy.

Kellan walked over, picked up his jacket, rifle, and backpack, and continued to marvel at his newfound toughness.

"Are you younger again?" Kellan asked.

Sen scoffed. "Yes. But just… a few years this time. It was easier than before."

"What's the cost normally?" Kellan asked. "Why not just do this the old-fashioned way, whatever that is? Why substitute your soul?"

"Normally, it requires me to damage my willpower. Or I need Crafting Clay. If I had *Langarren Clay*, this wouldn't be a problem. That legendary substance prevents *all* loss from exchange-based fleshcrafting."

Millie scooted to the edge of the booth, her eyes wide. "Do you have Langarren Clay?"

Sen dismissively waved his hand and sneered. "Of course not. If I did, I wouldn't *be like this*."

Her expression deflated, and she hunched over, her gaze falling to the floor. After a moment of silence, she finally asked, "Are you a high-ranked fleshcrafter? Someone who can… change people?"

"I'm not high enough rank to fix *inbred monstrosities*," Sen said with a huff. "Your problems are more than physical. It's baked into your very DNA."

Millie said nothing in response.

Irritated that Sen would be so callous, Kellan grabbed the man's shoulder. "Enough with the comments, all right? We get it. You don't like the Nexus residents. Let's just focus on the task at hand."

"Well, I think that my comments are—"

The restaurant door slammed open. Kellan leapt for his rifle, but a compulsion to remain calm came over him. They were still in an Oasis—he couldn't go blasting anyone who entered.

A rennic came stumbling into the dining room, his black fur matted with blood. The massive nine-foot-tall man crashed into a nearby table and sent the silverware clattering to the floor. He dug his claws into the furniture in an attempt to stand up straight, but his efforts were futile. The rennic eventually collapsed to the floor, breathing rough.

The number 33 was on the back of his left hand.

"Husker?" Kellan asked.

Sen hurried over to the rennic's side. He knelt and then placed a hand on Husker's bloody fur.

When Kellan made his way over, he took note of Husker's many injuries. He was burnt, slashed, and beaten. Although Xiang's illusions maintained themselves over the rennic, they were clearly adaptive. He was missing tufts of fur, and bullet holes in his legs were actively bleeding.

Sen's healing magic worked wonders. But halfway through, he stopped and gasped.

"I'm running low on mana," he whispered. "Husker, you said you gathered potions from the Exchange. Do you still have them?"

After a few moments of gulping down air, Husker finally managed to sit upright. He hung his head and shook it. "No. They're broken. And… we need to leave here immediately."

"Why?" Kellan asked. "This is an Oasis. No one can hurt us here."

"Other teams can't hurt us here. But the Oasis won't protect us from the Kuji."

Millie gasped and lifted her hands to her lopsided mouth. "Is a Kuji following you?" she whispered. "Does that mean you're the team's Straggler?" She buried her face in both her hands. "Oh, no…"

"The fight with Team 42 got out of hand," Husker said with a grunt as he got to his clawed feet. "I'm glad… you waited for me here. I was outnumbered before. Team 42, a master yami, and the Kuji… I couldn't handle them all."

Kellan just nodded along with his words. They *hadn't* waited for Husker, but Kellan preferred teaming up with the man. They needed to stay together as a team as much as possible. There were too many dangers to risk splitting up any more than they already had.

"Do you have any more mana?" Sen asked as he turned to Kellan.

"Five." Kellan walked to Husker's side. "Do you need more healing?"

Husker exhaled and then ran a hand down his body. "I can make do." He pulled back his lips in a half-sneer as he said, "I apologize. I tried to kill Brenner, but the man was too fast. I never managed to hold onto him long enough to use my hex. If I had, he surely would've perished, but it was as if he *knew* he couldn't allow me to touch him."

"What's your hex specifically?"

The rennic hesitated for a long while. Finally, after putting his ears back, he held out a clawed hand. Kellan placed his hand into Husker's, amazed at how much larger the rennic were compared to humans. Husker had pads on his palm and fingers, similar to a dog. They were calloused and cracked, making for a rough touch.

Kellan got the information he needed in an instant—but also more. It felt as though Husker trusted him, and thus, nothing was hidden.

Name: Husker Linis
Race: Rennic
Magics: Wyld, Magma
Rank: B, B
Armor Rating: —
Health: 11/11

Stats:
Strength—5 [Strong]
Dexterity—4
Fortitude—7 [Tough]
Charisma—3
Manipulation—2
Intelligence—2
Perception—4 [Keen Senses]
Wisdom—5 [Insightful]

Willpower—5

Abilities:
Personal—[Magic and Nature]—The mage is not killed when their health reaches 0. Instead, damage then harms their mana pool. If their health and mana both reach 0, the mage dies.
Training—[Mage Warrior of Rarn]—The mage has consumed Rarn's blood and has a 20% reduction to rank wyld magic.
Hex—[Reaper Touch]—The mage touches a magical target and activates this death sentence without the need for mana. Every six seconds, so long as the mage remains in contact with the target, they deal 20 automatic damage. This damage cannot be mitigated or reduced by fortitude, armor rating, or shielding. *Reaper Touch* has no energy type. As punishment, every time the mage activates this power, a blood relative of the mage instantly dies. If the mage has no blood relatives, the mage dies instead. If the mage dies (in any way other than the hex), this hex is passed to the nearest blood relative until none remain. For every blood relative who inherits this hex, a link of a chain is formed and tethered to the mage.

"Brenner only has fifty-five health," Kellan muttered as he removed his hand from Husker's. "You really *would* kill him if you managed to hang on."

Husker nodded once. "It's a potent hex… But one I never wanted to be saddled with. I inherited this burden."

"Why doesn't your hex have an energy type?"

"It means it won't be negated by immunities," Sen interjected with a smug smile. "Meta magic allows for *no type* effects specifically to get around mages who think they can block all magical attacks."

"It is a troll-y magic." Kellan thought over his own abilities. He only had access to E-rank in meta, and already there were bizarre powers that would cause other mages to rage. "Husker, how many times have you used this hex?"

But Husker didn't answer.

"Well?" Sen asked. "I'm also curious."

Despite that, Husker remained silent. He just stared straight ahead, his eyes wide, his ears back.

Ice dumped into Kellan's veins. Something was wrong. The hair on the back of his neck stood on end. Something was in the restaurant with them. Something that hadn't been there before.

Kellan didn't want to glance toward the back of the restaurant. He already knew what lurked in the Blue Bayou.

The Kuji.

Millie shrieked. Kellan didn't have any more time to think about the situation. He didn't know how the Kuji had gotten here, or whether or not the restaurant was surrounded by enemies. All he knew was that they couldn't be *here*.

He dove into the darkness and stepped out near Millie's booth. She wasn't screaming anymore. Her eyes were wide, her misshapen body locked in position. And Kellan knew why. The Kuji had a special ability—*Haunting Sight*—that paralyzed all who looked at it.

Which was why Kellan couldn't turn around.

He grabbed Millie and hefted her into his arms. Her completely stiff posture made it difficult, but it couldn't be helped. The moment her eyes were torn from the creature, she regained her movement. That was when she grabbed Kellan's shirt and held on for dear life.

Kellan braced for an attack—he thought the monster Kuji would surely strike at his back—but it never came. Instead, the Kuji stepped over the booth and continued through the restaurant, heading straight for Husker.

That was when Kellan managed to get a better look at the horror show monster.

The Kuji was a giant spider.

Not a normal spider, by any stretch of the definition.

A true monster straight from the darkest corners of a nightmare. It had a human face with needle-sharp teeth and eyes that bulged and jiggled like a dead fish. Its eight legs ended in human hands. Its fingers ended in curved fish-hook claws.

In total, it had to be the size of a bus, but the Kuji was so spindly and freakish. The legs were long enough to stretch across half the restaurant, and its spider-body appeared to be writhing. No, that wasn't right. The abdomen was covered in tiny spiders.

Tiny Kuji.

Each little spider was the size of a human hand. They had human faces as well, but while the mother Kuji had the visage of an old man, the little spiders all had the faces of human babies. Their small hands ended in the same hook-like claws, and they squirmed around at a much faster rate of movement than their mother.

Two flew off the mother Kuji and landed on the restaurant wall. They scurried up and onto the ceiling. Three more went to the floor and hurried toward Husker. Five more leapt to the nearby tables and booths.

The whole fucking restaurant was a swarm of arachnids.

As long as Kellan didn't look straight into the Kuji's eyes, he knew he wouldn't be paralyzed. With all the speed and strength he could muster, he leapt over the booth, Millie still in his arms, and went for the light switch for the dining room. He flipped the switches, blanketing the Blue Bayou in darkness.

The void provided him the extra physical stats necessary to act. Kellan kicked off the wall, damaging the structure of the building as he did so. He leapt over the booth, got in front of the Kuji and managed to turn Husker around so that his line of sight with the monster was broken.

Free from the Kuji's paralysis, Husker turned to flee. But two of the baby Kuji leapt at him. They landed on his arm and shoulder and dug their fish-hook claws into his flesh. They cackled with shrill voices, disturbing enough that Kellan shuddered as he ran for the restaurant door.

While in the Oasis, he couldn't take any violent actions toward the monsters. He couldn't even bring himself to swat the spiders off Husker.

Sen was already there, standing by the door. He opened it the moment Kellan and Millie drew near. Afternoon light spilled into the restaurant from the outside, draining Kellan of his enhancements. He stumbled out onto the street, Husker close behind.

Husker huffed and then breathed flames. Red, orange, and white fire flashed across the sidewalk, the door of the restaurant, and across his whole body. Kellan had to dive away to avoid the heat. The flames killed the small Kuji, but their hook claws were so embedded in Husker that their charred corpses hung from his shoulder and arm like fucked-up Christmas ornaments.

The Kuji reached a clawed hand out of the Blue Bayou and slashed Husker across the back, its claws effortlessly ripping open his flesh. Husker cried out as he stumbled forward. When he collapsed to the sidewalk, it was clear he wasn't breathing normally.

Kellan set Millie down held up a hand and used his laser, but he didn't use an extra mana to empower it. Four mana.

The bright light that emanated from his palm lit up the inside of the restaurant. It slammed into the Kuji—but to no effect. The monster wasn't even hurt. Kellan kept his gaze down, but even the notifications said that nothing had happened.

Instead, the laser beam killed several of the baby Kuji on the mother's torso. Their little bodies fell to the floor of the restaurant, their legs curled in on themselves.

The Kuji chattered its needle-point teeth together, creating a haunting song.

It sounded… odd.

Then a terrible pressure came over Kellan.

> **[The Kuji of Team 101] used *Chittering Madness*. All magical powers used by enemy mages in range (10 feet per wisdom point) require double the mana expenditure to use.**
> **[Alex Kellan] succumbs to *Chittering Madness*.**
> **[Sun Sen] succumbs to *Chittering Madness*.**
> **[Husker Linis] succumbs to *Chittering Madness*.**
> **[Team 33's Doll] succumbs to *Chittering Madness*.**

The Kuji never had that ability before!

Husker got to his feet and stumbled away, but just barely. The Kuji slowly pulled itself out of the restaurant, its movements shockingly quiet. Only the odd song it created with the clacking of its teeth echoed all around them.

Kellan picked up Millie. Then he took a second to glance around.

The new street was cold and empty, but Kellan knew that could be deceiving. Husker had said multiple enemies had been present. They were likely lurking nearby, he just couldn't see them.

Fortunately, this street had fewer places to hide. There were no trees, no mailboxes—not even any streetlamps. It was a barren road, with two signs on either end, both of which had obvious yellow and red warnings, but Kellan couldn't read the words.

Husker ran for a building across the way. Sen was close behind. The teen refused to glance back, which was a good thing. Kellan didn't need more people getting paralyzed.

Knowing they couldn't fight to go through the front door of the building, Kellan went for a window instead. Although it was awkward to hold Millie and fire, Kellan used his rifle on the glass, shattering it inward. Then he leapt over the sill in one graceful bound.

But the inside of the building didn't match the outside.

Kellan had landed inside a hellish cannery, where the red lights overhead gave the entire cold atmosphere a sinister element. Cans clattered down conveyor belts, twenty at a time, sliding toward a gigantic machine that filled them with blood to the brim before sealing a lid over top.

Husker and Sen busted into the cannery, their expressions just as shocked as Kellan felt.

"We have to keep going," Kellan shouted. "We have several blocks to go in this direction before we turn."

Husker ran forward as several baby Kuji hurried into the cannery after him.

—Chapter 29—
—The Rot—

Although Kellan had been hoping to catch his breath more before taking off toward the goal, he didn't have time to complain. He ran forward, Millie in his arms, and jumped over a massive conveyor belt, knocking over several empty cans in the process. The *Chittering Madness* of the Kuji followed them into the building. The gigantic spider crawled into the cannery, its claws scraping across the concrete floor and wall.

The baby spiders poured in at a frightening rate.

Kellan ran for a set of stairs that led to the second story. Husker took the steps two at a time, and they met at the top. Sen wasn't as fast. He struggled to maintain his speed up the stairway, and once he reached the top, he took several gasping breaths.

"Go," Husker said, motioning to the hall. "I'll stay back to distract—"

"No." Kellan grabbed his shoulder and shoved him forward. "You're injured, splitting up isn't helping us, and we just have to make it to the end of this game—take your pick, whatever reason you want, it comes down the same. We just need to go."

Husker twitched his large ears and then nodded. He rushed down the hall. The Kuji pulled itself up the stairway at a surprising clip. The monster was at the top of the stairs before Kellan was prepared.

Sen struggled to run forward, and Kellan tried to impose himself between the Kuji and the narrow hallway.

Which was all it took for the Kuji to consider Kellan a target. While the Kuji normally went for the Straggler of a team, apparently it would also do whatever it took to remove obstacles.

With hook-claws, the creature went for Kellan's neck. Since Kellan avoided looking the beast in the face, his ability to dodge was impacted. He wheeled to the side, but the hallway was too small for him to get much distance.

On instinct, Kellan activated his armor. The skintight armor slid over his body in an instant, shadowy and powerful.

But it cost double the mana.

He was down to two.

[The Kuji of Team 101] slashed [Alex Kellan] for 8 damage and injected him with *Kuji Infestation*.
[Alex Kellan] reduces damage of each hit equal to his armor rating of 2.
[Alex Kellan]'s shadow shell absorbs 2 points of damage.
[Alex Kellan] suffers a total of 4 damage.

Blood wept from Kellan's neck as he hurried away from the beast. Millie mumbled apologies, her face buried in Kellan's shirt, her own body splashed with Kellan's blood. She clung as tightly as she could, never bothering to look up at the conflict raging all around her.

As Kellan struggled to breathe, another set of notifications flashed across his eyes.

[Tyranny Worms] already infest [Alex Kellan] and prevent the *Kuji Infestation*.
[Tyranny Worms] restore [Alex Kellan] for 1 damage every 6 seconds.

The number of insects and spiders that wanted to use Kellan's body as a breeding ground was disturbingly high. Kellan knew he'd never see bugs in the same light ever again.

He dove into a nearby foreman office, slamming through the door and stumbling inside. Once he had cleared out of the hallway, the Kuji rushed forward, intent on killing Husker, the team's Straggler. The monster was relentless. Even the babies scurried forward, giggling as they went.

Little by little, the spaghetti-sized worms used their own bodies to patch up the damage in Kellan's neck. After a few seconds, he could breathe again. Millie briefly opened her eyes, her attention on his injured neck.

"Are you okay?" she whispered.

"I'll be fine."

Kellan straightened himself, steeled his mind to the reality of the situation, and then hurried back into the hallway.

"Shouldn't we rest?" Millie asked, tightly closing her eyes. "We shouldn't go after the Kuji. Never the Kuji…"

"I can't," Kellan replied.

He just couldn't bring himself to do nothing. He had to keep going. *He had to.*

The nightmarish spider practically filled the whole hallway with its abdomen and spindly legs. The scrape of its claws along the cannery walls mixed with its chittering, adding another layer of horror show to the encounter.

Although Kellan couldn't see Husker on the other side—and he didn't know if the rennic needed help—he decided to irritate the Kuji regardless. He hefted his rifle and fired.

Like before, the Kuji was unaffected, but its babies weren't so lucky. A couple dozen more died to the terrible barrage of bullets that filled the hallway.

The death of the small spiders *did* seem to get the Kuji's attention. It attempted to turn around, its body so large that the process was painfully slow.

Kellan didn't wait around for the creature to face him. He ran in the opposite direction and then flew down the stairs. With as much haste as he could put into his steps, he ran through the red-light factory floor, leaping over another conveyor belt, and heading for the front door. He would walk around the building and meet his team on the other side of the building.

I told them where to go, he reasoned. *We should be able to meet up.*

Kellan slammed out of the front of the building and gritted his teeth. He hated being out in the open, so he ran along the side of the gray building, his shoulder practically shoved against the outside wall.

He took steady breaths, but at a certain point, his body couldn't handle the never-ending physical demands he kept asking of it. When his muscles burned, Kellan swore he felt the Tyranny Worms writhing beneath his skin, protesting his actions—like they were angry at him for pushing his muscles to the breaking point.

Just a little longer.

Kellan's arms threatened to quit. While Millie wasn't heavy—she barely weighed a hundred pounds—the constant strain was taking its toll. Determined to make it further, Kellan pushed himself to the limit. He ran around the building and made it into a back alleyway. A gunshot echoed across the street, and a bullet hole exploding into the side of the building. Kellan had avoided the worst of the enemy teams.

In the comforting chill of the shadows, Kellan managed to relax, but only slightly. He knew he couldn't leave Sen or Husker for very long.

"You should rest," Millie whispered.

"We don't have that luxury," Kellan said between controlled breaths. Then he hefted her up further into his arms and continued to the back of the cannery. "Once this is all over, I'll have plenty of time to recuperate."

She didn't protest much after that, for which Kellan was grateful. He ran through the alleyway and spotted Sen and Husker not too far away. They were the epitome of beaten and tired, but still, they stumbled forward.

Where was the Kuji?

Kellan didn't see it, but that didn't mean it wasn't nearby. The creepy spider and its many babies were the masters of the *jump scare*, and Kellan wasn't about to be caught off guard.

Husker's ears perked up when he noticed Kellan. He motioned him over and then ran for the opposite street. Kellan did his best to catch up. Sen, on the other hand, leaned against the wall of the nearby building, his breathing ragged, his pace slowing.

When Kellan went by, he shot the teen a glare.

Sen responded in kind. Then he shoved himself away from the wall and hurried after Kellan, obviously determined not to be dead last. The Kuji wouldn't attack Sen unless he was actively in the way or hindering the spider, which meant

Sen probably wasn't as worried about his life.

But it still wasn't a time to relax.

Kellan was about to enter the new street when he noticed something strange about it. He stopped at the precipice, his heart hammering. Husker stood next to him.

The road, the sidewalks, the mailboxes—they were in various states of decay. Rust covered most metal objects, and the asphalt had cracked and broken away. Parts of the street had caved in, crumbling into the flooded sewer down below. Foul-smelling water gushed upward at some points, stinking up the whole block with the odor of a Porta Potty.

"The Kuji got stuck," Husker whispered. "But it won't be like that forever. We shouldn't linger here."

A dark fog hung in the air, more transparent than smoke, and with the same wet sensation as mist. Kellan gritted his teeth as some of it dappled his skin. Goosebumps formed, and then the pain set in. A terrible, stinging flare of agony. He grimaced away from the black mist, irritated.

On the map, this road had been marked with a skull.

Which meant this mist was the rot that everyone had warned about.

Kellan set Millie down and withdrew the two burgers he still had in his backpack. He handed one to Millie, and then he handed the other to Sen when he approached. His burger had gone to Jace. Would his improved fortitude be enough?

I guess I'm going to find out.

Husker withdrew his own burger from the pocket of his tattered coat. In practically three bites, the giant rennic downed his whole fast-food meal. Then he belched.

Using his last mana, Kellan reactivated his *Ignore Pain* ability. At some point, it had ended, but his adrenaline had prevented him from even noticing.

Now, he had no more mana.

Kellan cursed under his breath. Sen glanced over and frowned. "Why that expression?" he muttered. "What's wrong?"

"I'm out of mana," Kellan said.

"Do you have any hane?"

"The black cigarettes?"

Sen narrowed his eyes. He took another bite of his burger and then swallowed in a hurry. "Of course, *the black cigarettes!* Don't play dumb. If you have some, just smoke one. Mages can heal four mana in a day if they rest—but the hane gets around all that. If you smoke one, you'll have a few more mana, just in case."

Kellan had seen the description of the hane before. They did say they helped restore mana. He reached into his backpack and withdrew one. He hadn't smoked since high school, and he had hated it with a passion. The only reason he had even done so for a short period was to impress a girl.

Which ultimately didn't work, but Kellan didn't dwell on that.

Once he held the hane stick firmly between two fingers, he stared at the magical item.

Magical Item [Consumable]—Hane Cigarette
The mage gains +2 perception and mana recovery while the hane remains in the mage's system. Highly addictive.

The *highly addictive* part worried him.

"Do you have a light?" Kellan asked.

Husker offered his paw-like hand. A small flame burst from his palm. Kellan lit his hane and then brought it to his lips. Would it taste as bad as cigarettes did in his home dimension? He hoped not.

Kellan took a drag on the smoke, bracing for the choking sensation. But none came. The hane… It felt smooth and helpful. Kellan breathed the smoke in and didn't gag. It soaked into his lungs, warm and peaceful. Was this some sort of magical weed? Kellan hated it even more. Probably irrationally, he admitted that to himself.

But…

He closed his eyes and inhaled again.

Something about the hane was pleasant. It reminded him of a warm cup of cocoa on a cold winter's night. When he exhaled, the taste of the hane lingered in his mouth. Was it sugar he detected? Or cake? Something about it was sweet.

"I can tell why this is addictive," Kellan said, smoke escaping him with each word.

Sen finished his burger and then motioned to the street. "If you have mana, we should go."

[Alex Kellan] recovers 1 mana every minute for the next four minutes so long as he smokes hane.

"I'm ready," Kellan said.

To his surprise, the mist seemed different now that he had the smoke between his lips. Everything seemed to shimmer with black energy. The color seemed distinct—more than the dark fog. It was the color of the magic in the area.

Now that Kellan's perception was in the superhuman range, he detected the colors of the magic, which in turn, told him the exact magic being used.

Husker ran into the road first. His hamburger made him immune to the rot, but some of his clothes became worn and tattered. Sen followed afterward. Nothing happened to his body, but his clothes suffered the same fate as Husker's.

When Kellan grabbed Millie and headed into the street, his legs almost gave out underneath him. Although he had mana, he hadn't really recovered. The reality of the situation ate at him. With his hane on his lips, he pressed forward, willing his damn legs to just keep moving.

An *Entropic Rot* covers the nearby area. All objects, mortals, and mages with a fortitude of 3 or less take 2 entropic rot damage every 6 seconds. Objects, mortals, and mages with a 4 fortitude or greater

take 1 entropic rot damage every 6 seconds.
[Alex Kellan] succumbs to *Entropic Rot.*
[Sun Sen] is immune to *Entropic Rot.*
[Husker Linis] is immune to *Entropic Rot.*
[Team 33's Doll] is immune to *Entropic Rot.*
[Tyranny Worms] restore [Alex Kellan] for 1 damage every 6 seconds.

The rot tried to eat at his flesh, but the Tyranny Worms refused to allow Kellan to unravel.

From Kellan's experience, the worms couldn't continue on forever. They would eventually have to rest, and "repopulate" in order to keep healing him. Kellan tried not to think about it. If they could just get through the next couple blocks, they would be okay.

The quiet of the rot-filled road bothered Kellan. In the distance, the smash of glass and the destruction of concrete rose up from the city. But here… it was a graveyard.

Sen, Husker, Kellan, and Millie made their way through the wicked mist. Millie's designer mall clothing also faded and wasted at the edges. The rot wanted to consume her flabby skin, but her immunity prevented anything from happening. Despite her obvious safety, she trembled as she pressed her face into Kellan's shoulder.

The hane wasn't affected by the bizarre rot and rapid aging. Was it because it was magical? That was Kellan's working theory. His clothes weren't so lucky. They, like Millie's, suffered from the rot. Thankfully, his illusions remained in place. Even if his clothing failed him, he wouldn't really change in appearance.

Husker and Sen kept close together. They only slowed once they came to a literal war zone. Kellan managed to catch up, and he examined their surroundings with his superhuman levels of perception.

They were in the middle of a WWI-style battlefield. There were trenches dug into the streets—one close to Kellan, one three hundred feet away. They were like reverse speed bumps, completely across the streets, even through both sidewalks.

The no-man's-land between the trenches contained a battlefield's worth of barbed wire, wooden stakes, and claymore mines. Kellan smirked when he saw the English words FRONT TOWARD ENEMY on all the mines in the road. Only the military labeled everything as though an infant would be handling it.

"What is this?" Husker asked. He wiped his padded hands on his coat. "Nothing here is decaying."

Kellan took a moment to examine everything, exhaling a line of smoke as he did so. Husker was right. The barbed wire, silver and perfect, hadn't been touched, not even by enemy blood. The claymore mines, greenish-tan and pristine, looked as though they had just neatly been taken out of a box. Was this a sick joke constructed by the Arbiter?

"Those will explode," Kellan said, pointing to the mines. "They're detonated by remote, or with a tripwire. I think we should go around."

"Do we have time for that?"

"If someone is nearby who can trigger the mines, we won't survive. I don't think we have a choice but to go around."

Husker snorted and then motioned to the far side of the road, beyond the sidewalk. "We can go there."

They'd still have to jump over the trenches, but Kellan didn't mind. Together, his team hurried to the far end of the road. Husker effortlessly jumped across the trench. Sen awkwardly leapt, basically half-stepping as he did so. Then he flailed his arms like he might tumble backward. Once he was across, he stumbled toward Husker and sneered.

Kellan was about to jump, Millie in his arms, when he spotted something red and glittering in the middle of no-man's-land. Between two claymore mines, and tucked inside a nest of barbed wire, he spotted a body. The rotting, mangled corpse had seen better days. Hell, freshly dug-up corpses that had been chewed by dogs looked better than the bastard in the middle of the street.

But Kellan didn't care about that.

His attention landed squarely on the red arcana scattered around the body. Kellan counted at least ten crystals. The man must've been a powerful mage if he had that much arcana just sitting around.

Had the rot killed him? Or had he been running through no-man's-land and just gotten unlucky?

"Husker," Kellan said. "Take Millie. I'll be right back."

The rennic turned to him, his ears back, his fangs showing. "We should stay together."

"I need to get something. And since I'm the only one who can move with the ease of a shadow, I think I should go alone." He handed over Millie—who clung to his shirt a bit—and then stepped into the darkness.

Although Millie tried to hang on, it was useless. Submerged in the darkness, and wrapped in the cold comfort of power, Kellan slithered as a shadow across no-man's-land. Once he emerged, he would need to grab the arcana and leave as quickly as possible. Something told him that the mines would be remotely detonated by *something*.

And knowing the Nexus, it wouldn't be friendly.

—Chapter 30—
—The End of Game Three—

Kellan stepped out of the shadows in the middle of the bizarre road.

The combination of *business district* and *World War I* wasn't a pleasant sight. Parked cars were wrapped in barbed wire, their parking meters surrounded by landmines. The way the Nexus combined certain terrains never failed to amuse Kellan, but he wished he could view them all from the safety of the AVU Palace, rather than be up close and personal with everything.

Determined to avoid the claymore mines, Kellan shifted back into the darkness and moved with the safety of a shadow. Since he could only shadow-step ten feet at a time, it took him two more jumps before he reached the mangled corpse. The many mines, and rolls of silver barbed wire, made reaching for the body a difficult task. Kellan planted his feet firmly on the ground, and then hesitated.

Trip wires.

They weren't thick metal cord, like on claymores he was familiar with. They were spiderweb thin, and barely visible in the black fog. Thanks to Kellan's superhuman senses, however, he spotted them before he triggered them.

He took another long drag on his hane and exhaled smoke. It mixed with the dark fog. He had two mana now. In a few minutes, he would recover his max of four for the day.

Careful not to touch anything, Kellan knelt and scooped up the arcana from around the body. The red crystals felt warm to the touch, and each one offered a strange sensation and a fleeting memory. Something about… wanting to win…

[Alex Kellan] absorbed 12 arcana.

"That's an outrageous amount of arcana," he muttered to himself.

While Kellan rooted around the corpse like a vulture, he noticed something in the pocket of the man's rotted jacket. The moment Kellan touched the clothing, the fabric around his fingertips disintegrated. All that remained was a keycard.

Kellan's eyes gave him all the info he needed.

Magical Item [Reusable]—VIP Lounge Keycard (Floor 1)

The mage gains access to the first floor of the AVU Palace's VIP Lounge. Can be used multiple times. Only grants a single person access.

A VIP Lounge? Kellan hadn't even known that one existed within the palace. *Interesting.*

He pocketed the keycard, his own pants coming apart at the seams. His pants weren't worthless yet, but he'd have to be careful. Thankfully, magical items weren't affected. His armor would stay with him despite the corrosive environment.

Then the soft click of metal on metal drew Kellan's attention to the opposite side of the street. Someone was in a nearby building, and before anything could happen, Kellan dove back into the darkness like how a frightened bird took to the sky whenever there was a slight noise.

When he stepped out of the shadows, he was caught in the last half of a claymore mine explosion. Rubble flew through the air. The ground shook. The force knocked most of the barbed wire and wooden stakes from the road.

Kellan shielded his face as he grunted and leapt backward. There went his hane, tumbling away in the aftershocks of the explosion.

Part of his pants caught on the barbed wire. He thought he might fall—get tangled in the trap, like the sad sack before him had—but Kellan went straight back into the darkness to avoid the flame and chance of tripping.

When he emerged a second time, he was in a pile of barbed wire. The small metal bits cut into his shoulder and arms as he stepped out of the shadows. He felt no pain, though. Just as he felt no pain with the fog. But the worms…

The more damage Kellan's body received, the more the worms struggled to keep him together.

Was his *Mold Metal* ability still active? Kellan grabbed the barbed wire and hoped his thirty minutes wasn't up. To his delight, he shifted the barbed wire and freed himself from the deadly trap.

"Kellan!"

All the surrounding buildings had taken a beating. Claymore mines had a good two-hundred-yard range—fifty-five yards around the explosion was destroyed, but the rest was just damaged. The buildings were in the damaged category, their windows shattered, the outer façade cracked and charred.

"*Kellan,*" someone yelled out again.

Husker. The rennic was leaning against a nearby building, his fur covered in dust and debris. He bled from several injuries, including a few cuts from thrown barbed wire. He had pressed his body over Millie and Sen, shielding them from the attack.

Kellan shadow-stepped to Husker's side.

A man with black wings exited the building across the street. The man laughed as he took to the sky. He wore a jacket and jeans, but his shirt was ripped and bloody, like he had fought his way through a pack of dogs to even get here.

Name: Kin Line the Raven
Race: Niav
Magics: Storm, Wyld
Rank: B, B
Armor Rating: —
Health: 10/10
Stats: Concealed
Abilities: Concealed

The man had gotten strong since last Kellan laid eyes upon him.

"You're still *alive?*" Kin shouted. He pulled a handgun from the waist of his jeans. He was too far for Kellan to see the make or model, but it was a lighter—smaller—weapon.

Bullets blasted the nearby wall as Kin opened fire, clearly intent on ending them.

"I need the damn arcana!"

With gritted teeth, Kellan smirked. "Well, let's try this laser beam again, shall we?"

He held up a hand and unleashed a blast of light. He spent two mana—one to activate the laser beam, and one to empower it with his meta magic. The beam fired through the air, bright enough to cut through the dark fog around. It scorched through Kin's wing, Kellan saw the notification, but he ignored it in favor of watching Kin plummet. The bird-like mage hit the roof of a nearby building.

Was he dead?

Kellan wanted to find out…

But Husker placed a clawed hand on his shoulder. "We're running thin. We shouldn't."

Although Kellan hated the idea of missing out on arcana, he nodded once. Then he took Millie and headed down the street, his body constantly rotting a bit, and then being healed by the worms in his system.

With Sen and Husker in tow, they made it down two blocks and then turned. Kellan remembered the entire map—he thought about it constantly, bringing up the streets in his mind's eye, trying to plot the perfect path.

The closer they got to the goal, the tenser Kellan became. He spotted a couple mages fighting atop the nearby buildings. Bursts of lightning and fire streaked across the sky. Not even the black mists could fully obstruct all the destruction and commotion.

But once they turned down another street, Kellan's skin no longer knitted itself back together. The worms could no longer mend the damage.

[Tyranny Worms] are unable to restore [Alex Kellan] and return to *Infestation Mode*.

Of course, Kellan thought with a sardonic smirk.

His skin flaked and rotted off, leaving raw and exposed flesh behind. Although Kellan couldn't feel the pain, his mind played tricks on him. Every chunk of his body that fell off, withered and hideous, caused him to grimace or shudder. It reminded him of the nightmares he used to have of his teeth falling out of his head.

When he ran his tongue along his molars, the terrible mist had, in fact, loosened them.

He took one damage.

Then another.

Kellan tried to run faster, but the more damage his body took, the harder it became. With each breath, the mist invaded his body, rotting him from the inside out.

"Help!" Millie called out. She reached a hand for Sen. "You need to help him!"

Sen, who clearly hadn't been paying attention, rushed to Kellan's side. He placed a hand on Kellan's shoulder and healed him of three damage.

But the rot persisted.

The damage returned.

Another point of damage.

And another.

Sen healed him again, but the teen clenched his jaw and shook his head. "I don't have much mana left!"

"We just need to get out of the rot." Kellan pushed harder, his body threatening to give up. "Hurry!"

When Kellan tried, he easily outran the teenager, even with a person in his arms. But his breathing was strained and ragged. If he could feel pain, he knew his chest would be on fire. Kellan wheezed, and a small splatter of blood coated Millie's faded clothing.

The instant he made it out of the mist, Kellan smiled and slowed his pace. He barely had three health left. He almost collapsed to his knees, but he managed to keep on his feet. *Can't give up now. Almost there…*

After three deep breaths, Kellan took stock of his surroundings. His heightened perception made everything easier. He saw further, and with more detail, and his eyes seemed attracted to even the slightest movement. *This must be how superheroes feel,* he thought with a cough and a chuckle.

They were on the side of a roundabout—a circular road with a park in the middle. The wide street, with four lanes, was pristine and empty. The park contained a wooden platform. A small flag was planted next to the platform, waving in the gentle breeze. It had a picture of a mechanized dragon, and Kellan knew that had to be the safe zone.

But he didn't see any other mages there. Were they the first team to arrive?

Impossible.

So where was everyone? Were the teams teleported away the instant they stood on the platform? Or only when they brought their dolls? If it was the latter, Kellan and the others wouldn't be teleported. Millie wasn't their doll.

He shook his head, tired of indecision. They needed to leave. Everyone was low on resources.

Kellan briefly considered staying to help Xiang and Mavis, since they were the ones with the real cargo, but he didn't know where they were. And since he had no mana and barely any health, staying seemed like a poor strategy. Now wasn't the time to die.

Husker and Sen stopped next to him.

A single mage—a human wearing a black tunic and trousers—ran across the four lanes of the roundabout. He had dashed out from an alleyway between two nearby buildings, breathing heavy as he sprinted to the platform. The mage carried one of the Nexus residents in his arms. The deformed person, missing an arm and most of their shoulder, had a vacant expression. Blood waterfalled from their head, their gray hair matted with crimson.

The resident appeared to have a concussion. But they were still alive.

"Shoot it," Husker said as he pointed at the doll in the mage's arms. "If the doll dies, we'll deny the team a key."

Kellan couldn't see the mage's information or team number from so far away. But he also didn't care. He understood that knocking out teams before every game turned into a PvP match was a good play, but he also didn't want to murder innocents to do it. Shooting the mage in the head was preferable to killing the doll.

"He's not going to shoot anything," Sen muttered. He glared at the mage as he entered the circular park and headed for the platform. "Our warrior values honor more than I thought he would..."

"Ironic," Husker replied, half-smiling.

"Right? Tsk."

Between heavy breaths, Kellan shot them both a sideways glance. "I'm right here."

Husker snorted. "Your alternate-self wasn't the most honorable of fellows."

"I'm not my alternate-self." Kellan couldn't believe he had to say it so many times.

The mage and his deformed doll clambered up onto the wooden stage. The moment they got onto the platform, they disappeared. A blast of confetti from hidden cannons filled the sky with bits of colorful paper. It was a rainbow rain of celebration, even though there was no one around to celebrate.

Husker ran by Kellan and huffed. "That's it! That's the goal. Let's go!" He leaned forward and practically ran on all fours, his clawed hands helping with the traction. Husker bounded across the four-lane road and then went straight for the platform.

Even Sen managed to outrun Kellan as he dashed for the finish. The teen kept his arms over his head, shielding his noggin from any surprise attacks that may come for him.

Kellan still didn't spot anyone else nearby. He hurried as fast as he could toward the platform, his breathing labored. When he made it across all four lanes of the road, his heart hammered in preemptive celebration. Were they going to make it unmolested and undamaged?

Husker leapt onto the wooden platform. The moment his padded feet touched the surface of the wood planks, he disappeared. *Pop*. One second, he was there, then all Kellan heard was displaced air, and Husker was gone.

Another blast of confetti filled the air.

Sen was next. He leapt onto the platform and vanished.

More confetti. The cannons in the platform didn't seem to have any limitations to their paper ammo.

With barely any breath, and his body practically falling apart, Kellan slammed into the side of the platform, hoisted Millie onto it, and watched her vanish like the rest. Weak, and trying to muster the energy to step up the three feet to get onto the wooden platform, Kellan glanced over his shoulder.

A giant serpent moved between buildings in the distance, its scales gleaming in the red hue of the Net-tainted sun. The beast was something out of a Godzilla movie. When it moved, however, it took care not to smash the nearby buildings.

Kellan couldn't believe he and the others had missed the thing.

First bit of luck in this whole game.

With his high perception, and *Blitzkrieg Analysis*, Kellan saw everything he needed.

Name: Qin Bolo, Living Disaster of Alameda City
Race: Master Yami
Magics: Body, Wyld, Entropy
Rank: Impossible to Rank
Armor Rating: 30 [Scaled]
Health: 150/150

Stats:
Strength—30 [Strong Coil]
Dexterity—25 [Fast]
Fortitude—20
Intelligence—2 [Insane]
Perception—10 [Superior Senses]
Willpower—2 [Insane]

Abilities:
Undead—The yami is immune to poison and gas. The yami does not need to breathe or eat to survive. Additionally, the yami feels no pain.
Rebirth Growth—The yami gains +2 to all physical stats (strength, dexterity, fortitude), +10 health, and +1 willpower each time it revives after death. It also gains an additional head (max ten).
Tied to the Arbiter—If the Arbiter is alive, this yami cannot be fully killed. If its health is reduced to 0, it stops functioning, but does not drop arcana. After a short recovery period, the yami is revived at full health. If the Arbiter is dead, this ability doesn't activate, and the yami drops arcana as

usual and then ceases to exist.

"I'm just gonna nope on outta here," Kellan quipped to himself.

He climbed onto the platform, and the teleportation activated. He was ripped from the play arena, his insides twisting as he traveled. When Kellan's feet hit the ground, he stumbled around.

He was in the middle of the gambling hall inside the AVU Palace. The green rugs, beige walls, and hazy air were all painfully familiar. Screens with betting odds, and TVs showing footage of the game, kept the place well-lit. Only a few chandeliers hung overhead, and some of them flickered.

A message stating Kellan had returned to an Oasis flashed over his eyes. He patted down his body and examined everything. Xiang's illusions had dropped. He wore ragged clothing, and now he had the complexion of a leper thanks to the rot. As soon as Kellan received some mana, he'd be able to heal, but in the meantime, he had no choice but to wander around with the appearance of a sickly hobo.

A robot behind a bookie counter spun around. Its face was just a flat tablet with a pair of eyes and a mouth animated on the screen.

"*My apologies,*" it said in a childish, yet robotic, tone. "*You failed to procure a key for your team! You are no longer able to participate. Because there are still other members of your team in the play arena, the Arbiter asks that you wait here until they succeed or fail.*"

The robot had a small mechanical body—thin and mostly wires and gears. It had arms and legs, but Kellan suspected he could knock the robot over with a simple push. It didn't look very sturdy or steady, nor did it stand more than four feet tall.

The machine-person waved a hand at the room, gesturing for him to wait.

"Thanks," Kellan muttered as he glanced around. "Where's Millie?"

"*Who? No one fits that designation.*"

"Team 33's doll."

"*Oh. She has been transported to the doll room for the key extraction.*"

Kellan tensed. He couldn't grab the robot to demand anything—though he would've loved to do that. Instead, he forced himself to remain calm. "Will the key extraction kill her?"

"*Negative. Key extraction has resulted in zero deaths over the past fifty Nexus Games.*"

A bit of anxiety left him. Kellan offered the weird robot a quick nod before shambling over to a bench. He sat down, and then stared at a TV mounted to the far wall. Footage of the game—in Alameda City—was the only thing playing.

Where were Husker and Sen?

Kellan glanced around, but he didn't notice them. The gambling hall was practically empty, save for the few robots behind various counters. It was a large room, as well—at least a hundred feet long and fifty feet wide.

Instead of searching, Kellan's attention was drawn to the TV, and the two figures running through the ruined city. He scooted forward on his bench, his heart racing all over again.

Xiang and Mavis. He recognized them by their illusions. And they still had their team's doll illusioned like a giant hiking backpack.

The massive serpent… It blasted onto the road with them. Qin Bolo, the Living Disaster of Alameda City. The beast had red scales as dark as bricks, two heads, and eyes as dead and black as a starless night. There were no pupils, no recognition in its snake-faces. It moved almost like a zombie, jerking forward with its serpentine mouth wide, fangs flashing.

Two other mages stood on the street as well. They were rennic—both burly and covered in fur. One held up a hand and blasted the gargantuan serpent with a ball of flame.

It was turning into a real fight now.

The TV had no sound. Kellan just had to watch the battle, unable to participate. He clenched his hands into fists, hating the fact that he had stepped on to the wooden platform. *What if they die?*

If Xiang fell in battle, that would mean that all of Team 101 would fail.

—Chapter 31—
—Bred in Captivity—

The massive serpent, Qin Bolo, coiled itself and then struck forward. Although the TV offered no sound, Kellan's mind filled in the blanks. When a building collapsed, Kellan felt a phantom rumble travel up through his worn boots. When the serpent threw back one of its heads in a roar, Kellan heard the phantom screech as though he were mere feet from it.

The two rennic weren't cowards.

One charged forward, his claws oversized. He leapt from the street, shooting through clouds of debris and dust, and slammed into the side of the monster snake. The rennic's claws pierced the thick scales, but only slightly.

Dark energy swirled around the claws, corroding the beast's body.

The yami had thirty armor, yet the rennic was piercing through. Kellan was impressed—the bastard must have had high damage potential.

But Qin Bolo didn't give a shit.

The serpent slammed down onto the ground, squishing the rennic between the street and its massive body. Although Kellan couldn't see any notifications for the damage or status, he practically saw phantom notifications.

> *[Qin Bolo] struck [Some Random Delta-Bravo] for a metric fuck-ton of damage.*
> *[Some Random Delta-Bravo] prays his suffering won't last long.*
> *It's super effective.*

The serpent lifted back up and struck for the other rennic. But mid-strike, it jerked and shuddered, its four ear holes bleeding. Qin Bolo roared with both heads, enough that the buildings nearby shook. Kellan held his breath.

Xiang had used *Mind Blasts* in the past, which dealt phantasmal damage. It was a mental attack that went straight for a target's willpower. The lower it was, the more damage the mage dealt to their target.

And this serpent's willpower was *low*.

Qin Bolo thrashed, slamming its tail into another building. Then it smashed one head against the road, trying to cure its deadly headache through caveman methods. Its skull broke into the street, collapsing some of the road into the water-filled sewers below.

The city was a swirl of dust, falling concrete, and filthy water. It became difficult to see what was going on. The serpent smashed its way through the city, thrashing like only a mad beast could.

Kellan stood from his bench and approached the TV. Whatever was filming—likely an Eye of the Arbiter—didn't move or zoom in on the specific action. It just passively filmed the area, like a disinterested security camera.

The serpent's two heads exploded outward, its skulls cracking. Qin Bolo's blood didn't run like a normal person. It was chunky—similar to cottage cheese, just crimson. The thick "liquid" splattered down the side of the serpent's body, and onto the flooded street. Then the beast collapsed with a whine and whimper.

Was it dead?

Had Xiang blasted it with such a powerful mental blast that *both* its heads erupted in a spray of gore?

There was no other explanation. Unfortunately, she wouldn't be gaining any arcana for the endeavor.

The body of the massive serpent remained in the road as the debris and dust thickened around the battleground.

"Is there any way to see a different view?" Kellan asked the robot behind the bookie counter.

"*Negative.*"

The odds of the game flashed across a screen behind the little robot with the tablet face. Team 101 had its odds for success listed as 25:1.

Which wasn't good.

Kellan wasn't really a gambling man, but he understood that the house wanted to make money—or in this case, arcana—and with that kind of payout, the house didn't expect Team 101 to succeed.

When Kellan returned his attention to the screen, his eyes widened. The serpent lifted both of its heads—and then a third one burst out of its flesh, tearing through scales as it formed. The third head stitched itself together, first through bones, then through muscle, then through red scales that patched up everything.

Now the living disaster was even *more* formidable. Would Xiang and Mavis be safe? Even if Xiang could defeat it, time and time again, the monster would always return, stronger than the previous time.

"There's no way I can go back into the game?" Kellan asked.

The robot's face flickered on the screen, becoming a frown. "*I apologize. Once you exit the game, you're no longer able to enter. You need to sit and wait for the game to end.*"

"Where are my other teammates?"

"*Sun Sen and Husker Linis were taken by Pestbyters for questioning in front of the Arbiter.*"

"Why?" Kellan barked. He leaned against the counter. "Did they break the rules?"

"*Apologies! I do not know.*" The robot spun around, its arms up, its face still a cartoon frown. "*Please stay seated until the end of the game. It will conclude in five hours, or when all of your team either reaches the teleporter or dies.*"

Kellan pushed away from the bookie. The gambling hall wasn't really his desired waiting room.

Two more people popped into existence, though, instantly turning the room into a scene out of a sci-fi movie. One was human, but the other was nine feet tall and freakishly alien.

The alien's body was black and shiny, as though wet, even when completely bone-dry. The creature had no hair, no fur, no whiskers, just a hard armored exoskeleton, similar to an insect or crab. The alien stood on four limbs, the "feet" ending in points, sharp and practically ripping holes in the green carpet. The disgusting beast also had two spindly arms, and two muscular arms, giving it as many limbs as a spider.

Kellan was starting to develop arachnophobia. Every spider he came across in the Nexus was its own special brand of horror show.

The alien's four arms ended in hands. The smaller arms had delicate piano fingers, but the muscular arms had hands with claws on the fingers.

And the face…

Kellan grimaced when he stared directly at it. Was it the face of a crustacean? The alien had feelers and movable mandibles, with spines on the chin and head.

Although Kellan's *Blitzkrieg Analysis* gave him basic information on the alien, Kellan already knew who she was. Viniss Tarkin—a flestiss on Team 42. She was a powerful mage who had shielded Kellan from the terrible madness effects on Overseer Station.

Her info read:

Name: Viniss Tarkin the Vanguard Queen
Race: Flestiss
Magics: Mind, Metal, Travel
Rank: Concealed
Armor Rating: 10
Health: 20/20
Stats: Concealed
Abilities: Concealed

Despite the fact that Kellan couldn't see all her stats and abilities, the few he could see had improved. She was getting stronger—all the mages on the other teams were.

The man standing next to her was an odd human. His hair was shaved, and the side of his head sported a black mark that appeared branded straight into his flesh. The gnarled scar prevented any hair from growing. Kellan wasn't sure what the mark was. It seemed to be a word, or perhaps a number, in a bizarre language.

The man wore tactical gear befitting any high-ranking operative military agent. A utility belt, tactical goggles hanging on a strap from his small backpack, a thin vest, heavy cargo pants, and tight gloves. He also had a metal collar etched with the same writing as the brand on his head. The collar didn't seem to have any joints or locks or fasteners. Did it ever come off?

The most disturbing aspect of the man was his expression. His face was one marked with stress and scowl lines, and he started straight ahead without much thought behind his eyes. His complexion bordered on burnt.

Kellan's analysis gave him information on the man.

Name: HR-8, Bred in Captivity
Race: Human
Magics: Magma, Metal
Rank: Concealed
Armor Rating: 12 + 5 Shielding
Health: 14/14
Stats: Concealed
Abilities: Concealed

Bred in captivity?

That was the single most disturbing title he had seen on a mage.

Viniss clicked her front mandibles. The noise persisted for a solid minute. Kellan wasn't even sure if she was speaking, but then he remembered a bizarre fact about the Nexus.

Everyone here could understand the speech of others. Since the Nexus was a mesh of so many dimensions, the Arbiter made it so that everyone could understand everyone else. The *opposite* of the Tower of Babel.

But that only meant Viniss's clicking was just that—a strange noise.

Kellan went to walk around the flestiss and return to the TV to watch Xiang and Mavis, but the giant 700-pound alien stepped in his path. She was surprisingly quick for something her size. Kellan had to glance up to meet her crustacean gaze.

"*Human,*" she hissed, her voice somehow feminine but deep and gravelly. "*You have made an enemy of the Flestiss Dominion.*"

Kellan glanced at HR-8 and then back at the female flestiss. "I'm pretty sure you started it. I'm just here trying to end it."

"*Your statements to the Arbiter, and your pathetic attempts to sway the other teams against us, will amount to nothing.*"

"We'll see," Kellan quipped. Again, he tried to step around her. There was nothing to do here—and since they were in an Oasis, it wasn't like she could attack him.

Viniss threw out one of her muscular arms. She planted her hand on the wall, blocking his path like a crossing guard before a train. Her clicking became louder and aggravated.

"*No one will help you,*" Viniss stated. "*If you are wise, you will join the Dominion before the end of the games. Loyalty will be rewarded.*" She placed one of her smaller hands on top of HR-8's head and petted him gently.

The man didn't really react to the touch. He just allowed the alien to stroke him.

Kellan wanted to make a snarky reply to that, but it occurred to him that he didn't know much about the Flestiss Dominion. He had seen glimpses of their operations on Overseer Station—their jails and a factory that recreated arcana by drowning people—but nothing else.

"What kind of rewards?" Kellan asked. He had no intention of joining, but he wanted to hear the pitch first. He never wanted to pass up an opportunity for knowledge.

"*The Flestiss Dominion is unrivaled by any other. Our tech, magic, and military are supreme. If you serve, you will be given a place among the ruling class.*"

"You live in a class-based society?"

HR-8, who hadn't moved since appearing in the gambling hall, flicked his gaze over to Kellan, his eyes narrowed. He seemed… surprised.

Viniss's clicking slowed a bit as she said, "*The most powerful societies always utilize their population to its fullest potential. The Flestiss Dominion has perfected this. We judge the potential of beings once born and place them in appropriate roles.*" She tightened her grip on HR-8's head, her black slender fingers practically digging into his skin. "*This one here was designated as my retainer.*"

HR-8 nodded once. "Yes, my queen."

The creepy dynamic left a terrible taste in Kellan's mouth.

Then he realized something. The man's name was *HR-8*. Human Retainer Eight.

The brand…

"Let me guess," Kellan said as he motioned to the brand on HR-8's head. "People's roles are clearly marked."

"*So that there is no confusion,*" Viniss replied matter-of-factly. "*All but the mages who rule are labeled and sorted into their best position. Humans are simple creatures, lacking in grand drive and group cohesion. Left to your own devices, you destroy each other. Under the Dominion, they have become the perfect citizens for our multi-dimension empire.*"

A cold chill ran down Kellan's spine. He pieced together the puzzle on Overseer Station. The Flestiss Dominion had sent mages here to win the Nexus Games so they could use the magic of Zenith to finish their conquest of all the dimensions. Kellan hadn't known they enslaved humanity only to breed them into the perfect roles—to make them subservient beasts that worshipped the ground the insect-aliens walked on.

It was all too insidious.

"And if I join, I don't have to be branded?" Kellan asked.

"*Mages who rule are given other means to display their authority.*" Viniss stepped closer, looking Kellan over with her considerable size and weight. "*Your Earth tried to fight us. They were defeated and crushed. The only wise decision is to join us before we're forced to collect your arcana for our own mages.*"

"*My* Earth wasn't defeated," Kellan growled. "That was Brenner's Earth—the one he betrayed."

"*It matters not. The same will happen with your world. And the next. And all others until there are none left to conquer.*"

Kellan held up a finger. "Let me think about it." Then he lowered his hand. "I'm done. The answer is *fuck you*. If *I* get to Zenith, I'm going to use whatever overpowered magic is there to wipe out your whole fucking Dominion. And if that's not possible, I'll at least come back for *you* specifically. So, if you don't want to get on *my* bad side, I would suggest you crab-walk your way out of here."

The female flestiss clicked out a laughing noise. Kellan wasn't sure how the weird alien race emoted, but he was fairly certain this was a sign of amusement.

"*Arrogant and stubborn,*" Viniss stated. "*We bred those traits out of our humans, and they're the better for it. This is why your race can't be allowed to govern itself.*"

Kellan stepped around the beast and continued over to the TV, his rage causing his whole body to tense. If he wasn't constrained by the Oasis, he would've probably attacked the flestiss right there in the middle of the gambling hall.

The Flestiss Dominion had a whole stable of humans they bred for their own purposes? Like cattle? The mere thought enraged Kellan so much he found it difficult to think about anything else.

And the worst part was that no one seemed to care.

They were *other humans* in *other dimensions*. Just like the Nexus residents—the lack of anyone giving a damn was disheartening to Kellan.

He went to the TV, but the programming had shifted. Instead of showing footage of the Escort game, the screens now displayed shots of the *Spin and Win* game. A human woman stood next to a rickety wooden wheel in the middle of a vast room. A spotlight lit up the woman and the wheel, but the room was so gigantic that Kellan couldn't see the walls.

The woman hesitated.

She wore futuristic armor, and the number on her head read: 79. The same as Robbie the Friendly's. She also had a skull on the back of her hand. She was the team's Straggler.

Without any words, she reached up and grabbed the wheel. When she spun it, it clattered around, each peg snapping the dial as it went.

Click-click, click, click, click… click… click…

When the wheel stopped, it was on a picture of a diamond and a frog.

The woman's brow furrowed, and she glanced around. "What does that mean?" she called out, her voice fading into the distance. "I don't understand."

A Pestbyter floated over, its spherical machine body a bizarre sight. Its wire tentacles handed over two small pouches. One pouch had a diamond ring, and the other… contained a live frog. Kellan wasn't sure what to make of that. And obviously neither did the woman. She stared at her "prizes" and then glanced up at the Pestbyter.

Before she could get an answer, the TV flipped to something else.

Kellan found it difficult to concentrate, though. Viniss and her *retainer* paced around the gambling hall, wandering from counter to counter, speaking to the robots there about something. Kellan couldn't really hear from this distance, but he hated everything about them.

He returned to the robot he had spoken to before and leaned against the counter. "Are you sure there's nowhere else I can wait? Anywhere besides this room..." He glanced over at the alien. "I don't want to mingle with certain teams."

The robot tilted its tablet head from one side to the other. "*My information says you are in possession of a VIP keycard. If you wish, you may wait out the remainder of the game in the VIP Lounge.*"

Kellan's eyebrows both lifted. "Really?"

"*Correct! Really!*"

"Okay... How do I get there?"

The robot gestured to the nearest wall. "*Use your keycard on any wall, and you'll find yourself in the VIP hall. It'll take you to the lounge. Enjoy!*"

—Chapter 32—
—The VIP Room—

Kellan mulled over the strange information for a full minute. He could use the VIP keycard on *any* wall to access the lounge? How did that work?

He shook the thoughts away. How did all the dimensions collide together into one mishmash of bizarre death games? There were just some questions he would probably never know the answers to.

Kellan withdrew the keycard from his pocket and pressed it against the beige wall. For a short moment, nothing happened. Kellan almost turned to the robot with a sarcastic comment, but then a line formed on the wall, originating from the keycard. The line stretched up and down until it went from the ceiling to the floor.

After a short breath, Kellan removed the card and stepped back.

The line sank into the wall, and then it proceeded to open like an automatic door at a gas station. The wall slid apart to reveal a dark hallway filled with soft neon lights speckled across the ceiling like a psychedelic night sky.

Kellan glanced around, his eyes wide. He stepped into the darkened hall, his attention on the fantastical ceiling. The wall-door closed behind him with a gentle *swish*. The hall smelled of cologne or perfume, Kellan wasn't sure which, but it was pleasant.

He strode forward, taking note of the black walls and posh white rug underfoot. At the end of the hall, he found two doors. One was labeled LOUNGE FLOOR 1, and the other was labeled ELEVATOR.

Kellan's keycard gave him access to the first floor of the VIP Lounge, so he didn't give the elevator a second glance. He turned to the other door. It opened as he reached for it, swinging inward with a slow and steady motion.

The inside…

During his time as a Special Forces soldier, Kellan had been invited to several ritzy parties. Some of the super elite military officers thought the only way to thank some of their operators was to throw lavish parties. Kellan had been on more yachts and cruise ships than he'd like to admit.

The VIP Lounge brought back memories of all those things combined.

The room was U-shaped, with a bar in the center. The sides of the lounge were made of giant couches with silk curtains, and enough leather and soft-furred blankets to be comfortable no matter the person's preference. The temperature—Kellan hadn't even taken note of it before—felt cool without being cold, and a gentle breeze swirled around the area, taking with it a fresh scent of luxury.

Each sitting area not only had privacy curtains, but its own TVs, mini-bars, and servers. The waitstaff seemed made up of every sentient race—except flestiss—and they stood outside the curtains, waiting for requests or instructions.

The waitstaff also wore shirts with no backs, exposing their skin, and pants that hugged their thighs but flared at the bottom. Everything was black or gold, even the couches and curtains, so clean and vibrant, it practically glittered. Kellan didn't know why, but the color theming helped the feeling of posh relaxation.

He hesitated, taking note of the four sitting areas. One was occupied. Three were vacant.

A man stood behind the bar—a human with short brown hair, a gold vest, a black shirt, and a black ribbon tied around his wrist. He had the sleepy expression of someone who hadn't slept in five days straight.

Was this man the bartender?

Kellan's eyes didn't give him any info, so he assumed the man was mortal, and not a mage.

"Can I help you?" the man asked, his tone just as fatigued as he looked.

"I just need to wait for the end of the current game," Kellan replied.

The man pointed to one of the empty couches. "Kick your feet up and relax. The Arbiter wants everyone in his VIP Lounges to enjoy themselves."

Kellan slowly made his way over to the nearest empty couch. When he sat down, he marveled at how soft and comfortable the furniture was.

Magical Item [Permanent]—Dreamweaver Cushion

The mage who sits upon this comforter restores any missing stats for 1 per hour seated. The mage also recovers health at a rate of 1 per minute seated. If the mage has used their willpower, or lost it due to attacks, it is completely restored if the mage sleeps on the cushion, even for just a moment.

Kellan leaned his head back.

His body… His injuries faded at a slow rate, similar to how the Tyranny Worms operated, just slower.

One of the servers—a busty woman with red hair—bounded over, a high amount of energy in her step. She smiled as she approached, joyful and upbeat in all ways.

The woman had more jiggle than Jell-O.

Once she was near, she held out a glass of sparkling blue liquid.

Kellan's eyes gave him information on her.

Name: Stephanie #2
Race: Figment
Armor Rating: —

Health: 1/1

Stats:
Strength—2
Dexterity—2
Fortitude—2
Charisma—4 [Friendly]
Manipulation—2
Intelligence—2
Perception—2
Wisdom—2
Willpower—? [Varies]

Abilities:
Figment—[Created by the Arbiter]—This figment was created by the Arbiter. If the Arbiter ever ceases to be, this figment disappears along with him. This figment's willpower is based on the Arbiter's. The closer the figment is to the Arbiter, the higher the willpower score.

"Hello," Stephanie practically sang. "Welcome to the VIP Lounge. A full meal will be prepared for you immediately." She handed him the blue drink. "This is a glintberry wine. It should restore your mana."

Kellan took the drink. The glass sparkled. Was it made of actual crystal? He took a sip and savored the restorative properties of the drink. The liquid slid down his throat, spreading to his whole body like hot chocolate on a snowy day.

Within a few seconds, his mana went back up to twelve. He closed his eyes, enjoying the rejuvenating sensations. Why couldn't he have this wine all the time?

"Thank you," Kellan muttered.

Stephanie replied with a *tee-hee*.

Before anything else happened, Kellan asked, "You're a *figment*?"

"That's right. So smart you are."

"Uh-huh. What, exactly, is that? Are you a person? Or some sort of… illusion?"

Stephanie stood straight, her red hair bright under the neon lighting. "Figments are like constructs. We're made of illusions and telekinetic forces, so we have physical form and can interact with our environment." She patted the side of the couch to prove her point. "Does that bother you? Some guests don't like interacting with figments…"

"No, it's fine." Kellan hadn't ever really interacted with a figment before. He wasn't sure why anyone would send one away, though. Stephanie was beautiful, like fine art. Well, *Maxim art,* but still art.

She smiled, her face and teeth too perfect for a normal person. Then she bounded away to grab Kellan his promised food. Once she was gone, he reclined back, placed his glass in a cup holder, and glanced over at the TV. The screen was mounted on the wall, but the moment Kellan gave it his attention, it moved toward him.

Kellan lifted an eyebrow.

The TV flickered to life and even turned up the volume all on its own, like it anticipated Kellan's needs.

To Kellan's amusement, Bitso was on the screen. The bizarre newscaster sat at his usual desk, leaning heavily on his elbows as he slouched forward. His suit and blindfold were neatly in place, but his tie was wrinkled and flung over his shoulder.

The man pointed to a display screen behind him.

"Every team who decided to play through *Davie's Gauntlet* has either succeeded or failed. Why don't we watch some of the highlights, shall we?" Bitso chuckled as he turned in his chair to "watch" the footage, despite the fact his blindfold was still securely in place.

A rennic mage with white fur was inside a metal warehouse. At one end of the warehouse, there was a goal. The rennic mage waited at the opposite end. An overly deadly and dangerous obstacle course stood between the man and his destination. The rennic smoothed his fur and then ran for the first obstacle. He leapt over a series of saw blades, and then jumped on top of a platform that was suspended over a pit of nails and broken needles. The rennic then climbed up a rope, but for some reason, it broke while the man was halfway up.

The rennic fell onto the platform. It broke, and the rennic tumbled down into the nails and needles. His canine mouth opened in a howl, and Kellan suspected the scream was loud enough to be heard from the moon, but the newscaster's screen was muted to allow for Bitso's commentary.

Bitso just laughed. He pointed to the rennic thrashing about on the nails and needles. "Do you see this chump? That's what he gets for only developing animal and plant-altering magics."

The rennic waved his bloody hand, and the rope sprang to life. It grew green hemp leaves in an outward explosion, like a greenhouse grenade, transforming the whole warehouse into a garden. The leaves were so numerous and clustered that the mage was able to pull himself off the nails and roll onto a bed of plants away from the hazard.

"That isn't going to last long," Bitso said with a smile.

A fire in one of the many obstacles spread to the plants. Then flames raged out of control in the warehouse. The heat and smoke filled the room quickly, and Kellan couldn't stop himself from watching the inferno grow larger and larger. The rennic tried to flee the hemp-filled room, but panic had clearly set in.

The mage didn't make good decisions.

When Stephanie brought a tray of tiny appetizers, Kellan barely paid any attention. She spread a napkin out on his lap, and he didn't even have the presence of mind to thank her before she hurried away.

Right as the rennic mage was being cooked alive on screen, Bitso changed the footage to a different warehouse, one filled with similar obstacles, but in a slightly different arrangement.

"That was fun," Bitso said. "But I'm sure some of you are *anxiously* awaiting what Nosferatu did on his run." He held up a finger and waggled it. "So many of you have bet tons of arcana on Nosferatu to win, but I have to warn you... Nothing is predictable in the Nexus Games."

With another cackle, Bitso dramatically whipped his chair around to stare at the screen.

Nosferatu, the deformed Nexus resident, stood at one end of the death warehouse, and his goal stood at the other. He waited patiently for the game to begin, his piercing gaze only on his desired destination. Once the buzz saws started up, and the gears in the room turned into position, Nosferatu stepped forward.

Unlike the rennic, who had run as fast as possible, Nosferatu took his time. The first obstacle was a series of electrified wires. They were taut and crisscrossed around so that someone would have to carefully duck and step through each narrow hole between them.

Instead of ducking through, Nosferatu stretched out his hand and grabbed one of the wires.

Kellan scooted forward on the couch, barely able to believe his own eyes. Why would anyone do that?

The wire shocked Nosferatu, a spark flashing from his burnt palm, but it didn't last long. A second later, the wire snapped from the ceiling, breaking away from the source of electrical power. Once he had it under his control, Nosferatu used the broken wire like a weapon.

His metal magic obviously gave him control over twelve-foot-long wire. Nosferatu controlled it like a limb, moving it toward the buzz saws in the room. When it got close to the saws, Nosferatu threw the wire onto the other electrified wires, causing electricity to short out the saws. Once the wire collapsed to the ground, Nosferatu picked it up. He used it again to clear away another obstacle, and then another.

He even used the wire to sweep away all sharp objects on the floor and around on the ceiling.

Each team only had a few minutes to complete the obstacle course, but Nosferatu hadn't even really broken a sweat. He rearranged everything in the warehouse and then sauntered over to the exit without much difficulty. Only his burnt palm from the first electrical shock seemed to have had an effect.

His rennic teammate entered the obstacle course afterward. Since everything was cleared, he just ran through, no problems.

"What a *bore*," Bitso said with a groan. He slammed his head on the desk. "The leper found one of the few pieces of metal in the room that would answer the command of his magic. Normally the Arbiter uses his meta magic to create anti-magic objects, but occasionally he overlooks things... That's no fun. Maybe we should switch back to the footage of the rennic burning to death..."

Bitso sat up straight, smiling so wide his face seemed in pain.

"Perhaps we should focus on all the *good things* to come out of the third game so far. Like how many teams have been completely eliminated from the Nexus

Games." Bitso held up both his hands, his fingers fanned out. "Ten teams. Ten teams have been removed, and we're not even done with the *Escort* game. We could still lose people!"

Bitso laughed, his howling mirth practically shaking his newsroom. Then he stopped, smoothed his tie, and "stared" straight into the camera. "I'm so happy. It's moments like this that remind me of my father's last words. *Don't, Son! That gun is loaded!*"

Silence.

Bitso had no audience, no crew, no cameraman. He waited for laughter from *somewhere*, but it never came. After thirty seconds, Bitso laughed at his own joke, even going so far as to throw his head back and grab at his stomach.

Kellan could've sworn the man was crying bloody tears, but before he could confirm, someone sat down on the couch next to Kellan.

At first, Kellan thought it was Stephanie, but when he finally pulled his attention from the TV, he realized it was a human man.

—Chapter 33—
—Inside the Flestiss Dominion—

The man was strikingly similar to HR-8. Had he come from the Flestiss Dominion?

He had a brand on his scalp, one that was different from HR-8's, but not in a way Kellan could articulate. The man was dark tan. Bulky with muscle. Tall. Remarkably still when he was just sitting. But unlike HR-8, this man had grown out his hair. The gnarled scar of his brand didn't allow him to grow anything, but the rest of his brown hair was shoulder-length.

The number 80 was on the back of his left hand.

"Merry Christmas," the man said.

When Kellan turned his gaze up to the man, he got all his basic information.

Name: G-7894, Bred in Captivity
Race: Human
Magics: Storm, Metal
Rank: Concealed
Armor Rating: 5 + 5 Shielding [Wind]
Health: 10/10
Stats: Concealed
Abilities: Concealed

"I'm glad we have a moment to speak," G-7894 said. "I've been wanting to chat with you ever since the first game."

G-7894 wore a T-shirt, jacket, jeans, and heavy steel-toed boots. Kellan spotted his shoulder holster and pistol, both of which looked well-loved.

"What can I do for you, G-7894?" Kellan asked. The name didn't roll well off his tongue.

The man smirked and snorted. "Just call me *Gunner*. That's what my designation stands for."

"Your flestiss designation?"

"That's right."

Gunner laced his fingers together and leaned back on the couch. He fidgeted a bit and offered Kellan half a smile.

"When I was born, the flestiss overseer sorted me into the *gunner shock troop barracks*. I was raised to fight in their wars." Gunner touched the brand on the side of his head. "This is a reminder of my designation, so that the flestiss know my role even before speaking to me."

Kellan wasn't a fan of the cruel methodology. It reminded him of an older sci-fi novel written as a warning to problematic societies. The rigid class system and lack of choice made everything feel dystopian.

They sat close together, but Kellan hadn't bothered to really examine Gunner's hands until that moment. Besides the number 80, which designated Gunner as part of Team 80, there were a number of faint scars along his knuckles, fingers, and wrists.

"So, what did you want to speak with me about?" Kellan asked as he slowly brought his gaze up to Gunner's.

"I wanted to thank you personally for saving Hank Gardener during the first game."

"You already sent me a letter thanking me. You don't need to thank me twice."

Gunner's lips twitched. "Did you enjoy the egg?"

"Yeah." Kellan glanced at his shadow. "I have a familiar now. An albino wyvern named Vlaze." *I wonder if he's okay in the darkness?*

"Ah. Lucky."

The comment got Kellan curious. "Why? I figured you must've stolen from a wyvern nest or something."

"Those familiar eggs can be anything. Sure, you can breed familiars to get something specific you want—either type or magic or quality—but when you get an egg from one of the games, the contents are random. You had just as much chance to get a piñata as you did a wyvern."

The statement reminded Kellan of his blender theory. He had been convinced he would somehow get a sentient blender as a familiar, and it amused him that he wasn't far off. A piñata familiar sounded bizarre—on a whole new level. It fit the Nexus's strange world.

Gunner cleared his throat. He seemed in his late twenties, but it was hard to tell. The man's face was rather haggard.

"I also wanted to talk to you about what you said to the Arbiter." Gunner's expression hardened, and his voice lowered. "I sent you a letter because I didn't want anyone to know we were associated. I feared the Flestiss Dominion would target you."

"Why?"

"Because they don't allow runaways and defectors to live." Gunner pointed to himself. "I would be considered a runaway. And the flestiss don't take kindly to people who help runaways."

Kellan held his breath for a moment. When he glanced around, he noticed the TV had moved back to its place against the wall. It had shut itself off and was now just a simple black screen. Had it known they weren't watching anymore?

Kellan wished he had the talking of the screen to blanket their conversation.

"I'm surprised you're trying to rally people to fight against the Dominion," Gunner muttered. "Most mages from other dimensions know nothing about them, so they don't have any motive to fight the flestiss. And everyone who *knows* about the Dominion tends to stay out of their way."

"Everything I've heard about these lunatics makes me want to puke."

Gunner shot him a sideways glance. "I've noticed… that you've been going out of your way to help others." He scratched at his neck and then fidgeted with his hands again, as though he couldn't sit still for too long.

Kellan replied with a single nod.

"Which makes me think you're the real deal. You actually *want* to stop them. You *want* us to team up in order to stop the flestiss from enslaving more of humanity from other dimensions."

"That's right." Kellan glanced down at the tray on his lap. There were dozens of little pastries and finger foods, but he just wasn't hungry. He placed the tray on the couch next to him in order to better sit closer to Gunner. "Is that what you're doing here?"

Gunner glanced at Kellan and then positioned himself to match Kellan's posture. It was… odd. Kellan had never seen someone do that, and he was about to ask, but Gunner replied with, "That's right. If I get to Zenith, I'm going to use whatever magical powers I gain to free my people and stop the Dominion."

Finally, someone is talking sense.

"You want any of this food, by the way?" Kellan asked, motioning to the uneaten appetizers.

Gunner eyed the food, his eyebrows knitted. "I find it difficult to eat… normal human food."

The comment gave Kellan pause. Then he chortled and asked, "What kind of food do you eat? *Abnormal* human food?"

"I was bred and raised in the Flestiss Dominion."

Kellan waited for a follow-up statement that would explain what was going on. But nothing ever came. Gunner just stared at him with a cold expression.

"And?" Kellan asked. "Surely, they feed the humans in the Dominion."

Gunner's lips twitched again. He scratched at his neck, his nails digging deeper, and then he shifted around the cushioned seat. "I thought… because of the way you've been acting… you knew about the conditions in the Dominion?"

"I've never been there," Kellan stated. "I didn't even know the Dominion existed until I started the Nexus Games." He leaned in close, his irritation rising. "And everyone here is too damn busy with their own plans, schemes, and social orders to give me the time of day. I *asked* all the questions, but only a few people bother to answer."

The information settled over Gunner like an obvious wet blanket. He tightly laced his fingers together. "Well, I'll have to show you a few things, then. So that you fully understand."

"How?"

Gunner stood. It was sudden and dramatic, like a horn had been blown and now was the time for attack. He turned on his heel with military precision and walked out of the sitting area.

Confused, but intrigued, Kellan also stood. He followed Gunner to the back of the VIP Lounge, ignoring the other figments walking around. Since the lounge was U-shaped, they went to the very back of one side. There, Gunner stopped in front of a black door that matched the coloration of the walls. It was difficult to see from the bar, but Kellan noticed it the moment he drew near.

"What is this?" he asked.

Gunner grabbed the handle. "This is a Room of Manifested Dreams. Think of it like… a large magical item that you can walk around in." He pushed open the door and walked into a small ten-foot by ten-foot space.

The floor was flat marble stone, as were the walls. No windows. No decorations. A few lights were mounted into the ceiling, but that was it. If Kellan hadn't known any better, he would've said this was a giant, luxurious closet and nothing more.

But then he spotted a man leaning against the wall.

He was dressed the same as the bartender, with a vest, tie, and ribbon around his wrist. The man jumped to attention when Gunner and Kellan entered. Then he bowed at the waist, deep enough to form a perfect ninety-degree angle.

"Welcome to the Room of Manifested Dreams," the man said with fake cheer in his tone. "I'm your host, Bellz. The Arbiter wishes you all the fun in the world here." Bellz stood straight, his lanky frame awkward, like an older teen's. "The Arbiter understands you might be homesick. This room uses illusions to show you different worlds, creating images of places in other dimensions in *real time*."

Bellz used jazz hands for the last two words, like it was an amazing selling point.

"We can see other dimensions here?" Kellan glanced around at the plain walls and floor. "So, this is a Holodeck situation? Like in Star Trek or whatever?"

Bellz anxiously rubbed his hands together. "I don't know why so many people say that… But please understand that I have to *stay* inside the room while you use it. By command of the Arbiter."

"Uh-huh."

"I really don't want to know all the shameful things you mages do behind closed doors," Bellz whispered to himself. "But does anyone listen to me? *Nooo*."

"Don't get your panties in a twist," Kellan muttered. "We're here to see what's happening in other dimensions, aren't we?" He turned to Gunner. "You want to show me what it's like in the Flestiss Dominion?"

Gunner nodded once. But then he touched the brand on his scalp and stared at the floor. "Before we do that… Do you mind if we look around *your* dimension? I've always wanted to see… a world where humans were the only ones inhabiting it."

Although that sounded like a waste of time to Kellan, it wasn't like he could leave just yet. Xiang and Mavis still hadn't completed the game. He was stuck here anyway, and if Gunner wanted to see a plain-o-boring Earth, what was the harm?

"Fine." Kellan waved a hand around. "Can the Holodeck show us my dimension first?"

"It's not a Holodeck," Bellz whispered. Then he wore his fake smile and said in a loud voice, "Of course! The Room of Manifested Dreams will show you what you desire!"

The walls, floor, and ceiling shimmered and shifted with the consistency of a heat mirage. All at once, the room transformed. They were no longer in an empty black marble closet—they were in the middle of Fayetteville, standing on a sidewalk in the busier areas around brewpubs and local shops.

The scene almost shocked Kellan.

It was his home, but it was more than that… The details were more accurate than he had been expecting. The smells, the temperature, the sun in the sky—everything was identical to how he remembered it. Even the brewpubs nearby, packed with customers, some even eating at tables outside, were recreated with loving attention.

Green, red, and orange trees lined the side of the road, their branches swaying.

Kellan felt as though he could start walking his way to Fort Bragg, that was how well he knew this area of Fayetteville. He glanced around, smiling as he did so. He hadn't realized how much he missed *normal.* His Earth had none of the twisted madness found in the Nexus.

However…

In a lot of ways, Kellan now saw it as mundane.

The people eating burgers and sharing beer were all wrapped up in inconsequential conversations. They were obsessed with glancing at their phones, or talking about the newest TV show, and Kellan felt so far removed from their interests that it was like he was an alien in his own hometown.

The brick restaurants, beautiful trees, and fancy cars had little appeal to him other than nostalgia.

But Gunner seemed to be the exact opposite. The man spun around on the sidewalk, trying to take everything in all at once. Then he spotted the burgers and the beer. He wandered over, his eyes wide. At first, Kellan thought he was intrigued by the food, but Gunner wandered by all that and went for the restaurant.

With shaky hands, Gunner caressed the red bricks. Then he turned his attention to the window and touched that, too. When he started rubbing the windowsill, Kellan grew concerned.

"Can people see us?" Kellan asked Bellz, who stood just a few feet off.

"These people are all illusions," Bellz replied. "They won't ever react to your presence."

"That's good." *At least we won't have to explain to the cops why Gunner is molesting the building.*

Gunner stopped admiring the building and instead went to one of the tables. He sat with a couple, admired their plates and silverware, and then moved to another table where a man quietly fed his guide dog.

"Are you okay?" Kellan asked.

A gentle North Carolina breeze swept through the air. Kellan loved the sound of rustling leaves. It had been a long time since he had heard them.

Gunner stood from the table and walked over to Kellan. "I'm just… I'm in awe. I've seen ruins of human civilization in the Nexus, but I've never seen *this* before. Humans did all this by themselves? No magic?" He motioned to the people having a good time. "They're not constantly fearing for their lives?"

Kellan slowly shook his head. "Yeah. Humans built all this. No help from anyone or anything else. And no. Most people don't fear for their lives. At least, not here."

"That's just so… wonderful."

"The bar to impress you must be set real low," Kellan said. "This isn't even one of the most interesting cities."

Gunner watched a family with two children as they ate their meal. He didn't even acknowledge Kellan's statement. Gunner just stared, observing the father and mother as they spoke to their kids about school and how one of them had lost their lunch box.

It was nothing more than an innocuous conversation about what kind of lunch box would be a suitable replacement. Despite that, Gunner listened with rapt fascination.

"This is amazing," Gunner whispered. "I wish… I could've been born in a dimension like this."

Amazing?

Kellan crossed his arms, feeling odder by the moment. Nothing in front of him seemed particularly *amazing*. It was quaint. And peaceful. But nothing significant was happening.

"Thank you so much for this," Gunner muttered.

"Couldn't you have viewed this at any point?"

Bellz held up a hand. "The Arbiter restricts people to viewing their own dimensions. You can have guests—like you two—but you're not allowed to use this room to view *any* dimension your heart desires."

"Why not?" Kellan asked, a little baffled by the rule.

Bellz didn't answer.

His silence didn't sit well with Kellan. Something about the exchange felt off. Why *wouldn't* the Arbiter allow someone to view other dimensions? It seemed silly, but… Was the Arbiter trying to hide something?

Kellan couldn't shake the feeling.

"Enough," Gunner said, tearing his attention away from the family. "No sense dwelling on things that cannot be." He rubbed his palm over the brand on his hand, like he was trying to wipe it clean from his skin. "Return us to the room."

The images of Kellan's Earth faded away.

Another shimmer of mirages swirled around the room, shifting everything back to the black marble. The shiny, reflective floor was clear enough that Kellan could practically stare at himself on the black mirror surface.

"You've seen nothing of the Flestiss Dominion?" Gunner asked.

"I've seen arcana factories and a prison," Kellan replied. "But that's the extent of it."

The flestiss had been killing people at a fairly high rate in both locations. Kellan had found a soldier being slowly bled out, and cages of people being drowned to easily collect a mass of arcana from afterward. It had been those sights that convinced Kellan the flestiss—and Team 42—needed to be stopped.

What more could Gunner possibly show him?

"Take him to one of the designation facilities," Gunner whispered, his gaze on the mirror-like floor.

Kellan braced himself for a scene of hundreds of flestiss oppressing humans. For some reason, he pictured the flestiss whipping the humans into submission, forcing them to build starships or magic facilities—something out of 1700 BC Egypt.

But when the room shifted with images and colors, there were no sand dunes, whips, or chains.

Kellan found himself standing in a long rectangular room with no windows. Were they underground? The walls reminded him of a submarine. Doors, electronics, screens, and hatches were built so thoroughly into the building, they were all interconnected. And technology—the wires, computers, and keypads—was a leathery, fleshy black, somehow organic, pulsing with life despite the fact that it was all obviously tech.

Dog-sized pods lined two walls. They had glass covers, but the glass itself was reflective—Kellan couldn't see in, he could only see his own face. Hundreds of them filled the room, each perfectly spaced from one another.

No one was in the room. Machine arms, mounted on the organic-tech wall, reached for the pods and tapped at the controls, caring for everything without anything else's supervision or inputs.

One pod opened, and Gunner walked across the room to approach. He motioned for Kellan to follow. After a moment of hesitation, Kellan did as he was asked.

Bellz remained behind, quiet and smiling, obviously content to be left out of the tour.

"These are uterine replicators," Gunner stated as he motioned to the contents.

Kellan glanced inside to find clear goo and a human fetus. Not a mature fetus, but one only half-formed. It sat in the fetal position in the goo, attached to tubes and a few small wires. The pod monitored its growth.

"These grow fetuses," Gunner stated. "They're extracted from females and then gestated in vitro, rather than in a human body."

Kellan stepped away from the pod. "Like some sort of Matrix shit?"

The other man stared at him without a hint of recognition. Why would Gunner have seen the Matrix? Kellan sighed.

"What happens when they're done baking?"

"They're sorted and given designations."

Gunner pointed to one of the submarine-style doors. It unlocked, and then a flestiss walked into the room. It scuttled over to the pods with its four disgusting legs clicking the whole way. It checked on the contents of the pods, tapping on the computer screens with its small delicate hands. One pod opened, and the flestiss took out the fully formed child and cradled it close. The flestiss's black exoskeleton was smeared with goo as it ripped out the wires and tubes and then held the child up to view it fully.

"The readouts indicate this one has superior strength and dexterity," the flestiss said to the computer. "Fortitude is low. Sort this one as a vanguard shock trooper."

The machine arms went back into the wall and then emerged again, this time with an odd soldering tool. While the human child was unconscious, the machine took the tool and branded its scalp, burning the flesh away and quickly writing the human's designation in a place for all to see.

The baby didn't wake or move.

Once finished—with the skull burnt and bleeding—the flestiss placed the child back into the goo. With a quick tap of its clawed finger, the flestiss shut the hatch and moved to the next pod.

Gunner motioned for Kellan to follow again.

Although Kellan was slightly horrified, nothing here had seemed as disturbing as the factory or prison. Up until Gunner gestured to a much larger pod. This one didn't have a reflective hatch—Kellan could easily see inside. It was more of a vat—some sort of waste bin where black goo and chunks floated around inside.

"All the children who aren't suited for a designation are thrown in here," Gunner stated matter-of-factly. "They're ground up into an organic paste used for other purposes around the Dominion."

At first, Kellan wasn't sure what he was looking at.

But then it hit him.

This was human-embryo soup. He stepped back, an icy indifference settling over his thoughts, as if to shield him from the anger that was quietly building.

"What kinds of humans aren't suited for designation?" Kellan quietly asked.

"All the physically weak. Or those who are missing one of their major senses. Those with poor eyesight. Any prone to early death through cancer or organ failure."

The whole room felt chill and dark. Kellan glanced away, trying to imagine what it would be like to live in such a place.

"Once you're sorted, the pods are emptied into your facility, and you're raised by the flestiss tamers who teach you only the things you need for your role." Gunner spoke as though he already knew all of Kellan's questions. "If you're ever damaged, they send you to the arcana factory—they don't tell you that, of course. They say you're going to get healed, but then you never return."

Kellan didn't respond.

"Unless you're female." Gunner sighed. "All human females who are damaged beyond usefulness are brought to the breeding facility. Their eggs are harvested, or they're put in the pits."

Kellan feared asking, but he did so anyway. "What are the pits?"

"Facilities where they keep human bodies. They're… medically unconscious. Shock troops can do what they want to them. The bodies never know. They never wake up ever again."

Human bodies. Kellan suspected Gunner was trying to shield him from the horrific reality that was *the breeding facilities.*

"It's to reward good behavior," Gunner said. "The flestiss say they're being benevolent and resourceful because they never allow human bodies to go to waste. Either they're used for this… goo… or they're *recycled* in the pits for *entertainment.*"

Kellan glanced back at the organic soup.

Now he had seen three locations in the Flestiss Dominion. He had seen how they treated enemies of war. He had seen how they made their own mages stronger. And now he had witnessed how they treat their "lesser citizens."

Everything in the Flestiss Dominion—that wasn't flestiss—was a resource. Or cattle. Or something in between.

And they wanted to control *every* dimension.

After a hard swallow, Kellan asked, "Does everyone know about this?"

"Most people don't know." Gunner moved to the side of a pod and placed his hand on the hatch. "They don't want to hear it. I tried to tell them… I was raised in the Dominion… and that I never had a mother or father… and that I was trained to serve or perish. But the mages of the Nexus Games all come from other dimensions—ones without the flestiss. So they don't believe me. Or just don't care."

It now made sense to Kellan why Gunner had been so focused on the family back on Earth. Gunner had been designated a shock trooper at birth, raised inside a barracks, and had been told that if he ever became too damaged, he'd be ground up like hamburger for his arcana.

What a fucked-up existence.

"What kind of food did you eat?" Kellan asked, remembering Gunner's strange reaction to the appetizers.

"Nutrient paste. We were given tubes with paste to eat for every meal. Anything else… feels disgusting in my mouth."

Kellan frowned just thinking about eating pudding for every meal for his *entire life.*

"I escaped," Gunner whispered as he ran a hand over the pod. "During the *Season of the Conflux*. People are pulled into the Nexus from all other dimensions. I was yanked out of the Flestiss Dominion and brought here."

Kellan held his breath. He knew people came to the Nexus through weird means, but he didn't realize it had happened in the Dominion.

"At first, I was afraid that the flestiss would hunt me down for deserting my post." Gunner glared at his own reflection. "Thinking back at how frightened I was… I'm disgusted with myself. As soon as I realized I could gather arcana, and become my own mage here in the Nexus… I quickly jumped at the opportunity to participate in the Nexus Games."

"Why?"

"Well, first… if you participate in the Nexus Games, you can't be forcefully removed from any dimension—especially not the Nexus. The Arbiter has a *Dimensional Anchor* ability that prevents people from teleporting you away."

"Okay. And what else?"

"*And then I heard about Zenith!*" Gunner whirled on his heel to glare at Kellan, his whole body shaking, his hands clenched in tight fists. "You've heard the claims. It's all the other mages here talk about! Zenith is a dimension with infinite magic! No need for arcana—your magic is empowered far beyond anything you could hope for! You become a *god*. The *perfect* dimension."

"Well, some of these claims seem exaggerated," Kellan muttered, still skeptical, but becoming less so each new day. *Everyone* wanted into Zenith. Could they all be wrong?

Gunner stepped closer to Kellan, bordering on hysterical. His tanned face shifted to a dark red. Even the brand on his head had drained of color and became bright white. "Do you see what's going on here? We can't allow the flestiss to have god-like powers! They'll do *this* to *every* dimension!"

Kellan placed a hand on Gunner's shoulder and squeezed tight. For a prolonged moment, they said nothing to each other. It seemed to work—Gunner took a deep breath and then brushed Kellan's hand from his shoulder.

"I'm calm," he snapped. "I just… I apologize. I'm getting frustrated. No one ever seems to listen."

"I'm listening."

The statement rocked Gunner. He turned his attention to Kellan's gaze, searching his eyes like he wanted to make sure Kellan wasn't lying. "No one else will," Gunner finally muttered.

"Then we just have to make sure no one from the Flestiss Dominion wins the Nexus Games." Kellan crossed his arms. "We'll team up. Nosferatu, from Team 5, already proposed we make an alliance. He wants to help the people of the Nexus. Our goals don't have to perfectly align, we all just need to be on the same page about the Dominion."

"You… made an alliance with Team 5?"

"That's right."

The click of the flestiss in the room drew Kellan's attention. It scuttled over to another pod and had another baby branded. Although it was all an illusion, the sight still bothered Kellan. Somewhere, in another universe, this was taking place for real.

"I don't know… how to be a normal human," Gunner said through gritted teeth. He glanced away from Kellan and glared at his boots. "I… I want to thank you for agreeing to help me, but I'm not sure… what to do?"

With awkward movements—like he was a robot—Gunner stepped close to Kellan and slowly wrapped his arms around the other man. It was the most bizarre hug Kellan had ever experienced in his life.

Gunner even offered a couple pats, but only after he seemingly remembered that it was part of the "thanking" ritual.

Then Gunner stepped back and slowly lowered his arms.

"You've been thanked," Gunner stated matter-of-factly.

Kellan stared at the man, unsure of how to respond. He forced himself to smile and then nodded. "Well, that's one way to do that, I guess. Where did you learn that?"

"I saw a few other humans doing it." Gunner scratched at his neck. "I've watched the others for most of the games. I think we're supposed to shake hands for greeting partners, and embrace—like we just did—for thanks. And we press our mouths together right before we undress in each other's presence."

Kellan snorted. "That all seems to check out," he quipped.

Gunner waved his hand. "Take us out of here, please, Bellz." With a shudder, he just stared at the floor, even as everything shimmered and shifted back into black marble. Once they were back in the AVU Palace, Gunner glanced up. "I feel like the embrace wasn't enough to express my gratitude. Do humans… have a higher form of *thanks giving*?"

"Cooking turkey," Kellan said—because he couldn't help himself. Then he just slapped Gunner's shoulder and added, "Listen, don't worry about it. Just focus on becoming a stronger mage. Once we're done with the Nexus Games, and we've made it to Zenith, we can go back to my Earth together, and I'll show you everything you've ever missed out on."

Although they hadn't known each other long, Gunner shifted his weight from one foot to the other, half-inching his way over to Kellan as though he would offer another awkward hug. He was obviously emotional, though he didn't seem to have the tools to express it other than fidgeting and glancing around.

"Thank you," Gunner stated. "I swear as the leader of Team 80, you will have our unwavering support."

—Chapter 34—
—The Oom—

Kellan, Gunner, and Bellz stood in the empty square room. As Kellan mulled over the information, he tried to think of the Flestiss Dominion as an enemy nation. How would he react if he were a nation trying to bring about their downfall?

"Who leads the Flestiss Dominion?" Kellan asked. "What's their governing structure?"

Gunner snorted out a laugh. "They have a strict hierarchy based around magical power and skill aptitude tests. But… the entire Dominion is ruled by one mage and has been forever."

"Who is it?"

"It's… It's an Oom." Gunner rubbed at his arms. "I don't know if you're aware of them, but…"

"An Oom?" Kellan narrowed his eyes. "They're messed-up space whales, right?" He had seen an image of one in the Catacomb Maze.

"That's right, I suppose. They're… magical beyond reason." Gunner shot Bellz an odd glance. "Can we show him the Oom in my dimension? The one who runs the Dominion."

Bellz just shrugged.

The room shifted all over again, but this time, there were barely any colors. Black mixed with black, creating a void and then filling it with distant objects. As if they were standing in space, Kellan forced himself to look around.

They *were* standing in space.

Stars twinkled in the vast distance. Sol, the star of the Milky Way, shone with a blinding brilliance. Kellan covered his eyes as he tried to glance around it.

That was when he saw it.

The Oom.

He caught his breath, shocked at how *massive* the beast was. Kellan stood over a wrecked and twisted Earth, but there was the Oom, orbiting the moon like a creature straight out of a Lovecraftian tale.

The *cosmic horror* was, in fact, whale shaped, but it had six fins, holes along its spine, and eyes that were fixed shut. Its skin was an odd reddish-brown, and it moved more like an asteroid than a fish moving through water. The longer

Kellan stared, the more he realized it wasn't moving at all. The gravitational pull of celestial bodies was all the Oom needed.

Gunner pointed at it. "The Oom are a race of space-dwelling mages with a special ability they call *Dynastic Telos*. Their children are all born with the highest ranks of magics that their parents possess. Which means… Even an infant Oom typically has multiple M-rank magics. They've had generations to perfect their magics in order to breed themselves into unstoppable powerhouses—but they only have children once every few millennia. They're rare, but godly."

Kellan nodded along with the words, hoping he understood the significance.

"The Oom are almost as old as the primordial dragons," Gunner muttered. "They have a fierce rivalry. And since *this* Oom rules over the Dominion… I assume it's the one who orchestrated the plot to kill the Arbiter and take the magic of Zenith."

"Why didn't the Oom just participate in the Nexus Games?" Kellan quipped.

Bellz cleared his throat. He walked forward, stepping out of the darkness of space and holding up a single finger. "Oom and starkin aren't allowed to participate in the Nexus Games. That was decreed by the primordial dragons around the dawn of time."

Kellan was starting to see the full picture. "So this Oom rules everything with an iron flipper. Who rules things under it?"

"Flestiss queens," Gunner stated. "The flestiss operate similar to… well, I learned it as *bees*. They have a hierarchy they follow, with queens at the top."

More of the puzzle came together. If the *Oom* couldn't play the games to get into Zenith, then it would have its faithful minions—the flestiss—do all of its work for it. And in return, the flestiss were allowed to rule over everything else.

Insidious.

While all of this was fascinating, Kellan had heard enough. Anger and confusion raged within him. Why weren't the others upset about this? How could Team 42—made up of *four humans* and only *one* flestiss—think this was a good idea? What were their motives? They wanted to be the first slaves, instead of the one thousandth?

"I'm done with this," Kellan stated.

The illusions faded, returning them once again to the empty room.

Gunner frowned. "I apologize if it was too much."

"It wasn't too much. I just have a lot to think about, and now is the time to do it."

"Hm. Now is the time for rest. Game four will surely begin tomorrow. Come. Let's leave this place."

With a nod to Bellz, Kellan and Gunner exited the Holodeck. Kellan didn't care what its real name was, he thought it of it that way just to spite the worker who insisted on using the proper name.

The VIP Lounge was empty. The mages in the other sitting area had left. All that lingered around now were the figments.

"I'll see you in the games," Gunner said as he walked toward the front door. "If you have need of me, I'll be in the suites on the ground floor of the palace.

Stay safe until then." He headed out, his gait strong and militaristic.

Kellan wasn't sure if Xiang and Mavis had finished with the Escort game.

He returned to his sitting area to find the appetizers had disappeared, but all the cushions had been fluffed, and his empty wine glass had been removed. He took a seat, and the TV moved closer. The screen flickered to life and returned to the Nexus Games coverage—Kellan didn't have to lift a muscle.

Ice filled his veins. Kellan had never felt so much hate toward something. He didn't know what to do with his pent-up frustrations. He felt like ripping the VIP Lounge apart just for the hell of it. That wouldn't do any good, but maybe then he wouldn't feel so cold.

In an attempt to bleed some of the hate away, Kellan closed his eyes and forced himself to exhale. Then he reclined his chair. There were several hours before the third game was officially over.

Perhaps he could rest until then.

***

Kellan fluttered his eyes open.

He was completely healed, but the ice in his veins remained. How long had he slept? Kellan hadn't had any dreams, nor had he moved. The couch was so comfortable, and the room so mellow. Everything was relaxing.

Bitso and his bizarre news show appeared on the screen. Kellan forced himself to wake up enough to watch the show, hoping to see more of the other teams attempting to survive. He wanted to know more about his opponents—especially Team 42—and if he paid enough attention to the replay footage, he thought he could glean something of importance.

After rubbing his eyes and yawning, he focused on Bitso's words.

"Well, that's it, ladies, gentlemen, and everything in between." Bitso smiled wide, his white teeth streaked with fresh blood.

His clothes and blindfold showed no trace of struggle or conflict, but Bitso's lips were gashed, both top and bottom, as though he had fallen face-first onto a knife. Blood ran down his chin and dripped onto the desk at a surprising rate. As Kellan watched, some of it slid down Bitso's neck and finally stained the collar of his pristine suit.

"The third game is officially over."

The news sent a jolt through Kellan. He sat up and scooted forward, his eyes wide.

"That's right. Two more teams are officially out of the running. The lucky sad sacks couldn't handle the yami inside the Escort arena."

Bitso slammed his hand on his desk and laughed aloud.

"In other news, if you *didn't* get a key in the third game, you should be ashamed of yourself. Somehow, a team of five dead mages managed to secure themselves a key this round."

The screen behind Bitso's desk flared to life. It showed footage of five corpses, all of which were in a ditch, their bodies mangled, flies buzzing around their exposed innards.

Bitso pointed at them. "That's right. *They* got a key. The five dead guys. What the hell are the rest of you doing with your lives?"

After a laugh, Bitso smacked his desk again. "How did a team of dead men get a key? It's a hilarious story, really."

Bitso's cackling filled his newsroom. He laughed and wheezed and slapped his knee like this was the most hilarious joke he had ever heard.

After wiping an imaginary tear from his blindfold, Bitso said, "Team 33 *died* during the Escort game, but their doll was brought to the platform regardless." He pointed at the screen again. This time it showed new footage.

Kellan was on screen. It showed him running across the four-lane roundabout and placing Millie on the teleport platform.

"That's Alex Kellan the Void Knight," Bitso stated with a smirk. "He's illusioned as a member of Team 33, probably to avoid some of his friends out in the game arena…" Bitso touched his blindfold, his fingers pressing so hard, blood bloomed beneath his fingertips. "*He* secured Team 33's key, which means he's the best player on their team! Actually, he's the best player on *everyone else's team but his own!* Because Team 101 didn't manage to get a key at all!"

Kellan stood off the couch, his heart hammering.

Had Xiang and Mavis died? Was Bitso going to announce it? Should he run from the lounge and find out?

If Xiang is dead, that means I've lost the Nexus Games…

With a chuckle, Bitso added, "The real tactic is to tell the Void Knight a sob story. Then he'll move Heaven and Hell to see you through. It's happened at least twice now—maybe more, who fucking knows—so at this point, it's a valid strategy every team should be incorporating into their playbooks."

Bitso made fake teary gestures, and even sobbed like a little girl.

Kellan gritted his teeth, forcing himself to remain composed. The chill in his blood wouldn't leave him, though. His hate had no outlet, and now that Bitso was trying to mock him, Kellan couldn't help but feel that hate in his direction.

Bitso stopped his dramatic wailing and then stroked his bloody chin. "Huh. Maybe Team 101 should try that. I mean, it would've helped them here. Instead, the leader of Team 101 just wandered the play arena gathering resources."

The screen changed to show Xiang and Mavis wandering through buildings in the play arena. They still had their doll as they wandered around, so why hadn't they gone straight for the platform? The massive serpent, Qin Bolo, thrashed around in the distance. It had five heads and fought with other mages, their battle enough to shake the camera recording. While that took place, Mavis and Xiang entered a Prize Room…

But then the screen cut out.

What was Xiang thinking? Kellan shook his head. *That wasn't part of our plan!*

After running a hand through his sweat-soaked hair, Kellan headed for the exit of the VIP Lounge. He couldn't take it anymore. He needed to yell at *someone*, and if Xiang wasn't going to follow their plans, he supposed she would be the target of his frustrations.

—Chapter 35—
—Fate Magic—

Kellan rubbed at his head as he traveled the halls of the AVU Palace. The blazing red sunset outside filtered through the windows. The VIP Lounge had been dark and quiet, but the rest of the palace was once again filled with the sounds of partying. Despite the fact that they had lost twelve teams, the volume of the celebrations seemed to have intensified.

The music thrummed with the power of an overworked bass. The strobe lights filled most rooms and hallways. At a few points, Kellan spotted people carrying massive amounts of booze from one room to the other.

Everyone was having a grand ol' time.

It disturbed Kellan that no one seemed to care about everything happening *outside* the Nexus Games. Then again, if he failed to succeed in the games, what did it matter if the Dominion continued their conquest? Kellan would be dead.

He shook his head.

Failing isn't an option.

Although the palace could be an Escher-style painting of random doors, stairways, and architecture, Kellan was starting to get a feel for the place. He turned left, then right, and walked through a small library—a library that *also* had a party raging within. Two rennic were definitely going to town on the sole couch. They didn't bother stopping as Kellan shuffled by.

Once out of the library, he recognized the main hallway and headed for the stairs. His team's suite would be on the floor above.

After he ascended the steps, Kellan stopped. Someone was waiting in the hallway. They wore a cloak, with the hood over their head, their shoulders slumped.

Kellan approached at a steady rate, not intimidated by the mystery figure, not when they were in an Oasis. When he drew close, however, he realized who it was. Her flabby skin, bizarre black and blonde hair with occasional bald spots—the odd way she held herself…

Millie.

The doll for Team 33. *The dead team.*

For some reason, Millie had a black cloak wrapped around her whole body. She held it tight, and even flinched when Kellan got too close.

"A-Alex Kellan," she whispered.

The hallway was empty, devoid of people and barely affected by the music playing downstairs. Kellan could still detect the thump of rock music, but it was minor. The sunset filled the area with dramatic lighting, but Kellan knew the lights would soon turn on.

He slipped his hands into his ragged pants. Although he was physically healed, his outfit could've been stolen straight from a hurricane refugee.

"What're you doing here?" Kellan asked. He glanced around, hoping to find his teammates nearby, but they were nowhere to be found.

"I came to thank you."

The soft tone of her voice grated at Kellan's thin patience. For some reason, the thought of her giving him a single gold arcana for their performance in the last game felt like a joke. He didn't really deserve it. He should've stayed behind to help Mavis and Xiang.

"You don't need to thank me." Kellan grabbed the door handle.

"B-But…"

"Just stay safe, all right? Don't leave the AVU Palace until everyone disappears for the fourth game."

Millie rubbed her hands together.

When she said nothing, Kellan realized she might want something else. "I can always escort you home. Well, as long as it's somewhere close. I have to return before the next game begins."

"You'd take me home?" Millie whispered.

"To make sure you got there without getting killed, yeah."

"Oh. Um. That's not… that's not why I'm here."

Kellan waited. When she said nothing, he slowly cocked an eyebrow. "It's really okay if you go." Then he glanced back at the door. "I have a lot to think about."

"Y-You never really gave me your full attention during the game," Millie whispered. "Even now… I feel like you're not seeing me. I have something important to say. I just need to find the right words…"

Her statements grated him a second time. He had done everything to make sure she was safe during the game, but he hadn't *given her enough attention*? Kellan bit back some choice words. He let go of the door handle, turned on his heel to face her, and then focused his gaze solely on hers.

"What can I do for you?" Kellan asked, slow and almost cold.

Millie shifted her focus to the floor between them. Her skin hung off her chin like a hound's hung off its mouth. Somehow, her forehead had jowls. Despite all that, her skin flushed a deep red.

"I want to have your child," she whispered.

At first, Kellan didn't think he had heard her right. Then he mulled over the statement and realized that *yes,* she had offered to have his kid. Kellan glanced over his shoulder, inspecting the hallway to see if anyone else was around. This had to be a joke. Perhaps Bitso had a new segment for his news program, and it would involve pranks?

When he returned his attention to Millie, the many layers of her face were still bright red.

Oh my God.

Kellan ran a hand down his own face. "Listen. That's single handedly the weirdest, creepiest, and yet most flattering, compliment a woman has ever paid me, but—"

"You w-wouldn't have to do anything," Millie quickly interjected, the haste of her speech obviously fueled by her embarrassment. "Someone like you, who is so handsome and perfect, wouldn't ever… touch something like me." She pulled the cloak over her head further, blocking most of her face. "There are machines that can do it. They would just need a sample. Then I could… The point is, you wouldn't need to be involved."

"Okay, well, I don't know how they do things here in the Nexus, but where *I'm* from, it's customary for—"

"*I know what you're thinking,*" Millie blurted out, cutting him off a second time. "But the residents of the Nexus don't usually mingle with outsiders. When they do, mages always breed true, which means your child would have magic, even if, well…" She touched her face.

"That's not—"

"I asked the Arbiter for permission. He said he would allow it." Millie clung to her cloak, practically drowning in the black cloth. "I just want to make sure that… just in case you die in the Nexus Games… a small piece of you continues to live on."

Kellan raked his fingers through his hair, trying to grapple with the awkward situation in his mind before he spoke again. Why did everyone have to bombard him with a million different dramatic problems and requests? Couldn't he just focus on stopping one team from winning the Nexus Games? Why did he also have to deal with a woman trying to spirit away with one of his children?

Sweet Baby Jesus, only in the Nexus…

Kellan grabbed Millie by the shoulder. She glanced up at him, both shocked and slightly frightened. Kellan didn't let her go. He just stared into her eyes, hoping she would believe everything he was about to say.

"I'm not going to die."

Millie opened her mouth to retort, but Kellan tightened his grip.

"No," he said. "Listen. I'm not going to die. There's too much riding on this. I'm going to win the Nexus Games, save my dimension, stop the flestiss, and once all that is done, I'm coming back here to get Gunner—and now *you,* as well. I'll take you to my Earth, we can fix up your problems, and everything will be all right. Understand?"

"What if—"

"I'm not going to leave a child behind in the Nexus." Kellan smirked. "Have you seen this place? Not really kid friendly, if you ask me."

Millie rubbed at her eyes. They grew red at the edges, and her lip quavered. For a long moment, Kellan thought she might cry, but Millie held it all back. She took a breath to compose herself before she touched his hand on her shoulder.

"You're too kind."

"Not really. The bar is just *real* low."

Millie smiled a tiny bit. Then she gripped Kellan's hand tighter.

"I lied," she whispered. "The Arbiter didn't give me permission."

The statement caused Kellan to tense. Her tone sounded so… icy.

She stared at him, her gaze unflinching. "I went to the Arbiter and begged him to tell me if you'd live through the Nexus Games. He is a powerful fate mage, with magics able to see the most likely future… And he said you were going to die in the next game unless you found more gold arcana."

The news struck Kellan at his core.

Fate magic could see the most probable future?

And he was going to die?

"I wanted to help you," Millie finally glanced away, her gaze on the floor. "But… the Arbiter said someone you trust will fail you in your time of need."

"Did he say anything else?" Kellan asked.

Millie shook her head.

"And you wanted to have my kid to make sure something of mine lived on?"

She nodded.

"Well, that's still a nice compliment," Kellan muttered as he removed his hand from her shoulder. "But you don't have to worry about it. I won't die. I already told you what I'm going to do. I'm going to win the Nexus Games."

"The Arbiter's fate magic is powerful," Millie said. She grabbed his tattered shirt. "You don't understand. His future sight…"

"He said I'd die if I didn't get enough gold arcana."

"Yes…"

"So it'll be fine. You already told me what I need. I'll spend my evening looking for gold arcana."

His statement seemed to resonate with her. Millie slowly released his shirt and took a step back. Even though she hugged her cloak tight around her shoulders, she still offered him a slight smile.

"Do you really think you can do it?"

Kellan nodded once. "I've done weirder things."

He made his declarations, but at his core, Kellan had absolutely no idea how he was going to acquire a bunch of gold arcana before the fourth game. Unlike red arcana, which could be harvested through mass murder, gold arcana required time and trust, to a certain extent. It was much more difficult to amass.

Kellan turned to enter his suite, but Millie shifted closer. He stopped and glanced over one last time.

"If you don't find enough gold arcana before the fourth game, I'll find you some," Millie whispered.

Kellan still didn't want to take her one gold arcana. He doubted it would be enough. "You don't have to worry about me. Keep your arcana."

"*You* didn't have to worry about *me* during the third game," Millie said, her tone argumentative. "But you did everything in your power to help me regardless.

And now… you don't even want anything for it?"

"I'm fine."

"Maybe… But I want to help you. Can't you see that?"

He finally exhaled. "Fine. If you can find a way to help me, by all means—do it."

Millie tepidly smiled. "Well… There is one way. You see, the Nexus residents have an old tale." She lowered her voice to a whisper. "About a resident who admired an outsider and wanted to be with him. H-He was a powerful mage, and very kind. Like you."

"Do I want to hear this? I feel like it can't end well."

Millie ignored Kellan's question. "The Arbiter gave the resident a knife. A special knife. A knife that could cut away all their ugliness and leave them young and beautiful—but only for a few days. If the resident could convince the outsider to be with them, the change would become permanent, but if the outsider refused… the resident would become hideous once more."

Kellan already knew, because of the nature of the Nexus, that the story could not end well. He dreaded hearing the conclusion, but Millie was clearly intent on telling it, so he just waited for the sinister punch line.

She continued, "The resident used the knife to cut away all their imperfections and became gorgeous. Then the Nexus resident approached the outsider, but he said that he was already in love with another. No matter how beautiful a person was, it wouldn't sway him from his lover."

"Sounds respectable."

"Heartbroken, the resident returned to the Arbiter. He said… if the resident killed the outsider, the outsider's blood would keep the resident young and beautiful forever."

"Let me guess, this story ends in murder," Kellan quipped. Then he narrowed his eyes at her. "Or are you trying to say everyone would've just been happier if the outsider had just cooperated?"

"N-Neither," Millie mumbled. "The story doesn't end like that. It's…" She tightly closed her eyes. "I promise I'll help you in the Nexus Games. It's just… I'll need the knife…"

But she didn't continue her statement or the story. She just stopped talking.

Kellan wasn't even sure why she had started telling the story in the first place. His fatigue, and the obstacles of the Nexus Games, weighed heavily on his thoughts. He didn't have time for metaphorical analogies.

"Thank you," he said, jolting her out of her thoughts. "For telling me what the Arbiter said about my death. Once I win the games, I'll return. I promise."

Millie shook her head. "You're much too kind to someone like me."

"*The most beautiful thing you can wear is confidence*," Kellan stated, quoting one of his old commanding officers. "Don't talk about yourself like that—there's more to value than your looks."

"You saved my life… and you never despised me. Now you want to lift me up." Millie smiled genuinely. "Thank *you*, Alex Kellan. If… If I'm not a coward, I'll show you the end of that story with the knife. I'll help you with the games."

Before he could question her last statement, Millie fled the hallway. She sidestepped him and then ran toward the stairs, never bothering to glance back or even explain herself. Kellan watched her go, baffled.

For some reason, every interaction he had had in the last day or two had been the epitome of awkward.

I guess I just attract the type. Kellan snorted to himself and finally entered his suite. He just needed… to figure out what he was going to do about the next game before anything else happened.

—Chapter 36—
—Another Hex Won't Kill You—

Kellan entered the suite for Team 101 to find a strange sight.

Mavis stood in the middle of the living room with the couch held above her head. It was awkward, because she couldn't find the right leverage and angle, but she had clearly lifted the piece of furniture and was showing off her ability to do so. It was a three-person couch, and the decorative pillows tumbled to the floor as Mavis turned in a slow circle.

Her eyes went wide when she spotted Kellan. In her shock, she lost her balance with the couch, and she gasped out, *whoa, whoa*, before dropping it in the center of the room. The seat cushions went everywhere. Mavis cringed, her face slightly pink.

Husker leaned against the wall, his ears perked forward. With a frown, he said, "You should've increased your dexterity. That'll help you keep your balance."

"Where have you been?" Mavis asked, ignoring Husker and running over to Kellan. "We've been looking everywhere for you."

Kellan crossed his arms. "I was in the VIP Lounge just waiting for the games to end." When Mavis threw her arms around Kellan in a hug, it reminded Kellan of everything he needed to tell them. While returning her embrace, he said, "I found out some important details about our enemies."

Mavis quickly ended the hug and then lifted a finger. "Wait. I have to show you something first. Xiang and I got more powerful during the last game." She motioned to the collapsed couch. "Didn't you see that? I'm *actually* physically strong. Like a superhero."

"You grew strong during the last game?"

"No. Look." Mavis grabbed his hand.

Although Kellan's *Blitzkrieg Analysis* always showed him the status of everyone who wasn't concealed—Mavis included—Kellan had opted to ignore the info whenever he met people he had seen before. Clearly, that was a mistake. Mavis had changed.

Drastically.

Name: Mavis Cartwright

Race: Human
Magics: Magma, Metal
Rank: D, D
Armor Rating: 1
Health: 9/9

Stats:
Strength—6 [Strong Grip, Cyborg-Enhanced]
Dexterity—3 [Accurate]
Fortitude—5 [Cyborg-Enhanced]
Charisma—2
Manipulation—2
Intelligence—3
Perception—4 [Mystic]
Wisdom—2
Willpower—4 [Tough]

Abilities:
Personal—[Rebuilt]—The mage can develop their physical stats (strength, dexterity, fortitude) for half the arcana cost.
Hex—[A Light That Blazes Twice as Bright]—The mage gains triple the stat increase from all magical means. As punishment, if they don't increase at least one primary stat (strength, dexterity, fortitude, charisma, manipulation, intelligence, perception, wisdom) once every seven days (the counter starting after each stat increase), the mage dies.

Kellan jerked his hand out of Mavis's.

"You took a hex?" he asked.

Mavis furrowed her brow. "Yeah. But did you see my stats? I have superhuman levels of strength."

"But if you don't continue increasing your stats, you're going to die. What if you fail to get arcana or—"

"Xiang pointed out that we're going to probably finish the Nexus Games within a few weeks," Mavis interjected. "And if we lose, we're all dead regardless. But if we *win*, the hex will be broken. So what does it matter? Don't you see? This is perfect."

Kellan clenched his jaw. He didn't like this. Not because the hex ability was bad—far from it, the ability clearly synergized with Mavis's personal trait—but because hexes carried with them some sort of chilling taint. They were clearly derived from a twisted source. Kellan didn't know *what* source, but he knew it couldn't be trusted.

Normally, hexes could never be removed. It required the perfect magic of Zenith to end them. How was that not a major red flag? Something about them was off.

"Everyone is doing it," Mavis said. "You've seen the other mages. Even Xiang and Husker have hexes."

And she wasn't wrong.

But Kellan didn't like the sound of what was going on.

"So, you're going to continue to build your stats?" Kellan asked, keeping his tone neutral.

"That's the plan. Xiang told me all about how metal magic has cyborg abilities, which add stats. Look, I even have wiring and metal on the inside of my body. That's how I got a permanent armor rating."

Mavis pulled up the sleeve of her jacket and then brought her fingernails down on her skin like she was going to cut herself, but Kellan grabbed her wrist.

"I believe you." He kept his hand on her arm, squeezing harder to get her full attention. "And I'm glad you're getting the hang of your magic, but I have to tell you about the Flestiss Dominion."

Husker twitched his ears in Kellan's direction. Then he turned his head. He wasn't wearing his usual long coat. Instead, he just had on a pair of cargo pants. His chest, completely covered in fur, seemed muscular and cut. It was difficult to tell—Husker's red fur was rather uniform. Chains hung from his wrists, and one was around his neck, each just a few feet long. Since the man was nearly nine feet, they seemed tiny in comparison.

"You learned information about the Flestiss Dominion?" he asked.

Kellan nodded, thankful Husker was interested. In an attempt to sum up the situation in only a few sentences, Kellan said, "The Dominion is run by a space whale, and they breed lesser races—such as humans—as slaves in their bee-like society. They're going to kill all the primordial dragons and enslave every dimension so that the Dominion can control everything."

No matter how many times Kellan went over the information in his head, it always sounded ludicrous.

"Whales and bees," Husker mumbled as he scratched his canine snout. "I've never heard anyone describe them like that…"

"You already said we have to defeat Team 42," Mavis said. "I'm with you. We can't let the Dominion win."

Husker nodded once. "I agree. I can't let the Dominion harm my tribes. I'm a warrior of Rarn, after all. If anything were to happen to Rarn, what kind of rennic would I be?"

It was reassuring to know that both Husker and Mavis agreed right away without any more need to convince them further. He wished they had seen everyone on the flestiss-occupied Earth, though. Maybe then they'd be a little more gung ho to defeat Team 42.

"I also need gold arcana," Kellan said. "The Arbiter thinks I'll die in the next game unless I have a lot more."

"How much arcana do you have currently?" Husker asked.

"Fourteen. None of it is gold arcana, though… I've been finding nothing but red arcana."

Husker snorted. "Well, I'm not sure how you're going to gather a bunch of mysterious gold arcana." He folded his arms over his chest. Then he wrinkled his nose. "Why don't you spend time in the mana spring, then change into some new clothes, and we'll search around the palace? Perhaps we can find someone, or something, that can help us for the next game."

Mavis snapped her fingers. "Yes. I need to rank up. Once I reach C-rank, I can purchase more stat-increasing abilities."

Although Kellan wanted to tell them that acquiring gold arcana was much more difficult than red arcana, he kept that to himself. Most people didn't seem to understand the difference, or they just didn't care. He knew Husker would take any arcana offered, and from the sound of things, Mavis was in the same boat.

But the Arbiter had been specific. Kellan needed *gold* arcana. At least according to Millie.

"All right, I'll wash up," Kellan stated. "Then we'll head out."

Husker nodded. "I'll go get dressed as well."

"I'll fix the couch," Mavis muttered, glancing at the mess in the front room.

The suite's mana spring was out on the balcony. Kellan exited the glass doors and then stood on a narrow strip of stone, mere inches from the edge of the pink waters. The spring was built into the balcony itself, the edges overlooking the AVU Palace's garden.

Kellan wasn't alone. He glanced over and spotted Sen in the water. He wasn't a teenager, like he had been. Now he appeared to be twelve years old, on the cusp of puberty. His speckly beard was gone, his wiry frame nothing more than the physique of a child. He rested on the edge of the spring, both arms up on the stone, his chin resting on top of them.

Sen barely moved. He just stared out at the garden.

Kellan removed his backpack, rifle, torn jacket, and damaged shirt. He tossed them to the side but opted to keep his pants on. Sen wasn't naked—the kid wore a pair of pants, though he didn't have anything else.

After removing his boots, Kellan stepped into the waters. The warm and soothing sensation of the spring put Kellan at ease. His mana had already been restored at the VIP Lounge, but if it hadn't been, the spring would've done that for him.

"I thought you said you would remain a teenager, even if you gave me some fortitude?" Kellan asked as he swam over to Sen's location.

The mana spring was only four feet deep, but Kellan enjoyed submerging most of his body beneath the rose-colored waters.

"I *was* still a teenager," Sen said matter-of-factly. "But… I gave another part of myself to improve Mavis's fortitude. Now look at me." He pushed away from the side of the spring and slapped his hand into the water, motioning to his younger body with a frown.

"Why did you do that?"

"Her new hex makes each of my sacrifices all the more impactful," Sen said with a sigh. Then he returned to the edge of the spring, his shoulders slumped. "It's the obvious choice to help her. I mean… the only reason we've made it this far is because we're a team that's actually working together."

Kellan wanted to make a quip, but he held back. His old Delta Force team would've put this team's "cooperation" to shame. When Kellan had actually been part of a coordinated operation, he had never questioned the competency or loyalties of his teammates. Everything had run smoothly, and when things went south, he knew he could depend on his brothers-in-arms to have his back.

But…

"If it hadn't been for your shielding, we all would've died to Team 42 in the last game," Kellan said. "Thank you for that."

Sen's face grew pink. He poked at the side of the spring. "If you hadn't physically dragged me through the games, I probably wouldn't be here, either."

He said nothing else.

Kellan dove underwater, rubbed at his hair, and then stood up. The mana spring smelled of roses. Although he had no shampoo or soap, he knew he would smell elegant the moment he got out.

"So you were only a teenager for a day?"

Sen scoffed. "That's correct."

"That's rough. Did you at least take advantage of that one night alone?"

With a roll of his eyes, Sen said, "Of course."

Kellan chuckled at his own dark joke, but then his thoughts turned to Xiang. She had been the one to convince Mavis to pick up the hex. "Where is our fearless leader, by the way?" he asked, his tone cold. "I need to speak with her about everything."

"She's with the Arbiter."

"Wait." Kellan positioned himself next to the edge of the spring with Sen. "Why did you and Husker see the Arbiter?"

"He asked about why we took Team 33's doll," Sen said. With a frown, he added, "And he also asked me about the puzzle imp. I was afraid he would get angry, because we killed his imp, but the Arbiter seemed… impressed. It was a little confusing."

Kellan gripped the edge of the spring, trying not to show his anger. "Why didn't Xiang and Mavis bring our doll back? Did they just let the woman die?"

"Our doll didn't *die*," Sen snapped. "Didn't you see the post-game analysis? That madman, Bitso, explained that Mavis and Xiang ran out of time. Since our doll didn't die, we didn't lose a key, but since we didn't get it to the safety zone in time, we didn't get one, either. It's not the *worst* outcome, but my honorable sister was understandably upset by this turn of events."

"She was the reason we didn't get the key. Xiang has only herself to blame."

Sen shot Kellan an icy glare. "There were factors outside of her control, thank you very much."

"It was still her responsibility to get the key to the end goal, wasn't it?" Kellan just returned his harsh stare with one of his own. "Why did she decide to search around the game arena instead of focusing on winning the game?"

With a dramatic swish of his long hair over his shoulder, Sen turned away. "My sister understands that our opponents are becoming stronger. She's balancing urgent priorities here. You and Mavis are weak, and must grow stronger quickly, but at the same time, we can't be open with our ambitions since several teams are actively against us. You wouldn't understand the many choices she has to make."

"I think I'm plenty capable," Kellan stated.

"Then just know that my sister found a Prize Room while they were exploring." Sen huffed. "She got herself a powerful magical item, and along with Mavis's hex, we've substantially improved our luck for the next game."

"Do you know what the next game is?"

"Not yet. It hasn't been announced."

The conversation between them died. The party music from the AVU Palace wafted up from the garden below. Kellan took the moment to just relax. He leaned against the side of the mana spring, the warmth of the water soaking to his core.

The sun had set, and the night sky grew more confident with each passing minute. Stars appeared across the dark sky by the dozens, but a tint of red kept them from being comforting images.

Sen stared out into nothing. After a few minutes, his shoulders drooped again.

"Are you upset about being younger?" Kellan asked in a quiet voice.

"Of course," Sen snapped, his words increasing in volume. "Do you think I enjoy being made to look like an infant? My very manhood is being called into question."

Kellan mulled over Sen's personal ability and training. He remembered everything he could about the mage, and in an attempt to lighten the mood, he asked, "So you studied at a place called Norticum?"

"Norticum *University*," Sen added. "And yes. I did. It's very prestigious. Only mages who display exceptional talents are allowed to attend." He held his head a little higher as he made all his statements.

"Did Xiang study there as well?"

"Well, no." Sen gripped his hands together. "She wasn't allowed."

"Why's that? You're siblings, right? And I thought you said she was talented."

"She's *very* talented." Sen glared at the edge of the mana spring. "But it was a matter of birth. My mother got me into the university. We both have the same father—and he's human—but my mother is a lindalphon and Xiang's isn't, so she wasn't allowed into Norticum University."

"Did you just say your mother is a *dolphin*?" Kellan asked.

Sen stood straight, his frown deep, his shoulders bunched at the base of his neck. "*How dare you.* She isn't a *dolphin*, you buffoon! She is a *lindalphon!* It's clearly a different word. Entirely different. *Wholly different.*"

"So, you're *half* human?"

"No, fool! It doesn't work like that! It's not…" Sen exhaled, forced himself to take a breath, and then said, "Unions between humans and lindalphons result in babies that are one or the other, not half-breeds. So, I'm human. *Understand?*"

"Yeah, calm down." Kellan smirked as he gently splashed the kid with water. "So you got into the fancy school because of pedigree and Xiang couldn't because of bloodlines or something."

With his frown still in place, Sen rested on the edge of the mana spring. "Yes. *Or something.* So eloquently put." With a huff, he added, "Since I'm human, I wasn't entirely accepted, but exceptions were made. Xiang was shunned from *lindalphon* society, though. Which is why she sought human companionship. That was how she met Brenner Hawke, actually. You see, her mother is a travel mage, and if you're high enough rank, you can shift through dimensions—but only nearby ones."

Kellan held his breath and focused all his attention on the story. He knew next to nothing about Xiang. Anything at this point would give him some insight into her motives and thought patterns.

"Xiang's mother knew about the Nexus Games, and other dimensions that were both technologically and magically powerful." Sen sighed. "She showed Xiang a dimension where humans were the only race… To show Xiang that being human in a lindalphon society didn't mean she was lesser."

"What happened? Xiang wanted to live there?"

Sen nodded once. After a short sigh, he said, "And it was that dimension where she met Brenner Hawke. He was *so impressive*—" Sen made air quotes as he said the words, "—and he was a *decorated military mage*, and Xiang became fascinated. You see, in most lindalphon societies, they claim humans are weak and dysfunctional. Brenner was the exact opposite. Xiang liked that."

He was a decorated military officer?

Kellan frowned. Brenner's title was *Traitor to Humanity* because he had betrayed his Earth to the Flestiss Dominion. He was the essence of a delta-bravo. Perhaps worse. But if Xiang hadn't known many competent humans before meeting him…

"Did you like Brenner?" Kellan asked, hoping Sen would continue the tale.

Sen rolled his eyes. "I found him to be insufferable. Xiang spoke of him day and night and day and night, until…" He closed his eyes. "Well…" He didn't finish his statement. Then Sen turned to Kellan, his expression more melancholy than before. "We shouldn't be discussing this. Xiang told me not to say anything."

"She likes to remain a mystery." Kellan cracked his knuckles. "Does she know about the Flestiss Dominion? She must, since she spoke about it with familiarity."

But Sen didn't answer.

Obviously, Brenner knew about the Dominion. He was serving them—actively helping the Dominion enslave humanity and bring about the death of the Arbiter. Just thinking about it got Kellan angry all over again. And apparently Xiang was *supposed* to have been on Brenner's team for the Nexus Games. Something about the situation bothered Kellan.

Motivated to win the games all over again, Kellan swam to the other side of the narrow spring and climbed out. Sen whirled around, practically splashing water as he did so.

"Where are you going?" he asked.

"I need to gather some gold arcana before the next event."

—Chapter 37—
—A Bloodstained Perimeter—

To Kellan's surprise, new clothes had been laid out for him on his bed inside the suite. A new pair of cargo pants, a sturdy jacket, and a thick flannel shirt. He wasn't a fan of the shirt, but he wasn't picky, either. As long as the next game wasn't a fashion show, Kellan was sure the shirt would do just fine.

As he buttoned it up, Kellan paused for a moment.

What if we have a game based on appearance? So many people would die. Not Xiang. But the rest of us...

He chuckled to himself as he finished dressing. Kellan had no way to predict the nature of the games. He hadn't seen the previous ones, the rule book didn't mention the types of games that could be offered, and the Nexus was so *koo-koo-ka-choo* that he couldn't rule out the possibility of a fashion show.

Kellan made sure to grab his backpack and rifle. The pack was worn, and the seams strained. It hadn't handled the rot well. The gun, on the other hand, wasn't affected at all.

Then he exited his room and met with Husker and Mavis in the living room. Husker wore a new cloak, the color of faded brown. He kept the hood up, covering his ears. Mavis had her usual jeans, jacket, and T-shirt, but something about her energetic jovial demeanor really agreed with her.

The three of them left their suite. Kellan wished he could've spoken with Xiang. Hopefully, he would get to before the start of the fourth game.

Kellan rubbed at the stubble on his chin, his thoughts briefly wandering. He needed to rest at some point. With nightfall upon them, how much longer did they have before they were teleported away? Twelve hours?

"What are you thinking about?" Mavis asked as they traveled down the long second-story hallway of the AVU Palace.

"That if the next game is a fashion show we're all going to die," Kellan quipped.

Husker snorted and laughed hard enough to show his fangs. "I agree."

Mavis shot the rennic an odd glance. "Why's that? We're all just too frumpy for you?" She fluffed her dyed purple hair.

"Rennic standards of beauty and human standards of beauty are two wildly different things." Husker rubbed his padded hands together, still chuckling to himself. "And don't get me started about the other races. You all have bizarre preferences and desires."

"Okay. Let's hear what you look for. Describe a jaw-dropping female rennic."

Husker exhaled as they all descended the large staircase. It took him several moments to piece his thoughts together. "Decades ago, during my first training sessions with Rarn, a rennic's fur pattern mattered the most. Rennic with stripes or spots, or even two-toned faces, were seen as exotic and appealing. But now, it's all about the tail."

Mavis brought a hand to her mouth as she stifled a laugh. "Are you serious?"

They stepped off the final step and made their way to the two sets of double doors of the AVU Palace. Kellan slipped his hands in his pockets as he listened to the conversation, amused by the differences between races.

"Male rennic should have thin tails," Husker said, lowering his voice to a whisper. "And female rennic should have fluffy tails. The larger, the shinier, the more *voluptuous*, the better."

"Oh, so you're an *ass man*," Kellan quipped.

Husker straightened his posture and growled, "This is why humans would never understand. You don't even have tails. If we were ever forced to compete in a deadly competition of sexual appeal, we'd all die."

Both the double doors to the AVU Palace were impressive. Kellan stopped bothering with the conversation when he drew near. The doors were made of sturdy wood, each with dragons carved into them from top to bottom. Neon lights shone from the ceiling of the entrance hall, giving the dragon designs a futuristic look.

When Kellan got close enough, he placed a hand on the dragon etchings.

They were of the Arbiter.

The machines, cogs, wires, and gears were small details carved into the wood, but they were there. Both doors had the Arbiter? And once Kellan glanced toward his feet, he realized the bottom of the door was detailed with bone etchings. Bones from fish, people, and other animals lined the bottom of the massive double doors.

Not ominous at all.

Kellan pushed open the door and found himself standing at the top of a massive stone stairway. It led to the streets below, but there were so many steps and pillars, it felt like he was at his nation's capital, or the Lincoln Memorial.

Mavis and Husker accompanied him outside.

It was dark. The streetlamps and hanging lights around the palace had been shattered. The smell of copper and sweat lingered on the night air. Thanks to Kellan's *Pierce the Darkness* ability, he could easily see their surroundings.

The AVU Palace was a mishmash of buildings. There was a stadium dome, pillars, multiple-story towers, and even a sprawling garden. At the end of the front stone stairway, there was an asphalt street clogged with broken down and rusted vehicles. Fords, Toyotas—and even brands Kellan had never heard of before. Beyond that were deserted buildings, each in an odd state of disrepair.

Kellan felt like he was standing on the set of a post-apocalyptic movie, except for the rave music thumping through the walls of the extravagant palace just a few feet behind him.

He held up his arm, stopping Mavis and Husker from walking any farther.

Blood stained half the steps.

Fresh.

And so much of it. No bodies, though, which was both curious and concerning.

Not only that, but Kellan recognized the blast divots of bullets. Judging by the angle of the holes, they had come from slightly above.

"What is it?" Husker whispered. He glanced around as he pulled off his hood, exposing his ears. "The smell… Something isn't right."

Kellan held still. He stared at the rooftops of nearby buildings. When he spotted the first gunman, he almost pointed for the others, but that was foolish. Neither Husker nor Mavis could see in the dark.

"There are gunmen nearby," Kellan whispered as he stepped backward. He gently pushed Mavis and Husker toward the doors. "I don't know if they can shoot us while we're in an Oasis and they're not, but we shouldn't risk it. They're obviously shooting anyone who leaves."

Husker growled, his fur standing on end. "Those vultures. There are mages here in the Nexus who aren't bound by the rules of the Nexus Games. They like to target outsiders. They tend to linger near the edge of an Oasis."

"Random people can kill players in the Nexus Games?" Mavis asked, keeping her voice low.

"They can. It's frowned upon by the Arbiter, but the mages who linger in the Nexus are sometimes powerful and have been here for decades. If they have the permission of the Arbiter, they can do whatever they want."

Kellan cursed under his breath. He wanted to speak with the residents. They often offered gold arcana for assistance. And *he* actually knew where a fair amount of them dwelled. But he couldn't risk being gunned down on the streets of Nexus-Fayetteville.

The three of them reentered the AVU Palace.

"Those gunmen can't target individuals inside the Oasis," Husker stated. "They can't shoot us if we're still within the boundaries of the AVU Palace."

"Well, apparently the boundary is about ten steps down from the front door." Kellan stood under the neon lights, rubbing at his neck. He couldn't shoot the men from within the Oasis, either.

"We shouldn't go out the front. There are other ways for us to get out into the city."

"You know an easy route? One where we won't get caught?"

Husker nodded once. "There's a pal of mine here who—" He cut himself off, closed his eyes shut, and then growled. He rubbed a hand along his gut, scratching through his cloak with long claws.

"You okay?"

"I'm fine." Husker shook his head and then continued, "I'm friends with a man who knows the whole palace's layout. Let's speak with him, and then go out." He motioned for Kellan and Mavis to follow. With long strides, he went straight into the center of the palace—toward the most raucous of parties.

Kellan had tried his best to stay away from the cacophony of celebration. He didn't want to cheer until Team 42, and the whole Dominion, were stopped. And he wasn't one to celebrate tiny victories—like still being alive after three games. As far as he was concerned, he had a job to do, and he could rest once it was all over.

But if Husker knew someone, then it couldn't be avoided.

Mavis stuck close to him as they traveled beyond the entrance hall. The neon lights stayed the same, but the volume of the music grew louder. Husker went straight for a large wooden door—one with a circular window near the top—and shoved it open. More lights and music escaped into the hall for the few brief seconds the door remained ajar.

Kellan and Mavis ducked inside as quickly as possible.

It was a bar.

In the middle of the palace.

There was a long countertop that could accommodate a couple dozen people, three bartenders, a couple high-top tables, and for some insane reason, multiple Jacuzzis. Kellan had never seen so many spas indoors. The steam from the hot water gave the entire bar a humid feel. Within moments, Kellan's jacket and flannel shirt were soaked.

More than fifty people mingled in the bar. Human, rennic, rezrah, niav—every race except for the flestiss seemed to be present.

"Let me speak to my friend alone. Just wait here." Husker went for a human seated near the end of the bar.

"This place is interesting," Mavis shouted, her voice barely piercing the techno music. She pointed to the dance floor not far from the booths. "Care to join me for a dance while we wait?"

"You want me to dance while holding a backpack and rifle?" Kellan shouted back.

"You can take them off."

The thought of leaving his supplies and weapon in a public area where anyone could take them—and he couldn't fight to take them back—left Kellan uneasy. They were in the midst of a death game. Even if relaxing, and dancing, would be fun, Kellan really didn't think the benefits outweighed the risks.

"I'll just stay here," Kellan stated.

Mavis playfully poked him in the chest. "Are you afraid of dancing? Just sway with me. It'll be fun."

"Seems very *high school.*"

"Oh?" She placed her hands on his chest and pushed him until his backpack hit the wall. Kellan was a little shocked—her strength caught him off guard, despite the fact that he had just seen her lifting a couch—and she pinned him against the wall, though he didn't fight it.

Up close, with Mavis's breath on his chin, Kellan felt the chill of her hex. It was a little unsettling.

Mavis stared at him. "What's wrong? You look worried." She smirked. "I'm not going to bite."

"I don't think you should get any more hexes," he said. "Something is wrong with them."

"You already said that."

Kellan ran his hand up the side of her neck and played with some of her hair. "Yeah, well, I'd hate myself if something terrible happened to you."

"It was my choice," Mavis said, pushing away from him. Then she crossed her arms.

Kellan grabbed her shoulder. "Listen. Don't take this personally—just take it seriously. We need to be leery of quick power grabs. This is a place where that always comes back to bite you in the ass."

"Look, if you're so damn worried, why don't we talk to some people around here and gather intel, huh? It's more productive than bitching to each other."

Her irritation was so thick, Kellan could choke on it. He had obviously killed the mood for her, but was this really the time? They had a game to prepare for, and discussing whether or not they took hexes as a quick way to improve their power seemed like a relevant topic of conversation. Why was she so defensive?

"I'm going to talk to a bartender real quick." Without another word, she headed for one of the people behind the bar.

She had been a bartender in Fayetteville. Perhaps she wanted to quiz the Nexus workers. Kellan wasn't sure.

Still bothered from earlier events, and his thoughts circling back to dreaded realities, Kellan wandered over to the bar and took a seat. The cushion was pleasant, but the music rattled around in his ears like discordant bells. He didn't like it.

One of the bartenders—a human wearing a Mr. Rogers style vest and shirt—slid Kellan a drink.

"I don't have any money," Kellan shouted.

"It's on the Arbiter, sir."

The strange bartender moved down the line, handing out drinks to everyone who took a seat. Kellan glanced down at his own. His eyes didn't give him any information. That either meant the drink wasn't magical, or the magic was being concealed. With a frown, he picked up the glass and examined the contents. Clear liquid. Spherical ice cubes.

Seemed pretentious.

Kellan wasn't much of a drinker, so he didn't know how to judge any of it, but from what his commanding officer said, if it wasn't whiskey or rum, it was a child's drink.

Would someone here know what this was?

Kellan turned and found a female rennic seated next to him.

She wore a pair of capri shorts and a bright feathered necklace, and that was it. Her white fur caught all the colors of the neon lights. She was practically a living rainbow wolf, her ears up straight and her dark eyes piercing. The rennic swished around a giant fluffy tail, so large, it could practically engulf the stool she was sitting upon.

> **Name:** Centa Greeniz, the Lone Wolf
> **Race:** Rennic
> **Magics:** Storm, Wyld
> **Rank:** B, B
> **Armor Rating:** 2
> **Health:** 15/15
> **Stats:** Concealed
> **Abilities:** Concealed

On the back of her left hand was the number 80, same as Gunner. She was a member of Gunner's team? Kellan already liked her a little more.

When Centa finally noticed him, Kellan held up his glass.

"Do you know what this is?" he asked, shouting to be heard.

"They serve two types of drinks here," the rennic said, her voice deep and sensual. "One is called *For the Wicked*, and the other is called *Come to Me*. They're both quite good."

"Which one is this?"

Centa shrugged and then returned her attention to her own drink. It, too, was clear, and in a short wine glass. When she sipped it, Kellan was amused by how someone with a long mouth took a drink. He probably stared a bit too long, because Centa laid her ears flat.

"Sorry," he muttered. In an attempt to be social, he added, "I was just admiring your beautiful tail. It's very fluffy. Very majestic."

Centa sneered, flashing her fangs. "Oh, you're one of those *interspecies perverts*." She threw her drink in his face before Kellan could even process her words. The alcohol splashed across him, coating his face, shirt, and some of his jacket.

Then Centa stood, huffed, and flounced off to the opposite corner of the bar, her luxurious tail swishing the entire way.

One moment a woman wants to have my kid, and the next moment I'm the creepy guy at the bar. Why haven't I written a book about how to pick up ladies? Clearly it would be a smash hit comedy.

"Whoa, man. That was brutal."

Kellan flinched and then turned to see his least favorite person in the Nexus Games who wasn't in Team 42. It was *Robbie the Friendly*, the lanky man wearing a *Taco King* baseball cap. It was on backward now, and Robbie sported a pair of circular sunglasses, even though they were indoors, making him look like the biggest delta-bravo in the whole bar.

Robbie flashed a smile.

Kellan's *Blitzkrieg Analysis* told him that the glasses weren't for show, though.

> **Magical Item [Equipment]—Hydra Corp. Shades**
> The mage gains +1 perception and +1 dexterity while wearing these

shades. They also make the mage *hip to the jive*.

Kellan hated everything about the shades as well.

"I've never seen someone get rejected that hardcore, man," Robbie said as he swirled his own drink around in its glass. The music made it difficult to hear him, but Kellan managed.

Kellan licked the alcohol off his lips. It was rather sweet. Pleasant, even. Was there even alcohol present? It was hard for him to say. He brought his own glass up to his nose and attempted to smell.

"I've had worse rejections," Kellan finally stated. "I think I'll live."

"Hey, if you wanna find a place where the ladies are easier, I know this sweet room in the corner of the palace that's, like, a secret treasure trove."

"Never," Kellan stated.

He took a tiny sip of his drink. It was pleasant. Not sweet, like the rennic's drink, but savory.

He liked it.

"How's your familiar doin'?" Robbie asked, leaning on the bar and scooting closer to Kellan. "You makin' sure he gets enough to eat? Playing in the games can be whack."

Kellan almost choked on his drink. He set the glass down and turned to Robbie. "Wait, we have to feed our familiars?"

"Well, yeah. They're little animals. Of course you gotta feed them." Robbie grabbed a tiny straw from behind the counter and poked it into his drink. Then he took a delicate sip. "Haven't you ever had a pet before, bro? They don't live off good vibes."

Guilt and regret settled over Kellan in equal amounts. He hadn't thought to feed Vlaze *at all*. He figured it was a magical creature. What *would* it eat? Arcana? Normal food? What if he had gotten a blender out of the familiar egg? Would the blender have required food?

"You look like you saw a ghost," Robbie said, lifting an eyebrow so high it peeked over the rim of the sunglasses.

Kellan reached across the bar and grabbed a few olives and maraschino cherries. Then he glanced at his shadow on the bar floor. Vlaze lived in his shadow, didn't he?

"Vlaze," Kellan said, trying to coax out his familiar. "Hey, buddy. I have food for you." When his albino wyvern didn't appear, Kellan threw olives and cherries onto the floor. They landed with a few wet splats.

And then they just sat there.

The neon lights flashed, and the music thumped on, but Kellan's familiar didn't emerge from its shadow hiding spot.

Kellan slowly lifted his gaze to Robbie. The Taco King just sipped his drink, staring at the olives and cherries like they were the most fascinating things ever.

"Is my familiar dead?"

Robbie shrugged. "I dunno. I doubt it. He seemed tough, ya know?" Then the man frowned. "And, like I'm really sorry about trying to kill you back in the maze, but a game is a game, and I was told I have to kill as many other people as possible. You get it, right? No hard feelings?"

Out of all the people Kellan had met in the Nexus, Robbie took the cake for most confusing. He seemed completely out of it. Disconnected with the reality of the situation.

"Listen," Kellan said, still raising his voice to compete with the music. "Just target Team 42 as much as possible. They're going to enslave everyone and everything if they manage to win the Nexus Games. Understand me? Just target them."

Robbie slowly nodded along with his words. "Right on."

"You understand?"

"What was that? You're slurrin' hard."

"I'm not slurring," Kellan shouted, irritated with Robbie all over again. "You know what? Never mind. I'll probably see you in the next match."

"Wow, man. Are you even speakin' English anymore? Maybe you've had too much to drink."

Robbie's odd reactions had Kellan genuinely confused. He stared for a moment, and only then realized that the music didn't make sense. It thumped and rang and buzzed all out of order. Kellan couldn't keep anything straight.

Gripped by dread, Kellan attempted to stand. The barstool fell away, and then Kellan tumbled to the floor. It seemed as though everything happened in slow motion—like he was watching everything from a camera behind his eyes, rather than experiencing it for himself.

Robbie just sat at the bar, staring at Kellan in the same fashion he had for the olives and cherries.

The world blurred and faded from Kellan's vision.

And then everything went black.

—Chapter 38—

—It's a Secret to Everyone—

Kellan awoke with his face on a concrete floor. His eyesight remained blurred for a long while, even after blinking. Despite his awkward positioning on the floor, and his dulled sense of sight, Kellan felt well-rested. It was as if he had slept a full twenty-four hours, erasing any sleep debt he may have accrued over the past week.

He didn't hear any party music.

Something poked him inside the ear.

"Master," a voice whispered, boyish and energetic. "Are you awake now?"

Kellan rolled to his side, groaning as he did so. His head spun. It had been years since he had a hangover, but he hadn't forgotten the sensation. His stomach churned in protest at his movements.

"Master. You should get up."

Master?

Again, something poked him in the ear. Kellan swatted it away, surprised to find he whacked something scaly and cold. He rolled onto his back and stared at a gray ceiling.

He was in some sort of storage room. A closet. A pantry. Something. There were wire racks on either side of him, with boxes and jars stacked on one another. His vision was too blurred to read the labels.

Like a closed refrigerator, the closet had no lights.

"Are you okay, Master? You don't look so well."

Kellan rubbed at his nose and then peered down toward his chest. His familiar, Vlaze, sat on his chest. The little wyvern had gotten larger. His white scales were thicker, his wing-arms were longer, and his fangs were pronounced. His lizard tail ended in a sharp stinger, and his red eyes seemed more intelligent than before.

"Vlaze?" Kellan asked, his voice raspy.

"Yes?" the wyvern replied. Then he tilted his head to the side, giving Kellan a questioning glance.

"You can… talk?"

"Now I can, Master. I've ranked up."

Name: Vlaze
Race: Animal of Pure Magic [Albino Wyvern]
Magics: Eclipse, Body
Rank: 2
Armor Rating: 2 [Scales]
Health: 5/5

Stats:
Strength—2
Dexterity—3 [Flight]
Fortitude—1
Charisma—1
Manipulation—3 [Scary]
Intelligence—2
Perception—3
Wisdom—2
Willpower—2

Abilities:
Hidden—This Animal of Pure Magic hides its magical nature from divination abilities (of A rank or lower). It does not appear magical until it chooses to reveal its nature.
Nocturnal Hunter—This Animal of Pure Magic sees in all non-magical darkness.

Kellan ran a shaky hand down his face. The information on his eyes was almost as blurry as everything else. It took him a long moment to read everything. "Your rank is *two*? Not C-rank or B-rank or something?"

"Only mages have ranks of magic," Vlaze said, his boyish voice adorable. "Animals of Pure Magic rank like… well… levels? We get stronger the longer we're bonded to a mage. The higher the rank of the mage, the faster we grow."

"Oh, God. Sure. Equations." Kellan rested his head back down on the concrete.

Rate of growth for an Animal of Pure Magic was *time multiplied by rank of mage*. Fun. Kellan wondered how he had gotten sent to a dimension with numbers-based magic. He had never hated math, but he hadn't considered it very fantastical, either. Now it seemed he was seeing numbers everywhere.

Vlaze curled up and rested his little lizard head on Kellan's collarbone. "You should get up, Master. We've been here a long time."

"How long?"

"Hours, at least."

"*Hours*?"

Kellan pushed himself off the ground with such haste that Vlaze tumbled onto the cold floor. With his vision still blurred, Kellan stumbled into the nearest shelf. He grabbed the wire frame and steadied himself, his breath coming out as a slight fog.

Vlaze scuttled around the ground. Despite the fact that there was no light, he, too, could see just fine, thanks to his *Nocturnal Hunter* ability.

"I tried waking you," Vlaze said. "But you slept through my attempts."

"Why was I sleeping in the first place?" Kellan asked. He glanced around the room, trying to find an exit. The closet was much larger than he had suspected. Were they in a meat locker? Or some sort of freezer for a restaurant? "I don't understand how I got here."

"Apparently, you weren't supposed to drink both the drinks at the bar." Vlaze flapped his wings hard enough to leap onto a shelf close to Kellan's head-height. Then Vlaze wrapped his tail around one of the wire posts and clung there, much like a bat. "They caused you to fall into a deep slumber. And then Robbie had you removed from the bar, because you were in the way of other patrons."

Kellan gritted his teeth. "Robbie the Friendly had me *removed*? Where is that delta-bravo? I'll—"

"The bar staff put you in here," Vlaze said, cutting him off. "I don't know where Robbie went."

Finally, Kellan's vision returned in full. He slowly walked around one of the wire shelves and found that the freezer had three doors. Two seemed normal—they were marked as exits, actually—but the last one was tucked behind a wire rack. Kellan almost missed it—the door was the same dark gray as the walls—but at the last moment, he spotted the outline of the frame.

Why was there a hidden door in the freezer?

"And why am I in a freezer?" Kellan barked, his voice echoing around the jars and food containers. "Why would the staff put me here? Why wouldn't Husker and Mavis take me?"

Vlaze snorted. "I don't think they saw you fall unconscious." Then he lifted his head, his neck snake-like and flexible. "Don't worry, Master. I watched over you while you slept, and I made sure no one took your bag."

Kellan immediately grabbed at his shoulder. He wasn't wearing his backpack or carrying his rifle. Then he turned his attention to where he had been on the floor. All of his possessions were just a few feet away, tucked neatly onto a shelf.

"You did that?" Kellan asked.

Vlaze nodded.

"And you… can speak?"

"You already asked me that."

"Yeah, but, you know words? How? How did you learn anything?"

Vlaze half-snorted. "Rude."

Kellan smirked and shook his head. "No, I mean—when did you do it? You weren't speaking before. When did you have time to learn a language?"

"I learn things based on the arcana you absorb." Vlaze flicked out his tongue in a snake-like fashion. Then he said, "Memories and knowledge are trapped in arcana crystals, and since I'm bonded to you, the magic filters to me. I don't know who you've been killing, but I know words like *spuddle* and *gubbins*."

The information swirled in Kellan's thoughts, jumbling around as he mulled everything over. "You absorb the magic in me?"

"Yeah. Like a parasite." Vlaze shot his tongue out again. "But in exchange, I help you out. I follow all your commands, regardless of how bizarre they may be."

"You're harming me?"

"Well…" Vlaze lowered his head and frowned. "I'm more like the Tyranny Worms. What's the word? *Symbiotic*. Not parasitic."

Kellan rotated his arms. He felt stiff, but not in pain. With each movement, he loosened up and felt more like his old self. The rest had done him wonders—even if he had been resting on a cold concrete floor in the middle of a freezer.

The drinks cause people to fall into a coma-like sleep? So I basically got roofied. Fantastic. Only in the Nexus. Kellan pinched the bridge of his nose. *I can't trust anything here. I should've known better than to drink anything handed to me by weirdos.*

"We need to get out of here," Kellan muttered. He glanced around the freezer a second time, his attention returning to the hidden door behind a wire shelf. "Do you remember which door we came in?"

Vlaze motioned to one of the doors labeled *exit*. "That one."

"Wait." Kellan grabbed a jar of olives off the shelf. "Robbie said you need to eat. What do wyverns like? Surely we can find something in here before we go."

"Robbie is an idiot," Vlaze said in a flat tone. "Animals of Pure Magic eat magic. Being bonded to you… I'm eating your residual magic. That's how I rank up. I don't need physical food. Robbie doesn't know what he's talking about. Or maybe he was just explaining it poorly."

"I never should've listened to a man wearing a *Taco King* hat," Kellan muttered as he slammed the jar of olives down on the shelf. "Come on. Let's get out of here. I don't know how much time I have left before the next game, but it's not enough."

Vlaze leapt from the shelf and landed on Kellan's shoulder. It was awkward at first—Kellan flinched and almost punched the little lizard—but after a few tense moments, everything was fine. Vlaze dug his claws into Kellan's jacket and clung tight. His little red eyes stared into Kellan's.

"Let's go, Master."

Kellan grabbed his equipment and then started for the exit, but he stopped halfway. His curiosity got the better of him. He turned for the hidden door, intent on finding out what was behind it. If this had been a normal freezer, on normal Earth, Kellan wouldn't have thought much about it—some rooms are sealed off for a variety of reasons—but this was the Nexus, and every little secret was worth exploring.

Could the AVU Palace have prize and puzzle rooms? *Perhaps I can win a bunch of arcana before the fourth game starts.*

Well, hopefully I haven't missed the fourth game…

Vlaze stayed on Kellan's shoulder as he walked around shelves and made his way to the secret door. Then Kellan grabbed the shelf in front of the hidden door and attempted to move it to the side. With just a gentle shove, Kellan practically slammed the shelf into another. That shelf collided with the one next to it, and then all three shelves toppled over, spilling their contents all over the freezer and creating enough noise for a WWI reenactment.

Oh, right. My Void Knight ability increases my physical strength to superhuman levels.

Kellan slowly looked around, half expecting someone to barge into the freezer demanding to know what had happened. But no one came. Once the contents of the shelves stopped rolling around the floor, it became quiet once again.

"You're really bad at stealth," Vlaze said. "Just... so bad."

"Yeah, yeah. They call me the group's *warrior*, not the *rogue*." Kellan returned his attention to the door. The handle was flat and well hidden. Kellan had to turn it and then push the door forward in order to go through.

Once inside, Kellan was surprised to find a small bedroom. There was a cot, a dresser, a bookshelf—even a computer and wall-mounted TV. Kellan scratched his chin when he glanced at the opposite wall and spotted a long hallway. There was no door that led to the hallway—it was just a hallway that connected with the bedroom.

Squished in the corner of the room was a person. Were they hiding? Half their body was concealed by the bookshelf, but they were too large to properly hide. Although Kellan could only half see the person, he already knew it was a Nexus resident. Their skin had lesions, and one visible hand had six fingers.

The inbred residents just always had problems.

"Hello?" Kellan called out.

"G-Go away," the man muttered, never moving from his corner. "You're n-not supposed to be here."

The suspicious statement bothered Kellan. He stood at the doorway, debating whether he should just leave or ask the frightened man some questions. Then Kellan noticed small holes in the wall. He quickly pieced everything together. They were head height and came in pairs.

Eyeholes.

Was this Nexus resident spying on people in the AVU Palace?

Kellan turned his attention to the long hallway. More holes. Could this man see into all the nearby rooms?

"You're some sort of spy?" Kellan asked.

"I'm h-harmless!"

"I'm not going to do anything. We're in an Oasis."

The man didn't move from his corner. He wore a heavy coat and long pants, but Kellan wasn't getting many details. The man kept his face planted against the wall, practically making out with the paint.

"My name is Alex Kellan," he said.

The trembling resident stopped his shaking. After a few deep breaths, the man whispered, "You're the outsider who saved Millie? The outsider who... brought Alvo and Juan to Nosferatu?"

"Yeah. That's me."

The man still didn't venture from his corner. Instead, he held up a hand.

"This room is a secret from everybody. Take this and go. I… I want to help you. And Nosferatu."

A single gold arcana emerged from the palm of the man's hand. It glittered with inner power. Kellan held his breath for a moment, still in awe whenever he had a chance to really stare at the beautiful crystals.

Vlaze clung to his shoulder tighter. "What beauty."

Kellan walked over. The man never glanced at him, even as Kellan took the arcana from his palm.

[Alex Kellan] absorbed 1 gold arcana.

"Thank you," Kellan said.

One gold arcana wouldn't make the difference, but Kellan realized he shouldn't ever turn them down. When would be the next time he found any?

"Thank *you.*" The man muttered all his words straight into the wall. It was getting to the point that Kellan thought he might be incapable of moving. "If you go down the hall, you'll find doors to everywhere in the palace. Please take care not to mention my hideaway to anyone. No one can know…"

"I won't tell anyone."

The man went silent. While things in the Nexus Games tended to be crazy, Kellan hadn't expected to find a creepy guy living in the walls of the palace. It reminded him of far too many horror movies. If things ever started moving around in his bedroom, Kellan knew the first person he'd find to ask questions.

"Goodbye," Vlaze said as Kellan walked by the man and then entered the hallway. Light streamed in through the eyeholes. They were like sideways pillars of illumination, brightening the hall similar to a laser grid.

The faint sound of partying and music wafted down the hall. With a smile, Kellan went forward. He passed most of the holes, not even bothering to peer through. He didn't have time to investigate every room. He had to make it back to his team and gather more gold arcana. One wasn't enough.

But then he heard a familiar voice.

"That's right! The rules for the fourth game will be a little complicated."

Bitso. His showmanship and lunacy were impossible to imitate. He was giving an announcement about the fourth game. Was there a TV nearby?

Kellan glanced through the eyeholes, hoping to find the source of Bitso's broadcast. He couldn't miss anything—Kellan needed all the information he could get. Plus, everyone was so damn cagey with spilling the beans about *anything*, that Kellan couldn't rely on others to just tell him what was happening.

It didn't take him long to find the room. Kellan glanced through some holes and grimaced. Smoke stung his eyes briefly, but the glow of multiple TVs was hard to miss. There was some sort of lounge or club room on the other side of the wall. Kellan just needed to get there…

"Vlaze, you can go back into my shadow, right?" he asked.

"Yes."

"Hide there."

"Can I come out again later?" Vlaze tilted his head. "It's lonely in the shadow." With a frown, he widened his eyes to adorable levels.

Kellan half-laughed, half-huffed. "Yeah, yeah. Of course. I'll bring you out afterward."

With a nod, Vlaze dove for the floor, his wings spread. The little white wyvern disappeared into the darkness of Kellan's shadow. It was a little extra-dimensional space that seemed to store his familiar without a problem. Well, it was lonely, apparently. No other problems.

Then Kellan stepped into the darkness himself, using the void as his own mode of transportation. He slithered like a shadow through the peep holes, moving at a surprising speed. Then Kellan stepped out of the shadows, emerging in the smoke-filled room.

His heart nearly stopped.

The room was occupied. The inhabitants all turned to face him.

They were mages from Team 42.

—Chapter 39—

—The Fourth Game—

The massive lounge room was every hippie's dream. Mountains of pillows, plenty of drinks and smokes, tables with trays of cubed fruit, and gigantic TVs mounted to the walls. Bitso's insane smiling face was plastered across the screens.

The TVs provided the only light, but since the screens were so large, it was enough to illuminate everything with dramatic one-way lighting.

Ysa stood only a few feet away, her hands on her hips. She wore what appeared to be a neon-pink bikini. Or lingerie, Kellan wasn't sure which. All he knew was that it was barely a square foot of cloth in total, and she was an attractive woman.

Several other women were around, lounging on pillows and eating little cubes of food from trays sitting on small tables. They weren't mages—Kellan's analysis gave him nothing—and they all whispered and pointed in his direction. Each of them wore a similar outfit to Ysa, some less.

Brenner Hawke was in front of the TVs, his arms crossed, his cold gaze on Kellan, though there was a hint of surprise. He was shirtless, his dog tags on display. He wore pants, though. No socks, as though he had only recently gotten partially dressed.

"That's right, players, you'll have one extra hour to prepare for this game session. What a gracious gift!" Bitso laughed across both TV screens. He smacked his metal desk as though the statement were a classic joke. But then he stopped. "Only four of you need that time to think things over, though. The rest of you will be randomly assigned! How… deliciously fun."

Kellan wasn't sure what was going on, and his attention was divided, regardless.

Brenner and Ysa stared at him, their eyes practically drilling through his skull. But then Brenner exhaled and turned away, his expression aggressively neutral.

"Listen, *fuck-face*," Ysa finally said. "I don't know why you're here—unless it's to beg us to leave you alone."

Bitso's laughter remained the only music in the room.

When Kellan said nothing, Ysa sauntered over. She stopped mere inches from him and smiled. "Are you here to beg? Brenner and I will listen."

"He's here by accident," Brenner stated, his tone commanding, and with an edge of finality to it. "He got lost wandering the AVU Palace. Just point him toward the exit. We have things to discuss."

Ysa rolled her eyes. With her tongue, she poked at the piercing on her lower lip. Then her attention homed in on Kellan's flannel shirt. "Ugh. Why are you the Frumpy-Alex-Kellan? Is your home dimension devoid of fashion sense?"

She grabbed the collar of his shirt and examined it, all while sneering.

Kellan *wanted* to grab her wrist and break it, but the pacifying power of the Oasis stilled his hand. Instead, he slowly removed her hand from his clothing and took a step backward, closer to the wall.

He glanced over his shoulder and tensed.

The eyeholes…

He couldn't see them. Were they illusioned? Most likely. The Nexus residents liked to hide themselves away with as many illusions as they could.

But if he couldn't see them, how was he supposed to shadow-step through them? Unlike with other illusions that he could throw himself through, this required more precision, and he wasn't entirely able to see while doing it.

"Tsk." Ysa moved away from him. She threw herself down on a pile of pillows and playfully smiled. "We almost killed you in the last game. We saw it on all the after-action reports. I wish you pussies wouldn't illusion yourselves all the time. Not really as fun."

There were eight other women in the room—Kellan counted while Ysa made her statements. They were all human—none of them branded, none of them deformed. Who were they? Kellan's analysis gave him nothing.

They had almost vacant expressions, but they smiled when he stared long enough. It made Kellan uncomfortable. Like staring into the faces of semi-sentient sex dolls.

Not an ideal situation.

"You're still a D-rank mage," Ysa continued, regardless of Kellan's lack of participation in the conversation. "I don't know how you're getting so many weird abilities that I've never seen before, but I'm the better eclipse mage." She ran a hand through her Mohawk, slicking it over to one side. "I'm in a pretty good mood. Are you sure you don't want to ask me for an itty-bitty favor?"

Kellan continued to ignore the woman. He wasn't sure what she wanted, but it wasn't anything he was about to offer.

Brenner Hawke, seemingly unconcerned about Kellan's presence, slowly paced in front of the TVs. Bitso continued his speeches, but Brenner took a moment to mute the screens. The smoke-filled room became quiet. Only the whispering of the girls lingered in the background.

There was a single door out of the lounge. Kellan thought about running for it—to put as much distance between him and Team 42 as possible—but since they were in an Oasis, he knew they couldn't do anything to him.

Last time, however, Brenner had killed a pair of Nexus residents just to fuck with Kellan. That was what Kellan feared more than anything. That the lunatic would do something like that again—that Brenner would just massacre everyone Kellan ever associated with.

It was probably best to avoid him, but there was one question Kellan was dying to know the answer to.

"Hey," Kellan called out. He strode through the haze of smoke, the scent reminding him of hane—which made him wish he had a stick of his own.

Brenner stopped his pacing and turned. He had the military precision of someone standing at attention, but the hard *I don't give a damn* of someone who served too long.

The chill in the room…

It was from Brenner. The closer Kellan got, the icier it became, and it wasn't just from Brenner's cold demeanor. The man had so many hexes—each one a layer of frost over his soul, apparently.

His sandy blond hair was swept back, and his dark eyes were locked on Kellan.

The man was ripped, Kellan had to give him that, but without his shirt, Kellan also noticed the odd marks and protrusions just beneath Brenner's skin. Like something was underneath, threatening to burst outward. Wires? Or machines. According to Brenner's status information, he was filled to the brim with cyborg enhancements to give Brenner a physical edge.

Kellan could see that now, clear as day.

"You've come to speak with me?" Brenner asked as he slipped his hands into his pants pockets. "There's nothing to discuss."

"Why're you helping the Flestiss Dominion?"

Brenner narrowed his eyes. His expression never shifted, never betrayed any feelings on the matter. All he had was a look of mild contempt.

"I saw your stunt on Bitso's news program when you told the Arbiter about our plan," Brenner drawled. "Pathetic, as always. You should've known it wouldn't matter. The Arbiter sees and hears everything—but he never intervenes. The dragon deserves what's coming to him."

"The other teams might intervene," Kellan stated. "Now that they know you're a piece of shit."

It wasn't helpful to be antagonistic, but Kellan was secure in the safety of the Oasis, and he honestly didn't mind riling people like Team 42. No one ever stood up to them, and Kellan wasn't about to be one of the crowd. Not after what he had seen.

Brenner smirked, but there was little mirth in it. "You think the other teams are going to stop me? No one here is going to do jack shit." With a powerful exhale, Brenner stepped closer. "Listen. I know you've gotten lucky so far. You're all the way to the fourth game, and you're not dead. That's impressive."

Kellan said nothing.

"But your attention is all over the place." Brenner lifted his hands and snapped his fingers to Kellan's left, and then to Kellan's right. Brenner stopped and glared. "You run around attempting to save *everyone* and *everything*. You hang around with flestiss slaves, gathering information on the Dominion like you're little Sherlock Holmes about to solve a big case."

Brenner's condescension knew no bounds. But how did he know about Kellan's investigations?

With a forced laugh, Brenner said, "You're *never* going to win the Nexus Games if you don't pull your head out of your ass and focus. Rank up your magic. Stop saving people. Stop bothering yourself with information that's just upsetting."

"What sage advice," Kellan quipped.

Once again, Brenner slipped his hands in his pockets, as though the conversation wasn't of much importance to him. "You don't get it. You're in the Nexus Games. Either you're going to win, and get to Zenith, or you're going to lose and die. Forget. Everything. Else. It doesn't matter anymore."

"Is that what you think? Nothing else matters now?"

Brenner lifted an eyebrow. "I didn't say *nothing mattered.* I said your past, the Dominion, the inbred sacks of flesh you keep saving—*they* don't matter. Those are relics of the past. Drop your savior complex and see the games for what they are. A power grab. There's arcana for the taking everywhere, and only the powerful will make it to Zenith."

"I almost forgot what a delight you are," Kellan said.

"With power, you can do anything. That's the only law that spans all dimensions."

"Just *make out* already," Ysa said with a groan.

Her interjection caused Kellan to tense. He had almost forgotten she was in the room. When he glanced over, she was hanging out with the vacant-eyed women, eating little bits of fruit off the chests of the others.

Despite Brenner's bluster, Kellan still didn't really understand.

"I was told you were a decorated military officer in the United-Earth Defense Force," Kellan stated. "You received medals for your service, and now you don't care?"

"Medals are just chest candy," Brenner growled. "The moment I discovered there were *thousands of dimensions* that were near identical to mine… Service lost its meaning. And when I discovered there are beasts like the Arbiter—or like the Sovereign of the Dominion—I knew that everything I had worked for was just a shadow of importance."

Kellan didn't have an answer for any of that.

"I'm not going to play in anyone's game," Brenner stated, his words soaked in confidence.

"Except the Arbiter's," Ysa sarcastically chimed in. "You're playing his Nexus Games."

Brenner flashed her an icy glare.

She scoffed and rolled into the pillows, further away from the conversation, like a child that didn't want to be chastised anymore.

"You could've joined us," Brenner stated as he returned his attention to Kellan. "Now you're going to die to prove a point. A shame, really."

"I'm going to stop the Dominion." Kellan had no reservation in his statement.

"Does Xiang know about any of your plans?"

The question caught Kellan off guard. He crossed his arms and asked, "Why?"

Ysa couldn't stop herself. She laughed from her pile of pillows. "He doesn't know jack shit about Xiang, does he?"

"I think you'll find that Xiang doesn't hate the Dominion like you do," Brenner stated. "She's a snake, and she's just as willing to use whatever means she needs to get power. Remember what I said about staying focused? Maybe if you spent more time with your team, and less running around this maze of a palace, you'd know what I'm talking about."

Then Brenner turned on his heel and continued his pacing. After a few steps, he stopped, his shoulders tense. "Oh, just some friendly advice. Pick weak teams for the next game. Teams weaker than you."

"What?" Kellan asked. "What're you talking about?"

"You haven't seen the news?" Brenner motioned to the muted TV. "There aren't any options for game four. Everyone will be playing the same game. But those who managed to get a Summoning Chime have an extra advantage. So, when it comes time for you to choose who to play with—pick weak teams." Brenner glanced back and smiled. "Trust me. It's the best way to win."

Kellan still didn't know what the man was talking about. And Kellan almost wanted to pick all the *strongest* teams just to spite the man. He would have to watch Bitso's programming to really understand what was happening.

As if answering Kellan's unasked questions, Brenner unmuted the TV. Bitso was still on the screen, obviously detailing out the next game.

He was handcuffed to his metal desk with his wrists flat against the surface. He had no slack or leeway. When he had to scratch his chin, Bitso lowered his whole head to his thumb.

"I'll repeat that again," Bitso said as he lifted his head again. "The fourth game will be *Wave Defense!* Groups of four teams will be sent to their own personal play arenas. Once there, the teams will have thirty minutes to prepare for the wave of yami the Arbiter will be sending their way. The teams must protect their treasure from the yami, who are out to destroy it. And them, of course. Yami love flesh."

Kellan held his breath.

He hated the fact that they didn't get to pick a game. Part of the strategy Xiang had been using was to pick the correct game to match their strengths. If they were all forced into the same game, it just meant more people could mess with them.

"The four teams will be picked at random—except the teams who have a Summoning Chime. The individual who managed to find the Chime will be able to pick the other three teams they cooperate with."

"Wave Defense is a cooperative game?" Kellan asked, turning to Brenner.

The other man didn't answer. He just stared at the screen, his harsh gaze unblinking.

Bitso yanked on his hands but couldn't seem to free himself. He pulled harder, damaging his wrists. "But wait! *There's more!* This game will have *several ways to win!* Isn't that exciting? But don't get too excited. We wouldn't want you dying before the good parts arrive."

And here it is. The twist.

"There will be five waves of enemies—each wave more difficult than the last. More and more yami, until the last wave of enemies is a swarm. You'll get a few minutes between each wave to catch your breath, but the waves will be *so exciting*." Bitso giggled to himself. "I can't wait until you see the yami and the arena. It's amazing."

Ysa snorted and laughed. "That newscaster is something else."

"*Shut up*," Brenner barked.

Ysa went silent. No one in the room said anything. Even Kellan just focused his attention on Bitso. He wanted to know all the many ways he could win.

"If your team survives all five waves, you'll get a key!" Bitso attempted to clap his hands, but it was almost impossible. Instead, he tapped two of his fingers together in rapid succession. "If *all four teams survive*, you'll be given *two* keys!"

Ysa shot up. "Really?"

"One will be a Wave Defense Key, and the other will be a Heart Key, to prove you cooperated. That means that this might be the game, folks! *This might be the game that a team wins the Nexus Games!*"

Kellan furrowed his brow. If the fourth game gave away two keys, Bitso was correct. Someone *could* win. Kellan glanced over at Brenner—Team 42 already had three keys, didn't they? If they managed to win this game with the other teams, they'd win… and then the Arbiter would die.

Panic gripped him.

Kellan hadn't expected that twist.

"But wait! There's even *more*!" Bitso chuckled as he said, "If the leader of any team takes the treasure into their possession, their entire team will win, and they'll be teleported out of the arena, leaving the other three teams to fend for themselves!"

Of course.

"The team who steals the treasure only gets one key." Bitso shrugged. "But they also won't have to fight wave after wave of yami growing in power and number. So, ya know, tradeoffs." With a wistful smile, Bitso leaned to the side. "Unfortunately, the Arbiter has one last way you can win… If your treasure *is* taken, he has hidden three pieces of a silver ape statue around the game arena. Find the silver ape pieces, reassemble them, and it will teleport you to safety. You'll get a key, and you won't have to deal with the remaining waves of enemies."

Kellan tried to imagine the game arena and scenario. If there really were waves of enemies, the best bet for survival would be to set up a defensible position. Like the Spartans at Thermopylae, the best strategy would be to funnel enemies into a narrow choke point, so that the limited number of mages could deal with a larger number of enemies, so long as they had the stamina to endure.

But if one team teleported away with the treasure, leaving three others, the only way to get a key would be to run around looking for three pieces of a puzzle. If the waves of enemies hit, and rushed for the mages, they wouldn't have the advantage of a defended position, and would likely die.

Except for the four teams cooperating—where they all received two keys—

every other method of winning had some form of drawback.

Except taking the treasure and blowing out of the game super quick.

Kellan realized then that Brenner's advice was accurate. If Kellan picked three *weak* teams to join Team 101 in the fourth game, it would be easy to grab the treasure and leave. But then Team 101 wouldn't get two keys…

If I pick three strong teams—people I know will cooperate with me—we'll all receive keys. And since we didn't win a key in the third game, this would be a way for us to catch up.

"What happens if a team with a Chime wants to partner with another team with a Chime?" Ysa casually asked from her pile of pillows. "Like, could Team 42 and Team 101 partner up?"

"They'll have to agree to the partnership," Brenner stated, as though he had some sort of inside knowledge on the situation. "And I doubt *this* Alex Kellan will want to help us win."

Kellan didn't reply.

"We should team up," Ysa purred. "It would be fun. Probably pretty bloody. But definitely fun." She sat up and giggled. "Can you imagine Bitso reporting? He'd love it, too."

Brenner muted the TV, his gaze distant. He was clearly mulling everything over.

Why had Brenner offered Kellan advice on how to win the game? And why wasn't Brenner trying to convince Kellan to partner together? His motives seemed questionable at best.

"Who are you going to partner with?" Kellan asked.

Brenner smirked. "We'll try to find teams who will help us win. Definitely Team 10. Perhaps two weaker ones—people who won't betray us for fear of our might."

"Why tell me all this? Why offer me advice?" Kellan just had to know.

Again, Brenner paced, his attention on the floor. After a short moment of contemplation, he casually remarked, "I'm still human. *My* Alex Kellan is a good man, and you remind me of him. I thought Xiang was using you as some sort of substitute for me, but since that's not the case, I find your inevitable death a shame."

"But if I were porkin' your ex this would be a different conversation?"

Brenner grew tense and still. He stopped his pacing and balled his hand into tight fists. It was only the second time Kellan had seen him lose his tightly controlled composure.

With a snicker, Ysa said, "Oh, you're asking for it."

But despite Brenner's brief dance with rage, he calmed himself and returned to his silent pacing. No remarks. No gestures. Brenner was clearly done with the conversation.

And Kellan was done, too. He had heard everything he needed. Brenner was disillusioned and clearly lacking empathy, and Kellan had to think of three other teams to take with him in the game. Gunner's team seemed like an obvious pick—Gunner was happy to help.

Kellan headed for the one door out of the smoky, poorly lit room. The other women whispered as Kellan made his way around the pillows. Ysa snorted and smirked.

"Why are you so sour?" Ysa called out to him. "You're just like us, ya know."

"You're both psychotic," Kellan said as he offered a sarcastic wave goodbye.

"I'm going to be the one who kills you!" Ysa laughed again, darker than before. "I'll see you beg yet."

Kellan slammed out of the door and entered a hallway that he was semi-familiar with. His heart hammered in against his ribs as he turned and jogged for the main part of the AVU Palace. Once he was a few hundred feet away, the chill of Brenner's hexes no longer gripped him. But Kellan still felt the rush of anxiety.

Where is everyone?

His heart dropped into the pit of his stomach when he realized the sun was rising.

"I slept through the night," Kellan muttered.

Somehow, between each game, Kellan always found himself sleeping far longer than he wanted. It was like… the place itself was conspiring to steal as much time from him as possible. Kellan couldn't shake the feeling.

He ran through the empty halls, past rooms that still had music playing, and headed for the main stairway.

His shadow stretched out beneath his feet, and his albino wyvern leapt from the darkness and into the air. With his bat-like wings, Vlaze glided around and then landed, haphazardly, on Kellan's shoulder. He clawed himself into position and then whispered in Kellan's ear, "So much better out here."

Kellan patted Vlaze's head. "Just stay close."

Once he reached the stairs, Kellan took them three at a time. He could've used the shadows, but running was giving him at least some time to think over the situation. Since he had a Summoning Chime, he was going to be given a special advantage… But what game were they playing?

And the fact that he hadn't gathered that much arcana bothered him. Kellan needed ten arcana to unlock C-rank in eclipse. He only had fifteen total arcana at the moment. With five remaining arcana, what was he supposed to do? Get one power?

Kellan needed gold arcana to unlock the more powerful versions of his abilities—the ones that Ysa envied so much. But he had only gathered *one* gold arcana, and that had been from a frightened man in a creepy room.

Millie had said she would help him if he hadn't found more gold arcana by the time the fourth game had started. Would she come through for him?

"You seem tense," Vlaze said. "Do you want me to fight someone for you?"

Kellan smirked as he reached the top of the staircase. "I appreciate the sentiment, but some problems require more than just stabbing and punching."

"Lies."

"Let's just find the others and discuss our strategies. No more worrying."

Vlaze nodded his head. "As you wish, Master."

—Chapter 40—
—The Mermaid Knife—

Kellan walked the second-story hall until he came to the door of the suite. Outside, sitting on the floor, was a box. A brown box, with some tape and a simple piece of paper taped to the side. Normally, Kellan would find it suspicious, but this was the second time a package had arrived at his suite, so he scooped it up and glanced at the letter.

It was addressed to him, though the handwriting was shaky, as though written by someone with Parkinson's. Kellan read further, his eyebrows knitting as he tried to decipher the poor penmanship.

Then he realized who it was from.

Alex Kellan the Void Knight,

Thank you for saving me from the Arbiter's wrath. I was chosen to become a doll because the Arbiter was displeased with my existence. I wasn't born a mage, I'm weak, and I disobeyed his rules that govern the Nexus. I never thought I'd come to admire an outsider. I thought they were all cruel, as my mother had taught me, but I realize now that she was wrong. Some outsiders are just as gallant and amazing as the old tales say.

I didn't finish telling you the story with the Arbiter and the knife. The Nexus resident had the option to kill the kind outsider and remain beautiful forever, but the resident couldn't go through with it. The resident realized they loved the outsider, but that the outsider would never feel the same.

So the resident slit their own throat with the Arbiter's knife and became arcana for the outsider to absorb. They say it was the first gold arcana ever, but that's probably more fairy tale than reality.

Some people also say that providing arcana is all the residents are good for. I know you feel differently, which is why I want to help you win the Nexus Games. You said honor and compassion are some of the few things worth dying for, and that confidence was one of the most beautiful things.

I'm confident you'll win, and I'm certain whatever you do with the magic in Zenith will be worth all the sacrifices in the end.

Millie

Kellan read the message over three times. The tale of the knife seemed cruel and tragic. Although Kellan didn't much believe in fairy tales, he only really appreciated the ones that ended in clever solutions for horrific problems. Hansel and Gretel were a pair of abandoned children who tricked a witch into throwing herself in her own oven—that was the kind of revenge tale Kellan could get behind.

But the tale of the knife wasn't like that. It was a sad tale with no villains, just terrible circumstances.

Unless you count the Arbiter, Kellan mused. *The Arbiter apparently had the power to fix everything but decided not to.*

Wasn't that the reality of the Nexus?

Kellan briefly wondered why. Then he opened the box.

Vlaze gasped the moment the lid came off. The contents startled Kellan as well.

Inside was a pile of gold arcana—nine shimmering gold crystals, all the size of a thumb. Beside them was a black knife with a carved fish-tail handle. Kellan's analysis gave him more information.

Magical Item [Unique Weapon]—The Mermaid Knife

A mythical weapon created by the Arbiter himself.

When used against outsiders (any sentient race born outside of the Nexus), it deals strength + 3 damage (minus the target's fortitude). This weapon ignores all armor rating and shielding, no matter the source. Additionally, the Mermaid Knife steals 1 unspent arcana per strike. If the target has no unspent arcana, this doesn't trigger.

If the target is a Nexus resident, this weapon has no added effects.

If the Mermaid Knife is used to commit suicide, it triples the amount of arcana dropped afterward.

With an unsteady hand, Kellan picked up the blade. The Mermaid Knife wasn't like his rifle, which was semi-sentient on its own. Instead, the weapon felt cold and lifeless, and stained with so much blood that the handle had once been a much brighter color.

The nine gold arcana in the box…

It was Millie.

The realization caused Kellan to think over his slight interaction with her. She had seemed grateful at every opportunity, and speaking with her in the hall had been tense, but he hadn't imagined she was planning this. Were the Nexus residents so programmed to believe they were worthless that Millie thought herself only useful if she became arcana?

"It's so much," Vlaze said, wagging his tail. "You'll rank up in no time. That's so exciting, isn't it? Excellent."

"Yeah," Kellan said, knowing damn well that Vlaze didn't understand what had happened.

"Why aren't you absorbing it? Quickly! It's so beautiful. Look at that luster."

Kellan opened the door to the suite and stepped inside. He felt a clash of emotions. Millie's death, coupled with the warm presence of the gold arcana… It was hard to tell how he felt. He hadn't wanted Millie to kill herself. The damn arcana wasn't *that* important. Kellan almost couldn't believe she was gone.

Kellan wanted to participate in another game, not because he wanted a chance to die, but because he wanted something to distract him from his dark thoughts.

Millie's sacrifice weighed on him, even as he thought over his future options.

I need to think of anything else.

Kellan exhaled.

Eclipse was his primary magic, so he would have to rank that up first.

"There you are!"

Kellan glanced up as Mavis jogged over to him. The suite was quiet, but Husker and Sen were also around. They both sat on the large couch near the TV, their attention glued to the screen. Bitso was still repeating information, as always.

Mavis threw her arms around Kellan and squeezed. Kellan lost most of his breath, and his ribs flared with pain. He grimaced and cursed under his breath.

"Oh, sorry," Mavis said as she quickly released him. With a nervous chuckle, she added, "I keep forgetting my own strength now." Her eyes lit up when she noticed the shimmering gold glitter from within the box. "What's that?"

"Arcana," Kellan stated.

"It's gold. Just like you keep talking about."

Mavis reached into the box without another word. Before Kellan could pull it away, Mavis's fingers got close to the crystals. A mere inch from touching the crystals, the arcana shifted in color. They went from being gold, to a bright, almost harsh, crimson. Mavis jerked her hand away, obviously startled by the change.

Once her hand was out of the box, the crystals all returned to their lustrous metallic gold.

"Gold arcana is only good for the person it was given to," Kellan said. "It's given freely. You can't take it."

"Wow." Mavis just stared at the nine crystals. "Who gave you all that?"

"The doll I saved from the games."

"Really? The doll I carried around didn't give me anything. She just stayed quiet the whole time."

Kellan slowly nodded. "Yeah, well, I spoke with Millie a few times. Even after the game."

Mavis blinked. "You… did? Why?"

Kellan forced himself to avoid the subject. "Forget it. I need to spend my arcana, and then we can talk strategy."

"All right. But… where were you this whole time? Out just getting this arcana from Millie?"

"Yeah," Kellan said. "Sorry. I was unconscious for some of it after drinking something strange from the bar."

"Oh. Okay." Mavis stepped back. "I'm going to watch the rest of the rules. Hurry and rank up and then join us." She returned to the couch and took a seat next to Sen.

Before anything could happen to the arcana in the box, Kellan absorbed it.

[Alex Kellan] absorbed 9 gold arcana.

Just like with all the arcana, Kellan saw brief glimpses of images in his mind's eye. They were fleeting, but clearly involved the Nexus. Millie's memories? Kellan closed his eyes and tried to block out all the agony that haunted the edges of his thoughts.

After a shaky gulp of air, Kellan realized he had twenty-four arcana, ten of which was gold arcana.

And that… It felt different. Again, like he was touching something raw and powerful. It was different than the red arcana. It was pure.

Kellan immediately purchased C-rank of eclipse, which dragged him back down to fourteen arcana. Once he unlocked that rank of magic, several things happened all at once.

His total mana jumped to seventeen—base fifteen for C-rank, and two more for the D-ranks of metal and body, one each.

He also became aware of the C-rank eclipse powers.

Eclipse Magic Rank B Cost: 20 arcana

Eclipse—C-Rank Powers:

Laser, rank II [3 arcana]

Eclipse mages rely on "laser" energy in their attacks. This power is, weirdly, shared by metal mages.

The eclipse mage gains "laser" as an energy type and may spend a mana to shoot a destructive beam from their hand. The damage dealt is equal to metal magic rank (E = 1, D = 2, C = 3, etc.) + the mage's dexterity score. This stacks at half rate (round up) when added to any other light power.

Shadow Stepping, rank I [4 arcana]—[Included Within Mage's Focus]

The mage may step into the darkness and move nearly instantly from one location to another, so long as a shadow could travel the surface.

The mage spends a mana and moves at 10 feet times the mage's wisdom score.

Sphere of Darkness [3 arcana]

The mage's power of darkness allows them to create an orb of darkness, blinding all those trapped inside.

The mage spends 2 mana and makes an orb with a radius of 10 feet times the mage's wisdom. The mage can only create the orb in a location he can see.

Light Weapon [6 arcana]

The mage coats his melee weapon in laser, making it all the more deadly.

The mage spends 3 mana and adds his wisdom score + 2 damage to any melee weapon as well as the ability to ignore the first 4 points of armor rating. This enhancement to the weapon lasts 15 minutes.

The Sun's Rays [4 arcana]

The mage learns how to empower all their light-based attacks.

The mage gains +2 to all laser-style damaging attacks as a flat bonus after other calculations have been made.

Eyes of Light and Darkness, rank II [4 arcana]

The mage is simply better at noticing subtle things, whether it be a blush, a shifting of the eye, the movement of a shadow, or even the time of day based on the light.

The mage gains +2 perception.

Sentient Shadow, rank II [5 arcana]

The eclipse mage's shadow gains a significant amount of sentience as it's infused with magic. This power makes the shadow have a physical aspect, and it moves to help block and hold.

The mage gains +1 armor rating, and benefits when dodging and brawling, but they lose 10% to their familiar's growth.

Thick Shadows, rank II [Sentient Shadow, rank II] [3 arcana]

The mage's shadow jumps in the way of all damage, protecting their "person" at all costs.

The mage gains +3 "living shell" to their health. The shell must be broken before the mage can be harmed. The shell is reformed whenever the mage sleeps.

Empower Shadow, rank II [4 arcana]

The mage can "boost" their shadow.

The mage spends 3 mana, and a mana every 6 seconds to hold, and their shadow gains increased fortitude. This gives the mage +2 additional armor rating until their shadow is destroyed.

Shadow Sewing, rank I [Eclipse AND C-rank Body] [4 arcana]

An eclipse and body mage may use the shadows to deliver their healing abilities to others.

The mage's shadows (including abilities such as *Sphere of Darkness*) are now considered "touching" for the purposes of all healing abilities in body (such as *Heal the Body*, *Purge*, and *Purify*).

Infused with Magic, rank I [Eclipse, Universal] [2 arcana]

All C-rank mages may infuse their body with raw magic to become slightly stronger. While other magics offer more ways to grow beyond normal limitations, this ability helps a mage become as powerful as their racial limits will allow. When a mage purchases this ability, they must pick a benefit.

This power may be purchased multiple times, until the max stats have been achieved.

The mage gains +1 to any stat (to a max of 5) or +2 to their health (to a max of 11) or +1 to their willpower (to a max of 10).

It required *twenty* arcana to reach B rank?

Kellan hated the ever-increasing arcana requirements. At least with meta magic, he had a 20% reduction to ranking costs. If only he had that for eclipse as well…

And while Kellan found all that interesting, his mind hurt from the flood of information. He rubbed at his temples, trying to process everything. But then he was given one more set of options… The gold arcana had unlocked the D-rank of the apex magic, granting him unique and powerful abilities…

Eclipse—D-Rank Apex Powers

Neo Excalibur [10 arcana]

The mage understands that light is a deadly weapon. It burns and destroys and brings low even the sturdiest of mages and objects.

The mage spends 3 mana and enhances any bladed weapon with the power of raw laser light. This grants the weapon bonus damage equal to 2 x the mage's rank of eclipse, and the ability to ignore the first 15 armor rating. This will last for 15 minutes.

Once taken, the mage may never acquire "Neo Svalinn."

Neo Svalinn [10 arcana]

The mage understands that the darkness protects life from the harshness of light. Its cold comfort allows all to rest and dream.

The mage spends 3 mana and enhances any suit of armor with the power of pure void darkness. This grants the armor bonus armor rating equal to 2 x the mage's rank of eclipse as well as the ability to shield others the mage is touching for the same amount. This will last for 15 minutes.

Once taken, the mage may never acquire "Neo Excalibur."

A sword and a shield?

Kellan almost laughed to himself. For some reason, everyone on his team had told him to wield a sword instead of a rifle. Was it because eclipse magic had so many ways to enhance bladed weapons? That was the most likely reason.

Kellan understood there were advantages to both now. His rifle gave him range, and the laser blades gave him the ability to pierce through armor.

It still seemed like a lot of information to process, but Kellan had to make a decision. He had a build going—he could enhance his laser beams—but he had fourteen arcana to spend, and with Millie's sacrifice to help him through the games, he figured he should take one of the new apex skills.

The *Infused with Magic* seemed like an interesting way to increase power as well. Kellan could purchase it a few times and then use his body or metal magic to raise his stats beyond five, the human limit.

And health…

I need health like a cancer patient needs a cure.

But which abilities would he take?

"Are you okay?" Vlaze whispered in his ear.

"Yeah," Kellan said with a groan. "I just… need to know if I'm going to take a sword or a shield."

"Did you say you were a warrior and not a rogue? Seems like you should have a sword."

The shield seemed more prudent since C-rank of eclipse offered a weaker version of the sword ability… But *Neo Excalibur* did ignore the most armor rating. And Kellan had already run into a problem with that on a few enemies. Especially people like Brenner, who had an outrageously high armor rating.

Sevriss, his rifle, pulsed with a dark desire. Technically, it was a weapon that could shift shape. Kellan had originally found it as a sword, but it had transformed into a rifle to better suit Kellan's fighting style. Now it seemed to be aware of Kellan's direction…

Kellan had his laser beams for ranged attacks. Now he would have a sword.

I can't believe I'm actually going to wield a damn blade.

Closing his eyes, Kellan purchased *Infused with Magic* twice. He chose health twice, to increase his overall health to eleven, and then he purchased *Neo Excalibur.*

But he knew once he received more arcana, he would need C-rank of metal, and then he would need to purchase *Sun's Rays* and every laser-enhancing bullshit ability he could get his hands on.

"I need to specialize," he muttered to himself, trying to burn it into his thoughts. "That's what they all say, right? Hopefully this will be enough."

Kellan silently thanked Millie for her help. And then he briefly wondered…

if he spent the arcana, was the person who gave it to him gone? Or were they part of his magic now?

He supposed some questions he might never have the answer to.

—Chapter 41—
—Four Teams to Trust—

Kellan walked over to the couch in the massive suite. Mavis, Sen, and Husker sat in the center, their attention on the giant TV mounted to the wall. When Kellan sat down on the far end, one of Husker's fox ears twitched and faced in Kellan's direction. Then Husker turned his head and growled.

"Where have you been?" he demanded, his voice half a growl. "I went with you in order to help gather arcana, and you disappeared."

"Apparently you're not supposed to drink both the drinks at the bar," Kellan stated.

Husker snorted. "You fell asleep?"

"Yeah. You know, shit like this wouldn't happen if you warned me."

"I keep forgetting you came from a world without any magic." Husker leaned back on the couch and frowned. "My apologies. I should've kept a better watch over you."

Kellan shook his head. "Forget about it."

Although Bitso was in the middle of a rant about the fourth game—at some point he had tipped over his desk, and now he was lying over most of it, his hands still cuffed to the top—Sen muted the TV.

"I assume you heard the good news." Sen shot Kellan a glare. "*You* get to pick which teams join us in the games."

Today, Sen wore a child's red hoodie and a pair of cargo shorts. He was younger looking again. He had the rounded face of someone who had yet to experience puberty. He appeared to be eleven or twelve. Kellan preferred him older.

"I already know which teams I want us to play with," Kellan stated.

A door in the suite opened and shut, and Kellan leapt to his feet. He felt anxious—or perhaps *energized*—and the slightest of disturbances put him in the mood for a fight. He wanted to test out his new powers, after all.

Xiang walked into the suite's central room. She wore a dark-red leather jacket reminiscent of Carmen Sandiego, skintight black pants no better than spray paint, and heels that weren't for the faint of heart. Kellan wondered why she changed her outfit so frequently, but perhaps Xiang just got bored. She could illusion herself endlessly, at no mana cost. Who wouldn't constantly change their appearance?

One final detail caught Kellan's attention. Xiang wore a necklace—one made of bone and small black beads. It was a thin necklace, one that accentuated her elegant neck, but Kellan's Blitzkrieg Analysis gave him a lot more detail.

Legendary Magical Artifact [Equipment]—World Ender's Ring

A ring made from the skull of an Oom. This unique magical item was crafted by the rival dragon who ended the Oom's life. When worn, the World Ender's Ring enhances mind magic abilities.

The mage gains +6 willpower, +2 ranks of telekinesis (can surpass M rank), mana reduction of 2 per telekinetic attack, the ability to use the S-rank mind power *Crush* without mana cost, and +5 telekinetic shielding for the purpose of damage reduction.

"That's a ring?" Kellan asked, gesturing to the necklace.

Xiang placed her fingers on the World Ender's Ring. "It's originally meant for a dragon," she said. "But since I'm much smaller than a dragon, it can function as a necklace."

"Where did you get it?"

"I won a magical item in a Prize Room during the last game, and then traded that item at the Exchange for this." Xiang ran her fingers through her inky hair. "But that's not why I came out here."

Illusions wrapped around her new artifact. The bone and black beads became a dull silver—not unique or interesting in any way. Xiang's powerful illusions also hid the item from Kellan's analysis. He could no longer detect all the benefits the artifact gave her.

Was the World Ender's Ring worth losing a key? Kellan wasn't so sure.

"Did I hear you correctly?" Xiang asked. "You *decided* who we will be cooperating with? Without discussing it first?"

Kellan glanced at the clock. The games always started at the same time in the morning—9am—and it was 7:45am now. They had enough time to discuss things, but time always seemed to fly in the Nexus.

"I think we should do one of two things," Kellan stated. "Either we should team up with Team 42, or we should ally ourselves with teams we can trust and go for the two keys."

Mavis stood from the couch. "You told us we need to fight Team 42. Why would we team up with them?"

"To prevent them from getting two keys." Kellan pointed at the muted TV. "Bitso said that if the teams cooperated, they'd be rewarded with two. That means Team 42 will win."

"Really?" Mavis knitted her eyebrows and glanced over at Sen and Husker. "Is that right? What happens then?"

"What happens if Team 42 wins?" Sen repeated.

"Yeah." Mavis nodded. "Does everyone else keep playing the game or what?"

"Everyone has to wait until the end of the fifth game before they can be declared the winner. That's just standard rules. So, even if Team 42 gets all their keys, we'll have the fifth game to catch up with them. But if no one else gets five keys, then the games will end, and everyone else will lose."

Kellan wheeled on him. "Really? I thought multiple teams could win the games?"

"Yeah," Sen said, his volume increasing as he, too, leapt off the couch. "I just told you we'd have another game to catch up! And if *no* teams have five keys by the end of the fifth game, the Nexus Games continue all the way to the tenth game, regardless of key totals. You see, the fifth game is special. It's a way for people to end the games fast. Think of it like a *checkpoint.* It was Xiang's original idea to have five keys by the end of the fifth game—but since we missed the key in the third game, we'll probably not trigger an early victory."

Goddammit.

"So we *definitely* have to make sure Team 42 doesn't win."

"Teaming up with them won't help us," Husker stated. He motioned to the TV with a clawed hand. "Bitso already said the teams cooperating could fight each other. If we team up with his team, they'll attack us. And probably win. I might be able to kill the flestiss queen, or Brenner, but not before someone on *our* team is blown away—and they'll definitely aim for Xiang."

"But if we grabbed the *treasure* before they did, we would get a key and teleport from the game arena."

Kellan crossed his arms. Vlaze shifted on his shoulder, and then attempted to fold his wing-arms across his reptilian chest.

"It's a terrible idea to allow Brenner and his flestiss anywhere near us," Xiang stated. "The flestiss are talented mind mages by nature. They all specialize in *enslavement* and *domination* abilities. Such is the way of their culture. If Viniss uses her mind magic on us before we take whatever this treasure is, we'll lose immediately."

The new information fit in line with what Kellan understood of the flestiss. It also confirmed what Brenner had said. Xiang knew all about the Flestiss Dominion and didn't seem to care. Although it disturbed Kellan, he was just reminded that he was going to have to do this on his own. No matter what, he couldn't allow Team 42 to win the Nexus Games.

But he couldn't lose, either.

Kellan gritted his teeth. He'd just have to hope that Team 42 didn't get two keys. Or that Team 101 could get five keys before the end of the fifth game and somehow stop the Dominion from Zenith.

"Fine, we won't work together with Team 42," Kellan stated. "But we should work with Team 80, Team 5, and Team 77."

Mavis lifted both of her eyebrows. "You already have teams in mind? Why those ones?"

"Team 80 is run by a mage who escaped the Flestiss Dominion. His name is Gunner. I spoke with him a while back, and he seems trustworthy."

"Team 5 is led by Nosferatu." Xiang glared at him, her rage cold and quiet.

"I told you he isn't to be trusted. Taking him with us will be a mistake."

Husker snorted. "He has a Summoning Chime. That means he might decide to make his own teams, and not ally with us."

Kellan shook his head. In his heart, he knew Nosferatu would team up if Kellan suggested it. "I think we can trust him. He's a talented metal mage, and he's passionate about helping the Nexus residents."

The others in the room practically groaned all at once. Kellan almost couldn't believe his ears. Why did everyone hate them? Were they just *that* disgusting?

"They're the Arbiter's responsibility," Husker growled. "We shouldn't concern ourselves with the welfare of creatures as forsaken as them. We should focus on ourselves."

Which was the same advice Brenner had given.

Sen nodded along with Husker's words. "Yes. I agree. Stop associating with those inbred lunatics. The deeper you get into their ranks, the more they'll feel betrayed when you win."

"What does that mean?" Kellan asked.

"I'm just saying you're not going to win for their benefit. Leave them alone. Harvest arcana like the rest of us and stop overthinking everything."

Before Kellan could offer a counterargument to everyone's disapproval, Xiang held up a hand. The room went quiet. Then she turned her glower on Kellan. "Why Team 77?"

"Jace is on that team," Kellan stated. "I think… he'll help us. And he's powerful. And knowledgeable."

"You *think* he'll help us?"

Sen rolled his eyes. "Kellan gave that man a burger during the third game! I don't know why. I assume it's because Jace approached him at some point."

"I did find out he's Alternate-Kellan's son," Kellan stated. "But that's not the point. I think he's trustworthy."

"He stole the key from us in the first game," Xiang said.

"But he helped me during the second game. Without him, I probably would've been killed by Brenner."

Again, everyone went quiet. Sen, Husker, and Mavis didn't really have much to say about the situation. The three of them exchanged glances as though they didn't care one way or another, so long as they weren't saddled with Team 42. Xiang, on the other hand, folded her arms across her chest and gripped at the sleeves of her coat with white-knuckle force.

Perhaps her plan had been to steal the treasure and leave the game immediately? Which wouldn't work if they agreed to help the other teams.

It would be safer to steal the treasure, but there would be fewer rewards.

"We need to make up for the fact we lost the key in the third game," Kellan said, his words pointed. Xiang had lost them the key—couldn't she see that teaming up with others was their only choice now?

"Jace and I don't get along," Xiang slowly said. "And Nosferatu isn't to be trusted. Team 80… I don't see any problem with Team 80. If you want to ally yourself with a former Dominion slave, that's fine by me."

Kellan couldn't think of two other teams to ally with. The only other mage he considered a friend was Levvy, from Team 89, and she was the Straggler that no one wanted, apparently. He knew no one else from her team, and he couldn't rely on them if push came to shove.

If they weren't going to cooperate, they might as well pick weak teams and sacrifice them. But since so many of the weaker teams had already died in the first three games, there weren't many left. Anyone Kellan picked would be decently strong.

"You need to register the teams you want," Sen said. He gestured to the muted TV with a dramatic sweep of his arm. "I don't know if you were paying attention, but you need to go to the betting hall and present your Chime so that you can pick the teams."

Kellan glanced back at the clock. It was already 8:05am. They had less than an hour before the start of the game. He turned his attention to Xiang and then held out a hand.

"Can I get the Chime back? I'll go register our teams."

Xiang lifted a perfect eyebrow, her lips turned down in a slight frown. "Of course you can have the Chime back." She reached into her pocket and withdrew the spherical bell from her jacket pocket. It had no clacker and made no noise as she handed it over to Kellan. "And what have you ultimately decided? Will you listen to your team leader or are you just going to do whatever you want?"

Kellan shoved the bell into his own coat pocket. It was clearly powerful—the magic pulsed in his grip, and he could still sense it, even when tucked away.

"You know, you haven't actually offered me another solution. You just say *no* to everything." Kellan stepped closer to Xiang and asked, "So, if you were picking, what would it be?"

"I would pick teams we could overpower. I say we take the treasure and flee the game arena." She said each statement with no hesitation, her voice calculated.

"Even though we're down a key?"

Xiang opened her mouth to respond, but then quickly shut it without saying anything. Clearly caught off guard, she waited a long moment before answering. "I don't trust our team to make it through all five waves of enemies, even with Teams 5, 77, and 80."

Ah. Here's the problem.

"Nosferatu is an M-rank metal mage."

"He's the one I trust least of all," Xiang snapped. "And since he's the most powerful of us—and has a teammate who can also use a Summoning Chime—I think we'll be at his mercy. And I've learned, through painful lessons, over and over, that I should *never* be at anyone's mercy. They'll fuck me over every time."

Her last few statements came out heated. For half a second, Xiang was tense and almost livid. But she quickly calmed herself and turned on a heel. After a deep breath, she added, "I don't understand why you're so willing to cooperate with these other teams."

"We'll be stronger if we work together," Kellan stated. "That's the whole point of a team. Everyone else understands that *but you.*"

Kellan's anger rivaled Xiang's. They were practically yelling at each other. No one else in the suite offered any input. Even Vlaze lowered his head and tried to make himself as small as possible on Kellan's shoulder.

Since Xiang wasn't saying anything, Kellan added, "Everyone else on this team has fought together—or worked together for a goal—but you're always separating yourself. You've helped in a few games, but mostly from afar. I understand you have a hex, and it's tough for you, but that doesn't mean we shouldn't cooperate. If we don't work together, we're going to lose this damn game."

"My mother won on her own," Xiang stated, her voice low.

"And she also never came back from Zenith to help you, like she promised," Kellan shouted. "Is *she* really your role model? Because I've known trash cans that I could depend on more than her."

Sen stomped over and shoved himself between Kellan and Xiang. With as much rage as his little child face could muster, Sen glared. "*How dare you.* You know nothing of this world, or ours, and you think you can say such things?"

With a gentle touch, Xiang placed a delicate hand on her brother's shoulder. She gripped him tightly, and then released. "Enough, Brother. There's no need for this."

"But…" He whirled around, his brow furrowed. "You don't have to suffer through these insults!"

"Our *warrior* is correct. Mother didn't return as she had promised. Perhaps she never intended to, and only told me lies to placate me."

The statement caused Sen to go quiet. He turned his anger to the floor, his gaze practically drilling a hole through the carpet.

Xiang glanced over at Kellan, her expression neutral, her voice strained. "Pick your teams. If you want to cooperate—if you think we can win—prove it to me. Show me that I'm wrong. Dispel the doubts and return our team to the top of the ranks."

"Is that what you actually want?" Kellan asked. "Or is this just your anger talking?"

Xiang brushed her long black hair back. Then she turned away from Kellan and headed back to her room. "I've acknowledged that you made a fair point. I don't know our team that well. I haven't trained with you or fought alongside anyone to my fullest extent. I do think this game will end in disaster if we take mages stronger than ourselves. But even if it does, I trust myself to live through the mess… So, make your bet. Pick your teams. If we win, I'll rethink my entire strategy."

"All right."

"Plus, you've surprised me several times already. Perhaps this will be another upset."

"Really?" Husker asked as he stood a bit taller. "You're willing to cooperate with other teams?"

"Better than having their ire."

"I'll head to the betting halls right now," Kellan stated.

Xiang nodded. "I hope you're right about all this."
Heh. So do I.

—Chapter 42—

—Wave Defense—

Kellan exited the suite and headed to the first story of the AVU Palace.

The palace was surprisingly quiet. When he traveled down the stairs, Kellan spotted two Pestbyters hovering around the entrance hall, their machine-bodies always a disturbing sight. Their wire tentacles dragged across the carpet floors as they patrolled the area. When Kellan walked by, their camera eyes homed in on him for a moment before flitting over to other objects.

Kellan didn't know what they were searching for, but it was probably for people who had broken the rules of the Nexus. The Pestbyters were basically the dimension's law enforcement. Kellan typically liked the law, but he hated the randomness of the Nexus. It felt like nothing made sense, and ignorance was never a defense.

When Vlaze spotted them, he hopped off Kellan's shoulder and dove back into the safety of his pocket shadow.

Kellan made his way through the many winding halls and confusing rooms. The place was more trashed than usual. Food, garbage, and clothing covered everything. Kellan found a few spots of mustard on a large rug, and several candy wrappers thrown around an office space—it was like children had run wild through the AVU Palace, and the parents were too lazy to clean up.

When Kellan finally made it to the betting hall, he found that the other three mages with Chimes were already there.

Alternate Alex Kellan.

Robbie the Friendly.

And Wast, of Nosferatu's team.

They stood around one of the bookie counters. They weren't speaking to each other—they weren't even looking at each other. Robbie watched the TV, Wast stared at the betting boards, and Other-Kellan stared at the wall, his gaze vacant.

Wast and Other-Kellan had their finest equipment on. Heavy bulletproof armor, thick pants, and steel-toed boots. Each carried a variety of weapons and held himself like he was about to fight a horde of monsters.

Not Robbie, though. The man watched the nearest TV with a groggy expression. Every few seconds he yawned. Whenever Bitso screamed and laughed, Robbie chuckled to himself.

Kellan walked over to the robot behind the counter. Its tablet face lit up, and a smiley expression flashed across the screen.

"*Welcome, Alex Kellan the Void Knight,*" the robot said in a singsong voice that was still very *machine-like.* "*The Arbiter has allowed you to pick the teams you wish to cooperate with in the Wave Defense game. Have you made your decision?*"

"I have," Kellan said as he stepped up to the counter and leaned against it.

"Which team is your first pick?"

"Team 80."

The robot's face flickered as the expression shifted to something extra happy. "*Excellent! None of the other teams have picked that one. Team 80 will be forced to participate with you. Which team is your second pick?*"

"Team 77."

"*Excellent! None of the other teams have—*"

But before the robot could finish its many automated statements, Other-Kellan grabbed Kellan by the bicep and jerked him away from the counter. It wasn't hard enough to hurt, but it was shocking enough to get Kellan's full attention.

"What the hell?" Kellan asked.

His alternate-dimension counterpart glared, one of his eyes mechanical and glowing gold. The man appeared enraged, but since he couldn't speak, it was difficult to tell what had triggered him. Obviously frustrated by his lack of immediate communication options, Other-Kellan used a brief bit of sign language.

Shocked, Kellan watched the man make a few hand gestures.

But he didn't know what they meant. Kellan had never learned ASL or whatever form of hand language Other-Kellan was using.

When it became obvious that Kellan didn't understand, his alternate-self pointed to the dog tags around Kellan's neck.

"You don't want me teaming up with your son?" Kellan asked, taking a guess at the meaning.

Other-Kellan replied with a single curt nod.

"I'd ask you why, but I don't think we have time for you to find a pen and paper," Kellan quipped. "Look, maybe if you weren't helping Team 42 destroy everything, and enslave humanity, maybe I would have sympathy for you. But as it stands, you're just another delta-bravo that almost killed me during the third game. Fuck off."

Other-Kellan clenched his jaw. When Kellan tried to turn around, his alternate-self grabbed his bicep again. Then Other-Kellan tried signing something else. He did the actions slowly, as though that would help Kellan's understanding. It didn't.

"So if you ever used profanity, would your mother wash your hands with soap?" Kellan asked, sarcastic in all regards.

Robbie the Taco King laughed, his one loud *HA* enough to echo around the betting room. Wast watched with his ears back and his tail swishing in irritation.

Other-Kellan stopped his attempts to speak to Kellan with sign language and instead used gestures. He pointed to the dog tags, then to himself, and then to Kellan. With a glare, he pointed to the tags again.

None of that was helpful. Kellan wasn't sure what his other self was trying to say, other than he was displeased with everything that Kellan was trying to do.

"Let me guess, you're also upset I'm helping Xiang, and you'd rather I not get in the way of all these plans you had?" Kellan figured, given Brenner's reactions, he was probably correct.

Other-Kellan didn't reply.

Just to mess with him some more, Kellan added, "When you were with Xiang, did you have to use one hand to moan, or was it just all silent? It's difficult to picture."

Robbie couldn't help himself. He laughed again, this time more thoroughly. He had the comedic taste of a stoner with absolutely no other forms of entertainment nearby.

Other-Kellan let out a raspy scoff and then stepped away, obviously done trying to communicate. Kellan preferred it this way. Everyone on Team 42 was the enemy—and if they had their way, Kellan would've been dead ages ago.

The only thing that bothered Kellan was… why would his alternate-self ever do this? What had happened in *his* life that had turned him to Brenner? That had caused him to have a falling-out with his son? To the point that Jace wanted Other-Kellan dead?

Clearly, something was wrong, but it was far too late to do anything about it. The Nexus Games weren't going to wait for Kellan to solve another mystery. And Brenner was right—Kellan to focus.

"*We've registered your two desired teams,*" the robot said, drawing Kellan's attention. "*Which team is your final pick?*"

"Team 5," Kellan said as he glanced over at Wast. "I don't know if Nosferatu is willing, but I convinced Xiang to—"

"Perfect," Wast said, cutting Kellan off. "We were waiting to see if you'd ask to join forces." Wast pushed away from the counter and sauntered over to Kellan. His black fur had an almost-bluish hue to the ends. With a large canine grin, he patted Kellan on the shoulder. "Team 5 would love to fight with you in the Wave Defense game."

"Really? Excellent. I think we'll make a great team."

"Don't get so excited." Wast scratched his head with his claws. "The game will be difficult. We need to stay on guard."

"I understand."

Wast headed for the door. "I'll inform Nosferatu. Prepare yourself, and we'll meet in the game." He didn't wait for Kellan to answer. The rennic left the betting hall as fast as normal walking would allow, but Kellan suspected the man wanted to run straight back to his team leader to tell him the news.

Other-Kellan shook his head and also exited the room, his brow furrowed, his gait tense. Kellan wasn't sure what to say to his alternate self, but what did it matter? The man was an enemy.

Robbie walked away from the TV and offered Kellan a smirk. He fidgeted with his *Taco King* cap and then straightened his circular sunglasses. He reeked of hane and held himself with a slouch. “You didn’t want to pair up with my team? I mean, we’re pretty great. We would’ve said yes.”

“I’ve never believed in anyone as little as I do you,” Kellan quipped.

“Harsh, bro. That cuts deep.”

“You tried to kill me in the Catacomb Maze. And you killed your familiar in a sad attempt at messing with other people. Do I need to keep going? I could probably think of a few more examples.”

Robbie held up a hand. “Nah. It’s okay. I get it. I did leave Kenzo to die in those dark halls. That was my bad. It still bothers me.”

Kellan turned away from the man. “Well, good luck in the games.” His words came out sarcastic, even though he tried to sound serious.

With a tip of his baseball cap, Robbie replied, “Yeah, see ya.”

***

Kellan returned to his team’s suite without seeing a single other player in the games. When he entered the main sitting room, he was surprised to see everyone on the couch—even Xiang. She sat the farthest away from the others, but she was still there.

They weren’t talking, however. The TV was on, and Bitso continued his reporting of the game. Kellan slowly strode over and took a seat in the middle of the couch, between Mavis and Xiang.

The two of them didn’t glance over. Bitso’s speech was too loud and frantic.

“That’s right, every wave will get progressively harder!” Bitso’s desk was toppled over, and Bitso was just lying on the floor, his arms contorted since his wrists were still cuffed to the top of the desk. “And after every wave, you’ll be given some resources to replenish, *but each round you’ll be given less and less*, because it’s a battle of attrition!”

“Do we have many ways to restore mana?” Kellan asked.

Husker glanced over. He laid his ears back. “We’ve been running short on things to trade, but Xiang had an extra hamburger, so I managed to get us five mana potions. They’ll restore ten mana each. Not the greatest, but at least it’s something.”

“Is that it?”

“Some types of mages can restore mana through stranger means.”

Kellan nodded along with his words. One of the powers he had in eclipse was called *Photosynthesis*, and it allowed him to restore mana if he was in sunlight. He hadn’t taken the ability—he desperately needed more arcana—but Kellan was starting to regret that fact. There had been several instances in the games where mana depletion had been an issue.

“Do we have any other supplies?” Kellan asked.

The others remained quiet.

“Did Teams 5, 77, and 80 agree to help?” Mavis asked.

Kellan nodded. “As soon as 9am rolls around, we’ll be in the game arena.”

Bitso slammed around his newsroom, trying to free his wrists and failing. He grunted and then shouted as he lifted the metal desk up, and then kicked it onto its other side. The sharp edge of the desk slammed into the back wall, gouging out a chunk of the pretend studio he was in. One of Bitso's background screens fell to the floor and shattered.

Bitso gave up and just lay on top of the desk, breathing heavily. "Sorry, folks. We're having technical difficulties."

No one commented on Bitso's insanity. They glanced between each other, and then the clock on the far wall. Except for Xiang. She pondered for a long while, her attention on nothing in particular. When Kellan turned to her, she glanced back, her face beautifully smooth and without visible worry.

"If Nosferatu does betray us, what would you recommend we do?" Kellan asked.

She lifted an eyebrow. "I thought you trusted the inbred mage?"

"Well, I don't 100% trust the man. I just met him. He *seems* trustworthy, and I'd rather extend a helping hand than cower away because things *might* go south. That doesn't mean I can't have contingencies in place if he decides to betray us."

"We have a trump card," Xiang stated. "Your Summoning Chime. If Nosferatu, or any of the other powerful mages, for that matter, try to harm us, use the Chime to summon someone—and then order that someone to murder the other teams. We'll take their arcana, then the treasure, and exit the game as victors."

"Nosferatu has a Chime as well."

"Just make sure whoever you summon can win in a fight against whoever he summons." Xiang forced a smile. "Or be the first one to use the Chime."

"Seems like a waste to use it in this situation."

"I agree." Xiang smoothed her crimson jacket. "But better to be survivors than dead men with plenty of loot."

Kellan snorted a laugh. "Yeah… That makes sense." Then he hardened his expression. "But who should I summon?"

"Ygg'Exos Vain," Xiang stated. "My mother summoned him and won the last Nexus Games. He can win us this game for certain."

There weren't many options for Kellan. There were no mages in his dimension. His "Normal Earth" was filled with mundane people. And he didn't know the names of many powerful mages. He knew Ygg'Exos, because of the stories—everyone calling him the tyrant king, and how he was a master at fighting and killing mages, but that was all the information Kellan had on him.

Then there was the Immortal Rarn. She was a jungle werewolf, apparently. The rennic who ruled over Husker's tribe. Or tribes—Kellan wasn't certain. According to Husker, she was a fierce warrior and a benevolent ruler.

Kellan also knew of Zarr Mantis—a rezrah who went by the name *Councilor Zero*. Apparently, he and Ygg'Exos had a beef. But that wasn't the only place Kellan had heard the man's name. Councilor Zero's blood ran black with the power of eclipse magic. According to Bitso, he was an "edgelord" who was rather angry at everyone.

The last mage Kellan knew of was Megadonis. He was a human mage who conducted magical research. It was thanks to Megadonis that Kellan had meta magic. Would summoning a man like him actually help in the Nexus games? Kellan kept the information tucked away in his back pocket just in case.

But that was it.

Those four names.

Kellan scratched at his chin, wondering if he could walk around the palace and just ask for names of famous mages. Would that help him? Kellan wished he had more intel on everyone and everything.

The clock ticked over to 9am.

"It's time," Xiang said as she stood from the couch.

Then everyone was teleported from the suite. It was a relatively painless process, until Kellan appeared on the deck of an aircraft carrier.

He stumbled forward and almost face-planted on the laminated armored steel of the aircraft carrier's flight deck. Kellan managed to straighten himself and glance around, his eyes wide with shock. They were out in the middle of an ocean, the weather poor. The clouds wore black, like this was a funeral, and harsh wind whipped over the flight deck, bringing with it the salt water off the tall waves.

The Net formed around the aircraft carrier—a giant scarlet bubble enclosing the entire game arena.

—Chapter 43—
—The CVAN Renegade—

Kellan ran both his hands through his hair, shocked by his surroundings.

Aircraft carriers were gigantic. They were often referred to as *floating cities*. The largest of carriers—and Kellan suspected they were standing on the flight deck of one such vessel—was about three American football fields in length. The flight deck itself was over four acres, with several hangars under the deck capable of housing eighty aircraft.

This mass of metal defied the waters, displacing one hundred thousand tons, floating when no mountain its size should.

Kellan turned in place, taking everything in.

Sen, Husker, Xiang, and Mavis were all around him, each baffled or confused. Husker immediately lowered himself. He pressed his hands flat on the flight deck.

"What is this?" Husker asked. "Such a foul contraption."

The wind howled, and Kellan shielded his eyes. "This is a supercarrier. It's a military vessel for transporting helicopters and fighter craft into war."

"It's deserted."

Kellan cursed under his breath. No one was around. The flight deck, the control tower, the radar, the hangar elevators—Kellan didn't see a soul. But that didn't mean it was deserted. The Nexus residents were always about. Kellan had learned that the hard way. They were probably on the ship as well.

"Are you familiar with this boat?" Sen asked. "I… I've never seen anything like this."

"Neither have I," Xiang said.

Mavis glanced between them, her mouth hanging open in disbelief. "You both knew about a goddamn space station during the second game! How do you *not* know what an aircraft carrier is?"

"We're familiar with Brenner Hawke's version of Earth," Sen said matter-of-factly. "The United-Earth Defense Force didn't have *water boats*, they had *space boats*, woman! I know about things that fly through space… Not this! It's like… a street in the middle of the water."

Kellan turned to Husker. "And you live in a weird jungle society in your dimension? No cars? No aircraft carriers?"

Husker clung to the flight deck, his claws practically digging into the thin layer of laminated asphalt. "I only know of technologies that Xiang has taught me…"

Which meant everyone on Kellan's team—except Mavis—didn't have a clue about their surroundings. They either knew of future tech or medieval warfare. Somehow, they skipped over the middle part of history and technological advancements.

"Everything will be okay," Kellan said, the salty winds stinging his eyes. "Aircraft carriers are almost impossible to sink, and they're armored and fortified. I'm not sure what kind of monsters we'll be facing, but the carrier is a safe place."

The crackle of a speaker system flared to life over the flight deck. Husker flinched, lowering himself further until his stomach was flat on the ground. Xiang, Sen, and Mavis all stepped closer to Kellan as they glanced around for the source of the static-filled speaker.

After a few moments, the irritating noises stopped. Then a voice boomed out over the flight deck.

"Welcome, boys, girls, and everything in between," the voice of Bitso shouted.

Kellan didn't spot any speakers, but he suspected it didn't matter. Bitso was broadcasting to remind them of the rules of the game. They just had to listen.

"Welcome to *Wave Defense!* Get it? Waves? Because you're on the ocean. *It's clever.*" His own laughter boomed out over the aircraft carrier. Once he quieted himself, he continued, "There will be five rounds of enemies. They'll emerge from the waters and invade your little boat. It's your job to protect your lives and the *treasure*. The treasure should be in the dead center of the carrier. I'll give you thirty minutes to find it and fortify your defenses. After that, the first wave will begin!"

Kellan clenched his jaw, his heart beating at rapid and almost uneven rates. The ship was gigantic. There were at least twenty-five decks, perhaps more. They had *thirty minutes* to get to the center? That was almost a challenge in and of itself.

"Once the first wave is over, you'll have only ten minutes to rest and prepare for round two."

"I hate this," Husker growled, his eyes closed tight. "I don't feel well… My stomach hurts."

"It's just seasickness," Mavis commented.

Bitso's voice boomed louder than before. "And since this is an *even-numbered* game, the Kuji in this round will be more fearsome than usual. They won't stop until they kill the Stragglers. The Arbiter has given them enhancements to make sure they're even more deadly than before!"

The cackling was the worst part of the announcement. The wind added to the haunting mirth, as though the ocean was howling with laughter.

Once he calmed down enough to speak again, Bitso said, "Remember—there are four ways to win. First, survive all five waves with all four team leaders still alive. You'll be rewarded with two keys! Second, survive all five waves, even if other teams die. You'll get one key. Third, steal the treasure! You're immediately teleported to safety, and your team gets a key. And lastly… search the aircraft carrier for three pieces of a silver ape statue. Assemble the statue, and you'll be teleported to safety! And get a key!"

That was a lot of ways to win.

It was a trick, though. The aircraft carrier was too gargantuan. They could be searching the ship for days and still not find pieces of a silver statue. Surviving all the rounds was their best bet.

"There're also a few *surprises* that the Arbiter has placed around the game arena! The first is the dragon… Watch out. While waves of enemies are rushing the boat, the dragon will become hostile. Don't worry, though. When the waves are over, it'll cease its aggression."

Kellan turned his attention to the flight deck. Several fighter jets were parked around the edge of the landing pad. Chains from the deck secured all the aircraft in place. Then Kellan noticed a pile of machinery near the end of the runway. It wasn't a plane or a car or even a helicopter.

His analysis gave him additional information.

Name: Aspect of the Arbiter #12
Race: Semi-Sentient Construct
Magics: Eclipse, Metal
Rank: Impossible to Rank
Armor Rating: 40
Health: 100/100
Stats: Concealed
Abilities: Concealed

The "pile of machinery" wasn't unorganized garbage. It was a dragon. And it stirred from its resting place, moving at a slow rate, lifting its head first and then standing up on four legs. Large blades lined its spine, and its claws were practically swords. The machine beast was as large as a school bus, its shiny chrome body a mix of pistons, gears, and shafts.

The dragon's eyes glowed red, and the inside of its mouth was a bright neon green, like the Arbiter's. When it moved, the sound of each footfall boomed across the deck.

On its shoulder was a display screen. It read: DOCILE.

No doubt the word would change once the wave began.

"The second surprise is… You can't sink the ship!" Bitso said over the speaker. "And I don't mean you *can't physically* sink it, because you *can*. I mean, *if* you sink the ship, you'll lose the game, *and your key*. And probably your life. The Arbiter really doesn't want you sinking his beautiful little boat. These guys came through dimension rifts during the Conflux! The Arbiter loves them like a child loves their puppies."

Kellan wasn't too worried about that. Sure, some mages had magical abilities that could sink the ship, but he didn't have those. *Yet*.

"The other surprises will come later!" Bitso shouted. "For now, you must find the treasure and prepare your defense. Good luck. I can't wait to see how many of you lukewarm IQ types end up as corpses."

Kellan took a deep breath.

Where were the other teams? Were they on different decks of the aircraft carrier? Kellan didn't have time to search for them. He motioned for Team 101 to follow him, then he headed for the operations tower. Every aircraft carrier had hangar elevators to store their aircraft beneath the deck.

As Kellan started to walk away, Sen leapt to his side and grabbed the side of his jacket. Kellan glanced down at him and frowned.

"I just, uh, don't want to get too far away from you." Sen frowned at the waves in the distance. "Besides, it's good to have me close. I can shield you, remember?"

"Oh, I remember."

Xiang walked to Kellan's side. Despite her impractical heels, her speed wasn't hindered. Mavis helped Husker to his feet. He was nine feet tall and had to hunch down to hold on to Mavis's shoulder.

Kellan jogged to the tower, his eyes searching for the carrier's designation. It was typically written in several places, specifically for emergency personnel. In theory, if the aircraft carrier was in danger, and needed outside assistance, maps, designations, and warnings were set up near the command centers to assist outsiders.

The designation for *their* supercarrier was: *CVAN Renegade*.

Kellan stopped dead in his tracks and ran both his hands through his hair a second time. "Shit."

"What's wrong?" Xiang asked. The wind played with her long hair, and she struggled to keep it under control.

Her brother was the same way.

"This is a nuclear-powered attack carrier," Kellan muttered. "That's what the *CVAN* stands for. That means there's *two* nuclear reactors on this goddamn boat. Two of them."

Which meant it would be a little easier to accidentally sink. What if an explosion of magic went off close to one of the reactors? Kellan wasn't sure how they would react. He didn't want to think about it.

"And these *nuclear reactors* are… bad?" Husker asked, his eyes squinted, his tail tucked between his legs.

"They're just not something we should touch. They're something we stay away from."

The control tower on the aircraft carrier was similar to an airport's. There were satellite dishes mounted to the roof, and large viewing windows around the highest floor. Unlike with normal airports, there were *Sea Sparrows* mounted to the side—guided missile systems capable of firing several missiles at once.

Kellan found the large elevator down into the hangar. The elevator itself was practically four thousand square feet of space with no railing or sides. They used them to drag planes up and down, as well as plenty of missiles and other armaments. It looked like a piece of the runway—asphalt-coated steel with only a few numbers painted on the side for its designation.

"Get on this platform," Kellan said pointing to the elevator.

The team did as he instructed. Kellan walked over to a manual control bench and hit the button that would take them to the center hangar. Kellan then jumped on the elevator as it descended into the depths of the massive carrier. The grinding of wheels and the hum of motors accompanied them the entire way down.

"This place feels like it might be larger than the space station," Mavis muttered as she glanced around the elevator shaft.

Lights had been fixed into all corners of the carrier. Although it was gloomy outside, and the weather was threatening to turn on them, the inside of the ship was bright, warm, and inviting, even if industrial.

After descending one more floor, however, Kellan was reminded this was Nexus. The first deck had been normal, but the second deck was a scene straight out of a depressing dystopian movie. The metal of the carrier was rusted, there were random elementary school desks thrown down the hallways they passed, and someone had taken spray paint and tagged most flat surfaces.

When they made it to the third and fourth decks, things became oddly sea-themed, with decorations of sailboats, anchors, and oars everywhere. Kellan wasn't sure if there was any rhyme or reason, but suspected not. The Nexus didn't care—everything was just a jumble of every dimension ever.

When the elevator finally arrived at the central hangar, Kellan knew they had found the correct location. The hangar was practically an oversized gymnasium. The ceiling was tall, the jets and helicopters were pushed to the walls, and the open space in the center was empty except for a single glittering gemstone.

The rock put all diamonds to shame. Its many facets shone with iridescent colors, like the surface of water covered in oil.

Magical Item [Unique]—"The Treasure"

The treasure for the Wave Defense game. This magical item attracts yami to it. If the treasure is broken by any means, all teams instantly lose the game and die.

If the treasure is touched by a team leader, the treasure teleports the team to safety, outside of the game arena.

Kellan pointed to the diamond. "There. We need to protect that in order to win the game." He jogged over to the treasure, Sen close behind him.

Mavis, Husker, and Xiang stayed a bit behind, lingering near the elevator. The inside of the hangar was colder. A chill wind blew in from large open windows on both the starboard and port side of the carrier.

It would rain soon.

Kellan picked up the treasure. The diamond rock was nearly the size of a basketball, but it didn't weigh much. Kellan turned the glittering gemstone over in his hand, admiring the way his face reflected across the many surfaces.

"Gaudy," Sen said with a sneer. "I can see why the yami would want to destroy it."

"We need to take this somewhere deeper into the carrier," Kellan muttered as he tucked it under his arm. "Someplace with choke points. We can't defend it here—it's too wide open. We'll be killed for sure."

Kellan glanced around until he spotted a door at the far end of the hangar. He motioned for the others to join him.

"Shouldn't we wait for the other teams?" Mavis called out, her voice echoing between helicopters.

How much time did they have left before the first wave was upon them? Kellan didn't want to take any chances.

"Put a mark on the ground so they can find us. We don't have time to wait."

"That's not necessary," a voice boomed out from the other side of the hangar.

Kellan whirled around on his heel. The other teams—77, 80, and 5—all stepped off the far elevator.

—Chapter 44—
—The Team of Teams—

Kellan recognized most of the mages. Team 5 was obviously led by Nosferatu. The man had lesions and pockmarks across his skin like an Irish person had freckles. Although he wore a suit—seemed silly for a death game, but Kellan wasn't going to comment—the man was still hideous. Nosferatu held himself with regal confidence, though. Kellan respected that.

Team 5 also had Wast, the black-furred rennic. He was geared out like a one-man army. And like Husker, Wast was damn tall. Almost ten feet. That alone made him one of the most intimidating people in the whole group.

The last person on Team 5 was someone Kellan hadn't seen before. A small human woman with pixie-cut hair. She was just barely over five feet, making her the shortest in the group. Kellan couldn't help but compare her to Wast. The two made for a hilarious odd couple.

She was blonde, her skin wan, and her posture weak. Her team mark—the number 5 on her left hand—also had the skull. She was Team 5's Straggler.

Kellan paid attention to her analysis, whereas he ignored Wast and Nosferatu.

Name: Jayna Guerrero the Hidden
Race: Human
Magics: Storm, Eclipse
Rank: Concealed
Armor Rating: 1
Health: 10/10
Stats: Concealed
Abilities: Concealed

Jayna was clearly a stealthy and quick type. *No wonder she's the team's Straggler. She can avoid the Kuji.*

Team 80 also only had three members. Kellan recognized Gunner immediately. The brand on the side of his head made him stand out from the rest of the group. No other person here had been a flestiss slave. Gunner wore his gear well, and he walked with confidence, even if he had a few nervous tics. He constantly glanced over at Nosferatu and Wast, his eyes flitting over for half a second before returning to the hangar.

The Straggler of Team 80 was Hank Gardener. The skull on the back of his left hand was rather visible. He appeared to be in his early twenties, and he wore a simple T-shirt, jeans, and a pair of hiking boots. The man had brown hair, cut short. He wasn't the most confident, which worried Kellan. He needed people who would be able to hold their own.

The last member of Team 80 didn't surprise Kellan, but he almost wished it had been someone else. It was the beautiful white rennic from the bar—the one with the poofiest tail Kellan had ever seen. Centa Greeniz, a B-rank storm and wyld mage, her wolf-like features prominent. She was shorter than Husker and Wast at only eight feet, but still rather impressive. When she walked, her tail swished back and forth behind her, long enough it was like she was sweeping the floor of the hangar.

Both Husker and Wast gave her the occasional glance, though it was fleeting.

Centa turned her wolf-like gaze on Kellan. "Oh. It's *you.*"

"The feeling is mutual."

She sneered and turned away with a huff. Kellan didn't bother dwelling on it. He focused his attention on the last team.

Team 77 had only four members, and they dressed as though they all belonged to the same damn motorcycle team.

Jace was easy to spot. His glowing mechanical eye could be spotted in the middle of a rainstorm. It glowed with an intense blue. He was about as tall as Kellan—a little over six feet—and he was muscled enough to look dangerous. His short dark hair and alert gaze were things Kellan shared with the man. They *looked* like they were related to anyone paying attention.

The human next to Jace was nearly seven feet tall and had a shaved head. He had piercings on his eyebrows and lower lip and walked with a hunch. He, too, was muscled enough to be dangerous, and his dark tanned skin carried a few knife scars.

The man had a skull on his left hand near his number. He was the team's Straggler.

> **Name:** Nasir Warren the Butcher
> **Race:** Human
> **Magics:** Entropy
> **Rank:** B
> **Armor Rating:** 2
> **Health:** 12/12
> **Stats:** Concealed
> **Abilities:** Concealed

Kellan had met Nasir before. He hadn't been the Straggler then, which meant Team 77's Straggler had died at some point.

The next member of Team 77 was one of the bird people, the niav. He had black raven wings with a fifteen-foot wingspan, the feathers shimmery and clean.

He kept his gaze down and his shoulders bunched near the base of his neck. Nothing about the man screamed confidence, and Kellan worried that he could be a weak link.

Name: Kin Line the Raven
Race: Niav
Magics: Storm, Wyld
Rank: B, B
Armor Rating: 2
Health: 10/10
Stats: Concealed
Abilities: Concealed

Kin… The delta-bravo who shot at me during game three. Hopefully we can rely on him.

The last member of Team 77 had to be the team's leader. It was a woman—or so Kellan thought—but she was one of the rezrah, the dragon-like people with scales. She was mostly human looking, except for her arms and legs, which were covered in silver scales. Her darker skin complemented the metallic tones—it made everything pop. In Kellan's opinion, she was more striking than even Centa, the bushy-tailed wolf.

The rezrah woman had a long, scaled tail, the tip flitting from side to side as though she were irritated. Her hands and feet ended in claws, and it reminded Kellan of old-world gargoyle statues.

Kellan allowed his eyes to tell him the rest.

Name: Vora Tanner the Silver Crusader
Race: Rezrah
Magics: Soul, Metal
Rank: B, B
Armor Rating: 6 + 4 Shielding
Health: 15/15
Stats: Concealed
Abilities: Concealed

Vora? She seems like she's seen her fair share of battles.

She wore cargo pants, a protective vest, and carried a large backpack. No boots—her clawed feet didn't look like they'd fit into anything. Her black hair was shoulder-length, but she kept it held back in a tight ponytail. When she met Kellan's gaze, Vora frowned slightly.

All three teams approached Team 101.

Together, they had fifteen mages. The team leaders—Nosferatu, Xiang, Vora, and Gunner—would have to be protected at all costs. The team Stragglers—Husker, Hank, Nasir, and Jayna—would be pursued by deadly versions of the Kuji. Was it wise to keep them with the rest of the group? Or would it be prudent to send them to other parts of the carrier while the waves of yami were attacking them?

Gunner walked up to Kellan and smiled. "Merry Christmas. I'm glad to see you're still alive."

"Yeah, Merry Christmas." Kellan patted the side of his shoulder. "Let's make it through this."

Gunner nodded once in acknowledgement. Then he stood close to Kellan and remained silent.

Then Kellan turned his attention to Team 77. "We don't have much time. I know you might be confused, but I thought we could work together. If all four team leaders live through this, we all get two keys. That's our goal—everyone surviving."

Vora scratched her claws along the silver scales of her forearms. "You're Jace's father? Or one of his fathers?"

"An alternate-dimension version of my father," Jace muttered in correction. "I'm not trying to kill this man."

Vora huffed. "Heh. Yes, well, I've seen you a few times on the news reports. You're the weaker mage who continues to live. The one helping the Nexus residents."

"That's right," Kellan said.

"Why am I speaking to you? Why aren't we listening to your team leader?"

Xiang—clearly and unequivocally the most beautiful person in the room—smiled as she said, "Our warrior gave a passionate speech about how we should *work together* and *friendship is magic*." She added sarcastic jazz hands to the last few words. "I told him it was a terrible idea, and that none of you are to be trusted, but he believed very strongly in the opposite. This is *his* gambit. If I had my way, we would take the treasure and leave."

She motioned to the diamond in Kellan's grasp. If she wanted, Xiang could grab it and end the game for Team 101 immediately. But she didn't. Xiang shot Vora a piercing stare, as if challenging her to deny any of Xiang's claims.

Vora glanced from the treasure to Xiang, and then over to Nosferatu and Gunner. "You all agree to this? We're going to aid one another during the game?"

Nosferatu replied with a tight smile. "I agree."

"It must be this way," Gunner stated. He stepped closer to Kellan.

The rezrah woman swished her reptilian tail. After a short moment of contemplation, she stared at Kellan. "Rezrah don't just trust other mages easily. We have rituals and ceremonies."

Kellan glanced at an imaginary wristwatch and then sarcastically looked up at Vora. "Well, we have ten minutes. Hit me with your best ritual."

The others in the group chuckled darkly. Vora swished her scaled tail a few times before replying, "If you get two keys, will that bring you to five?"

"No. We didn't get a key during the third game."

"Neither did we." Vora exhaled. "Very well. Let's work together. Perhaps we'll make it through this." Then she turned her attention to the hangar. "But I'm not sure where we are or where to find suitable defenses."

Kellan pointed to the far door. "Follow me. I think there's a mess hall down that way, perhaps one deck lower. It'll have narrow hallways leading to a larger room. If we position ourselves in the room, and block off most of the hallways, we can force the yami to attack us through one or two directions."

"You know where we are?" Jace asked, narrowing his eyes. "You know this boat?"

"We're on an aircraft carrier. I haven't been on this particular one, but I've been on others. They have similar layouts, and even if they don't, I know where to find us some maps."

All the other teams glanced between each other, mumbling reassurances and hopeful statements. Apparently, no one else knew much about the carrier, not even Jace. That wasn't helpful, but Kellan didn't really care. So long as the others listened, he figured they would be okay.

"*Let's get going,*" Sen hissed. "We haven't much time! Quickly!"

Kellan guided the four teams across the hangar and to the far door. The heavy metal of each of the carrier's interior doors was reinforced and could be shut and locked down to prevent water from passing through. There were so many redundancies and safety measures in place to prevent the ship from sinking, which would normally be helpful, but Kellan feared they wouldn't withstand magical damage from monsters.

The narrow corridor was only wide enough for two people at any given time, and even then, they would be bumping shoulders. The halls would definitely limit the movement of the yami.

"Was this vessel designed by humans?" Gunner asked. "*Only* humans? No other races or aliens involved?"

"It was completely designed and built by humans." Kellan patted the cold gray steel. "They're some of our most impressive creations. On a ship, the walls between rooms are called *bulkheads.* A navy officer once yelled at me for calling them *walls,* and now I have PTSD about it. Figured I should tell you now."

"It's the same for a starship." Gunner half-smiled as he examined their surroundings. "It's just… I've never seen anything created by *just* humans. All the starships I've been on were flestiss designed, and the cities I patrolled were built by multiple conquered peoples. I was told humans weren't capable of designing anything great. At least, not on their own."

"What a delta-bravo," Kellan quipped. "In my experience, whenever someone says, *somebody isn't capable of blank*, they have no idea what they're talking about. They're just afraid they're not the smartest person in the room, and that soon everyone will figure it out."

"I'll try to keep that in mind." Gunner rubbed at the brand on his head. "Is that a human saying? I want to learn more about our culture."

Kellan chuckled. "Well, I'm a human, and I'm saying it, so I guess it's an official human saying now."

"And *delta-bravo* is a term humans use for people they don't like? Is that right?"

"Sure. Yeah. Knock yourself out. Also, the official dance of humans is *twerking*, and we all love *cat memes*. Commit both of those to memory."

"*Kellan*," Mavis snapped, though she was snickering at the same time. "What's wrong with you? Don't tell him stuff like that. *Let's just focus on finding the mess hall.*"

Sen threw his little arms in the air. "Yes! Thank you. *Finally*."

Kellan hadn't forgotten their primary goal. He had been following the instructions written on the bulkheads. Mini-maps and schedules were posted on most corners, and he had used the information there to find his way.

He considered himself lucky—everything on the *CVAN Renegade* was written in English. It made the whole process easier.

Kellan led everyone down the corridor and into a nearby mess hall and café combo. Aircraft carriers were so large that most had several amenities normally only found on land. Carriers had gyms, chapels, restaurants—even stores that sold basic clothing and supplies. Most carriers even had their own firefighting crew complete with their own "firehouse" inside the ship.

The mess hall and café were large enough for all fifteen people to fit inside. There were six doors that connected to the room, and one kitchen built into the back end. Several tables and chairs were scattered around the hall. Some were normal, others were nautical themed, and a rare handful looked as though they had been colored on with crayons.

"We need to prepare this place," Kellan said. He placed the treasure in the back corner of the room and then turned over several metal tables. "The yami will be coming for this."

Kellan spent a mana to *Mold Metal* and then shaped the legs of the metal table. His magical ability made the metal seem like clay between his fingers. He attached the table to the far bulkhead of the ship. When he placed his fingers on the wall, he was surprised to see he could mold that steel as well. He had thought the carrier would be immune to magical effects, but clearly, he was mistaken.

Without saying another word, Kellan built a protective cage around the treasure. He "stitched" the metal together, forming a box around the diamond and keeping it in place. This way, the yami would have to get past them, and then the sturdy steel alloy of the table before they could damage the gemstone.

"What're you doing?" Husker asked. He glanced around the mess hall. "*This* is where you want to put us? Shouldn't we be up on the deck?"

Kellan shook his head. "If the creatures are coming out of the water, the deck would be a terrible place to fend them off. We need to control the route they take. That's key to strategy."

"This place is a steel coffin. If disaster strikes, we won't be able to escape."

"I've got good news, *asshole*," Nasir said. He rubbed his hands together and then wiped them off on his leather jacket. "You, me, the kid, and the girl should all leave this place. Maybe we can find those silver ape statues."

"Why would we leave?"

"You want the Kuji breakin' in here?" Nasir shouted as he waved his arms around the mess hall. "*Huh*? The Kuji will only come after us, and the yami will only be heading for the giant *diamond brick* over there. If we stay, everyone will have to deal with the Kuji, and we'll lose. If we leave, the yami won't bother us, because we won't have the diamond. That way our teams *only* deal with yami, and we *only* deal with Kuji, understand?"

"Don't assemble the statue," Kellan commanded. "If one team leaves, we all won't get two keys."

Nasir scoffed and then rolled his eyes. "Don't tell me what to do."

"He's right," Vora stated. "We want both keys. Gather the statue but don't put it together. That way if something happens to one team, we'll have our escape route prepared."

But who would use it? Kellan didn't ask the question because he'd rather not think about it. They didn't have time to argue.

"Go with them," Xiang said to Husker. "We'll be fine here."

There was a short moment of silence. Finally, Husker lowered his head and sighed. "Fine. We'll explore the carrier… But I'm not happy about it."

"Don't go anywhere near the nuclear reactors," Kellan said.

"What do they look like?"

Nasir scoffed a second time and even laughed. "God, you dogs are dumb. Don't worry about it. I'll keep us away from any dangers."

Nosferatu and Gunner both nodded to the Stragglers on their teams. There wasn't much of a discussion. They had no time for that. Kellan didn't protest when they left, though he did worry about Husker. The rennic held his stomach as he ducked his head and headed into the narrow corridor. The carrier was built for humans. Husker had to shuffle his way forward, following Hank, Nasir, and the tiny girl, Jayna.

"We need to seal off four of these doors," Kellan said, motioning to the exits off the mess hall. "The doors can be locked, but I don't know if that's enough. Yami always have some sort of bizarre abilities, like *acid spit* or *rot touch* that can probably waste away the steel of the ship. We'll need to make barriers—something with multiple layers so we have time to deal with the yami as they attempt to get to us."

The more obstacles the monsters had to chew through, the more of a chance everyone in the mess hall would have to prepare. The worst-case scenario would be a surprise attack from an enemy that broke through.

Kellan hated the fact that he knew little about the yami that would be attacking. He knew they were beasts made of corrupted magic and controlled by the Arbiter, but he didn't know their capabilities, which limited the amount of prep he could do before their attack.

The bird-man, Kin, attempted to spread his wings. The black feathers collided with the ceiling and two of the bulkheads. He grimaced as he tucked them tightly against his back. "Listen, most of my magic benefits me flyin' or attacking from range. *This* isn't helping me. I can't do anything here."

"Do you have any magical beams or bolts?" Kellan asked.

Kin slowly nodded. "Takes a bit of mana, though. You want me doin' that right away? Wave one?"

"Just stay near the treasure. If something does break through, use your beam to kill it, all right?"

Vora flexed her fingers, extending her claws a few inches. "You talk as though you've been in situations like this before."

"No, I've never been in a magical death game where monsters were thrown at me in waves," Kellan sarcastically commented. "But tactics from other situations I've been in—or learned about—can be applied here. If *you* have any better ideas, I'm all ears, but *a* plan is always better than *no* plan. We hold this room together, focusing our fire down two hallways. Anyone who isn't useful in this situation, like Kin, stay back and guard the treasure."

"I like your attitude. It's very *rezrah*."

"I'm glad we're on the same page. Now either take a position at the front lines or back." Kellan glanced around at the others. "I don't know what kind of magics you all have. Just sort yourselves—if you can't do that much, we're all probably going to die."

"How should we block the hallways? With chairs and tables?"

Nosferatu placed a disgusting hand on the bulkhead of the carrier. He glanced at the others and shook his head. "Leave the defenses to me."

Nosferatu was an M-rank metal mage, and the moment he pumped mana into the ship, the steel answered his every whim. Four of the six hallways twisted and contorted, the ceilings melting down to the floor and then hardening partway through, creating walls. One after another, after another—Nosferatu made it so that the yami would have to destroy several before they ever got close to the mess hall.

The other two hallways also twisted, but no walls were formed. Instead, a single set of bars melted into place in the middle of the hall, and then the floor shifted and formed into razorblades, all pointed upward, so that anything that walked over it would be thoroughly sliced up.

The perfect choke point.

"You can alter the ship?" Kellan balked.

"The Arbiter didn't infuse this vessel with anti-magic," Nosferatu said matter-of-factly. "This is just normal metal. Mundane electronics. My M-rank metal magic allows me to control buildings and facilities so long as I'm touching a small part of them. This is the perfect environment for metal mages, such as ourselves."

While Kellan had *some* metal magic, he didn't really consider himself a metal mage. Two abilities were hardly anything to write home about. He could shape metal in his hands, and he could determine the function of devices by touching them. Woo.

Vora nodded once. "Metal mages will have the advantage here, for sure." She, too, touched the metal of the wall and molded it.

"We should rearrange the room," Xiang said as she glanced between the tables. "Press them against the sides of the wall or use more to barricade the treasure."

The others nodded.

Mavis, with her new superhuman strength, shoved the tables and chairs with ease. The steel scraping against steel practically made Kellan's ears bleed, but he didn't protest her actions. He turned his attention to the overhead lights, wondering if he could smash a few to lower the number of lumens. If it was dark enough, his *Void Knight* ability would activate, but the rest of the mages would be hindered. Was it worth the trade off?

It's probably more beneficial if everyone can see what's going on.

Even Sen helped out with the room. He dragged one chair at a time, like a child trying to assist his parents. When Sen noticed Kellan staring, he went red in the face and grumbled under his breath.

"I'm plenty capable, *even in this body, gah.*"

Once the room was prepared, everyone did as Kellan asked. They positioned themselves near the doors, or near the treasure.

Nosferatu, Kellan, Mavis, Xiang, Vora, Gunner, and Jace were all in the front, prepared to fight the yami in the halls as they rushed for the mess hall. Kin, Centa, Sen, and Wast were the only ones who stayed by the treasure.

Only Kellan, Mavis, Jace, and Gunner had any firearms; the rest seemed to have thrown weapons or relied on magic for ranged attacks.

Anxiety dominated the mess hall.

The silence between them was thick. Sen coughed, and everyone turned to glare. He ducked down a bit, half hiding himself behind a toppled table. When it was quiet again, everyone returned their attention to the choke point halls.

But nothing came.

The creaking of the carrier as waves battered the sides was their only music. Kellan leaned against the wall, wondering if there was a possibility this was all a joke. Would Bitso do that? Just give them a handful of rules and then film them panicking?

Kellan turned his attention to the ceiling. He spotted one of the Eyes of the Arbiter in the steel beams overhead, its half-organic camera eyes watching without blinking. Observing. Recording. Bitso would surely show all of this after the game.

The minutes marched on.

The first round had already begun, hadn't it? Were the yami just taking their sweet-ass time getting out of the water? Or were they searching the ship for the treasure? Kellan wasn't sure. The mystery ate at him.

No matter what happens, I can't leave this room. We have food and water in the kitchen—there's certainly a bathroom around here. There's no reason to leave. Investigating on my own would mean certain death.

To help distract his thoughts, Kellan turned to Nosferatu. The man stood tall and proud on the opposite side of the door. His thinning hair, and flaking skin, obviously bothered him. Nosferatu pushed his hair back and then cleared away the pus and blister mucus from his forehead with a handkerchief.

"Nosferatu," Kellan said.

The man glanced over. "Yes?"

"Who would you recommend summoning with the Chime?"

"It depends on the situation." Nosferatu smoothed the sleeves of his suit jacket. "One metal mage isn't identical to another metal mage. It depends on the abilities they purchase. If I needed a fighter, obviously someone like Ygg'Exos Vain is ideal. He's a powerful mage, most of his abilities are focused on combat, his master abilities are impressive, and he's not participating in the Nexus Games."

"Master abilities?"

"The special power you get for achieving M-rank in a magic. It's like your *focus* when you hit D-rank, only much more powerful. Some mages even get combo master abilities—for reaching more than one M-rank in different magics."

"And what if you wanted to summon someone for protection?" Kellan asked. "Not killing people but protecting them."

"Hm. I'm not certain."

Kellan waited, hoping the man would elaborate, but he never did.

Another few minutes ticked by. Kellan listened to every creak and groan of the carrier. Were the yami on their way? How long would they have to wait?

The wait twisted around his insides.

"Do you know much about fate magic?" Kellan asked.

Nosferatu glanced over with a frown. "I know some things."

"It can predict the future?"

"Fate magic has domain over time. Past, present, future—speeding time up, slowing time down. And luck, for reasons unknown to me. The visions of the future are not written. They're just *most likely situations* and *probable paths*."

"So, what's the probability future predictions are correct? Like 50%? Or lower? I'm hoping lower."

Nosferatu narrowed his eyes. "Have you recently received an ill-fated vision?"

"You shouldn't listen to the predictions of fate mages," Xiang interjected. She stood near the other door, her back to both Kellan and Nosferatu, but obviously she had been listening. "I spoke to a fate mage about what would happen in the Nexus Games. The fool said I would be part of Team 42. Clearly, he was wrong."

Jace, who paced between the two doors, his blue mechanical eye glowing bright, just snorted a laugh. "I've spoken to a fate mage. He predicted I would die if I faced my father. I haven't yet seen if that's true or not."

"You have a local street-corner fortune teller in your dimension?" Kellan quipped.

"No. Only the most powerful of mages can learn fate magic—no street corner mages can handle such power. The mage I went to was one of the few United-Earth Defense officers left after my Earth fell to the flestiss. I spoke to her before she died defending Overseer Station."

Xiang shot him a glare. "You suspect your father will kill you, yet you pursue him anyway? I told you to abandon your revenge. Your mother wouldn't want this."

"Feh." Jace dismissively waved away her comment. "Stay out of this, whore. I wasn't speaking to you."

Sen barked an insult and toppled a chair as he tried to rush over to his sister.

Vora, Kin, and Wast all chuckled, their laughter adding fuel to the metaphorical fire. Even Mavis moved from her position to step closer to Xiang and Sen, like the scene was about to turn into a rumble. Nosferatu tensed as he placed a hand on the steel bulkhead.

Kellan interjected himself between Jace and Xiang. "Jesus Christ, keep it together. We've only been in the same room for two fucking seconds. Let's pretend like we're good buddies and just fight some monsters."

Jace said nothing. He stared down the twisted hall, no emotion in his expression or mannerisms.

"Are you okay?" Kellan whispered as he faced Xiang.

She glanced up at him through her eyelashes, her eyebrows knitted. "You're concerned about my wellbeing? Jace didn't attack me."

"Maybe not *physically*. I just wanted to make sure you're okay."

Obviously taken aback, Xiang hesitantly nodded. "I… I'm fine. Thank you for asking."

Their conversation was cut short when a loud screech echoed through the corridors of the massive aircraft carrier. Then another. Followed by another. The screeching sounded inhuman and sent a shiver down Kellan's spine. An odd grating noise lingered at the end of each scream.

Kellan returned to his original position. The clack of metal on metal followed the screeching. Hundreds of *click-clacks, click-clacks* filled the ship.

"They're coming," Kellan said as he hefted his rifle. "Prepare yourselves."

And then the first of the monsters appeared at the end of the twisted corridor.

—Chapter 45—
—The First Wave—

Giant deformed crabs. Monsters the size of large dogs. Their shells were black, their eyestalks tall, and their eyes red.

Hundreds of them.

They clawed and scuttled their way in waves toward the mess hall, hissing the entire way. Their legs were the source of the *click-clack*. Each time one of them stepped forward, the needlepoint of their legs clicked harshly on the steel of the floor. Were the crabs themselves as hard as metal? Their shells had a metallic sheen.

The monsters lifted their two claws—one larger, one smaller—as they hit the barrier in the middle of the hallway. Their claws were tough enough to damage the steel, and the first five yami crabs to reach the bars snapped their claws on the metal and tried to cut through.

Kellan lifted his rifle and took aim.

"Kill them," he commanded.

His eyes gave him the information he needed.

Name: Krilli #24,654
Race: Lesser Yami
Magics: Storm, Entropy
Rank: Impossible to Rank
Armor Rating: 5
Health: 6/6

Stats:
Strength—4
Dexterity—4
Fortitude—4
Intelligence—1
Perception—1
Willpower—1

Abilities:

Abyssal—The yami breathes underwater and is immune to entropic damage.
Claw Crush—The yami's claws deal double their strength score for the purpose of damage.

Kellan, Mavis, Jace, and Gunner all opened fire. The hail of bullets filled the corridor as much as the monster crabs. Unfortunately, the metal shells of the crabs reduced the damage they took from the barrage. Thankfully, they were small, and even after their armor rating came into play, they were gunned down one after another.

One crab.

Two crabs.

Kellan kept counting every time he killed one.

Three. Four. Five.

Each crab that died dropped between zero and two arcana. It mixed with the blood of the monsters, filling the hallway with crimson gore and glitter.

Ten.

Fifteen.

Kellan's rifle didn't run out of bullets. He didn't know where the weapon got its ammunition, but it wasn't from a magazine or belt, that was for sure. Mavis, Jace, and Gunner, however, found themselves slowing down their rate of fire. They had to take careful aim, and only fire at crabs that managed to claw their way through the mountain of dead bodies and get close to the door.

Twenty.

The amount of yami was more than he expected. Their bodies clogged the hall, and Kellan had to wait for the rest of them to tunnel through. The razorblade floor didn't seem to make a difference. The crabs had no feet to rip up.

Both halls were wastelands of corpses.

If they *hadn't* been in the mess hall, Kellan had no idea how they would've handled hundreds of crab monsters.

We would've died on the first wave.

Xiang used her mind abilities to pop the brains of crabs who got too close. Nosferatu threw metal, and it sharpened into knives just before striking beasts. Vora did the same thing, just a tad weaker.

The aircraft carrier rumbled. Kellan held his rifle close. The bodies of the dead crabs trembled and shook. Then they were sucked out of the corridor and thrown aside. A monstrous eel-yami the size of a car slammed its way into the hall.

It had the long body of an eel, the claws and eyestalks of a crab, and a mouth filled with teeth. It screamed and hissed as it easily tore through metal. The *krilli yami* had only four strength, but the eel-crab had *fourteen*. It smashed through the metal bars and headed straight for the mess hall, its red eyes glowing bright.

Nosferatu placed his hand on the bulkhead and manipulated the metal of the carrier. The steel shot up from the floor and shot down from the ceiling, like teeth chomping on the monster. The eel screamed as it was impaled, but that didn't stop it. The monster clipped the steel with its claws and then rushed for the mess hall.

The monster lunged for Kellan.

Xiang turned to face it and lifted her hand. A burst of telekinetic force smashed into the yami's crab shell. The beast's body cracked, its teeth shattered, and then its legs folded in the wrong direction. Xiang closed her hand into a tight fist, and the monster balled up in response, crushed by a powerful invisible force. Xiang's telekinesis thoroughly squished the monster until all its blood was squeezed from its eel body.

She dropped the monster in the blood-soaked hall. Five arcana spilled out of its body as it twitched and writhed. Both eyestalks were broken, and its eyes were nothing more than vacant orbs.

Kin, Centa, Sen, and Wast stood close to the treasure. None of them had involved themselves in the fighting. When no new crabs appeared or attacked, Centa stepped forward. She patted at her beautiful white fur and fluffed her tail.

"Impressive," she said. "I thought some of the yami were sure to break through."

Gunner lowered his rifle. "None made it to the doors."

"Is the wave over?"

"I think so," Kellan muttered. "But until we hear from Bitso, it's not official."

As if to answer his implied question, speakers in the mess hall flared to life. After an electronic crackle, Bitso's voice echoed all around them.

"And that concludes wave one! If you're hearing my voice, that means you survived. Sorry about that! Maybe the sweet embrace of death will find you during wave two, but as of right now… you're still, unfortunately, alive."

"That seemed short," Kin said. Once Centa was far enough away, the man spread his wings a bit. "I thought we were going to be fighting for hours."

"We have ten minutes until the next wave hits us," Kellan snapped.

Bitso laughed. "Remember—you only have ten minutes until wave two!" he unknowingly repeated. "So rest and recuperate while you can. Supplies should appear around your treasure in a few short seconds."

Although mana was typically a problem for him, Kellan hadn't spent any during the fighting. He had spent one to *Mold Metal* their surroundings, but none during the first wave.

A few seconds later, objects popped into existence around the treasure. Ten vials of pink liquid, a few sandwiches wrapped in wax paper, and a whole tin container of hane. While Kellan considered the vials and sandwiches more valuable, Kin and Wast immediately dove for the hane. The two of them fought over the container, but Wast—who was significantly larger—easily tore the tin from the bird-man's grasp.

"We shouldn't be fighting one another," Kellan said.

"You can share the smokes," Kin said with a hiss on his breath.

Wast pulled a stick of hane out and held it in his canine mouth. "Make me."

"Don't tempt me, *fool*," Sen said from his side of the mess hall. He rubbed at his upper arm, and the Tyranny Worm there, though Kellan wondered if anyone else knew that.

Kellan ran a hand down his face and prayed to Baby Jesus for the strength not to shoot all of his "teammates." Why couldn't they just get along for an hour or two? Just a little bit. *God, it would be so pleasant.*

After Wast lit up his hane, and the smoke wafted through the mess hall, Sen grabbed the other supplies and passed them out. The hane restored mana, but so did the pink vials. Each was a mana potion worth ten mana restoration. The sandwiches—which were ham and mayo—healed an individual of five damage after consumption, as well as curing any poison or purging any toxin.

"This is gonna be easy," Kin said as he unwrapped a sandwich and nibbled it.

"Save those," Kellan snapped. "You don't have to eat it now."

Kin frowned. Then he wrapped the sandwich back in its wax paper. "What're you so butt hurt about? You were right. This is a good place to defend. Those creatures didn't get anywhere near us."

"The waves get progressively more difficult. Did you see the last beast that tried to get us? It almost reached the doors."

No one said anything. They generally nodded. The eel-crab was in plain view—right in the middle of the distorted hallway.

The arcana from the first wave was scattered in the hall and throughout the carrier beyond. The bodies had been flung around, after all, which spread out the arcana. They needed those crystals, though. Kellan knew they couldn't leave them.

"Jace, help me collect the arcana," Kellan said.

The man turned and straightened his leather jacket. "Yeah, all right."

"We're not going to let you have all the arcana," Wast growled, his black fur standing on end. He stomped over to the exit, his claws scraping against the floor as he went.

"They'll bring it back," Nosferatu said as he held up a hand.

The others all gave each other quick glances. While no one else said anything, Kellan felt the tension in the room. Everyone wanted the arcana, sure, but they couldn't risk just leaving the room to search the ship.

Mavis walked over to Kellan. In a low voice barely above a whisper, she asked, "You want me to join you? Just in case?"

"No, I want you to stay here and watch the treasure. Just make sure nothing happens to it, and that no one touches it, not even one of the other players."

"Why?"

"I'm just worried," Kellan muttered. "Better safe than sorry."

Mavis nodded once. "You can count on me."

He offered her a short smile. "You're the only one I can count on here."

The statement made her honestly blush for a moment. She brushed back her dyed hair and smirked. "We'll get through this."

With that, Kellan headed for the door. Jace moved to his side as they stepped into the gory hall. The insides of crabs decorated everything. The floor, the bulkheads, the ceilings—if Kellan had some butter, they could all eat well for several weeks.

Jace took off his jacket as he knelt. A couple arcana glittered in a pool of blood. Instead of picking it up with his bare hands, Jace used his jacket to pluck it out of the carnage.

Kellan went ahead and kicked the body of the eel-crab over. The five arcana was still there, shimmering with power. He wanted to pick it up for himself, but he knew they needed to count everything first. There were eleven mages defending the treasure—*eleven*—and seven of them had actively helped in the fighting. They would need to split the arcana seven ways at the bare minimum.

Jace and Kellan scooped up stray arcana all throughout the twisted hallway. Then they turned a corner and found the dozens of crab bodies strewn about. The eel had thrown them aside to make way for its giant body.

The arcana lit up the halls with an eerie red glow. The glow from the crystals reminded Kellan of Christmas lights, but the scarlet hue was anything but festive.

Jace collected a couple, always using his jacket to pick them up. Kellan used his shirt and the sleeve of his jacket. Neither of them touched anything.

When they were a good distance from the mess hall, Kellan asked, "Why do you want to kill your father?"

Jace continued collecting arcana as though he hadn't heard the question. His mechanical eye glowed blue, a harsh juxtaposition to the crimson hue of the hall.

"I think my curiosity is justified," Kellan said as he grabbed another thumb-sized crystal. "I mean, your father is *Alternate-Me*. I'd like to avoid the same mistakes as my other-self."

"You're not going to make the same mistakes." Jace's words were so cold and curt, Kellan almost didn't recognize him. "You're *obviously* a better version of my father. Well, except for magically. My father has years of experience as a mage. And you don't."

Kellan kicked over a crab corpse and grabbed another arcana. "Yeah, well, no one is perfect."

Jace knelt, and then stopped searching for arcana. He just stared into a puddle of blood, his blue eye reflecting across the liquid surface. "My father… He betrayed the United-Earth Defense Force."

Kellan stopped collecting the arcana in order to better pay attention.

"When the Flestiss Dominion attacked, he joined Brenner Hawke's defectors. They helped the invasion force." Jace glared at the blood. "Me, my sister, my mother… He didn't care about us. He didn't warn us or help us. It was *his* division of defectors that attacked our sector. My mother and sister didn't make it out alive. I almost died as well."

Jace slammed his hand in the blood. It splattered across his jeans and boots and soaked his palm. Then he lifted his hand and stared at his red fingers.

"It was a pretty bad day," he intoned. "To say the least."

"Why'd he do it?' Kellan asked. What would've possessed the man to act like that?

"To save his own life, probably," Jace said as he stood up. He wiped the blood off on his T-shirt, leaving a handprint straight out of a horror show. "What does it matter? I promised my sister and mother I'd see him pay for what he did. So here I am."

"You're not in the Nexus Games to get to Zenith?"

"No." Jace shrugged. "Well, that's not true. I think… Maybe Zenith has the power to change things. I don't know." He shrugged and forced a chuckle. "I mean, Zenith's capabilities are so vague. But things like *fate magic* exist. You can't travel through time, but what if the people of Zenith can? And if I can't—at least I'll have the magic to kill my father if I fail to get him in the games."

"Seems petty," Kellan stated.

Jace shot him a glare. "Yeah? Well, you can fuck off. I don't have anything left. I don't have a home. I don't have a family. And I certainly don't have a father. It's either *this*—" Jace held up his arms and motioned to the bloodbath, "—or *nothing*. I might as well go with petty."

Kellan held up a hand. "No. I get it. Sometimes revenge burns so hot, it chars away all other thoughts and feelings." He grabbed another arcana and walked over to place it in Jace's jacket. "Forget I said anything."

After a prolonged moment of silence, Jace said, "I was surprised when I saw you were part of the games. I mean, I figured Xiang would do something shocking, but including you was a new low I didn't think her capable of."

"It was actually her brother who brought me here," Kellan muttered.

"Still. I guess I'm trying to say…" Jace turned around and grabbed another arcana, his back to Kellan. "I'm glad a different version of my father exists. Someone I got to meet and see and speak to. My father… He just doesn't care about anything except himself. You're the exact opposite. You're so insane—you've been saving everyone for almost no damn reason."

"Sorry about that."

"Don't apologize." Jace smiled to himself. "I just said it was a good thing." He stood and then offered a one-shoulder shrug. "If you had been on Earth when the flestiss attacked, I think you would've done everything in your power to save your family."

"Of course."

"And that's all I really wanted from him."

Kellan wanted to ask more—to talk about his alternate-self in more detail—but their conversation was cut short. The speakers flared to life again, Bitso's voice booming louder than ever.

"You have two minutes remaining before the next wave begins! Prepare yourself now, because you won't get another chance."

"We should get back to the others," Jace muttered. He glanced down the hall. With a wave of his hand, the shadows sprang to life and acted on their own. Tentacles lifted up, grabbed arcana, and slithered over to him, dumping everything they had missed into Jace's jacket.

"Why didn't you do that from the start?" Kellan asked.

Jace shrugged. "It uses up mana. I figured we'd have enough time to collect things by hand, but you decided we should have a heart-to-heart instead. This one's on you."

With that, the two of them headed back to the mess hall. By Kellan's estimate, they had one hundred pieces of arcana—which wasn't a bad haul.

—Chapter 46—
—The Second Wave—

Jace set his jacket full of arcana in the middle of the mess hall floor. Kellan's estimates had been correct. They had one hundred arcana. The pile of glittering crimson drew everyone's attention. The many mages of the four teams moved closer, though no one made any sudden movements. A few shot suspicious glances around the room.

"That's *all* you found?" Centa asked. She scratched at her wolf ear and flashed her fangs. "How do we know you didn't just absorb some?"

"We really don't have time to cast doubt," Kellan stated. "Since we have eleven people, and this can't be divided evenly, I'll take the hit so that everyone else gets the same amount."

"Why would you do that?" Centa showed even more of her fangs. "It only proves your guilt."

Kellan wanted to run a hand down his face. Dealing with certain people just wasn't worth it. There was no winning.

"That's my best offer," Kellan stated. He turned his attention to Nosferatu, Xiang, Gunner, and Vora—the team leaders. "Does that sound okay to you all?"

Nosferatu held up a finger. "I suggest we give arcana to those who participated only. I'm not in favor of subsidizing larger teams of mages if some of them did nothing."

"Who would you suggest gets the arcana?" Xiang asked, politeness in her voice.

"If it weren't for my metal magic, this entire tactic wouldn't have worked as well as it did. And if it weren't for Alex Kellan's planning, we still would've been bickering in the hangar. We should get the majority of the arcana—twenty each—and those who fought should split the rest."

Xiang crossed her arms and narrowed her eyes. "I love how you preach teamwork, but then passive-aggressively berate everyone who isn't at your skill level. Not the fastest way to foster cooperation."

"But it will instill a sense that *hard work is to be rewarded*." When Nosferatu frowned, his skin twisted. "I know murderers like yourself prefer to farm the helpless citizens of the Nexus for your arcana, but that won't be the case here."

Kellan understood why parents loved the *Quiet Game* so much. Literally no one could open their mouth without stirring the pot.

He stepped into the middle of the room, near the arcana, and held up a hand. "Listen, we don't need to attack each other with snide remarks. We have literal monsters to worry about. All of this is small time compared to that."

"My people aren't *small time.*" Nosferatu turned on his heel and stood next to one of their open hallways. He placed his hand on the bulkhead and warped the metal to fit the bars back into place. "I keep careful track of how many have died at the hands of the Nexus Games players… Xiang's mother, the winner of the last games, slaughtered hundreds. She's following in her mother's footsteps well."

No one said anything.

Kellan glanced around. Most people—except for Nosferatu's teammate, Wast—seemed disinterested in the conversation, or were too busy staring at the arcana in the middle of the room. How many of them had killed Nexus locals?

Mavis and I might be the only ones who haven't just outright murdered all the people we've come across.

The bird-man, Kin, fluttered his raven wings. A black feather fell to the floor. "I'm pretty sure the Arbiter said we could kill the locals. You can't blame us for that."

Nosferatu didn't reply. Once he was done rearranging the hallway, he removed his hand from the wall and remained silent.

"It's either *get arcana* or *get yourself killed.*" Kin scoffed. Then he tightly folded his wings to his back. "The Nexus locals are all messed up anyway."

"*Enough,*" Kellan said, interjecting himself into the conversation. "We're splitting the arcana evenly, to avoid this bullshit. Everyone take ten arcana, and let's shut the hell up until the next wave."

The group didn't protest. One by one, they walked over to collect their crystals. Since there was only one hundred, and there were eleven mages in the room, Kellan had opted not to take any to make sure the others felt they were justly compensated. However, when it came time for Sen to take his arcana, he absorbed only five.

"You should take the rest," he said with a dismissive wave of his hand. "You're a lower-ranked mage than me, and Nosferatu did make a point. You were the one with the plan." Sen turned on his heel with a huff before Kellan could respond.

When Xiang went to absorb her arcana, she only absorbed five as well. She gave Kellan a quick glance, but otherwise said nothing about it. No scene. No fuss. She returned to her position near the choke points, her statuesque posture something out of a modeling magazine.

When Wast approached, he nodded to Kellan. He said nothing, though.

Mavis absorbed her arcana and then frowned. "Why would you give up yours?"

"I prefer gold arcana in general," Kellan stated. "And arguing at this point is foolish." He smirked. "Besides, my CO always said a good leader makes sure his troops are happy before making himself happy."

"We're your troops now?" Mavis playfully asked.

"That's right. We have infantrymen, and strategists—" he motioned to everyone near the choke points, "—and we also have the platoon mascots." He pointed to everyone standing near the treasure, especially Centa and her large tail. "The perfect team."

She stifled a laugh and shook her head. "Are you just always making jokes in your head? We're in the middle of a death game, ya know."

"That's when you need jokes the most." Kellan could only muster half a smile. "I told you that you'd get sick of me."

"I'll be the judge of that."

The rest collected their arcana, including Nosferatu, without another word. Once it was all said and done, Kellan had ten arcana all for himself, even though he had tried to give it away to the others.

[Alex Kellan] absorbed 10 arcana.

Kellan immediately used four arcana to purchase *Sun's Rays*, a C-rank eclipse ability that added a flat two damage on top of all his light attacks. It would enhance his laser beam, and his new sword ability, though it wasn't the strongest enhancement. Still, he liked stacking the bonuses.

He had six arcana remaining.

I still don't have a bladed weapon. Kellan turned his attention to his rifle. *Sevriss, my gun, can become a sword. Somehow.* He slung his backpack off and rummaged through the inside. He still had the Mermaid Knife that Millie had used. It was an odd weapon—one that worked well on everyone but the Nexus locals. It was just a knife, though.

The speakers crackled and popped with static. Then Bitso's voice rang out loud and clear. "I know what you're thinking. *What if one team takes the treasure and disappears? The yami won't have anything to be attracted to.*" A loud bang thumped over the speakers. "Wrong! The yami will be attracted to all life once that treasure is gone. Players, Stragglers—everyone. It'll be a mess, trust me."

Kellan sighed. He really didn't want to think about nightmare scenarios. He stared at the treasure locked behind the makeshift cage. It was just a shimmering diamond out of everyone's reach.

"Oh!" Bitso said. "Look at the time. The second wave is about to begin. Good luck, chumps! Perhaps you'll shuffle off your mortal coil this time."

The speakers cut out, leaving the room with only the groaning of metal as the aircraft carrier tilted slightly with the waves. Kellan held his breath. The monsters had to storm out of the water and make their way to the mess hall. They had a few minutes of silence until then.

Everyone returned to their previous positions. They remained still and antsy. When Sen sneezed, several people jumped, including Mavis.

The wait was excruciating.

Kellan could think of nothing but the attack, and what they would do afterward. He tried to mull over his six arcana, and where best to spend it, but he didn't have the focus necessary. His heart hammered with each passing second.

When the sounds of the yami filled the distant corridors of the carrier, everyone tensed. Kellan positioned himself next to Nosferatu, hoping the wave would be just as easy as the first.

The first yami appeared.

It was an eel-crab hybrid, just like before. Eel body, crab claws, and crab legs to help it move across the ground. The eyestalks stretched up a good foot in length, and the whole creature had to weigh as much as a car. It whipped down the hall, some of its eel body catching on the razorblade floor. The monster tore itself up as it ran into the steel bars. Then its claws snipped through the metal, and the beast slammed through.

Nosferatu had seen the previous yami cut their way through—why hadn't he made the bars thicker this time around to compensate? Kellan cursed under his breath as he opened fire with his rifle. Was *everyone* incompetent? Or were they just *that* terrible at combat tactics?

The eel-crab took several bullets to the body, but it wasn't until its head exploded from Xiang's *Mind Blast* that it finally slumped to the floor of the hall and died. Arcana emerged from the pool of blood forming around its amalgam body.

Before anyone could get settled, several more of the creatures entered the two choke point hallways. Gunner and Mavis opened fire, but they tried to conserve their bullets. Reloading took time.

Nosferatu used the metal of the carrier to his advantage. He crushed some of the eels, but their strength and claws proved superior to the steel. They sliced through, hissing the entire time, their red eyes gleaming with hate.

No matter how many obstacles Nosferatu made, or how many spikes he created to jut down from the ceiling, impaling the monsters in the head, more arrived, and they destroyed his fortifications.

They still died before making it to the room, but each time a new one arrived, it came with another buddy. Three rushed the corridor at once, their slender bodies mashed together as they tried to squeeze their way into the mess hall. It made it easier to hit them—they were just a writhing mass of flesh—but it made it difficult for Kellan to focus on one.

An eel-crab almost busted into the room, simply because it was lucky enough to live all the way to the door. Once again, Xiang's *Mind Blast* killed it.

Vora attacked a few by throwing bits of sharpened metal. Her metal magic made it so the steel bits shifted shape after striking the enemies. They dug around the insides of the beasts, damaging them over time.

The steel-alloy ceiling groaned in protest.

No one else seemed to hear it—not through the screech of the yami or the constant barrage of firepower. But Kellan had. Just faintly.

And it wasn't the ceiling in the hallway that was groaning—it was the ceiling in the mess hall. Kellan glanced over his shoulder just in time to see the metal above them corroding and rusting. A yami rotted its way through the ceiling and crashed into the middle of the mess hall. It wasn't an eel-crab, like the others…

It was some sort of lamprey. A disgusting fish with a snake-like body. It, too, was the size of a car. Its mouth was like a blender of sharp fangs. That was how Kellan knew it was a lamprey—they had circular mouths used for suctioning themselves onto larger fish. Lampreys drilled holes into the fish and then consumed them from the inside out.

Truly horrid creatures.

Kellan's analysis gave him more information on this one.

Name: Juvel #1,090
Race: Greater Yami
Magics: Storm, Entropy
Rank: Impossible to Rank
Armor Rating: 10
Health: 50/50

Stats:
Strength—16
Dexterity—12
Fortitude—8
Intelligence—1
Perception—1
Willpower—1

Abilities:
Abyssal—The yami breathes underwater and is immune to entropic damage.
Rotting Bite—The yami's bite deals entropic damage to its target and inflicts a DOT (damage over time) that deals 1 damage every six seconds for a full minute.

Kellan pointed to the four people standing near the treasure. "*Kill it!*"

Sen didn't really have any way to attack. He was small—a child—and backed away toward the cage with the diamond inside. He used his shielding on the others, but otherwise didn't really have a means of attacking.

Centa used her natural weapons. She leapt forward like only a wolf could and dug her black claws through the body of the lamprey monster. It hissed and attempted to bite her, but it wasn't fast enough. Wast dove around the other side of the creature and also used his wolf-like claws. He slashed at the creature's tail and back.

Kin held up a hand and blasted the monster with electricity so powerful it arced from Kin's hand and almost jumped to the chairs and tables. The crackling of energy created a cloud of static that fizzled everyone's hair.

The lamprey roared, but for a few seconds after the attack, it seemed stunned. Centa continued to slash at the beast, cutting into its body like she was digging for buried treasure and just about to reach the chest.

Kellan couldn't help with the lamprey. He was too busy shooting at the eels in the hallway, watching as they tore through the steel environment like scissors through paper. Why were they so strong? When one got too close, Kellan spent two mana to use his laser beam—eighteen damage when he took into account his new C-rank eclipse and *Sun's Rays* ability. The eel squealed as it died.

The lamprey thrashed its snake-like body, slamming into the tables and chairs stacked against the bulkhead. It hit Wast aside and then it bit Centa, its circular mouth clamping down on her shoulder, its hundreds of tiny fangs drilling into her beautiful white fur. Blood wept from the many injuries, splattering across the floor.

With a burst of magical power, Centa's claws elongated and sharpened. She gouged the lamprey monster in its head, scooping out its brains in one brutal attack. The monster went limp, but its teeth remained hooked in Centa's shoulder.

Sen hurried to her side and used his body magic to heal her. The entropic rot continued to damage Centa, but Sen managed to heal her again before she could die.

Once again, the sheer number of yami during the fight was insane. Their bodies clogged up the halls. And Kellan kept his eye on the hole in the ceiling, fearing a second lamprey would use the entrance as well.

Between crushing some of the eel-crabs, Nosferatu turned his attention to the hole. He pressed his fingers harder on the bulkhead of the carrier, and the steel of the ceiling stitched itself together, repairing itself before any more monsters could plunge in.

Jace controlled the shadows to stab into more eels, and Xiang telekinetically crushed some of the yami trying to force their way inside. It didn't take long before the number of monsters waned. Little by little, the wave ended, only this time the halls were so filled with blood, guts, gore, and arcana, that no one would be able to fit.

The stink of death filled the mess hall. Anyone looking to eat would have to have an iron stomach.

Jace, Mavis, and Gunner all put their guns down.

"I'm out of ammo," Mavis muttered.

"I'm almost out." Jace tucked his handgun into its holster. "Not enough for three more waves, that's for sure."

Gunner nodded once as he slung his rifle back onto his shoulder. "I should last through another wave, but that's it." He glanced over at Kellan. "This is a military vessel?"

"Yeah." Kellan pointed to some of the navy markings. "I thought it was from the United States, but I don't recognize the flag symbol on most of the crew instructions. It's some sort of alternate-Earth carrier, but these ships are *only* made for military purposes. No one books a cruise on an aircraft carrier."

"So there might be supplies around."

"There are missiles somewhere," Kellan said with a chuckle. "But we don't have time to search for them."

The others glanced between each other before sighing.

Centa sat down on the floor and pried the dead lamprey from her shoulder. Then she sighed, her wolf-ears laid back against her skull. “Dammit.”

“What’s wrong?” Sen said as he circled her. “I’ve healed you of all your damage! There shouldn’t be anything wrong with you.”

She growled and flashed her fangs. Then she held up her left hand. Her number, 80, was prominent on her white fur. But underneath it was a new marking.

A little skull.

“Hank died,” she said through clenched teeth. “I’m our team’s new Straggler.”

—Chapter 47—

—I Hope You're Okay—

Hank Gardener had been with Kellan in the first game. Technically, Kellan had saved Hank from the Kuji that round. It seemed a shame that the Kuji would catch up to him only three games later. But Kellan couldn't worry about that.

"Hank was a good human," Gunner muttered. He rubbed at the brand on his head. "Hank taught me a lot about how humans lived on his world. It was a fascinating place. Unfortunately, we won't be able to bury his body like he requested..."

Centa snorted. She stood and then attempted to wipe some of the blood from her white fur. "The Kuji are more fearsome in this round. Hank was clearly the weakest one among us. It makes sense he died."

"Let me help you with that," Wast said. He patted down her beautiful fur, using his own jacket to do so. At one point, he even fluffed part of her tail, his own tail wagging.

She growled and jerked out of his touch. "Keep it to yourself, asshole."

The speakers crackled as they sparked to life. Bitso's voice chimed through loud and clear. "The second wave is over! Prepare your bodies for the third wave. It's my favorite."

Bitso had no other words of advice or descriptions of how the game would proceed. He cut off early, leaving the teams in silence.

More healing items appeared around the treasure, but fewer than before. They gained one sandwich and only three vials of pink liquid. They still had their supplies from the first wave, but this told Kellan valuable information.

They were going to get fewer and fewer recovery items, despite the fact that each wave would become progressively more difficult. If they didn't ration out their recovery, they might not have enough.

Kellan cursed under his breath when he remembered that Wast had already smoked one of their hane.

"I need two of the mana potions," Xiang said. She walked over and grabbed one off the ground. "Using my *Mind Blast* and *Telekinesis* requires a decent amount of mana." She threw back one of the vials, drinking it in a single gulp. When Xiang went for another vial, Wast stepped in her way.

"You can't have them all," Wast growled, his fur on end. "Nosferatu needs mana as well." He snatched up the other two vials and brought them over to Nosferatu. The hideous man drank both.

Xiang wore a neutral expression during the exchange. She neither fought nor complained. Instead, she went over to the original ten vials near the treasure and picked up another one. "Since I'm one of the mages constantly using my abilities, I think it's only fair I get one extra."

"*We need to save them,*" Wast barked.

No one else interjected.

Kellan knew about Xiang's extra hexes, though. She had one that required her to have mana at all times. If she ran out, she'd die.

"She can have my share," Kellan stated. "Xiang's magical attacks are powerful. We need to have them ready."

"Your laser is rather impressive," Nosferatu said matter-of-factly. "I see you've been using meta magic to empower your attack."

The others in the room raised eyebrows. Even Gunner seemed a little more interested than before. They hadn't been able to see his magics due to Xiang's protection. Just as Kellan sometimes got the word *concealed* when glancing at someone's abilities, they apparently couldn't see his.

Why would Nosferatu reveal to everyone that Kellan had meta magic? It was rare—most people couldn't learn it—and Kellan had wanted to keep it a secret so that enemy teams couldn't prepare for his magic ahead of time.

Wast gathered up the sandwiches and the vials and brought them all over to Nosferatu. He didn't seem interested in Kellan's unique magic.

These are supposedly our allies, Kellan thought with a sigh. *In theory, I should be able to trust them all. But…*

Millie's warning rattled around in his head. Was he going to die here? No. He had gathered enough gold arcana to pick up another apex ability. He would be fine. Or so Kellan hoped.

While Kellan thought over his situation, Sen walked to his side. The kid looked him up and down, and even frowned at his clothing. "Why aren't you wearing your magical armor?"

"It requires a mana to activate," Kellan said.

"You should have it on! You never know when someone will burst through the walls or floor next. Clearly, most of these yami aren't stopped by metal. Haven't you been paying attention?" Sen's voice went louder with every word.

Kellan smirked. "I like to live on the edge."

"You have the life expectancy of a trout on land!"

"*Shh.*" Kellan leaned down closer to Sen. The others were giving them sideways glances. "I know what I'm doing." Kellan tousled Sen's hair.

Sen flailed his arms and ripped his head away from Kellan's touch. "How dare you. I'm a full-grown man who deserves respect." Then he flounced over to the treasure cage, grumbling something under his breath.

Although Kellan hated—with a small passion—the Tyranny Worms in his body, they *had* kept him alive through impossible circumstances. Kellan would never admit it. Ever. The fact that they could semi-control his body was too much. He hated them, even if they wanted to keep him alive through a war zone.

"How are we gonna get our arcana this time?" Centa asked as she walked over to a choke point hallway. She stared at the pile of gore and then huffed. "There's arcana in there… I can smell it."

"I'll get it," Jace said.

He waved his hand through the air. The shadows answered his summons, the darkness in every corner slithering out as a physical tentacle to search through the dead bodies and bring them arcana. The shadows weren't sentient, though. Jace had to stand at the front of each choke point and use the darkness like a tool. He carefully picked through the bodies of the eels, pushing the guts aside in order to find the valuable crystals underneath.

Vora paced back and forth in the room, her clawed feet making a clicking sound with each step. Her silver scales were quite striking. The room was made of metal, but the metallic sheen of her body had a luster unrivaled by the cold steel.

Vora caught Kellan staring. "I know you've seen rezrah before," she said. "You helped out my kind when you saved Levvy from the Arbiter's wrath."

"You're interesting," Kellan stated.

"Be careful," Centa whispered. "He's a weirdo. One of those inter-species pervs, I'm tellin' you."

"I prefer humans, thanks," Kellan sarcastically replied.

"Uh-huh."

Vora exhaled. She watched Jace collect the arcana in his leather biker jacket. "Rezrah are natural-born warriors." Vora seemingly spoke to no one, but Kellan understood that it was for his benefit. "Most rezrah value physical and magical strength. The Nexus residents claim they're descended from a primordial dragon—the Arbiter—but rezrah believe the same thing, just with Malcibur, the primordial dragon of Eveon."

Kellan slowly nodded along as he drowned in *Proper Noun Soup*. He sometimes found it difficult to imagine there were so many mages, places, mythologies, and magics—just so, so many. If he managed to live through the Nexus Games, and actually see Zenith, he'd use whatever magic he got there to visit all the other dimensions.

"It's a lie," Nosferatu muttered. "Only the people of the Nexus are true descendants of dragons."

Vora glowered in his direction. "You're a little high and mighty, aren't you?"

"My people have been killed for far too long. Decades of watching their blood fill every river, lake, and ocean will change a man."

After motioning to the scales on her arms and legs, Vora said, "I look the part of a dragon. Unlike you. You look like a dumpster."

A few chuckles circled around the room. Kellan didn't catch who all laughed, but he knew it wasn't Wast. The rennic growled at everyone, his fur on end, his claws slightly protruding from his fingers.

Jace finally finished plucking the arcana from the carnage. He set the pile in the middle of the room using his shadows. The sparkling red crystals killed all other conversation. Unlike last time, where they only had one hundred, this time they had closer to one hundred and fifty.

"I think we're going to make it," Jace said with a smirk. He rubbed at his forehead, clearing the sweat away from his machine eye. "I'm surprised. Two rounds in, and none of us have died. I know the Stragglers are having a hard time… But not *us*."

Centa sighed. "I'll need to leave." She glanced at the hallway. "Is it clear enough for me to get out?"

Jace nodded. "Yeah. You should be able to get out. Be careful, though. You don't want to be on your own too long."

The two exchanged a quiet stare. They weren't on the same team—Jace was 77, and Centa was 80—but for a brief moment, it felt like they were comrades. Centa even acknowledged it with a toothy smile.

"I don't get arcana before I leave?" she asked with a purr in her voice.

The one hundred and fifty arcana stared back at everyone. If Kellan took a hit to his own arcana, everyone else would get thirteen, and he would get seven. That wasn't too much of a drop, and it was certainly better than arguing over who got what.

But if Centa left, and then they divided everything, everyone would get fifteen arcana each.

Wasn't fair to Centa, however.

"Wait," Kellan said. "We have to talk tactics for a moment."

Everyone gave him their attention, though they had varying levels of irritation. Kellan didn't care. He was going to figure the damn game out whether or not anyone gave him any help. If it came down to it, he would drag everyone over the finish line kicking and screaming.

"The first wave had tons of smaller yami, the crabs, and one large yami, the eel. In the second round, we saw *no* crabs. The second round was tons of eels, and then a single even larger yami—the lamprey. Which means—in all likelihood—the third wave is going to be tons of lampreys and one *even larger* creature."

No one replied, but the dawning realization was easy to see across their faces. Had no one thought of this? The only people in the room who *weren't* surprised by the info were Xiang and Nosferatu. They listened with hard expressions, never indicating their true feelings on the matter.

"The lamprey could rot through the metal," Kellan said as he motioned to the ceiling. "Which means wave three is going to complicate things. We need to figure out how we're going to corral the yami, and we have to do it fast. Either Nosferatu needs to shape this whole area with thicker patches of metal or we need to make a hole in the ceiling ourselves so we can control where the yami enter from."

"You want a hole in the ceiling?" Sen asked.

"We can't have the yami surprising us in the middle of the fight." Kellan pointed to the heaps of dead bodies. "But thankfully, the monsters are stupid and animalistic in their desire to destroy. They clearly charge forward without any planning or tactics. The lamprey rotted through the ceiling because the hallways were blocked, not because it was a master strategist. That means if we make a hole, the lampreys likely won't create their own. They'll use the pathways provided, so long as they aren't blocked."

Jace frowned. "But then they'll be inside. The last one almost messed us up."

"Sen, Wast, and Kin will just have to be prepared for the monsters. They'll deal with the hole, and we'll deal with the hallways. Perhaps we should even open one other hallway, to make sure the monsters always have someplace to travel. The real trick will be resource management and making sure we have a way to kill the yami without running out of mana or bullets in the middle of a wave."

"Do you really believe this will allow us to win?" Gunner asked.

Kellan shook his head. "The escalation from the first wave to the second means the third wave will probably be the last one we can just stand here. Once the third wave is done, we should search the hangar for warheads. Those missiles can be detonated. We can use them to clear a large amount of yami."

"And damage the ship?" Sen practically shouted. "What if we accidentally sink the ship? We'll lose the game!"

"Aircraft carriers are difficult to bring down. We can damage the ship a little before we need to worry." Kellan motioned to Nosferatu. "And we have a master metal mage. You can repair it, right?"

Kellan remembered seeing a power like that at D-rank of metal magic.

> **Repair [1 arcana]**
>
> One of the most common and most useful abilities, this power allows a metal mage to return something to its proper, ordered state, taking the inherent structure of an object, and returning it to that base.
>
> The metal mage spends a mana, and any single, non-magical object of up to person size is repaired.

Kellan figured some rank above D would have a stronger version of the power. And if there wasn't one, Nosferatu always had thc ability to rearrange the metal in the nearby area and fix damage from a missile strike. They didn't need the carrier to last forever—just until the end of the game. One missile wouldn't sink the ship. Everything would be okay.

"You're really thinking this through," Wast muttered. He turned his attention to Nosferatu. The two just stared at each other for a long while.

"I like this plan," Gunner said. "The Arbiter probably put us in this location for a reason. The ship is clearly meant for war purposes, and we're in a war with the monsters. We might as well take advantage of the natural supplies the carrier offers."

Kellan replied with a curt nod. "Look, none of us here have died yet. We can prevail that if we cooperate and stick to a plan. Nothing will kill a team faster than a single person deciding mid-operation that they want to do something else. So, as long as everyone pulls their weight, we'll be fine."

The statement seemed to resonate with the others. They nodded slowly and gave each other cooperative glances. Except, again, for Xiang and Nosferatu. The two of them exchanged cold looks.

"What does this have to do with me?" Centa said with a frown. "I'm a Straggler now."

"You should go to the others and tell them the same thing," Kellan stated. "If the four of you cooperate, there should be less death."

"I don't know where they are."

"Go to the operations tower on the flight deck. Since the carrier clearly has power, and the speaker system functions, you might be able to tell them to meet you in a specific place."

Centa's frown grew more prominent. Although Kellan had spoken a language she could understand, the concepts were clearly too much to handle. She was a rennic, after all. Had she grown up in some sort of tribal society away from technology as well? Kellan didn't have time to describe how to use an intercom system to someone who knew nothing about it.

"What about the one hundred and fifty arcana?" Centa asked. "I want some of that before I leave."

The speakers flared to life again, cutting her off. Bitso's voice, more monotone than Kellan had ever heard, echoed throughout the mess hall. "The third wave will begin in one minute."

Then silence.

Was Bitso okay? Kellan worried about the man probably more than he should. He was an insane newscaster, after all. He would probably be okay. Probably.

"When this game was announced, I thought for sure we would fail to have all four teams live through it," Nosferatu said. His odd statement garnered everyone's attention. "But it seems fate has smiled upon us. Not only did our combination of teams give us someone familiar with the setting, but it gave us someone to manipulate the setting as well."

"But that disappoints you," Xiang stated. She remained tense as she said, "You haven't been pleased with the setup since we arrived here. You haven't even been using your abilities to their fullest extent."

"We only have a minute before the next wave begins," Kin muttered. He frowned. "We don't have time to keep arguing."

Nosferatu smirked. His twisted features and grotesque appearance gave him a sinister expression, even when jovial. "You haven't been using your abilities to their fullest extent, either. If you wanted, there could be illusions up and down these hallways—illusions powerful enough to trick the yami. But you didn't offer up a single one."

Kin half-flapped his wings. "Less than a minute, really. What's wrong with you all?"

"Illusions wouldn't be as useful," Kellan stated. "Obviously, the monsters will go through walls to get to us if they think they have no other option. All the illusions would do is slow them from getting to us. We need to—"

"The way you defend her is contemptible," Nosferatu said, cutting Kellan off.

With a sneer, he added, "You're a good man, Alex Kellan, but you've been roped together with a murderous witch. She doesn't deserve someone like you on her team."

"The name calling isn't helping. We only need to pretend to be friends for just a short while longer. For the love of all that's holy, can we please just cooperate?"

Nosferatu placed his hand on the bulkhead, his fingers digging into the steel of the carrier. "I had assumed the Arbiter's yami would've been too numerous and too powerful for a grouping of four random teams. I thought you all would die without my assistance. I had *planned* on saving you, Alex Kellan, and asking the Arbiter to make an exception to have you join my team once the rest of yours was dead. You're the only one who has treated my people with respect, unlike these other *dogs* and *murderers.* But now I must do things differently."

The ship's metal rippled like water.

In a matter of seconds, the entire mess hall rearranged itself. Nosferatu's magic acted so quickly, and without mercy, that Kellan couldn't react to the first of the attacks.

A portion of the ceiling slammed down on Kin, while a portion of the floor under his feet lifted, crushing the bird-man in one brutal blow that sent blood, organs, and arcana splattering across the room.

At the same time, Centa turned, perhaps to run, but it was too late. Steel spikes shot up from the floor, piercing her feet, legs, and torso. She screamed as she tried to pull herself free, but the ceiling formed into spikes as well, shooting down and piercing her head. Her scream died with a gurgle as her wolf-like body was skewered in place. More arcana and blood spilled onto the floor.

Gunner lifted his rifle and fired on Nosferatu.

But Nosferatu had twenty armor rating and ten shielding. Most of the bullets bounced off a magical shimmer—the shield—and those that broke through didn't have the power to rip through Nosferatu's metal-infused skin. The bullets ripped up part of his suit, but nothing else.

Kellan turned his gun on the lights in the room.

He shot out all ten bulbs within a single breath, casting the whole mess hall in darkness. The only spots of light came from the glittering red arcana. The pile in the center of the room was a swarm of fireflies, the crimson hue adding to the murderous atmosphere.

Although the others were mostly blind, it didn't stop Nosferatu. The room contorted, and Kellan's foot slipped into the metal, similar to quicksand. Mavis, Sen, Jace, Vora, and Xiang were in a similar situation, trapped by the steel of the carrier.

Gunner continued to fire. The blast of his rifle gave away his position.

The ceiling and floor turned on him, the spikes slamming through his body from multiple directions, dealing so much damage that he died nearly instantaneously. The arcana that spilled out with his blood added to the growing red illumination.

But there weren't enough lumens to stop Kellan from being empowered.

Perhaps out of fear, perhaps out of desperation, Nosferatu tried to collapse the whole ceiling down on most of the room—even over Wast, his teammate. But the metal groaned in protest, and only collapsed *half* the way.

Xiang held out a hand, and using her telekinesis, stopped the steel in the room from moving. The metal fought against her. It was Nosferatu's abilities versus Xiang's. Fortunately, Xiang's artifact necklace gave her extraordinary power—obviously more than Nosferatu could muster. When more spikes tried to form, Xiang stopped those as well, the pressure of her magic filling the mess hall with an almost high-altitude atmosphere.

By stepping into the shadows, both Kellan and Jace freed themselves from the clutches of the steel around their feet. Once capable of moving around the room, Kellan reached into his pocket, hoping to grab his Summoning Chime.

But that was when Wast attacked.

—Chapter 48—
—Using the Summoning Chime—

With claws glowing white-hot, Wast swiped at Kellan. Not only did his claws brighten the area, but they also sizzled in the air. They were so hot, they cooked everything they touched, even little flakes of dust floating all around them.

Wast's claws sliced through Kellan's flannel shirt and jacket. Kellan used a mana to summon his armor. The future-tech spread from his spine and covered most of his body in a thin, protective layer.

He was down to thirteen mana.

Kellan searched his pocket, his movements frantic as Wast swiped again. This time, the massive ten-foot-tall werewolf caught Kellan's arm, searing through his bicep. Kellan grunted as he was knocked to the ground. He only took one damage thanks to his armor rating, and Sen's shimmering protective shield. Kellan ignored all the notifications, even the Tyranny Worms, as he tried desperately to just focus on the fight in front of him.

Kellan's Chime fell from his pocket and rolled across the floor.

No one else could use it, but in the glowing red light of the blood-soaked mess hall, Wast saw what Kellan's intention was.

The rennic reached into his own pocket as Kellan dove for his Chime.

"Ygg'Exos Vain," Wast said.

A *ding* reverberated through the aircraft carrier, sending a shudder through the very environment. Then Wast's Chime shattered into a puff of dust.

Kellan grabbed his Chime. "*Ygg'Exos Vain.*"

His Chime also sent a reverberation through the ship. But unlike Wast's, Kellan's only cracked a little.

Invalid Target

Kellan caught his breath.

He couldn't summon someone already under the control of another Summoning Chime.

"*No!*" Nosferatu roared. "We needed our Chime! *Not now! You shouldn't have used it!*"

But it was too late. Kellan's heart raced as he remembered the video footage of Ygg'Exos Vain descending from the sky to help Xiang's mother. It had taken him a moment to arrive, but once he did, he had destroyed everything in a nearby radius. Wast would surely order the Tyrant King to kill them all.

Mavis unleashed a wave of fire through the room. It washed over Wast, but the giant rennic just ran through her flames and attacked her directly. His white-hot claws sliced through her face and chest. If not for Sen's shielding, Mavis would've likely lost her lower jaw.

Shadows lashed out from all directions. Tentacles, shadow claws, blobs of darkness—they all attacked Wast, tearing at his fur, ripping flesh, and even smearing across Wast's eyes, actually blinding him. Jace moved to the corner of the room, obviously trying to kill Wast, but keeping his distance.

Wast's burning claws tore right through the darkness, and the rennic slashed at everything around him, his frantic thrashing enough to send embers through the air.

Vora managed to free her clawed feet from the floor of the mess hall by molding the metal away from her ankles. She leapt up and then lunged for Nosferatu, but the Nexus resident had too much armor. Vora's claws were razor sharp—obviously enhanced through her magic—but they wouldn't pierce his skin. His clothes were shredded. Then Nosferatu slammed a bit of steel from the ship straight into her chest. Vora gurgled a scream as she staggered backward.

A magical *presence* settled over the aircraft carrier.

Although Kellan didn't know for certain, he suspected it was Ygg'Exos Vain, the legendary killer mage, finally arriving. Was he on the flight deck? Did it matter? He would soon be *here*, and there were only a few options to save them all.

Kellan reached into his backpack and withdrew the Mermaid Knife.

He needed a bladed weapon. *Any* weapon.

Then he activated his *Neo Excalibur* ability. It cost him three mana. He was down to ten.

The Mermaid Knife was only eight inches, but then light flared into existence all around it. The knife became a sixteen-inch short sword. The extended length of the weapon was completely gold laser-light crackling with inner power. The weapon weighed next to nothing. It was just a knife—the empowering magic over it added nothing to the heft. When Kellan swung it, the laser blade made a *swish* noise.

Wast growled as Kellan swung again. This time, Kellan hit Wast in the arm.

The Mermaid Knife originally dealt strength plus three, minus the target's fortitude. Kellan's strength was nine. But *Neo Excalibur* added double his eclipse rank—six—on top of that. And then *Sun's Rays* added an additional two.

And if the Mermaid Knife was used against non-residents, it ignored all shielding and armor. Plus, it stole unused arcana.

The weapon cleaved through Wast, sending his blood, and a single arcana, across the room.

Kellan had dealt sixteen damage and stolen an arcana. At this rate, he'd win the fight in a few swipes.

But Nosferatu must've known. While he was in a fight of willpower with Xiang—the two of them trying to control the entire ship either through metal molding or telekinesis—Nosferatu opened a hole in the middle of the mess hall. Xiang attempted to close it, but her telekinesis wasn't as fast as Nosferatu's fluid ability.

Wast tumbled down to the deck below.

Nosferatu was trying to protect him.

Kellan *could* give chase—if Wast died, perhaps Ygg'Exos would be released from service?—but they didn't have time.

The *presence* was upon them. The killer mage was here.

The far door to the mess hall didn't open—it folded outward, the metal completely warped from something on the other side. A man stepped into the mess hall, a mix between a *roided-out* gladiator and an Old Testament angel. He had long blond hair, dark tanned skin, and white wings that barely fit in the area. And the man only wore pants—his arms, feet, chest, and neck exposed, all bulging with muscle. It was enough to make most bodybuilders feel inadequate.

Name: First Councilor of Psi, Ygg'Exos Vain, Tyrant King
Race: Lindolphan
Magics: Mind, Body, Soul, Metal
Rank: M, M, M, S
Armor Rating: 10 + 25 Shielding
Health: 100/100 [Body Mastery]

Stats:
Strength—25 [Body Mastery, Zen Combatant]
Dexterity—22 [Swift, Accurate]
Fortitude—28 [Body Mastery, Tireless]
Charisma—15 [Regal]
Manipulation—8 [Dark]
Intelligence—5
Perception—10 [Insightful]
Wisdom—8
Willpower—20 [Indomitable]

Abilities:
Personal—[Mind Over Matter]—The mage adds half their willpower to all defensive checks against enemy magical abilities and powers.
Personal—[Descended from Zenith]—The mage has the raw magic of Zenith in their blood and has no rank maximum. The mage can also develop one "unknowable" magic.
Personal—[Superiority]—The mage grants temporary +1 to 3 random primary stats (spread out, can't be the same) to all lindolphan citizens under his rulership. The mage also imposes a one stat penalty on all

> rezrah under his rulership. These stat fluctuations disappear when the mage's rulership ends.
> **Personal—[Royal Bloodline]—**The mage's children all have an additional +1 to their willpower.

With stats and abilities like that, it didn't matter how well Team 101 fought. Kellan only had one option.

He slipped into the darkness and then emerged near the makeshift cage that held the treasure. His *Mold Metal* was still active, but when Kellan touched the cage, his magic couldn't seem to overpower Nosferatu's—the man's ability still had hold of the ship. Kellan instead used his laser sword to cut the bars. The Mermaid Knife effortlessly sliced through the steel. Kellan grabbed the giant diamond and then threw it as hard as he could.

His aim was true.

The treasure smashed into Nosferatu's face. But the man's bones weren't damaged—not with his shielding and armor. He probably wasn't even hurt *that* badly. Kellan didn't care. In the next moment, Nosferatu and his teammates, Wast and the Straggler, were instantly teleported away.

Ygg'Exos Vain vanished along with Wast.

Jace's eyes went wide. He whipped his attention back to Kellan. "You sent him away?"

"I had to." Kellan took in a ragged breath, trying to regain his composure. "They used their Summoning Chime."

Sen crawled out from under a table. "You could've used that treasure to send *our team* to safety, you buffoon!"

Kellan didn't respond. If he had thrown the treasure at Xiang, he *could* have saved Team 101. But then he would've left Team 77 to die at the hands of Nosferatu and their summoned ally. Since *he* had been the one to bring them here, Kellan couldn't bring himself to just abandon them.

With the help of the Tyranny Worms, Mavis's face was completely healed by the time she leapt to Kellan's side. "Do you hear that? The ship… The yami are on their way. I'm surprised they haven't gotten to us yet."

"We should go to the hangar." Kellan turned to the others. "We'll use the warheads there."

They only had six people.

Xiang, Mavis, Sen, Jace, Vora, and Kellan.

They weren't enough to hold the mess hall, not when they didn't have Nosferatu's ability to completely shift the environment. If they used explosives, perhaps they'd have enough strength to destroy the yami during this wave.

"I can't believe Nosferatu betrayed us," Sen said, his volume set to *shout*. "That inbred bastard! *We were going to win!*"

Jace chuckled darkly. "I've never liked those Nexus residents. Something about them is always off. Like this whole damn dimension."

"He's a fool! An ingrate! We had this in the bag… It's not *our* fault the Arbiter doesn't care about his kind! Nosferatu should be enraged at that lunatic dragon, not us!"

"Quiet down," Kellan shouted. "We need to leave. *Now.*"

"Grab arcana before you leave," Jace said. His glowing blue eye homed in on the dozens of arcana shimmering all around them.

Kellan did exactly that. He headed for the door, but on the way he grabbed several crystals.

[Alex Kellan] absorbed 27 arcana.

He didn't stop to grab any more. Kellan headed down the bloodstained corridor and then for the hangar. The groan of metal, and the hiss of distant monsters, rang in his mind. When he turned down the hall, a yami leapt at him. The giant lamprey monster hissed as it flew for his face.

Kellan swung the light sword, slicing the beast in its giant circular mouth. The yami collided with him, and they both hit the floor. Xiang held up a hand and used her *Mind Blast*, exploding its brains in a mere instant. Then Mavis grabbed Kellan's arm and jerked him to his feet. Mavis's superhuman strength made the task effortless—Kellan was practically flung upward, his shoulder sore after the encounter.

They continued on, Kellan's mind racing.

When they entered the hangar, Kellan turned his attention to the giant openings that overlooked the ocean. A storm raged outside the aircraft carrier. Wind. Rain. The waves… The ship was too large to toss around, but the ocean was trying its damnedest.

Salt water sloshed into the hangar from the two giant openings. The holes in the side of the ship were used to load planes, helicopters, and cargo without having to place everything on the flight deck first. The openings could be closed, but Kellan didn't have time to figure it out. Instead, they would have to deal with the weather getting into the ship.

Lamprey yami shot out of nearby hallways, and a few even slithered up the side of the carrier and entered through the large cargo holes. At least a dozen headed their way, each with a ravenous hunger, their mouths open, their circular rows of teeth flashing.

Xiang gritted her teeth. She crushed one with her telekinetic power—like a bug in an invisible hand, being slowly squished by balled-up fingers—and then used her *Mind Blast* on another. When it became clear she couldn't just kill them all in an instant, she created illusionary walls between the yami and everyone else, confusing the beasts and stalling for time.

The walls appeared like the rest of the carrier—steel and riveted. The yami screamed and attempted to destroy them or go around. Xiang had to create more and more illusions, leading them in a circle as they tried to attack.

"There!" Kellan shouted.

The warheads were kept in cargo containers marked with warnings. He ran over and struggled with the crate. It was locked. Using his *Mold Metal*, Kellan destroyed the hinges, and then with his super strength, slid the lid off. It hit the floor with a loud *clang*. Inside were at least two dozen missiles, the types loaded into fighter jets—*air-to-air missiles*.

Which meant they were filled with fuel and their own rocket motor.

"*Xiang*," Kellan called out. "Can you move these? If you crush them with enough force, you'll cause them to explode. But we can't be near them."

Xiang stood in the middle of the hangar, breathing hard. The yami were slowly dying, but more had burst into the hangar from the far hallway. At least eight new lampreys hurried through the hangar, one even crashing into a helicopter in its haste to get ahead of the other monsters.

"Sister!" Sen called out.

She finally turned. With a shaky hand, she motioned for the crate of warheads to move. Her telekinesis was so powerful, the whole steel alloy box of two dozen missiles scraped along the floor of the hangar, screeching with metal-on-metal as it went from the cargo area to the center of the hangar.

The whole crate had to weigh multiple tons, yet she moved it anyway.

Once it was in place, Xiang forced herself to jog over to Kellan. She was breathing heavy, her whole body shaky. Then she altered her illusions to funnel the yami toward the crate. The massive lampreys shot straight for them, some crawling over the crate of missiles.

Kellan dragged Xiang to the nearest door and threw it open. Everyone ran inside. Then Kellan pointed back to the crate. "Crush it now!"

Xiang didn't argue. She lifted her hand, used her *Crush* ability, and the box of warheads exploded.

Not a subtle explosion. It rocked the whole carrier with an apocalyptic rumble that could be heard from land. Kellan threw himself into the corridor and shut the door, but even that wasn't enough to save them from the violent shaking of the ship. The explosion sent a wave of force through the hangar, smashing several planes and helicopters, and even ripping holes in the decks above and below.

Kellan gulped down air as he steadied himself. Xiang kept the door in place with her telekinesis. Once the quaking was over, everyone took several breaths.

"Is everyone okay?" Kellan asked.

Sen, trembling, nodded his head once. "I don't think we're going to make it."

Jace brushed himself off. Then he stopped, his attention on his left hand. Right underneath the number 77, a skull had appeared.

Which meant Jace was now his team's Straggler.

"Oh, fuck me," Jace whispered.

Kellan immediately glanced at his hand. No skull. None on Sen's or Mavis's either. Husker was still alive somewhere. But now that the treasure was gone, the yami would be attacking anything and everything. The Stragglers would have to contend with the monsters *and* the Kuji.

Kellan's knife faded and returned to its normal self. He tucked it back into his ragged backpack.

"Did we kill all the yami this round?" Mavis asked. "How can we even tell?"

"Bitso will tell us," Kellan muttered.

"So, what're we going to do now?"

Everyone turned to Kellan, their eyes wide. Kellan grabbed at his bloody and ripped-up shirt. They were all waiting on *him* for a plan? He closed his eyes, calmed himself, and remembered his emergency training and protocol for ship emergencies.

There was a control tower…

The intercoms.

"We need to get to the flight deck," Kellan stated. "We'll head to the control tower and use it to tell Husker to meet us there."

"We want to bring *another* Straggler to us?" Vora asked. She glanced between everyone, her expression one of shock and disbelief. "We need to form a plan to stop these monsters."

Kellan shook his head. "We might as well all be together. Husker has a hex that can kill damn near anything. We might need it."

—Chapter 49—
—The Third Wave Continues—

Kellan, Sen, Mavis, Xiang, Jace, and Vora made their way through the narrow corridors of the *CVAN Renegade.* At one point, Xiang stopped and leaned against the bulkhead. Everyone else slowed and turned around.

"What's wrong?" Sen asked.

Xiang reached into the pocket of her red leather jacket and withdrew another small, pink vial. She drank the contents and then exhaled. "I apologize. All the magic use has taken its toll."

Sen whirled around on Kellan. "Carry my honorable sister!" His words were almost a command, but the Tyranny Worms didn't react.

With a sigh, Kellan turned his attention to the overhead lights. Without his added fortitude and strength from his *Void Knight* ability, carrying Xiang would be a toll.

"I'll do it," Mavis said. She pushed aside the others and strode over to Xiang. For a moment, it seemed as though Xiang would protest, but Mavis scooped the other woman into her arms before Xiang could say anything. Like any good superhero, Mavis carried Xiang like a new bride, one arm under legs, one under her back.

Xiang wrapped her arms around Mavis's neck. "I would've preferred Alex."

"We all would," Mavis quipped. "But he's too busy carrying *two whole teams* through this game, so here we are."

Jace and Vora both chuckled to themselves. They were the last remaining members of Team 77. Somehow, through everything, Team 101 had yet to lose a member. The longer they were away from Husker, though, the more worried Kellan got for the man.

"We need to keep going," Kellan said. He motioned toward a door. "If we go through there, and then up the ladder, we'll be back to the flight deck. We need to cross the deck and head for the control tower. That's where we can use the intercoms."

Normally in an emergency, Kellan was supposed to use the radio to call for help. But this was the Nexus Games. There was no help, and the Net around the game arena would prevent anyone from getting in, even if there was another ship out there.

The others remained silent as Kellan opened the door, headed up the ladder, and then emerged on the deck of the ship. The massive aircraft carrier was being beaten by the rain. Buckets of water fell from the sky, the white noise of the storm so loud it made it difficult to hear anything else.

The storm kept everything dark. Kellan preferred it that way. Once he was out on the night-covered deck, his enhanced strength returned to him.

At the far end of the carrier was the machine dragon. It stalked the ship with its mechanical wings spread wide. The display on its shoulder read: DANGER. Which meant they were still in the third wave of the game.

But where were the yami?

Kellan glanced around. He didn't see any. None rushed for him from the ocean, and they didn't see any in the corridor. Was there a weak and injured yami somewhere? Was it dying a slow death? Or perhaps one was hunting down Husker…

After a short exhale, Kellan jogged over to the control tower. It was rather tall, and the lights were on inside, creating a fishbowl effect. Kellan opened the door to the tower and motioned for everyone to follow him. Sen, Mavis, Jace, Vora, and Xiang all hurried across the flight deck, with Mavis still carrying their team leader. Once inside, Kellan stepped in and shut the heavy metal door behind him.

The sound of rain became a dull patter barely heard through the thick walls of the carrier's control tower.

They stood in a large entrance room with several desks and computers. They had enough space to spread out, and most everyone leaned on something.

Soaking wet and shivering, Mavis placed Xiang down on her feet. With a wave of her elegant hand, Xiang's appearance shifted from *pathetic survivor of a hurricane* to *runway model with beach hair*. She removed all blood and damage signs and fluffed her shimmery black hair until it looked as though she had just exited a shower commercial.

Then she glanced over at Kellan, her eyes narrowed.

For a long moment, no one said anything.

"Let me guess," Kellan said, his voice terse. "This is all my fault. This is what I get for trusting people. You knew better."

Xiang just smiled. "I was going to thank you for getting us out of that mess."

"Is that right?"

"The fact of the matter is—your plan would've worked. The teams were cooperating, we had the situation under control. But Nosferatu decided his grudges were more important than our collective victory. While I hate being put into a situation where I had to fight for my life to get out, it was satisfying to see his Summoning Chime disappear, and for him to lose all that arcana. He obviously thought we would roll over and die, and he would walk away with over two hundred arcana for his trouble."

Kellan rubbed at his chin as he pictured all the arcana in the mess hall. If everyone but Nosferatu and Wast had died, there really would have been more than two hundred there.

"I improved my telekinesis for this exact situation," Xiang said with a more genuine smile. "Phantasmal damage is better against individuals with low willpower, which means mages like Nosferatu are basically immune to that attack. He couldn't handle my new levels of telekinesis, though. And if I hadn't needed to protect everyone, I suspect I could've crushed him. Well, given enough time. He's rather *tough* for a wrinkled and disease-ridden bastard."

After mulling over what he knew about Xiang's magical capabilities, Kellan leaned in close and asked, "Why didn't you use your travel magic? You could've teleported him away."

Xiang shot him a glare. When she glanced over her shoulder, it seemed as though none of the others had heard. Sen was busy healing everyone, and Jace was pointing to a map on one of the bulkheads.

"I still don't want them to know," she whispered. "And my teleportation wouldn't have affected Nosferatu. He has too many defenses. He would've had to have consented to the teleport, and I doubt he would've allowed me to teleport him into the ocean."

"Why not teleport us around the ship? It'd be faster than walking."

"If we *need* it, I will. But I'm low on mana as it is, and teleportation requires a mana per person shifted."

Ah. The real reason Xiang wasn't teleporting them around. She couldn't afford to zero out her mana.

The speaker in the control tower flared to life. Kellan tensed and glanced upward, though he still couldn't spot any speakers around.

"Oh, good news," Bitso said with a chuckle in his voice. "The third wave *is over*. That means if you're hearing this, you're still in the running! You could still get a key. You just need to hang in there. Wave four will soon commence. Ten short minutes. Use them wisely."

The speakers died out with a *zap*.

Had Husker defeated the last of the yami? It was the only explanation. Kellan sighed as he crossed his arms. What was their new plan? How could they survive two more rounds? What was the best strategy that would ensure that they would all live?

Gunner and all of Team 80…

They had died during Nosferatu's betrayal.

The thought of their deaths sent a lance of empathic agony through Kellan's chest. He rubbed at his shirt, his jaw clenched. Their deaths were Kellan's fault. He had invited them into the game. He had invited Nosferatu.

Xiang placed a hand on the side of his arm. "I don't know what you're mulling over, but it's not the game." She removed her hand and then ran her fingers through the locks of her hair. "Focus. Everything else can be dwelled on in the future."

"Heh. Sometimes I think I might be defined by my mistakes, rather than my successes." Kellan still couldn't move on from the death of his former Delta Force teammates. What if it happened again, in the twisted dimension of the Nexus? What if he was just doomed to repeat it, over and over, and this was some sort of hell he couldn't escape?

"I think that a lot," Xiang whispered. "But I refuse to let it be reality. You're strong enough to pull yourself out of this. So do so."

Mavis broke away from the others and walked to Kellan's side. She patted off his wet jacket and offered a smile. "Are you okay?" Then Mavis held his arm close. "You have a look on your face that says something's wrong."

He glanced down at her and forced a smirk. "I just need to think of a plan."

"We'll think of something. Maybe we can find a helicopter."

"The Net won't allow us to leave. And I don't think anyone here knows how to fly a helicopter." Kellan thought over his magical abilities and then shook his head. "Actually, I take that back. I have a metal power that would allow me to fly helicopters just fine." He snapped his fingers. "We need to find the intercoms. Husker needs to know we're here."

Mavis nodded right away. "Okay. They're probably in the observation room. It's only two floors above us." She pointed to the map Jace had found. "We should do that as soon as possible."

The two of them headed to the narrow stairway. Xiang, Sen, Vora, and Jace allowed them to leave without another word. Kellan preferred it this way. He needed time to think, and having multiple people speak to him would only be a distraction.

Together, Kellan and Mavis made it all the way up to the observation room. All four walls were gigantic windows. Rain pelted the glass, creating a waterfall curtain that distorted their vision of the flight deck below. The machine-dragon was clear as day, though. The screen on its shoulder read: DOCILE.

Kellan went straight for the intercoms. He tapped the controls and set the communication to *ship wide* before grabbing the microphone. "Husker," he said. "This is Alex Kellan. We abandoned the mess hall. I repeat, we abandoned the mess hall. Team 5 betrayed us and has left the game. Team 77 is still our ally. We're holed up in the control tower on the flight deck. I repeat, we're holed up in the control tower on the flight deck. Please make your way to our location as soon as possible."

Then Kellan clicked off the microphone and turned to Mavis.

"Do you think he's still alive?" she asked.

"He has to be. None of us are the Straggler." Kellan glanced at his hand again. He still didn't have a skull, and neither did Mavis.

She placed a hand over her heart. "Thank goodness." Then Mavis frowned. "We still have two waves to get through, though… Do you have any ideas? Maybe more missiles?"

Kellan glanced out the large windows that overlooked the flight deck. The downpour made it difficult to make out any details, but he knew there was damage to the carrier from the massive explosion of warheads. They couldn't keep doing that going forward. And it wouldn't guarantee that every yami would die. Just some.

"We need another plan," Kellan muttered.

"We have fewer mages. And fewer resources. The treasure is gone… We didn't get any sandwiches or vials."

"Hm."

"You… You think we'll make it through this, right?" Mavis furrowed her brow. "I mean, you think it's possible?"

"Yeah. It is."

"Say it with more confidence. Please."

Kellan slowly pulled her close. She was cold and wet, and Kellan wrapped his arms around her, hopefully in a comforting way, even if his mind was elsewhere. He had to devise a plan. What *could* they do?

"We'll make it through this," he said with as much confidence as he could muster.

Mavis exhaled and pressed her forehead to his chest. "Thank you."

After a prolonged moment, where Kellan counted the seconds, realizing they had wasted two whole minutes, he said, "We have several options, but I think we're going to have to use the Summoning Chime."

Mavis frowned. She pushed away from Kellan and stared up at him with her disapproval written in every facial feature. "I thought it only lasts fifteen minutes? That's not long enough."

"It is if I use it once wave four is underway. If we can gather the creatures, and then have a powerful mage kill them all, we'll wait another ten minutes, and then have the mage do it all over again. We'll be cutting the timing short, but hopefully it will work."

"Who will you summon?"

Kellan reached into his pocket and withdrew the Summoning Chime. "I think I have an idea. But we need to tell the others first."

—Chapter 50—
—Arrival of the False Sun—

"You want to summon *Councilor Zero*?" Sen balked.

Everyone sat on the tops of nearby desks. They weren't standard wooden desks found in homes or schools. They were sturdy desks meant to withstand the devastation of war. Each was made out of heavy metal parts fastened to the floor and wall to prevent it from sliding around. The computers had been shoved to the side to allow everyone a better sitting area.

Sen was the only one with his legs crossed in front of him. He looked like a child on a field trip when compared to everyone else.

Jace leaned back on his desk, supporting most of his upper weight on his posted arms. "I don't know who that guy is, but if he's strong, he has my vote."

"You don't know who Councilor Zero is?" Vora scoffed. She sat up straight, her scaled tail hanging off the side of her desk, the tip flicking back and forth. "He's one of the most talented rezrah mages of all time. He fought Ygg'Exos Vain and lived to tell the tale."

"But he didn't win," Sen muttered under his breath.

Vora's claws extended from the tips of her gargoyle-like hands. "What was that?"

"You heard me."

Vora leapt down from her desk, her tail fully swishing around. "Ygg'Exos is a cheat and villain. A rezrah would never stoop to his level of tactics. Councilor Zero protected his kith and kin."

Kellan held up a hand. "Listen, all I need to know is... Will Councilor Zero win two waves of this game all by himself?"

"Certainly," Vora said as she crossed her arms. "I'd bet my life on it."

"You are," Jace quietly quipped.

Xiang half shrugged. "I'm not so certain. I've never actually seen him in battle."

The door to their control tower opened with a loud creak and the screech of metal scraping against metal. Kellan tensed as he turned on his heel. To his surprise, and delight, Husker stumbled into the room. His reddish fur was soaked through and hung heavy over his massive nine-foot-tall body. His fox ears were low, and his mouth remained open as he panted.

Mavis was the first to rush to his side. She helped him over to a desk, and he braced himself on the edge.

"Are you okay?" Mavis asked.

Husker shuddered. His clothing was ripped up enough that his chains were exposed. The sheer amount of water his fur was holding made it seem like he was twenty pounds heavier. "I'm not…"

"You look sick."

"I barely made it here," Husker said through gritted teeth. "The Kuji… It's protected. It had some sort of helmet. And shield…"

The crackle of the speaker was like music to Kellan's ears. He glanced up, hopeful to hear good news from Bitso. Instead, the insane news anchor just laughed.

"You have exactly one minute before the fourth wave begins! Good luck."

The madman chuckled for a solid thirty seconds before the speaker cut out. Although that wasn't exactly the news Kellan was looking for, it was good enough. He walked over to Husker, gently patted the man on the back, and then asked, "Are you going to be okay?"

"I think so," Husker said between strained breaths. "My stomach… It's ached since we arrived."

Sen slid off his desk and hurried over. "It has? And you said nothing to me? Have you lost your mind? I know all there is about healing!"

"I'm sorry… I didn't have time." Husker reached into his coat and pulled out two silvery objects. He placed them on the desk, each one clattering around until it came to a stop. "I found… these…"

They were two pieces of the silver ape statue. One was the base, and the other was the midsection. The statue was no longer than a person's arm. If they found the last piece, one team could leave. But only one.

Sen touched Husker and used his body magic to heal the rennic. Husker seemed to breathe easier afterward, but it was clear he wasn't completely better. When Sen attempted to heal him a second time, Husker pushed the kid away. "Enough," he growled. "You need to save your mana… I'm good for now."

Kellan wanted to ask Husker about his thoughts on using the Summoning Chime, but the rennic was clearly not in the mood to entertain such discussions. Xiang had offered very little input. Did she care if they lost the Chime? Or was she more concerned with living and winning the game? Kellan couldn't tell.

Their minute came and went.

The storm outside ceased.

No more rain. Even the wind seemed dead.

Kellan gritted his teeth, his anxiety greater than before. He hadn't seen the new type of yami for the fourth wave. Whatever it was, he was worried for everyone's safety. He wanted to make sure everyone else made it through the game—no matter what. He couldn't allow the others to die just because he had trusted Nosferatu.

"I'm going to handle the wave," Kellan said to the group. "You all wait here and defend this position."

The others stared at him with wide eyes. Kellan headed to the control room door and exited, the screech of metal his only goodbye.

When he got out to the flight deck, his attention went to the dragon. It stood at the far end, its shoulder lit up with the word: DANGER.

"No shit," Kellan muttered to himself. Then he reached into his coat and withdrew the Chime. He clenched it in his hand, his heart beating hard.

The waves of the ocean roiled and crashed against the side of the ship. From the depths rose squid creatures, their tentacles grasping for the edge of the carrier. They were the size of a large school bus, their skin dark purple and black. Each had a bulbous head covered in human eyes. When one pulled itself up onto the flight deck, Kellan got more information.

Name: Tintly #56
Race: Greater Yami
Magics: Storm, Entropy
Rank: Impossible to Rank
Armor Rating: 5
Health: 80/80

Stats:
Strength—18
Dexterity—14
Fortitude—12
Intelligence—1
Perception—5 [Multi-Eyed]
Willpower—1

Abilities:
Abyssal—The yami breathes underwater and is immune to entropic damage.
Crushing Grab—The yami deals double damage to anything it has wrapped in two or more of its tentacles.

The yami thrashed its way around the flight deck, smashing fighter jets that were chained down. At least four of the squids were dragging their way to the control tower. The flight deck was gigantic, however. Kellan had a minute or so before they reached him.

"Of course," Kellan sarcastically muttered. "Well, let's see how this works…" He clenched the Chime close. "Councilor Zero—real name, Zarr Mantis—I hope to god you're not an invalid target."

The Summoning Chime rang out with a resonating *ding* that shook Kellan to his core. Then the Chime disappeared. It shattered and puffed away as brilliant dust. Somehow, deep in Kellan's soul, he knew the Chime had worked. He felt another *presence*, just like when Ygg'Exos had entered the game arena.

The disgusting squid yami pulled themselves closer and closer. Kellan hefted his rifle as he waited for his *summoned mage* to arrive. Kellan took aim and shot one as it hurried in his direction. The bullets ripped through the soft body, but it only seemed to agitate the monster.

Kellan held up his hand and shot one of his lasers at another. It ripped a hole through its bulbous head. Kellan was down to eight mana.

But then something strange happened. The shadows across the whole aircraft carrier stirred. They moved as one, lifting up from the darkness and grabbing the yami before they could reach Kellan. They weren't aggressive or attacking—the shadows, all of them, just latched onto the yami like spiderwebs. Four more yami exited the water, and they were grabbed too.

The monsters screamed and thrashed. Their tentacles slapped across the deck. A few pulled at the bindings. But nothing worked.

That was when the mechanical dragon started its ominous march down the flight deck. Each step it took, a loud *clang* rang out over the ship and ocean. It had a long way to reach Kellan, since it was at the end of the runway, but Kellan knew it would light up everything with its laser breath if it managed to get close enough.

Then a mage rose out of the darkness only inches from Kellan. Then the mage hovered in the air a foot off the flight deck.

Kellan flinched, shocked at how silent the arrival had been.

The mage was a rezrah with scales and skin as dark as night. His irises were red, but he didn't have white sclerae, like normal individuals. His sclerae were as black and void-like as his scales.

Raven wings adorned his back. Not normal bird wings, but feathers made of liquid ink that dripped at the tips with each and every movement. Even the man's clothes were born of shadows and rippled as though pure liquid. He wore armor, tight to his body.

Kellan already knew who this was, but his analysis insisted on giving him more information regardless.

Name: Councilor Zero, Zarr Mantis, Reborn from the Void of Black Stars
Race: Rezrah
Magics: Eclipse, Metal, Entropy, Fate
Rank: M, S, M, S
Armor Rating: 20 + 15 Shielding + 10 Shadow Shell [Metallic]
Health: 67/67 [Cyborg-Enhanced]

Stats:
Strength—22 [Cyborg-Enhanced, Powerful]
Dexterity—16 [Cyborg-Enhanced, Swift]
Fortitude—22 [Cyborg-Enhanced, Reserves of Strength]
Charisma—3
Manipulation—16 [Dark, Occult]
Intelligence—5
Perception—14 [Cyborg-Enhanced, Keen-Sighted]

Wisdom—18 [Mystic]
Willpower—12 [Determined]

Abilities:
Personal—[Nullify]—The mage nullifies the personal abilities of any mages that face them as an opponent in battle.
Personal—[Descended from Zenith]—The mage has the raw magic of Zenith in their blood and has no rank maximum. The mage can also develop one "unknowable" magic.
Personal—[Void of Black Stars]—The mage has been reborn within the ultimate darkness and ranks their eclipse magic at only 50% the normal cost per rank. Additionally, the mage's affinity for eclipse is doubled, and the mage's wisdom score is tripled for the purpose of eclipse abilities. The mage's blood now runs black.
Personal—[Magical Oath]—The mage has sworn themselves to a cause. They have vowed to eradicate all mages with the last name of *Vain*. If this mage comes across such an individual, the mage will be compelled to carry out their oath.

Kellan looked the man up and down. His tail had scales practically made of obsidian. His claws were scarred and chipped, but still sharp in the places that mattered. If anyone was descended from a dragon, it was Zarr Mantis.

A chill breeze from the ocean reminded Kellan that he was under time constraints.

"Councilor Zero," Kellan said.

The rezrah turned to him, his red eyes something haunting. They reminded Kellan of arcana.

When Zarr didn't answer, Kellan said, "Can you kill all the yami, please? The squids. All of them. As quickly as possible."

The rezrah returned his attention to the monsters. They were helpless—stuck in a trap of inky tar and shadows. When Zarr waved his clawed hand, a powerful magical force took over the area.

[Zarr Mantis] used *Arrival of the False Sun*. The eclipse and fate combo power slows the time around all enemies and speeds up the time around all allies. Enemies with a 14 or higher wisdom score can ignore the slowing effects. While the *False Sun* is present, all light-based eclipse powers in the area are doubled. The *False Sun* remains for 24 hours.
[Alex Kellan] is empowered by the *False Sun*.

Kellan held his breath as he turned his attention to the sky.

The storm clouds parted as an orb descended toward them. The orb itself was a sphere of darkness with a ring of brilliant gold shining all around. The glowing halo of light was enough to create an afternoon glow over the entire aircraft carrier. Somehow, deep in Kellan's soul, he knew this power was one of the apex abilities.

Councilor Zero had collected enough gold arcana to improve his master power.

The False Sun hung overhead, larger than a blimp, shining with an eerie, but powerful, glow that altered the colors of everything nearby. The black of the flight deck, the white of the control tower, and the purple of the squids were all muted and distorted, practically hazy around the edges.

Zarr waved his hand a second time.

The darkness dragged the yami under, pulling them into a void. The squids shrieked the entire way, fighting against the dark prison, but in slow motion. Even their voices were warped by the slow way they did everything. They lacked the magic or tools necessary to free themselves.

Once they were pulled into the shadows, they never emerged again.

As the mechanical dragon slowly drew near, the shadows ensnared the beast as well. But unlike the monstrous squids, the dragon wasn't pulled into the darkness. Just as Kellan had suspected, the dragon opened its mouth and evoked a beam of laser that cut through the void. It tried to free itself, but the more it struggled, the more the darkness fought to keep it in place.

Kellan glanced away, relieved they had such a powerful mage on their side.

"Thank you," Kellan said.

Zarr didn't acknowledge him. He stared at the far dragon with his glowing red eyes. When more squids crawled their way onto the deck of the carrier, the shadows and void dragged them away.

Kellan couldn't help but take note of Zarr's personal abilities. "I see you really hate that Ygg'Exos guy. He was just here."

"I know," Zarr said, his voice much deeper and colder than Kellan had imagined. "I can smell Vain's lingering stench."

The yami couldn't approach. A shark dragon managed to haul itself onto the flight deck, but it met a similar fate as the squids. Would a wave of sharks attack them next? Kellan was confident that was the plan.

"Thank you," Kellan said again. "I really appreciate you helping me with this."

Zarr spread his wings and held them out. He continued to just hover in place—not flying, but he wasn't touching the ground, either. "Do not thank me. You've summoned me against my will to the twisted domain of the Arbiter. You are forever my enemy. I will remember your name and face and curse it for all time."

"Wow," Kellan muttered. He folded his arms and clicked his tongue in disapproval. "I hadn't been expecting that response."

"You must be young. The Summoning Chime is a horrific item of oppression."

"Huh." Kellan tightened his grip on his own arms. He *was* forcing Councilor Zero to help him with the games. For some reason, he thought the mages who were summoned would be excited to serve. It seemed foolish now that Kellan gave the situation critical thought. "When you put it like that… I apologize. I didn't have much of a choice."

"The fourth wave is over!" Bitso's voice rang out over the flight deck. "That was fast. Much faster than the previous rounds. It's almost like… Someone had some help." His laughter punctuated his statement. Then he added, "You have ten minutes before the final wave. Use it wisely." Bitso laughed again, but after a few seconds, his voice was cut off, the speakers dying mid-chuckle.

The machine-dragon roared as the display screen on its shoulder shifted from DANGER to DOCILE. The shadows released it, and the beast stomped its way back to the bow of the ship. It didn't seem to care about Kellan or Zarr anymore.

Cold winds rushed over the aircraft carrier. Kellan shivered, his mind on the incredible power that both Ygg'Exos and Zarr had. They were already M-rank in several magics, and it was clear that Zarr had gone to great lengths to develop powerful skills.

"Can I ask you a personal question?" Kellan rubbed at his arms.

"I cannot refuse your questions."

"Why aren't you in the Nexus Games? It seems like you could effortlessly win."

"Tsk." Zarr's already-icy expression seemed harder and more distant than before. The glow of his eyes practically dulled as he focused on the distant waves. "Centuries ago, the Nexus Games were used to test mages—to find those worthy of magic's ultimate glory. But the Arbiter has gone mad, driven insane by unknown means and forces. Now the Nexus Games aren't meant to *test*, they're meant to *torture*."

Kellan chuckled. "You're tellin' me."

"Those who enter the games are killed off at an alarming rate, and the last few winners of the games haven't been worthy of Zenith. Only fools and masochists participate in the Nexus Games at this point. I would never willingly join this bloodbath disguised as an honest competition."

"I didn't have much of a choice."

Zarr said nothing. He didn't seem to care or have any sympathy for Kellan's position.

The False Sun hung in the sky overhead. The golden halo around the dark orb spoke to Kellan at a deeper level. It was shimmering, beautiful. It had the same hue and warmth as the gold arcana.

"When the Chime's time expires, I will abandon you," Zarr stated. He glared at the ship, and then at Kellan. "Command away. Your minutes dwindle."

"I have another question." Kellan shaded his eyes as he glanced upward. "Why the light? You seem like a mage focused on shadows."

Zarr ran his obsidian claws across his dark body. "There is little difference between the light and the dark. If there is a powerful source of light, you are blinded. If there is a powerful source of darkness, you are blinded. If there is too much light, life withers. If there is too much darkness, life withers. They are of the same kind—forever woven together. A powerful eclipse mage will master them both."

"Interesting. I hadn't thought of it like that."

After a short moment of silence, Zarr stared at Kellan. "Your title of *Void Knight*… It is rare. You have acquired gold arcana."

Kellan nodded once. "That's right."

"Perhaps my hate for you is not as thorough as I suspected it would be."

"I get that a lot," Kellan quipped.

Zarr, clearly unamused, simply asked, "Did you summon me here for knowledge?"

"We just need to live through the next wave. When the yami attack again, you should kill them."

"Heh."

Kellan stared at the inky darkness that ran off Zarr. Any mage who consumed some of Zarr's blood would be able to rank eclipse magic easier. However, Kellan couldn't ask Zarr to harm himself, nor could *he* harm Zarr. If he did either of those, the Chime's power would end. The ability to rank quickly would be useful, though…

They still had free time.

"Do you see that dragon over there?" Kellan asked.

Zarr glanced at the Aspect of the Arbiter. His wings remained outstretched, his hovering body seemingly held by on invisible strings. "It is a construct created by the lunatic Arbiter."

"Can you defeat it?"

"It will take effort."

Kellan smirked. "Perfect."

—Chapter 51—
—The Fifth Wave—

Zarr, sped up by the time-warping powers of the False Sun, flew over to the mechanical dragon. His wings dripped darkness the entire way, even under the golden glow of his powerful magic. The dragon didn't attack. It stood, waiting, its steel claws sheathed, and its machine-wings tucked to its side.

Without warning, Zarr attacked with his claws. His opening strike to the dragon's head was like a blast of time and entropy. Rust sprouted from the gouge Zarr rent in the side of the beast's steel skull. The monster rapidly aged, the gears and servos in its neck corroding. But it wasn't enough to stop the dragon. It roared and attempted to bite Zarr.

But the dragon was slowed by the impressive power of the False Sun.

Zarr managed to slash at the beast three more times before the dragon could open its jaws once again. Instead of biting, the dragon unleashed a blast of laser light. The sun empowered that as well. The beam was so fearsome and powerful, it blew a hole through the flight deck, and then through several decks below.

The door to the control tower opened. The others cautiously walked outside, their eyes wide, their attention on the glowing golden halo around the black sun.

A whisper near Kellan's ear asked, "You commanded him to fight the dragon construct?"

Kellan glanced around and saw no one nearby. But Jace was a mage with invisibility. "That's right," Kellan said. "He was bored. Might as well."

Jace's disembodied voice said, "Will he be done in time for the final wave?"

"Hopefully." Kellan slipped his hands into his pockets. "But I suspect so."

"It's not a *real* dragon. You won't get to claim one of its eyes."

Kellan wanted to laugh. Why would he want a dragon's eye? But then he remembered Jace's mechanical eye—and Other-Kellan's. *Those* were dragon eyes. And Jace's had the ability to make his magic-use easier. Specifically, his mind magic.

Perhaps a dragon eye would be useful… Kellan made a mental note of it.

Zarr and the machine dragon continued their fight, Kellan watching their every move. Zarr moved so much faster than the beast that it was a one-sided beatdown. Which was, honestly, fun for Kellan to watch. He would've given anything to see an all-powerful mage rip through the Nexus and completely destroy every spooky and deranged thing that crossed their path.

Sen, Mavis, and Vora walked over to watch Zarr fight the machine dragon. The clang of metal as the monster attempted to dodge was a chorus of destruction that rang out off the ship. Thanks to the afternoon light of the False Sun, everyone could see the gory details.

"That's Zarr Mantis?" Vora asked, breathless. "I've never seen him in person…"

Xiang and Husker stood near the control tower. The rennic leaned against the wall of the tower, his shoulder pressed up firmly against the steel. He breathed heavy, but not raggedly. Husker and Xiang seemed most interested in the False Sun, their gazes upward.

Before Kellan could walk over and ask Husker if he was okay, the dragon's sword-like claws managed to just barely strike Zarr's wing. The chip damage was enough to splatter some of Zarr's black blood onto the flight deck.

Smirking as he went, Kellan dove into the shadows and slithered across the deck. He emerged from the darkness near the blood droplets. The dragon hadn't managed to do much. Three spots of blood were all that had been splattered onto the carrier.

Kellan knelt, dragged his fingers through all three drops, and then lifted them to his mouth. Never in his life had he ever been excited to consume someone else's blood. Yet here he was, reflecting on his own elation. *The Nexus really messes with a person…*

Kellan licked the blood off his fingers. He closed his eyes as a shudder overtook him. The inky blood tasted of fish and cooking oil. Kellan half-gagged as it went down, but once it settled, a chill coursed through him.

He gained something new…

> **Training—[Dark Star Bloodline of Councilor Zero]—**The mage has consumed Councilor Zero's blood and has a 20% reduction to rank eclipse magic.

Which meant it would now only take *sixteen* arcana to achieve B-rank instead of *twenty*. Kellan chuckled to himself as the dragon slammed around the flight deck, its hate focused entirely on Zarr. Kellan didn't care if the dragon was defeated or not—all he had wanted was Zarr's blood.

"You're doing a great job," Kellan sarcastically called out. "Keep it up."

Zarr didn't reply. His rot and rapid-aging attacks were rusting the dragon to the point it was entirely red and falling apart at the edges. When the dragon roared, it sounded like a broken megaphone, screeching and cutting out.

A bit of silver glinted in the false light. Kellan perked up, surprised by what he spotted at the bow of the ship.

Another piece of the ape statue. It was the third and final portion—the head. The dragon had been guarding it. *Of course. I should've known.* Kellan held his breath as he dove into the darkness and then emerged next to the statue at the tip of the bow. The statue was held in place with chains.

If the False Sun hadn't been hanging in the sky, Kellan doubted he would've noticed the statue. The glitter of its lustrous silvery outside was magnificent. Kellan unchained the statue, scooped it up, and then went back into the darkness. He slithered across the flight deck, jumping in and out of shadows as needed, until he made it back to the control tower.

The ape statue could only work for *one* team.

"Jace," Kellan called out. "*Jace.* Come here."

The man allowed his invisibility to drop and seemingly emerged from thin air. Although his leather jacket was cut up, and blood soaked his jeans and shirt, he somehow had the swagger of a man in his prime, ready for anything. His blue machine eye glowed bright as Jace glanced down at the statue piece.

"What's this?" he asked.

"We have all three pieces. You and Vora should take this and go."

Jace lifted his gaze to meet Kellan's. "Are you serious?"

"We have a ticket to leave. Someone might as well use it."

"Don't be an idiot. We still have one wave left."

Kellan jutted his thumb out and motioned over his shoulder. "Zero back there will handle it."

"If that's true, then there's no harm in stayin'."

Kellan caught his breath. In truth, he was worried. Councilor Zero would only be here for fifteen minutes, and the ten-minute waiting period between rounds was the majority of that time. It always took the yami several minutes to claw their way out of the ocean… What if Zarr wasn't around for the entire length of the fifth and final wave?

After a short sigh, Kellan shoved the ape head into Jace's arms. Then Kellan walked over to Husker. The rennic still wasn't well enough to stand straight. When Kellan held out a hand, Husker seemed to know what he wanted. Husker reached into his coat and withdrew the other two pieces of the statue. It wasn't big—altogether it was no longer than a person's arm.

"Thank you," Kellan said.

Xiang eyed the statue and then glanced over her shoulder at Jace. In a whisper she said, "He's not your actual son, you realize that, right?"

"Yeah, I know." Kellan huffed as he walked around the woman. "Trust me. It's been hammered in."

Xiang gently grabbed his arm. Kellan stopped and stared at her.

With a frown, she said, "Giving Team 77 a key, and having them leave right before the toughest part of the game, isn't a tactical decision. It's emotional. You don't have to protect them."

Kellan allowed her words to sink in. She was right. "Half their team died because of me."

"Half their team died because of *Nosferatu*. Never forget it." She tightened her grip on his arm for half a second before letting go. "But do as you like. Their presence might not even matter if Councilor Zero helps us."

Kellan nodded and then returned to Jace. The man stood around with the silver ape statue in his hand, his gaze distant. When Kellan approached, Jace smirked. "Vora."

The woman turned and walked over, her clawed feet scraping across the runway as she went. With a huff, she crossed her arms. "What is it? I was enjoying watching Zarr dismantle the construct."

When Kellan turned his attention to the battle, he realized it was long over. The dragon was nothing more than a pile of rust. Zarr stood over the corpse with an uncaring expression—almost bored.

"You have all three pieces of the ape statue?" Vora asked. She grabbed the head from Jace and then frowned at Kellan. "You want us to leave?"

"I figured you two should get to safety," Kellan muttered. "Team 101 can handle the rest."

Vora snorted. "What an insult."

"An… insult?"

"A rezrah soldier doesn't abandon their post, their team, or their unit. *They fight till the bitter end.*"

Vora gripped the silver ape head tightly in both her clawed hands, and then threw it as hard as she could toward the side of the ship. It sailed through the air at an impressive speed, only hitting the flight deck once before bouncing and falling into the troubled ocean. When she turned back to Kellan, she wore a frown more prominent than any before.

Jace lifted an eyebrow. "I had absolutely no idea she would do that."

"Wow." Kellan rubbed at this temple. "All right."

"This is fine," Jace said with a sigh. "I was going to suggest we stick it out anyway. It just would've been nice to have the option to leave in case the rest of you were killed."

"Yeah, probably not the best move."

Vora growled at the both of them. "Cowards. We've made it this far, haven't we? What more could possibly go wrong?"

As if the universe wanted to spit in their faces for daring to suggest things had gotten easy, Husker doubled down and hit the deck on his knees. He growled and gurgled at the same time, his massive body shaking. Everyone turned to see the commotion.

The speakers flared to life at the same time. Bitso's voice sounded over the carrier. "You have one minute until the last wave begins. Not too much longer and the game will be over."

Husker groaned. A waterfall of saliva gushed from his canine mouth. With both arms wrapped around his stomach, he retched.

"What's happening?" Sen asked as he hurried over to Husker. "What is this? I thought you said this was some sort of sea sickness!"

"Get back," Husker said after a wheeze. "It's…"

He vomited across the flight deck, his saliva mixed with blood. Lumps of flesh spilled out, each spherical and the size of a golf ball. There were dozens. Husker retched again, and more spilled out, his whole stomach emptying onto the aircraft carrier.

The little flesh lumps jiggled and writhed around. Then cracks formed.

Then spiders rushed out.

No—not spiders. Baby Kuji.

Kellan practically gasped when he realized what had happened. The Kuji in round three had tried to infest Kellan with eggs, but the Tyranny Worms had prevented that from happening. Had the Kuji infested Husker? The baby spiders were proof that had happened! Why hadn't Husker done anything about it? Had he forgotten? Had the notification not reached him?

The Kuji…

As if drawn by the birth of its kind, a massive spider crawled out of the hangar elevator. Its many long legs were the length of a train car, each one ending in a twisted human hand. The claws on the fingers scratched the steel as it moved, the noise enough to make Kellan's skin crawl. The Kuji normally had the face of a human, but this time it was covered by a helmet made of tarnished brass. A contorted face was crafted into the mask, giving the spider a permanent smile.

Its eyes were visible, though. The helmet had a window for the paralyzing gaze to see through.

Kellan glanced away, shocked the Kuji would just show itself. Under the light of the False Sun, the massive spider moved at a slower pace. Apparently, its wisdom wasn't high enough to avoid Zarr's fate magic.

"Councilor Zero!" Kellan pointed in the monster's direction. "Handle that!"

But just as Kellan issued the command, waves crashed into the side of the carrier, the salt water splashing over the deck. Yami clambered up the side of the carrier, brought by the massive waves. They were four-legged dragons, but with no wings. Their heads—and their thick skin—were like a shark's. Each one had a mouth loaded with sharp fangs, their fat necks lined with gills.

The shark dragons lumbered across the flight deck, huffing in excitement.

—Chapter 52—

—The End of the Fourth Game—

Zarr Mantis turned away from the pile of rust and glared at the Kuji. The paralyzing effect of the monster spider didn't seem to grip him. He spread his inky wings and flew across the carrier without the assistance of the wind, and without even the need to flap. He seemed to glide through the air untethered by gravity.

Five of the shark-dragons charged for the control tower, each running in slow motion, all of them affected by the fell sun. Husker was too busy vomiting up the rest of his organs. He couldn't stand, he couldn't fight—the man could barely breathe.

Xiang exhaled and then straightened her posture. With a resigned expression, she held up a hand. One of the sharks stopped mid-run. Then its body slowly collapsed in on itself as Xiang crushed the beast with her powerful telekinesis. When she turned her gaze on a second yami, its brains exploded out of its ears—her *Mind Blast* was powerful when the creatures had one willpower a piece.

Kellan reached into his backpack and withdrew the Mermaid Knife a second time. He activated his *Neo Excalibur* a second time, spending three mana in the process, and then had the blade at the ready as a shark-dragon approached. Because the beast was so slow, Kellan had no problem rushing it and slashing.

He wasn't an expert swordsman, but he knew that the sharp end went into the enemy. He used the knife's ability to bypass all shielding and armor to effortlessly slice into the belly of the yami. He cut along its underside, spilling its guts onto the flight deck.

And the light of the False Sun empowered his laser sword as well. He dealt more than thirty damage a strike—*way* more than he had ever done before.

When the yami swiped at him with a fin-like claw, Kellan effortlessly dodged around it. The yami was so slow, and Kellan felt so fast…

Jace and Vora ran for another yami. Vora took point. She rushed ahead and slashed the beast with metal claws. Jace went invisible and then controlled the harsh shadows created by the False Sun. They lashed upward, whipping the shark dragon as Jace shadow-stepped behind it and opened fire with his handgun.

Even though Zarr was busy with the Kuji, he still managed to slice up a charging yami with his control over the darkness. The tendrils of darkness dug deep gouges in the shark. The False Sun seemed to weaken shadows a bit, but nothing slowed down Councilor Zero.

Except…

A *ding* rang out across the *CVAN Renegade*. It reverberated and rumbled through the steel of the aircraft carrier.

Kellan leapt away from the yami and turned his attention to Zarr. He *had* been fighting the Kuji, but after the powerful *ding*, the rezrah glanced at Kellan. "This was interesting, Void Knight. Good luck. May we never meet again."

Councilor Zarr disappeared in the blink of an eye. A pop of displaced air was all that was left. His False Sun remained, though.

"*He left us?*" Sen shouted, his voice so loud, everyone could hear him, even the dead. "*In the middle of the wave?*"

It was just as Kellan had feared. The man hadn't lasted through the final wave. Instead, another wave hit the carrier, splashing water onto the flight deck despite the fact that it was so high up above the surface of the ocean. It brought with it three more shark yami.

Thankfully, the False Sun still lingered overhead. It hadn't disappeared when Zarr had. It just remained to hinder the yami.

Mavis and Sen stayed close to Husker. When a yami came slowly stomping in their direction, Mavis lifted a hand and blasted it with fire. Sen protected her with his shielding, and the two attempted to char the beast to oblivion.

But Mavis's attacks were too weak. The fire washed over the shark dragon with little effect.

Kellan held up a hand—and after spending two mana for the laser and to empower it—unleashed a laser beam from the palm of his hand. The blast was so bright, it hurt his eyes. It seared the air, brightened the area further, and exploded a hole through the shark dragon as though it had been hit by a javelin missile.

The False Sun sure did love boosting light effects.

The dragon still didn't die, though. It wobbled on its four feet, stumbling around as though drunk. The damage had been great, but the beast was a damage sponge with its one hundred health.

"Vlaze!" Kellan yelled. "Help us!"

He hadn't summoned his familiar before, because he was so small, and weak. But since everyone's life depended on this, Kellan decided they needed every little bit of help.

The albino wyvern leapt from his shadow and took to the sky. Then he took one good look around and groaned. "Oh, Master… Why are you like this?"

Without needing any direction, the wyvern flew over to the yami that Kellan had blasted. Vlaze slammed into the shark's face and clawed at the monster's eyes, tearing and shredding like he was a cat with a new scratching post.

Kellan took a deep breath and then blasted another shark dragon with a beam of his superpowered laser. The hole it charred through the beast was large enough to ride a bicycle through. Kellan couldn't believe the difference in power.

Damn, we need to start using more buffing powers as a team, he thought, his teeth gritted as he smiled. *We're missing out on some potent options.*

With his laser sword, Kellan slashed at the nearest dragon. It swiped at him, but Kellan managed to stumble away. The claws were nearly as large as his whole body. One slice and he knew he'd lose an arm. Would the Tyranny Worms fix that? Kellan wasn't sure.

No longer harassed by Zarr or anyone else, the Kuji scurried forward. It would've moved dangerously fast if it weren't for the False Sun. Instead, it crept along, its head protected by the bizarre helmet, its eyes locked on Husker.

The rennic was still vomiting up baby Kuji, their little child-faces contorted and crying, like any normal infant. Husker couldn't stand. He couldn't defend himself.

Kellan stopped fighting the dragon to slither through the darkness and emerge next to Husker. But what could he do? Last time he fought the Kuji, all of his attacks had done nothing.

But the monster had gotten angry when its children were killed…

Kellan stomped on the babies, their bodies exploding like giant grapes. Each one made a sickening *crunch* noise as it died. Some of the baby Kuji cried out, their distressed screams almost enough to stop Kellan's onslaught.

The adult Kuji turned to face Kellan, just as he had hoped. Instead of looking the beast in the face, Kellan kept squishing the babies, hoping to build the monster's rage. Kellan wanted to draw all attention away from Husker—the rennic clearly couldn't defend himself.

The Kuji sped up. The False Sun still worked its awful magic, but somehow, the Kuji empowered itself to move a little quicker. Its fishhook claws practically dug into the flight deck as it scrambled forward, anger clear in its movements.

Once Kellan stomped on the last of the egg sacs and babies, the Kuji was almost on top of him. He shifted into the darkness as the Kuji swung with one of its spider legs and human hands. Kellan emerged ten feet away, but the Kuji was smarter than the yami.

One of its other spider legs was already in full swing.

[The Kuji of Team 101] slashed [Alex Kellan] for 11 damage.
[Alex Kellan] reduces damage of each hit equal to his armor rating of 2.
[Alex Kellan]'s shadow shell absorbs 2 damage.
[Alex Kellan] suffers a total of 7 damage.
[Tyranny Worms] restore [Alex Kellan] for 1 damage every 6 seconds.

The fishhook claws caught on Kellan's flesh. He grunted as the monster yanked him closer. Kellan attempted to fight back, but he wasn't empowered by his *Void Knight* ability. His strength wasn't as great as the Kuji's, but when he brought his laser sword up and around, he managed to slash through the monster's leg.

And it dealt damage.

The Kuji shrieked as one of its eight limbs fell to the flight deck. Blood gushed from its injury, but that didn't stop the monster from craving Kellan's death. It swung with another claw. Kellan ducked under it and rolled away, his shoulder and chest burning.

He grabbed at the injury, his hand shaky. The yellow Tyranny Worms squirmed under his skin, attempting to heal him as fast as possible. It was like they desperately didn't want him to perish, lest they lose their beloved home.

But seven damage…

If Kellan hadn't taken the improvement to his health, he would've died from the single attack, even with his armor. He clenched his jaw, his heart hammering.

The Kuji slashed again. Kellan stumbled away, almost tripping on his own feet. He kept his sword raised, ready to dismember the Kuji a second time if he could manage it.

In a surprising rush of speed, the Kuji lunged forward and smashed its brass helmet into Kellan's chest, sending him slamming to the deck of the ship. His head collided with the ground, and his vision went momentarily white. Had the Kuji been holding back? Hiding its real strength and speed to catch someone off guard?

"Face me, *monster*," Husker managed to choke out. He lunged for the spider monster and grabbed on to its abdomen, his claws digging into its flesh.

Normal magics didn't seem to harm the Kuji, but Kellan's *Neo Excalibur*, and now Husker's hex, seemed capable of piercing whatever mysterious defenses the creatures had. Husker's *Reaper Touch* disintegrated the monster's body at a hideous rate. The Kuji's legs, body, eyes—and even its brass mask—fell apart as though string being unraveled. An entropic rot-like effect spread across its body as dark energies crackled around Husker.

With its weakening arms, the Kuji reached back and dug its fishhook claws into Husker's back.

Kellan forced himself to stand and then slashed his weapon across the Kuji's face. The laser blade cut through the armored faceplate.

"Husker, run!"

But the rennic didn't. He remained on the Kuji, allowing his hex to take its toll.

It killed one of his family members every time he activated it, though…

With its claws deep in Husker's back, the half-rotted Kuji yanked the rennic away. With a powerful throw, the Kuji hurled Husker into Kellan. The collision sent Kellan to the deck once again, this time with Husker on top of him. He struggled to breathe, his chest twisted in agony. Husker rolled to the side, and Kellan forced himself to stand.

"C'mon," Kellan rasped. "Let's do this."

But just as he prepared himself to attack, an odd sensation came over him. He was pulled from his spot—teleported away—as though tugged to a new location by something far more powerful than himself.

Kellan stumbled backward and then found himself inside the AVU Palace. He gulped down breaths, confused and still on edge. He whirled around in place, his weapon held tight in his hand.

Mavis, Sen, Husker, Vlaze, and Xiang all appeared next to him.

They stood in the middle of a hallway, the crimson carpet, poor lighting, and odd pictures of dragons on the wall telling Kellan they were on the first story, somewhere between the techno dancefloor and the eighteenth-century kitchen.

"What happened?" Kellan demanded.

Xiang placed a weak hand on the wall and then slowly sank to her knees. Her long black hair fell over her shoulders and face as she exhaled. Her brother hurried to her side, his lip quavering.

"X-Xiang? Sister? Will you be okay?"

He placed his hand on her shoulder and attempted to heal her. But his body magic didn't seem to do anything. Kellan wasn't sure what was wrong. He knew her mana couldn't hit zero—or she would die—but what else was happening? What had she hidden from him?

"Xiang killed them," Mavis said, answering Kellan's question. "She killed all the yami while you and Husker were fighting the Kuji. She used… her mind magic. The monsters couldn't withstand her attacks."

Vlaze flapped his bat-like wings. "Yes. It's as she said. The yami died to phantasmal attacks." He scurried to Kellan's side, rubbed his head against Kellan's leg, and then dove into the darkness as though he couldn't wait to hide himself in the void's safety.

"The game is over?" The tension in Kellan's body slowly bled from him. The worms in his body healed the last of his injuries, bringing him back to his normal healthy self. "We did it? We won?"

Mavis nodded in response. "Yeah… All five of us. We made it through game four."

—Chapter 53—
—How Many Keys Do We Have?—

Sen and Xiang didn't speak. The brother and sister remained quiet.

There were no other mages in the long hallway of the AVU Palace. Jace and Vora were nowhere to be seen. Had they been teleported to safety as well? If so, where were they?

Husker, shaken and obviously still unwell, rubbed saliva from his canine mouth. He turned to Kellan, his ears down and his tail so droopy that it practically dragged on the floor. "Thank you."

"Don't mention it," Kellan muttered. "I'm sorry you had to use your hex."

"I… I will have to grieve." Husker shook his head. "But for now… I want to imagine it was worth it."

Windows lined the hall, giving Kellan a good view of the outside. The sun was on its way down. It would soon be evening—the time of celebration in the AVU Palace. Kellan ran a hand through his hair, his first thought on Nosferatu.

Was that resident bastard somewhere in the palace? Kellan couldn't believe the man had betrayed them, but after everything he had seen, Kellan had his name at the top of his *kill list.*

Kellan walked over to Xiang. He held out his hand, offering to help her to her feet. Xiang took his hand and struggled to stand. Kellan leaned down, giving her his shoulder, and then carried half her weight.

"Thank you," she whispered.

Mavis gave him a sideways glance but didn't say anything. She could've helped Xiang just fine. Kellan wanted to help, though. His guilt compelled him to.

As a team, they walked down the long hall, made their way to the grand staircase, and then traveled up to the second story of the palace. The strange architecture was becoming home to Kellan. He thanked whatever bizarre gods were listening that he was within the comforting aura of an Oasis. No one would harm them here. No monsters would emerge from the floor or the ceiling—or someone's insides. They could finally get some rest.

"I'll take you straight to the mana spring," Kellan said.

Xiang tightened her grip on him. "Thank you."

They made it to their suite without running across a single other mage. How many of them had lived through the Wave Defense? Kellan suspected it wasn't many.

Their suite was just as he remembered it. A large central living room with couches, chairs, and a massive TV. Beyond the sliding glass doors was the glorious pink mana spring. Kellan headed straight for it, Xiang holding on to his shoulder and saying nothing.

Sen hovered around, fussing with her clothes and attempting to heal her. When it still wouldn't work, Sen turned his attention to Husker instead.

"You were incubating Kuji eggs?" the kid yelled. "Why didn't you say anything to me? Why didn't you let the team know of the infestation?"

Husker growled. "I wasn't aware. Do you think I *wanted* to surprise everyone with Kuji babies? Trust me, I did not."

"You should be more careful! *Extra careful!*"

Husker snorted and then hobbled his way over to a couch. He sat down with a heavy *whump*, his body stiff, his clothing shredded, and his expression one of deep fatigue. Mavis sat next to him. She placed a hand on the reddish-brown fur of his arm. He didn't seem to mind her touch. The tip of his tail wagged a bit.

With a sigh, Kellan opened the sliding glass door and stepped out onto the balcony. His body and mind remained in *fight mode*. He wanted to kill something—finish the battle with the Kuji—but there was nothing here to destroy. The hollow feeling of being unfulfilled bothered him as he stepped into the pink water. He remained fully clothed, not giving a shit about his state of dress as the warm water came up to his hips.

Xiang was the same. She didn't mind the water or the clothes she wore. She seemed at ease the moment the spring worked its wonders and restored her mana.

Kellan was back up to seventeen. He relaxed and slid into the water until it reached his chin. Xiang clung to him, allowing herself to sink into the waters as well.

For a long while, there was no talking, no discussions, no arguments. Just silence. Just the mana of the waters soaking into Kellan's clothes, flesh, and bones. He closed his eyes, exhaled, and allowed the frustrations of an interrupted fight to leave him.

Thank goodness we made it.

Xiang released him, and Kellan moved to the edge of the spring. He propped his arms up on the stone, keeping his head out of the water and resting his weight forward. Then Kellan closed his eyes, his breathing even.

No one inside made a fuss. Even Sen quieted himself down as he took a seat on a chair.

The TV remained off, the black screen reflecting the quiet sitting room of the suite.

"Alex," Xiang whispered.

He glanced over. "Yes?"

"If Team 42 acquired the Wave Defense Key and the Heart Key for surviving with four teams, they'll trigger the end of the Nexus Games. The fifth game will be the last. And since we only have three keys, we may not… have a chance to win."

Xiang lifted a hand out of the pink water. In her palm was a black USB drive. It was the Wave Defense Key. Their third key of the game—with two more they could win. But unless the Arbiter offered another chance to win two different keys in a single game, they weren't going to have five by the end of the fifth game.

"Team 42 might've only gotten one key," Kellan said as he returned his chin to the cushion of his arms.

She closed her eyes. "Brenner doesn't typically fail."

"But he also doesn't play well with others." Kellan snorted and half-laughed. "I'll bet you my thirty-three unspent arcana that Team 42 didn't complete the game with all four team leaders."

"Even so. If Brenner's team gets a key in the fifth game…"

"He won't," Kellan stated. "We'll just have to make sure it doesn't happen. That way we go another five games, right? The checkpoint is only at game five? If no one has collected five keys, we'll continue till the end?"

Xiang chuckled, her inky hair swirling around the water around her like oil. "Extreme optimism is a sign of insanity."

"This is *the Nexus*. It was bound to happen sooner or later." Kellan yawned. He couldn't find the energy to move away from the edge of the spring.

His thoughts—what few he had—lingered on darkness. Gunner and Team 80 had died. And so violently. Their deaths replayed in Kellan's mind, haunting him. How could Nosferatu have done that? Why couldn't they have just banded together to fight Team 42?

"It's not just Team 42," Xiang whispered. "Nosferatu will be looking to end the games. If *he* gets a fifth key, he'll—"

"That man isn't getting anything," Kellan stated.

"You sound so confident. But Nosferatu is a powerful mage."

"Yeah, well, the Nexus has all sorts of surprises. Whatever the fifth game is, I'm sure we can turn something to our advantage. He doesn't have his Summoning Chime anymore. He's lost a significant advantage."

"So have we."

Her grim tone wasn't helping the mood, but Kellan refused to be somber. Somehow, they had made it this far, and he wasn't about to let *depression* be the monster that finally got him.

"We'll figure something out. Maybe we'll find another Prize Room. Or we'll complete a challenge. Or maybe we'll just get so much arcana we all rank up to M. I don't know—but we'll just roll with the punches as they come."

Kellan hated not having a plan, but one thing the military had taught him was not to give up. He could improve a bad plan, but he couldn't improve *no* plan. It was always better to do something in a situation like this.

After a long exhale, Kellan relaxed. The warmth of the spring, combined with his quiet surroundings, made the chaotic world of the Nexus seem tranquil. Kellan slipped into a light sleep, his mind remaining alert to his surroundings, even if the images in his thoughts played out like a dream.

Or maybe they weren't a dream…

Scenes of the aircraft carrier flashed in Kellan's thoughts. Scenes that involved him. Like watching himself from the eyes of another. Were these fragments of memories? Kellan dwelled on how arcana sometimes did this to him. Memories… It was as if Kellan had stolen the experiences of others. Their souls powered his magic. The disturbing thoughts rolled through his mind, tainting the images with sorrow.

Kellan tried to think of home. His tiny apartment in Fayetteville. Nothing about it comforted him. Would he return once he found Zenith? Or would he go somewhere else? Surely, he wouldn't live in the Nexus after the games were over.

Or perhaps…

He would help the Nexus residents escape the bizarre alternate dimension. Kellan would stop the Flestiss Dominion, the Arbiter, and help the residents…

It seemed impossible. There were just too many things to do. They didn't even have five keys. How could one mage—someone who barely knew anything about magic—hope to achieve so much?

But Kellan defiantly shook his head, his body tense all over again, even as he half-slept. He wasn't the type of person to give up before the challenge started, just because it sounded difficult. There were several instances in human history where a single person had made the difference. Hell, a single Serbian farmer had shoved a bottle wide-end first into his rectum and caused the dissolution of Yugoslavia. If that could happen, anything was possible.

Xiang swam over and rested on the edge of the spring next to him. "Thank you." Her voice was quieter than before. "I distrusted Nosferatu, and figured he would betray us, but the fact of the matter is… If we as a team had more trust for each other, we wouldn't have arrived at this situation. I should've… done many things differently. For that, I apologize."

Kellan said nothing. He drifted in and out of the gentle sleep, half wondering if Xiang's words were even real. If they had been more of a team, situations like what had happened in the fourth game *wouldn't* have been a problem. Would they work together better in the future? Kellan hoped so.

"I've made a lot of terrible decisions in my life," Xiang whispered. With a sigh, she added, "I've always felt great pressure from everyone around me to do things as *they* wanted. If I wasn't perfect, I was worthless." She chuckled, more to herself than for anyone else's benefit. "I know you don't care, but… I admire your drive. No matter how many times everyone tells you the path you're on is foolish, you push forward regardless."

Kellan forced himself to open his eyes. He wasn't sure if she was insulting him or trying to compliment him. But her gaze seemed softer, and her words easier. Was this her terrible way of saying something nice?

"Pushing forward regardless of opinions and obstacles is the essence of duty," Kellan said. "And I'm not the type to ignore my responsibilities."

"Your alternate-self isn't so honor bound."

"My *alternate-self* is a delta-bravo who abandoned his family and left them for dead." Kellan gripped the side of the mana spring, his anger returning in full force. "Everyone on Team 42 is our enemy. I'm disgusted I share the same name as that guy."

The glass door slid open.

Sen and Husker stepped out onto the balcony. Husker immediately walked into the mana spring, not bothering to undress. His reddish-brown fur fluffed in the pink waters. With a groan that sounded like a soft howl, Husker closed his eyes and relaxed. "My guts hurt."

"Well, you *did* give birth to hundreds of baby Kuji," Kellan quipped. "You should be proud."

With a snort, Husker replied, "Sorry I wasn't more help during the game…"

Kellan didn't want to discuss it. As long as he didn't think about the many deaths, his chest wasn't twisted with guilt.

After hesitating a few moments, Sen finally stepped into the spring. His child-sized body wasn't suited to the spring. He clung to the edge, his feet unable to reach the bottom.

The door opened a second time.

Mavis stood there, gripping the balcony door handle tightly. She glanced at Kellan with a frown. "Kellan. There is a Pestbyter at the door. It says it needs to take you to the Arbiter."

—Chapter 54—
—Look What You've Done—

Kellan stepped out of the mana spring and headed for the glass door. Mavis stepped aside and pointed to the front door of the suite.

A Pestbyter hovered in the hallway. Its spherical body was only a few feet from the floor. Antennas on the top of its body nearly reached the ceiling, while the wires hanging from its underside brushed along the red carpeting.

"*Hello,*" it said in a robotic little girl's voice. "*Alex Kellan the Void Knight has been summoned to speak with the Arbiter. Please, come this way.*"

Soaking wet, and still in need of much sleep, Kellan shuffled his way through the living room. Mavis, Sen, Husker, and Xiang watched him go. The Arbiter summoned people all the time to answer for things that happened during the games. It wasn't uncommon. And no one wanted to defy the Arbiter, not while they resided in his Oasis.

Kellan stepped out into the hall with the Pestbyter. Its camera eye swiveled, stared at him for a moment, then turned to face the hall. The machine hovered forward, its engine *rum-ver-rumming* as it went for the stairs. Kellan dripped water onto the rug as he walked along, his boots squishing with each step.

They went down the stairs, through the halls of the first story, and through a massive library. The Pestbyter said nothing their whole trek, its one-minded focus machine-like in all regards. Kellan easily kept up with it. He almost asked questions, but he knew it would be pointless. The Pestbyters had never really spoken to him about any matter worth a damn.

Then the Pestbyter arrived at a smaller spiral staircase.

"*Up these steps,*" it said sweetly.

Kellan took the stairs to the second story and found himself in a small and narrow corridor. No windows. No rug. There was a single door at the far end, one made of redwood. A single light hung overhead, flickering with the sporadic intensity of a horror movie prop.

Kellan walked to the door and opened it.

He had been here before.

It was a singular room—square, windowless like the hallway—with a sole desk and a couple of chairs. The ceiling was lined with giant head-sized eyeballs. They were the half-machine Eyes of the Arbiter…

Bitso stood in the middle of the room, right in front of the desk. He leaned against the single piece of furniture, his arms crossed, his blindfold tightly wrapped around his head. It was so tight, the skin around the edge of the blindfold seemed red and irritated. Bitso combed his dark copper hair forward, his nails scratching along his scalp.

The door shut behind Kellan, leaving him alone in the room with dozens of eyes and Bitso.

"Sit down," Bitso commanded, his voice curt.

He didn't laugh or joke. Kellan tensed, uncertain of what was happening.

"I said, *sit down*," Bitso said, more forceful than before.

Kellan held his breath as he cautiously strode across the room. He took a seat in one of the cushioned chairs. Bitso's suit wasn't stained or marred with blood. The man seemed a little more *confident* and *put together*.

"Is everything okay?" Kellan asked.

Bitso smirked. "The Arbiter gave you one *simple* instruction. Now look what you've done. *Look. What. You've. Done.*" His words were strained, almost shaky. They weren't like his normal self at all. Bitso gripped his arms, his jaw clenched.

Kellan racked his mind, trying to remember the Arbiter's instruction. Had the Arbiter ever even spoken to him? Kellan was certain that he had never heard the dragon's voice, not once. Bitso had relayed all sorts of information—but what instruction had Kellan missed?

"Well?" Bitso asked. "What do you have to say for yourself?"

"I don't know what you're talking about. Remind me—what was the instruction?"

Bitso shook his head. Then he brought both hands up and yanked at his hair, practically growling and grumbling the entire time. He pulled so hard on his hair, Kellan thought Bitso might actually rip some of it out.

Kellan sat forward, right at the edge of his seat. "Are you—"

Bitso kicked the other chair, sending it tumbling to the floor. Then he turned around and slammed his hands down on the top of the desk. "You don't remember?" Bitso took in a deep breath as though on the verge of hyperventilating.

Kellan went to stand, but Bitso whirled around on his heel, so tense that Kellan thought the other man would attack him.

"*Did I say you could stand*?" Bitso swept a hand through his hair, his palm coming back with blood. His scalp had been bloodied from his attempt to rip everything out by the roots. Bitso took one controlled breath and then forced half a smile. "Just… stay seated."

Kellan remained in his seat. He had never seen Bitso so coherent. Or upset.

"The Arbiter told you to gather gold arcana. You remember that, don't you?"

"Yes," Kellan muttered. "I remember. Is *that* why you're upset?"

Bitso's lip twitched—just once. Then a squeaky giggle escaped him. It was more unhinged than normal.

"*Is that why you're upset*?" Bitso repeated in a high-pitched tone. In a cold and calm voice, he said, "Yes. That's why I'm upset. Very upset."

"I've been gathering gold arcana," Kellan stated. "I mean…" He thought back to Millie, his thoughts tainted by the odd sadness mixed up in the event. "I gathered more."

"And then you gathered *thirty-seven* red arcana from the last game!" Bitso let out a frustrated growl and then paced around the desk. He tapped the tips of his fingers along the top of it, and Kellan realized this one was made of the same redwood the door had been constructed out of.

"Is that wrong?" Kellan asked. "Because the Arbiter never said to *not* gather red arcana."

Bitso stopped once he had returned to the front of the desk. With a chuckle, he said, "Oh, you're getting smart now, huh? Think you're clever?"

"Look, I'm happy to do what the Arbiter wants, but he can't be vague." Kellan glanced up at the eyes on the ceiling. "What the hell do you want from me? Just tell me!"

Bitso grabbed Kellan by the front of his ripped-up jacket, dragging Kellan's attention back to the deranged newscaster. In a low whisper, Bitso hissed, "*Don't yell at the Arbiter!* He won't like that! *I* won't like that!" Bitso pulled on Kellan's collar. "If you don't get gold arcana, the Arbiter will blame *me* for not delivering his instructions carefully enough. Don't you see?"

Kellan narrowed his eyes. "Okay. Well, next time you should give me clear instructions."

Bitso released Kellan with a shove and then walked back to the desk. "I *did*, you sad sack! I gave you perfectly clear instructions. *Gather gold arcana.* The Arbiter likes that. But when you gather *that much* red arcana, you're practically undoing all your hard work! *Look where that leaves me!*"

Kellan rubbed at his chest. Nosferatu had said that the more red arcana someone had, the more their soul was *smudged.* The more gold arcana, the cleaner and clearer their magic. Did that mean Kellan would have to gather more gold arcana to make up for the thirty-seven red arcana he had collected?

"I'm sorry the Arbiter is upset with you," Kellan stated. "But it's your own damn fault. Maybe if you weren't so obtuse, I'd know what's expected of me."

Bitso ground his teeth so loud, Kellan felt it in his own jaw. Then Bitso placed his hands on the top of the desk and just leaned most of his weight forward. For a prolonged moment, Bitso said nothing. The Eyes of the Arbiter on the ceiling shifted—they moved down the walls, slowly getting closer to the confrontation, unblinking and intensely focused.

Kellan gripped the side of his chair. "Bitso?"

"I'm so… tired," Bitso murmured.

The statement caught Kellan off guard. "Yeah. I feel that."

"And the Arbiter gets so… *angry.* His punishments are worse than death." Bitso trembled, his nails scratching across the redwood.

Kellan wasn't sure what to say. The Eyes got closer and closer, staring from the wall, all two dozen of them.

"You understand, now, right?" Bitso turned around, his voice and posture slumped. "Don't go ignoring the Arbiter's instructions. For *my* sake… Please."

Kellan nodded once. "All right. I'll help." He glanced at the Eyes and then back to Bitso. "I've been trying to gather more gold arcana in general. It's… powerful. And the magic I get from it is better than the magic I get from the red arcana."

"Good." With a shaky hand, Bitso patted his suit, smearing blood everywhere. It gave him back his normal lunatic appearance. "Very good. I'm glad we had this touching conversation."

Touching?

Kellan hesitantly stood from his chair. Bitso didn't yell or shout or tell him to sit. But before Kellan attempted to leave, he asked, "Are all the teams done with the fourth game?"

Bitso fidgeted with his blindfold, making sure it was secured in place. "Hm? Yeah. Of course."

"Did Team 42 win two keys?"

With a snort and laugh, Bitso shook his head. "Oh, no. Definitely not." Then Bitso poked Kellan in the chest with a single finger. "Looks like you've influenced some people. The other three teams tried to wreck Team 42 during the final wave. Almost killed one of their members. But then the leader of Team 3 died. So, ya know how it goes. Team 42 only got *one* key."

"Do *any* teams have all five keys?"

Bitso shook his head. "Nope."

Which meant they still had time. As long as no teams gathered five keys by the end of game five, they would be okay.

"If no one has five keys by the end of game five, the Nexus Games still continue, right?"

Bitso half-shrugged. "Until game ten." He leaned forward. "It's confusing, I know. People don't understand you need a key *per member of your team*. The teams with ten people technically need ten keys to win, and they keep asking me things like *but what if we have five keys*?" Bitso laughed. "Next time, we're just going to have the *Nexus Race*, that way it's over in one wham-bam-thank-you-ma'am moment. None of these confusing contingencies."

"All I want to know is—how many games do we have to attempt to gain the appropriate number of keys?"

"You'll either have five games or ten. After game five is the first checkpoint. If no teams have won, we go into overtime, so to speak. Five more games for a total of ten." Bitso smacked Kellan's shoulder. "I'm not really into sportsball, but you get the analogy, right? Sure you do. You're clever enough."

"Right…" Kellan waited for a few moments. Bitso said nothing. The Eyes of the Arbiter did nothing. "Can I go now?"

Bitso picked at his back teeth. Each molar was just as sharp as his canines. When he was done, he asked, "You used your Summoning Chime already?"

"Yeah."

"On that goth vampire wannabe?"

"Councilor Zero?"

Bitso chuckled. "Yeah. *Him*."

"That's right." Kellan glared. "You once told me I should get his blood. So I did."

"I saw that." Bitso rubbed his blindfold until blood appeared. "Very interesting. The Arbiter liked that, by the way. It amused him. He was hoping that you'd made a good impression so that Zarr left you some gold arcana. Instead, Zarr just left you a little orb of light. Pfft."

"Is Nosferatu in the palace?" Kellan asked, since Bitso seemed in a helpful mood.

Bitso smiled wide. "Yes. He's here. *Like always.* Stinkin' up the place with his boils."

"If I wanted to kill someone like him… What would be the best way to go about it?"

The question seemed to catch Bitso by surprise. "You want him *dead*?" He playfully smacked Kellan again. "That's so unlike you." With a giggle, he added, "I thought you liked the Nexus residents? You're always helping them."

"Not this one." Kellan balled his hands into fists. "I assume you saw what happened in the fourth game? Nosferatu betrayed us."

Bitso shrugged. "Oh, boo-hoo. It's the Nexus Games. Everyone betrays everyone else eventually. Is that the only reason you're mad? Or is it because he said such nasty things about you behind your back?"

"Wait, what?" Kellan asked.

"Xiang, too. Such horrible things. It was rather entertaining." Bitso leaned in close and lowered his voice. "If I were you, I wouldn't listen to the man's thoughts. They'll paint a picture that your mind's eye can never unsee."

"They're that bad?"

"Oh, yes. And I've read things like *erotic fan fiction.* When your thoughts are worse than *that*, you definitely need mental help. Nosferatu is one such person." Bitso laughed as he took a seat on top of the desk. "I've been really enjoying this conversation, by the way. Not too many people just chat it up with me. Well, besides the Arbiter. But he doesn't want to gossip about the players of the Nexus Games. He's *too important* for any of that."

Kellan rubbed at his chin, trying to grapple with the bizarre information he had been handed. It wasn't helpful, so he decided to ignore it for the time being. "I just need a way to kill Nosferatu," Kellan stated. "Can you help me or not?"

Bitso leaned back. "Oh, you're bloodthirsty now? I see. Well, how about this. If you collect *twenty more* gold arcana, I'll help you find a way to easily kill Nosferatu, how does that sound, hm? That way, we'll be helping each other." He motioned to himself, and then to Kellan. "Hm? What do you say?"

Last time Bitso had made a deal with Kellan, the madman had come through. Kellan had gotten meta magic, and at a reduced price to rank. "Fine. I'll work on that."

And it would give Kellan time to think over the situation. There were other ways to deal with Nosferatu. Perhaps he could catch Nosferatu off guard in one of the games. Or trick him in some way with one of the many deadly objects in the Nexus…

"You know, when you first started the games, you wanted everyone to hold hands and win together," Bitso said with a wistful tone. "Now look at you. Plotting everyone's death. Mages grow up so fast."

"Team 42 is actively going to destroy everything, and Nosferatu betrayed me, even though I was willing to help him. I think my bloodlust stems from a logical place."

"I'm sure that's what every murderer says."

Kellan chuckled. Then he headed toward the door, his steps slow. The Eyes watched him the entire way, the pupils tracking him as he walked. Kellan suppressed a shudder. What did the Arbiter want with him? Why wasn't the bizarro dragon demanding *everyone else* get gold arcana?

"Wait," Bitso said.

Kellan stopped, but he didn't turn around.

"The next game… There's only one key. For everyone. So, if you're still desperate about making sure Team 42 doesn't win, you'll get your chance."

"Really?" Kellan glanced over his shoulder. "Only one key for every team involved?"

Bitso smiled wide as he nodded, his white teeth bright in the otherwise-dull room. "Mm-hmm. But don't tell anyone I told you. I'm not supposed to give out hints and secrets to the players."

"Trust me. I won't tell."

"Good." Bitso waved his hand. "Then get out of here. I have a news show to film, and you'll probably want to pay attention to all the details."

END Book II

THANK YOU SO MUCH FOR READING!

Please consider leaving a review—any and all feedback is much appreciated!

But who will win the Nexus Games?

To find out more about Shami Stovall and the Nexus Games,
take a look at her website:
https://sastovallauthor.com/newsletter/

To help Shami Stovall (and see advanced chapters ahead of time)
take a look at her Patreon:
https://www.patreon.com/shamistovall

To chat with Shami Stovall (and see a bunch of writing memes) chill with
here at her Facebook group:
https://www.facebook.com/groups/capitalstationlounge/

ABOUT THE AUTHOR

Shami Stovall is an author of fantasy and science fiction (which you probably know because you just finished one of her books… Derp.). Before that, she taught history and criminal law at the college level and loved every second. When she's not reading fascinating articles and books about ancient China or the Byzantine Empire, Stovall can be found playing way too many video games, especially RPGs and tactics simulators. She loves John, reading, and writing about herself in the third person.

Favorite RPG: Mass Effect 1 and Super Mario RPG
Favorite 4X: Stellaris
Favorite Monster-Catching Collectathon: Azure Dreams

If you want to contact her, you can do so at the following locations:

Website: https://sastovallauthor.com
Twitter: @GameOverStation
Facebook: www.facebook.com/SAStovall
Email: s.adelle.s@gmail.com

And please help this group grow!
https://www.facebook.com/groups/LitRPGsociety
https://www.facebook.com/groups/LitRPGGroup
https://www.facebook.com/groups/litrpglegion
https://www.facebook.com/groups/litrpgs

"To learn more about LitRPG, talk to authors including myself, and just have an awesome time, please join the LitRPG Group at https://www.facebook.com/groups/LitRPGGroup."

www.ingramcontent.com/pod-product-compliance
Lightning Source LLC
Chambersburg PA
CBHW030345310726
48979CB00001B/196
* 9 7 8 1 9 5 7 6 1 3 7 5 8 *